A Rumor of Gems

A Rumor of Gems

ELLEN STEIBER

TOR®

A TOM DOHERTY ASSOCIATES BOOK

NEW YORK

A RUMOR OF GEMS

Copyright © 2005 by Ellen Steiber

This book is printed on acid-free paper.

A Tor Book
Published by Tom Doherty Associates, LLC
175 Fifth Avenue
New York, NY 10010

www.tor.com

Tor® is a registered trademark of Tom Doherty Associates, LLC.

Library of Congress Cataloging-in-Publication Data

Steiber, Ellen, 1955–
    A rumor of gems / Ellen Steiber.—1st ed.
       p. cm.
    "A Tom Doherty Associates book."
    Includes bibliographical references (p. 463).
    ISBN-10: 0-312-85879-5 (acid-free paper)
    ISBN-13: 978-0-312-85879-7
    1. Antique dealers—Fiction. 2. Gems—Collectors and collecting—Fiction. I. Title.

PS3569.T3425R86 2005
813'.54—dc22

                                                                2004063752

First Edition: June 2005

Printed in the United States of America

0 9 8 7 6 5 4 3 2 1

To my mother,
MURIEL L. STEIBER,
and to the spirit of my father,
SAM STEIBER

"Speak to the stones, and the stars answer.
At first the visible obscures:
Go where light is."

—THEODORE ROETHKE,
"Unfold! Unfold!"

PART I

A Scattering of Stones

"When you touch topaz
topaz touches you . . ."

—PABLO NERUDA,
Stones of the Sky, "*XXV*"

$\mathcal{O}ne$

THERE WERE RUMORS of gems appearing in the city: topaz turning up in the sneaker of a three-year-old; discarded emeralds found glittering on a restaurant dish that a waiter was about to clear; a convenience store cash register filled with opals instead of dimes; the dark soil in a window box suddenly shining with bits of polished lapis and garnet—enough to make necklaces for every woman in the tenement.

There was no confirmation of the rumors. No one came forward with a coffee cup filled with rubies, and who could blame them? Except for a woman who'd won the local lottery, no one displayed sudden wealth. No one reported stolen jewels. No one fenced them through the underground. And yet the rumors continued—a girl in the park spilling out a sack of marbles and watching spheres of aquamarine and moonstone roll out in their stead; a punk pulling a knife on a onetime friend only to find he held a small, obelisk quartz crystal in which the image of an even smaller tiger roamed. (He kept the crystal and the tiger. The onetime friend fled.) Not all such appearances were welcome. An old man opened his cigar box to find no cigars but a rod of dark green tourmaline. He junked the stone and bought himself another box of cigars.

They were just rumors. And yet they persisted. Winter was finally releasing its hold, the sky held more light, and the people of Arcato began to walk with a sense of hope that had not been present for years. Although few admitted to believing the tales, there was hardly a soul who did not secretly hope that he would open his refrigerator door and see a topaz in place of a tomato, or that she might pour from a bag of cat food and have a cache of diamonds tumble out. The promise of riches was in the air.

Riches, however, were not what the appearance of the gems betokened. They were messages of a sort, calling cards. They were left by one who could not help himself. Alasdair scattered gems wherever he went, even when trying to be discreet. They fell from his pockets, trailed from his sleeves, hid in the brim of his hat, and brushed his eyelashes as they fell. He knew this for a problem and so he did not move about much during the day. When he did he wore layer upon layer of clothing to keep the showy little things concealed. And still the gems came. They had a penchant for escape. They liked the light of the sun. They were impossible to contain.

To the people of Arcato the rumors of the stones were an infusion of hope, a promise that what was desired might one day be met. To Alasdair the stones in their irrefutable reality were a sign that he could not stay long in the city, even under the cover of darkness. He would have to return to the place he had come from though he had left, swearing up and down that he would have nothing to do with it again. Even then he'd known his words for a lie. He was as bound to the place as the moon to the earth. He could feel its pull moving along his skin, streaming through his blood like a tide, whispering to him when he slept. He would have to go home. But the rumors were still considered the stuff of children's stories. No one took them seriously. He still had time.

In an apartment on a granite ridge near the top of the city, he closed thick velvet curtains and shed the layers of clothing for a simple robe. He pretended not to notice as the gemstones tumbled to the carpet. He turned on a lamp, knowing its narrow spectrum would annoy them. Their reaction was predictable. As if to show him just how inadequate lamplight was, the diamonds arranged themselves on his desk, sending out streams of rainbow-colored light, inviting him in their most dazzling fashion to be seated. And write a letter home, of course. The rubies took themselves off to the kitchen where they sorted themselves into various corners so that the white appliances glowed with the warmth of high mountain sunsets. The sapphires gathered in the bedroom, darting deep blue fire against the wood-paneled walls, reminding him of rooms he'd grown up in, of the chamber where he'd first made love.

For Alasdair the stones outdid themselves. They went beyond reflecting available light. They drew energy from their very centers, sent out colors beyond those normally seen by the human eye—colors he would recognize, colors he would long for. They were determined to please him. They were bound to seduce him. They were his only to lead him back. He turned on the old TV set, welcoming the black-and-white screen.

Beside him a tiny jade dragon climbed from the end table to his shoulder, its claws sinking into his robe as it climbed. It settled contentedly on his collarbone, where it blinked its eyes once and then watched the sitcom. Although he did not find the show funny, the dragon did. He could tell by the occasional amused flutter of its pale green wings.

LUCINDA DE FRANCESCO had never had patience for stories of the Easter bunny, the tooth fairy, or gemstones appearing in teacups. She took the rumors for mass hallucination, a phenomenon that she believed explained a great deal of the stupidity around her. It was the only thing that could account for the enduring popularity of certain politicians, religions, and hairstyles. Then again, odd and inexplicable things had been happening in Arcato for some time now. Quite a number of people claimed to see things that simply weren't there—a full crew loading an old steamboat that had been drydocked for years, a busker in a doorway where a building no longer stood, a line of stilt walkers striding across the surface of the river's grey-green waters. Lucinda gave no real credence to any of these claims. She trusted that what she saw was real and that the gems were not. She refused to look for the glitter of sapphires beneath streetcars or pearls pouring out of vending machines. So when she found a piece of pale green jade carved to look like a small, perfect dragon—complete with wings, scales, claws, and a long, curled tail—she thought only that someone had been fool enough to lose something valuable. She tucked it in the pocket of her shirt, wondering if she should advertise it, deciding immediately that she didn't want to be bothered with the phone calls or letters that would come in response. Besides, it was a pretty thing.

At home she put the dragon on top of her bookcase. The carving was so small, she couldn't see it up there unless she walked right up to it. This bothered her. Before she went to sleep she took the dragon down and set it beneath the Chinese lamp on her bedside table. In the glow of the electric light the jade was translucent. It made her think of early spring, of clouds and water, of things that flowed.

Lucinda stripped off her clothing, leaving on silver bracelets and rings, anklets and earrings, necklaces strung with lockets and beads, milagros and charms. She hated sleeping in clothing and couldn't sleep without jewelry. Her last lover had complained that her earrings kept sticking him in the jaw. She'd shrugged and told him she didn't see why she was the only one who should be penetrated. They'd had angry sex and she'd left his bed before dawn, vowing he'd never see her again.

She got into bed and opened the book she'd been reading for the last three months, a novel about a man and a city and how the two wore each other down. She never could seem to get very far into it. She read another page, too tired to stay with the story, too restless to stay in bed. Resigned, she got up, went to her bookshelves, and began to skim through books of poetry, but tonight none of them soothed.

She got dressed again and though it was nearly midnight, she left the apartment and went down to the streets. A light rain had fallen, and the sidewalks smelled damp and chalky. Shallow pools of water, coated with a film of rainbow oil, caught the reflections of the street lamps. In one she thought she saw the image of a small green dragon.

She wound up on Consolación Street, walking past the Teatro Descardo to Indigo, one of the smaller clubs. It was a chilly weeknight and the street, usually crowded at this hour, was deserted. Indigo's bouncer barely glanced at her before opening the door; she wondered if there was anyone he refused tonight. "Maxine here?" she asked, before stepping over the threshold.

He nodded. "She'll find you."

Inside a band played half-heartedly and discordantly on the stage. Lucinda bought herself a shot of tequila at the bar and sat down in an empty banquette, her attention roving between the band and the audience. She couldn't remember ever seeing this place so empty. She could actually count the number of people dancing. The most noticeable were four young women dancing directly in front of the stage, seeming oblivious to the fact that the music barely had a beat.

Lucinda lifted her glass to a tall, gaunt woman, holding a drink in one hand, a lit cigarette in the other, who came toward her, hips swaying. Maxine, who owned Indigo, bent, kissed Lucinda's cheek, and took a seat at the table. "How are you, girl?" she asked.

Disturbed would have been the correct answer, but Lucinda settled for "Restless. I couldn't sleep," she added more honestly.

Maxine shrugged. "No sympathy here. You're talking to the queen of insomnia. Why do you think I run a club? Still, it's a lousy night to be out."

"Better than staying home."

"It's too subdued for my taste." Maxine wore rings on every finger, dark stones all. Faceted onyx, garnet, peridot, black tourmaline, and what she'd told Lucinda was an alexandrite glittered as she pointed her cigarette toward the sparsely populated dance floor. "I should have closed an hour ago. Don't know why I'm paying a band for this."

"You've got customers," Lucinda said, nodding to the girls.

"Those four don't count. The band comp'd them."

"They're sleeping with the band?"

"Or hoping to." Maxine took a drag on the cigarette. "Look at them. Can you remember when going home with the lead guitar player was everything?"

"I always had better luck with drummers." Lucinda swirled the tequila in her glass, her silver bracelets clinking together softly. "Drummers do lovely things with their hands."

Maxine gazed at her through heavy-lidded eyes, and Lucinda wondered how old Maxine was. She wore her hair in the same glossy black bob she'd worn twelve years ago when Lucinda first met her. And she still had the slouched, decadent silhouette that reminded Lucinda of the women in Aubrey Beardsley drawings—thin, beautiful, elegant creatures who seemed somehow hollow inside.

"The boys in the bands, they're all bastards." Maxine spoke without rancor. "Not that they mean to be. But they're young and self-involved and they've got all the energy of the music streaming through them so they think they're golden."

"We thought so, too," Lucinda reminded her.

Maxine blew a smoke ring. "Illusions, darling. Illusions who can give you the clap."

"Speaking of illusions . . ." Lucinda realized that she'd come to the club seeking out Maxine because Maxine was too cynical to be taken in by rumors, too hard-headed to give anything but a straight answer. She was also notoriously well-connected; very little went on in Arcato that Maxine didn't know about. "You haven't found any of these gems everyone's talking about, have you?"

"Yeah, I've heard about those." Maxine tilted her head toward the stage. "But *they're* as close as I come to diamonds—in the rough, that is. I know it doesn't sound that way tonight, but they actually have talent."

"So . . . nothing . . . strange has happened to you recently?" Lucinda asked, finding that she didn't want to mention the jade dragon.

"There's *always* something strange going down at a club," Maxine corrected her. "This afternoon I came in to find that painted Japanese screen in my office—the one my grandmother left me—and the ivory brocade on the love seat slashed." Maxine's tone was cool and detached, as always, but Lucinda caught a flash of pain in her dark eyes. "Oh, and the stack of handbills I'd copied, advertising these sweet young things, was shredded like confetti. That's why no one's here tonight." She ground out her cigarette in a glass ashtray. "Think someone's trying to shut me down?"

"I don't know," Lucinda said, envisioning the damage. Maxine, despite her aversion to sentimentality, had filled her office with eclectic, graceful antiques. Lucinda had always loved the contrast between the rough club space and Maxine's elegant office.

"Nothing else in the club was touched, nothing missing or broken. Cops weren't even interested enough to show up. But someone hurt the things I loved."

"Who would want to—"

"Probably the same lunatic who took a knife to the old velvet stage curtain at the theater next door. Now the Teatro's gotta buy a new curtain and they have less of a budget than I do. Who knows, maybe some sicko's trying to shut down the whole street." Maxine ran a hand through her glossy hair. "It seems pointless to me. I figure, if you're going to go out of your way to vandalize a place, you ought to at least get something for your trouble."

"Yeah, well, you've always had a larcenous heart."

Maxine lifted her glass, gave a toast, "To larceny," then put the glass down without drinking. Her hand was shaking violently.

Lucinda clasped Maxine's hand between her own but couldn't still the tremor. "Hey," she said softly. "What's going on? Are you all right?"

Maxine pulled her hand back. "Things are changing, 'Cinda," she said. "No one's ever broken into my club before." Her hand still trembling, she lifted the glass and downed the drink. "I'll tell you something. Soon no place is gonna be a haven anymore."

HOURS LATER LUCINDA returned to her rooms and slept. She dreamed she'd left Arcato. She was traveling into the mountains that bordered the city. Standing on one rugged peak, looking out into an apron of others, she saw dwellings cut into the surface of the rock, entire towns she'd never known existed. Then she was on a steep granite slope, climbing surely and steadily. Following a vein of pale green jade.

She awoke disturbed by the fact that she remembered the dream. Normally, her dreams went through her like a train boring through a tunnel. They took her into a racing darkness whose rhythm shook her to her core. She never knew what happened in her dreams, who peopled them, what their landscapes looked like. Only the rhythm of the dream stayed with her through the day, leaving her waking body jarred and confused. There'd been a time when she'd thought she had some say in the matter, when she told herself that the rhythm was like the breath, a variable that could be controlled. She'd tried yoga. She'd tried hypnosis. She'd tried downers. Nothing worked. The dreams themselves vanished with the dawn, but their pace sped through her for hours on end.

And now she'd dreamed of a granite mountain striped with a vein of jade. The mountain had been serene, the skies above it a tranquil, luminous blue. She could still taste the air of that place. It tasted like something that could wash her soul clean, a possibility that had never occurred to her before. She sat up in bed and closed her eyes, letting the images return, seeing them vividly in her mind. She opened her eyes, alarmed. The dream had been so clear it didn't feel like one of hers at all.

Lucinda's hand went instinctively to the tiny jade dragon, still resting beneath her lamp. What occurred to her was absurd and yet self-evident. "That was your dream," she told the dragon.

ALASDAIR DIDN'T NOTICE the dragon was gone until late one evening, and then he realized it had been several days since he saw it last. It could take care of itself, he knew. Though it frequently went off on forays of its own, it rarely stayed away long. He wondered briefly if it had somehow hurt itself or become trapped. No, he would have known if it were in trouble. He couldn't imagine not knowing; they'd been together too long.

When a week had passed and the dragon still had not appeared, he knew he had to search for it. For three nights he walked the streets of Arcato, sending out a call that could only be heard by ears of jade. Gems fell in his wake and he cursed the troublesome serpent. And yet the nights were not unpleasant. The city still amazed him. He was delighted by the movie marquees and brightly lit streetcars, by all-night markets and Laundromats, by the colored lights of the midway Ferris wheel, by clubs whose doors stayed open until dawn. There was so much in the city that nearly succeeded in lifting the cloak of night, a feat his people had never tried. It simply would not have occurred to them.

Three nights of searching told him that if the dragon were to be found, it would be found when it chose to show itself. Perhaps, he thought, it had returned home. He didn't blame it; he'd told it not to follow him. And it had not only followed him here but had kept him company on an ocean crossing and a desert sojourn before that, which was really far more than loyalty demanded. He knew the dragon longed for the mountains; it had sent him its wistful dreams often enough. The dragon would return to cool limestone caverns and pools of pale green water, and there it would happily mate with its kin. It was such a small dragon, he had not thought it would feel confined here. Once again, he'd been wrong.

THE MORNING AFTER she dreamed the dragon's dream, Lucinda did not go to work. She took whatever the inverse of a sick day was. She lay in bed for as long as she could keep the dream with her. Then she dressed in petticoats and a top she'd made from Belgian lace and she went down into the streets of the city, the tiny jade dragon pressed into her fist. She stopped as she passed the St. Agnes fair because it felt for a moment as if the dragon's wings had fluttered. She opened her hand. The dragon lay perfectly still. But she felt the fluttering sensation again as she reached the riverfront and a third time as she passed an outdoor café. This time when she opened her palm the dragon sat up, flexed its wings, and flew. It set down a few feet away from her on the shoulder of a man wearing a deep blue robe, who seemed not at all surprised to see it.

Lucinda studied the man curiously. He was tall, his black hair streaked with strands of silver. His face was unlined, tanned skin over high, chiseled cheekbones, a wide generous mouth, and a fine white scar that dropped in a straight diagonal from the outer corner of one eye to the corner of his mouth. Even to Lucinda, who'd been with many beautiful men and found their beauty quite beside the point, it was an interesting face. It was his eyes, she decided. The grey eyes looked as if they had seen their way through entire lifetimes, as if there was nothing that would ever surprise them.

Lucinda found that she wanted to know who he was. "What's your name?" she asked.

He'd had many. He debated a moment on which to use and then gave her the most recent. "Alasdair."

"Alasdair." She took that in. "How old are you?" she demanded, a little startled by her own question. Normally, she didn't ask such things. Normally, she didn't give a damn.

One corner of the man's mouth curved up. "It doesn't matter," he said. "I'm no wiser than I was ten years ago."

"Just more evasive?" Lucinda guessed. She noticed that he wore a leather thong around his neck with a single oblong crystal on it. She didn't recognize the stone, couldn't even tell what color it was; the slightest shift in light or shadow seemed to change it from black to green to purple to deep blue.

The jade dragon walked delicately to a point on his collarbone, flexed its wings, closed its eyes, then settled comfortably into what looked like a long-overdue nap.

"That's your dragon?" Lucinda asked.

"He often chooses to stay with me," the man answered. "Though I suspect he's stayed with you lately."

Lucinda nodded, then ran a hand through her long, disordered hair. This man, whoever he was, seemed to find nothing odd in a creature that was inanimate stone one moment, a living, breathing being the next. "When I first saw it, it was just a carving," she said carefully.

The man removed the dragon from his collarbone, gently lifted her wrist with his other hand, and set the dragon on her palm. It was an intricately carved piece of translucent green rock. A tiny scaled serpent with wings, claws, and a curving tail. It lay on her hand, cool and still and no more alive than any other bit of rock.

She handed it back with a shudder. "I haven't been sleeping well lately," she said. "My dreams have . . . gotten all mixed up in my days. And—"

"And you think the dragon was a dream?" he probed gently.

"Are you going to tell me it's alive?"

"Not if you're unwilling to hear it."

She was suddenly furious with him for standing there so calmly and asking her to believe that she was losing her mind. "Does it breathe fire?" she taunted.

"Not this particular dragon, no," the man answered. "He has other abilities. For example, he led you to me."

"No," she said, stepping back from him. "No one leads me anywhere." She studied him again. If she knew nothing else, she knew men. She could see through any man's charms to his weakness. This one was different though. There was something inside him she'd never seen before, something she had no words for and whatever it was frightened her. "I think there's something wrong with you," she told him.

He smiled humorlessly and his reply was almost a whisper. "Most assuredly."

She was on the verge of telling him to fuck off but she didn't quite dare. Instead, she spun away from him, walking rapidly toward the fair, losing herself in the crowds.

Alasdair's eyes followed her until she was out of sight. He gazed down at the jade dragon curled up in his open palm. "You are causing trouble," he told it.

In his palm the dragon opened one golden eye and winked.

LUCINDA STRODE BENEATH the wrought-iron arch whose lettering spelled out ST. AGNES FAIR, with barely a thought for the name that used to give her the willies. Her mother, who had taken up devout Catholicism after Lucinda's illegitimate birth, considered the martyred Agnes "a saint among saints" and had repeatedly told Lucinda about the young girl who "joyfully let the Romans cut off her beautiful little head rather than lose her virginity." Lucinda had always thought it one of the sickest stories she'd ever heard and concluded early on that virginity as a virtue was highly overrated. Then again, there was nothing about her mother's religious devotion that made sense; as far as Lucinda could tell, it hadn't ever done either one of them a shred of good. What, she couldn't help wondering, would her mother make of the man with the jade dragon? Paintings of St. George happily impaling dragons came to mind, and she decided it was better not to pursue that one.

Lucinda lost herself in the fair. There were booths selling silks and silver. A small man with fair hair and a reddened nose hawked old glass bottles. A rumpled, heavyset woman who reminded her uncomfortably of her mother sat behind baskets of pastries and meat pies, their scents mingling with the aromas of honeyed nuts and popcorn. A teenage boy with bad skin and a killer smile caught her hand and asked her to dance to the band that played by the water. Lucinda gave him a dance, determined to banish the images of the man in the cloak and the jade carving that came to life. It was the dreams, she told herself. They left her weakened and confused, vulnerable to believing just about anything.

When the teenage boy offered to take Lucinda on the Ferris wheel, she told him he was crazy and left him standing in the middle of the dancers. She continued to wander through the fair, afraid for the first time to go home on her own. Her apartment would seem empty without the little dragon, she realized, and then further realized that that was the most absurd thought she'd ever had. She wound up at the Dome, a small bar with a dome-shaped ceiling, drinking apricot liqueur and eating dark chocolates she'd bought at the fair.

At nearly three in the morning she let herself into her apartment. She was safe—too bleary and exhausted to dream or miss a small piece of jade.

In the middle of her unmade bed she found a rectangular cloisonné box, whose turquoise enamel work made her think of dragon scales. *I am losing my mind,* she thought as she stared at the unfamiliar box. She thought of Maxine, wondered briefly if someone had broken into her apartment, and found she didn't much care.

Lucinda stared at the box a long time before lifting it from the rumpled bedclothes. It was heavier than she'd expected, tarnished brass beneath the enamel. She lifted the lid, half-expecting one of those mysterious cascades of gems that everyone was talking about. Instead she found a single oval moonstone, glowing against a bed of midnight-blue velvet.

WHEN HE'D LEFT his home in the mountains Alasdair had taken nothing but the clothes on his back and the small leather pouch he'd been given on the day he came of age. The pouch had been white then, soft white deerskin.

Now after years of being carried, it was an unnamable shade, yellowed, with bits of grime rubbed into the finely creased skin—oils from his hands, dust from the mountains, whatever the dark particles were that floated through the city air. Only what was within the pouch remained unchanged as they had been for millennia—ten stones, the ones he'd been given to use and had called on ever since.

This night he returned to the apartment knowing there were only nine. He emptied the pouch, letting the stones roll into his palm: quartz, coral, turquoise, lapis lazuli, black opal, sapphire, emerald, golden topaz, and aquamarine. The moonstone was gone. It made him far more uncomfortable than he would have guessed, as if without it he could no longer be sure of its properties. His people believed that the stones you were given on the day you came of age were your life stones, companions of a lifetime. As far as he could tell, his people were wrong.

It was not the work of a thief, Alasdair reasoned. In Arcato, moonstones were not worth much money. Besides, a thief would have found more valuable baubles lying most anywhere in the apartment. The vacuum cleaner bag alone rattled with rubies. (They'd made themselves a little too plentiful the night before; he'd gotten annoyed and vacuumed them up.) The moonstone had not been vacuumed. And he had not lost it to carelessness. Alasdair could no more lose it unknowingly than he could lose an eye.

He examined the leather pouch a second time, still unwilling to believe that one of his life stones was gone. The moonstone's gifts were quiet ones, and yet there were times when he valued it more than the others combined. It was, among other things, the stone of tenderness. It scared Alasdair to think of himself bereft of its qualities.

A shift in the air made him look up. The dragon appeared on a window ledge. Extending one delicate clawed foot, it stepped into the room.

"You little thief," he said, understanding where the moonstone was and why. She had more need of it than he, and the dragon had always read needs very clearly. "Did you wrap it properly?" he inquired, unable to keep the anger out of his voice.

Though he'd come to Arcato with only the leather pouch and the clothing he wore, other objects had followed him from the mountains. One morning he returned to the apartment to find an oil lamp made of blown glass that had been in his mother's house. Another day he woke to see an iridescent crystal goblet given him by his first lover. He was grateful that it wasn't filled with her wine. A blue cloisonné box had followed the goblet, and that, too, was now missing he realized. The dragon had wrapped it properly indeed.

LUCINDA TOOK THE moonstone from its bed of midnight-blue velvet. She could not even feel the weight of the moonstone on her palm. There were many things she had not been able to feel lately—a bit of crystallized honey dissolving on her tongue, the last man who'd been inside her—and she wondered curiously if her prayers were actually being answered. Not that she worshipped the gods, but for years now she'd sent up one devout wish on a daily basis to any entity that might listen: She'd prayed to feel nothing at all. She ran her other palm along her hip, somewhat reassured that she could still feel the worn cotton of her petticoat. Then she ran her thumb along the cool, smooth surface of the stone. She should have known. She had, after all, been born out of favor; from the day of her birth it had been ordained that the gods would be deaf to her prayers.

It was nearly four in the morning and she was exhausted and half-crazed and staring at a small piece of translucent rock. She held it up beneath her lamp. The moonstone had a slight blue tint, as if she were holding a drop of seawater perfectly contained. A narrow arc of light gleamed near the top of the stone. She glanced out through the glass doors of her bedroom and then, curious, opened them and stepped out onto the narrow wrought-iron balcony. Below her the lights of the fair still burned, casting lines of gold in the river's black waters. Above her the waning moon was more than halfway through the night sky, its pale sliver of light a twin to the arc in the stone.

So what? Lucinda asked herself. What did it matter if the stone reflected the moon, the stars, or tiny dancing giraffes? She was too tired to wonder about the implications or how the moonstone had appeared on her bed in the first place. Back inside, she shut the doors that led to the balcony and set the moonstone on its bed of midnight blue.

That night Lucinda dreamed of being held in a man's arms, of being carried, of rolling through the darkness, his body fitted to hers. He held her, caressed her, read her needs as if he knew her heart. She never saw his face or heard his voice. But she knew his scent and taste and the cool lines of his limbs. She was enveloped and yet there was infinite space surrounding her. He was different from any man she'd ever been with. No man had ever been that gentle with her. No man had ever made her feel as if she'd been taken up by the sea.

THE WIND CHIMES woke Lucinda. A dry storm was sweeping away the night. The winds came down from the granite foothills, tore at the sides of her building, and whipped down through the narrow, curved streets to the flat, broad stretch of the Candra River. In the city the wind always ran to the

Candra, and Lucinda knew that when the storm had pulled the night after it
and taken it into the river's depths, the people of the city would wake to a
clear-washed morning.

But now the lavender glass in the fan-shaped window above her bed rattled in its frame, and on her balcony the thin metal cylinders of the wind
chimes crashed against each other until she was sure they would shatter. She
lay in bed listening to the storm, thinking that somehow it was a natural
conclusion to her dream. She drifted again, going into one of the old
dreams, its momentum driven by the winds.

AT FIRST SHE took the pounding on her door for more of the storm. The
wind, they said, belonged to Boreas, and she had cursed him just last week
when a milder storm had taken one of her scarves. It was not unheard of in
the city for the gods to take their revenge in most direct ways. And while
Lucinda had never had any sort of contact with the gods, she would not have
been surprised if one of them materialized for the sole purpose of avenging
himself on her.

She opened her eyes. It was still dark out, the winds still howling. Her
clock read 6:17. The pounding on her door continued, then developed a neat,
insistent, four-four rhythm. It had to be Tyrone.

Briefly, drowsily, she considered ignoring him. It would serve him right.
She didn't like being awakened before dawn on two hours' sleep. But she
knew Tyrone and she knew he wouldn't go away and she couldn't take
much more of his infernal pounding.

She slipped on a robe and opened the door. Tyrone leaned casually
against the door frame. He was wearing a tan linen suit, a pinstriped shirt,
and a Panama hat. An ebony fica hung from a gold chain around his neck.
As always, he looked as if he'd just returned from some tropical island
where one did nothing but drink frothy drinks laced with rum. How, she
wondered, had he managed to keep a hat on in the storm?

"I thought you had to be dead, girl," he told her, entering without invitation. He smelled of almonds today, a scent he varied with coconut.

Lucinda stepped out of his way. "Did you come to view the body?"

"I've already seen your body." Tyrone glanced around the untidy apartment and began tying back the heavy velvet curtains. "The storm's almost
over and the sun is rising," he announced. "Time for you to greet the day."

Lucinda sank down in a wicker chair draped in brocade and sullenly
took in the view. The winds were quieter, the sky a pale opalescent blue. It
did nothing to improve her mood. "Tyrone," she said in a flat voice, "get out
of here."

Tyrone lifted the phone. "I thought so. Unplugged again."

"Did you try to call?"

"Girl, you kept me waiting for four hours yesterday. I called you every twenty minutes. You're lucky I don't fire your sweet ass."

"Go ahead." Lucinda yawned, then favored him with a saccharine smile. "Since you just fired me, I think I'll go back to bed now."

"And deprive me of the pleasure of telling you how I've been up all night, sick with worry? Child, I looked for you all over this city. I checked every bar and seedy hotel. I chased down that no-good drummer you used to see, I called the morgue, I—"

"Spare me." Lucinda slumped deeper into the chair. She glanced at him curiously. "I did call in, you know."

"You mean, you called in the day before. Gave me some story about your dreams and how you needed a day off. And I, being the soul of generosity, said, 'Go ahead, babe. If you need the time, take it.' I didn't expect you to stand me up the very next day."

"I didn't stand you up."

Tyrone took off the Panama hat, revealing dozens of braids that fell along the sides of his face, making him look vaguely leonine. "Yesterday, I had three buyers at the studio," he informed her. "No one thought they were coming to a runway show complete with gossip columnists and caviar, but they did expect *someone* to model the skirts I spent the last three months draping over your bones."

"Yesterday is the day I called you," Lucinda said.

Tyrone shook his head slowly and emphatically, and Lucinda had the same sensation she'd had when she'd seen the jade dragon stir and take flight: that the solid ground beneath her had been quietly stolen, leaving her on a phantom surface that dissolved frequently and without warning. "Yesterday morning I called you," she repeated. "Last night I went to the fair and the Dome and came home late. I fell asleep around four. I had all of two hours' sleep before you started pounding on my door."

Tyrone shot her a look of contempt, sauntered into her kitchen, and began to make coffee. He didn't speak again until he tried to find a clean cup, and then it was only to say, "Girl, don't you ever wash your dishes?"

He rinsed a mug, filled it with coffee brewed to kick, and handed it to her.

She made a face at the mug. "I don't drink it black. I need cream."

"Not this morning, you don't. You drink that, and then we're going to try and understand how you managed to lose an entire day of *my* life."

Lucinda sipped judiciously at the black coffee, and Tyrone made an enormous effort to be patient and rational, although neither quality came easily to him. But in the end all they could figure out was that Lucinda had just slept straight through the last twenty-eight hours. She did not mention either the jade dragon or the moonstone in its cloisonné box.

"You using again?" Tyrone asked.

Lucinda glared at him from narrowed eyes.

"All right, no drugs. Then what's going on?"

"I don't know," she said honestly. "I've been feeling a little . . . strange."

He gave a hard, dry laugh. "'Cinda, baby, *I'm* strange. Always have been. *You* walked in from another place altogether."

Lucinda massaged her forehead with her fingertips, then made a last, futile attempt to drink the bitter coffee. "Will you please get out of here?"

"All right, babe." He reached for the Panama hat. "But I expect to see you in the studio today at ten."

She saw him to the door. "Didn't anyone ever tell you expectations are just setups for disappointment?"

"Ten A.M., girl, or I'll come make you coffee every morning at dawn."

"I'll be there," she said with a groan.

"I know you will." He kissed her on the forehead and disappeared down the stairs with a fluid wave of his hand.

Lucinda closed the door behind him and began to run a bath in the old claw-footed tub. She scented it with lavender, cedar, and rosemary. Then she sank into the steaming water and closed her eyes.

ALASDAIR LEFT THE apartment at midnight, well into Hekate's hours. She was present tonight. He had felt her from the moment the sun sank beneath the horizon, had seen her in the waning crescent of the moon, had heard her owls calling from the hills. Normally, Hekate preferred to stay in the wilds or with her dead. But she'd come into the city just last week at the bequest of a boat full of sailors from her native land. And it made sense that she'd be comfortable here. The city was, after all, a crossroads of sorts, and she a goddess of crossroads.

Arcato, he reflected, drew a strange choir of gods, nearly as many as there were types of goods shipped into the harbor. They sailed in with the boats, asleep in freight compartments or prancing along catwalks. They took the sails for trampolines and did balancing acts on crows' nests. They reclined in old steamers, playing endless, dissolute hands of cards. Most of them left again with the merchants and sailors who'd brought them, but some took an extended shore leave. At the moment the city was practically teeming with deities. He could walk ten consecutive city blocks, and each would have a different feel to it; each would be under the influence of a different god. It was causing a certain amount of commotion among the people. The gods themselves were doing what they normally did when too many of them gathered in one place—they were enjoying the resulting chaos, contributing to it as a sort of divine recreation.

Hekate was a different matter, for when she walked all others belonged to her. She was the night and absorbed them all. And while Alasdair had spent enough time under her cloak to have lost most of his fear of her, he knew what she did to others. Since her arrival he'd watched the papers carefully, to see if there were outbreaks of nightmares or prophecies, hauntings or worse. But there was no real shift he could detect. Everyone was too busy uncovering small caches of gems. He was, despite himself, providing a distraction of sorts. And she was, he decided, treading delicately.

He wound his way down to the riverfront, ignoring what sounded like an owl calling from the foothills. It was a weeknight, and except for the fair and the occasional howling of dogs, Arcato was quiet. The dark silhouette of a freighter pushed through the water to the pier. Idly, he tried to sense what it carried. Spices of some sort as well as items small and electronic. To him it was a cargo of exotica, goods that had never been known in his mountains.

Over the centuries his people had found their way to the city to trade. They appeared one at a time with goods of their own. Usually they posed as antique dealers, purveyors of rare oils or hand-loomed fabrics, often trading the very objects they'd traded for decades ago. Rarely did they barter the gems.

Alasdair walked down to the water's edge where he stood studying the reflections of the city's electric lights, elongated gold script on a black, viscous tablet. A wave of irritation went through him as he felt a familiar sensation: stones falling—rather, springing—to the ground. Hematite, this time: shiny, polished bits of black and blood-red metal, a stone that had always belonged to the god of war. He wondered if, when the stones were found, anyone would recognize them for what they were. Aggression, he reflected, was not what the city needed.

He knew he shouldn't leave the stones lying there. He would have gladly cast the glittering orbs into the water if it would have done any good. He knew that more would only fall. The hematite wanted out tonight; it was as simple as that. Still, he tried calling them back. They ignored his call, preferring to bask under the night sky, taking in the sounds of the waterfront, winking back at the electric lights. He had lost the moonstone and was now surrounded by hematite, of all things. It depressed him no end.

ALASDAIR LOST TRACK of how long he stood by the Candra. Long enough to see the lights of the fair go out one by one. Long enough to leave a square of waterfront newly paved with hematite, to feel the entire city breathing in rhythm with Hekate. She was growing stronger by the second. Her power would wax until the night had reached its darkest hour. And as the night drew on, the ghosts of her dead would stir. He'd seen Hekate's dead before and had no wish to repeat the experience tonight.

He sketched a slight, respectful bow to her and he turned to go. He stopped himself, remembering that it was wise to leave food at her cross-roads. He reached into his cloak and found only a candy bar he'd purchased from the five-and-ten. It was hardly a magnanimous offering but better than nothing.

He turned back to the water as he heard a faint clicking sound that he identified as hematite traveling across the pavement. Indeed, quite a number of the stones were rolling to one particular point on the riverbank. They were congregating, he realized, magnetized by something that was hovering at the water's edge.

Years ago he had been taught to identify patterns of energy, and now he could just make out wire-thin traces of color against the charcoal night sky. He'd seen patterns like this before and they never boded well. This one was a faint but distinct reverberation of something that had happened here in the past. Quite some time ago, he guessed, and yet the event had had tremendous energy, so much so that years later traces of it remained. In some cases, he reflected, it was a great pity that energy could not be destroyed. He watched it hover at the water's edge. It was as distinctive as a fingerprint and more conclusive, a perfectly preserved remnant, woven of the event itself. It was difficult for him to read exactly what had occurred, but it involved blood and iron—which explained why the hematite was making itself at home. Someone had been murdered here.

Drawing up the collar of his cloak, he began the steep ascent from the waterfront. A young boy ran past him, racing for the river, disturbingly familiar. The boy was no more than eleven, pale and thin with straight brown hair that covered his eyes. It still surprised him that children here roamed on their own so late at night. He'd seen this one the other day at the fair, he realized, when he was searching for the dragon. Concerned for the dragon, he hadn't really been paying attention to the crowds. He'd registered the boy in his peripheral vision, noting only that the child was nearly hollow with hunger and that the hunger had little to do with when the boy had eaten his last meal.

THE BOY, WHOSE name was Michael Fortunato, didn't even see the stranger in the cloak. He'd been running clear from the other side of the city. His breath was coming in short, hard gasps, and a searing pain blazed through his side. His mother said that meant his liver was slamming against his rib cage. "Running ruins your liver," she'd said, meaning her gin and vodka and whiskey didn't. Michael thought his mother was full of shit, but something inside him was definitely getting bruised. Maybe destroyed. He'd figured that one out. That sometimes when he thought he was just getting hurt, he was really getting destroyed.

He slowed to a walk. He didn't even know why he'd come to the river to-night except that there wasn't any other place he wanted to be. He looked out across the water, waiting for his heartbeat to return to normal. The Can-dra was black and still and full of secrets. He wasn't afraid of it; he'd hid out down here before. Michael shivered as the night wind tore through his jacket and stuck a hand right up between his ribs, cool and knowing, going straight inside him. It eased the ache from running. It filled the part of him that always seemed empty. He sucked in a lungful of dank air smelling of garbage soaked with river water. Anyone else would say he was warped, but he liked that smell. It was more honest than his mother's perfume, sicker than her cigarettes.

Something was shining on the ground, right next to the toe of his sneaker. He shook his head in disbelief. Just like all the bullshit stories about jewels. The whole damn city acted like it was in the middle of some kind of fairy tale. Rubies in restaurants, pearls in church pews. It was enough to make him puke. Everyone telling themselves stories and then telling everyone else. It was a city of liars. Not one of 'em would know the truth if it punched him in the face. At least *he* didn't go making up stories about finding sapphires in his socks.

But something was glittering on the pavement. He looked down and around, and when he was convinced that no one was watching, bent and scooped up a handful of stones. He held them up under one of the lights. They weren't diamonds, that was for sure. He ought to just throw 'em in the river. But he didn't. He rolled the bits of shiny red and black rock along his palm. Then he slipped them into his pocket. The night was still inside him, easing the fire, filling him with something cool and dark and strong. For just a second the lights along the riverfront dimmed. It was as if the night had suddenly dropped a thick, soft cloak of darkness over everything, a black-ness so dense it muffled even electricity. Michael wondered uneasily if this night was really darker than others. And then he had a crazy thought—that it was and he might never see daybreak again. He felt himself trembling as a wave of pure terror swept through him. He didn't know where it had come from or why, but the fear was so strong, so overwhelming, that he *knew* that something was out there and it wanted him. It had been after him all along. Tonight it would get him.

Then the terror passed, easing into a familiar, vague sense of everything being off, skewed, screwed. He pushed it aside. Something else was shimmering at the edge of the river. It was like the outline of a person, almost as if a figure had been sketched in the black air and was now hovering there over the water. He rubbed his eyes. The outline was still there, clear against the night sky—it was an older boy, maybe seventeen, bare-chested and barefooted, wearing a bandanna tied around his neck and a thick gold ring through one ear. His eyes studied Michael as if to say, "I know you." He was not real, and he was more real than anyone Michael had ever seen.

"Michael, you sleaze." The voice was a quavering whisper. "On your knees, asshole. Confess your sins and say good-bye 'cause this is the end."

Fear faded into irritation. He knew that voice, and it wasn't anything to be scared of. "Very fucking funny," he said. "Spook, that you?"

The outline at the edge of the water disappeared, and a boy his height, his skull covered with fine white fuzz, stepped out of the shadows, one skeletal finger pointing at Michael.

"You know what you look like?" Michael said. "This picture in one of my mother's prayer books. It shows the Angel of Death. He's this skeleton dude, all dressed up in a hooded robe. And he's pointing a bony finger at this guy who's cowering on the ground."

Spook acted like he hadn't heard any of that. He stooped down and picked up a candy bar that was lying on the pavement.

Michael wondered briefly if Spook felt that angel pointing at him. Spook was supposed to die a year ago. Had some kind of cancer. For two years now he'd been cruising downhill on the slide of his own death, reckless and cruel and unafraid. Nothing scared him, because there wasn't anything anyone could do to him that was worse than what was happening day by day. He said he didn't even believe death could get him anymore.

Casually, Spook unwrapped the candy bar and ate it. Then he crumpled the wrapper into a ball and tossed it into the water. He stepped toward Michael. His eyes were runny, and there was a brown crust around the edges of his mouth. "You're not on your knees," he said.

"How come you're not dead yet?" Michael shot back.

Spook smiled briefly. He had a smile that never lasted more than a quarter of a second, even before he got sick. "I'm not gonna die." He reached into the pocket of the jeans that hung loose on his frame and pulled out a plastic bottle. He opened it and tiny red pills spilled into his palm—tiny red pills and an oval faceted white stone that caught the light of the streetlamps and sent it back, sparkling.

"It's not real," Michael said at once.

"Is too."

"Then you stole it and put it in that bottle. You're as demented as everyone else in this city." Michael walked away from him, headed toward the water where he'd seen that shape. Spook didn't interest him, but he wanted another look at whatever had been flickering there above the Candra. Some kind of ghost, he decided, a notion that both scared and intrigued him.

"This diamond's gonna save me," Spook announced loudly. "I'm gonna sell it and get out of this damn city and then I won't be sick no more."

"Right," Michael said. "Whatever you want to believe." Somewhere inside he knew that taunting Spook with his own death was cruel. But he couldn't help it. They all did it. It was what you did when Spook was around.

Spook caught up with him and grabbed him by the shoulder. "I told you, *you're* the one who dies tonight."

Michael pulled away easily. "Fuck off," he told the other boy. "Find someone else to haunt."

Spook's hand shot out, cupped the back of Michael's head, and pulled it close to his own. Michael swallowed hard, forcing himself not to gag. The other boy's breath stank of medicine and decay. "You and all the others," Spook said. "You treat me like I'm already gone."

Michael jerked away. "You are."

"*You* are," Spook said quietly. He held out his other hand, extending it toward the Candra. And Michael saw something he didn't believe. That figure that had been there dancing over the river came back. He was still just an outline; Michael could see the black water right through him. But in his hand was a knife, the kind you use to slit open fish. Casually, the figure tossed the knife to Spook.

Spook caught it with one of his lightning smiles.

Michael backed away, talking fast. "No—Spook, come on, man. Listen, I wasn't serious. I was only—"

But the white-haired boy wasn't listening. One thin hand shot out, grabbed Michael's jacket, and pulled him close. Spook's face was calm, his expression almost blank, as he ripped the blade in a short, hard line, straight across Michael's bare throat.

Michael felt a line of fire around his throat then blood streaming down his neck. It burned like hell. Somehow he never really thought that getting cut would hurt. And everything was going weird. That thick, solid darkness was back, the lamps by the waterside gone. All he could see were Spook's eyes, a pale blue against the black night, like he had some kind of light glowing inside him. And right behind Spook, the see-through man dancing on the water. Michael cursed as he felt something he hadn't felt since he was five—a hot, stinging stream of piss soaking his pants leg as his bladder lost control. He was shaking now, trying to banish the terror with disbelief. This wasn't happening, any of it. It couldn't. Spook's eyes got paler, lighter as he raised the blade again. And in their light Michael read that all of this was for real.

$\mathcal{T}wo$

LUCINDA SHRUGGED OUT of her clothing and ran another bath. She had gone to the studio today, had soothed Tyrone's ruffled feathers, had even bought fabric for him at a good price. She had a far better eye for fabric than he did, though he was too vain to admit it. Afterward she'd gone back to the Dome where she met a man who told her he had a boat and was setting sail for an island near the equator. He told her, with a look of frank, lusty appreciation, that he could use a good woman on board. She told him she wasn't a good woman, and she wasn't interested in being used. She went home with someone else, a young, underweight student-type who worked in a laboratory fooling with weather instruments. To her surprise he talked of Boreas; of thunder sent by Thor; of Agni, the Hindu god who was, among other things, lightning; and of Chac, a Mayan deity, who liked to be offered the hearts of wild animals in exchange for the gift of his rain, and was not getting his fill in the city. The young man said, rather apologetically, that he knew such presences existed, but he had trouble providing his fellow scientists with empirical proof. Lucinda told him he worked too hard, and had him take her to his pristine apartment. He'd watched astounded as she'd ripped the blanket and sheets from his tightly made bed and thrown them into the air, so they'd landed in a great unruly mound. Then she'd settled in, making herself comfortable. He was a decent lay, sweet and considerate, but there was something inside her that he would never match or even reach, and they both knew it.

Now as she sank beneath iridescent foam scented with jasmine, she thought of his long, pale hands as they lay across her belly. *I've been with worse,* she thought.

The jade dragon flew in through the open bathroom door and perched on the rim of the tub. The pale green reflection of his wings shone on the white enamel.

The heat of the bath combined with the aftermath of sex made her drowsy, too relaxed to be startled by an animated piece of rock. "Where've you been?" she asked it. "With the guy in the blue robe?"

The dragon opened its wings, hovered above bath water, and settled on a large soap bubble, which it proceeded to ride around the perimeter of the tub.

Lucinda watched it with amusement. "I'm glad you're back, you know."

The dragon knew. It left the bubble to sit on her knee.

"Who is he?" she asked it. "Alasdair."

She half-expected the dragon to begin speaking and to be a fast-tongued wicked gossip, besides. But the dragon just gazed at her with unblinking golden eyes.

The bathwater was getting cold. Gently, Lucinda set the dragon back on the rim of the tub. She could feel drops of condensation on the cool jade. It sat unmoving, lifeless stone again. She reached for a bath sheet, wrapped it around her, and stepped out of the tub, mindful not to upset the little statue. But as she walked barefoot to her bedroom, she felt tiny claws take careful hold of the skin on her shoulder. She fell asleep with the dragon curled up on the pillow beside her.

JUST BEFORE DAWN broke, Alasdair left his apartment and walked the ten blocks to the newsstand on Pennington Street, where he purchased his morning papers. There was another newsstand closer to his flat, but he liked the cheerful, middle-aged woman who ran this one. He knew nothing about her other than she managed to greet everyone who came into her shop with a warmth so genuine and expansive that his daily visit with her always left him feeling as if he'd received some sort of benediction.

"And how are you this morning?" she asked as he handed her the coins to pay for the paper.

"Well, thank you," he replied. "And you?"

"Splendid," she told him, sounding as though nothing could please her more than to be peddling newsprint at five in the morning. Her glance slid to the paper in his hand. "Though the news could be better."

Alasdair nodded noncommittally. As usual, he'd folded the paper, not daring to look at it until he was back home. He walked uphill swiftly, aware of the rounded bits of chrysoprase trickling from his coat to the street, and telling himself all the while that it was all right. Chrysoprase, often confused with green plastic, did not look particularly valuable. Apple-green and slightly fluorescent, it was a stone usually in need of proper craft. He'd spent hours working it—cutting, setting, even carving it once, as he'd learned to carve cinnabar. The chrysoprase was, of course, more than three times as hard as cinnabar and ten times as stubborn. It had a good deal to say about what it was he carved. (He'd wanted a ship, it had wanted a plum tree; they'd compromised on a cypress wood at the edge of the sea.) And yet for all that, it was a merry stone, a gift in times of joy. It wasn't such a bad thing to put into the streets of Arcato.

He let himself back into the flat, shed his coat and a last obstinate chunk of the chrysoprase. Standing at his window, he watched the sun rise over the hills behind the city. It was very different from the mountain sunrises he'd grown up with, and yet there was a sameness—the way the hills became a flat black silhouette, all their definition gone, with only the very top of the ridge clear against the new light.

Today the sky went from grey to a gentle coral tinged with streaks of gold. *Perhaps it will be a good day,* he told himself. He opened the paper still in his hand, and an unutterable heaviness went through him as he saw what he'd been expecting for a while now. WATERFRONT KILLING ran the banner headline. With a growing sense of dread, he read the account of a twelve-year-old boy knifed to death the night before. The killer was eleven. When asked why he'd done it, he'd replied, "I was scared. He was trying to kill me. And he was gonna die anyway."

The victim, identified as Kevin "Spook" Williams, was dying of bone cancer. A photograph showed a painfully thin boy, his nearly bare skull covered with white-blond fuzz. His killer, one Michael Fortunato, claimed that the other boy had eaten a candy bar he'd found on the ground, then he'd pulled a knife and went for his throat. The police confirmed that Fortunato's throat had been cut, through not deeply.

The article became more unnerving. In a pill bottle in the dead boy's pocket, a single brilliant-cut diamond was found. *Which did what?* Alasdair wondered. Probably gave the boy some sort of false hope, perhaps even the illusion of power. The other boy, the killer, had some sort of red and black stones on him; he said they'd been on the ground by the waterfront. He'd just picked them up. That one was self-evident.

Alasdair read on. Two rust-covered fish-scaling knives were found at the scene of the murder, one embedded in the dead boy's chest. When asked where the knives came from, the boy who killed him answered, "Someone gave 'em to us."

Strangest of all was the earring. The boy who survived had handed the police a thick, gold earring, saying, "It's for Spook's family." A police specialist had appraised the earring. It was soft, heavy gold, nearly pure, of a consistency common about two hundred years ago. The earring was the sort sailors used to wear to pay for burial at sea.

The police were holding onto both the earring and the diamond, as both were obviously stolen. The killer, who showed no remorse, was being remanded to a juvenile facility and child psychiatrists. The article concluded with the usual rhetorical breast-beating: What kind of city is this in which children commit murder? Where are we going wrong in raising our young? What could possibly make a child kill?

Alasdair let the paper drop to the floor. He could think of quite a few things that made children kill. He wondered how many of them the boy hadn't mentioned to the police. He thought about what the boy had told them.

He'd been scared. Of course. The cement pilings beneath the pier probably trembled at Hekate's presence last night.

He'd picked up the hematite. In doing so he'd aligned himself with Mars, a killer if ever there was one.

Spook was going to die anyway. He'd even eaten Hekate's offering. He'd belonged to her well before the knives. Alasdair was willing to wager that not only the knives but the earring had arrived on the scene courtesy of Hekate. It would be typical of the goddess to supply the murder weapon and then thoughtfully offer payment for the funeral. Hekate never hesitated to take what was rightfully hers, nor did she act without honor.

Alasdair opened his hand and sent out a silent call. Within seconds his palm was covered with small bits of metallic black and red, catching the light of the early morning sun.

He held them, considering. To him hematite had always been an aggressive stone. Like most rock, it held history and memory. He concentrated on the stones in his hand, wondering if perhaps these might yield something different. With the ease of long practice he opened what he thought of as the hearts of the stones, then read their memories as others read books. It was the same as always. In even the smallest bit of hematite he heard swords clashing and the screams of the dying. In each he saw rivers of dark red blood soaking into the earth.

He let the hematite run from his hand onto the floor. "Take yourselves somewhere," he told them, and was relieved to see them dispersing to other parts of the apartment.

There were those, he reflected in an effort to be objective, who claimed hematite for a medicine, healing diseases of the blood and of the eyes. Personally, he'd never known that to be true, yet even he could not blame the stones for what had happened last night. The hematite only accelerated things. Some would say it opened a door. But it was no more the cause than the diamond. The death would have happened one way or another.

Still, the stones had played their part. *He* had a played a part. Could he have stopped it, he wondered. The dragon, who'd materialized sometime in the last half hour and now reclined in a shallow alabaster bowl, gave him a look that clearly said, "Oh, don't be ridiculous."

Alasdair knew full well there was nothing he could do to counter Hekate. But he could have intercepted the boy who ran past him. He could have turned him back, coaxed him into going home. Or perhaps he might have sat up with him in a coffee shop, pretending the child was an adult or someone who interested him—anything to keep him from the event that was.

Most of all he regretted that the boy had been so scared. That was the part Alasdair wished he could undo. Hekate had not only claimed her dead, she'd spawned a young killer to serve him up. It had been a swift delivery, he was sure. Those born from the womb of terror moved with uncanny speed.

"Was that necessary, Lady?" he asked softly. "Will you use him to kill again?"

Alasdair read the article a second time, and made a mental note of where and when Spook's funeral would be held. The dragon fluttered down onto the newspaper. The tip of its jade tail pointed to a line he'd ignored. "Oh, all right," he said, and made another note, this one of where the boy who'd killed was being held.

ALASDAIR HELD A brief conference with the stones, asking them this once to contain themselves. Then he went to see Michael Fortunato, explaining to the child protection services that he was the boy's Uncle Ivor. Apparently, the boy's mother, his only parent, had not yet shown up, and after making his statement to the police the boy refused to talk to anyone. Uncle Ivor was welcomed with a brisk, clinical air that did little to conceal the social worker's profound relief.

A stout woman dressed in a nubby red sweater and tan pants led him from an office to a large adjoining building, enclosed by barbed wire. Michael was locked in a room by himself. The room had a metal door with a tiny window made of wire sandwiched between layers of glass. Alasdair peered through it and saw a thin boy with a bandaged throat slumped on a narrow cot. The long brown hair that had covered his eyes was gone, shorn as short as his victim's. He was staring at the wall, as if waiting for a television to materialize. He didn't look up as Alasdair was let into the room. But he did wait for the door to swing shut before saying, "I don't have a fucking uncle Ivor."

"Yes," Alasdair said. "I'm well aware of that."

"Then who are you?"

"I'm someone who believes that you told the police less than half the truth."

The boy continued to gaze at the wall, studiedly ignoring him.

Undiscouraged, Alasdair continued, "Who was the 'someone' who gave you the knives? He wasn't your average sort of fellow, was he?"

Michael shot him an annoyed look, which Alasdair took to mean that he was getting warm.

"Whoever gave you the knives also gave you the earring," he went on. He stopped as he saw that the boy was glaring at him now, his thin body rigid with fury. "Why so angry?" he asked. "I thought you'd be relieved to know that there's at least one person in this city who knows what you saw down there."

"What?"

" 'Ghost' is probably the closest word for it," Alasdair told him. "He was transparent, right?"

The boy nodded, his eyes still wary.

"He not only gave you the knives, but he gave you the earring and—"

Michael cut him off with a low hiss. "Who told you?"

Alasdair shrugged, feeling like a third-rate charlatan. Any moment now, the child would expect him to pull a rabbit from a hat. "Perhaps I've seen a few ghosts in my time." When the boy was silent he went on. "I know, for example, that the ghost not only gave you the earring, he told you to give it to Spook's family. I doubt it was something you would have done on your own. You didn't like Spook very much, did you?"

"He tried to kill me," Michael replied.

"Yes," Alasdair said, "I believe that, too." He looked around the small, bare cell. "This place is ugly."

"It's okay," the boy muttered. "At least it doesn't have all those damn calendars with saints staring down at you from every wall." He gave Alasdair a calculating look. "Spook was gonna die anyway." The sentence had the flat ring of an official statement, one that had been repeated too many times.

"Yes," Alasdair agreed. "Spook was claimed by Hekate, goddess of night and darkness and queen of ghosts. The ghost you saw was one of her dead, calling for another. And those rocks you picked up . . . they stoke aggression."

"You actually believe all that?"

"I should think you would, too, after what happened by the river. Didn't you know that was no normal night?"

The boy was silent for a while as he reached the inevitable conclusion. "You're saying it wasn't my fault. It was the stones, right?"

"No," Alasdair replied firmly. "It's never that simple. Another person in your place would not have been the agent of death. Someone else would have fled or talked Spook out of it or tossed the knife back to the ghost. There were, as always, many possibilities. You chose the bloodiest. On the other hand, there were certain conditions that made it easy for you to do so."

Michael made a show of being absorbed by a scab on his arm, which he began to pick.

Alasdair tried again. "Hekate also rules crossroads and hidden things. Whether or not they are conscious of it, people who find themselves at Hekate's crossroads—as you were—are often there because they have a choice to make. I've never understood why, but sometimes we need to go into darkness and chaos in order to make certain choices. You have another choice before you now, and as you've blundered into Hekate's most negative aspect, you have the right to ask that she show you her more benign aspect and help you in seeking what's hidden. If you are aware—"

"I don't believe in that Hekate shit," the boy broke in. "I killed Spook because he was going to kill me first. I'm not sorry. I'd do it again."

Alasdair sent up a fervent prayer for patience, a quality that eluded him when confronting those who asserted their right to cruelty. "Spook's death can't be undone," he said at last. "And I do know you'd do it again. That's why I'm here."

"Why?" Michael asked, his tone bored.

"Because you've got to choose now. Unless what you *want* is to be a killer, you are going to have to choose deliberately, consciously not to kill again. Do you understand?"

A sudden glimmer of interest flickered in the boy's eyes, and for a moment Alasdair believed he was listening. But what he asked was, "You can get me out of here, can't you?"

"I don't know," Alasdair told him honestly. "But I won't even try if I think you'll take another life."

"What if I say I'll be good and then I kill again?" Michael taunted. He had to push him, Alasdair knew. He had to see how far he could go. "I mean, some of those stones just might show up again, or there could be another weird Hekate night or more knife-throwing ghosts or—"

"If I get you out," Alasdair said softly, "and if you kill again, I'll find you and I'll end you. I give you my word."

The boy gave him a disturbing feral smile. "You've killed, too, haven't you?"

Alasdair stood up and knocked on the door, signaling that he was ready to leave. He hesitated. "I almost forgot. I have a gift for you." From within his coat he took a cloudy yellow stone. A white line gleamed inside its smooth rounded surface.

He handed it to the child who made no move to take it but said, "What is it?"

"It's called cymophane or chrysoberyl cat's eye."

"What's it worth?"

"I have no idea. Probably not very much. Chrysoberyl is somewhat rare but this one isn't what's considered gem quality."

"Then why are you giving it to me?"

Alasdair hesitated, sensing it wasn't wise to tell the boy of the stone's protective qualities. Nor could he explain that the stone was useful for centering and calming the mind, opening into one's sense of self-worth, intensifying empathy, and allowing forgiveness. All of that, he knew, would simply draw the boy's ire. So he said only, "Take it."

Michael reached for the stone and glanced at it briefly. "Great. I'm locked up for murder, and this weirdo I've never seen tells people he's my uncle and gives me this stupid rock that's not worth anything."

"You have need," Alasdair said gently. "And it's a far better gift than the knife that killed Spook. Hold onto it for a while and see."

He rapped on the door and waited for the woman in the red sweater to fetch him. He offered the boy one last explanation, doubting it would do any more good than the others had. "The stone was not given to you for commerce," he said. "If you try to sell it, it will leave you."

The woman opened the door and he left the cell. Michael's screams followed them down the hall, "He's a liar! I don't have an uncle Ivor! I don't have any fucking uncles!"

She turned to Alasdair with a weary, questioning glance.

He shrugged and stated the obvious, "The boy needs help."

ALASDAIR TOOK HIMSELF to Josefina's, a badly lit bar that served fresh sandwiches, decent beer, and excellent cappuccino. Though the neighborhood was industrial and depressed—the juvenile detention hall was less than a block away—Josefina's was clearly a home away from home for the elderly men who gathered there every morning to sit at the small, square tables and play endless games of chess, dominoes, or cards.

Alasdair ordered a cappuccino and counted himself fortunate when he found an open table. He took a seat, aware that a garnet and a peridot had chosen to remain on the counter when he'd placed his order. No one seemed to be paying attention; even the waitress had barely acknowledged his presence, which allowed him to hope that perhaps no one would link the stones to him. And if they did? They'd probably be as impressed as Michael Fortunato had been with the cymophane. The visit with the boy had left the bitter taste of failure in Alasdair's mouth. To Michael he was a fraud, and at the moment he could think of no evidence that might prove otherwise.

"Gideon!" A strong hand clapped him on the shoulder, and then a bulky form wearing a thick sheepskin jacket made his way around the table and pulled out the other chair. "Would I be imposing?"

"Not at all," Alasdair responded, more from surprise and innate good manners than from truth. One of the reasons he'd chosen to live in Arcato was because almost no one in the city knew him. It was hard to be gracious about having his anonymity breached, especially by one who seemed almost perversely hale and cheerful.

Something in Alasdair's tone must have betrayed his feelings. The big man took a step back and said softly, "I see I would be imposing. I'll find another seat."

"No. Please, Johari, join me," Alasdair said quickly. "I was just—preoccupied. I didn't mean to be rude." Johari, whose people, like Alasdair's, lived in the mountains, was an acquaintance from his boyhood. And gauging by the fact that Johari had addressed him by one of his earlier names, Alasdair realized it had been a long time since they'd seen each other.

With a somewhat doubtful look, Johari settled himself in a chair. He had coppery skin and a lined, weather-beaten face, and when he placed a thick arm on the table, the table wobbled on the uneven floorboards. Observing the etiquette of the mountains, he and Alasdair each established that the other and his relations were well. That taken care of, Johari said, "Our elders were right; there is, indeed, a great deal that can be foreseen if we only pay attention. I should have known I'd run into you here."

Alasdair stiffened imperceptibly. Did Johari somehow know that he'd been to visit Michael Fortunato? Did he suspect him of being connected to Spook's death?

"Why?" Alasdair kept his voice neutral. "Why would you think I'd be here?"

"Not in this bar necessarily but in Arcato," Johari explained. "And not you necessarily, as much as one of your kind."

Johari took a bright blue polished turquoise from inside his jacket. He laid it on the table between them. He fished into the pocket again and this time set down a jagged aquamarine crystal. "Found the first in front of the library, the second in a stairwell. And you know I'm not the type who normally stumbles on gems."

Alasdair did know. His people referred to Johari's as the Sinpiedras, those "without stones." The appellation was both a crude jibe, remaining from a time generations ago when their peoples had been enemies, and a statement of fact. The Sinpiedras, who had many esoteric skills, had no ability at all for working with the stones. It was typical that the amulet that Johari wore around his neck looked like an ancient stamped bronze coin, rather than the stone amulets Alasdair's people favored.

A waitress appeared at their table with Alasdair's cappuccino. Johari asked if she could bring him a glass of tomato juice with a slice of lemon and a stick of celery.

"Still an ascetic," Alasdair observed as the waitress moved off. "You do realize that you're depriving yourself of the best cappuccino in the city?"

"It's not a matter of deprivation," Johari assured him. "We just find it easier to do our work when we keep things simple. Caffeine, alcohol, grains, some of the herbs your people have been known to ingest, they tend to cloud things, confuse the frequencies."

"Undoubtedly," Alasdair agreed, amused. Whereas Alasdair's people tended to understand the world through what they learned from the stones, the Sinpiedras worked with tone frequency and harmonics.

"So what will turquoise and aquamarine do for me?" Johari asked with more interest than Alasdair would have expected.

"Well, many things. Turquoise is often considered a protective stone. It's been known to protect a rider from falling from a horse."

Johari gave a derisive snort. "If I fall from a horse, that's my own fault for not controlling the beast, now, isn't it? I don't need a piece of blue rock to keep me safe." This statement did not surprise Alasdair. The Sinpiedras, who had once been a raiding nomadic people, were still exceptional riders. Johari pushed the turquoise across the table to Alasdair. "I'll take my chances without."

Alasdair shrugged and took the turquoise. It was, he could tell, indignant at having been so rudely dismissed. "The aquamarine," he went on, "is a good stone for travelers. It's also potent against demons and dark spirits."

Johari grinned and turned the stone over with rough, callused fingers. "Now that might be useful. I can always use help when it comes to wrestling with the spirits."

"Many demons around lately?" The question was only half-facetious.

"You know we don't discuss our rituals." Johari became silent as the waitress set his juice and celery stick on the table. He waited until she had gone before asking, "What are you doing here, so far from the Source Place? I mean, aside from adding to the mineral content of the city."

"I've—" Alasdair hesitated, searching for the right words. "I needed to be out of the mountains. I've been gone nearly six years."

"You stayed away by your own choice?" Johari's tone indicated that he found this nearly unthinkable.

"It was necessary. I've only been in Arcato this last month. Before that I was traveling."

Johari held the aquamarine up to the small candle that flickered on the table. "And now that you're here, you leave your stones everywhere."

"I try not to," Alasdair said, sounding more apologetic than he meant, "but the stones have a will of their own."

"So do animals," Johari said, "and yet we control them."

It was, Alasdair thought, one of the root differences between their peoples. The Sinpiedras sought to master what they encountered and usually did so quite successfully, while his people tried to work with their surroundings and were often far less precise in their outcomes.

"When I was a boy," Alasdair said, "there was a time I threatened to run away and join your people."

"Did you?" Johari seemed to find this humorous.

"Working with the stones had gotten very frustrating," Alasdair remembered. "I told my mother I was going to join your people and learn to break a horse and then I'd have something that came when I called and carried me when I tired."

"I don't remember you in our camps. She stopped you?"

"No, the stones did. Jade did."

"Ah, that's when your little companion came into your life."

Alasdair nodded.

"Is he with you still?"

"At times. He's another one who can't be commanded. He's always had an agenda of his own."

"Like the spirits." Johari chewed meditatively on his celery stick. "I'll tell you this much. I've sensed some sort of . . . disturbance . . . in Arcato."

"One disturbance? From what I can tell, there's something going awry at nearly every corner."

Johari didn't take offense. "Yes, well, there are many influences. Some of it can be ascribed to the gods behaving badly, as they are wont to do. But some of it—" He looked up at Alasdair and for the first time in the years they'd known each other, Alasdair saw fear in Johari's eyes. "Some of it feels familiar to me. Things that should be used for good turned to another purpose."

"Such as . . ."

The big man spread his hands. "I can't be more specific than that. I've been calling up what information I can and that's all I get." He picked up the aquamarine. "Maybe this will help me, though I doubt it." He squeezed the lemon into the tomato juice, drained the glass, then looked at Alasdair again. "Care for a game of chess?"

"No," Alasdair said quickly. "I'm not up for being beaten at the moment. How long will you be in the city?"

Johari gave him a regretful smile. "I have passage out on a boat this afternoon, the first leg of what will be a long journey. I've been called to teach at a sanitarium in the Pyrénées." Though he looked as though he wrestled bears for a living, Johari was a healer adept whose reputation had spread far beyond his own people. He glanced up at the clock on the wall, muttering, "Cronus and his confusion, it's later than I thought. I'd better go."

Getting to his feet, Johari pocketed the aquamarine then left a few bills on the table for the waitress. "I wish I could be more help to you." He extended both hands, clasping Alasdair's wrists in his powerful grip. "Take care of yourself, Gideon. I hope we'll meet again in the mountains. The gods be with you."

"And with you. Safe journey," Alasdair replied, finding he was glad that Johari had kept the aquamarine.

He watched as Johari made his way out of the crowded bar, seeming a giant among the stooped figures of Josefina's elderly patrons. Why, he asked himself, did Johari think he needed help? An odd, irrational flicker of fear went through Alasdair, and he quelled an urge to go after Johari and ask to travel with him.

THE PHONE WOKE Lucinda. It was nine in the morning. She was due in the studio in an hour. She sat up on the edge of the bed, noticed without surprise that the dragon was gone again, and picked up the ringing phone.

"Tyrone here, baby."

"I'll be there in an hour." Lucinda started to hang up.

"Will you hang on a second? I'm not calling to hassle you about coming in. I got the flu or something. Nasty cough, a fever of one-oh-two, and my stomach is doing things that are positively obscene."

"I don't want to know," she assured him.

"Lucinda," Tyrone said, "this is the day."

She lay back on the bed. She was still half-asleep and in no mood for his guessing games. "Okay, what day?"

Tyrone's voice lost its normal good-humored boom. "You know what day," he said quietly. "It's the day Winston died. I'm in no shape to leave the house. I was calling to ask if you'd take some flowers to the cemetery for me."

Winston was Tyrone's son. He'd died when he was four, a year before Lucinda met Tyrone. Tyrone didn't talk about it, and she'd never had the courage to ask him how it happened.

"Sure," she said awkwardly. "I'll go."

"Get some tiger lilies," Tyrone told her. "That kid was mad for tiger lilies—kept expecting them to roar or something. Just put them on his grave and tell him I'm sorry I couldn't get there myself today, but I'll catch up with him as soon as I can. Got it?"

Lucinda saw no point at all in talking to a dead child and even less in leaving perfectly good flowers on a grave, but knew this was not the time to explain that to Tyrone. "Go back to bed," she said. "I'll take care of it. You okay?"

"No," Tyrone said, and hung up.

LUCINDA TOOK THE hill with long, fast strides, determined to get her errand over with. Ahead of her at the top of the cobblestoned street, she could see the elaborate wrought-iron gate that led into the cemetery, and beyond it, the green dome of the graveyard hill. She was in Genesia, the oldest part of Arcato where the first houses—narrow three-story sand-colored buildings with red tile roofs—still clung to the steep streets. But they were fewer than they had been, and those that still stood were in need of serious repair. Great sections of the sand-colored walls seemed to have simply dislodged themselves, and now their bricks lay scattered in alleyways among broken bottles and ripped mattresses. It was all dismal, Lucinda thought, quickening her pace. She was walking so quickly that she almost missed it—a curved shard of red tile filled with translucent blue stones. Without thinking about how the moonstones had gotten there or to whom they might belong, she stopped just long enough to scoop them up and put them in her pocket. Then she hurried on.

She was breathing hard by the time she reached the cemetery gate. She stood there for a moment, staring at the neatly trimmed lawns that stretched out in front of her. Except for Oasis, the city park, which had been taken over by dealers, the cemetery was the only area in the city that was still green. It was typical, she thought, that the city's only grasslands were the domain of the drug dealers and the dead.

Pushing aside a mild sense of trepidation, Lucinda passed through the gate. She didn't believe in ghosts or spirits. And if they existed, she couldn't believe they'd hang around a place as boring as a cemetery. There was nothing here to be frightened of. Still, she fingered the moonstones in her pocket, taking comfort from their cool, smooth touch.

She followed a gravel path to a small wooden house marked ADMINISTRATION. Inside, she gave the woman behind the counter the name of Tyrone's son. The woman, in turn, gave Lucinda a photocopied map, then marked an X on Linden Lane.

According to the map, Linden Lane was at the very top of the hill, so Lucinda resumed her ascent. She found it vaguely amusing that the cemetery depicted itself as a city within the city, with its own avenues, lanes, streets, and clusters of buildings. The buildings were, of course, mausoleums. A light snow, a last holdover from the departing winter, was falling, melting the moment it touched the grass-covered ground. But it clung to the bronze plaques, marble headstones, and crosses. It gave soft white cloaks to the shoulders of cherubs, saints, and a number of statues that could only be gods from other lands: a snakelike creature with its tongue sticking out, as if to catch the snowflakes; a woman dancing with skulls in her hands; a merman whose tail curled round the top of the gravestone; a slender human body with bracelets on its arms and a falcon's head.

She consulted the map again, turned left, and arrived at her destination. The grave was marked by a small white headstone beneath a maple tree. It was the only maple in sight. Tyrone or someone else related to the child must have planted it here. There were other plantings—the broad green leaves of iris plants and taller stems like those of the lilies she held in her hands. Sometime in early summer the small grave would be surrounded by flowers.

Lucinda set the bouquet beside the headstone and read the simple inscription, the dates of the boy's birth and death beneath a two-line epitaph:

Winston Dessalines
—four sweet years—

It took her by surprise, the four sweet years, because it made her feel what she'd always refused to allow Tyrone to make her feel: grief for the boy she never knew. She wondered if the child had looked like Tyrone or his mother. She wondered who the mother was and what woman would ever put up with Tyrone, much less agree to bear a child of his. And what had come over Tyrone? As far as Lucinda knew, Tyrone didn't do women.

She stopped herself. She'd always thought it rude to wonder about the things friends wouldn't tell you. If Tyrone didn't want to talk about it, then it was none of her business. Not that Tyrone had ever respected *her* privacy.

She stood a moment then began speaking to the narrow little plot of earth. "Your daddy, Tyrone, said to tell you he'll be up here as soon as he can. He's got some kind of cold or something and couldn't come today."

She stopped, feeling foolish talking to a tombstone. So she knelt a moment and rested her hand on top of the grave. She felt only cold earth, still wet from the snow.

There's a child's body beneath this ground, Lucinda told herself, and was relieved when the thought left her unmoved.

She stood up. She'd done it. There was nothing more to stay for.

Feeling lighter, she made her way back down the hill. Her right fist was closed around the moonstones, and she found herself thinking of the one that had found its way into her room, of the dreams it had given her.

Lucinda was almost to the bottom of the hill when she saw a crowd of people gathered around a freshly dug grave. It was another small one, not as small as Winston's but obviously made for a child. Lucinda began to backtrack. She didn't want to be anywhere near grief. But she stopped as she saw, on the very edge of the mourners, a face she recognized. It was the man in the blue robe, Alasdair. Today he wore a long black coat, and his hair was brushed back, making his face look harsh and worn.

She wanted nothing to do with the funeral. She wanted to leave the cemetery. But she didn't know when she'd see him again. And she knew that she wanted to.

Lucinda sat on a granite bench inscribed with the names of two sisters, and waited while the group huddled round the grave and a minister spoke. She watched while a woman who was clearly the child's mother caressed the coffin. While others held her as it was lowered into the ground. While each of the people who stood by the graveside dropped a handful of dirt onto the coffin. While the sobbing mother was led away.

A figure standing a short distance from the grave caught her attention, mostly because she couldn't tell whether he was part of the crowd or not. He was tall, very thin. She couldn't see much of his face because he wore a hooded sweatshirt, but from the way he held himself she guessed that he was in his late teens or early twenties. He wore loose, oversized pants and his hands were thrust into his pockets, but there was a kind of animal alertness to the way he held his body. The interesting thing was he seemed to have no interest in the deceased. Everyone else seemed bent beneath a mantle of grief. It didn't touch this man at all. Instead, he studied the other mourners, and if she wasn't mistaken, his gaze kept returning to Alasdair.

Alasdair was the last to leave. He shed no tears but watched silently as the gravediggers began to fill the pit from the mound of dirt that had been unearthed. He opened his hand over the still-open grave, and she thought she saw a clear red stone fall. And then he raised his head and looked directly at her.

As if she'd invited him, he came to stand before her. "Were you here for the funeral?" he asked.

"No," Lucinda answered. "I don't even know who died. I came here for something else—to put some flowers on another grave. For a friend."

He nodded, his eyes like obsidian, dark and glittering and sharp enough to cut.

"Did you—lose someone?" she asked awkwardly.

"I've lost a great many people," he replied.

"I meant the funeral."

"Ah." He glanced back toward the grave. "No, I didn't know him."

"His family?"

"I didn't know them either."

"Then why were you at the funeral?"

"Paying my respects," he answered, and began walking away from the grave.

Lucinda caught up with him. He glanced at her and slowed a little, so that she didn't have to walk so quickly to match his stride.

Lucinda was aware of the sound of her heels coming down on the damp earth, of the light metallic sound of her bracelets hitting against each other. She couldn't remember the last time she'd walked beside a man who was silent. Men were invariably eager to either tell her about themselves or to ask questions designed to tell them whether she was already "taken." Alasdair, however, seemed to have no interest in impressing her or determining her state of availability. He walked with her as if they'd signed an agreement to remain forever silent.

So it surprised her when he stopped, took off his coat, and held it out to her. "You're cold," he said. "Take this."

"No," she said, though the jacket she wore was thin and she was shivering. It seemed important that she not take anything from him, not be beholden to this man.

He nodded at her refusal, as if he'd expected it, and slipped the coat back on. "The dragon was gone this morning, wasn't it?" he asked casually.

"Was the dragon with you?" she countered.

"No," he replied. "I haven't seen him for a while."

The dragon is a him, she noted, having never given any thought to the matter of the dragon's gender. "He'll come back to me," she said. She had no evidence that this might be true, but she wanted to see if Alasdair agreed.

"Will he?" She couldn't tell if he was mocking her.

"Could you stop him?" she asked, genuinely curious.

"Perhaps if I tried."

"And will you?"

His eyes, which had seemed black just moments before were now a mild grey. "The dragon is quite capable of taking care of himself. It's been a long time since he's needed my protection. I think he's decided that it's I who need his."

"Do you?"

His eyes studied her, as if measuring how much he could tell her. "We could all use protection," he said at last. "There is a great deal in this world that would do any of us harm." He nodded in the direction of the new grave. "That boy hadn't had any protection for years. He was wide open."

"And that's what killed him? Being open?"

"Cancer was killing him. But his life was actually ended by another boy with a knife."

"And you could have protected him?" she guessed.

"Possibly from some things. Not at all from others. I couldn't have stopped his death, only—perhaps—the way it occurred."

"And that's why you came to the funeral."

"More or less."

Lucinda pulled her useless jacket more tightly around her. He was playing games with her, but she was curious enough to be willing to play a while longer. "Why did you drop that stone into the open grave?"

"I arrived at the funeral too late to place it inside the coffin," he said simply. "The casket was already closed."

"But why put a red stone in a casket?"

"An old tradition."

"Which is?"

"To send carnelian with the dead," he told her. "To Isis," he added almost reluctantly.

They passed a row of headstones, each topped by an eternal flame that flickered madly in the wind. To Lucinda, it looked like a macabre birthday celebration. "I suppose sending carnelian with the dead makes as much sense as leaving flowers on a grave," she allowed.

"The Egyptians considered carnelian the blood of Isis and gave it to the dead as an aid on the road to rebirth."

She couldn't keep the skepticism out of her voice. "So you think you just helped that kid on his way to another life?"

Alasdair's eyes flickered with something that might have been pity, but he only said, "I've answered enough questions for now."

They continued to walk. She felt a distinct sense of relief as they passed through the cemetery gate and out onto the city streets. "What will we talk about if I can't ask you questions?" she wondered aloud. "We don't know any of the same people, so we can't gossip."

"There's the weather," Alasdair offered politely.

"I hate talking about the weather," Lucinda informed him. "And I refuse to discuss homes, clothing, horoscopes, sex, pets, art, politics, finances, education, or what anyone does for a living."

"It should be a fascinating discourse then, with so much to discuss."

"Who was the guy who was watching you at the funeral?" she asked abruptly.

Alasdair came to a halt but didn't respond.

"You didn't see him? He stood across the grave from you. Maybe late teens, early twenties. Thin, tall, taller than you. He wore a hooded sweatshirt and it looked like you were the one he was there for." She wasn't even sure that last statement was true but she found she wanted to rattle him.

He seemed to weigh her words with some sort of internal truth meter before saying calmly, "No, I didn't see him. I was focused on the grieving mother and on the boy who died."

Again the image of his dropping the stone into the grave came back to her. There was something in that moment that she should have understood. She took the moonstones from her pocket and held them out to him. Overhead a swath of dense white winter clouds blanketed the sky. Beneath the cloud cover the moonstones' blue was lost; they glimmered silver-grey in the afternoon light.

"Are these yours?" she asked.

He gave her a wry smile, and murmured, "So much for no more questions."

"Are they yours?" she pressed.

"It would help if you'd stop thinking so possessively," he said with a trace of exasperation. "There really isn't a yours or a mine involved here."

She closed her fist over the stones. "Then I'll keep them."

"That could be a good thing," he said, and his voice softened. "You seem like a woman in need of moonstones."

Lucinda didn't trust the kinder voice. "What does that mean? I have a feeling I've just been insulted."

"Not an insult. Just an observation."

She slid the moonstones back into her pocket. "Which is?"

"That you have not been treated very gently or with much tenderness."

Lucinda wasn't prepared to be read so clearly or for the reading to cause her so much pain. She turned from him, her breath drawn in and her eyes shut tight.

"You don't have to be ashamed," he said even more gently. "It's not your fault that you were not well loved. Nor is it too late to claim those gifts for your own." He took a step toward her and she whirled to face him.

"Stay away from me." Her voice was shaking. "You don't know the first thing about me or my life. And I'd bet the fucking city you don't know the first thing about love. So don't presume to tell me who am I or what I need."

"I—" He held out a hand toward her.

"Stay away. Don't you ever come near me again."

"I didn't," he said. "I didn't even get close."

LUCINDA WAS NOT ready to go home. She had a horrible feeling that after insulting Alasdair she'd never see the dragon again, and she couldn't quite bear to find her flat so permanently empty. She managed to catch one of the infrequent streetcars down to Charlot Street, where she got off and walked to the small redbrick building whose brass sign read DESSALINES PRODUCTIONS. She let herself in through an iron gate then went around the back to an outside stairway that led to the second floor. At the top of the stairs, she pounded on a metal door. "Tyrone, you in there?"

Several minutes later she heard a shuffling sound followed by the sound of the locks being unbolted. The door opened and Tyrone stood scowling at her, swathed in layers of robes whose thick shawl collars made him look as if he had no neck at all. His mane of braids was hidden beneath a green knit cap, and he smelled of menthol and eucalyptus.

Lucinda grinned and patted the top of his cap. "Has anyone told you that you look like a bad-tempered turtle?"

Tyrone's scowl deepened into a glare as she pushed past him into the part of the loft that served as his living space. "Just what is so all-fired important that you had to get me up out of my deathbed?" he demanded.

"You're not dying."

"And how do you know that?"

Lucinda sank into his overstuffed couch. "You're too much of a pain in the ass to die. Pains like you go on forever."

"Perhaps I'm a god," Tyrone said, sounding as if he liked the idea very much.

"You're not," Lucinda said firmly. "I'm certain of that."

Tyrone folded his arms over his chest, trying to look stern. The effect was ruined by a massive sneeze. "Are you *trying* to get sick?" he asked, after fishing a handkerchief out of a pocket and blowing his nose loudly. "The last thing I need is both of us running this fever. We're already two weeks behind in orders. Go home, girl!"

"I can't," Lucinda said. "I'm in a lousy mood. You have to humor me."

"I will get you one cup of nasty-tasting decongestant tea," Tyrone said. "Then I'm throwing your ass out of here."

Lucinda waited while he bustled about in the kitchen. She shifted uncomfortably in the depths of the white leather sofa that always made her feel as if she were trapped inside a giant marshmallow. "How do you live with such abominable furniture?" she asked when he returned with the tea.

Tyrone sat down across from her on a black slatted wooden chair that was, in its own unyielding way, even more uncomfortable than the sofa. "You are a joy to be around," he observed. His eyes took in her thin black jacket and the lavender sheath dress she wore beneath. "Don't tell me *that's* what you wore to visit Winston?"

Lucinda shrugged. "I've never been to a cemetery before. I didn't know what to wear."

"I suppose it doesn't matter," Tyrone allowed. "Besides, Winston liked purple and black. And orange. He wanted me to make him pajamas that were those colors."

"Did you?"

Tyrone gave her a bitter smile. "Me, make something garish? You ought to know better. Especially since that was the period when I was obsessed with neutrals: If it wasn't taupe, *it wasn't.*" His voice became nearly inaudible as he said, "I told him I couldn't find the right fabric." He took a sip of the tea. "So how was it?" he asked quietly. "Visiting the cemetery."

"I did what you asked," Lucinda said. "I went up there and put the tiger lilies on the grave. I told him you'd visit yourself as soon as you got better."

"And?"

"And what?"

"What else happened?"

"Nothing." Lucinda tried to straighten her spine, only to sink deeper into the white leather folds.

"Something else must have happened," Tyrone insisted.

Lucinda considered telling him about Alasdair. Wasn't that why she'd come to Tyrone in the first place? Tyrone would hear her out and then neatly, scathingly, dissect and classify Alasdair as yet another deplorable male she ought to steer clear of. Tyrone guaranteed instant character assassination and post-mortem all in one succinct session. So why didn't she tell him?

Lucinda shook her head. "Nothing."

Tyrone stood up and walked over to the window. The river couldn't be seen from his loft. In fact, the window he stood at looked out on a trompe l'oeil mural of a brick wall painted on the cement wall of the brewery next to him. He liked the brewery, though, said living so close to the smell of beer saved him the trouble of ever having to drink.

"I meant with Winston," he said. "Something must have happened with Winston."

"He's dead," Lucinda said before she could stop herself.

Tyrone turned to face her. "You think I don't know that?"

Lucinda silently cursed her own tactlessness, her stupidity in having come here in the first place. "I'm sorry," she said. "Shit, Tyrone, I told you I was in a lousy mood."

"Winston's dead," Tyrone said. "But that doesn't mean he's over."

With effort, Lucinda pushed herself out of the sofa. It felt good to stand again, as if now she might steer this conversation out of the pool of weirdness and pain that was threatening to drown them both.

"Tyrone," she said carefully, "I never knew Winston. And I don't know a whole lot about death. I've never had anyone die on me. So I can't pretend to know what goes on for you at the cemetery. I left the flowers and told him you'd be by. And I touched the ground on his grave. That's all."

Tyrone turned back to contemplate the wall through the window. "I appreciate you going up there for me," he said stiffly. "It means a lot to me that he knew someone was there."

Lucinda held her tongue, restrained herself from asking how "he" knew, and whether "he" was a ghost, a spirit, or just a sentient dead body. She set the unfinished cup of tea on the white marble coffee table and came to stand behind him. "I'd better go."

He turned back to face her, his eyes unreadable. "I told you that when you walked in."

"You did." She leaned forward and kissed him on the tip of his swollen nose. "Rest up."

"Don't you dare call in sick tomorrow. I am not going to forgive you if you come down with my cold." Tyrone gave her his imperious look, the one designed to make her feel like a clumsy imbecile with excruciatingly bad taste. At the moment it cheered her immensely; it meant Tyrone was on the mend.

"You know," Lucinda said, "you give a lot of orders for someone wearing four bathrobes. I mean, don't you think that look is a bit . . . much?"

He caught her wrist as she reached the door. "Oh, no you don't. You came here for a reason. You don't get to sashay on out before you tell me what it is."

She hesitated, then reached into her pocket and pulled out the moonstones. "What do you know about these?"

Tyrone held out his hand, and she dropped the stones onto his palm. They were blue again, seawater and sky.

"Moonstones," he said. "Feldspar, semiprecious, not worth much."

"That's it?"

"People say all kinds of things about moonstones," Tyrone went on after a suitably dramatic pause. "I heard one story that says they were formed out of the rays of the moon. My granny used to say that you can see the future in a moonstone during crone time."

"Crone time?"

"When the moon wanes, of course."

"Crone time," Lucinda murmured. "Where do you get this stuff?"

"I'm not done," Tyrone said testily, then continued in the tone of a congested professor. "The moonstone is also a very propitious stone for lovers. Supposed to make the wearer faithful—" His eyes narrowed. "That's it, isn't it? You came here to tell me about another disastrous relationship. Excuse me, they're not even relationships—another disastrous encounter. Or shall we just save time and call it a fuck?"

"You're amazing, you know that? Even when you're sick, you have to twist the knife."

"Oh, Lucinda, baby, I'm trying to be kind here," Tyrone protested. "When are you ever going to develop some taste in men?"

"When you develop manners," Lucinda told him. Leaving him holding the stones, she let herself out of the loft before he could make things worse.

ALASDAIR FOUND SIMONE Fortunato sitting at the bar of the Lucky Diamond. He asked if the seat next to her was taken, and when she indicated that it wasn't, he sat down beside her. She looked exactly like the woman whose photograph had appeared in the paper along with an interview. If the article was to be trusted, then Michael's arrest had elicited nothing more from his mother than an enormous wave of self-pity.

Mrs. Fortunato had been pretty once, with small, even features and thick-lashed pale blue eyes. Now her blond hair was brown at the roots and teased to look full. She wore a tightly fitting dress made of a shiny magenta fabric and black patent leather heels. Makeup couldn't disguise the dark circles under her eyes or the alcoholic's web of broken blood vessels. She was nursing a shot glass filled with clear liquid.

Alasdair ordered a whiskey for himself and noted with interest that although he'd made no attempt to restrain them, as he had at the jail, gemstones were not dropping from his sleeves. They didn't like her.

"You're Michael Fortunato's mother, aren't you?" he began.

She gave him a sideways glance. "My famous son. For years no one in this city remembers my name. Now they all know me as the mother of the eleven-year-old killer." Her voice was grainy with years of drink and smoke. It was also weak, as if she didn't have quite enough breath to complete a sentence; he could catch her words but they were faint and seemed to slip from the air between them.

"My name is Ivor," he said. "I'd like to help your son. If you'll let me."

She swung around on the bar stool to face him, and he saw that the magenta dress was cut low, her breasts nearly spilling out of it. "How are you going to help him?" she demanded. "Are you going to get him out of that place? Pay for his defense? Get people to stop calling him a killer?"

"He *is* a killer," Alasdair said. "But I thought I might visit him."

She concentrated on lighting a cigarette, the act made difficult by a tremor in her left hand. "You got a thing for killers? Or maybe just young boys?"

Was everyone in this city so impossible to approach, he wondered. Or was it him? Was there something he said or did that made them all so defensive and angry?

His eyes lit on the oval saint's medal that hung from her neck, and he recited the age-old rhyme: "Dear Saint Anthony, please come around. Something's lost and must be found."

The rhyme made her smile. "I say that every time I can't find my keys. Works like a charm."

"It is a charm," he said. "I would think that you might try it now. Your son is quite lost, you know."

She held out her empty glass to him. "Buy me another?"

He ordered the drink for her, and her eyes roamed his body. "What are you?" she asked. "Some kind of social worker?"

"Hardly. I read about your son in the paper, and . . . I have an idea of what he went through that night. It seemed to me that he could use a friend."

She leaned toward him and enunciated each word very clearly: "What's in it for you?"

"Grief and frustration, I expect."

The bartender brought her drink, and she toasted Alasdair with her glass. "All right then, what's in it for me?"

"Shouldn't the question be, what's in it for Michael?"

"Let me tell you something," she said. "You're right. Michael's lost. I lost Michael years ago." For the briefest moment, he saw sorrow in her eyes. "But not you or St. Anthony or anyone else is going to bring him back to me."

Alasdair finished his whiskey and stood up. The city was beginning to tire him. If he had another place to go, he'd be on his way by now. Perhaps that was what he should do: go back to the flat, pack what he needed, and set sail on the next ship out of the harbor.

He left some coins on the bar and nodded to Simone Fortunato. "Good night," he said. "It was kind of you to talk with me."

She caught up with him as he reached the door of the Lucky Diamond. When he'd first come to the city, the bar had been called the Lucky Shamrock; he had a dreadful feeling that he had something to do with the change of name.

"Wait a minute," she said. "You already saw him, didn't you? He told me some fake uncle showed up. I could tell them," she threatened. "I could tell the police that you went in there under false pretenses."

"You could," he agreed, and again turned to go.

This time she caught the sleeve of his coat. "Michael showed me that yellow rock you gave him. You have any other rocks? Maybe some that are, you know—" she actually winked at him "—worth a little more?"

"No," he said quietly. He could see that her life had been rough and often grim, that she'd had very little luck. He could change that. All it would take was one stone. And yet, he could not envision her doing anything with such a stone that wouldn't be wholly self-serving.

"I'll tell them you're his uncle," she bargained. "I'll tell them to let you visit any time you want. If you could, say, leave another kind of stone with him next time—maybe something blue, like a sapphire. I always liked sapphires."

Gently, he extracted his sleeve from her hand. "I'm sorry, Mrs. Fortunato," he told her. "I can't help you."

MICHAEL FORTUNATO SAT in the narrow room that had been his home ever since the night Spook died. He sat on the floor, his knees drawn up to his chest, and stared at the cinder block walls. His social worker, a balding man named Bob, had just left. Bob talked about a hearing and possibly a trial. From what Michael could tell, he'd probably wind up in a prison school with other kids like himself. That had to be better than this stupid room. He'd never been so bored in his life. He took the yellow rock from his pocket. He couldn't decide if it was ugly or not. The color was cloudy yellow-grey, but the white line inside it that seemed to expand or shrink with the light was kind of cool. He could see why it was called a cat's eye. He could also see why it wasn't worth squat. It wasn't nice enough for jewelry. About the only thing it was good for was throwing at the cinder block walls. He'd give it that—it was hard, little bugger; it didn't chip or crack. He threw it against the wall again, wondering briefly about his "uncle Ivor." The man had never returned. He was probably a pervert, Michael decided. Still Ivor had been his only real visitor. His mother didn't count. She only showed up if a newspaper reporter accompanied her; then she'd spend the entire visit telling the reporter how hard this was on her. Bob didn't count. Bob treated him like another form that had to be processed. Ivor had talked to him, had given him a rock to throw. Big deal.

There was something more that came into the tiny cinder block room. It came at night. And it was connected to the see-through man. Michael didn't know what to call it or even how to describe it. He knew no one would believe him if he tried. But after lights out, he'd be lying there in the dark. And suddenly the dark in the room would get darker. So thick and black he could almost touch the darkness. And he'd feel the way he felt that night before he saw the see-through man, like he might never see daylight again. And his whole body would go rigid with terror, because it felt like Spook's death was going to happen all over again. That was one thing he'd figured out: The darkness had come for Spook. And now in this tiny cell of a room, he knew it had come for him, too.

But Spook never came back and the see-through guy didn't show either, and lately Michael had started wondering if that darkness wasn't a part of *him,* something he breathed out into the night. He was fairly certain now that the darkness wouldn't take him away, that it would leave him alive on the metal cot. Still, it frightened him. Each time it came he could feel something inside him changing, and he didn't know what it was. Or what it would make him do. And always when it left he dreamed of Spook and the see-through man.

He learned one trick: If he held onto the yellow rock when the darkness came, then after it left he'd stop being scared a lot faster. He'd still dream about Spook and the see-through man, about that night when he felt the darkness for the first time. But if he held the yellow rock, then he didn't feel like he had to scream out his terror. He'd screamed every night before Ivor came. Not that anyone noticed. He'd woken every morning with his throat raw and his pillow drenched with tears. Now he made it through the darkness and the dreams without screaming. And he thought that if they ever set him free, he'd find the see-through man and ask him to just get it over with and take him, too.

HERE ON THE banks of the city the Candra River was still tidal and carried a faint salt tang borrowed from the ocean that it fed. Lucinda stood in the outdoor market, surrounded by open trunks filled with fabrics, aware that the tide was in now and of the low overcast skies that held in the scent of the river, and of how that smell was seeping into the cloth, clinging to it, making itself as much a part of the weave as warp and weft. The city was invasive. Give it even an hour of your life and it worked its way into your clothing, got inside you, transformed whatever was open and vulnerable, and claimed you for its own. She'd lived in Arcato all her life, and she still felt it working on her. She'd fucked a sailor once who told her about going through sea changes: how he boarded his first ship a boy and disembarked two continents later a man. City changes were subtler, she knew, more insidious. And unlike so many things observed from the vantage point of a ship, they were impossible to chart.

She began a quick, practiced inspection of the trunks. She reached into the soft mounds of cloth, examining texture and resilience, searching for whatever touched her skin and brought pleasure. From the depths of the trunks she drew up a delicate batik—purple flowers on green vines against a white background. She found forest-green water silk, ivory linen, pearl-grey damask, lavender tulle, and yards of black taffeta. She bought them all with Tyrone's money, enjoying the thought of how outraged he'd be when she told him what she'd spent. And how, after giving her his usual grief, he'd make them into the finest clothes in the city. Clothes that knew how to hang on a body and move with it. Clothes that looked good no matter how long they'd been worn. Clothes that felt like a caress.

She reached for the velvet pouch where she kept her money, and a stranger's voice behind her said, "Do you have to take that green silk? You're buying all that other beautiful cloth. Don't you think it would be kind to leave some for someone else?"

Lucinda turned to a face a man with thick, straight red hair brushed back from a narrow, fine-boned face. He had a pointed chin, high arched brows, and dark blue eyes that danced with life.

"I'm not kind," Lucinda told him, and went to find the woman who owned the booth so that she could pay for her fabrics.

He followed her.

"There's plenty left in the trunks," she told him.

She looked at him again, and this time she noticed the shirt woven of a soft dusk-blue wool, the faded black jeans, and the fine leather boots.

"As a matter of fact, there isn't," he said. "I checked. I've been searching for that particular shade of green silk for the last six months, and I haven't found it, and now you're holding it in your hands. Let me buy it off you?"

Lucinda paid the woman who owned the stall. "You're serious?"

"How much do you want for it?" he countered.

She tripled the figure she'd just paid for the lot.

He handed her the money at once.

"Tell me something," she said, reluctant to part with the cloth. She had wanted Tyrone to make a sheath of it, a slim green dress that would make a woman look as though she were a forest spirit. "Why is this particular silk so important?"

"It's like this," he said, as if he were about to reveal a great confidence. "I've got a lamp from the twenties. It had a gorgeous green fringed silk shade—exactly that color—but the fabric's moth eaten and falling apart. I have to replace it."

"And if you don't?"

"Then I've broken my trust."

"With—?"

"The objects I buy and sell." She didn't ask, but he told her anyway, "I'm an antiques dealer."

She handed him the green silk. "Well, I certainly wouldn't want you to disappoint your lamp."

He accepted it with a flourish. "My lamp thanks you."

She turned to leave. She had one more dealer to visit, a woman who sold glass and crystal beads. She knew that Tyrone would be horrified by the idea, but she intended to persuade him to bead the black taffeta.

The stranger appeared in front of her, walking backward so that he faced her. "Have coffee with me?"

She bit back a laugh. "Why would I?"

"Because it would make me very happy to spend some time with you."

She gazed into his eyes, searching for sarcasm, irony, or manipulation. She saw none. Only a guileless transparency. As though he were inviting her to gaze into the depths of his heart, sure that what she would find was good, clean, even merry. He was not her type, her type being well-heeled bad-boy scum, and therefore she was safe. "All right," she told him. "One cup of coffee."

HE BOUGHT TWO coffees from a stand by the market then led her to one of the warehouses. "It's owned by a friend of mine," he explained. They climbed a wide steel staircase, passing men stacking great wooden crates on the first floor and answering phones and adding up invoices on the second. The third floor was empty. Afternoon light filtered in through grimy windows and streamed across a vast, dust-filled floor.

He knelt in front of one of the windows, used his sleeve to clear a patch of glass, then sat down on the dusty linoleum to watch the river traffic go by. "Arcato's best view," he told her.

Lucinda wondered if he were oblivious to the dirt or simply didn't care. She decided that it didn't matter. "How come this floor is empty?" she asked, settling down beside him.

He shrugged. "Another company used to have offices up here, but they moved out. Giorgio, my friend who owns the place, says they'll take the space back. Just haven't gotten around to it, I guess."

Lucinda sipped her coffee. The warehouse was unheated. Steam rose from the cup, and the hot liquid warmed her. "So your friend's name is Giorgio," she said. "What's yours?"

He looked startled, surprised that he hadn't told her.

"Sebastian. Sebastian Keane."

"That sounds like a fake name," she said. "Like something from a bad novel."

"Tell that to my mother. I always wanted a normal name like Jim or Nick. Believe me, it wasn't easy growing up with Sebastian." He looked at her curiously. "And you are . . . Evangeline? Viveca? Natasha? Klotilde?"

"Lucinda," she admitted, trying not to smile.

"Better than Sebastian. *And* Klotilde." He gazed out at the river. "That red boat there coming into port is owned by a rug merchant named Madana. He brings in the most extraordinary carpets from the East. Remind me to take you aboard sometime."

Lucinda found it extraordinary that Sebastian assumed that there would be a sometime, that he would see her again. She had to set him straight. "Listen," she said. "I might sleep with you once, but that's it. Don't expect anything."

His blue eyes regarded her with amusement. "You cut straight to the chase, don't you?"

"That's what this is, isn't it?"

"Maybe. I hadn't really thought that far ahead."

"What were you thinking?"

"That it's nice to sit here with you, drinking coffee, and looking at the river. And because I know you like beautiful things, I thought you'd appreciate Mr. Madana's rugs."

She studied him, searching for the lie. When she didn't find it, she sat beside him in silence, content to watch the river, at least until she finished her coffee.

"I have to go." She set down her empty cup and picked up the bag filled with fabrics. "I bought these for someone else. He's expecting me."

"Your husband?" Sebastian asked.

"The gods forbid! I work with Tyrone. He's my friend," she added.

Sebastian stood up beside her. He took her free hand in his, then covered it with his other hand, as if he were holding something infinitely precious. "Do you have any interest in looking at carpets tomorrow?"

She thought about it. "Maybe."

"Mr. Madana usually docks at the north pier. I'll be there tomorrow at one."

He was hitting on her, she was sure of it. But he was doing it in a low-key way that she didn't find offensive. "Maybe I'll see you there," she said. "But—"

He grinned and finished her thought, "Don't count on it." He turned her palm up and swiftly kissed her hand. She pulled back, startled as a deer caught unawares.

"Thanks again for the green silk." He let her go with another invitation. "Maybe later, if you don't mind the chase, I'll invite you round to see the lamp."

She started down the stairs of the warehouse. She had no doubt that he'd invite her to see the lamp. She might even accept. But first to make sure that he posed no danger, to convince herself that there was no chance he'd get too close, she'd find someone else to sleep with tonight.

"YOU HAVEN'T SEEN Boris, have you?" Mrs. O'Donnell, Alasdair's land-lady, stood on the stoop of their building, surveying the street with an anxious gaze.

It took Alasdair a few moments to recall that Boris was his landlady's Russian wolfhound, an animal that always looked half-starved despite the fact that its mistress seemed to devote her life to cooking for it. Alasdair didn't know Mrs. O'Donnell well, but it didn't take much to see that Boris was the center of her days, the source of love in her life.

"No, I haven't seen him. What's happened?" Alasdair asked.

"I don't know what happened, do I? If I did, I wouldn't be asking," she snapped. An appalled look crossed her face seconds after she spoke. "I'm so sorry," she said quickly. "It's only that I'm deathly worried about Boris. We were right here. We'd just gone to the market and I tied him to the railing, so I could unlock the front door and bring my cart inside. You know how it is. He's such a big dog, and the doorway is too narrow to fit the cart *and* Boris. So I always get the cart inside first and come back out for Boris. And I had just opened my door when there was this ghastly shriek and I ran back out-side and—" She pointed to the railing. Alasdair saw part of a leather leash still tied to it. "Someone cut his leash. When I came out Boris was gone."

They both called for Boris loudly. Still calling, Alasdair did a quick search of the neighborhood, then returned to the building and stood there with Mrs. O'Donnell for a while, offering as much sympathy and comfort as he could. At last he left her there, an arthritic widow waiting tearfully for her dog to return.

He climbed the stairs to his apartment, which took up the top floor of the building. He stopped on the landing, his senses prickling. As a matter of habit, he'd put protections on the door, calling on the energies of the stones inside the flat to keep anyone from entering. No one had touched the door; the pattern of energy that surrounded it was exactly as he'd left it. But in front of the door . . . he stood perfectly still, concentrating, seeing faint lines of light vibrating furiously. No, he wasn't misreading. There'd been some sort of disturbance. Someone had tried to get in.

Alasdair let himself inside to be greeted by a bevy of stones in a state of excitement that rivaled Mrs. O'Donnell's. The rubies, always aligned against destruction, were vibrating so hard they were nearly hopping. The lapis and rutilated topaz were working together to maintain a shield that even now they were reluctant to drop. But Alasdair focused on the rods of black tourmaline that had arrayed themselves in a kind of U in front of the door. They were crackling with energy, giving off a deep green light, ready to repel anything that might harm him. Tourmaline was particularly good at countering negative spells, he reflected; their being so charged meant that whoever came to his flat had come with powers well beyond the ordinary. "Thank you all," he told the stones. "I'm grateful for your protection."

He poured himself a glass of water and sat at the kitchen table, trying to order his thoughts. Was the person who tried to enter his flat the same one who'd cut the dog's leash? Could it be the hooded man at Spook's funeral that Lucinda had described? Alasdair hadn't given much credence to her story, coming as it did from a defensive young woman who was obviously trying to unsettle him. But maybe he should have paid closer attention. For the first time he considered the possibility that someone might be trailing or stalking him. A ripple of unease went through him, and he examined it dispassionately. It was animal wariness at territory broached, no more, no less. And yet someone with a good deal of power had alarmed the stones. And Boris was missing.

Alasdair closed his fist and summoned faustite, a green stone that was mineralogical kin to turquoise. Faustite was not something he often used but it had a particular aptitude for strengthening communication with animals. His fingers closed over something smooth and oblong. Opening his hand, he saw that what had answered his summons was a hand-turned bead, its deep green color perfectly even.

Clasping the faustite bead between his hands, he began to send out calls to Boris. It took a while—there was a good half hour when he wondered if the dog was still alive—but he finally felt the animal's consciousness responding. Boris was frightened but not far away and not, as much as Alasdair could sense, in any danger. Alasdair pictured Mrs. O'Donnell, her entire being fraught with worry, and tried to send the image to Boris. He would never know whether or not the dog actually received it, but as he sat there holding the faustite, he felt Boris steadily moving closer, on his way home.

ALASDAIR WAITED UNTIL nearly midnight for moonrise. He left the apartment and walked to where the city streets vanished into the foothills of the mountains. There he found a flat shelf of gneiss, sat himself down on the smooth, white rock, and waited until the sliver of the waning moon arched over the city's skyline. He noted that the horns of the moon curved down; rain wasn't far off. And the crescent was thin, only a day or two away from the dark of the moon. Crone time.

He made himself very still, opening his senses, searching for any trace that someone might be following him. An owl called and a hare darted out in front of him, so frightened he could hear its heartbeat. Hekate was moving through the scrub oak, in no particular hurry, hunting for those who rightfully belonged to her. She, however, was not the one who'd come calling at his flat; of that, he was certain. Here, on the threshold between the mountains and the city, he felt no threat.

Gazing down, Alasdair picked out the lights of the fair and of the docks and warehouses that edged the river. The lights were still a marvel to him, points of gold against the blackness. They made him nostalgic for something he'd never quite known—a sense of enclosure, a world that was warm and familiar and safe, proof against the darkness.

Before leaving his apartment that evening, he'd summoned a moonstone, half-hoping that the one that was given to him as a life stone would appear. Instead a smooth circular stone, nearly as large as a magnifying glass, had rolled toward him from somewhere beneath the refrigerator.

Now he drew it from the pocket of his coat and held it in his palm. It reflected the moon as cleanly as a mirror. He gazed into it, concentrating on the luminous white crescent. He let himself feel all that the translucent stone knew of light and shadow, tides and currents, births and deaths, and the particular sort of madness that is tied to the moon.

And in the silver-blue circle of the stone he saw the boy, Michael, in the cinder block room. The boy was frantically pacing the perimeter of the tiny cell, an animal confined. As Alasdair watched, Michael slowed his pacing. He suddenly bent and picked up something from the center of the floor—a ring of tarnished brass skeleton keys.

The boy examined the keys. And then he did the obvious. He used one to open the cell's steel door. It did not matter that when Alasdair had been in the room, there had been no keyhole on the boy's side of the door.

On this night other forces were at work. Michael fitted a key to the keyhole, pushed open the heavy door, and walked out of his cell. There were no guards or social workers. The boy walked out of the jail as easily as he'd walk between rooms in his own home.

Michael never looked back. He pushed open the steel doors of the building without setting off alarms. The high outer gate swung open at his approach. And he headed straight for the river.

This was not the future that Alasdair had wanted to see.

Three

TYRONE WAS PINNING the black taffeta on Lucinda, and Lucinda was fidgeting.

"Tyrone, I need to take lunch," she said.

"You can take lunch after I figure out how to do the shoulder on this dress," Tyrone told her through a mouth full of pins. "And after I sketch it so I don't forget exactly what this burst of genius created."

Lucinda groaned. "You've barely started. Why don't we take a break now and pick up again after lunch?"

"Because I just got this material to drape around your hips in a way that is not identical to every other evening dress I've ever designed." He swatted her on the butt. "Now stay still, girl!"

Lucinda made do with an indignant scowl. She hadn't definitely decided that she wanted to meet Sebastian on the dock until about three minutes ago. And now Tyrone was being difficult. She should have expected it. Tyrone was as possessive and territorial as any tomcat.

He continued to lecture her. "You were the one who was so keen for me to cut a dress out of this stuff. Which, incidentally, slides out of place every time I try to put a pin in it. You'd think you'd be grateful that I'm following your suggestion."

"Oh, undying gratitude," Lucinda told him.

"Well, then act like it. What's with you anyway?" he muttered. He looked up at her. "Oh. I see. Another man who wasn't so hot in the sack last night?"

"Let's just say he wasn't memorable."

"Well, then what was he?"

"A graphic designer," she reported, trying to be gracious about missing her date with Sebastian. Tyrone, after all, did pay her a full-time salary for very part-time work. "He had these huge posters of letters on his wall. An S over the sink. A giant C over the couch."

"And a T over the toilet?" Tyrone guessed.

Lucinda smiled sourly. "And an apartment filled with furniture made of industrial steel and black leather."

"Sounds kinky."

"*That* might have been interesting. It was just fast. And hard. It went on too long, actually."

"You are a difficult woman to please," Tyrone said. "Too long, too hard. Pray tell, what exactly is the perfect fuck?"

"I didn't say it was too hard," Lucinda protested, trying to keep a straight face. "I said it went on too long. And it wasn't memorable."

"I should have such problems. I don't want to tell you how long it's been since my last. At this point, I'd remember a handshake." He frowned at the mirror and adjusted the shoulder of the mock-up. "Turn around, babe. Let me see what the back looks like."

Lucinda turned.

"So who are you so hot and bothered to have lunch with?"

"What makes you think I want to have lunch with anyone?"

"You don't get all urgent about lunch just 'cause you're hungry. You've never been that interested in food."

It was true. She saw food as sustenance, nothing more.

Behind her Tyrone tugged on the black taffeta, added a few more folds and pins, and stepped back. "The shoulders are a bore," he declared. "Got to do something with those shoulders." He pulled a ribbon of fabric from the floor and began pinning again. Ten minutes later he grabbed a sketch pad and a charcoal pencil. "Now if you will stand very still," he said, "I'll try to get this part over with quickly, so you can go have your little rendezvous."

Lucinda gave a long-suffering sigh and did as he asked. She'd tried to convince Tyrone to simply take photos of his mock-ups, but Tyrone claimed that the sketching was an integral part of the process, that as he drew he saw the finished piece, made changes, took the design in through eye and hand until something inside him knew just how the fabric was supposed to fall.

She glanced in the mirror. The black taffeta was draped in a series of subtle folds that looked as if it were the natural inclination of the material to cling to her body that way. The dress was stunning.

"No beads," Tyrone said, not looking up from his pad.

"Not on this one," Lucinda agreed.

Tyrone sketched the back of the dress with quick, fluid strokes. "I want the back coming down in more of a V," he muttered. He rubbed at the sketch pad, drew some more, and then sighed. "All right, let's get you out of this, then you're a free woman."

Lucinda's eyes went to the clock on the wall. It was one o'clock. She'd be late. She closed her hand over the memory of Sebastian's kiss. She had a feeling that Sebastian would still be waiting when she got there.

Behind her, Tyrone was removing pins and carefully folding the black taffeta.

"Get out of here," he told her as he finished. "And just because you ain't said anything yet, doesn't mean I don't expect a full report."

THE NORTH PIER was the one farthest from Tyrone's studio. Lucinda took her time walking, as it violated her most basic beliefs to hurry for any man. Yet she was curious about Sebastian, wondering if she'd like him as much the second time as she had the first. She doubted it but the possibility intrigued her.

She wound her way through the maze of narrow streets that led to the waterfront, stopping in a shop that sold herbs and essences to buy a tiny vial of sandalwood oil. She touched a drop to her neck and each of her wrists then continued toward the wharves. She thought about the designer she'd been with the night before. She could still see his face—serious brown eyes behind wire-rimmed glasses, thin lips, straight brown hair, and a long, straight nose—but his body was already vague in her memory, blurred with others. She couldn't remember if his arms were muscled or fleshy, whether wiry, dark hair covered his chest, whether he smelled of salt or musk-scented cologne. And yet when she spent the night or even part of a night with a man, she didn't have the dreams. It was worth it for that alone.

She took a shortcut through the curving alley where the gold merchants kept their shops. She lingered a few moments in front of her favorite window, savoring the jewelry, the plates and statues, the masques and vases and candlesticks all in gold. She'd once slept with a man who brought her to this shop the following day, and told her to pick out anything she liked. She'd chosen a necklace strung with disks so bright she was sure they were stolen from the sun. She'd watched as the necklace was set in a velvet-lined box and carefully wrapped, as the salesman wrote out an exorbitant bill, and the man by her side casually reached into a fine-grain leather wallet and extracted five exceedingly large bills. He'd been a nice man, really. She knew that he gave her the necklace not to impress or hold her but because she had seen that he was still mourning a dead wife, and she had been gentle with him, had allowed him to grieve his dead and return to life inside her. She had not found it odd or off-putting that he wept the entire time they made love. She still had the necklace. She had never worn it.

Lucinda's heels clicked along the wooden boards of the north pier. It was one of the older piers, in need of serious repairs and yet heavily used. She stepped carefully over rotted-out boards, glimpsing the cold, grey waters of the river below.

She didn't know the name of Mr. Madana's boat but she recognized the wide, flat-bottomed scow painted bright red. Up close she could see that the red paint was weathered and the boat was a good deal larger than it had looked from the factory window. The deck was empty. Lucinda stepped around heavy coils of rope, assorted lanterns, and a large rust-covered anchor then knocked on the door leading to the cabin. The boat rocked gently beneath her.

"Come in," called a heavily accented voice.

She opened the door to a short stairway and descended to a room lit by oil lamps. Carpets covered the walls and floors. Everywhere Lucinda looked intricate designs were woven in reds and blues and golds. The patterns were endless—geometric and swirling, pictorial and abstract. She made out bits—birds that edged one carpet, deer another, medallions that circled a dragon, flowers faded into leaves. Her eyes couldn't take it all in.

A warm spicy scent filled the room, and when Lucinda's eyes finally adjusted she saw Sebastian sitting at a low wooden table across from a man with a thick black mustache.

Sebastian's eyes lit with pleasure. "I just lost my own bet," he confessed happily. "I bet you wouldn't come."

"That's the first thing you should know," she told him, smiling. "I'm never a good bet." She turned to the man who sat beside Sebastian. He had coffee-colored skin, dark hair, and even darker eyes. A bright blue parrot sat on his shoulder, its feathers a gaudy contrast to the subtle tones of the rugs.

"Lucinda, this is Mr. Madana," Sebastian said.

Lucinda found Mr. Madana fascinating. He was far from striking—a small, portly man with a round belly and a balding pate. But something about him compelled her. As if he and she were familiar to each other. And yet she knew she'd never laid eyes on him.

"You are most welcome," Madana said in formal tones. He indicated a cushion next to the table. Lucinda took a seat, and Mr. Madana lifted a brass samovar and served them each thick, creamy tea flavored with anise, cumin, coriander, cinnamon, and a spice Lucinda couldn't name.

"You have lived in this city long?" he asked her.

"Too long," Lucinda replied. "I keep telling myself I'll leave, and I never seem to go."

Madana shrugged. "It's a port city. Many things will come to you here, so it is not so necessary to leave home."

"And you?" she asked.

"I am from India, originally. A tiny village. Nothing came to us there. I had to leave," he said with a smile. "Since then, I found that I could not stay in one place. I like to live in many places. So now this boat is my home."

She glanced at Sebastian, waiting for him to volunteer his birthplace, but he held out a wrist to the parrot who stepped onto it and made its way to his shoulder with a rocking, sideways gait. There the parrot rested, its head tucked beneath Sebastian's chin.

"It likes you," Lucinda said.

"We've met before," Sebastian explained. He stroked the bird, his hand gently enclosing and sliding the length of its brightly feathered body. Lucinda wondered why she hadn't noticed his hands before. He had well-shaped hands with long, slender fingers. She could easily imagine them playing a stringed instrument or repairing a fragile lampshade or running the length of her body.

The parrot opened its eyes, ruffled its feathers, then made its way back to Mr. Madana who said, "This city of yours, strange things are happening here now."

"You mean the gemstones?" Lucinda asked.

Madana nodded. "I've only been docked here one day and already I've heard stories." He gave a low chuckle. "I keep hoping to find rubies in my engine room but, alas, I am disappointed. And what about you?" he asked. "Have you found any of these miraculous gems?"

Lucinda thought of the moonstones and of Alasdair, realizing that this was the first time she'd thought of him since meeting Sebastian.

"I found a few moonstones," she admitted. "Nothing valuable."

"There you are wrong," Madana told her. "A moonstone may not be worth much in monetary terms, but it has other value. For years India's astrologers have used moonstones to befriend the moon."

Lucinda sipped at the fragrant tea. "So the moon needs friends. . . ."

"Maybe it's the other way around," said Sebastian. "Maybe we're the ones who need the moon's friendship."

Lucinda rubbed her eyes. Here in this dark little room with the tea and scents and rugs, she could almost believe him, could believe almost anything.

Madana passed his hand over the steam rising from his cup. "Sebastian tells me you have an eye for beautiful things. May I show you some of my rugs?"

She nodded, wondering if this was all a calculated sales pitch. Any prospective buyer who'd spent this much time in Tyrone's studio would have already seen three portfolios and half a dozen samples from the racks.

The merchant stood up and ambled over to the far wall, matching his gait to the swell of the water beneath the boat. He chose one of many rolled-up rugs and unrolled it. Its colors were faded to soft tans, oranges, yellows, siennas. Lucinda could see where the weave was worn, could almost feel the generations who had lived with it.

"This one," Madana said, "is seventeenth-century Turkish, when they were still using geometric patterns. It has been in my family a long time. Do you like it?"

"It's beautiful but not to my taste," she admitted.

"Nor mine," Madana said. He winked at her. "I like an honest woman. Let me show you another."

This time he unrolled a carpet woven with deep reds and blues and the browns of desert sands. It made Lucinda think of red wines and rubies, of dark seas and sapphires, of mountains glinting with topaz.

"This one must be newer," she said.

"The same age, but from Persia," Madana said. "This one is silk which, as you must know, holds color better than wool." He turned over the edge of the carpet so she could see the weave of its back. "Twenty-five hundred knots to a square inch. This carpet, a very unusual one, has also been in my family for many generations."

Sebastian raised a skeptical eyebrow. "Are there any that have *not* been in your family since the dawn of time?"

Madana ignored him. He turned over the rug again. "This is the border," he told Lucinda, running his hand along the edge. "And this"—he swept his hand toward the center of the carpet—"is the field. Touch it," he told her. "You should feel the silk. It is the very finest."

Lucinda ran her hand along the border. "It's a garden," she realized. The pattern, which moments before had seemed flowing and abstract, now defined itself before her eyes. She pointed to the very edge of the carpet. "These are flower beds and urns." Her hand moved across the silk threads, tracing patterns. "Trees, a deer grazing, and these paths . . . they all lead to—"

"It is possible," Madana said, "that if you look carefully, you may follow what you see."

In the garden a parrot, bright blue with a streak of yellow across its wings, flew among the treetops, teasing her with harsh cries. Lucinda looked up for a moment to see if the bird's coloring was the same as Madana's parrot and found that she was no longer on the boat, no longer in the hold whose walls were covered with rugs, but in the garden. She was standing barefoot on rich black earth and the parrot was flying above her.

She fought a wave of dizziness. The soft black earth seemed to be summoning her, asking her to give it her weight, her anger, everything in her that had grown hard and bitter. She grasped a sapling and held herself upright.

Sebastian was gone, as was Mr. Madana, and yet she could hear Madana's voice clearly. "There was once a young woman who found herself in a beautiful garden where the earth was dark and fragrant and the birds called to each other and the sun streamed through the leaves in a clear green light. The young woman, who had never been in this garden before, saw that there were paths for her to follow. So although she had no course or direction, she was not lost."

The dizziness passed. The air smelled of cinnamon and orange blossoms. Lucinda saw that her own bracelets and earrings were gone, and she now wore a sleeveless grown of white silk. A clear, rectangular stone suspended from a white-gold braided chain hung from her neck. The water-clear stone, the white gown. A ridiculous notion occurred to her—that she had somehow become an innocent.

"She followed the paths that the deer had followed for centuries before her," Madana went on. "The same paths that the tigers still followed when they needed to drink. She moved through the jacaranda trees and entered a garden of lilacs, another of lilies, and yet a third where all the flowers were white so that beneath a full moon, the garden glowed.

"She then passed beneath arches wound with blue wisteria. And the parrot called to her, and she felt that everything in the garden—the flowers and the spices, the trees and the water, the very earth itself—was calling out to her, drawing her to its center where water tumbled from jagged cliffs into a jade-green lake.

"As she moved toward the water, the path became overgrown with thick trees and high grasses. This discomforted her, for she had been sure that the trails would open to the lake. Instead she caught glimpses of statues glimmering between the trees, dancing figures sculpted in gold. And of tigers padding through the grasses just ahead of her."

Lucinda felt her heart stop as she saw three of the great cats only a short distance away. They walked calmly, as peaceable as everything else in the garden, gleaming orange pelts that caught the sun; muscles that moved so smoothly, they seemed creatures without bones. And yet she knew that they thirsted for blood. She could feel their thirst and it was different from her own, a need wound through with the easy assumption that other lives must be taken.

"Yes," Madana went on, "there were tigers all around her, but in truth they had always been there. She understood that it was only now that they made themselves visible, and she could not honestly feel surprise."

"Are they hunting?" Lucinda heard herself ask aloud.

"Always," Sebastian answered. He stepped from a copse of tamarinds, barefoot and bare-chested. Blood welled from four long cuts along his rib cage. He gave her a wry grin. "I got between a tiger and a deer. Bad place to be."

"Why didn't it kill you?"

His grin widened. "You sound disappointed."

"No." She felt flustered. "I mean, how did you get away?"

"The garden has protections, as well as dangers."

Lucinda tried to shake herself from the unreality of it all. "You need to put something on those gashes," she told him.

Madana's voice returned. "In the garden she saw one whom she'd seen before and yet not fully seen. Now she saw him as he truly was. Wounded, like most mortal creatures, and yet unbowed by it, willing to walk through danger for her and with her."

Sebastian stepped closer to her and Lucinda put out an arm to stop him. "I don't know what this place is," she said. "Or what it will do to us or how we get out. But if you want to take even one step closer, you've got to promise me something."

"What's that?"

"That you won't get cute or oblique on me. No metaphors. Nothing poetic or even sarcastic."

"What options are you leaving me?" he asked, amused.

"The truth," Lucinda said. "I want whatever you say to me to be the truth."

"Ah, our young woman has asked a boon of our young man." Madana sounded enormously pleased. "And how will he respond?"

"Okay," Sebastian said. "You've got it."

"She has asked that he speak his heart," Madana went on, "and now he cannot do otherwise."

"You are beautiful in any world," Sebastian told her.

"And no flattery," she added.

"It's the truth!"

"This is useless," she told him. "I want to get out of this garden."

Sebastian shook his head, and she noticed that his hair had grown longer and the blood on his chest had dried. "Not yet," he said. "I want to show you something."

Sebastian led her to a path strewn with petals, all in pastel shades of rose, ivory, coral, and gold, so that she felt as though dawn had fallen to the earth and she was being given the gift of walking through its colors, knowing what it was to have the morning sky whisper round her ankles.

Ahead of her Sebastian moved silently. She realized that Madana had not spoken for some time. Was he gone, no longer narrating her journey? Was he still watching?

As if he'd heard her question, Sebastian turned. He reached for her hand. "What happens between you and me is our choice," he said. "Our choice only."

"Our?" She pulled her hand from his.

He touched the necklace she wore. "You have protection here."

"From a piece of quartz?"

"Quartz?" He was laughing at her now. "That, my lady, is a Jaipur diamond of the first water, perfectly transparent and flawless. It's the original crystal as it was found, never cut, only polished for a Mughal prince."

She touched the smooth planes of the stone. ". . . And it's protection against what?"

"*From*. From wild beasts, among other things."

"From you?"

"Do you think you need protection from me?"

"No," she answered. "But then I thought I was wearing a piece of quartz."

"We're almost there," he said.

The petals beneath their feet had thinned and the sound of rushing water filtered through the trees. She caught her breath as they rounded the side of the hill and the path opened to a lake fed by a waterfall. The top of the falls was so high that she couldn't see it—only the heavy, cascade of water pouring over pale green translucent rock and crashing into white foam.

Wordlessly, Sebastian led her toward the water and then across a bridge of slippery rock that ran behind the falls. They stood together, held by translucent green rock, curtained by the water.

Sebastian leaned toward her, said something into her ear, but she couldn't hear anything above the roar of the falls. A fine mist clung to her hair and soaked through the thin silk gown. Colors danced from the diamond; Lucinda watched them play along Sebastian's skin. She leaned forward, licked a band of purple from his throat, a ray of green from his chest. The water tasted surprisingly sweet.

She felt a ripple of pleasure go through him, then his hands were on her waist, sliding down her butt, cupping it, and pulling her to him. His face was in her hair, then he was kissing the side of her face, her neck, her throat, pulling the soaking white silk from her body.

There goes my innocence, she thought, but she was wild with happiness, believing for the first time that nothing could be lost, nothing could be taken. This was for giving only.

Then she was lying on the translucent green rock, feeling none of the jagged edges. It was cradling her. And she was in Sebastian's arms, their bodies pressed close, his fitting hers as perfectly as any of Tyrone's clothing. As though they'd been made for each other.

She knew he couldn't hear her above the sound of the water, but she said it anyway, her voice hoarse with emotion, "I want you inside me."

"It is done," Madana's voice said quite clearly.

And then she was kneeling on the old silk carpet in the hold of the boat. She wore her own clothing, her own bracelets. The diamond was gone.

Sebastian and Madana sat at the low table. A small bronze statue of a many-armed goddess stood on the table between them. She reminded Lucinda of the dancing statues in the garden.

"Are you sure you're willing to part with her?" Madana asked.

Sebastian shrugged. "I still owe you on that rug."

"For that, my friend, you will owe me for the rest of your life. All the precious knickknacks in this city cannot come close to the value of that rug."

Lucinda watched them, stunned. Had they been haggling the whole time she was in the garden? Had she even been *in* the garden or it was some bizarre daydream?

She got to her feet and Madana glanced over at her. "It is done," he repeated softly. "The carpet can pull you inside, no? But it always allows you to return. Unscathed."

"I'm not so sure about the unscathed part," she said.

Sebastian stood, crossed the small space to her and offered her his hand. When she took it, there was something new between them, a connection of sorts that she'd never felt, never allowed, with any other man.

"You look like you could use another cup of tea," he told her. He drew her back to the table and poured another cup of the hot spiced drink.

Lucinda concentrated on the warmth of the terra-cotta cup. Then something occurred to her and her hands started shaking so badly that she nearly dropped it.

"What is it?" Madana asked.

"Nothing," she said. "Just a silly idea."

"Which is?"

She didn't answer but she knew where the tea came from. The scent of the spices was identical to the scent of the garden, the taste identical to the taste of waterfall on Sebastian's skin. The tea couldn't have come from any other place.

She set the cup down carefully on the table. "I need to go now," she said. "I have to get back to work."

Madana nodded. "Of course. It was a pleasure meeting you," he told her. "You are welcome back here at any time."

"Let me walk you," Sebastian offered.

"No," Lucinda said. She managed to keep the alarm from her voice.

Sebastian got to his feet and helped her up from the table. "Then only as far as the dock?"

She couldn't refuse him that without creating a scene. She nodded and started out of the hold. Moments later, she stepped onto the boat's deck, incredibly relieved to once again be under the grey skies of the city, to be surrounded by the river's familiar salty tang.

Sebastian spoke just before she stepped onto the dock. "Will I see you again?"

She turned to face him. "It's not a good idea."

"Don't be so sensible."

"Good-bye," she said gently.

He held out his hand. "Can we at least part friends?"

She smiled and gave him her hand. And felt it again, the visceral current between them, both alluring and disturbing.

"Are you sure I can't show you what good use I've put that green silk to?" he asked.

She didn't answer.

"Maybe tomorrow night?"

"I'm busy."

"Then you pick the time. Any evening."

She hesitated, searching his eyes. Again, she saw only a guileless sincerity. And she felt the way his body had met hers behind the waterfall. Would he really feel that way if she gave him the chance? Was it possible for any man to feel so right in her arms?

"Next week," she finally said.

"When?"

"I don't know."

He reached into the pocket of his shirt and pulled out a plain printed business card. "Let's do it this way. Here's my address. Show up any night you like. I'll be there. Okay?"

Lucinda thought for a moment and nodded. "Maybe." She turned and started back toward Tyrone's studio. "And maybe not."

MORNING WASHED THE streets of Arcato with pale golden light that looked as though it had been filtered through the citrine that Alasdair held in his hand. It was the second morning after the new moon, and he'd woken with the piece of golden quartz cupped loosely in his palm. It had come to him during the night, positioned itself beside his coffeepot as he made coffee, then rolled into the folds of his cuffs as he picked up the mug.

He finished his coffee, doing his best to ignore its presence, but it kept prodding him, the point of its crystal sharp against his skin.

"Did the dragon send you?" he finally asked, extracting the stone from his sleeve. "You share a similar persistence."

He examined it closely, reading its heart, and found that it loved the sun and had an affinity for honeycombs and amber but no apparent connection to the jade dragon, who was still missing, probably playing pet to that bad-tempered young woman. And of course, it had its own agenda. The citrine kept pricking him, nudging him, urging him out of the apartment and onto the city streets. There was somewhere it wanted to go with him. He knew it was more than capable of appearing at the destination of its choice on its own. But it was quite insistent that there was a place they needed to go. Together.

Ever since seeing the vision in the moonstone, Alasdair had been reluctant to go out. He knew that Michael Fortunato would soon be set free, and he didn't have the first idea of how to stop it. The day before, he'd returned to the holding facility but hadn't been allowed to see the boy. He'd even swallowed his distaste and sought out the boy's mother again, only to find her passed out from drink. To go back out into the streets was to be reminded of how ineffective he was in Arcato, of how little power he held in this place.

The citrine cared nothing for that. It was satisfied only when he left the flat and then at its prodding, walked up and down the city's steepest streets, as if in training for an endurance race.

At least the dragon usually knows where it's going, he thought irritably. The last thing he needed was a pushy piece of rock with navigation problems. And yet he sensed that the stone's proddings were not random. It was searching for its destination. They simply had not stumbled onto it yet.

The sun continued its ascent, and the morning grew warmer, and the piece of golden quartz still had not found what it sought. Each time Alasdair slowed, he felt the point of its crystal sharp against his skin.

At last the citrine sent him in a switchback pattern toward the uppermost reaches of the city. And when the buildings had nearly stopped, when he was nearly back in the foothills of the mountains, the stone sent him through a narrow alley between two abandoned brick factory buildings.

The alley opened onto what had once been a plaza of sorts, its center a square paved with mosaic tile. Only bits of colored stone and glass remained, the original pattern gone. On each corner of the square stood the remains of a rounded column. Alasdair gazed upward, guessing that the columns had supported a roof. Now there was only bare sky and the surrounding walls of the factories.

He took the citrine from his robe. "Are you happy now?" he asked it. "Is this where you were so desperate to go?"

The rock sat quite still in what he took for contentment. Alasdair looked around, puzzled. Was he standing in the ruins of an ancient temple, a market, or perhaps just a public square? A marketplace would make sense, as citrine was known as a merchant's stone. In any case, he should be able to feel echoes of the past—the people who'd been here, the gods they prayed to, the objects that connected and divided them. And yet the feel of the plaza was curiously empty. As if its past had been erased, swept clean. It was impossible, he knew, to remove all traces of what had been. Something always lingered.

Although he'd been trained to keep fear at a remove (his people considered it counterproductive, unless sown in enemies), Alasdair felt it closing around his heart. How could all traces of the past be gone from a place that had been used for so long? And yet the citrine seemed content to be here, and he'd found nothing in the stone to make him think it untrustworthy.

He placed his hands on one of the columns. It was carved of a dark granite not found in these mountains. Which meant the columns were imported, he reasoned, brought in on ships then carried up through the city. But the granite yielded no information. When he tried to read it, he could sense no resonance, saw no images. He felt his fear give way to an old, familiar arrogance, a trait he'd once believed himself cured of. Something in this place would yield to his touch; something had to open. It could not continue to conceal itself from him.

Alasdair knelt to study the mosaic. Perhaps he could make out the original pattern. He caught a curved line, a patch of bright green tile and another of sapphire blue, but most of the mosaic had crumbled into the dirt of the foundation. When he ran his fingers across the bits of broken tile he found they were neither hot nor cool to the touch. Even that had been taken from them.

The citrine slid down into the palm of his hand and then fell—or to be more accurate, jumped—onto the mosaic floor. It rolled to a stop, the point of its crystal resting between two broken turquoise-colored tiles. He could sense it aligning itself with the sun, basking in its warmth.

The shape of the citrine crystal was roughly the shape of a diamond, he noted. And now he saw that surrounding the citrine was a much larger mosaic diamond made of golden tiles. Diamond within diamond? He ought to know the significance of the pattern if there was one. At the moment he saw only a pleasing design element.

"Thank you, that was most illuminating," he told the piece of golden quartz. "Now do you mind if I return to my flat?" He reached down and as his hand closed on the crystal he felt resistance; it wanted to stay. He rested his fingertips against its smooth planes. It was home. It had been here in the past and wanted to return.

He released the citrine and stood. "As you wish—" he began. He started to walk away, then stopped at an anguished shriek pitched so high and shrill as to be almost inaudible. A series of images went through him. It was almost like seeing one of the moving pictures in the city—the images flickered by so fast he couldn't separate them. But he felt them and the pain of what they conveyed was so intense, it brought him to the ground.

He crouched low, drenched in sweat, shaking. He felt as though red-hot wires were being laced around his guts, his spine, his heart. He willed it to be over and instead screamed in agony. His bones. A series of blows smashed into him until every bone in his body broke.

And then it was over. The images gone as suddenly as they'd appeared, leaving him curled on the ground, drained, and trembling. Slowly, Alasdair worked himself to a kneeling position and tried to make sense of the "information" he'd just received. There actually wasn't much he understood beyond the fact that this was neither a good nor a safe place to remain.

"If you stay, you'll be in danger," he told the citrine. "This place was—" he couldn't think of words to accurately describe it "—shattered . . . and I think blanketed with a magic that damped down all memory of what was. And whatever did this is not gone. Something that powerful does not just disappear. If it covers you, you'll not be able to feel the sun again or—"

The citrine returned to his palm as quickly as it had fallen. He tucked it safely in his robe and got to his feet. He still wasn't sure whether this had been temple or marketplace or central square, only that something of tremendous power had destroyed it. Why? The question made his head throb. He backed out through the narrow alley, his every move stiff with tension. It was silly, he knew. Something that powerful was not going to jump him from behind like a street thug, and yet he couldn't bring himself to simply walk away. The fear was working his body like an arthritic puppeteer.

The tension didn't begin to ease until he was several kilometers away. Until he'd reached a grimy, crowded little waterfront coffee shop where he ordered black coffee and a doughnut. It felt good to be in the midst of so many others. He sat, taking in the scents of coffee and bacon and fried fish, the voices of a harried waiter and a disgruntled longshoreman. He marveled at the greasy fingerprints on the piece of red vinyl that covered his table. Normally, this place would have struck him as crude. Now, however, it seemed vibrant, wonderfully awash in scent and texture and sound. Here, he almost felt safe from whatever it was that had gone through him in that plaza. He still couldn't fathom what it was, only that it held tremendous power, and that its nature frightened him. To strip a place of all traces of its past and identity—it was not only nearly impossible, it seemed a great crime against life.

He lost track of how long he stared blankly into the warm, muggy air of the coffee shop, but at last his eyes focused beyond the window and he realized that there was an unusual bustle outside. Awnings were unfurling over windows. Banners were being raised on the piers. Colored lanterns were being strung between the shops.

"What's all the preparation for?" he asked a burly man who was leaving a tip on the table beside him.

"Carnival," the man grunted. "Starts tomorrow tonight. Gonna be a big procession of boats in the harbor. And everyone in the city'll be out in the streets."

Alasdair refrained from asking whether that was a good thing.

The man, who smelled of fish, shut one eye and stared at him sharply. "You're not from here, are you?"

"Is it that obvious?"

"Yeah. You come in on one of the boats?"

"Yes," Alasdair said. "Did you?"

"I wish. I haven't left this city in forty years."

"Why not?" Alasdair found himself curious. It was assumed among his people that they would travel, that to spend your years solely among your own was to be uneducated.

The man gave a broad-shouldered shrug. "That's the way it worked out," he said. "I grew up, I got married, I got a job on the docks. Worked the boats for a while. Now I work at the fish market. Never had the kind of money to go traveling."

"Would you like to?" Alasdair asked.

The man snorted with amusement. "Doesn't matter if I do or don't. And I ain't wastin' time thinking about it." He pulled a wool knit cap over his wiry grey hair. "Take care of yourself," he told Alasdair, and strode out of the coffee shop.

Alasdair silently sent a summons to the large, well-cut sapphire he'd seen nestled in his soap dish that morning. Caught up in dealing with the citrine, he'd barely paid it any mind. *Follow him,* he now told it. *Give him the means to do as he likes. If he chooses not to travel, let it not be because he never had the chance.*

Feeling vaguely ashamed, he paid his tab and left the coffee shop before he was tempted to do another good deed. Interfering was never wise. He had no way of being sure that what he had just done would cause more good than harm, or any good at all. *So why did I do it?* he asked himself as he started back toward his flat. *Because I couldn't stand feeling as powerless as I was in that plaza? There's an altruistic motive for you.*

What more proof did he need that it was time he left Arcato?

$\mathscr{F}our$

"YOU SHALL BE a water nymph!" Tyrone proclaimed grandly, holding up a shimmering, filmy gown in shades of azure-blue and sea-green.

Lucinda spun around on the tall drawing-table chair. "As in river water?" she queried. "You'd have to dress me in sludge."

"No one ever said a Carnival costume had to be factually accurate."

She kept spinning. "It's got *sparkles* on it. What do you think I am—a five-year-old in her first ballet recital?"

Tyrone's expression wavered between being mortally offended and simply annoyed. "Look, I wouldn't offer you this dress if I didn't know it was going to stop traffic. Now will you please quit messing with my chair? You're making me dizzy."

"Maybe I don't want to stop traffic."

"Lucinda—"

She brought the spinning chair to a stop. "I am not going to be a water nymph," she said plainly. "End of discussion."

Tyrone scowled at her but went into one of the studio's many walk-in closets and returned with a tiered dress made of crimson taffeta.

"Do I look like I want to open a bordello?"

"It's a costume, babe, not an employment application."

He returned the red dress to the closet. Lucinda heard the sound of hangers knocking against each other and Tyrone cursing. Finally, he emerged holding up a slim black satin man's suit.

Lucinda raised one eyebrow. "I'll try it."

"I'm forever in your debt," Tyrone assured her.

She took the suit from him and hung it on a hook next to one of the mirrors. It was her size, of course; most of Tyrone's samples were. She stripped down unself-consciously, wondering why—when it was so beautifully made—she'd never seen the suit before.

The jacket fit her snugly, the two long, narrow lapels meeting just below the hollow of her breastbone. The pants, too, molded to her body perfectly—Tyrone's trademark fit.

"Beyond androgynous," he proclaimed. "Very male but makes you look maddeningly female. Every gay and straight man in this city is going to want you."

She pulled her hair to the top of her head and twisted it into a loose knot. With the right hat, she'd pass for a pretty young man. It was interesting, different from the extravagant gowns she'd worn at other Carnivals. "Who'd you make this for?"

"For a lover," Tyrone answered. "Who wasn't."

"When?" she demanded, surprised that he hadn't told her. If Tyrone was an incurable gossip about her love life, he was even worse with his own. Although, she reminded herself, he wasn't exactly forthcoming about the relationship that had produced his son.

"Before your time." Tyrone adjusted the suit's left shoulder a fraction of an inch. "I'll let you wear it," he said magnanimously. "Looks good on you. Wicked dark."

She frowned at her reflection. "Maybe that's the problem."

"Lucinda, please don't tell me you want me to make you a nun's habit."

She laughed in spite of herself. "Now that'd be a change."

"The suit looks good. Wear it," Tyrone told her.

"I don't want to."

"You crazy?"

She gave a confused shrug and took off the jacket. She wasn't even sure of why she was refusing the black suit. Except that like everything else, it felt wrong.

"Fine. Make your own damn costume," Tyrone muttered.

Lucinda judged it time to change the topic. "So what are you going to wear?"

Tyrone's eyes lit with delight. "Excuse me," he said, and disappeared behind the white lacquered French doors that led to his bedroom while Lucinda pondered why none of the costumes felt right—especially the suit, for which she would have gladly traded her first-born child only a week ago. If she didn't want the sea nymph or the queen of the bordello or the androg-yne's suit, what did she want?

Then she knew. She had a vision of herself in the simple white silk shift, the diamond pendant resting against her chest.

That was what she wanted to wear, *all* she'd wanted to wear since she'd left Madana's boat. Every day since then she'd put on her own clothes and Tyrone's designs, and all of it felt wrong, an offense to her skin. What she wanted was that slip of white silk. And if she told Tyrone? She could de-scribe it to him. Tyrone would whip up something close, if not identical, in an hour. And yet she couldn't bear to tell him about it and risk him laughing at her, at her desire for an innocence that she'd never felt before or since.

The French doors opened, and Tyrone stepped toward her. He was a vi-sion of peacock-blue silk and gold lamé. Lucinda blinked in astonishment, taking in the layered, triangular skirt, the breastplate, the golden headdress in the shape of an inverted crescent, the slingshot in one hand, the club in the other. The outfit was gaudy, ridiculous, and strangely beautiful.

"What are you supposed to be?" she finally asked.

"Magnificent, am I not?"

"Yeah, but what—"

"Just call me Ilyap'a. He's an Incan weather god, who was known for his shining garments." Tyrone lifted the slingshot. "When he hurled a stone from this contraption, the sound of the sling snapping was thunder. And the lightning was the reflections off his clothes." Tyrone positioned himself be-neath a track light so Lucinda could get the full weather effect.

"And the club?" she asked.

"Haven't got a clue," he confessed. "But this Ilyap'a, he takes water from the Milky Way, keeps it in a jug, then he breaks the jug with a stone and it rains. Isn't that poetic?"

"A god, Tyrone? Are you sure you're not letting that colossal ego of yours run away with you?" She immediately regretted her words as she saw hurt in her friend's eyes. She tried again. "It's just that with all the gods who are supposed to be in residence in this city, how do you know you're not go-ing to offend some deity in that getup?"

"You are offending *me,*" Tyrone told her in a dangerously low voice. "I am sure that if Ilyap'a is here, he will be flattered to see himself so gloriously represented." He whirled in front of a mirror, admiring his reflection. "Now this would look so fine, parading alongside that water nymph gown I have for you. Are you sure you won't reconsider?"

Lucinda reached for her bag, this one a patchwork of velvet scraps that Tyrone had discarded. "I'd better go," she told him.

He reached out one gold-banded arm, holding the door to the loft shut. "You haven't settled on a costume yet. How are you and I going to do the parade together?"

"I don't know." She found herself looking at the black-and-white tiled floor, reluctant to meet Tyrone's eyes.

"You getting moody on me, girl?" he asked in a tone that was surprisingly gentle.

She leaned back against the door, thinking she'd never seen him look quite so absurd—or quite so dear. "Nothing I try on feels right," she explained. "I don't know why, but I don't think I can do a costume this year. Would you be terribly mad if I asked you to do the parade on your own?"

"It won't be as much fun."

"I know." She put her arms around him. "I'll call you tomorrow morning and let you know for certain."

Lucinda left the studio, certain she'd just ruined Carnival for Tyrone. She started toward her flat then changed direction and headed for the waterfront. Ever since that afternoon on Madana's boat, she'd felt a peculiar restlessness. It drove her out into the streets of the city. It made the hours at the studio nearly unbearable. She considered returning to the rug merchant's boat. She considered calling on Sebastian. She put both thoughts on hold. When she'd been on the boat, when she'd emerged from that vision in the carpet, she'd been vulnerable in a way that she was usually proof against. And she wasn't at all sure she could risk that again.

IT WAS NEARLY midnight when Lucinda returned to her apartment. After leaving the studio she'd gone into a riverfront café owned by one of Tyrone's clients, only to be drafted into helping with Carnival preparations. She'd strung lights and glass beads and tiny paper lanterns. She'd made flowers from colored tissue paper, and draped the tables with cloths that matched the deep reds and purples of the flowers. Altogether it was more of an arts and crafts project than she could stomach; she returned to her building tired and cranky and wondering if she'd agreed to all the work in the café as a penance for disappointing Tyrone. Or as a distraction from her thoughts of Sebastian.

She pushed open the door to her building and crossed the area that the owner of the building liked to refer to as "the lobby" and she thought of as "Mugger's Delight." Two small lamps with colored-glass shades lit the cavernous space; it was all dark corners, shadowed alcoves, and stained marble columns that disappeared into the gloom of a vaulted ceiling.

The building had no elevator. She took the wide marble stairs that wound to the fourth floor. The hallways were as dim as the lobby, though Tyrone had installed a sconce outside her door, claiming that was the only way he'd find her. Now in the pool of light from the sconce she saw two soft-sided packages, wrapped in brown paper and tied together with a silver string. She picked them up, looked for a note or a card, and when she found none, took them into the flat with her.

She set the packages on the side table in her living room, then began the search she now did whenever she entered the apartment—but there was no sign of the jade dragon. Why it had vanished, why it had come into her life in the first place, remained mysteries.

Using her pocketknife, she sliced through the string that bound the two packages then opened the top one. Lucinda's breath caught as she lifted out a dress of shimmering white silk. It couldn't be and yet it *was* identical to the dress she'd worn in the garden. She'd wanted it so badly and now it had appeared at her door. She pressed it against her body and felt a rush of memories: being held by the translucent green rock behind the falls, being folded into Sebastian's arms with only the white silk between them . . .

She sat down on the edge of the bed, trying to sort through a rush of conflicting feelings. She had no doubt that the gifts were from Sebastian, and Sebastian set off warning signals in every fiber of her being. She knew she ought to stay away from him; he was dangerous—to her equilibrium at the very least. And yet, all her life she'd been drawn to beautiful things. Though she would never admit it, there was a childlike part of her that hoped that by surrounding herself with what was rich and beautiful, she'd banish ugliness from her life. What she'd seen on Madana's boat and had felt with Sebastian was the promise of that shimmering richness, a realm of beauty that she'd always secretly hoped existed but had never quite found or created on her own. So was it wrong of her to want—okay, to delight in—something from that world? Maybe that wasn't the question. More concretely, was it perverse to accept a gift from a man she was so wary of? But wasn't it also equally perverse to turn away what you'd been aching for?

And why, now that she had it in her hands, was she curiously reluctant to put on the dress? She ran a finger along the smooth, shimmering fabric, so white it was almost pearlescent. She couldn't wear it for Carnival, she realized. It would be wrong. Tyrone liked to talk about how every dress had an essence, be it seduction or sophistication or playfulness. The essence of this dress, Lucinda knew, was connected to something pure and untainted, and on Carnival Night the very air dripped mockery.

Curious now, she opened the other parcel and lifted out a second dress— a delicate web of silver crescents and stars, connected at their points with silver beads. Whatever the silver fabric was, she didn't recognize it but she knew instinctively that this dress was made for Carnival. She took off her own dress, a soft, funky flower print that Tyrone considered one of his mistakes, and slipped on the silver dress. One glance in the oval mirror and Lucinda started laughing. The dress fit as well as any of Tyrone's, clinging to her body exactly where it should, revealing just enough skin between the stars and moons. She looked back at the open wrapping and saw that beneath a layer of pale blue tissue paper there was more: a pair of silver dancing slippers, a silver mask, and a necklace of perfectly round moonstones suspended from a silver chain. *Well,* she thought, *I suppose I'll have to tell Tyrone I have a costume, after all.*

ALASDAIR HAD ARRIVED in Arcato with money enough to rent a flat and cover expenses for a month or so. He was running low now and unwilling to trade any of the objects that had been arriving unbidden from the mountains. If he was going to buy passage on a boat out of the city, he would have to shore up his finances. Which was why, dressed in a long black coat, he was now standing in front of the window of a jewelry shop called Manjusha, debating the wisdom of actually going inside. He needed to sell a few stones and do it without being taken for a jewel thief. Of course, there was a black market for gemstones in Arcato and he probably could have tapped into it without too much trouble, but he liked what he saw in this particular window. The pieces were extraordinary, not in rarity or price—there were semiprecious as well as more expensive gems—but by virtue of the fact that every stone was superbly cut. Deceptively simple settings showed off the stones' color and shape and let the light stream through them. Rings and necklaces and bracelets and earrings, every piece seemed to glow. If he was going to trade stones, Alasdair mused, he wanted them to be well served.

A chime rang as he entered the shop. A heavyset woman, who sat in a high-backed chair, gazing out the window, didn't even glance at him. The fastidiously dressed man who stood behind the counter hovered at a polite distance as Alasdair studied the contents of the glass display cases, noting that the pieces in the store were even finer than those in the window. Only when Alasdair had looked through every case did the man speak up. "May I show you something?" he inquired. His hand swept over a collection of gold and emerald pieces arrayed on black velvet.

"Actually that was my question for you," Alasdair said. "I was wondering if you buy stones."

The man raised a skeptical brow. "What sort of stones?"

Alasdair hesitated. "They're blue." He took a small glass vial from his coat pocket and poured the contents onto a black velvet pad that sat on the counter.

"May I?" said the man as he strapped on a head loupe. One by one, he examined the stones through the magnifying glass, muttering, "Blue topaz, oval mixed cut; two aquamarines, step cut, matched: blue tourmaline cabochons; opal . . ." He removed the loupe to gaze at Alasdair. "Where did you get these?"

"They've been in my family," Alasdair said, coming as close to the truth as he dared.

"We'll need some sort of proof of ownership if we're going to buy them from you."

"I'm afraid I don't have any," Alasdair admitted, reproaching himself for not thinking to come up with some sort of documentation. He'd never understand why cities all seemed to have this obsession with officious-looking pieces of paper. "I give you my word, though."

"I'm afraid that's not enough. We can't afford to risk our reputation."

"I see. Well, thank you for your time." Alasdair was scooping the stones back into the glass vial when the woman in the high-backed chair got to her feet.

"I'm Rudelle Udovitch, the owner," she announced. "Let me see those stones." She made her way over to them, moving with a slow, slightly lopsided gait.

Alasdair again displayed the cache of gems. Rudelle Udovitch didn't bother with the head loupe. She fingered the stones, held a few up to the light, then said, "These were in your family?"

Alasdair nodded.

"Then you've inherited gems of remarkable quality."

"Yes."

She inclined her head toward her employee. "My associate has a point. These won't do me any good if the police show up a week from now and confiscate them as stolen goods."

"No one will confiscate them. They weren't stolen," Alasdair said, glad that he hadn't added any sapphires or blue diamonds to the mix. "How much will you give me for the lot?"

A sly expression came into Rudelle's eyes. She named a figure far less than the stones' value but enough to get him out of Arcato. For form's sake—and to avoid arousing further suspicion—Alasdair doubled the price.

Rudelle didn't even pretend to consider it. She gave a deep, throaty laugh and said, "You've got a deal. Joseph, get him his money."

A disgruntled-looking Joseph retreated to a back room and emerged a few minutes later with an envelope. At Rudelle's insistence Alasdair counted it. "It's all there," he confirmed. "Thank you."

She gave him a brisk nod but as he handed over the stones she said, "My gut tells me you know exactly what they're worth. Why were you willing to let them go for a price like that?"

"Because the jewelry you sell is beautiful," Alasdair said. "And I'm thinking that there's at least a chance that you'll see that each stone will be given a setting that's worthy of it."

She gave him a long, shrewd look. "Well, at least your lies are pretty ones."

Alasdair smiled and bent his head to her. "It was a pleasure doing business with you."

"Yeah," she said. "Come back when you have more to sell."

DUSK WAS FALLING when Tyrone showed up at Lucinda's flat the next evening. He'd covered his face with gold paint to match the gold lamé in his costume. Iridescent-blue glass beads were braided into his hair. Even in the dim hallway he was luminous.

"A sky god, indeed," Lucinda murmured admiringly. "You are a sight."

"So are you." He stepped into the apartment, staring at the dress of silver moons and stars. "Who made that sexy thing? And what, may I ask, is it made of?"

"Don't know and don't know. It was a gift."

"From who?"

She shrugged. "Mystery admirer?"

He caught a bit of silver fabric between his fingers. "Some gift. I don't know anyone in Arcato who does work like this."

She nodded. Music was beginning to filter up from the streets. A samba followed by drumming.

"It fits you like I made it," he told her, frowning.

"Does that mean you approve?"

"When I'm not being consumed with jealousy. I tell you, whoever de-signed this dress better not open shop in this city. I'd be out of business fast." He snapped his fingers. "Good-bye, Dessalines Productions."

"Don't you think you're overdoing the modesty—or is it the melo-drama?"

"It's envy, girl, pure bile-green envy. And I'll tell you something else. This mystery man is one serious suitor. Better watch your ass, babe."

"I'll remember that," she said as she returned to her room to finish dressing.

Tyrone trailed her into the bedroom. "I suppose I ought to be grateful," he conceded. "After all, whoever gave you this frock—"

"*Frock?*"

"Frock. As I was saying, whoever gave it to you, got you to go to Carnival, and I'd have been woesomely bored without you."

The phone rang. Lucinda made no effort to get it and her answering machine clicked on. "*Hello, Lucinda, are you there? Lucinda, this is your mother. If you're there, pick up the phone.*"

"You heard her," said Tyrone. "Pick up the phone."

Lucinda didn't move.

"*Lucinda, where are you? You never answer your phone and I worry about you. I don't know why I bother, I know you won't call back, but I'm your mother and it's Carnival Night, with all that craziness. Not that I think you're using drugs again. You're not, are you?*"

Lucinda sighed, bracing herself for the usual guilt-inducing monologue.

"*I wouldn't worry so much if I knew you had something healthy in your life, something like church,*" her mother went on. "*You know, I saw Father Vincente the other day, and he told me you'd be welcome back any time. He said the Holy Mother herself would open her arms to you. He says she helps all sinners, Lucinda. So maybe you should come to church with me on Sunday. Then I wouldn't worry so much.*" There was a silence, her mother presumably waiting for her to respond, then, "*Okay, I just wanted to say hello. Call me.*"

The sound of her mother hanging up came through the answering machine's speaker, and Lucinda relaxed. She grabbed a handful of hair and twisted it up in a loose chignon. "Up or down?"

"Forget your hair for a minute," Tyrone said. "Why won't you talk to your mother?"

"Didn't you hear that message?"

"So what? You don't have take it so personal."

"Tyrone, she hasn't approved of anything I've done since I was nine."

"Nine?"

"Okay, since she got pregnant with me and my father-to-be took a boat out of the city and never came back. I ruined her life."

"You think that's true?"

"Well, I'm not the one who got her knocked up but you notice, I'm the sinner. Or at least a disaster in need of rescue."

"You know," Tyrone drawled, "you could disabuse her of that idea by letting her see you as you are. Why not invite her into your life now and then? Why don't we invite her to one of our shows?"

"Because she'd probably bring Father Vincente and try to get me to take communion on the spot." Lucinda took a pair of silver filigree earrings from her jewelry box and put them on. "My mother has never gotten over the idea that she did a terrible thing when she got pregnant. She's been trying to expiate it—and me—ever since."

"Because she was unmarried?"

"Essentially. That's when she renounced the other gods and turned to the church."

Tyrone regarded Lucinda thoughtfully and when he spoke his voice was soft. "When she got pregnant she was left on her own, right? So maybe she found some comfort in the church. Don't be so hard on her. Talk to her next time she calls."

Lucinda frowned at her wrists and removed two thick silver bangles, replacing them with more delicate bracelets. "And say what? When we do talk all she does is tell me how much she worries over me and how I should go to church because that will make everything all right. And I sit there with a glazed look, wondering why on earth I ever gave up drugs."

"Doesn't have to go that way," Tyrone pointed out in an equable tone. "Maybe if she really understood something about your life, she wouldn't be putting it down."

"Oh, please. She won't listen. She needs someone to disapprove of. Makes her feel righteous."

"Then let her," Tyrone said. "She's the only mother you're going to get in this lifetime."

"Thank you for that sage advice," Lucinda said, trying to keep her voice as even as his. "Now could we get back to the matter at hand?" She strode back to the mirror and lifted her hair again.

"Are you going to call her back?"

"The truth?" Lucinda stared at her reflection. She looked nothing like her mother, which was the only source of comfort in their relationship. "No," she told him. "And you can't change that. So if you want to get down to the streets tonight before Carnival ends, tell me: Should I wear my hair up or down?"

"Down," said Tyrone with a theatrical sigh of resignation. "Oh. I almost forgot." He reached into the peacock-blue costume and removed from some hidden pocket a fine chain strung with silver stars. "Stand still and I'll drape this through your hair."

"You just happened to bring that with you?" she asked. It seemed too much of a coincidence; the silver chain looked as if it had been made for her costume.

"Booty," he explained. "I found it on the street on the way over here. Someone lost their Carnival bauble. No reason not to put it to use."

"I suppose," Lucinda agreed, letting him pin the chain of stars through her hair. When he'd finished she put on the silver mask. She held out her arm to him then drew it back. "One more thing." She took the moonstone necklace from her dresser and put it on.

"Mystery man give you that, too?"

She nodded. The stones glowed softly, and for just a second she could see a spill of silver moonlight across a pale blue sea.

"And you're not the least bit suspicious?"

"Of what?"

"Of why some anonymous someone went to so much trouble so you could shine like the night sky at Carnival. And this necklace . . . it's a fine piece. I'm guessing Victorian, maybe older."

Lucinda was tempted to tell him that that was because it came from an antique dealer, but she resisted the urge. "Let's go," she said, and headed for the door.

Tyrone folded his arms across his chest. "That can wait. Ever since you disappeared on that lunch break last week, you've been dreamy eyed and restless, looking like a lovesick teenager. Now what is going on and who is he?"

"None of your—"

"What? None of my damn business? Lucinda, you *are* half my business. I don't even like to think about where my designs would be without you. Come on, babe, you and me don't keep secrets from each other." When Lucinda didn't respond, he added, "You don't have to worry. I give you my solemn word, I won't steal him away from you."

Lucinda looked at Tyrone through the silver mask. "I never gave him my address," she said. "And I'm not listed. So how'd he know where to find me?"

FOR THE ZILLIONTH time, Michael Fortunato tossed the yellow chryso-whatever at the cinder block wall and watched it fall to the floor. Listlessly, he got off the cot and retrieved the rock. The white line that gleamed and sometimes seemed to wink inside it, the thing that made it look like a cat's eye, was sort of cool but nothing to get worked up about. He threw the stone again. It was the only thing to do in this crappy cell. He couldn't figure out what was going on with his case. He was supposed to have some sort of hearing, tests, a trial. And then either he'd get out or he'd get locked up someplace else. Whichever it was going to be, he wished it would happen already. He hated all this waiting. If it weren't for the guard who brought him tasteless meals twice a day, he'd swear the world had forgotten he existed. His mother's visits had stopped weeks ago. She came once after his fake uncle showed up, and then the newspaper reporters moved on to other stories and she seemed to lose interest as well. No one had visited him since then. He still wondered about "Uncle Ivor," who he really was, what he wanted. And he half-wished he'd show up again, just to break the monotony.

It was weird how his mind kept circling around the same tired memories. He thought about his room at home, how it was cramped and cluttered and a mess, and how the whole place reeked of his mother's cigarettes and the knock-'em-dead perfume she wore to mask the alcohol on her breath, but how it was still so much better than this place. Michael thought about the day before Spook died. That afternoon Michael and a girl from his class cut school and snuck into a movie together. After, they walked along the riverfront. She'd squeezed his hand and that felt nice. He thought about the river, about the way it drew him; how, no matter what else was going on in his life, he always wound up down by the water. Sometimes he thought about Spook. Okay, he thought about him a lot. And what he thought was that it wasn't right that Spook got such a raw deal; it wasn't fair that he had to get cancer and die so young.

MICHAEL TRIED NOT to look too interested as he heard the bolt on his door slide back and a key turn the tumbler. The door opened and the guard, a sad-looking, overweight man named Carl, came in with another tray of slop.

"Cheer up, little buddy," Carl said. "Tonight's the start of Carnival."

"I'm so excited," Michael replied in a flat tone. He pushed away the tray. "I'll really enjoy the view. Soon as you cut me a window in the cinder block."

Carl shrugged and turned to go, and Michael found that he didn't want to be left alone so quickly. "Hey," he called out, "do you know when I'm going to have my hearing?"

The guard scratched at his thinning hair. "Didn't see your name on the court schedule."

"Can't you ask someone?"

Carl smiled at him for the first time, and in that instant Michael knew the man hated him. "It doesn't look like there's anyone too interested in getting you out," Carl said. "If I were you, little buddy, I'd get used to this place."

"I'm not your fucking little buddy," Michael muttered.

"What did you say?" The guard's eyes gleamed with interest, and Michael knew he'd just given the man an excuse to hurt him.

"I mean, that's really good advice," the boy said quickly, but couldn't stop himself from adding, "Thanks a whole hell of a lot, douche bag."

Carl took a step toward him. "You watch your mouth, boy. 'Cause no one here would be too upset if I took my belt to you. They'd probably give me a raise if I beat your ass."

"Yeah? What would they give you to kill me?" Michael knew he was acting crazy now, but he couldn't stop. He was bored and furious and he didn't care what Carl did to him. Anything would be better than sitting here, staring at the walls.

Carl unbuckled his wide leather belt and began to slide it out of the belt loops. He stopped as he noticed the cat's eye on the floor. "What's that?"

"It's mine." Michael dived for the stone but Carl got to it first.

"It's mine now," the guard said. He held the dull yellow stone up to the room's bare lightbulb, squinting at it. "What are *you* doing with a diamond?" he muttered. His brows knit together. "You lifted it off someone, didn't you?"

Michael worked hard to keep a straight face. "A diamond? You really think that's a *diamond*?" He gave a low whistle. "Just goes to show how even prison guards can be dumber than they look."

Carl backhanded him across the mouth and Michael landed hard on the floor. He felt a dull stab of vindication along with the pain. The man was an asshole, ridiculously easy to bait. He had to work harder to get a rise out of his mother, and she was the neighborhood hysteria queen.

Carl swaggered over to him. "Don't try to give me any of your juvenile bull. I know a yellow diamond when I see one. And I sure as hell know it don't belong to you. Guess we'll be adding robbery to your charges."

Michael stayed where he was on the floor and rubbed his jaw. "Maybe you're not stupid," he said. "Maybe you're just going blind. Did anyone ever tell you, you ought to get your eyes checked?"

But the guard wasn't listening. He was staring at the cloudy yellow stone like it was giving off rainbows. Michael remembered the diamond Spook had shown him, glinting with white fire even in Hekate's black night. No one who'd ever seen the real thing could mistake this piece of rock for a diamond. No one in his right mind, that is.

Carl gave the boy a sly look, buckled his belt, and pocketed the stone. "You're in luck, little buddy. I'm going to take this with me for evidence. So we'll save your beating for another time. Besides, it's Carnival. Knock yourself out!"

The door clanged shut and Michael heard the familiar sound of the bolt being shot, the lock turning. *What just happened?* he asked himself. *Is he trying to set me up?*

Deciding Carl was nuts—who else would take such a dumb-ass job?—Michael returned to his cot with a sigh. Now he didn't even have a rock to throw. Figures that douche bag would take the one thing in here that was his.

He shut his eyes, and this time he remembered last year's Carnival when he caught a ride on one of the boats in the flotilla. Standing on deck, feeling the river moving beneath him, feeling the night sky all around without buildings breaking it up, it had been . . . okay. Out on that boat, he hadn't felt scared and he hadn't felt angry. He just felt like it was a good place to be, so good that he hadn't wanted to go back ashore. He hid out in the engine room and fell asleep. He woke up the next morning—and nearly died of embarrassment—to find himself in the arms of a burly sailor, being carried back to the empty city streets. He'd wriggled out of the guy's arms and disappeared down an alley. But he could still remember what it felt like to be on that boat—part of the city and Carnival itself, but free of it all, too.

Something restless clawed inside him. Michael got up and began to pace the cell, feeling like the caged animal that he was. *It's not fair,* he thought. *I haven't even been convicted of anything and they've got me locked away. The least they could do is let me go to Carnival. Just for one lousy night, they could let me out.*

Right then, a split second after he thought about getting out for Carnival, something metal skittered across the cell's cement floor. Michael blinked, not believing his eyes. Then he dove for it.

A ring of tarnished brass skeleton keys. Something was listening, answering his wishes. Which would be a first for him. " 'Bout time," he crooned softly as he started toward the door.

His jolt of excitement faded at once. What a joke. There wasn't even a keyhole on his side of the door, let alone one that would work with keys from some other century.

Disgusted, he threw the useless key ring on the floor.

How the hell had they gotten into this locked box anyway? He glanced up at the tiny wire-reinforced window in the door. Nope, no entry. And he knew Carl hadn't left them.

They'd just appeared out of nowhere. And not burning hot or ice cold or anything remotely strange. Just a ring of tarnished brass keys. He picked them up. They were heavy. They made a nice jangling sound when he shook them.

He stood in the center of the cell, holding the key ring and considering.

Then he shrugged. *Why not?* He walked over to the steel door. Despite the fact that there was no keyhole on his side, he held one of the keys up to the general area where he thought the lock was. He poked around a bit, the brass tip of the key scraping the metal door. And then, quite suddenly, the key sank into the surface of the door, almost as though it had been sucked in.

Michael gripped the head of the key. His hand was shaking now. This was too fucking weird. All of it. The cat's eye that was a diamond, the key ring appearing from nowhere, and now this one skeleton key, melting into a door of solid steel. He bit down on his lip until he tasted blood. Okay, the blood was salty and real; this wasn't a dream.

It got weirder. He turned the key, heard the tumblers drop, felt the bolt push back. The door swung open into an empty hallway, glaring white beneath fluorescent tubes. The boy looked both ways, saw no one, made his way cautiously down the hall. Expecting alarms to sound at any second, he followed a sign to a stairwell then took the stairs down to the street. The outer door was locked, but one of the skeleton keys took care of that too.

Michael stepped outside and let his eyes adjust to the night. The river's cold, damp air bit into him, made him shiver with pleasure. Just being outside felt great. The detention center was on the very edge of the city. It was industrial here—warehouses, a power plant, a lot filled with the long, motorized platforms used for transporting the port's cargo through the city, a graveyard for rusted-out ships, none of it decently lit.

That's good, the boy told himself. The shadows would hide him. He figured he was about four klicks from the waterfront. Briefly, he debated whether it was smart to even go near the heart of the city. *Tonight's Carnival,* he reminded himself. *I'll get a mask. No one's going to notice me.* Besides, he felt the river calling him again. And he had to answer that call; it felt like hunger.

Keeping to the shadows, Michael started walking. He'd gone less than three blocks when he heard footsteps close behind. "Shit," he muttered, "where they'd come from?"

Michael turned, instinctively choosing to bluff rather than bolt. He relaxed a little as he realized it was someone in a costume and mask. Actually two Carnival masks—a man's bearded face in front, a smooth-shaven head facing the back.

"Hey," Michael said.

"Hey, yourself," a voice replied.

"Cool costume." Michael let the guy walk ahead of him. The guy was carrying a big, heavy-looking staff in one hand but that didn't faze Michael. Something was helping him, he realized. Something was out there tonight, removing every obstacle. It occurred to him that he could help himself to one of these masks—after all, the guy had two. Besides, he was a criminal now with an official jailbreak to his credit. Might as well act the part.

Moving quietly, he began to follow the masked figure. All he needed was a weapon or something that would feel like one. His eyes skimmed the ground and found a broken screwdriver lying against a rusted-out oil drum. Michael scooped it up, barely stopping. He'd poke the guy in the back with it, say, "This is a holdup! Your mask or your life!" What a joke.

He never got that far. The masked figured passed beneath a street lamp, stopped, and very deliberately opened the hand that wasn't carrying the staff. As if to show Michael what he held. A ring of brass skeleton keys lay in his open palm—the same keys that were no longer in Michael's hand.

The boy froze, his chest tight with fear. This was too much. This was getting to be every bit as strange and sick as the night of the see-through guy. *And you know how that one ended,* he reminded himself. He pocketed the screwdriver, let the masked figure disappear into the darkness up ahead. For a heartbeat he considered returning to the detention center. But he could see the river in his mind, almost feel it—the black expanse of water, the sound of it swelling against the piers, the boats all lit up. Maybe tonight he'd get himself on a boat. But this time he wouldn't let himself be found.

That was it. He knew what to do. The river was his friend, a promise that there was always someplace else to go, always a way out. It was calling to him. It would give him refuge. And it would take him away. He began to run toward the water.

PART 2

Carnival

"For stone gathers seed and clouds,
skeleton larks and wolves of penumbra . . ."

— FEDERICO GARCÍA LORCA,
"Lament for Ignacio Sanchez Mejias"

$\mathcal{F}ive$

"DAMN," LUCINDA SAID. She came to a halt in the lobby of her building just a few steps from the front door. "I have to go back upstairs," she told Tyrone.

Tyrone shot a longing glance out toward the street. "Lucinda, it just took me an hour to get you *out* of your apartment. There is no way I'm going to let you go back up there again."

"Fine. Wait here for me," she said distractedly. "I forgot to bring a bag, and now I have no place to put my keys."

"Let me guess. That marvel of a dress doesn't have a pocket? I tell you, if I'd designed it, I would have found a way to put pockets in there."

Lucinda kissed Tyrone on the cheek. "Yes, darling," she said, imitating the magazine editor who'd interviewed him that morning. "You are without question the most brilliant designer in Arcato."

"Until her next issue," Tyrone agreed. "Here, let me have those keys." He slipped them into one of his costume's many pockets and held out his arm to her. "Time to party, girl."

They stepped out of the building and into the crowded street. Lucinda inhaled deeply, savoring the damp night air and the tantalizing blend of smells that was Carnival: coffee and pastries, cigarette smoke and beer, grilled seafood, bodies covered in sweat and perfumes, incense rising from sidewalk shrines—and all of it riding the salty tang of the Candra.

Fireworks thundered against the sky then rained streams of colored light down over the harbor. The doors to every shop and bar and restaurant were thrown open. *Everything open, everyone concealed,* Lucinda thought as she brushed shoulders with harlequins and courtesans, witches and angels, executioners and nuns and sideshow grotesques.

Tyrone pointed to an altar—a circle of shells and smooth white stones surrounding a painting of a voluptuous green-skinned goddess. "I swear that wasn't there when I walked over to your place," he said. "What is with this city? We've got altars springing up everywhere."

Moving slowly at first, they eased their way into the throng of revelers that filled the street. Halfway down the block, as they neared a masked percussion band playing on a wooden platform, the crowd began to move more quickly, surging forward, backward, then forward again in time to the band's insistent rhythm. The drummers danced as they played, their drumsticks whirling overhead, behind their backs, spinning across the makeshift stage, never missing a beat. Lucinda felt the rhythm go straight into her bloodstream. It captured her pulse, made her hips sway and her feet dance. A sideways glance told her that Tyrone had already given in. He was dancing with the infectious beat, arms spread wide, fingers beckoning, as if inviting legions of fans to join him in celebration.

"What are we going to do with you?" Lucinda asked him. "You're such a shrinking violet, it's scary."

"Take a right at the corner," Tyrone told her. "The parade starts on Grand and Barrow."

Good thing that they were heading toward the waterfront, Lucinda thought, because that's where the crowd was taking them whether they wanted it or not. The crowd was an entity unto itself—a creature both animal and fey—with what was, in this city, a rare spirit of reckless generosity.

"Hey, pretty lady," called an old man, leaning forward on his cane.

"Ooooh, it's a moon goddess!" said the young girl beside him.

A man in a rotund pumpkin costume knelt before her and said quite solemnly, "Lady of the Night, bless me."

Lucinda shot Tyrone a helpless look.

"Bless him," he snapped, "before the fool gets himself trampled."

Feeling awkward, Lucinda mumbled an impromptu blessing: "Bless this pumpkin—I mean, the man inside—with . . . with strength and serenity."

"Strength and serenity?" Tyrone echoed when the blessed one had gone on his way. "Where'd you get that? And I would like to know why you're the one being treated like a goddess when I'm the one who's dressed up as a god."

She tried not to grin. "No accounting for taste."

The crowd swept them onto a block where the scent of jambalaya filled the air and calypso set the beat.

Tyrone took her hand and spun her into his arms. Lucinda let him lead, comfortable with his being the flashier dancer, the flashier everything, the male bird with his glorious plumage. Dancing with Tyrone wasn't really about the two of them dancing together anyway. It was about Tyrone strutting his finery and taking her along for the ride.

A large silvery paw came between them, making it clear that the reveler in the wolf's costume not only wanted to break in but that it was Tyrone he wanted to dance with.

"Be my guest." Lucinda stepped back, amused. Despite the clumsiness of the costume, the wolf danced nearly as well as Tyrone. Moments later the song ended. The band took a break, and Tyrone and his partner sought her out in the crowd. The wolf lifted her hand and lasciviously licked the back of her wrist.

"Uck!" Lucinda yanked her hand away.

"Lucinda, it's Marcus!" Tyrone told her, as if that made it any less repulsive.

Marcus Tuttle and Tyrone had been in art school together. For years now Tyrone had struggled valiantly to find plausible reasons not to buy Marcus's god-awful sculptures, which always reminded Lucinda of giant, demented spiders. Recently though, Marcus had caught on with one of Arcato's more influential art critics, and his prices had become so insanely exorbitant that Tyrone was officially, gratefully, priced out.

Marcus lifted off the wolf's head. "No one warned me it was going to be a hundred degrees inside this costume!"

Any fool could have figured it out, Lucinda replied silently. She studied the two men. Though Marcus's head was shaved smooth, he and Tyrone looked enough alike to pass for brothers. They were about the same height with similar light, lithe builds. They had the same cocoa-colored skin and nearly identical straight, full-lipped mouths; but there was a good-natured belligerence in Tyrone's eyes, something calculating in Marcus's.

Marcus draped an arm around Tyrone's shoulders and fingered the gold lamé. "And who are you supposed to be, my shiny friend?"

"Ilyap'a, Lord of Lightning." Tyrone dramatically pointed to the sky. His eyes widened in alarm as a crack of thunder shook the ground and jagged lightning flared above the fireworks.

Marcus laughed. "Don't look so surprised, man. You always could sew up a storm."

Tyrone smiled but the cocky attitude was gone, and in his eyes Lucinda saw doubt and the first glimmerings of fear. "Coincidence," she told him.

The calypso band began another number. "Do you mind if I steal your man again?" Marcus asked Lucinda. He didn't give her a chance to answer but whirled Tyrone into the dance.

"Lucinda, don't get lost!" Tyrone shouted to her. "Meet me at the Dome in an hour!"

"Maybe!" Lucinda called back. If Tyrone was going to go off dancing with that no-talent canine, she wasn't making any promises.

She glanced up at the sky again. It was hard to tell with fireworks dissolving against the night, but the skies seemed clear, of a piece with the smooth black surface of the river. Rain, thunder, lightning—they belonged to another night.

In the harbor the line of boats was slowly making its way across the water. She decided to skip the parade. She'd head down to the riverwalk and at least be closer to the Dome in case she decided to forgive Tyrone. Maybe she'd even catch a glimpse of Madana's boat in the flotilla.

With some effort Lucinda pulled herself out of the main flow of the crowd and onto one of the alleys that cut between the streets. She liked this particular alley because its ancient stucco buildings no longer stood straight but leaned against each other comfortably like old friends. Tonight the alley was decked out, colored lights strung between the buildings, garlands of flowers draping each door, and in the niches in the walls, more shrines—statues of austere saints and mirthful gods, all of them lit by votive candles flickering in colored glass. Tyrone was right, she thought. There'd always been shrines in the city, but lately they seemed to be multiplying exponentially.

She followed the trickle of revelers who were taking the same shortcut down to the waterfront, where she managed to work her way through the crowd toward the railing that overlooked the water.

A crowd was pressed up against the railing, the equivalent of being in first-row seats for the fireworks that were being set off from a barge. Yet amid all the costumes Lucinda recognized a tall, slender figure wearing a long, blue robe.

It did not for a second occur to her that it was someone in costume. She knew exactly who it was. The only real question was, should she talk to him or melt back into the crowd. They had nothing to say to each other. They never had, and yet he always managed to shake her to her core. Then again, the last time she'd seen him—the day she'd gone to the cemetery for Tyrone—was before she'd met Sebastian, before he'd sent her the white dress.

Somehow knowing that Sebastian was in her life, sending her gifts even, made her proof against Alasdair. Besides, she still wondered about the dragon.

She waited until a man standing close to Alasdair gave up his spot, then she made her way between the press of shoulders and hips until she stood by his side.

He did not look at her. He kept his gaze on the illuminated boats of the flotilla and the fireworks above them, but said quite clearly, "Your people are so fascinated by light. I shall miss that about them."

"And your people?" she inquired, automatically falling into the verbal fencing that had become their pattern.

"Different fascinations." He finally glanced down at her, his grey eyes gentler than before. "I'm sorry. I'm not trying to be oblique. But I can't talk about it."

She nodded. She'd never really expected an answer. "You're not in costume," she observed. "Or are you *always* in costume?"

He shrugged. "Whichever way you prefer to see it."

For the first time she noticed the cloth satchel at his feet, and what he'd said about missing her people registered. "Are you going away?"

"Yes, I'm leaving Arcato."

She wasn't sure whether she felt regret or relief. A little of both, she decided. "Where are you going?"

"I haven't decided yet. My plan was simply to go down to the docks and see which ship would be kind enough to let me book passage."

"None of them will set sail before morning," she said. Now that she knew he was leaving the city, it was suddenly easier to talk to him. "The harbor's closed tonight. And tomorrow—you really don't want to be at the mercy of a boat crew on the day after Carnival. None of them will be in shape for navigation."

His mouth turned up in a brief smile. "Bad timing yet again."

She inclined her head as a familiar red flat-bottomed boat passed in front of them. "I know the man who owns that boat," she offered. "He's a rug merchant. Maybe you should talk to him."

"Do you know his name?"

"Madana. Mr. Madana. He has a very friendly parrot."

"And you said he's from India?"

"I didn't but he is."

"You weren't the only one on his boat, were you?" Alasdair asked.

Lucinda's easy mood vanished. "What do you know about him?"

Alasdair turned to face her. "Take off your mask," he said. "It's difficult to talk to someone who's hiding."

She ripped off the silver mask. "Why do I always feel like I'm playing guessing games with you? I barely know you, and yet every time we talk there's some piece of information that you deliberately dangle just out of reach. Does it make you feel superior? Powerful?"

"No." He sounded genuinely surprised. "Nothing like that."

"Then tell me. What is it you know about Mr. Madana?"

He gave her a long, measured look then said, "That in India Madana is another name for Kama, the Maddener, who is usually accompanied by his parrot."

"The Maddener," she echoed stupidly.

"Also known as the god of desire, or Eros. When you are under his influence, you must expect to lose your heart."

She didn't want to run from him again, but she turned away and shut her eyes. Sebastian. If what Alasdair said about Madana was true, then Sebastian had not only set her up for seduction but had called in divine reinforcements.

"Are you all right?" Alasdair asked.

She opened her eyes. "You're telling me that little, round man on the boat is a god?" The erotic had never seemed divine to her or even benign. Earthy, sometimes down and dirty, often a channel for anger that ripped everything to shreds.

"It might be easier to think of him as an incarnation of an eternal energy."

"For me, Eros has always been the fleeting type," she disagreed. "Intense but doesn't tend to stick around long. Besides, Eros isn't about the heart. Cunt and cock maybe, but not the heart." She watched to see if her profanity shocked him.

It didn't register at all. "Are you really able to keep them so neatly separated?" he asked.

"Men do it all the time."

"Then that would be a very diluted version of what Madana has to offer. His energy is sacred. It will connect everything if you let it."

Lucinda pushed herself away from the railing, trying to make sense of why she felt so betrayed. After all, she barely knew Sebastian. And other men had used other means to seduce her: drugs, alcohol, jewelry, extravagant stays in the city's most luxurious hotel. But Madana and his magic carpet were in another league altogether. With the other men she'd always had the power to refuse; she'd thought she had that with Sebastian. She glanced at Alasdair. "So betrayal is sacred now?"

"Betrayal?" He was silent for a beat then said, "It sounds as if whoever brought you to Madana's boat . . . it sounds as if you'd already let him in more than you realized."

"Don't," Lucinda said. "Don't second-guess me. Besides, this is not a conversation I want to have with a stranger."

"We're not exactly that."

"You're strange enough." The truth was, Alasdair was the last person she wanted to discuss Sebastian with. Because Alasdair himself confused things even further with the jarring blend of attraction and animal-fear she felt whenever she was in his presence. And tonight she saw clearly that attraction had always been a component of what Alasdair stirred in her. How had this happened? She wasn't used to feeling this kind of attraction for one man, let alone two men who were so . . . other. She softened her tone. "In any case, arguing over Eros is not how I want to spend Carnival Night."

"Don't feel tricked."

"Don't pity me."

Another round of fireworks went off—blue chrysanthemums dissolving against the black sky—and she found she was reluctant to walk away. He was leaving Arcato. She would never see him again.

"I hate not knowing," she confessed. "I hate it that he didn't tell me."

"Gods rarely wear name tags. They have a particular sort of hubris; they expect *you* to recognize *them*."

"That may be but I've never prayed to the gods. I couldn't begin to tell you which one was which. The gods and me, we don't really make time for each other."

"You ignore them? In this city?" He was laughing now, a full-throated laugh whose richness caught her by surprise. "I didn't think that was possible in a place where you can't walk three feet before tripping over a shrine."

"It's possible," she assured him. "They just don't—apply—to me."

"I see."

She found herself staring at his throat—the tanned skin against the dusk-blue robe, the long, clean lines of his neck, sweeping up to his jaw. His skin was smooth with no hint of a beard. There was that faint diagonal scar running down to the edge of his mouth, a wound that must have healed years ago. A few strands of silver ran through his black hair, but she could detect no other signs of age. It was his eyes, she decided. His eyes seemed to look out of a past so far away, she could barely fathom it.

"How did you get that scar?" she asked.

"That's a very personal question. I'll answer it if you'll let me ask one."

She considered the terms of the deal. "That's not fair. You already know what the question is, and obviously you don't mind answering it. What if you give me a question I don't want to answer?"

"Then I'll try another."

A teenage couple now stood beside her, the girl dressed all in black, the boy in white. They were kissing wildly, passionately, oblivious to everything and everyone around them. Lucinda felt an angry jab of envy. Only when she'd been behind the waterfall with Sebastian had she been able to lose herself so completely. And that had been a setup, a sham.

"I was cut with a knife." Alasdair was answering her, and she was grateful for the distraction.

"In a fight?"

"That's your second question."

"It was an incomplete answer."

The warmth was suddenly gone from his eyes. The grey of his irises actually dulled until they were the cold dead color of tarnished pewter. "I was cut by someone who was trying to kill me."

"And?"

"I stopped her."

Lucinda felt sick to her stomach but had to be sure. "You mean, you killed her?"

He nodded. "Is that enough?"

"More than enough." Unconsciously, she wrapped her arms around herself and stared out at the water. At least she knew she wasn't paranoid or a fool. There was good reason to be frightened of him.

"You're not in danger from me," he said.

"That's very reassuring coming from a confessed killer."

"The odds are in your favor," he pointed out calmly. "You could vanish into this crowd and I'd have no chance of finding you. So why aren't you running?"

She turned back to him. "Is that my question? I don't know the answer."

"Then let me ask another." Alasdair's voice was gentler than before. "Who was on Madana's boat with you?"

Lucinda winced. "I don't want to even think about that bastard right now."

"He brought you to the boat," Alasdair guessed. "You know, Madana himself is neither good nor bad. He's just what he is. But when Madana so blatantly aids another—that's something to be wary of."

"If you conveniently happen to know who Madana is," she agreed. "I suppose I should have. I've certainly given enough of my nights to Eros. No wonder he seemed familiar." She ran a hand through her hair and the web of stars came off. She let it dangle from her fingertips for a moment and flung it away. It hit the water, floated on the surface of a black wave, tiny silver stars shining all too briefly, then vanished.

"An offering to the river gods." Alasdair seemed pleased. "May it stand you in good stead."

Lucinda blinked, suddenly losing her fear of him. "That wasn't an offering. It was an act of disgust. How do you manage to get everything so completely wrong?"

The wry smile was back. "That's what I've been asking myself ever since I came to this city. I'm hoping that somewhere else I won't be quite so inept."

"Will the dragon go with you when you leave?"

"I have no idea. I haven't seen him for a while."

"But you'll see him again?"

"If he so chooses. You miss him, don't you?"

"Yes," Lucinda admitted. "I keep hoping he'll come back."

"He might. He's loyal to those he likes." Alasdair's eyes narrowed as a slight figure wearing a one-eyed monster mask pushed past them. "I know him," Alasdair muttered, and took off after the little Cyclops.

He'd only gone a few yards when he stopped, turned briefly, and gave her a look that might have been regret; then he disappeared into the crowds as completely as a drop of rain disappears into the river. For once he was the one who'd bolted, but the thought gave her no satisfaction.

It occurred to her that she'd promised to meet Tyrone in an hour and had no idea of how much time had passed. Moon goddesses didn't wear watches. She still had time, she told herself, but decided she'd head toward the Dome anyway. Besides, she needed to be away from the water. Knowing what she did about Madana, looking at the flotilla made her uneasy, as though each of the boats contained hidden worlds in which she might be seduced and betrayed. Fireworks cracked into the night again, and were followed by a sly, almost soft ripple of thunder. Lucinda felt it move through the water and the black fabric of the skies.

She slid the mask over her eyes and started toward the Dome, heedless now of the costumes and revelry around her. A young man with coppery skin, pale hazel eyes, and a long, slightly crooked nose stepped in front of her. He wore pants made of a soft leather—deerskin, perhaps. Strands of colored glass beads covered his bare chest. Straight black hair fell to his waist. He gave her a half-smile, as if there were already some understanding between them, and her breath caught. *Thank the gods he wasn't on Madana's boat,* Lucinda thought. *I'd still be there.*

"Nice moonstones," he said.

She'd forgotten she was wearing them. Her fingertips went to the smooth cabochons that lay against her collarbone, and a serrated line of lightning flared overhead, and in its light she could see into the heart of the young man who stood before her. She had a sudden vision of him welcoming his lover to his bed, and felt a keen, almost aching, desire to be so longed for.

She let herself be drawn into his eyes, mesmerized by his beauty. A wave of pleasure went through her as she imagined her hands running along the smooth skin of his chest, his mouth on hers. It would be so easy to touch him. If it hadn't been for what she'd just learned about Sebastian, she would have pulled him to her, kissed him thoroughly, found a way to spend the night in his arms. Instead she wondered if he, too, was friends with Madana; if his eyes, the moonstone necklace, the night itself, were all meant to put some kind of spell on her.

"'Scuze us. Coming through." A woman dressed as the Queen of Diamonds shouldered her way between them, and Lucinda felt something warm and sleek press against her hip. She glanced down. A full-grown tiger, connected to the Queen of Diamonds by the thinnest of leashes, padded placidly after her, rubbing against Lucinda as it walked.

"Pretty cat," the young man said admiringly.

But all Lucinda could think was: *The tigers in the garden.* Had this one stepped off Madana's boat into the city streets? Probably not, she told herself. The Queen of Diamonds didn't seem to be a figure from the garden. Still, everything evoked Sebastian, and how could it be otherwise? Here she was in the moonstone necklace, the mask, the silver dress and slippers— dressed by him, her skin enclosed in his gifts. Suddenly, she could no longer bear to have any of it touch her.

She backed away from the young man then turned and began pushing impatiently through the crowds toward the Dome. Tyrone should be there by now. She'd tell him she was going home to change. And if she didn't find him, she'd go home and change anyway.

LUCINDA STOOD AT the top of the flight of marble stairs that led down into the Dome, scanning the room for Tyrone's peacock-blue and gold lamé. You'd think anyone dressed that garishly would be easy to spot but the place was packed, every table and inch of floor space filled with costumed bodies. A blues singer stood on the square stage, emoting hoarsely into the mike.

Her voice barely carried above the din of giddy toasts, and shouted conversations. The vaulted glass ceiling was completely obscured in a haze of smoke, and the air was thick with the scents of tobacco, cloves, and sweet hashish.

"Tyrone, where are you?" Lucinda muttered. "I don't plan to stand here all night searching for your flashy butt." Her eyes came to rest on a familiar silver wolf sitting on a red velvet banquette, his hairy legs spread wide.

Lucinda made her way to the wolf. He was sipping a blue drink through a straw that went into the mouth of his mask.

"Marcus," she said loudly, "where's Tyrone?"

The wolf removed the straw from its mouth, and gazed around the room with glittering golden eyes. "I don't see him, do you?"

"He said he'd meet me here," she reminded him.

The mask was extraordinary. The wolf's black lips curved upward in a smile, revealing white, pointed teeth. "Maybe I had a better idea for him."

Lucinda could not believe how much she despised him. She grabbed the wolf's muzzle and yanked it upward, pulling the mask off Marcus's smooth shaved head. "Where's Tyrone?"

Marcus jerked the mask out of her hand. "That is my property, bitch."

She grabbed the drink from him and tilted it nearly horizontal. "Unless you want me to spill this all over your 'property,' I suggest you tell me where Tyrone is."

Marcus's eyes gleamed with excitement and she knew she'd made a mistake. All she'd wanted was an answer, and instead she had him thinking she wanted to play power games. "What's it worth to you?" he asked, his eyes locked on her breasts.

It would be so gratifying to pour the drink down the open collar of his costume. But she could almost foresee the sequence of events that would follow: he'd curse and grab her and she'd have to fight him off. She'd get away, maybe even do a little satisfying damage in the process, but it would be nasty and her resisting would probably get him hot and hard, and she'd hate herself for giving him that much.

She handed him his drink. "If you see Tyrone, tell him I went home to change," she said, and left the Dome.

Outside, the streets were even thicker with revelers than they'd been before. Lucinda edged her way into a crowd that was moving in the general direction of her building, and let herself be pushed along. Flowers rained down from an open window above her.

"It's spring!" A slight man dressed as a unicorn caught the blooms in his open arms and inhaled deeply. He seemed delirious with joy and oblivious to the thunder rumbling through the chill, damp night. The skies were heavy with humidity now, and the lights of the flotilla shone dimly through a thick fog. Lucinda could almost feel the rain clouds nestling over the city, hovering on rooftops, cloaking the harbor, turning the direction of the night.

The crowd rounded a corner and packed itself more tightly into a narrow street lined with warehouses. Two young men in bloodied headbands stood on a loading dock, pounding a giant taiko drum; and the crowd picked up the beat in a heavy, furious stomping that only intensified Lucinda's sense of foreboding. Where was Tyrone, and why hadn't he been in the Dome like he'd promised? Did Marcus really send him off somewhere and if he had, would Tyrone actually have gone? No, she decided. It wasn't Tyrone's style to take orders or desert her, especially on Carnival Night.

The high, sweet notes of a wooden flute penetrated the drumbeat. Lucinda turned toward it and found herself facing Sebastian.

Her body stiffened with fury. "You bastard. You manipulative, lying—"

He took her wrist. "We've got to get away from the drum," he told her. "They're using it to call up—" Then without finishing his sentence or giving her a chance to respond, he turned and pulled her from the crowd. She tried to wrench her arm away but he was surprisingly strong, and she found herself being hauled toward an alley between the warehouses. Trying to pull away, Lucinda's heel accidentally came down on a woman's instep. The woman didn't hesitate. She cracked Lucinda hard across the face. The silver mask took the sting out of the blow but shock brought Lucinda to a dazed standstill. This wasn't the usual Carnival madness. The earlier mood of antic, generous chaos was gone from the night. And in its place was something she had no name for.

"Let's go!" Sebastian yanked hard on her, and she stumbled toward him. The drum grew more insistent, the crowd's stamping louder and more frenzied.

"Get your goddamned hands off me!" She was running after him now, pounding him with her free hand. But she felt a surge of relief as they broke free of the crowd and Sebastian pulled her into the alley.

They stood facing each other, both of them breathing hard. Sebastian looked down at his hand clamped on her wrist and seeming startled by it, released her.

"I hate you," she said. She was trembling with it.

His eyes darted beyond her to the mouth of the alley where the crowd was swelling, pressing toward them. They were chanting, words that Lucinda couldn't make out but that matched the drum's insistent fury.

"Hate me later," Sebastian told her, then grabbed her and began running again.

This time she didn't resist, sensing that to fight him now would get them both killed. He led her through a tangle of alleys and down a series of short stairways that tunneled beneath a building, then up into the night again, and through another alley, this one lined with fabric shops. Lucinda glanced at the windows as they raced past, wondering how it was neither she nor Tyrone knew about this area. The shops looked as though they'd been here forever—how had they missed them?

They rounded another corner then climbed a steep lane whose shops were given entirely to oil and gas lamps; glass shades of every hue glowed in the windows. Another stretch of the city she didn't recognize. She was still disoriented when they emerged from the lane into a twisting cobblestone alley where Sebastian finally slowed his pace and released her. He dropped his hands to his knees and drew a few deep breaths. "We should be safe here."

She waited until her own heartbeat slowed before asking, "From what? What was going on back there?"

He straightened, shrugged. "You never know with taiko drums. They've been used to call soldiers to battle, to cause frenzy in the enemy, even to signal storms. Some people say there's a god inside them. All I know is the one in that alley was calling up something dark." His blue eyes flickered over her. "And you belong to the moon's light. That dress looks beautiful on you."

Was he oblivious or just shameless? "I know who Madana is," she said. "Do you always get the god of desire to arrange your seductions?"

"Never before."

"Why was I the lucky one?"

"You probably won't believe this, but it wasn't my idea. The Lord Kama already knew you. He told me about you, said that the garden held gifts that you needed. He asked that I serve him and bring you to his boat."

"And you said, 'Sure thing. I'd be happy to help with a mind-fuck.'"

"That's not what it was."

"What was it, then?"

His eyes held hers, that clear guileless look that meant nothing. "What passed between you and me was real. What we felt—that would have been the same with or without Madana."

She found herself laughing. "You are such a liar. It was a complete setup, right up to the package delivered to my flat. And how, by the way, did you find out where I lived?"

"I didn't."

She tugged at the shoulder of the dress. "Then where did this come from?"

Sebastian raised one eyebrow. "My guess is Kama. I wish I could take credit for it, but those aren't a mortal's gifts you're wearing."

The wind rushed down the alley, carrying a swirl of flowers on a gust of air so frigid and sharp that she instinctively stepped closer to Sebastian, only to recoil when he reached out to draw her into his arms.

He saw it and stepped back, then draped his jacket, a soft black wool, around her shoulders. "Maybe the drum *was* signaling a storm," he said, "because I swear the sky was clear just a little while ago."

As if responding to his cue, a streak of blazing aqua lightning split the sky, releasing fine, cold needles of rain. Lucinda ducked beneath a doorway and Sebastian stepped in beside her. Although she'd only been in the rain a few seconds, her hair was sopping, her teeth chattering. Sebastian reached into his pants pocket and removed a ring of tarnished brass skeleton keys.

"You live here?"

He nodded.

She began to laugh again, the sound shrill, nearly hysterical. "Don't tell me. After getting Kama to help seduce me, you had the Drum God bully me toward your doorstep, and now the Rain God conveniently shows up, forcing me into your building?"

"Do you really think I'm that manipulative? Or that I have the gods at my beck and call?" His hand brushed against her wet cheek. "Or that I'd want you to do anything against your will?"

"Now that's the question," she agreed. "Would you?"

Something that looked like pain flashed through his eyes. "No." His voice was soft, fierce. "No, never that."

Lucinda pulled his jacket more tightly around her shoulders. Ten minutes ago she'd hated him. Now she found herself half-believing, *wanting* to believe him. "I must be mad," she muttered.

"Look," he said, "I think we should get out of the rain. You don't have to come to my flat. I can go upstairs, get something warm and waterproof for you. Then I'll walk you wherever you want to go or let you go on your own. Or you can come upstairs, and I'll make you a cup of hot tea."

"Like Madana's tea?"

He had the grace to look embarrassed. "Nothing like that. Plain mint tea. I've got chamomile, too. You pick." He smiled with a warmth that nearly undid her.

She blinked, breaking eye contact and reminding herself that she hated him. "You think I'm going upstairs for a friggin' tea party with you? *You set me up*. Maybe you were trying to curry favor with a god. Maybe you just wanted an easy lay—"

His hands clamped down on her shoulders, gripping her tightly, as though he wanted to shake her. "Those are lies." She could feel the effort it was costing him to keep his voice even. "I didn't invite you onto the boat for my benefit. Madana told me the garden had gifts for you. That means there was something you needed, something that the gods themselves saw as yours. I couldn't refuse that summons. It would be like taking a mother's milk from her infant. Whatever he gave you is yours by right and is necessary to your survival."

"A Carnival costume? Oh, I can't think of anything more essential."

Sebastian released his hold. "That's not what was in the garden," he reminded her.

"No." The white silk dress. That was the gift of the garden. Which meant what? Lucinda's head was spinning. She dropped down into a crouch, her arms around her knees.

She stared at the delicate silver slippers on her feet. They seemed untouched by wear or rain or even those in the crowd who'd stepped on them. Faery gifts. She'd been dressed up for the ball only there was no prince. Just this freak who'd brought her to his friend, drugged her, seduced her, and was now babbling nonsense about gods and their gardens, trying to seduce her once again.

She stood up. She was bone weary, as though she'd been awake for days. "I don't need Madana's gifts to survive."

"He's been part of you for so long, and he's obviously cost you pain. Why won't you let him be kind to you now?"

"Kind? Eros? That's a contradiction in terms. You obviously don't know him at all."

Something in his eyes changed. Moments ago there'd been a kind of determination. Now she saw only regret. "I'm sorry," he said. "I never meant to hurt you."

"Too late." Lucinda removed Sebastian's jacket from her shoulders and handed it to him. "But I've got a tip for you. If you don't want to hurt people, don't invite any other girls onto your friend Madana's boat."

Without thinking, she reached out a hand to his cheek, just one last touch, and he took her hand, kissed her palm, and she felt the keen sense of loss that was cleaving him apart. Stunned, she ran her hand down the side of his face, then turned away and set off into the rain. It was coming down harder now, a full-out downpour, the rain drilling into her skin through the open weave of the silver dress. It figured that a dress given to you by Eros would offer no protection from the elements, just leave you exposed and vulnerable as hell. And lost. She felt as though she'd just lost something that breathed deep inside her. She didn't even know what it was, and yet there was a new grief that ripped at her, made her heart fold in on itself, aching.

Then Sebastian was standing in front of her again. "I can't let you walk away in this," he shouted over the storm. Without asking, he lifted her into his arms and carried her into the doorway of his building. The skeleton key was already in the lock. He pushed the door open, reached down, grabbed the key, and carried her up three long flights of metal stairs. And she let him. Because she was cold and wet and aching, because the night scared her, and also because there was still a glimmer of a chance that something real—a genuine connection—existed between them, and if it did, she had to find out what it was.

On the top floor, he set her down, unlocked a metal door, and wordlessly held it open for her. He lit a hurricane lamp on an Art Deco end table, then a silver candelabra on a marble pedestal. They were in a vast room filled with inlaid chests, overstuffed sofas, brocade- and silk-upholstered chairs, dining and side tables, crystal bowls and goblets, statues in jade and bronze and stone. Huge tapestries covered the rough brick walls. Lucinda stepped inside, her eyes unable to make sense of the confusion of textures and objects.

"It's home, warehouse, and showroom for me," Sebastian explained a bit sheepishly. "Everything, or nearly everything, is for sale."

"Where do you live?"

"There's a kitchen of sorts through that brick arch in the far wall. And through that oak door, the room where I sleep. The bath's behind the door with the stained-glass panel on top."

"Office?"

"That mahagony monster over there," he said, pointing to what looked like a massive creature with thick legs, a winged back, and dozens of drawers, each featuring a carved eye.

"Cozy," Lucinda murmured.

"I figure I'm not in any danger of anyone making me an offer on it." Sebastian's blue eyes studied her with concern. "You must be freezing." He went over to a squat cast-iron stove, fed it some kindling, and lit a fire. "We'll have heat soon enough. Will you let me lend you some dry clothes?"

She nodded and he opened a large wooden steamer trunk, dug through it and emerged with loose corduroy pants, a flannel shirt and a thick, nubby wool sweater. Lucinda was relieved to see that the outfit could not in any way be construed as suggestive or sexy or even mildly attractive.

"I'll change in the bath," she said, crossing the warehouse floor to the door with the stained-glass panel.

The bathroom, she found, featured a large, claw-footed enamel tub and a sink carved from rough grey stone. A full-length mirror in an elaborate gold-leaf frame reflected back her sodden hair and an angry red mark across her cheek, her souvenir from the Carnival crowd.

She peeled off the wet silver dress and gave herself a long, hot soak in the tub. Sebastian had no scented oils but did have a jar of mineral salts from the Dead Sea. It felt good to be out of the dress, to let the madness and chill of Carnival dissolve in the delicious heat of the water.

A while later she dried off with a thick Egyptian bath sheet and began to dress. She put on the flannel shirt, loving its softness and warmth, then pulled on the sweater and the corduroy pants, rolling up their cuffs, since the pants were clearly made for someone six inches taller. She left on the moonstone necklace, but slipped it beneath the shirt and bulky sweater. She checked her reflection in the mirror. The red mark was fading. The homely outfit wasn't her look at all; Tyrone would have been horrified. But she felt warm and protected, and it had been a long while since she'd felt either of those things.

ALASDAIR MOVED FORWARD and occasionally backward, held in place by the Carnival crowd, as if caught in a surging sack of fluid whose walls he could not break. He knew he'd lost the boy. Michael had darted out of sight several blocks ago. He could be anywhere in the city by now. The boy couldn't have picked a better time for a jailbreak, Alasdair mused. Or more accurately, a better night couldn't have been picked for him. The question was, who had picked it? Alasdair thought of the vision he'd seen in the moonstone. Had Hekate set Michael free or was some other being aiding him? Alasdair could almost hear Johari's riddle-like warning—something good being turned to another purpose—and he wondered just what was loose in Arcato.

With much careful maneuvering, Alasdair worked his way to the edge of the crowd and was finally disgorged by it, breaking free and finding himself on a fairly quiet, undistinguished street. By the light of the street lamps he saw that there were no shops or businesses here, just an eclectic mix of narrow three-story apartment buildings. One was built of brownstone, another of yellow brick, another of white stucco. Shrines to the gods filled windows, and some of the stair railings were wound with Carnival ribbons, but the pounding music was a distant thrum and there were very few people on the street. Six black mongrel dogs were tied to the brownstone's stoop. Like Boris, they looked half-starved, though these had a dejected air that would have been alien to the pampered wolfhound. The windows in the brownstone were dark. Alasdair sat down on the step next to the dogs and obligingly scratched one mutt behind the ear. "Just waiting for someone to come cut your leashes, aren't you?" he asked sympathetically.

He was distracted by two nearby voices and turned to see a woman in her late forties with a younger woman, perhaps in her twenties. The older woman he recognized; she was the cheerful lady who ran the newsstand on Pennington Street. He didn't recognize the other. Neither woman was in costume. The older woman wore a knee-length dress. Her brown hair was carefully swept up and her face was alight as she said, "Oh, Johnny, they told me you were never coming back, and now you have. Do you know how long I've waited for this?"

"Please, Ma." The younger woman put a gentle hand on her mother's arm. Her hair was the same brown as her mother's but she wore it cropped short and there was a deliberate plainness in her appearance that Alasdair sensed had something to do with her notion of truth. "Come back inside. I'll make you a nice cup of tea."

The older woman seemed not to hear. She broke rapidly from her daughter, as if following someone down the street. "I knew you'd come back to me. Do you remember how we used to go dancing at the Chanticleer?"

Alasdair's eyes narrowed as he tried to read the energy pattern of whatever it was she was talking to. But he couldn't sense anything—not ghost or spirit or god, certainly not any sort of mortal being. He glanced down quickly at the dogs, knowing that dogs were usually quite good at seeing spirits. None of them were even paying attention. There was nothing there.

"You want to go dancing again, Johnny? The Chanticleer is closed now but there's plenty of places we can go—"

"Ma, stop it!" The young woman caught up with her mother. Stepping in front of her, she grasped her by the shoulders. "Da's not here," she said in a steady voice. "He's been dead twelve years now. You know that. He's not coming back."

Her mother looked past her, gazing into the distance. "Hear that, Johnny? That's what they've all been saying." She gave the phantom a fond smile. "And you just proved them wrong."

The younger woman gazed around with a frantic expression, her eyes locking on Alasdair. Alasdair sighed, surrendered to the inevitable, and got to his feet. Amethysts and aquamarines rolled to the ground, but the women, one preoccupied with distress, the other with bliss, didn't notice. "Do you need help?" he asked.

The woman who ran the newsstand was still talking to Johnny, and didn't acknowledge him, but her daughter said, "Can you help me get her back into the house?"

Alasdair nodded and took the older woman's arm. Gently, they guided her back into the ground-floor apartment of the stucco building. The younger woman hesitated after she opened the door to the flat. "I don't usually do this," she said, "but would you like to come in?" Alasdair began to politely refuse and then stopped. The older woman was waltzing around the kitchen, her hands set, as if resting on the shoulder and waist of an invisible partner, her smile intoxicated.

"Perhaps I'd better," he said, and stepped inside.

"I'm Adrienne," the younger woman said, holding out a hand to him. "And that's my mother, Irene."

"I never knew her name but I buy my papers from her newsstand," Alasdair said. "Your mother is a very kind woman."

"Normally, yes. What you're seeing now isn't normal. Can I offer you some tea, Mr.—"

"My name is Alasdair," he said quickly. "And yes, thank you, tea would be fine."

Adrienne began filling a kettle with water. "I don't know what's gotten into her," she said as Alasdair took a seat at their kitchen table. "My da's been dead for years now. She knows it. She even stopped wearing the rings he gave her. Then this evening, some sort of alarm went off in the street—we both covered our ears. The next thing I know, my mother is sure my dad's back and wants to take him dancing."

Her mother looked at her reproachfully. "It's disrespectful to talk about your da like he isn't here." She took a small mirror from her purse and reapplied her lipstick. Her movements were quick and agitated, as if something were shaking her. She closed the lipstick case and returned it and the mirror to her purse. "I have to go now," she said. "Johnny's waiting for me."

Outside the black dogs howled. Alasdair shut out their cries, attuned to something stirring in one of the flat's back rooms. He let himself feel the subtle pulse inside it. The pure, clear vibration was like a signature; it was a diamond, the only gemstone composed solely of one element. And it was giving him an idea.

"Your rings," Alasdair said to Irene. "Is one of them a diamond?"

"My engagement ring. Johnny saved for a year to buy it for me."

"Would you consider putting it on now?" Alasdair asked.

Adrienne's eyes hardened with suspicion as she set mugs of black tea on the table. "What's this about?" she asked sharply.

Her mother smiled. "What a good idea. Johnny will be pleased to see me wear it again. He always said I had the prettiest hands."

"He was right about that," Alasdair agreed.

"You're encouraging her," Adrienne said in a furious undertone.

"I'll get it," Irene announced. She stood up, pivoted with a defiant flounce, and headed toward the back of the flat. Adrienne rose from her chair to start after her mother, but Alasdair said quietly, "Let her put the ring on."

Adrienne rounded on him. "Are you after my mother's jewelry?"

It took all of Alasdair's self-control to resist dropping a cupful of jewels on the table to put an end to that accusation. Instead, he studied Adrienne. She seemed a younger, plainer version of Irene. Her shoulders were stiff with fear and worry lines creased her forehead.

"I know that your father didn't come back," he said. The dogs were howling again and he had to raise his voice. "But I don't think that either one of us can convince your mother of that. So I thought we might try another approach. Wearing something he gave her, in real life, might ground her, let her see the difference between reality and illusion."

"What are you, a therapist?" the girl asked derisively.

"It's just a hunch," Alasdair said. "Don't you think it's worth a try?"

Adrienne never replied because Irene returned to the kitchen then, holding out her right hand on which a small, round, brilliant-cut diamond sparkled. "Isn't it beautiful?" she asked.

Adrienne said nothing but her face had reddened, and Alasdair sensed she was ashamed of her mother being so proud of such a small stone.

"It's lovely," Alasdair said sincerely.

As Irene took her seat at the table Alasdair opened the heart of the stone. The first thing he read was that the diamond was very pleased to be worn again after so many years of being shut in a drawer. Small though it was, it was already happily refracting the light from the overhead fixture. Silently, Alasdair asked it if it would help protect Irene against illusion. The stone responded affirmatively, sending out a steady band of rainbow light.

His gaze traveled to Irene's face. She was sipping her tea, looking at the ring but without the agitation that had been in her earlier. She held out her mug to her daughter. "More tea?"

"Sure." Adrienne got up and poured the second cup of tea. "You?" she asked Alasdair.

"No, thank you," he said. "I really must be going." He turned to Irene again. "Will you be all right?"

She gazed at the ring on her finger. "I'm fine. Just a little tired. It's late, isn't it?"

"What about Da?" Adrienne asked her.

Irene looked at her in surprise. "What about him?"

"Just a little while ago you were talking to him," Adrienne reminded her. "You said he was back."

"Oh." For a long moment Irene gazed intently at the ring on her finger. She looked up at her daughter, her eyes brimming with unshed tears. "Johnny's gone."

"Yes, he is," Adrienne said softly, and went to hug her mother.

Alasdair let himself out of the flat, making no effort to hold back the three rubies that dropped from his robe and nestled in a candy dish in Irene's living room. A cold, heavy rain was falling from the night skies. He had left his coat, along with other possessions he didn't deem vital, in the flat in Mrs. O'Donnell's building, the one he would never return to. He passed the brownstone. The dogs were gone but he didn't see any cut leashes so he assumed that someone had taken them in, out of the rain. Wishing he'd waited another night before telling Mrs. O'Donnell he was moving out, he reconciled himself to a night without shelter. Besides, he had to find the boy before he did more damage. Where would a cocky eleven-year-old running from the law head in the middle of Carnival, Alasdair asked himself. Resigned, he headed back toward the center of the city to search for Michael Fortunato.

Six

IN THE MAIN room of the loft Lucinda found Sebastian pouring boiling water into two mugs. "Mint or chamomile?" he asked.

"Mint. If you swear that's all it is."

"I swear."

He gave her a cup of tea and she settled herself in the curve of a deep striped chair. Sebastian sat across from her in a rocker. "Are you warm enough?"

She nodded.

"Still hating me?"

"Not actively at the moment. But that's subject to change."

"I expect." The inside of the loft flared white with lightning, and the clap of thunder that followed made the floor and ceiling shake. The prisms on a crystal chandelier hit lightly against each other. "Will you at least wait out the storm here?"

"Maybe. If you don't give me reason to flee."

"I won't. I promise."

"I don't trust you," she said.

"Do you trust anyone?"

"One friend. We're used to each other. And we need each other," she admitted without quite meaning to. She had no intention of discussing Tyrone. "Who do you trust? Madana?"

"In a way. He's a man—or being—of his word. Whatever else you may accuse the gods of, they usually do what they say they will." Sebastian grinned at her. "Except for the tricksters, of course."

She stretched out her legs on the striped ottoman. "If Eros isn't a trickster, I don't know who is."

"Oh, they're everywhere," he agreed softly. "Sowing disorder whenever possible and reveling in it."

"Tonight? Do you think that's what was going on in the streets?"

"Are you surprised? Something like Carnival, a public celebration of chaos—it's like throwing down a welcome mat to tricksters."

She shivered in spite of the warmth of the room. "So what are we supposed to do?"

He gave her a rueful smile. "Work hard, say your prayers, and follow the rules."

"If you know what the rules are in the first place," she mused. "Not that it matters in my case. Rules and prayers don't work for me. I was born out of favor."

"Which means?"

It suddenly occurred to her that he couldn't be from Arcato, as everyone in the city knew exactly what being born out of favor meant. "Where are you from, anyway?" Lucinda asked.

"No place in particular. My mother was born in the Celtic Isles, my father in the Mediterranean, and the only things they agreed on were wanderlust and a complete indifference to each other. They handed me off to each other, as often as possible, and I grew up on three continents and half a dozen islands. My family was such a mess that I took all my comfort from objects." He waved a hand toward the expanse of the loft. "And that gave me my calling. . . . So, what does it mean to be born out of favor?"

"That because of the time and place of my birth, and because my mother allegedly spurned a blessing from Kwannon—a goddess who's supposed to be compassionate—I have no protective spirit and no god with whom I'm aligned, who's disposed to listen to my prayers. So I don't pray. They ignore me and I do my best to ignore them. It simplifies life."

"Kama didn't ignore you."

"You'd call his attentions a blessing?"

"Now I've never actually seen them, but like Eros, Kama carries a quiver filled with arrows," Sebastian began.

Lucinda snorted then burst out laughing. "I'm sorry. It's a little hard to picture rotund Mr. Madana as an archer."

"Some things are metaphor," Sebastian said easily. "That doesn't make them any less true. It's said, there are five kinds of arrows in Kama's quiver: *Harshana,* which means Joy of Living; *Rocana,* which means Attraction; *Shoshana,* Languor; *Mohana,* Illusion; and *Mârana,* Bruiser."

She sipped at her tea. "Clever names for what wounds you. I've felt them all, I think, all except the first."

Sebastian leaned forward and took the tea from her hands. "But that's the most important one of all. I can't believe Madana would be so miserly with his arrows and hold that one back from you."

She drew farther into the recesses of the chair. "Then perhaps you don't know him as well as you think. What are you anyway—his errand boy? How did you get so chummy with a god?"

Sebastian gave her a wide-eyed humorous look. "When I was younger, much younger, I had a bad habit of falling madly in love with nearly every girl I set eyes on."

"You broke a lot of hearts?" Somehow Lucinda wasn't surprised.

"And had mine broken. Repeatedly," Sebastian assured her. "After a while it occurred to me that Eros was taking special delight in tormenting me, and I decided to seek him out. I was determined to confront the little bastard face to face."

"And?"

Sebastian shrugged. "He's a god. He was elusive. Showed absolutely no interest in answering my prayers, challenges, or demands. Everything just got worse. I was caught in such a relentless dance of bliss and grief that I decided to renounce the material world and become an ascetic. I made a great nuisance of myself to a poor, beleaguered monk, who did his best to convince me that I was not suited to take orders."

Lucinda found herself smiling. She hadn't a clue as to whether Sebastian's tale was true or false, but at that moment she didn't care. The rain was pounding against the loft's windows, and the story seemed a good one with which to pass a long, stormy night.

"So he finally convinced you?"

"Not at all. I'm stubborn as they come. I badgered the poor man to the point where he was so desperate for some peace and quiet that *he* began praying to Kama for relief. And since he was a genuine holy man with one of those rare pure hearts, Kama found himself bound to listen."

"So that's the secret," Lucinda said. "Find yourself a holy man to intercede."

"Easier said than done," Sebastian told her. "In any case, Madana appeared to me soon after and very courteously invited me to sail with him on his boat. Naturally, he refused to discuss the sorry state of my heart. Instead he gave me intensive schooling on the weaving, buying, and selling of Oriental carpets. He'd take me to the markets with him, and I would wind up buying lanterns and samovars and silver boxes set with jewels. Everything *but* carpets." Sebastian got up and poured himself a second cup of tea. "I was hopeless as a rug merchant. Had no talent for it at all. But Madana and I have been friends ever since."

"He no longer torments you?"

Sebastian's gaze swept over her with an almost tangible warmth. "I didn't say that. No one's fully immune from Kama's arrows, but now I try to see them as blessings."

"Then he's cast a spell over you," Lucinda said.

"To be sure." He sipped at his tea, his eyes focused on hers, as though searching for the answer to a question he hadn't asked. When she gave no response he went on, "Seems to me, if you're going to wind up enspelled by a god, better Kama than Ares or Loki or half a dozen others I could name."

"I was enspelled on the boat," she said. The memory of it was so embedded in her senses that just thinking of it was enough to bring the scents of the garden to her, make her feel as though she could turn around and find herself walking its paths. "I didn't like it."

"Didn't you?" There was the barest hint of mockery in his tone.

"No, but that's not the same thing as saying I didn't enjoy it," she admitted. She'd wanted him so badly then, and now she could feel that same desire flickering through her. She wanted to touch him, to be held in his arms, to feel him inside her. It should be easy. They were sitting all of three feet apart, and yet she couldn't imagine how she'd cross that distance.

Sebastian leaned forward, forearms on his knees, and studied the planks of the hardwood floor. "You don't trust anything that happens between us now. Because you're afraid it might be Kama manipulating things." He lifted his head, his eyes calm. "That's always a possibility."

"You don't mind being Kama's puppet?"

He shrugged again. "Who isn't? The gods themselves are helpless before him. Shiva once took great exception to being the target of one of Kama's arrows. He incinerated him on the spot with a bolt of lightning from his third eye."

Lucinda laughed. "Good for Shiva."

"Didn't make a difference," Sebastian told her. "Kama's arrow had done its work, and Shiva fell in love with Parvati, the Lady of the Mountain— though he resisted her mightily."

"And Kama?"

Sebastian smiled. "To hear him tell it, while he was dead love disappeared from the earth, and the earth became a barren, desolate wasteland. Even the gods couldn't stand it, so they went to Shiva and with Parvati's help, finally persuaded him to allow Kama to be reborn."

"So you can't get rid of him?"

"Impossible," Sebastian assured her.

She got up and began to walk through the loft, examining the pieces he'd collected. A tall armoire, carved with suns and moons. A bronze lamp with a mica shade, shedding amber light over a side table made of rough sandstone. Clocks set in mahogany and brass. A fan-shaped vase blown from lilac glass. A rosewood cradle. A rectangular box made of banded onyx. A woven basket filled with colored glass beads. All of it, with the possible exception of Sebastian's desk, was beautiful, and something deep inside her hummed with pleasure at being surrounded by so many beautiful objects.

"You can open anything you like," Sebastian offered. "Any box, drawer, chest. Everything here is open to you."

Lucinda didn't reply to that, mostly because she didn't believe it. But she opened the onyx box and found twelve tiny crystal elephants inside.

"They're a family," Sebastian told her. She couldn't even see him from where she stood. He was still in the rocker, separated from her by a tall armoire and a three-panel lacquer screen. She closed the onyx box, and opened the armoire. It was filled with kimonos, and she couldn't resist touching the silk. It was different—both heavier and somehow finer—than the silk that came through the city.

"They're from the beginning of the Meiji Era," Sebastian explained.

"How do you know what I'm looking at?"

"I recognized the sound of the wardrobe's doors being opened. And the onyx box."

"You have ears like a fox," she said.

"I know the things in this loft," he explained. "I'm their keeper. At least until I find them their proper homes."

She made her way to a wall of tall windows. Their glass panes rattled as wind and rain beat against them. Lucinda stared into the black night. The storm wasn't easing; if anything, it was getting worse.

Sebastian came to stand behind her. Though he wasn't touching her she was acutely aware of him—his body, his warmth, his pulse, his breath. It was as if the storm were moving through them, connecting them on a current of electricity.

"That isn't a natural storm out there," he said. "It was called up by a storm god, perhaps Thor or Tlaloc."

"You mean, there are storms that *aren't* called up by storm gods?" she asked, unable to keep the sarcasm out of her voice.

"Some are just part of weather systems," he acknowledged. "But this one has been summoned."

"It's got a rhythm," she said. "I can almost hum it."

"Maybe that's because you heard it before. It's the same rhythm they were playing on the taiko drum."

"That's not possible."

"Listen," he said, and she did and knew he was right.

"So, those drummers called up the storm?"

"My guess is they helped call up the storm. They were . . . acting as agents for a storm god."

Not quite ready for whatever was going to happen between them, Lucinda focused on the window. Its glass seemed a thin and fragile membrane between them and the fury of the storm, and the storm seemed a living thing with a will and a destiny of its own. "You said what they were calling up was dark."

"This storm is about destruction," Sebastian told her. "It's going to take things down, shatter things."

As if to confirm his prediction, the loft glared bone-white then shook with a crash of thunder. Lucinda felt the electricity through the floorboards, a low-grade shock that traveled through her cells and left her nerve endings vibrating.

The thunder faded and the wind lashed the windows again. Lucinda heard a clear, hard snap. She looked up. A long jagged crack ran through one of the upper panes. Rain began to drip down in a steady line then splatter against the floor. The storm had found its way in.

"I'd better get a bucket," Sebastian said. "Here, I brought this for you."

She turned to him then and saw that he was holding a silk kimono. It was deep blue, a muted sapphire. "To sleep in," he went on with an endearing touch of awkwardness. He tilted his head toward the oak door in the back wall. "You can have my bedroom. I'll sleep out here on one of the couches. You'll have as much privacy as you want."

"Um—" She had no doubt that they'd have sex tonight—that had been clear to her from the moment she'd entered his loft—but she hadn't let herself think ahead to actual sleeping arrangements. Now she wasn't sure what to make of his offer to let her sleep on her own. Was he trying to disarm her or—

"I've got to get something for that leak," Sebastian said, frowning at the stream of water that was seeping across his floor. He started off toward the kitchen, leaving her holding the silk robe.

Lucinda opened the oak door and stepped into a large room whose sole light came from a glass hurricane lamp on a bedside table. In the shadows cast by the lamp she could see another wall of windows. The bed stood against a brick wall. Two diamonds were carved into its headboard, one set inside the other. The room itself was simply furnished, almost spare. There was the bed, a square night table beside it, and a graceful Crafts rocker in front of a small woodstove, which was radiating warmth.

Lucinda took off the borrowed clothing and fastened the kimono around her. The thick fabric was slippery and cool against her bare skin. A faint scent of sandalwood clung to the silk. *This is his robe,* she thought, *what* he *wears against his skin.* The thought intrigued her, and she found herself remembering what he'd looked like under the waterfall and wondering if that were real. Was that what a naked Sebastian actually looked like? Or was that a vision conjured by Kama for reasons only a god could fathom?

A polite two-beat knock on the door broke her reverie. Flushing a little, she opened the door and saw Sebastian standing there, still fully clothed.

"Well, I've got a bucket under the leak," he reported. "Anything I can get you before I turn in? A glass of water? Whiskey? Warm milk?"

She made a face. "I hate warm milk."

"Okay. Let me know if you need anything." He stepped toward her and placed his fingertips on the side of her neck. Curious as to what he'd do next, she remained still.

He rested his fingertips there, as if he what he wanted was to feel her blood pulsing through her artery. "Sleep well," he said, then his touch was gone and he was turning back into the main room.

Lucinda closed the oak door, not sure what to make of Sebastian's tactful retreat. She sat in the little rocker by the stove. The heat from the fire was making the windows steam up, and she could no longer see the rain beating against the glass. But its rhythm was relentless. She forced herself to concentrate on other sounds: the wood crackling inside the stove, a creaking in the outer room that sounded like a trunk being opened. Was he taking out bedding for himself? Through the crack beneath the door she saw the outer room gradually grow darker. He was turning out the lights, though it seemed he was leaving at least one lit.

The bedroom was growing hot. Lucinda slid the rocker back, away from the wood stove. A line of sweat was trickling down the hollow of her breastbone, another down her spine.

Getting to her feet, she started out of the room then stopped as lightning blazed again. In its glare she thought she saw something bolting across the wooden floorboards, something tiny enough to dart beneath the door. Could it be the dragon? Was that even possible?

She stepped out into the main room, but it was too dark to see anything as small as the jade dragon. She moved toward the one source of light and saw Sebastian, stretched out on a couch, a wool blanket draped over him. He was reading a book beneath a lamp with a fringed green silk shade.

"You were right," she said. "That lamp needed that green silk."

"And grateful it is to have it," he said, sounding both drowsy and welcoming. "I didn't think I'd see you again before morning. Trouble sleeping?"

She nodded, not quite trusting herself to speak.

The blanket slid to the floor as Sebastian got to his feet. He was wearing a grey river driver's shirt and flannel pajama bottoms, the soft, formlessness of the clothing somehow emphasizing the long, lean lines of his body. "Why don't I make that chamomile tea?" he suggested. His eyes narrowed as he studied her. "And why does that robe look so much better on you than it does on me?"

Lucinda blinked, suddenly aware that she'd belted the kimono too loosely. She drew it closer, tightening the silk sash. "I don't really want chamomile tea," she admitted. "I don't think I want to sleep."

"Ah." He studied her again and she could almost feel the intensity of his gaze traveling along her body. "I'm not sleepy either."

He reached out, took her hand, and led the way through the maze of furniture to a small hexagonal area defined by two leather armchairs, a teak side table, a mirror framed in lapis and gold leaf, a Chinese apothecary's cabinet, and two guardian lions carved from green stone. A delicate crystal candelabrum hung low in the center of the area over a kilim.

Lucinda, feeling uncertain and uncharacteristically shy, settled in one of the armchairs. Sebastian sat in the other. He seemed perfectly calm and yet she could feel that current of connection between them, and both of them just waiting to fully open into it. She wondered if she should mention the dragon, wondered if she'd really seen it.

Lightning flared, bleeding the deep colors from the woods and leathers. For an instant it all seemed bleached, bone-white, overexposed. Even Sebastian, who sat with his long legs comfortably stretched out in front him looked, for an instant, spectral. Repressing a shudder, Lucinda stood up. She put a hand on the cool stone of a lion's mane. "Where did these come from?"

Sebastian laughed. "From a manor house owned by my mother's great-uncle."

"Your family was wealthy?"

"He was. I was only at his house once. Got lost in a corridor that connected the wings. He lived in thirty-five rooms, most of them empty and shut-up, with three aging servants who slept in the unheated attic."

"Sounds like a lovely man."

"I hated him," Sebastian said. "He said something to my mother—I can't even remember what—that made her cry."

"So why do you live with his lions?"

"The lions weren't to blame. Besides, I always wanted to find them a happier home."

"He willed them to you?"

"He didn't will me a damn thing. But his house fell apart and he went mad—most mysteriously—and when he died soon after, various relatives showed up to pick at the bones, and no one else wanted to be bothered transporting the lions."

Lucinda walked over to the second lion, and as she did she passed the mirror edged in lapis and gold. She stopped, her hand going to the moonstone necklace. "I forgot I was wearing this."

Sebastian arched one red brow. "How could anyone so wary of Kama's gifts have forgotten that she was wearing one?"

"Don't ask annoying questions." Lucinda reached behind her to unhook the clasp.

Sebastian came to stand behind her. "Don't," he said softly. "The robe brings out the blue in them. And moonstones are meant to be worn at night."

"You mean on a night with a moon. This doesn't happen to be one of them."

"The moon is always there," Sebastian said. "She doesn't disappear just because we can't see her. Even during new moon you can feel her in the tides."

Lucinda stared into the mirror. He was a good head taller than she was, his face narrow, cheekbones sharp. He was not as handsome as many of the men she'd been with, but his eyes, like Madana's, danced with life. They belied the calm that radiated from his body. In his eyes she saw merriment and curiosity and the kind of quick, instinctive intelligence she'd only seen in animals.

She needed to know what he was like without the moonstones on her. "I want to take the necklace off," she said.

"Then let me do it," he answered. She felt his hands lightly touching the back of her neck as he undid the silver clasp. The current between them was as alive and electric as the storm.

The necklace was open now. She took it from him and felt his hands on her shoulders. For a long moment they stood like that, his hands resting lightly on her shoulders, their eyes meeting in the mirror, each studying the other. She liked the distance of watching their reflections. It allowed her the illusion that this was happening to someone else.

His hands slid from her shoulders down the length of her arms. She watched him with a peculiar heightened alertness, feeling the silk press against her skin beneath his hands, feeling his breath warm on the back of her neck, knowing that she was only moments from being inside his embrace.

"I want to put the necklace down," she said, stepping away from him.

He let her go but said, "Why? Was I doing something that you didn't want me to do?"

"No. I don't want to think that whatever happens between you and me happens because I'm wearing Madana's gift. I don't want to feel like he's sitting in his damn boat, pulling the strings and laughing."

"That may be the case whenever two people—or even two gods—come together," Sebastian told her. "There's no way you can safeguard yourself against that. But from what I've seen, even when the gods interfere we usually have choices. We can act on their gifts or spurn them."

Lucinda set the necklace on the flat spot between the ears of the closest lion. She turned back to Sebastian with a self-mocking smile. "This is a first for me. Fucking preceded by a discussion of metaphysics."

"Fucking? I was hoping we'd make love."

"Is that what it was behind the waterfall?"

"You're still angry about that."

"I can't believe you're not. But then men just like to get it, don't they? Any way they can."

Taking her hand, he sat on the edge of the side table and drew her toward him. "Please don't come into this with so much bitterness. That's not what I want between you and me."

"How do I get rid of it?" She was mortified to hear her voice trembling.

"Let me take it from you."

"Can you?"

"I can try." He lifted her hand, kissed her open palm. "You ever hear that old Biblical expression 'to know someone'?"

"You mean that old Biblical metaphor for fucking."

He gave her a look of mild reproof. "I was thinking . . . coming together, making love, that's exactly what it is . . . learning and finally knowing each other."

"Maybe that's why I prefer a simple fuck."

"I don't. I want to know who you are. I want to know what pleasures you and what excites you and what makes you feel safe. I want to know what it's like to fall asleep with you in my arms."

She shook her head. "That's asking too much."

"Seems reasonable to me." His hand caressed the side of her face then slid to the back of her neck, working the tension from her muscles. "Why don't we start with what pleasures you and take it from there?"

Lucinda felt his hand move to the base of her hairline, then cradle the back of her skull with a tenderness that took the breath from her. He ran his other hand from her temple through the length of her hair to the small of her back. She pulled away, but only for a moment, to stand upright, loosen the knot in her sash, and draw his hands inside the silk kimono. She was trying not to rush things. She was trying to go slow, to savor every second. But she had a hunger burning through her; she craved his hands on her skin. All her life she'd been wanting their warmth. Hand and heart, brain and cunt—everything inside her ached for him.

He hesitated, asking, "I'm not imagining this?"

"No." The word came out hoarse, broken, her voice suddenly incapable of speech.

Sebastian pulled her toward him and ran one hand the length of her back; the other traced the bones of her rib cage up to her breasts. And all the while his eyes held hers, alight with the kind of fire she'd only seen in cats' eyes. *He has eyes like jewels,* she thought wildly. Thunder broke against the building, shaking it so violently that a vase skittered across the teak side table and crashed to the floor. The skies were opening, falling. They were shattering the invisible skein that held her together. She was caught in the heart of the storm and it was taking the bitterness and fear from her. The world fell away as Sebastian drew her into his arms.

Seven

"OH, A FORTUNATO is a most fortunate man. A most fortunate man is he . . ." Michael sang to himself. It was a nonsense song his mother made up when he was little. Bullshit, really. "Mary Had a Little Lamb" made more sense, and probably had more truth to it. Here he was, on the night of his big prison break, when he was supposed to lose himself in the Carnival crowds and then get his butt onto a boat, and he couldn't even get near the river. Instead, he was huddled in a doorway like some pathetic homeless mutt, waiting out a storm that had been going on for hours and showed no sign of letting up. The crowds were gone, the Carnival booths hurriedly shut down. He should have stolen something to eat before the rain broke. Now he was drenched and cold and hungry. Plus for the last hour or so he'd been coughing. At least if he'd stayed in that crappy little cell, he wouldn't be coming down with pneumonia. He wrapped his arms more tightly around himself, trying to stop himself from shivering. *Spook was always going all shivery and trembly,* Michael remembered. *Probably because he was so thin and weak. Shivering was for wimps.*

"Shit," he muttered as the wind shifted, driving the rain straight into him. Hunching over, he ran back out into the storm. He'd have to find another doorway, facing another direction. He jumped as thunder crashed all around him. It felt like he was caught inside some giant drum. A giant wet drum. His sopping clothes were sticking to his skin. His shoes felt like they weighed five pounds each. He darted into a doorway on the other side of the street, but the wind shifted again, driving needles of rain into his skin. If he were the paranoid type, he'd swear the storm was after him.

Forget doorways. They're too shallow, he decided. He'd find something else. The problem was, all the street lamps had gone out when a blazing bolt of aqua lightning forked down near the power plant. Except for a few glimmers of candlelight in windows, the city was black. He couldn't see a thing. He didn't even know what street he was on.

He made his way out of the second doorway, fighting a blast of wind that tried to pin him there. He bent into the wind. Maybe if he could make his way down to the docks, he'd find a cargo container or something to hide out in. At this point he'd settle for a Dumpster.

"Did I give you permission to mow me down?" a voice asked indignantly.

Michael straightened up as he felt two hands grip his shoulders. Lightning flickered and he saw a man with long braids, a shiny gold costume, and crazed eyes. An initial moment of fear subsided as Michael realized the man was swaying unsteadily.

Great, a drunk, the boy thought. How many times had he watched his mother do the same sick dance? Better not get into it with him. Reaching up, Michael began to pry his wet shirt free of the man's grip.

"Don't you know who I am?" The man sounded outraged. "You are messing with Ilyap'a, god of lightning and thunder!"

"Sorry," Michael mumbled, finally shrugging himself free. The guy was not only drunk, he was deranged.

"What's a kid like you doing out in this storm?" the man demanded irritably. "Don't you know what I turned loose on this city tonight? Why aren't you home?"

"I don't have a home. I—" Michael broke off the lie as another coughing fit doubled him over. He had to get out of this friggin' storm before it killed him. "Piss off," he muttered, then turned toward the river, determined to find that nice, dry cargo container.

The drunk grabbed his arm and spun him around, shouting over the gale, "I am hungover and soaked and too damn tired to deal with the problems of homeless waifs—"

"Who asked you to?" Michael wrenched his arm free.

The drunk gave him a sorrowful look, said, "I've lost my moon goddess. You see, the wolf separated us," and started to walk away. But he hadn't gone two steps before he stumbled, toppled at a crazy angle, and nearly fell.

Cursing, Michael grabbed the guy's arm and held him upright. "What a joke. *You* thinking you can deal with my problems. You can't even walk."

The man held out his arms for balance and stooped a little, so his face was level with Michael's. "Come with me," he said, sounding almost sober. "I need you to help me get home. You need a dry place to spend the night. Even deal."

The boy fought back a cough and stared at the weird vision in front of him. Rain was streaming down the man's braids and running down his nose into the folds of the shiny costume. He was ridiculous, drunk, maybe even a pervert. Most of all, he was pathetic.

Michael felt for the broken screwdriver in his pocket. He still had it. Besides, this guy was too far gone to be a danger to anyone except himself. So okay. He'd go home with this guy, dry off, raid his refrigerator, disappear as soon as the storm let up. It was a plan.

"Well?" the man demanded.

"Okay, deal," Michael agreed.

"Okay." The man held out a shaky arm, and the boy took it. The wind was at their backs as they moved off into the storm.

SOMETIME DURING THE night Sebastian had covered the kilim with a thick mound of comforters and quilts he'd taken from one of the loft's many trunks. It was, Lucinda thought, the most divinely comfortable bed she'd ever been in. A single candle flickered on the top of the apothecary's cabinet, and in its light she memorized Sebastian's face, wanting to hold onto this night forever. At one point she'd glanced up, thinking she'd seen a fluttering of jade-green wings, but there were only shadows, wavering slightly with the flame, playing along the lines and curves of their bodies. They'd massaged each other with a light oil scented with amber. There was no part of her that hadn't been held, kissed, caressed, cherished.

And yet when he entered her she felt that one irremediably stubborn part of herself holding back, unable to be touched by anyone. He'd sensed it, too, had held himself still, saying, "You've got a sliver of ice deep inside, don't you? You can let it melt now. I promise you it will be all right." She hadn't been able to meet his eyes then—no one else had ever seen that cold, thin shard that floated between her heart and spine—and she couldn't do as he asked. Still, she had arched toward him, welcoming and glad, matching his rhythm, reveling in every thrust, and releasing in the same wild instant. When the pulsing inside her finally slowed, she found that she felt curiously light—as if she might float up to the ceiling buoyed by pure pleasure. Now, hours later, Lucinda's body still hummed with the warmth of his touch. As she drifted off to sleep, curled in Sebastian's arms, only the tiniest doubt tugged at her: Would she ever be able to give him her whole self?

"DAMN LIGHTS DON'T work." The drunk guy kept turning the light switch on and off anyway.

Michael rolled his eyes. "You didn't notice the city's blacked out? The storm did something to the power."

"Oh." The man slumped against the wall and rubbed his forehead. "Candles. I got candles somewhere."

Michael gave in to a coughing fit as the man lurched through the dark apartment, stumbling into furniture in his search. At last the boy heard the sound of a match being struck and saw a glimmer of flame, reflected in the man's shiny headdress. The guy was lighting a silver candelabra. *Shit, he's gonna burn the whole place down,* Michael thought as the man started back across the room, the candelabra swaying wildly.

"You'd better let me carry that," the boy said. But when he crossed the room and reached for the candelabra, the man gave him an indignant glare. "I'm not gonna steal it," Michael assured him. "I'll just hold it for now. 'Cause you're not exactly capable at the moment."

Sullenly, the guy handed over the candlestick. Michael lifted it high and gazed around. The loft was huge, at least five times the size of the cramped apartment he shared with his mother. But this place had floors tiled in fancy black-and-white squares, white leather furniture, and tables carved from marble. Everything was sleek and gleaming and perfect, and Michael had a feeling that none of it came cheap.

"You live here?" he asked.

"My name is Tyrone Dessalines," the man answered in a grand tone, "and you are in the headquarters of Dessalines Productions."

"Yeah? What does it produce?"

"Clothing. I design clothes for women."

"Oh." This time Michael remembered to cover his mouth as he coughed. He could feel the beginnings of a fever spiking through him. At least he was out of the rain.

"You're not interested in clothing?

"Not particularly."

"Dull boy."

"Don't do that to me!" Michael winced as he realized he was using the same half-angry half-pleading tone he used with his mother.

"Do what?"

"Make me sound stupid." Now he was just angry. "*I'm* not the one who got so drunk at Carnival, he couldn't walk home."

"This is true." The man seemed to be struggling to focus his gaze on him.

"You're soaked." He gestured toward shiny white double doors. "Let's find you a change of clothing."

Michael followed as Tyrone opened the doors into another huge room, his bedroom. The boy hesitated. *Was* the guy a pervert?

"I do not feel good," Tyrone mumbled as he wove across the floor to a tall chest of drawers.

Me neither, Michael thought. The skin on his face felt hot, but his hands were icy and he had the chills.

Tyrone began pulling things out of drawers. "Shirt, sweater, pants, socks. They'll all be too big for you but they're dry." He handed the clothing to Michael. "You're probably hungry, too. Help yourself to whatever you find in my kitchen. I am going to get myself some sleep."

With the clothes in one hand, the candelabra in the other, Michael waited for Tyrone to find his way to the bed. But the man moved shakily toward a closet door, reached in, and pulled out a blanket. "You can sleep on the couch out there," Tyrone told him, draping the blanket over Michael's shoulder. Finally, Tyrone lowered himself to the edge of the bed and began to remove the ridiculous shiny headdress. He looked up at the boy. "Bring me a glass of water?" he asked, sounding helpless.

"Yeah, sure," Michael replied, having no intention of doing so. He knew drunks. Tyrone would be passed out by the time Michael found the kitchen. Still, he was relieved the guy didn't expect him to share his bed.

Taking one candle with him, he left Tyrone in the bedroom, dropped the blanket and clothes on the couch, and looked around for the kitchen. The guy really did make clothes, he decided as he padded through an area where a dressmaker's dummy stood beside a sewing machine, and sketches of skinny women in skimpy dresses lined the walls.

He found the kitchen beyond that and helped himself to a thick slice of chocolate cake and half a roasted chicken, and washed them down with milk. He hadn't eaten anything except jail slop for weeks now, and he couldn't believe how good the food tasted. Feeling surprisingly grateful for the meal, he decided he'd bring Tyrone his glass of water after all.

Michael knocked on the white double doors that led to the bedroom. When he didn't hear a reply, he cautiously pushed one open.

A single candle burned on the bedside table. Tyrone was sitting up in bed, propped up against two rows of pillows, the covers drawn up to his chest. "You knocked and I didn't answer, so you took that as an invitation to come in?"

"You said you wanted water."

"Oh. Sorry." Tyrone nodded to the table. "Just leave it there. Thank you."

His eyes narrowed as the boy walked toward him. "How come you're still in those wet clothes?"

"Stop worrying about my clothes," Michael said irritably. "I don't need another mother."

"Don't you? How old are you anyway?"

"Thirteen."

"The hell you are."

"It's none of your business."

"I had a boy named Winston," Tyrone told him. "He would have been about your age, which I'd bet my last dollar is closer to eleven than thirteen."

"What happened to him?" Michael asked, curious in spite of himself.

"He died when he was four."

"Oh." Michael didn't really want to get into it.

Apparently, Tyrone didn't either because he said, "You ever hear of an Incan storm god called Ilyap'a?"

"I don't believe in gods. My mother's been praying to Jesus and Mary her whole life, and they've never done her any good."

Tyrone leaned back against the pillows. "I know what you mean. Felt a little like that myself until tonight when I royally pissed off Ilyap'a. He didn't take kindly to a human walking around, claiming to be him. That storm tonight, he sent it through me. Can't believe I didn't die of electrocution with all that lightning shooting through my fingertips."

"You're drunk," Michael said. "You should go to sleep."

"Wise counsel, indeed," Tyrone agreed. "I should have stayed home and slept. I never should have gone out into Carnival tonight. I let myself get tricked by the wolf, I lost my moon goddess, and I angered a storm god. So why did he give me this?"

He opened his hand and Michael drew closer. In the candlelight the boy saw a clear oval stone. All the colors of the rainbow blazed in its facets, fiery points of blue and red, lavender and yellow and green, dancing almost as though there was something alive inside. It was like the diamond Spook had but better. This one was bigger, more beautiful. "It's a diamond," Michael said reverently.

"Is it?" Tyrone wondered. "One second I was standing there, lit up like a firework, lightning sizzling through me, knowing I was a dead man, and the next it was over and I was still on my feet but holding this rock, like a piece of that lightning had somehow gone solid in the palm of my hand. What this rock is . . . I think it's from Ilyap'a, his little souvenir, his way of reminding me I got no business messing with the gods, of making sure I don't forget just who holds the power in this town."

"That's what you're telling yourself?" Michael rubbed his head. It ached from all the coughing. He felt like shit. Why was he even having this conversation? "You're just fucked up. You probably lifted it off someone but were too drunk to remember."

"Even when I drink—which, by the way, I rarely do—I do not steal," Tyrone replied in a tone of injured dignity.

"Yeah, whatever you say." Michael started out of the room, but another coughing fit doubled him over.

"Boy, get out of those wet clothes," Tyrone told him, "before you catch yourself a death."

Michael didn't want to change into anyone else's clothing. He just needed to lie under a blanket long enough to stop feeling so chilled. Then he'd get away from this crazy drunk who thought he could tell him what to do.

DROWSY AND WARM, Lucinda woke slowly to the smell of fresh coffee brewing. Her body was still purring with contentment. She could hear Sebastian stirring in another part of the loft. A few minutes later he returned, carrying a tray with two steaming mugs. He set them on the side table and knelt down on the bed beside her. "Good morning. Did you sleep well?"

She nodded, pulled him down to her, nibbled on his ear for a moment, then kissed him thoroughly.

"Maybe I shouldn't have made coffee yet," he murmured. He took off his robe and got back under the covers. His skin was cool against hers as he curled around her and began to kiss the back of her neck.

"Is the storm over?" she asked.

"Still lots of dark heavy clouds out there, but the rain and thunder and all the drama have stopped."

She relaxed against him, wonderfully content to remain exactly where she was. Sebastian turned her to face him, began to kiss her eyelids, her cheeks, and then her neck and breasts. She began to laugh deep in her chest.

"You find this humorous?"

"Very."

"Good. I like to see you laughing." He kept kissing her, moving down her body, kissing her belly, the tops of her thighs. He spread her legs and she felt his lips press against her cunt, then his tongue tasting, exploring, entering her, making something inside her stir until she was writhing in delight.

It was much later when she sat up. Sebastian lay beside her, one arm curled loosely around her waist. She felt worn in the nicest possible way, like a piece of flannel that gets softer and softer with use. Gently, she brushed a shock of reddish hair from his eyes. "I suppose the coffee's cold by now?"

"Mmmm," he said happily. "Want me to make another pot?"

Lucinda watched him leave the bed, this time without putting on a robe. He had a very nice back, she decided. And butt and legs and arms.

She had to pee. So much for lusty thoughts. The sapphire-blue kimono was lying on the foot of the bed. She stood up and slipped it on, her eyes coming to rest on the moonstone necklace that still lay between the stone lion's ears. Feeling surprisingly amicable toward Kama's gifts, she put it on then stepped into a more open area where she could see the windows that lined the east wall of the loft, framing a dark grey sky. She wondered idly if she'd go out into the weather. Maybe Sebastian would invite her to spend the day here. After all, it was the day after Carnival. The city would be sleepy and shut down. Tyrone wouldn't expect her at work.

Tyrone. Lucinda winced as she remembered that she was supposed to meet Tyrone and never had. He'd probably spent all of last night looking for her in that hellacious storm while she and Sebastian were blissfully fucking their brains out. He'd be worried sick. By now he probably had half the city out searching for her.

She detoured into the kitchen area where Sebastian was pouring hot coffee from a glass carafe into two mugs. He looked up at her, smiling. "Am I taking too long?" he asked. "I realize some people get very impatient about their morning coffee."

"It's not that. It's my friend. I was supposed to meet him last night. And then the storm broke—"

"And I absconded with you to my loft," Sebastian filled in.

"I need to call him," she said, smiling at the memory of their absconding. "Can I use your phone?"

"I don't have one."

"You what? How can you do business here and not have a phone?"

"Arcato's postal service is quite good," Sebastian told her. "My clients either write for what they want or they send their messengers. Sometimes Madana or the other boats bring me word."

"You're serious?"

"Completely."

She stood for a moment, stunned. "Well, that's charmingly old-fashioned, but I have to get in touch with my friend. Tyrone's a worrier. He's probably been looking for me all night."

"Not likely in that storm," Sebastian murmured and then asked, "Does he live here in the city?"

"Yes." She ran a hand through her tangled hair. "I'd better go to his loft."

"Now?"

She nodded.

"Do you want me to come with you?"

"No." She wasn't ready to expose him to Tyrone's barbs and she wasn't ready to bring him fully into her life, which were nearly one and the same. What she had with Sebastian was something apart. It belonged to another place entirely. It felt newborn, fragile, woven of a sweet gossamer enchantment that she couldn't bear to break. Still, she owed him more of an explanation. "I'm sorry," she said carefully. "I don't want to leave, and you don't know how rare that is for me—I never spend the night with anyone. But I have to go."

Sebastian set down the carafe and walked over to her. He lifted her chin and gazed into her eyes, as if making certain she was telling the truth. Then he kissed her forehead and mouth. "Just promise me that I'll see you again."

"Promise."

He kissed her mouth again. "What about your clothing? It's still wet."

She thought about Madana's dress. "It can stay here until it dries." She gave him a half-smile. "There. Now I have an excuse to return. I'll have to come get my costume."

"I can live with that."

"Can I borrow the clothes you lent me last night?"

"You? You're really going to walk through the city looking like a lumberjack? Let me dig through one of the trunks. I'm sure I can find something more suitable."

"Don't. I'll be fine in those clothes."

She made a quick trip to the bathroom to pee, and noted that her clothes were indeed still wet. Which pleased her. Lucinda liked the idea of coming back to reclaim them.

In Sebastian's bedroom she grabbed the baggy pants and flannel shirt and began to put them on. She might have to borrow some shoes, she realized. She was twisting her hair back into a knot when her eyes fell on Sebastian's night table, where a sphere of polished blue crystal rested on a silver stand. She could swear it hadn't been there the night before.

Rolling up the sleeves of the flannel shirt, she walked over to the night table. It was just a clear, blue glass sphere. She picked up it, enjoying the smooth weight of it in her palm. A bit of color flickered in its depths. Lucinda peered at it more closely, expecting to see a reflection of something in the bedroom, and instead saw Sebastian's kitchen. Sebastian wasn't anywhere in sight but a large red fox sat there, its thick tail curled round its feet, its tongue licking its lips as though it had just feasted.

She bit back a gasp and nearly dropped the crystal ball. With an effort, she managed to set it back on its stand, half-expecting the thing to bite her.

The door to the bedroom swung open then, and Lucinda whirled to see Sebastian standing in the doorway. He was holding up thick wool socks and rubber boots. "Thought you might need these," he said.

"I—" She turned back to the crystal, but when she glanced at it again she saw only a sphere of clear blue glass.

Sebastian stepped toward her and something flashed in his eyes, something that was no kin to the lover's sleepy indulgence that had been there moments ago.

Lucinda felt a tremor of fear ripple through her. It made no rational sense. She wasn't entirely sure that she'd actually seen a fox in the crystal— it was simply too bizarre—and there was nothing in Sebastian's manner that hinted at any kind of danger, but she was suddenly certain that she needed to be out of this place. She took the socks and boots from him and forced a smile, murmuring, "And I was wondering if I ought to go barefoot."

"Let me walk you down to the street," he offered as she pulled on the boots.

She saw no way out of it, and nodded. He handed her a thick wool jacket, then he unlocked the metal door of the loft and walked her down the stairs.

Outside, she gazed up at his building, wanting to be sure she'd recognize it. The building itself wasn't terribly distinctive, one of dozens of three-story cast-iron factory buildings, but the street was unusual, paved with cobblestone. She hadn't realized that there was still cobblestone left in Arcato. She remembered when she was a little girl, watching workers tear up the uneven grey stones and replace them with smooth red brick.

"I don't recognize this part of the city at all," she confessed.

"It's a bit of a maze up here."

"Will I be able to find my way back to your loft?" she asked, though she was feeling more certain by the second that finding her way back was not a thing she'd want to do.

"If you don't, I'll find you. Sure you don't want me to walk you to your friend's place?"

She shook her head, and with a resigned sigh he pointed to the right. "This is Montague. Follow it downhill. It will curve into Luminaria. Take that down another block, and you'll see a little alley on your right, which is Arellano Alley. Follow Arellano to where it forks, then take the left fork— Castleton Way. It snakes around but eventually you'll see the steps we took last night. They'll lead you back down to Delahanty."

She nodded, not sure she'd taken it all in but wanting to get away from him.

Sebastian brushed her lips with another kiss. Despite her mind warning her to keep her distance, she moved back into his embrace and the current danced between them, filling her with a rush of warmth. He ran a hand along her cheekbone as he released her. "I'll see you again," he said.

"Mmm," she agreed, then she was off, hurrying downhill, past tiny shops whose windows were crowded with lamps and fabrics and porcelain. Lucinda still couldn't imagine how it was that this part of the city was new to her. She had lived here all her life. As an adolescent, hating the depressing flat she shared with her mother, Lucinda had taken to the streets as though they were her first love. From her early teens she'd spent days and nights roaming the streets and wharves, hiding out in abandoned buildings and, when she had the money, passing hours in cafés. From the waterfront up to the foothills of the mountains she knew every street and alley of Arcato. So how had Sebastian managed to find an entire neighborhood that had eluded her? Even the names of these streets were completely unfamiliar. It was as though she'd wandered into another city tucked into her own.

She stopped as she realized she'd been following a curving alley for a while now, and it hadn't forked. Or was it a street that was supposed to curve and the alley that was supposed to fork? What had Sebastian said? Did he really friggin' expect her to remember all that? Or had he been counting on her to forget?

She cursed him for not drawing a map, and herself for not writing down the convoluted directions. In any case, she seemed to be facing uphill when she wanted to go down. She was lost, which was simply something that did not happen to her in *her* city.

Lucinda quickly ran through her options. She could ask for directions, but the narrow houses here were shuttered, and it was never wise to wake people on the morning after Carnival. She could retrace her steps to Sebastian, but she was terrified she might wind up in his arms again. So she just stood for a moment, trying to fend off a rising panic. The air was heavy and cool and still, a lull between storms. The streets were silent, as though muffled by the cloud cover. She'd keep wandering, she decided. It seemed the only viable choice.

She turned so that she faced downhill, toward the river, but when she'd walked another ten minutes or so, she found herself again facing the foothills. The whisper of fear that had started with the vision of the fox turned into a full-blown alarm that was ringing through her body. She was beyond lost. She was caught, without the first idea of what it was that held her.

Lucinda was drawing deep breaths, trying not to give in to tears, when she felt a strange fluttering in the pocket of the flannel shirt. She peered into it and gave a hoot of amazed laughter as she saw the jade dragon gently opening and closing its wings. It flew out of her pocket and hovered in the air in front of her, its jewel eyes gleaming.

"Where did you come from?" she asked it softly. "You *were* in Sebastian's loft last night, weren't you? How long have you been hiding out in my pocket?"

The tiny creature turned and began to fly away from her.

"Oh, no, you don't," she muttered. "You're not leaving me here all alone." She began to run after it, her boots slapping against damp cobblestones. She followed the dragon down a crook in the alley that she'd missed the last two times she'd come this way, then around several corners and across a footbridge to another series of alleys and shuttered streets where the houses all tilted at the same angle, looking curiously windswept. At last the dragon came to rest on a lamppost, snorting tiny puffs of pale green steam.

"What is it?" she asked, irritated. "What are you trying to say?"

The dragon craned its delicate neck. Following suit, she glanced around and realized that she was on a street that was filled with familiar brick buildings.

"Oh, my goodness," Lucinda said, finally understanding. "You came to lead me back."

IT WAS STILL early, only a few hours past dawn, and Alasdair was in a foul mood. He'd caught sight of Michael again, down by the waterfront, and had been led on a merry chase through Carnival crowds and alleys ripe with the smell of rotting fish. Was it four or five times he'd come up short at the river's edge—as if the boy had darted straight out across the water—only to then catch a glimpse of the little Cyclops shoving someone aside or knocking into a stack of crates on his frenetic, clumsy run? Alasdair tried calling to the cat's eye he'd left with Michael, but all he got from the stone was that it had cast an illusion in an effort to protect him and was no longer in the boy's possession.

At one point, in the moments before the sky opened and the rains began, Alasdair had actually caught hold of him. Michael had cursed him fluently, twisted out of his costume, then disappeared into the crowds. Alasdair hadn't seen him since. Or had he? In the charcoal light of a murky sunrise he'd glimpsed a boy about Michael's size helping a drunk through the streets, but the act seemed so completely out of character that Alasdair had passed them by. Now the storm was over, the glistening city streets were bathed in a weak morning light, and Alasdair was sodden and exhausted and profoundly annoyed to have been outwitted by a slip of a boy. If he hadn't been convinced that Michael Fortunato was a disaster waiting to happen, he'd gladly have given up the chase.

He forced himself to keep walking, wishing he could call on the dragon for help. The dragon had an uncanny talent for locating those it wished to find. Unfortunately, it had an equal talent for concealing itself. Alasdair knew he'd only see the little jade serpent when it chose to grace him with its presence, which could take some time. Although it was an intrinsically loyal creature, the dragon was also moody and easily offended. It hadn't quite forgiven him for coming to the city in the first place.

Alasdair came to a halt as he felt the black opal stirring in the deerskin pouch. He drew it out. Known as the thief's stone, the opal could make the one who held it invisible while simultaneously sharpening his sight. This one was a rare black opal, a polished blue-black stone with rivers of red, orange, green, and a deep blue. It was the most dramatic of his life stones, the colors inside it dancing fire. The iridescent lines of color were flickering wildly now, wanting him to invoke the stone's protection.

Alasdair gave silent assent and in the chill morning air he felt an aura of warmth surround him as the opal's fire began to oscillate out from the stone. He knew the basics of how the opal worked: It both absorbed and reflected light; it had often made it impossible for others to detect his presence in the play of light and shadow it cast. Now, though, the life stone was working its protective powers in a completely different way. The black opal's fire was drawing a net of its own colors around him, its fibers fine yet layered so thickly that they formed a cocoon of light invisible to the mortal eye. Alasdair was literally being wrapped and hidden in the stone's energy. His first reaction to this was a kind of pleased sense of wonder; he hadn't known the opal was capable of such a feat. His second reaction was more unsettling: the opal wouldn't be concealing him this way without reason. He thought of the stranger who'd visited his flat, and Lucinda's telling him that there was someone at Spook's funeral watching him. He was being followed.

Wrapped in the cocoon of light, Alasdair studied the streets around him. Only a few people were out. One was an elderly woman, another a thin, middle-aged man in a turban. Two teenage boys passed, all lanky grace and good-natured insults. An alley cat skittered past. Alasdair let his concentration rest on each one, even the cat on the chance that he was being followed by a shape-shifter. He detected nothing out of the ordinary, saw no one who seemed to be other than they appeared. Yet he trusted the opal, knew it was incapable of overreacting. Despite the fact that Alasdair couldn't see anyone who seemed even remotely suspicious, someone was hunting him.

It took the better part of an hour before the opal saw fit to let its protective netting dissolve. When it did Alasdair realized he'd been on this same street earlier that night. But he hadn't seen the footbridge. Had it been obscured by the crowds or one of those gaudy floats? Had he been distracted by a glimpse of the boy or had he simply not looked in the right direction? He would have noticed the stone bridge, with the gentle arch spanning a shallow stream. He would have remembered. Because the stones had the soft grey-blue iridescence of labradorite, which was an unusual material for a bridge. Unless one wanted to connect two realms.

MICHAEL HUDDLED BENEATH the comforter, trying to muffle the coughing that convulsed him. Even here in Tyrone's ritzy apartment, even with Tyrone's hokey table lamp on, he could feel that thick velvet darkness coming for him again. He didn't want to fall asleep because he knew he'd dream of Spook. He was in bad shape and he knew he couldn't stay here. They'd be looking for him. He might even be in the morning paper, which Tyrone probably had delivered to his door. How was he ever going to sneak onto a boat? He wouldn't exactly be inconspicuous, coughing his head off. He burrowed deeper into the couch. His wet clothes were damp and clammy. And his head hurt. He couldn't think straight. Maybe if he just got a few hours' sleep, he wouldn't feel so lousy and he could figure out a way to get himself down to the river and out of Arcato.

It figured, sleeping on Tyrone's fancy leather couch was a bust. The combination of the comforter and his fever had him so sweaty he was slimy. And the cushions on the sofa were too deep and squishy. His butt and head were sunk lower than the rest of his body, with the leather pressing its sticky surface against his neck and face. *Tyrone should have given me a pillow,* the boy thought resentfully. *He only has about a dozen of them on his bed.*

So is Tyrone asleep? Michael wondered. *He ought to be passed out by now if all my coughing didn't wake him up.* He listened for a few minutes, and when he didn't hear any sounds coming from the bedroom, he decided he'd slip in and get one of those pillows. Tyrone would never notice.

Michael got to his feet. Without the comforter around him he was suddenly chilled again, but he made his way into Tyrone's room. The single candle still burned on the bedside table. Tyrone lay stretched out on his back, snoring loudly. Sure enough, he was propped up on three pillows, but there were at least three more on the far side of the bed.

Michael started across the room on his tiptoes. He didn't have far to go. Just to the other side of that friggin' huge bed, but the fever was dancing up his spine and he felt himself swaying slightly with every step. He caught a shadowy glimpse of himself in the full-length mirrors that covered the closet doors. He looked like some cartoon burglar; all he needed was a mask over his eyes and a sack over his shoulder.

He held his breath as he reached the other side of the bed. It wasn't like he was doing anything criminal, borrowing a pillow. He just didn't want to wake Tyrone and have to get into boring explanations. He reached out, grabbed one of the soft pillowcases, and pulled the pillow toward him. Easy. He reached for a second pillow and became aware that there was a night-stand on this side of the bed, too. In the room's dim candlelight, he could see that a small, glassy, oval object lay on top of it. The diamond.

Michael stared at the stone. It was just lying there on the end table. He couldn't believe it. *If Tyrone really cared about that diamond, he wouldn't leave it lying there like that,* he told himself. How come Tyrone, who didn't care and who didn't need to be any richer, got a diamond? And how come Spook, who wasn't even going to live, got one? It wasn't right that they had diamonds, and all he'd ever gotten was a crappy yellow cat's eye. He could change that, he realized with a shiver that wasn't entirely the fever. He could just help himself to the diamond, and then at least he'd have something that would take care of him when he was out there on his own.

PART 3

After the Storm

"See the rain in the street,
lament of stone and crystal."

— FEDERICO GARCÍA LORCA,
"Madrigal to the City of Santiago"

$\mathcal{E}ight$

ALASDAIR STARED AT the city streets beyond the footbridge. It certainly looked like a continuation of the same city except that the streets were paved with cobblestones rather than brick, and the buildings were older and not packed together so densely. He didn't really think the boy had come this way, didn't believe he had the kind of power necessary to find the labradorite bridge. Still, Alasdair hesitated just a moment before crossing it into the Arcato of an earlier time.

The streets had a different smell here. Coal furnaces and wood fires heated the buildings. Peering into the window of a tea shop, he saw gas lamps being lit and concluded that he hadn't traveled much more than a hundred years into the city's past. In the distance he could hear a man calling out that he had fresh eggs and cream to sell, and someone else hawking "tonics for the morning after Carnival." He cast a cautious glance around, wondering if whoever had been stalking him had followed him across the bridge. He sensed nothing, though. Resolved to remain wary, he continued on.

Alasdair walked the streets, enjoying their quiet. In this older city the buildings were separated by yards and courtyards; in one a tame white goat grazed. Some were even covered with a thin growth of grass and flowers that Alasdair recognized from the mountain foothills above. The birds must have carried down the seeds, he thought.

He stopped as he saw a lot filled entirely with doors. Most were made of wood and hung from posts and lintels: rough, heavy courtyard doors from Mexico; intricately carved doors from Bali; doors bearing delicate inlays from India; doors once painted in bright colors, the colors now so faded that one could only guess at their original hue.

At the back of the yard a set of barn doors opened wide to reveal a high-ceilinged room furnished with a desk and two chairs, where the purveyor of doors kept shop, Alasdair supposed. There was no one inside. The only other person on the lot seemed to be a customer—a tall, broad and powerfully built man, carrying a staff in his right hand and still wearing a double mask—one face bearded, the other smooth-shaven. At first Alasdair assumed the man was still in his Carnival costume, which seemed odd. That morning the few people who'd been out on the streets were scrubbed clean of makeup and wearing ordinary clothing, be it contemporary on the other side of the footbridge or here, the clothing of a hundred years ago. The last person he'd seen in costume had been the drunk at dawn. Alasdair studied the mask that faced out from the man's back. Its eyes were closed, the clean-shaven mouth composed and serene, as though meditating.

The masked figure moved among the doors, examining them intently. *He's reading them,* Alasdair realized, *the way I read stones.* Curious, Alasdair moved toward him. He stopped, frozen by his own stupidity as the eyes of the back "mask" snapped open, fixing him with an outraged glare.

"You no longer recognize me?" the god demanded.

Alasdair dropped to his knees and pressed his forehead to the ground. "Good my lord Janus," he murmured.

The god did not respond. Alasdair remained on his knees, acutely conscious of the muddy ground seeping through his robes.

"Do you like my doors?" Janus asked.

Alasdair dared a glance up. He should have known. Of course, the god of entries and all passages would be drawn to a display of doors. Either that, or it was he who'd set them there.

"They're . . . intriguing," Alasdair answered carefully.

"Stand up," Janus told him, and Alasdair obeyed. Standing, he was perhaps a head shorter than Janus, though he had the peculiar sensation that he often had when in the presence of a god: that he was an infinitesimal being whom the god towered over like a colossus. Admittedly, he had no idea of Janus's real height or even his form. The gods allowed only glimpses of their true nature. Shape, dimension, perspective—the gods played with them all, seeming to delight in leaving mortals dizzy and disoriented.

"How long has it been since our last meeting?" Janus inquired in a polite, conversational tone.

"I don't know, my lord."

"Time enough for three generations in this city to have traveled from infancy to adulthood," the god calculated.

Alasdair nodded. It had been at least that long.

"And what might you be calling yourself this time?"

"Alasdair."

"Last time it was Aesig, wasn't it? And Ivor and Gideon and Stefano times before that?"

"Yes, my lord. All those names have been mine."

"Show me your life stones," the god commanded.

Alasdair complied, drawing out the deerskin pouch. "The moonstone has gone missing," he explained, pouring the nine remaining stones onto his palm.

Janus raised one dark brow. "What happened to it?"

"I don't know. I think there was one who had more need of it than I."

"It was careless of you to let it go," Janus chided him. "You will miss it sorely."

"I already do."

Janus turned so that Alasdair now confronted the bearded face that stared out from the front of the god's body. This face was severe, the eyes so hard and unyielding that Alasdair wondered if Janus, who was among the most ancient of gods, had once been born in stone.

"You were made for a purpose," Janus told him. "And you've been fortunate enough to have that purpose made clear to you. So why do you run from what you are?"

"Cowardice?" Alasdair suggested.

He never saw Janus's arm move. He only felt the oak staff smashing into his face, driving him down into the wet ground.

"I would have thought you'd have sense enough to be respectful," the god told him.

"Forgive me. I'm sorry, my lord."

"You're not." Janus watched him, his ancient eyes dispassionate. "And if one more lie escapes your lips, I'll end your life now. Or is that what you've sought all along?"

"No," Alasdair said, finding it was true.

"Then get up, and this time I'll have the truth."

Alasdair forced himself to his feet, fighting a wave of blazing pain and trying to ignore the blood that was dripping from his temple. He wondered if any of his bones were fractured.

"Why are you here?" Janus demanded.

"I came looking for someone. I don't expect he's here, but I saw the labradorite bridge and—"

"And it was as though someone had sent you a personal invitation?" the god finished. "I see. And whom is it you seek?"

"A boy. He escaped from a prison here last night. He's already killed once. I'm afraid he'll kill again."

"And you believe you are responsible?"

"Indirectly, yes."

"Don't blame yourself for his escape, Aesig." The god sounded almost compassionate. "I aided him in that."

"*You?*"

Janus held out his ring of keys. "It was Carnival, a time of beginnings and endings, a night to open doors. How could I resist?"

"You didn't have to open the *prison* door!" Alasdair's instinct for self-preservation dissolved in molten fury. "You *had to* have known what he is. That he's already been Hekate's pawn, and she turned him into a killer. That he's angry enough and callow enough to—" Alasdair caught himself mid-tirade and stopped, bracing himself for the next blow.

But the god's response held no ire. "It pleased me to do it. I was petitioned by a supplicant. A fine sacrifice was made to me to listen to his prayers. And so I answered."

"Who was it?" Alasdair demanded. "Who bought your favors and how much did they pay?"

Janus smiled at him for the first time. "So righteous in calling the gods to account. At last the true Aesig, or whoever, emerges."

Alasdair ignored the jibe. "Tell me now," he insisted. "Has the boy killed again?"

"Not that I know of."

"Where is he? I need you to take me to him."

"The boy or the supplicant?"

"By all that is sacred," Alasdair swore, "if you don't stop playing me like a—" His words choked off as Janus reached out one immense hand and closed it around his throat.

"How is it that you've never learned to fear us?" Janus wondered.

Alasdair fought his own instincts to try to break free. To struggle against the god would only make things worse. Instead he tried to thin his own breath, so that it became like a thread that could slip through the vise that held him.

Janus saw what he was about and tightened his hold until Alasdair, choking, began to writhe. He couldn't breathe. There was no air left in his lungs and the edges of his vision were going black. His eyes bulged in their sockets, his head throbbed, his limbs were going numb. And then the god released him and he again slammed against the ground.

For a long while he lay there, sucking in long, delicious inhalations. The air tasted damp and sweet with the promise of spring, of seeds stirring beneath the damp earth, of new life coming into being. It occurred to Alasdair that Janus, a god who embodied dualities, was sending him visions of beginnings—as a sort of prelude to the coming vision of his own end.

"Well?" Janus said.

Alasdair hadn't realized he was supposed to speak. He cast a wary eye up at the god's stern countenance and though his throat was raw, he forced out words. "Is that what you want from me then? My fear?"

"You were born into power," Janus said softly. "Use it for something other than defying your own destiny."

Alasdair rolled himself onto his knees, his head again pressed against the soggy ground and spoke in the low murmur of the faithful. "Then I kneel before you as a supplicant and ask you to hear my prayers. On the other side of the bridge, at the very top of the city, I found the ruins of a temple or a marketplace, I'm not sure which. And I sensed the thing that had been there, my lord. It destroyed everything in that place. It stripped the memory from the stones, leaving only echoes of unbearable pain. It still exists. It's somewhere in this city. And *it* frightens me. So I ask for your help and your protection—"

"Now is not the time for this battle." Janus cut him off, his tone bored and dismissive. "Find the boy instead. Come on, get up. You're wasting time."

MICHAEL CLOSED HIS free hand around the diamond and felt a familiar rush. This was just like when the skeleton keys appeared in his cell and got him out of jail. His luck was holding. Something was helping him, clearing the way, giving him exactly what he needed. He'd be stupid if he didn't take it.

Now all he had to do was get out of here before he started coughing again. Rising up on tiptoe again, he began to make his way around the bed to the door. This time when he glanced at his reflection in the mirrors he was grinning.

"Not so fast, little man." Tyrone lifted his head and squinted at him. "Didn't anyone ever tell you it was wrong to go walking off with other people's possessions?"

Michael didn't hesitate. First line of defense when someone attacked was always to take the offense. "I wasn't stealing anything. I was only *borrowing* two of your precious pillows. 'Scuze me if you need to sleep on all twenty of 'em."

Tyrone pushed himself up to a sitting position. "I have no problem with you borrowing pillows," he said way too clearly for someone who was supposed to be sleeping off a hangover. "I'm talking about that diamond you got tucked away in your other hand. Believe me, that rock is not a good thing."

"You're crazy," Michael told him. "I help you get home—you never would have made it if it wasn't for me—and look how you treat me! Are you always this paranoid?"

"Oh, you are good," Tyrone said with a soft laugh. "Do you work this kind of guilt routine on your parents?"

"I don't have parents," Michael spat back.

"I'm sure." Tyrone crossed his arms over his chest. "Well, to answer your previous question, I'm only this paranoid when someone's stealing from me. And I have a real problem with that. So why don't you put the diamond back where you found it?"

Michael gave him an indignant scowl and promptly ruined it by breaking into yet another coughing fit.

Tyrone sighed heavily. "You need some cough syrup and probably a doctor, too."

Michael definitely didn't need some doctor asking questions, checking records. "I don't need anything from you," he told Tyrone. "Here, take your damn pillows!" He walked over to the end of the bed and smashed the two pillows down on it.

Moving faster than Michael would have thought possible, Tyrone lunged across the bed and caught his arm. "Now you can give me the diamond."

Michael tried to pull away and found he couldn't. It was the damn fever, he realized. It was making him weak, trapping him.

"Give me the diamond," Tyrone insisted.

"Why?" Still trying to twist out of Tyrone's grip, Michael found himself half-crying. He couldn't help it. He didn't feel good, and now Tyrone was ruining everything. "Why should I give it to you? You don't even know where you got it. That means you stole it from someone else, so what makes you think you get to keep it? And you just left it lying on your night table. You don't need it. You already got this fancy apartment. I'm the one who needs it!"

"You're burning up with fever. What you need is a doctor. Stop thrashing around and let me help you."

"Let go of me!" Michael screamed. He began pounding on Tyrone's arm with his fist, and when that didn't work, he dug into his pocket and pulled out the broken screwdriver.

"You little punk. I ought to call the police—" Tyrone grabbed for Michael's other hand, pried it open, and grabbed the diamond.

"No!" Michael couldn't let that happen. "You can't have it! I need it!"

He drove the broken end of the screwdriver into Tyrone's gut, heard the man grunt and curse in pain. Waited while the blood pooled and the man's grip on the stone relaxed before he yanked the screwdriver free and stuck the bloodied end back in his pocket.

"I need it," Michael repeated, taking the diamond.

ALASDAIR GOT TO his feet as Janus waved a regal hand toward the doors in the yard. "Find the boy," he said. "If you are lucky, one or another will open and show you what you seek."

This, Alasdair knew, was about as accommodating as he could expect the god to be. Resigned, he began to examine the doors, wondering which would lead him to Michael. He had to find a way to read them, as Janus had, though doors were not his specialty. He stood quietly for a moment, simply paying attention to what he felt. That did him no good. What he felt was the resounding pain from Janus's blow. He would have to circumvent it.

He closed his eyes and in his mind's eye he saw the cool sheen of blue chalcedony. If he could only hold a piece of the stone in his hand, it would stir something inside him, probing gently but persistently until it opened a pathway that was now closed, a pathway that would allow him to read the doors, sensing what they concealed.

Alasdair opened his eyes as he felt a tug on his robe near his knees. He glanced down to see a young girl—she couldn't have been more than four—dressed in a rough blue smock and holding a basket. She had straight butterscotch-colored hair that framed her face and large brown eyes. She seemed utterly unaware of Janus and spoke with the urgency of one who'd worked hard to memorize her message. "Mum says, it's early for Easter but these are for you. You must take them."

"Must I?" Alasdair asked softly, but he reached down for the basket. Two teardrop-shaped pearls rolled from his sleeve, one pink, one silvery gray. "Give these to your mother with my thanks," he told the child. She nodded solemnly and walked off clutching the pearls, leaving Alasdair wondering whose child she was and to whom he was now indebted.

"Charming," he muttered as he examined the contents of the basket: half a dozen eggs dyed in bright pastels nestled in a bed of fragrant grass. He lifted a lavender one, shook it, didn't hear liquid moving inside.

"Care for an egg?" he said to Janus. "They seem to be cooked."

The god raised a dark brow.

Alasdair returned his gaze to the basket. At the very bottom was a pale blue egg made of polished chalcedony. "I believe this one is for me."

"The stones always find their way to you, don't they?"

Alasdair grimaced. "Haven't you seen the havoc that's caused on the other side of the bridge? Half the city expects to wake and find sapphires in their breakfast cereal. And the stones may have played a part in the boy's taking a life."

He set the basket down, cupped the chalcedony egg between his palms and gave himself to it. Though his eyes remained open, he could no longer see the yard or the doors or even the god. He'd surrendered his vision to the stone, and now he could only see what it gave him, a wash of its own translucent blue. He felt a gentle surge of its pale blue essence hovering at the edges of his eyes, removing something that felt like grains of sand, something that obscured. He still saw only the wash of blue but he knew his vision had been altered. Then he felt its essence within him, the stone's cool probing and his own body opaque and resistant. He tried to open himself, to dissolve his own ignorance. It was like trying to open one of Janus's bloody doors without the god's aid. He was only halfway there. Thanks to the chalcedony, he'd now see the doors differently, but choosing the correct portal would remain a guessing game, and he was well aware of how dangerous it was to guess incorrectly where Janus was concerned.

"Good my lord, Janus, help me," he murmured. "Help me open what remains shut inside me so that I may read your doorways for what they are."

"You had only to ask, you stiff-necked lout."

Alasdair felt the cool touch of chalcedony somewhere near his heart and then what felt like a thin needle of bone dissolving at its touch. Involuntarily, his hand flew to his chest. He sensed nothing broken, but something had changed. The wash of pale blue dissolved. He could see the lot again, and the god watching, obsidian eyes flickering with contempt, infinite patience, and strangely, love.

"Focus on the doors, Aesig," the god instructed him, "and whether or not this child you seek might be behind them."

"I will, my lord," Alasdair murmured, and did as he was told.

The doors, or perhaps his eyes, had changed. It was as if each portal had come into sharper focus. He could now see the grain of the wood beneath paint, the mark of the woodworker's chisel; he could sense each doorway's beginnings, how its parts had come into being and been shaped and fitted to-gether into the whole. And there was something else; as if recognizable scents and imprints came from them, he could now sense what most of the doors concealed—or more accurately, what they opened to.

He quickly discounted a set of Balinesian temple doors, a pair of arched doors that led to a scriptorium in Janus's own city of Rome, and the red lac-quer doors of an opium den. He was tempted by the lattice gates of a Japa-nese moon-viewing garden, but to walk through those would only have satisfied his own selfish desire for tranquility.

"Oh, you are slow," Janus taunted him.

Alasdair shrugged, not about to be goaded into a choice that might land him on the other side of the globe, possibly in another millennium. There was always the danger when crossing one of Janus's thresholds that you might cross space and time as the gods do but, because you were not one of them, never be able to retrace your steps. Often there simply was no route back. Alasdair suspected this was because Janus, the great Initiator, was far more interested in beginnings than in endings. So he walked slowly through the lot, measuring each portal against what he knew of the boy.

He halted as he reached a pair of highly polished wooden doors inlaid with turquoise. It was the pattern of the turquoise that stopped him and sent a sudden wave of panic sweeping through his body. One diamond set within another, the same pattern he'd seen in the mosaic at the top of the city. The pattern he should recognize and yet couldn't, the pattern that was somehow connected to whatever haunted that place.

Alasdair pushed aside the fear that gripped him. Did the diamond pat-tern conceal the boy? Though he sensed power behind the diamonds, he sensed nothing that indicated any connection to Michael.

"At some time you may choose to enter this portal," Janus interceded. "But this is not that time."

Alasdair kept walking, the fear ebbing as he put distance between him-self and the diamond pattern. He stopped as he came to a pair of French doors coated in glossy white lacquer. These were not old and imprinted with generations of those who'd touched them. In fact, these were rather new and bore the faint scents of cleaning fluid overlaid with a man's cologne. Alas-dair rested his hand on one of the rounded brass knobs, which were a good hundred years older than the doors themselves. He could sense a life well provided for, love twined with grief, a strange sense of resignation, and above all a desire for what was beautiful and an irresistible impetus to create it. None of this spoke of the boy. Alasdair started to move on when he felt something else behind the French doors, something so familiar it nearly hit him between the eyes. There was a desperation here that had nothing to do with whomever the doors belonged to, a desperation and a furious, whirling panic that could only belong to Michael Fortunato.

He returned to the French doors. "This is the portal I choose," he told Janus, and was rewarded with the god's smile.

"Very good. Perhaps your talents are not a complete waste, after all. Go through then, Aesig, and use them wisely."

Alasdair wondered briefly if the dragon would be able to find him in whatever world he was about to enter. Hoping that it would, he turned the brass knob, opened the glossy white doors, and stepped into the bedroom of a dying man who was being robbed.

"WILL YOU COME with me?" Lucinda asked the dragon. It remained perched above her on the lamppost. "I've got to go see a friend. To get my keys back and assure him that I haven't died. And then . . . I need to figure out what happened last night. You were there, weren't you—in Sebastian's loft?"

The dragon gave a solemn blink of its topaz eyes, which she took for a yes.

"Was . . . was I in danger?"

The dragon blinked again, and Lucinda felt her stomach churn and an acid taste fill her mouth. "Oh, hell," she said. "I was an idiot. I should have known nothing could be that sweet." She ran a hand through her hair, wishing desperately she could just go home and crawl under the covers and not come out until she was so old and decrepit that there was no chance in the world that she'd ever wind up in bed with another man. "I need to find Tyrone," she said, trying to keep her voice steady. "And I'd really appreciate it if you wouldn't disappear on me right now."

The dragon flitted down from the lamppost and settled itself on the shoulder of Sebastian's flannel shirt, and together they set off through the rain-washed streets. A heavy, lethargic mist seemed to hang over Arcato. The sidewalks were deserted, the shops closed, as most of the city's inhabitants were sleeping off Carnival.

Lucinda's pace quickened as Charlot Street and Tyrone's redbrick building came into sight. She should have called him the night before, not that she could have from Sebastian's. Then again, she shouldn't have been at Sebastian's in the first place, a fact that Tyrone would doubtlessly have been clear about. She wasn't sure how it had wound up this way, but over the years she and Tyrone had each become the other's self-appointed protector. He was probably out of his mind with worry by now, and she was going to have to hear about it. In detail.

"Oh, Tyrone, I really am sorry," Lucinda muttered as she climbed the stairs at the back of his building. "You'd think I'd know better." The dragon gave a emphatic little snort of agreement.

Lucinda reached the top of the stairs and knew that something was wrong. The loft's steel outer door was ajar. Tyrone was a security fiend, always locking and double locking doors, always trying to persuade her to move because he was sure that one day someone would mug her in her lobby. She pushed open the door and walked into the living room, where she saw a rumpled comforter spread out over the couch. She gave the dragon a quick, surprised glance. Tyrone had a guest who slept in the living room?

But as she neared the couch she realized that it was currently unoccupied. Maybe whoever it was, was in bed with Tyrone, she told herself, trying to counter her growing dread with an almost-reasonable explanation. The white French doors to his bedroom were also slightly ajar. Lucinda hesitated, torn between feeling like a snoop and being certain that something was terribly wrong. It was the dragon who confirmed her fears, prickling with alarm then darting into the room.

Lucinda yanked open the French doors, and fear ricocheted through her body. Everything inside was wrong. Tyrone should have been sleeping in his extravagantly loud way—no one snored like that man—with or without a guest. Instead the dragon hovered anxiously over a bizarre tableau: Tyrone lay on the edge of the bed, his body terribly still, his eyes glassy. For some reason Alasdair was there, kneeling beside him, pressing a compress made from one of Tyrone's fine-weave Egyptian cotton sheets to Tyrone's stomach. The sheet was rapidly becoming soaked with dark red blood.

"What have you done?" she demanded, rushing toward the bed. "Get your hands off him!"

"I'm trying to stop his bleeding," Alasdair replied in his usual level tone. "He's been stabbed. He's breathing but unconscious. Can you summon help?"

It occurred to her that Alasdair was not the one who'd hurt Tyrone. "I—" she began, but there was a wet metallic smell to the blood that hung over the room and made her feel stricken and numb. It slowed her responses, gave her time to notice the pale, skinny boy who stood in a corner of the room, his eyes intent on Alasdair. "Who the hell are you?" she asked. "And what are you doing here?"

"Just get a physician," Alasdair told her. "I'll answer questions later."

Dazed, Lucinda picked up the phone and dialed the emergency number. "I'm at—on Charlot Street," she began, momentarily blanking on the address. It didn't help her concentration when the boy started to edge away from the corner, and Alasdair's voice snapped out at him like a lash. "Stay where you are!" The boy stayed.

"I'm going to have to ask you again," said the woman on the other end of the line. "What's the problem there?"

"Um—someone's been stabbed. He—he's bleeding badly and—"

"He's in shock," Alasdair told her. "Give them the street number, then get off the phone and help me. I'm afraid to take the pressure off the wound, and the boy is useless."

Forcing her mind to a place of practicality, Lucinda managed to relay the information and hang up. Then she remembered some of what one was supposed to do in cases of shock. She put a pillow under Tyrone's feet and tucked a quilt around him. She started shaking as she watched it quickly absorb the red stain of blood.

"Tyrone, Tyrone, honey, it's Lucinda." She put a hand on his forehead and was appalled by how cold his skin was. As though the life had already left him. "Listen, you can't die," she told him. "You've got to get better. *I need you.*" She stopped her pleading, realizing she was making a fool of herself in front of Alasdair. What was he doing here anyway?

The dragon, meanwhile, was clinging to Alasdair's robes near his hip, tugging furiously. Alasdair glanced down, murmured, "In a moment," then grabbed more of the sheet and folded it on top of the already blood-soaked compress that covered the wound. "Can you hold this and keep pressing down on it?" he asked Lucinda. "There's something I should try."

As Lucinda moved to take Alasdair's place the boy doubled over, coughing. "What's he doing in here?" she wanted to know. "He's going to make Tyrone sick."

"He's already done that," Alasdair assured her, giving the boy a warning look. "No, he stays. He's going to see exactly what he's caused."

Lucinda turned on the boy, rage burning through her as clean and hot as fire. "You did this to Tyrone?" Only the fact that she was still trying to staunch Tyrone's bleeding kept her from flying at him.

"We'll address that later." Alasdair reached into the folds of his robe, took out a drawstring pouch made of white leather, and removed a smooth but uneven deep-red stone. "Coral," he said, answering the question in Lucinda's eyes. "It's been known to be effective against excessive bleeding. Here, let me back in there."

He held the coral close to the wound and began to sing a strange, lilting melody. Lucinda couldn't tell whether it was words he was singing or just a pattern of sound; the song was utterly foreign, like no music she'd ever heard, and yet it made her think of waves washing into shore, of tides moving swift and deep, of a world beneath the sea she'd only imagined. She could see branches of oxblood coral on the sea floor, iridescent fish darting among them. And she could see the diaphanous water spirits who sang to the coral as it as grew, songs of hunger and need, danger and haven, of birth and death and growth and healing; all this the coral drew in as it drew nutrients from the sea. . . . Lucinda blinked, surprised to find herself still in Tyrone's bedroom, following the melody as though it were a lifeline. The dragon, who was perched on Alasdair's wrist, seemed equally intent, its translucent wings beating in perfect time to the rhythm of the song.

The boy in the corner gave in to another fit of coughing, muttered, "Screw this," and started out of the room. Alasdair paid him very little attention. He continued with the song, but held out one hand.

Inches from the door the boy stopped. His right hand was clenched over his left fist, and he was struggling against his own body, trying desperately to hold his fist closed. His struggles were futile. The clenched fist opened and a clear, sparkling stone jumped halfway across the room into Alasdair's outstretched hand.

"No!" the boy howled as Alasdair pocketed the stone. "That's mine!"

"The bleeding's better, I think," Alasdair said to Lucinda, and she saw that it was. It hadn't completely stopped, but Tyrone's blood was no longer soaking through the sheet so rapidly. "Keep the compress on the wound," he said, then turned to face the boy who was advancing on him, holding a broken, bloodied screwdriver. Tyrone's blood, Lucinda realized.

"Give it back!" The boy's voice was shrill and hysterical. "It's mine!"

"Only since you stabbed this man and took it from him," Alasdair countered. "That hardly grants you the right of possession."

"You gave me that lousy yellow stone—"

"Which cast an illusion and protected you from someone who wanted to do you harm," Alasdair pointed out. "Or were you too busy breaking out of jail to notice that?"

"You know him?" Lucinda interrupted. "Who is he?"

"His name is Michael Fortunato," Alasdair replied, then returned his attention to the boy. "You are not wholly to blame," he said in a steady tone. "You've been used by forces who are so much more powerful than you that . . . it is a grief." He broke off to ask Lucinda, "Is there another way out of this apartment?"

"The fire escape from the kitchen." She regretted the words as soon as she spoke them, sure that the boy was going to run, but the boy was still advancing on Alasdair. "I said, give me the diamond. Or I'll hurt you like I did him."

Alasdair, who seemed not to have heard any of that, said, "Swear that you'll do no more harm, and I'll let you go. Before whoever she called arrives."

"Are you out of your mind?" Lucinda demanded. "He's a fucking sociopath! He needs to be in jail!"

"He was in jail," Alasdair told her. "He escaped. He's had help, the kind that all the police in your city can't counter." He continued to talk to the boy in that maddeningly calm tone. "But know that if you break your word—with even the smallest blow—I will end you."

The boy was now trembling so hard he reminded Lucinda of a plucked guitar string. Still, he held onto the screwdriver and moved toward Alasdair until they were only inches apart.

"I see you need proof," Alasdair said, sounding regretful. He removed a large hexagonal crystal from the leather pouch. To Lucinda it looked like a piece of plain quartz. Alasdair stroked its glassy surface, murmured a few of his strange words, and a miniature jaguar appeared inside its clear walls, pacing the length of the crystal, its tail lashing angrily.

It's like the fox in the crystal ball, Lucinda realized, a sickening wave of recognition rippling through her. Here in Tyrone's loft, where the night with Sebastian should have dissolved into memory, it seemed as though she'd stumbled straight back into the world of his magic. And yet she was becoming so numbed to marvels that she wasn't even surprised when Alasdair muttered another word and the jaguar walked straight through the walls of the crystal and settled itself on the center of his palm. "He hates being enclosed," Alasdair explained.

Michael blinked, looking as though he were seconds away from passing out. "Is—is he real?"

"As real as the dragon," Alasdair assured him. The dragon now sat on his shoulder, topaz eyes blazing at the boy. "Put down the screwdriver."

Michael shook his head stubbornly and the tiny spotted cat sprang, landing on his collarbone. With a low but distinct growl it sank sharp white teeth into his neck, drawing blood.

The astonished boy slapped at the miniature cat but succeeded only in slapping himself. The jaguar had already leaped to safety on Alasdair's knee. Michael rubbed his neck. "It bit me!" he said in an injured tone.

"You're in no danger of bleeding to death," Alasdair assured him. He ran a gentle hand across Tyrone's forehead. "Unlike the man you attacked."

Michael gave Tyrone a cursory but calculating glance. "Listen, I'll leave," he said. "Just give me the diamond. I need it, okay?"

Instead Alasdair murmured another of his words and the cat began to grow, as no natural animal grows. It doubled then tripled then quadrupled in size until it had grown to the size of a small housecat. It sprang to the floor. Seconds later it was the size of a bobcat, the tips of its ears level with Michael's chest, its golden coat gleaming.

"He's hungry," Alasdair told the boy.

The cat continued to increase its size, quickly and effortlessly, until it was easily three times the weight of the boy with a thickly muscled body, powerful, heavy shoulders and a large, rounded head. Michael began to edge backward, and the cat padded after him, its eyes glittering with predatory fascination.

"I'd avoid any sudden movements," Alasdair advised. "Now that he's grown to his usual size, he won't go for your neck. He'll go for your head. The jaguar kills its prey by biting through the skull."

"Okay!" the boy said quickly, and dropped the screwdriver. "Keep the diamond. Just call off your cat."

"Give me your word."

"You're going to believe him?" Lucinda asked, outraged.

"Your word," Alasdair repeated.

"I—I won't hurt anyone else," Michael stammered.

"Swear it!"

"I swear," he said as the jaguar stalked toward him. "I won't—do harm again. Ever."

"Be bound by your word," Alasdair told him, and Lucinda sensed she was witnessing the sealing of a sacred covenant, a pact that could not be broken without consequences that would reverberate throughout time. The boy just nodded, his eyes on the cat.

Alasdair turned to Lucinda. "Your people have a medicine for fever, don't they? The sort of thing you all keep in your homes?"

"Yes," she said, startled by the question.

"Well, find some and give it to the boy. I'll watch your friend."

Lucinda quickly got an analgesic and a glass of water from Tyrone's bath. When she returned to the bedroom Alasdair was addressing the jaguar who was in the process of shrinking. It made her woozy to watch, so she handed the pills and water to the boy, then turned back to Tyrone. "Just hang on," she told him. "We're getting you help, so please, Tyrone, just hang on."

"The jaguar goes with you," Alasdair told the boy, "with the power to resume his full size whenever necessary. Don't be fooled and don't forget. He's tasted your blood and he has your scent. You will never lose him. The instant you break your vow, you're his. Do you understand?"

"Yes." Michael's voice was barely audible.

"Do you know how to use this kitchen fire escape?" The boy nodded again. "Then go in peace, Michael Fortunato, and may you find the help you so desperately need."

Lucinda watched the boy leave the room then heard the sounds of his opening the kitchen window. Alasdair tucked the coral and the quartz crystal back into the leather pouch. The dragon remained on his shoulder, its wings folded, its golden eyes closed.

With Alasdair still watching Tyrone, Lucinda grabbed another sheet from Tyrone's linen closet, folded it, and replaced the bloody compress. The bleeding had slowed considerably, but was that because Tyrone was doing better or because he'd already lost so much blood that his heart no longer had much left to pump?

"Is he dying?" she asked.

Alasdair's fingers circled Tyrone's wrist. "His heartbeat is very faint. Where is this physician you summoned?"

"I don't know," Lucinda said, frustrated. Ambulances and fire engines were the only true vehicles allowed in Arcato, and both had trouble getting through the narrow streets and alleys, which were all built well before the invention of the automobile. "Someone should have been here by now."

"Perhaps you should call again."

For lack of a better idea, Lucinda went to the phone but before she could dial she heard pounding on the metal outer door. She ran to it, let in the two emergency technicians, then stood at the foot of the bed as they began working over Tyrone.

"I found him like this," Alasdair said in answer to a question. "No, I didn't see who did it. When I found him he was already unconscious." She noticed that Michael's screwdriver was no longer in sight. Nor were the diamond or the dragon. "No, I'm just an acquaintance," Alasdair went on, lying smoothly. "His friend—" he indicated Lucinda "—let me in."

Lucinda would have set the record straight, but the shorter of the two emergency workers, a burly man with thinning hair, began asking her a string of questions about Tyrone's allergies and medical history, and she found herself striving to remember the lengthy list of ailments Tyrone was forever detailing for her. She'd always pegged Tyrone for a healthy hypochondriac. She couldn't even begin to guess at how much of what he'd complained about over the years might be true.

The questions stopped as the emergency workers lifted Tyrone onto a stretcher. "We're going to take him to Mercy," said the one who had a full head of white-blond hair. "The police should have been here by now since you called in a stabbing. But we've had so many calls since last night's storm—" He pulled out a pocket radio. "I'll try them again, tell them you two will be here for questions."

"If the police have questions, they can wait," Lucinda said. "I'm going to the hospital with Tyrone."

"I'll stay to speak with the officers," Alasdair offered.

The blond-haired worker finished his call to the police, shot Lucinda a wary look, and bent to help carry Tyrone out of the loft.

"Is Tyrone going to be all right?" Lucinda asked, following close behind.

"You'll have to ask the doctors," the balding one answered.

Lucinda followed Tyrone's body out of the building. The feeling of dread she'd had for so long now, the surety that something terrible would shatter her world, was all being borne out.

LUCINDA SAT IN a hallway of Mercy Hospital, waiting for the verdict on Tyrone. Mercy, she reflected, was the most depressing building she'd ever been in, an old behemoth of a civic edifice, built early in the last century. Its badly lit, dank halls seemed to have sponged up years' worth of pain and suffering, all of which were now slowly but steadily seeping back out. She reminded herself that of the two hospitals in the city, this one was supposed to have better medical care. Still, it was hard to think of Tyrone behind the closed doors at the end of this hall, lying on an operating table with doctors slicing into him.

Alasdair walked toward her, holding two cups of coffee. In his long blue robes he looked both wildly out of place and oblivious to that fact. She'd seen him wear a coat, but she couldn't imagine him in pants and a shirt, couldn't imagine what the police had made of him or what he'd said to them. When he'd first shown up at the hospital and she asked, he'd replied, "I told them what I told the emergency workers."

"And they believed you?"

"Of course," he replied, and had gone off in search of coffee.

Now he offered her a lukewarm cup. "I already tried mine," he reported in a discouraged tone. "For coffee it is—a travesty."

"You've become very discerning," she told him, grateful to have an excuse to stop thinking about Tyrone for a few seconds. "Or are your people coffee drinkers?"

"We have herbal teas. It's not the same. Coffee has been one of the pleasures of your city."

She sipped hers and made a face. Travesty was generous.

"You haven't heard anything from the physician yet?" he asked.

"Nothing."

Alasdair nodded and sipped his tasteless coffee, leaving Lucinda to brood on the countless questions that were clawing at her. She didn't know where to start, didn't expect to get any real answers, but there was one thing she had to ask. "Why in the world did you let that little bastard go?"

"You'd rather I'd turned him over to the authorities? They wouldn't be able to hold him. He's being used by the gods."

"Putting him in jail is not what I wanted," she said honestly. "I wish you'd killed him."

"My but we're bloodthirsty," Alasdair murmured. "I'd have thought you'd had enough of that for one day." He made another attempt at drinking the coffee. "The boy isn't evil, you know. He's eleven and he's terrified and he's got no one who truly cares about him."

"Maybe that's what evil is," Lucinda said. "Being young and alone and scared, with a weapon in your hand."

"No, that's circumstances combining in one of the worst possible ways."

Lucinda massaged her forehead. She was wrung out, exhausted, and sick with fear for Tyrone. "Well, whatever you choose to call it, he's going to attack someone else and it's going to be your fault."

"He won't," said Alasdair. "The jaguar will take care of that."

"Oh, of course. How could I forget? Alasdair and his menagerie of miniature magical animals!"

A smile flitted across his face so quickly she almost didn't catch it. "I don't have a menagerie. The dragon is a friend, not a pet, and the jaguar is the spirit of the crystal. I simply summoned him and asked him to act as a sort of guardian."

"A rock has an animal spirit?"

"It can take that form, yes."

"What *are* you?" she asked, finally getting to the real question. "A conjurer? A charlatan? Or maybe," she said, thinking of the coral, "a healer?"

"If I were a healer, your friend would not be in the middle of surgery now," he said quickly, bitterly. For at least the hundredth time since he'd entered Tyrone's room, he wished that Johari were still nearby. Johari would have known what to do. Johari would have healed Tyrone. "I apologize if I've given you the impression that I'm either a conjurer or a charlatan. I know how to work with the stones. That's all."

"Right."

He shrugged then went to toss his coffee cup in a garbage container.

Too nervous to sit still, she twisted one of the silver bands on her wrist. "When I saw you last night at Carnival, you ran after someone," she said as Alasdair started back to her. "It was Michael, wasn't it?"

He nodded and sat down, careful to leave a good amount of space between them.

"So you knew he was dangerous then. Did you follow him to Tyrone's?"

"Not directly. I tried to follow him and lost him in the crowds. But yes, I knew he was a danger so I kept looking."

"Then how did you wind up at Tyrone's?"

Alasdair gave her a weary look. "Let's just say I had help from the same god who helped Michael out of jail, and don't ask me to explain that because I can't. There's something else I can't explain," he went on. "Around dawn, just after the storm let up, the streets were empty but I saw two figures. One may have been your friend. He was wearing some sort of shiny costume and he seemed inebriated, unable to hold himself upright. The other was a boy about Michael's height and build. And it looked like he was helping him walk. You may not want to believe this, but initially, I don't think Michael planned to harm Tyrone."

Lucinda was quiet for a few moments before saying, "For Carnival Tyrone dressed up as some Aztec god named Ilyap'a. Lots of gold lamé."

"Ilyap'a is an Incan storm god, originally worshipped in Peru," Alasdair corrected her. "His name means 'thunder and lightning.' And yes, he was pictured as a man in shining garments."

"Tyrone was so proud of that costume. He thought he looked magnificent," she mused, then something occurred to her. "Is Ilyap'a the one who let Michael out—"

"No. But he's probably the one who sent last night's storm and left Tyrone with that diamond Michael wanted so badly, and—hounds of hell," he swore, looking stricken. "How could I have missed that?"

"What? What are you talking about?"

"The black dogs," he said, his voice hoarse. "Not hell hounds, but the Incans used to leave starving black dogs tied up to howl until Ilyap'a took pity on them and sent rain. And I saw them last night but I didn't put it together."

"Forget the dogs," Lucinda said impatiently. "You're saying, Ilyap'a liked Tyrone's costume, sent the storm, and gave him the diamond as a reward?"

Alasdair gave her a pained look, stood up, and said, "I'm going to get more of that vile coffee. Can you stand another cup?"

"Tell me what happened last night."

"I don't know for certain, but I suspect Ilyap'a was anything but pleased at seeing a mortal impersonating him. I think he sent the storm in anger, as punishment, and the diamond was his parting gift." Alasdair sat down again on the bench. "In India the name for lightning is *vajra,* the same word for diamond. One and the same, do you see?"

"No." It occurred to her that asking Alasdair to explain anything was like asking to be set down in the middle of a maze, blindfolded.

"Most diamonds come into being far beneath the surface of the earth, in kimberlite," he went on with obvious patience. "I believe your scientists have proven that. But there are exceptions, a few stones that come directly from the gods." He drew the oval diamond from his robes. "This is one of them. It was born as Ilyap'a's lightning and bears his curse. It's no accident that your friend was nearly killed for it. Which is why I couldn't let the boy walk off with it. This stone can only draw misfortune to whoever holds it."

"But you're going to keep it."

Alasdair considered the diamond, looking perplexed. "I'm not sure what I'll do. I've got to either find someplace to hide it where it can't do any harm or find a way to remove the curse."

A doctor in surgical scrubs came toward them then and Alasdair quickly pocketed the diamond. "You're friends of Tyrone Dessalines?" asked the doctor.

"I am," Lucinda said, standing up. "How is he?"

"The wound itself isn't that terrible—fortunately, broken screwdrivers don't slice through tissue the way a knife would have—but he's lost a lot of blood. We haven't been able to get him to regain consciousness."

"Because of the blood loss?"

"Because of something that seemed to occur before the stabbing," the doctor said, sounding uncertain. "His body was subjected to—well, the sort of thing you see with an electric shock or a lightning strike. He had a few minor burns on his skin, his lungs were slightly inflated, and there's been some heart damage."

"Heart damage," Lucinda echoed.

"Do you know if he suffered from amnesia before he lost consciousness?" the doctor asked.

"No." She glanced at Alasdair, who said, "When we found him he was already unconscious."

"We'll do everything we can for him," the doctor told them. "You can see him in a few hours when he's out of recovery."

Lucinda nodded blankly as the doctor suggested she get some rest. He touched her shoulder in a brief gesture of sympathy then left them.

"Whatever happened to Tyrone before the stabbing was caused by Ilyap'a," Alasdair told her.

"I'm sure the doctor would find that information very helpful." She sank down on the bench again, her legs suddenly shaky.

"Are you all right?" Alasdair asked.

She nodded. "It's just that I was counting on Tyrone getting better. But what the doctor said—"

"He didn't say he wouldn't."

"It wasn't his words. It was his tone. He was warning me not to have too much hope."

"Why don't you take the doctor's advice and get some rest now?" Alasdair suggested.

"No, I don't want Tyrone to be alone when he wakes up."

"That doesn't mean you can't take a break. If you like, you can go home and I'll stay here until you return. You'll do him more good if you're not half-dead yourself."

"You know what I keep thinking? That the really sad thing is that Michael went to the right place. Tyrone's still mourning his own son. If that kid needed help, Tyrone would have found a way to help him."

Alasdair gave her a sideways glance. "As I'm sure you know, needing help and being able to accept it are not necessarily compatible. For example, right now you need to rest and—must I go on?"

Lucinda arched her back and stretched her arms overhead. Her body was stiff and aching from sitting on the bench for so long. "Maybe it's not a bad idea," she allowed, realizing that she hadn't washed off Sebastian. She could still smell his scent on her skin. At least she'd found her keys in Tyrone's loft. She could go home, take off these ridiculous clothes . . . "All right," she said. "I'll be back soon."

"I'll be here," Alasdair promised.

She started to walk away, but something Alasdair had said earlier tugged at her. She turned back to face him. "The diamond," she said. "You're holding on to it. Sort of for safekeeping, right?"

"I hope so. That's the intent, anyway."

"Then I want to give you something else. Because I don't trust it."

She took off the necklace of moonstones and held it out to him. He didn't take it. Instead he asked, "Where did you get this?"

"It was a gift."

"From whom?"

"I don't want to talk about that." He had warned her to be careful when she told him about Madana. She wasn't about to give him the chance to say, I told you so.

He took the necklace cautiously and laid it on his open palm. "I once told you that you were in need of moonstones, but these—"

"What's wrong with them?"

"They've been enspelled. Nothing exotic. The spell simply heightens the moonstone's powers. It both allows you to sense what's in the heart of another, and softens your own heart, opening you to the other."

"Meaning?"

"These moonstones will make you more receptive to a lover."

The sick spinning feeling of betrayal wrapped itself around her again, and she bit down on her lip, not trusting herself to speak. Which didn't stop her from hurling her coffee cup at the wall. There was very little coffee left inside, but she got a small hum of satisfaction from the spider-shaped splatter.

Alasdair watched her with narrowed eyes. "Are you sure you won't tell me where you got the necklace?"

"No," she said with a measure of control. "I'm going home to take a nice, long bath. Then I'm coming back here to take care of Tyrone. You can keep the necklace. I don't want to see it again."

She started to walk away once more, then turned back a final time. "Alasdair, I don't pray," she confessed. "Don't know how and wouldn't know whom to pray to if I could. So if you can, would you please send up some prayers for Tyrone?"

ALASDAIR SAT ON the bench in the empty hospital corridor, puzzling over the moonstone necklace in his hand. Who had given it to Lucinda? She'd told him she'd met Kama, but that only circled him back to his earlier question: Who was it that Kama was helping?

He started as the dragon swooped toward him and landed on his wrist. "And where've you been?" Alasdair asked it. He realized almost at once what the answer was. The dragon had been watching over Tyrone. "Then how is he?"

The dragon peered at him solemnly, its wings still.

"He hasn't died?" No, the dragon would be far more upset if that were the case. "But he's not doing well, is he?"

The dragon gave an affirmative flutter of its wings.

"I suppose it's miraculous he survived Ilyap'a at all, to say nothing of the boy," Alasdair mused. "Let's hope his luck holds."

The dragon hopped to the hand that was holding the moonstone necklace. "So have you seen this particular necklace before?" Alasdair asked. The jade wings fluttered again.

"You have." Alasdair peered at the dragon more closely. "Then you know who gave it to Lucinda?" The dragon's topaz eyes stared back at him, unblinking. One had to be careful when questioning a dragon. They were very sensitive creatures and would only respond if they felt a question was properly phrased. It was possible that the dragon felt his last question implied some sort of wrongdoing on its part, and therefore was refusing to answer.

Alasdair tried again. "I only want to know, since you can't give me a name, was this person familiar to you?"

At that the dragon began flying about in an agitated pattern that Alasdair could barely decipher. All he knew for certain was that whoever gave the necklace to Lucinda was someone the dragon recognized. And someone who scared it.

Nine

LUCINDA SANK INTO the hot bath water and closed her eyes, willing her body to relax, but the steaming water only brought back memories of her last bath, in Sebastian's loft, and how even then something inside her had known they'd be lovers and how the bath itself was one in a sequence of acts in which she opened herself to him. She pushed herself upright, grabbed the loofa and soap, and began a frenzied scrubbing, determined to scrape herself clean of Sebastian and all that had followed.

After, wrapped in a thick cotton robe, she stepped out onto her balcony. The skies were still overcast. A heavy swath of clouds hung just above the tallest buildings, muffling the noises of the streets and turning the river lead-grey. Lucinda watched trash collectors picking up debris and city workers removing strings of colored lights. The vestiges of Carnival always disappeared quickly, and this year it seemed a mercy. It wasn't enough, though. She wanted to make the whole night and the bloody morning after disappear; at the very least she wanted to undo what had happened to Tyrone.

The warmth of the bath was leaving her body, being replaced by the chill from the damp air. It was time she started back to the hospital anyway. She'd been gone nearly two hours. And then there were other things that she had to take care of.

Trying to keep her panic at bay, Lucinda went back inside and jotted down a list. She'd have to go back to Tyrone's loft, check the schedules and see where the orders were, call clients, pay bills, find a way to keep the studio running until he returned. But as she pictured herself going into the loft she realized that even before she touched the business details, she'd have to get rid of the blood-soaked bedding and scrub the splattered blood from the furniture and floors. The thought made her stomach lurch. She made a note to call a cleaning service. And she'd have to be prepared to deal with Arcato's police, who were generally acknowledged to be even more incompetent than they were corrupt. It was possible, Lucinda realized, that they had actually taken Alasdair at his word.

Adrenaline was ticking through her now, propelling her through a series of staccato movements that almost convinced her that she was accomplishing something. She dressed quickly, choosing a cropped lavender sweater, a long, swirling water-silk skirt of a slightly deeper hue, and amethyst earrings. Maybe it was a bit much for a hospital visit, but it was one of Tyrone's favorite designs, an outfit that he said did his eyes good, and she desperately needed to do something that would do him good. She twisted her hair into a knot, slipped a pad, a pen, and a pocketknife into her purse, then wrapped a pearl-grey shawl around her shoulders. She grabbed her purse, keys for her flat and Tyrone's, then stopped and went back into her bedroom where she opened the cloisonné box. The moonstone lay on its bed of dark-blue velvet, a translucent drop of seawater gleaming against the night sky. This was the first moonstone that had come to her—before the ones she found near the cemetery, before Madana's necklace. She suspected that she probably ought to get rid of it, as well, except for some reason she connected this one with the dragon. Maybe she was being a sentimental idiot but, because of the dragon, she found she couldn't let it go. She closed the enamel box gently. Then she snatched up Sebastian's borrowed clothing from her floor and the white silk dress from her closet. She stuffed them into the incinerator chute on her way out of the building.

Lucinda hurried through the damp, chilly streets, chiding herself for not having called the hospital from her flat. She should have at least checked to see if Tyrone's condition had changed, but she'd been too much of a coward, afraid of what they might tell her.

" 'Cinda, is that you?"

She slowed, not having seen the woman sitting at the outdoor café but recognizing Gabrielle Oculara's sandpaper-and-honey voice. Gabrielle was another designer, one of the few in the city whose talent rivaled Tyrone's. Five years earlier Lucinda, Tyrone, and Gabrielle had all worked together on a costume ball that raised money to restore one of Arcato's remaining riverfront palazzos. The benefit had been a success—the palazzo now housed the art school—and she and Tyrone and Gabrielle had formed a friendship born of giddy, late-night work sessions fueled by too much caffeine and other substances deemed inspirational at the time. Lately, Lucinda and Gabrielle hadn't seen much of each other—Dessalines Productions and the Oculara line were competitors, after all—but the warmth of the friendship remained.

Gabrielle, who never wore her own designs, was dressed in loose black wool pants, topped by a man's black silk shirt, its elegant tailoring a contrast to her wild mane of hair.

She studied Lucinda with a critical eye. "My, but you're dressed up for the day after Carnival. That's from Tyrone's last collection, isn't it?" She gestured to the empty tables and chairs around her. There were a few customers inside the café, but Gabrielle was the only one mad enough to be sitting out in the soggy weather. "Come keep me company."

"I'd like to," Lucinda said honestly, "but I can't. I've got to meet someone." She was tempted to tell Gabrielle about Tyrone, but she wasn't about to let anyone in the business know that Dessalines Productions was in trouble.

"Oh, you can spare five minutes to help me recover from Carnival," Gabrielle said. "Come on, sit down and have a chat."

Gabrielle never took no for an answer. Realizing that giving in would take far less time and effort than refusing her, Lucinda perched on the edge of a chair.

"So how was your Carnival? Andrew and I dressed up as salmon." Gabrielle went on, not waiting for an answer to her question. "Don't look at me that way. It was his idea, and you know I like to indulge my boys."

Gabrielle, who was in her late fifties, was famous for having a string of younger lovers, all of them ravishingly pretty. Most of them stayed at least a year, none seemed to want to leave; it was always Gabrielle who chose to move on. Lucinda found it all very mysterious and intriguing. Gabrielle had never been beautiful. Even in photographs taken in her twenties, she looked spent and jaded, with a small, pouty mouth, dark hollows beneath her eyes, and unkempt waves of ash-brown hair.

"Poor Andy had far too much to drink," she went on. "He became positively convinced that the two of us had to jump into the river so we could spawn. Thank the gods the storm blew in. If the rains hadn't soaked him, conveniently reminding him that he can't swim, I'm sure we both would have drowned. Tell me," Gabrielle didn't even pause, "what did Tyrone dress you up as?"

"He didn't."

Gabrielle's eyebrows rose. "Was that a snit on his part or a rebellion on yours?"

"Neither. Someone else sent me a costume."

"My, my. Tyrone must have been chartreuse with jealousy."

"It was a bad idea," Lucinda admitted. "I should have let Tyrone dress me."

"Well, don't ever tell him that. He'll never let you forget it. And what was Himself wearing?"

"A lot of gold lamé."

"Subtle as ever." Gabrielle's eyes, heavily lined in kohl, widened as she said, "Oh. I *thought* that was Tyrone I saw with . . . who is that abominable sculptor who's always so desperate to get himself written up in the gossip columns . . . Marcus someone?"

"Was he dressed as a wolf?"

"Not much of a costume if you ask me. I'd say it's his human form that's the disguise."

Lucinda found herself smiling. Gabrielle might be pushy but she didn't miss much. "Where did you see them?"

"In that little bar on Grand Street. Marcus had his wolf head sitting on the table. And he was holding a glass to Tyrone's lips."

"I knew I shouldn't have let Tyrone go off with him." Lucinda began imagining ways to inflict pain on Marcus. "That slimy son of a bitch. He deliberately got Tyrone drunk. Or maybe even drugged."

"Tyrone's a big boy," Gabrielle reminded her. "Though, I tell you, I don't know how someone who has such exquisite taste in clothes can have such wretched taste in men."

Lucinda let that one go, asking, "Did you see where Tyrone went after that?"

"I didn't stay long enough. Andrew was feeling the call of the river. And I was trying to avoid one of my exes." Gabrielle gave a low, throaty chuckle. "You never know what kind of weird shit you're going to walk into on Carnival night."

"Which is why we all should have stayed home," Lucinda said more to herself than Gabrielle. She rested her chin in her hand. "Gabrielle, did you ever run across an antiques dealer named Sebastian Keane?"

Gabrielle snapped open a gold lighter and lit a cigarette. "Not by that name, no. But if he's young and sexy, probably. What does he look like?"

"Tall, slender, reddish hair, blue eyes, sharp cheekbones, maybe early thirties—"

"No, and believe me, I've had my eye out for a redheaded boy. A fortune-teller once told me I'd find great passion with a man with red hair."

"Poor Andrew," Lucinda commiserated.

"Andrew is very well taken care of at the present," Gabrielle said with a wink. "He'll have nothing to regret."

"How about a rug merchant? He comes into the city on a run-down red barge, a Mr. Madana."

"Oh, that smooth bastard. Ten years ago I wandered on his skewed little boat and bought a rug. Leo was there—you remember Leo? No, he was before your time. Well, Leo was there, also shopping for a rug, and Madana insisted on introducing us. Next thing I knew—I don't even think it was twelve hours later—Leo moved in. Love as cataclysm. He stole from me, told lies I'm still unraveling, and nearly bankrupted my business. But he was absolutely scrumptious in bed."

"And?"

"The day after I threw Leo out, I sold the rug. I lost money on it but I didn't care. I didn't want any more reminders beyond the ones Leo left."

"What did he leave?" Lucinda asked, thinking of the moonstone necklace.

"That man got into my pores, into my bones. Sometimes I wake up and I can still feel his body curled around mine. Even when I'm with another man. And it's not like I ever confuse the new with the old. No, I always know it's Leo I'm craving."

"Did you ever see Madana again?"

"I'd spit in his eye if I did. Introductions like that, I don't need. When I was on his boat it was like—" Gabrielle broke off her story, looking embarrassed.

"Like what?"

Gabrielle exhaled a thin stream of smoke. "It was like I fell under a spell," she said quietly. "I've never felt anything like it, before or since."

"I know what you mean," Lucinda murmured.

Gabrielle's gaze sharpened with interest. "Let me guess . . . you've met Madana, too, only in your case he introduced you to this Sebastian."

"Actually, Sebastian introduced me to Madana."

Gabrielle made a *tsk*ing sound. "I'd watch my heart if I were you."

"You know," Lucinda said, feeling the heat of a long-simmering anger, "all I've done for years now is watch my heart. I've made an art of the fuck-and-run. I've slept with more men than I can count, and I've made sure that not one of them ever really touched me, and that"—she shouldn't be admitting this to anyone, and yet she felt impelled to finish, to get out the whole lousy confession—"and that just left me hollow and aching. So for one night I dropped my guard, and now everything's so—" Lucinda broke off, shaking, unable to even begin to find the words that would describe how thoroughly she'd been betrayed.

Gabrielle got to her feet and put an arm around her. "Hey," she said gently, "we all get burned sometimes. And sure, it hurts, but it's not the end of the world. You're going to be fine, 'Cinda. Come on, let me order you a nice hot chocolate."

Lucinda shoved her arm away. "I don't want hot chocolate, and I don't want anyone telling me I'll be fine, because the truth is, no one knows. Everyone's stumbling around, trying to find a little comfort, maybe even passion, hoping like hell they won't get their hearts cut up for trying. But it's just freak luck if they don't. None of us understands the first thing about sex or love, so don't pretend that you do."

"My apologies," Gabrielle said, taking her seat with a slow, regal motion. "I wouldn't dream of getting between you and your precious pain."

Lucinda got to her feet. "Shit," she muttered. "I knew stopping to talk was a mistake." Lifting the hem of the long silk skirt, she hurried up the hill toward Mercy Hospital.

LUCINDA FOUND ALASDAIR where she'd left him, sitting in the hallway outside the operating room. "Where's Tyrone?" she asked.

"Still in recovery," Alasdair reported. "I spoke to a nurse a few moments ago. He hasn't woken up yet."

"Oh." Lucinda sat down on the metal bench again. "So nothing's changed."

"Are you feeling any better?" Alasdair asked.

"No," she replied bleakly. "I just blew up at someone who didn't deserve it at all."

Alasdair made no reply to that, and for a long while they just sat, watching nurses and doctors and the occasional patient go by. Finally, a harried-looking young woman in a uniform came up to them and said, "They sent me to tell you Mr. Dessalines is in his room now." She had no information on his condition but gave them a room number on the other side of the hospital.

Lucinda trailed Alasdair through a series of long, depressing corridors. On his numerous coffee runs, he'd apparently gotten the lay of the place because he now walked up stairways, through unmarked wards, and across bridges connecting wings, unerringly leading her to a long, rectangular room with six beds. Barely sparing a glance for the other patients, Lucinda hurried straight to Tyrone. Alasdair, however, greeted each of the other men in the room with the decorous courtesy one would bestow on visiting dignitaries.

Tyrone lay in the narrow hospital bed, his eyes closed, his skin chalky in the wan light. Lucinda was afraid to touch him, he looked so small and fragile. All the ornery vibrancy that made him Tyrone seemed to have bled out of him.

"Tyrone? Tyrone, sweetie, can you hear me?" She wasn't surprised when he didn't respond, but she kept talking. "You don't have to say anything. Just open your eyes or blink or—" She shot a frustrated look at Alasdair who was now deep in conversation with a small, elderly man in plaid pajamas. "Can you go find a nurse and ask whether he ever regained consciousness?"

Alasdair made apologies to the man and left the room.

Lucinda perched on the edge of Tyrone's bed, careful not to disturb the tangle of tubes and wires that connected him to an array of monitors. She stroked his arm gently. "You're going to be all right," she said. "You've just got to rest and let yourself heal." And then she couldn't go on because she was sure she was lying to him and she couldn't bear that. She held his hand—it was so cool and still—and waited for Alasdair to return with someone who might make her believe that Tyrone wasn't dying.

"He hasn't moved since they brought him in here," the man in the plaid pajamas spoke up. "You his wife?"

"No, his friend."

"The last guy who had his bed died just after dawn," continued the elderly man. "About six A.M. his monitors started beeping, woke me right up, and just like that"—he snapped his fingers—"he's got doctors and nurses all around his bed. Only time I ever seen 'em show up when someone actually needed 'em. Lot of good it did. In the end they rolled him out of here, stiff as a board. Could be that bed has a ghost now. I wouldn't be surprised if—"

"Will you stop it!" Lucinda said.

The man gave her a wounded look and murmured, "I was only trying to help."

Alasdair returned then. "The nurses said they'll send someone to talk with you as soon as they can. Their staff is exceedingly busy right now."

"Forget it," the little man advised. "They won't show up."

Lucinda whirled furiously on him but Alasdair stepped between them, saying, "Don't. He's not the one you want to hurt."

"He'll do," she said, but she backed off, half-resentful, half-ashamed. "Will you stay here with Tyrone?" she asked Alasdair. "I'm going to find some answers." Alasdair looked skeptical but nodded.

In the hall she walked until she found a nursing station. It was deserted. She waited a while, fidgeting restlessly, but the only one who approached was a patient in a wheelchair. He had a wide bandage wrapped around his rib cage, and both legs were in casts from the knees down. Lucinda squinted at him, realizing he looked familiar, then strode toward him, propelled by a new rush of anger.

"Marcus." He seemed startled to see her and nervous as she stepped behind him and took the handles of the wheelchair. "How did you manage to wind up here?"

He rubbed his clean-shaven skull. "Don't know. Don't remember. But they tell me I passed out in the streets last night, and one of those big old Carnival floats rolled right over me."

"Poor baby. How unjust." She began to wheel him toward a door marked EXIT.

He glared up at her. "Let go of the chair, Lucinda."

"Mmm . . . no, I think you and I are going to go for a walk, and you're going to tell me what you did to Tyrone last night."

"Ask Tyrone," he said with exasperation.

"I would but there's a problem." She pushed the chair through the exit, stopping at the top of a landing. "Tyrone is unconscious, maybe dying."

"What the hell are you talking about? You think I did something to Tyrone?"

"Very good. You're catching on." She nudged the chair forward until its front wheels were halfway off the landing. "So why don't you tell me what it was you did to him last night, before I send this chair down the stairs."

"You are blaming me for something I've got nothing to do with!" Marcus proclaimed. "When did you turn into such a crazy-ass bitch?"

It was a valid question. Part of her couldn't believe she was actually threatening to send a wheelchair-bound man hurtling down a flight of stairs; part of her couldn't wait to see him fly.

She pushed the chair a few inches farther. Marcus grabbed onto the banisters, stopping the chair with a groan. Lucinda let him hold himself there. "What did you feed Tyrone at the bar on Grand Street?"

"Now you got spies?"

"Friends, who saw you giving him something to drink. What was it?"

"*Un petit apéritif.*"

She began to tilt the chair forward.

"Would you calm down? It was just a liqueur."

"Then why wasn't he at the Dome when he said he'd be?"

"How the hell should I know?"

With a wrench, Lucinda spun the chair around then let go of the handles, so that Marcus faced her, his back to the stairs. She pulled him toward her, holding onto the chair by its armrests. "Just tell me," she said, weary of threats and her own anger. "What happened last night?"

Marcus sighed heavily and rolled his eyes, making it clear that he considered the subject an utter bore. "Okay. After we left you last night, Tyrone and me were heading toward the Dome. Just like we said we would. And we started to come up on Guthrie's—the bar on Grand—and this crowd of people came dancing out the door on this ribbon of music and each and every one of them looked like they'd just found paradise. And Tyrone and I kind of looked at each other and shrugged and decided to go inside. You know the place—it's tiny. Barely room enough to look over your shoulder, let alone dance, and that's on a normal night. Thanks to Carnival, it was packed. A cat couldn't have moved a whisker in there. So about two seconds after we got wedged in, I said, 'I gotta leave this place,' and Tyrone, who was already very irritable about having his shiny costume bent and crushed into some new origami creature, agreed. So we're trying to turn toward the door, still not understanding all that wild dancing we'd seen, and I feel someone tug at my elbow, and say, 'Brother.' "

"Brother," Lucinda echoed, wondering if any of this was true, or if Marcus was simply spinning one of his grandiose creations.

"He said in full, 'Brother, I have something you want to try.' "

"And he corrupted your innocent soul," Lucinda said with a groan. "Marcus, you seem to be forgetting what a precarious position you're in."

Marcus's nostrils flared with indignation. "You asked for the truth. Now I'm telling you!"

"Go ahead," she said, but she gave the wheelchair a slight nudge.

"Well, I turned my head, and the person who had my elbow was wearing a wolf costume, just like mine."

"A character recommendation, if ever I heard one."

"Lucinda, I'm trying to tell you that I didn't buy or rent that costume. It showed up at my front door two days before Carnival with no return address. I still don't know who sent it."

"What?" she asked, stunned. Marcus let out a high-pitched yelp, and she quickly grabbed the chair, having let go in surprise. "Sorry," she said. "I didn't mean that one."

"The hell you didn't." Marcus glanced over his shoulder at the steep flight of stairs behind him. "If you want me to tell you what happened, then get me out of this stairwell."

"I hate to admit we have anything common," Lucinda said as she rolled him back into the hallway. "But my costume showed up the same way. Did you ask this other wolf where his costume came from?"

"Never got the chance, though now that you mention it, I'd like to know.

Anyway, I was staring at this other wolf, and he tugs me toward the back room of the bar, and the crowd just parts for us. And I yelled to Tyrone and he followed. And we sat down at this table, just the three of us. And the other wolf says, 'Be right back.' He vanishes into the crowd and returns a few minutes later with this skinny little red glass bottle.

" 'Nectar,' he tells us. 'This is the heart of Carnival.' Then he pours me a glass, just me. Tyrone's watching the whole time, and I'm watching the wolf fill the glass with clear liquid. I smell it. Smells like some sort of cherry liqueur."

Lucinda made a face. "Sounds like cough syrup."

"My thoughts exactly, but being an adventurous soul, I took a sip. And it didn't taste anything like that. It was barely even sweet. Or it was sweet and tart and had another taste deep inside it that was like the sweetness you always long for in a lover but never quite find."

"Oh, Marcus, don't go poetic on me."

"It made me hear the music they were all dancing to," Marcus said. "The music that is the soul of pleasure, you understand me?"

Lucinda wasn't sure but she didn't say so. She waited for him to go on.

"So I gave some to Tyrone, because clearly I couldn't leave him out of this, and he heard the music, too, and we went out into the street, dancing to it. And we got caught in the crowds and got split up. I went to the Dome, figuring he'd meet me there, but he never did show. I waited there for him a while, had that lovely little visit with you, then went back out when I heard that music again. The last thing I remember before waking up in the hospital was dancing out on the streets, heading to the river."

"You drugged him," Lucinda said.

"I was sharing the fun."

"Where's your room?" she asked, disgusted. "I'm going to take you back there, so I don't have to look at your smug face anymore."

Marcus gave her directions and she pushed him back to his room where she stood with her arms folded while he struggled to lift himself out of the chair. "You know how cautious Tyrone is," she said. "He almost never drinks anymore, and when he does he's so careful, he barely empties a glass. Why'd you have to give him something that pushed him over the edge?"

"You should know the answer to that one, girl." Marcus painfully levered himself up onto the bed, then bared his teeth in a grin. "I like seeing people fucked up."

AFTER ANOTHER FRUITLESS search for medical personnel, Lucinda returned to Tyrone's room. She found Alasdair still keeping watch by his bed while the monitors flashed numbers and graphs in a serene rhythm.

"There's been no change," Alasdair said before Lucinda could ask. "However, a physician did come by. She told me that they sewed up Tyrone's wound, gave him blood, and replaced a valve in his heart. They're hoping he'll recover."

"But she didn't actually say he would," Lucinda guessed.

"No, nothing that definite. Did you speak to anyone?"

"Only Marcus, one of Tyrone's more vile acquaintances. He told me he gave Tyrone some sort of liqueur last night, something that drugged them both. Marcus said it was like drinking the essence of Carnival, but then Marcus has always been full of shit." Alasdair hadn't reacted at all when she'd mentioned the liqueur but she asked anyway. "Do you have any idea of what that drink might have been?"

"No. I have very little knowledge of herbs and toxins. Did this Marcus tell you where he got the potion?"

"From someone else in a wolf costume, identical to his."

Alasdair seemed mildly interested in that, but only said, "And why is Marcus in the hospital?"

"Apparently, he got run over by one of the Carnival floats. It looks like he's got two broken legs and maybe broken ribs. He deserves it." Lucinda looked down at Tyrone's still form. "I hate talking over him this way, as if he weren't here."

"Then talk to him," Alasdair suggested. "He might hear you." When Lucinda didn't respond he said, "Would you rather I left you alone with him?"

She glanced around the room. The little man in the plaid pajamas was watching her with a raptor's keen interest, but the others paid her no mind. "Yes," she told Alasdair. "It would be easier to talk to him if you weren't here."

"I'll try to look in on you later," he said, getting to his feet.

"Is the dragon going with you?"

"He's already gone. While you were seeking information, he flew off through the window. It seemed he had some pressing matter to attend to."

"So you don't know where he is now?"

"I haven't a clue. But I suspect he's still in the city." Alasdair's face lit with that fleeting smile. "And I expect you'll see him again."

ALASDAIR BREATHED IN great lungfuls of damp river air, grateful to be freed from his watch at the hospital. It amazed him that anyone was expected to recover their health in such a dreary setting. Among his people the sick were always tended in the gentlest, most comforting places. Yet even among his people Tyrone's chances would not be good. And if Tyrone died, what would become of Lucinda? How much more bitterness could she hold without being poisoned by it? That, he reminded himself, should not be his concern since there wasn't much he could do about it. Besides, he couldn't get too close to her; there was the risk that whatever was after him might take notice of her and also put her in its sights. Alasdair weighed his own sense of duty. He felt a certain obligation to help Lucinda, but the most helpful thing might be to keep distance from her. Reflexively, he glanced around for any sign of his mysterious pursuer but saw and sensed nothing beyond the usual riverfront traffic—boats coming and going, pedestrians walking along the shoreline or making their way into the streets. Perhaps he should focus on things he could understand, such as who'd sent her the moonstone necklace.

It had begun to rain again, a light but steady downfall without any of the previous night's theatrics. Alasdair took himself into the first café he saw, craving coffee that would actually taste like coffee. He sat down, ordered, then drew out the necklace.

The moonstones, a pale silvery blue, shone with a radiance that went beyond the natural properties of the stone itself, almost as if they were star sapphires or had somehow taken on the incandescent sheen of pearls. He touched their smooth polished surfaces, asking a silent question: Who enspelled you?

The reply he got—Kama—was no surprise, but it didn't begin to answer his earlier question: Who brought Lucinda to Kama's boat? Kama, like many of the gods, was often notoriously deaf to mortals' pleas. So who had managed to gain the god's favors?

Alasdair considered the necklace again, then summoned the waiter and asked if he could have the coffee to go. Moments later, cup in hand, he started toward the Candra, wondering if Kama had already set sail.

A short time later he stood on the north pier, only semi-relieved to see that the red scow Lucinda had pointed out to him was still at dock. He walked toward it, feeling the familiar sense of apprehension that twisted his gut whenever he approached a god. He hoped Kama would be more civil than Janus had been.

He was debating stepping onto the boat when the door to the hold opened and a well-dressed couple emerged onto the deck. Kama, looking round and cheerful, followed them saying, "I will have the carpet delivered to your home first thing tomorrow. I know you will be delighted with it."

The couple turned to thank him, beaming, as nearly everyone did in Eros's presence, then stepped off the boat.

Alasdair waited on the dock as the warmth of Kama's glance settled on him. A feeling that belonged to his youth, a boundless sense of hope and promise, filled him and nearly brought him to his knees with its sweetness, but he pushed it aside, knowing it was only Kama's gaze.

"My old friend," Kama said. "It's been too many years since we met. Please, visit with me."

Alasdair found himself smiling like an enraptured teenager as Kama led him below deck. The décor was much as he'd expected; the floors and walls of the hold were covered with carpets whose colors were so vibrant, they made Alasdair's heart ache. He sat at the brass table but declined the offer of tea, holding up the take-out cup. "I just got some coffee when I decided to seek you out," he explained. "May I?"

"Certainly, I understand." Looking amused at the refusal of his offer, Kama sat down on the other side of the table and poured himself a cup of tea. The scents of coriander, anise, and cinnamon wafted through the air, and despite his determination to remain wary and alert, Alasdair felt himself relaxing.

"So much time has passed since I was last with you," Kama chided him. "Do you really think it wise to go so long without a lover?"

"I don't know," Alasdair answered. He noticed that the gemstones, which had restrained themselves from appearing in the hospital, were now tumbling to the carpet and table, eagerly arranging themselves in glowing circles before Kama. "It's seemed . . . appropriate."

"You shut me out." The god sounded more disappointed than angry. "But I forgive you." He smiled, his dark eyes filled with light. "And now you are here because you are ready for change?"

"That's not why I've come." Alasdair sipped his coffee, grateful that it had given him a polite way to decline the Maddener's tea.

"Then perhaps you want to buy a carpet? You know I carry only the finest, and for you, I will make an excellent deal."

Alasdair grinned. "That's not why I've come, either, and you know it. I have something that I think belongs to you."

He drew out the moonstone necklace and set it on the table between them. The stones grew even more lustrous, radiant with delight at having returned to the god's presence.

Kama didn't touch the necklace. "It's not mine. It belongs to a young woman."

"But you enspelled it before you gave it to her."

Kama lifted his shoulders in a barely perceptible shrug. "Moonstones are fairly soft stones, you know that better than most. They can absorb certain, let us say, influences."

Alasdair groaned. "Influences?"

"Me." Kama settled himself more comfortably on his cushion, looking exceptionally pleased with himself. He gestured to the gemstones that surrounded him. "The moonstones were in my presence. Like lovers, they drank me in."

Alasdair didn't doubt it for a second. The god had turned his radiance on the stones and they'd bathed in it, soaking in his energies they way they drew in the light of the moon. They hadn't been enspelled as much as immersed in the god's power, and now they shone with his essence. To wear the moonstone necklace was to invite Kama straight into the heart.

Alasdair understood that this was something he couldn't lift from the stones. All he could do was see that the necklace didn't fall into the wrong hands. He chose his next words carefully. "Why did you give the young woman the necklace?"

Kama chuckled. "You would have the secrets of the gods?"

"Just this one," Alasdair said, then added more respectfully, "if you would."

Kama eyed him shrewdly. "Are you in love with her? No, you could be but won't allow it. Really, Stefano, are you determined to complete your years without joy?"

"That's not the question."

The parrot materialized, hovering above the table then landing on Kama's shoulder to preen its feathers.

"And you used to give yourself to love so wholly. When you were with a lover you always honored me. I was always there with you."

"I know and I'm grateful. And," Alasdair hesitated, then admitted the truth, "I've missed your presence in my life. But this young woman—I think the necklace may have been used to betray her. I don't think that what happened under its influence honored her or you."

The boat began to rock wildly, as if a storm had just risen beneath it. Kama regarded him coolly. "So now you presume to know what happens between those I favor."

"My apologies," Alasdair said quickly, thinking that he was besting his own record for irritating the deities. In the span of a day he'd managed to offend both Janus and Kama.

"You haven't missed me enough," Kama said in the tones of a wounded lover. No, in the precise voice that had belonged to Gioia, Alasdair's lover. The door to the deck opened and she descended the stairs, wearing the same white silk gown she'd worn the last time he saw her. She even wore the same flat-cut diamond pendant, suspended from two strands of braided white gold. Alasdair felt light-headed with desire and wrenched apart with grief.

They could be lovers again, here, now. That would be Kama's gift. And then he would have to watch her die again. That was the cycle of their fate that even Kama couldn't undo.

"Please." Alasdair's voice faltered. "Don't make me go through that again. I can't lose her twice."

The vision of Gioia faded and Alasdair felt the searing pain recede.

"You are crossing into places where you have no right to be," Kama told him, his voice gentle. "I see that you are trying to help another. Your instincts are commendable if misguided. Do not meddle here, Stefano. You will only cause more grief than you are now trying to avert."

Alasdair drained the last of his coffee and crushed the paper cup in his fist. "Janus berated me for not using my power. You tell me it's better I do nothing."

"That's the problem with being a familiar of the gods. You are inevitably subject to conflicting information." Kama stroked the parrot's brilliant feathers. "We can't help it, you know. It's just that we so rarely agree."

"Perhaps I'd better go." Alasdair got to his feet, casting a wary eye at the gemstones. They were still arranged in front of Kama in what could only be adoration. "Are you coming?" he asked them, more sharply than he intended.

Citrines, amethysts, aquamarines, turquoise, and topaz all returned to the folds of his robe. The rubies, sapphires, garnets, and pearls chose to remain. An emerald wavered indecisively before nestling itself between the rubies and sapphires.

Kama beamed at him. "You leave me with gifts."

"Their choice."

"It's kind of you not to interfere. Others who command them might."

Alasdair shrugged. "I've never found forcing the stones to be very effective."

"Please," Kama said, "sit down." Wary of angering him a second time, Alasdair obeyed. "It is only fair that I give you a gift in return," the god went on magnanimously, "even if it is not truly mine to give." With a graceful gesture he handed Alasdair the moonstone necklace, its stones more luminous than ever.

Alasdair couldn't hold back a snort of laughter. "You're giving me this— the guarantee of heartbreak and grief?"

"Don't be arrogant, Stefano," the god warned softly. "The moonstones open you to all the risks of love, but also to its transcendence."

"Is that what it is, transcendence?" Alasdair muttered as he took the necklace. He shook his head, resigned. "I seem to have become a repository for troublesome gems."

"You have others?"

Alasdair summoned the diamond he took from Michael. "Have you seen one like this before?"

Kama's eyes widened in something that might have been recognition, but he didn't answer. With the parrot peering intently from his shoulder, he held the diamond beneath one of his oil lamps, turning it, examining it from every angle, watching rainbow bands of light flash from its facets. "Very pure, this one, and very dangerous," he agreed with an odd kind of relish. "As it is a diamond, it would not be easy for me to influence it."

"Would you care to try?"

"It would be a challenge," the god mused.

"You might succeed." Eros was one of the more insidious gods; persistent, pervasive, and eventually irresistible, he had a talent for penetrating the most unyielding of beings. "On second thought," Alasdair said, "your influencing the diamond is not much comfort. Even if the diamond became as drunk with you as the moonstones, it might be just as dangerous. Maybe even more so."

Kama set the diamond on the table and folded his hands over his round belly. "You were not thrilled with my gift of the moonstone necklace, although you should be. So I will add another gift. I'll take the diamond off your hands with the promise that it shall cause no mischief to you or any who cross your path."

"Or anyone in this city?" Alasdair added. He knew he was pushing it, but if he kept the diamond, he'd find a way to safeguard it. He couldn't let Kama do less.

Kama poured himself more tea and caressed the parrot, whose eyes were closing. "Very well," he said at last. "Leave the diamond with me, and you may consider the city safe from its ill effects. I think I will leave for another port soon, anyway."

"Thank you," Alasdair said, wondering just what it was he was feeling grateful for. Kama hadn't given him a shred of the information he sought. Instead, Kama handed him a necklace that he never wanted, and took the diamond, promising to do no more than Alasdair himself would have done. Additionally, Kama, who appreciated both material beauty and a good bargain, was getting a small cache of jewels. And *Alasdair* was grateful. It was typical of the kind of insanity that took place whenever one was in Eros's presence. *In the end,* Alasdair realized, *I'm no different than the stones. To be in Kama's radius is to be enchanted.*

Kama rose from his cushions with surprising agility. "Let me walk you to the dock," he offered.

The parrot flew up and out of the hold as Alasdair got to his feet, a flash of bright blue. Kama followed, the wooden stairs that led to the deck creaking beneath his weight. Alasdair smiled wryly. Some gods manifested themselves in human form but were shoddy on the finer points. They had no weight when they walked. There was no warmth to their flesh. If nothing else, Kama got the sensory details right.

Alasdair blinked as they emerged into the dank grey air of the waterfront. It was almost a relief to be outside again under the muted sky and away from the riotous swirl of color and sensation that was Kama's hold. The city seemed austere by comparison, and for once Alasdair welcomed the austerity, the harshness that cut through Kama's illusions.

Kama looked at him fondly. "I don't know when I'll see you again," he said, and the possibility that it would be a very long time before they next met made Alasdair unutterably sad. He gazed at the god, willing himself not to forget what it was to be in his presence.

Unexpectedly, Kama put his arms around him and held him close. "Till the next time, my friend."

Alasdair found himself near tears as the god released him. He stepped back onto the dock reeling, trying to reconcile the elation of a man who for one extraordinary moment has known the pure essence of love with the bittersweet surety that he would never know its like again.

Ten

MICHAEL WALKED AWAY from the docks, discouraged and pissed at having been booted off another boat. He'd sneaked on board and when he was caught, he'd offered to work, do anything if they'd only take him with them. He knew that if the police caught him again, it would be bad. Even if he got a trial and they said he didn't murder Spook, which he didn't really, they'd get him for breaking out on Carnival Night. And what if Tyrone died? . . . He wondered if the guy in the blue robe or that skinny bitch ratted him out. Maybe now he was wanted for two murders. He wished he'd never gone home with Tyrone. He wished he'd never seen the diamond. He wished he still had it. If he had the diamond, he could buy his way onto a boat. But now, how was he going to get food and where was he going to hide and how was he going to lose that friggin' jaguar? The cat gave him the willies. It wasn't big on being seen. Lots of times he'd just glimpse it out of the corner of his eye, following him like a shadow. Even when he couldn't see it, he could feel it at his back. It never left. It never slept. It watched him every second. At first he'd tried talking to it, acting like they were going to be friends. Obviously, he'd seen too many dumb animal movies. The jaguar wasn't interested. When he tried to pet it, it raked a gash down his arm. He thought about trying to trap it, get it in some kind of box and then toss it in the river, but the second he'd have thoughts like that he'd see this scene: his body lying on the ground and the jaguar, full-size, biting through his skull; he could even hear his bones crunching in its mouth. He figured it was his own sick imagination, playing on what Ivor had said. Ivor had no right to sic a jaguar on him. He had no right to scare him that way.

Michael had had one piece of luck since fleeing Tyrone's. He found a hooded jacket in the trash. It was a wimpy baby-blue and thin; a bandana would have kept him warmer. Still, it sort of worked as a disguise.

Now he drew the hood over his head as he stepped off the pier and into the crowds along the riverwalk. *Don't attract attention,* Michael told himself. When he was younger, about five, he used to pretend he was invisible. He thought about doing that now, but he was too afraid he'd believe it and get careless. He couldn't make any more mistakes.

He kept his head down, eyes on the ground. The smell of a street vendor's fried sausages and potatoes made his mouth water. It had been more than a day since he had had that feast at Tyrone's. He wondered if swiping some food would count as doing harm. Would the jaguar eat him if he stole a candy bar? It wasn't exactly worth finding out.

Michael dropped down onto one of the benches along the riverwalk as another chain of coughs ripped through him. On one of the boats he tried to sneak onto, the cough was what gave him away. It was not helpful for lying low, and it was not getting better. It made his chest ache and his head throb. He was practically used to running a fever; feeling crappy felt normal. What he really ought to steal was some cough medicine and maybe more aspirin.

"You enjoying this?" he asked the jaguar as he got to his feet again. The cat didn't answer. "Fuck you," he told it, then told himself to find food.

He set off again, heading away from the waterfront. Della Rosa Street was one hole-in-the-wall restaurant after another—Greek, Italian, Indian, you name it. Michael wasn't feeling fussy when he turned into the alley that ran behind the restaurants, but something in him recoiled when he saw the Dumpsters. Jesus, they smelled. Rotting food, dead cigarettes, and who knew what else. He forced himself to open the nearest one, reached in a tentative hand, and began scrounging. This was sick, not to mention gross and pathetic. He gazed around, ashamed, making sure that no one besides the damn jaguar was watching.

He wasn't alone. A large, red fox sat at the end of the alley, circled by a cloud of green fireflies. "Weird," Michael breathed, leaving the Dumpster. He edged toward the fox, fascinated. He'd never seen fireflies during the day or this close to winter. He'd certainly never seen any that glowed bright green. Summer nights, when he was little, he used to chase them. The kids on his street used to catch them, seal them in glass jars to make lanterns. The insects were always dead by morning, so Michael never kept his. But he used to like to catch them, to hold them in his hand and watch them light up, then send them back into the night. Now sick and half-starved and running from the police, all he wanted to do was catch one of the glowing green bugs. It was stupid and he knew it and he couldn't help it.

Michael approached the fox slowly. The fox sat motionless. The fireflies hovered around it, like a glittering green scarf that swept through the air.

"How come these fireflies like you so much?" Michael asked the fox. Okay, it was a dumb question but the fox made him nervous. Plus somewhere behind him the jaguar was making low, cranky sounds. He ignored it. "Listen, I just want to catch one and look at it, okay?"

The fox opened its mouth and panted. It had very sharp white teeth. Michael stopped. He ought to just get the hell out of this alley. And he would. As soon as he caught one of those fireflies.

The swarm lifted into the air above the fox, high above Michael's reach, then vanished over the rooftops. Except for three. Three fireflies dropped to the ground in front of the fox. They sat there, not moving but glowing so brightly that Michael rubbed his eyes. He had to be imagining this, didn't he? The three fireflies weren't bugs anymore. They were oval stones with so much green fire inside them that rays of green light danced out from them and glimmered across the pavement. The fox glanced down at the stones unimpressed, as if it saw fireflies turn into emeralds every day.

"Come on, Mary," Michael prayed to his mother's favorite saint. "You can't let this be a dream. This has got to be real."

Just to be sure he shut his eyes quickly and opened them again. No, the fox and the emeralds—he was sure they were emeralds—were still there. Michael kept inching forward, curiosity warring with caution. Weren't wild animals, like foxes, supposed to run when humans got close? What was wrong with this one? Maybe it had rabies and was waiting to bite him. Somewhere near Michael's shoulder, the jaguar began to growl, louder now and steady.

"What?" Michael asked irritably. "I'm not doing anything wrong. I just want to look at these rocks." That gave him a tickle in his throat, which turned into a coughing fit. When it was finally over, he expected the fox to be gone, but the animal was still there, watching him from wary blue eyes.

"Mind if I look at these?" Michael asked the fox.

It didn't seem to object, and it didn't seem to be drooling or doing anything disgusting, so he knelt down. He didn't quite dare touch the emeralds, not with the fox so close. What if it was guarding them? Did foxes guard things?

He glanced up. Maybe the fever was getting to his brain, but he could swear the fox was grinning at him. It was so bizarre that for a second it spooked him, but then he said, "Yeah, you and me, fox, we won't tell anyone else about these emeralds."

Michael took a step closer and a bolt of yellow and black fur streaked past him. "No!" he screamed as the jaguar, grown to full size, sprang at the fox.

The cat came to a sudden, confused halt on bare pavement. The fox was gone. Michael doubled over, laughing, which made him cough some more, but it was worth it.

"He got you good," he taunted the cat. "That fox vanished before you could even jump. And you thought you were such hot shit."

The jaguar growled again, then cuffed him with a heavy paw, knocking him to the ground. The cat stood over the boy, its golden eyes staring down into Michael's brown ones.

"Don't look at me," Michael muttered. "I don't know where the fox went." Still, he didn't move until he saw the jaguar shrinking again. Without hesitating, Michael scooped up the three emeralds. He cupped them in his palm. They weighed next to nothing, but their color made him think of clear mountain pools and wild grasses in the first weeks of spring—things he'd only read about. He wondered how much the stones were worth.

LUCINDA JERKED HER head upright as she realized that she'd nodded off. She was in the hospital ward, sitting beside Tyrone's bed. The elderly man in the plaid pajamas was propped up against his pillows, watching her with a disapproving expression. "You were out for over three hours," he told her.

Ignoring him, she turned back to Tyrone and the window. Morning light was coming through the blinds. She'd been here in the hospital for the last day and a half. And Tyrone looked exactly the same. Lying so still, breathing only because of the machines. She wondered how much of him was still in the world with her, how much of him already in the process of leaving it. She massaged the hollow between his thumb and forefinger. "Don't leave yet, Tyrone," she whispered. "I need you to come back."

" 'Cinda?"

She turned to see Gabrielle Oculara walking toward her, a deep-red wool cape draped around her shoulders. Gabrielle seemed large and vibrant, almost shocking in the midst of the sickly men beneath white sheets. It was as though she contained all the life and strength in the room.

" 'Cinda, sweetie, why didn't you tell me?"

"I—" Lucinda held out a hand toward Tyrone, unable to find words. "How'd you find out?"

"Word travels. It's not a big city." Gabrielle stood beside the bed and stroked Tyrone's forehead. "Oh, Tyrone. How did you wind up like this?"

"I don't think he can hear you," Lucinda said bleakly. "He hasn't responded to anything. He's in a coma."

Gabrielle's eyes narrowed. "This have anything to do with Marcus?"

"Maybe. He's here, too," Lucinda told her. "In another room. Do you want me to show you where?"

"Me visit Marcus? Don't be absurd. Actually, it's you I came to see. You're still in the same clothes you were in yesterday morning. Haven't you been home to sleep?"

"I slept here."

"Not very well, from the looks of you. Come on, I'm going to take you home, make you some breakfast, and put you to bed."

Lucinda waved her off. "No, I can't leave him. I—"

"Tyrone's not going anywhere for a while," Gabrielle assured her. "And he's got a hospital full of doctors and nurses looking out for him. You're the one in need of some attention." She put a comforting arm around Lucinda's shoulders, and this time Lucinda didn't push her away. "Come on. Let's go to your place."

"I *hate* being mothered," Lucinda said as she was herded out of the room.

"Really," Gabrielle said. "I never would have guessed."

LUCINDA GOT GABRIELLE to detour with her to Tyrone's loft. Somehow it was easier going back there with Gabrielle at her side. She supposed it was lousy business to bring one of your chief competitors to the office with you, but Gabrielle helped her return phone calls, order fabric, placate an irate distributor, and dispense with a callow, young police officer, all in a brisk, matter-of-fact manner. She even helped Lucinda with Tyrone's room.

"This doesn't turn your stomach?" Lucinda asked as she watched Gabrielle wring a blood-soaked rag into a bucket of water.

"I raised three kids," Gabrielle told her. "In the days before my boys, of course. When you're a mother you get a strong stomach."

"You've got kids? I never heard anything about that."

"Well, you wouldn't have. I didn't raise them here. This city warps kids. I had my children in Marrakesh and raised them on Mykonos. They're still in Greece. One's a shipbuilder, one runs a *taverna,* and my youngest is a goldsmith."

Lucinda regarded Gabrielle with amused respect. "And I thought you were just a decadent designer."

"That's my reward. I get to sell my clothes and play with my boys, and even though the business is a bitch, it is infinitely easier than raising children." Gabrielle mopped up the last of the blood. "What about you, 'Cinda? Is working with Tyrone enough for you?"

"It was."

Gabrielle dropped the stained rag into the bucket and got to her feet. "Come on," she said gently, "let's get out of this room."

"I need to put fresh sheets on the bed first," said Lucinda. "For when he gets home."

If he gets home. Gabrielle didn't say it, but Lucinda saw it in her eyes. Still, Gabrielle waited patiently while Lucinda changed the bedding, and Lucinda, grateful for all the help she'd given, didn't try to send Gabrielle away.

Later, in Lucinda's flat, Gabrielle bullied her into putting on a nightgown even though it was barely five in the evening. Then she cooked for her, poured her a stiff drink, and put her to bed. Lucinda was out before she even finished the drink.

SEBASTIAN CAME TO her in her dreams. Or rather she'd come to him. They lay together in his bed. The room itself had changed orientation. It had shifted at who-knows-what angle, and perhaps the building itself had relocated, so that the wall of windows now looked out over the river. Warm and sated, she lay curled in Sebastian's arms, watching Madana's red scow leave the harbor in a gentle rain.

"You see?" Sebastian pulled the velvet patchwork quilt higher, so that it covered Lucinda's bare shoulders. "Now you can stop worrying about being manipulated by a god."

"I burned the white silk dress he sent me," she told him.

He dropped a kiss on her hair. "Doesn't matter. It was just a dress."

"And I gave away the moonstone necklace."

His thumb traced the bones of her rib cage. "It was just a trinket. I'll bring you other dresses, other necklaces. We can dress you in necklaces if you like."

"Did I do something terrible—irreversible—by getting rid of his gifts?"

"Will you give me away, too?"

"I don't know."

She felt the quilt being lifted then his kisses dusting the length of her spine. "The only thing that matters is that you came back to me."

When Lucinda surfaced from the dream she woke drowsy and warm and peaceful, in her own bed; and the flat-cut diamond necklace she'd worn in the garden lay on her pillowcase.

CLASPING THE THREE emeralds in his fist, Michael headed for the pier near the art school. It had been rebuilt and had a fancy glass shelter called a pergola where you could wait for the passenger boats that ran up and down the Candra. People who looked like they had money came into the city there. Michael thought it would be a good place to sell one of his emeralds.

He was disappointed to find the pier empty. He went over to the pergola, read the schedule that was posted, and realized it would be a while before the next boat came in. Well, he could wait. It wasn't so hard being hungry now that he knew he'd have money soon. Someone was going to give him a lot of money for an emerald, and his whole life would get easy.

He sat down on the bench beneath the pergola and glanced up. A light rain fell on the curved glass panes, and he watched the raindrops bead up, grow fat, and then glide down.

He wasn't even aware that a man was sitting next to him until he heard him ask, "Waiting for the next boat?"

Michael stiffened as he realized it was the guy in the blue robe, Ivor or Alasdair or whatever the hell his name was.

"Are you following me?" the boy demanded.

"No." The man's eyes were a cold slate-grey.

"Then what are you doing here?"

The man didn't answer, just stared out at the river.

"I want you to take back the jaguar," Michael said. "He doesn't like me, and I don't like him."

"Liking each other isn't necessary. Or even desirable. I didn't give him to you to be your pet."

"He makes me nervous," the boy confessed.

"You'll get used to him."

Michael coughed loudly, not bothering to cover his mouth. He hoped he gave the guy all his germs.

"You're holding three emeralds," the man said.

"The jaguar tell you that? Now he's spying on me, too?"

The expression in the man's eyes was no longer cold. It was pitying, which made Michael even angrier.

"The jaguar isn't a spy," the man explained. "He simply watches you to ensure that you keep your word."

Michael's fist tightened around the emeralds. This guy knew he'd had

Tyrone's diamond, had made it leave him. Now he knew about the emeralds. Michael wasn't about to lose them the same way.

"I want to ask you something," the man went on, his tone calm and even. "When all this began you were down by the water and a mysterious figure, the one you called the see-through guy, gave you a knife that you used to kill Spook."

"I didn't kill him," Michael said.

"You did. Let me finish. Then you were in jail and quite mysteriously you were given keys to escape. That led to you going home with Tyrone, trying to steal a diamond from him, and stabbing, perhaps killing him."

"I didn't kill him, either!"

"Not yet. There's still a chance he may survive. But if Tyrone dies, his death will be charged to you. Now you've been given three emeralds. From what I can tell, they've appeared every bit as mysteriously as the knife and keys." The guy in the blue robe turned to face Michael, his eyes snapping with anger. "Hasn't it occurred to you that using these gifts is not a good idea?"

Michael scowled up at him, refusing to be intimidated. "What do you want me do? How am I supposed to get food, find a place to stay? It's not like I can apply for a job, with the police after me. There isn't any place for me unless I buy it. So that's what I'm going to do with these emeralds. I'm really supposed to give a shit if you think it's a bad idea?"

The man shut his eyes and massaged his forehead; when he opened his eyes again he was no longer angry. "What if I simply give you money?" he asked.

Michael looked him over suspiciously. "You don't have enough. And how is taking something from you any better than taking emeralds from a fox?"

"A fox?"

"Well, they were fireflies first, green fireflies flying around this fox and—" Michael stopped. "Forget it. No one would believe me."

"I do," the man reminded him. "I've believed you from the start. Tell me how the fireflies became emeralds and what the fox had to do with it."

Michael told him what had happened. The man listened without interrupting, then for the longest time he was absolutely quiet. He just kept staring at the river, like it was going to tell him a secret. At last he said, "My name is Alasdair and I come from a place where we're taught to read the stones, that is, to understand what's inside them. So they tell me things."

"You mean, rocks talk to you?"

"Not literally, no. But they . . . communicate with me. That's how I knew you had the diamond at Tyrone's. It's how I know you're holding three emeralds now. The stones let me know. But there are things they can't tell me. These emeralds can't tell me about the fox, for example, because the fox or some other being has seen to it that the information remains locked inside them."

One side of Michael's mouth twitched into a grin. "Guess you're not such a know-it-all."

"Apparently not," Alasdair agreed. "Since you've given me valuable information that I'd have a hard time uncovering on my own, I'd like to propose a trade."

"A trade?"

Alasdair surprised him with a quick smile. For just an instant he looked younger, not so severe. "Emeralds are not a bad stone for you to hold," he said. "They're the gem of spring and rebirth, and it would be a very good thing if you were reborn into a healthier life. They're also a protection at sea and will serve you well if you leave the city by boat. And they're an antidote to certain poisons; they're capable of destroying some of the influences that bring on disease."

"Great." Michael stood up and started edging away from him. "Then I get to keep these."

"The three that you have came to you through a fox's magic, and I suspect he's tainted them. Let me give you others that will bear no curse."

"You'll give me three other emeralds? Worth as much?"

"Worth more," Alasdair promised. "In fact, I'd suggest you not barter them away. I'll give you other stones you can trade for food and shelter, and money for your passage on the boat. But I must have the three from the fox."

Michael hesitated.

"You know I can call them to me the way I called the diamond," Alasdair said softly. "It's much better if you give them freely and get something in return."

Reluctantly, the boy opened his fist. The three emeralds rested on his palm, glinting spring light under grey wintry skies.

Alasdair opened his own hand, holding out three other emeralds, larger and even more beautiful. "And these," he said, holding open his other hand. "Garnets, pearls, turquoise, tourmaline, and two rubies for trade. Use them wisely, and they'll provide for you for a good stretch of time. And—" He dug into a pocket and fished out the roll of bills he'd gotten in his trade at Manjusha. He gave Michael half of them. "Use this money to buy passage on a boat and for when you first get to a new place. You want to be careful of whom you're dealing with when you trade the stones."

Again the boy hesitated, sure on some level that he was being conned.

"Start your new life with a fair exchange," Alasdair urged him. "Instead of just taking."

"Will you take back the jaguar?"

"No. But if and when you are no longer a threat to others, he will leave you of his own accord. That's the best I can offer."

Michael nodded, traded the stones, and quickly pocketed what he got. Then while Alasdair watched he walked toward the boat that was docking at the pier.

ALASDAIR REMAINED ON the bench at the pergola, staring up at the pearl-grey bands of sky alternating with slightly darker bands of clouds. It had looked like this for hours. It was impossible to tell what time of day it was, or even whether time was actually passing or he was mired in some sort of endless present where there would be no dusk or darkness or dawn. *Assume that time is passing,* he told himself. *It's probably the one assumption you can safely make.* But there was a quiet in the city that unnerved him. Even the river was unnaturally still, the water so calm that the boats appeared to glide across it as if on ice. A lone heron flew low, skimmed the glassy water, and extracted a fish, it seemed, without actually breaking the surface. It was as though the fish voluntarily slipped out and up into its captor's talons.

He turned suddenly, sensing a shift in energy behind him. But he saw no one, not even the pigeons or gulls that were so common on the waterfront. Still, he wondered if he was being followed again, and if he'd been too preoccupied to notice. Was it possible, he wondered, that someone in Arcato had connected him to the appearance of gems and was trailing him, hoping for riches? It was possible but it wouldn't have been very profitable. These gems, which appeared on his behalf, had a habit of disappearing when they didn't want to be found, and they'd never been partial to those who wanted to appropriate them.

Do something useful, Alasdair instructed himself. He got up and started toward the labradorite bridge. He knew he should be seeking out the ruined mosaic square at the top of the city, but the pain he'd experienced there gave him pause. The diamond-within-diamond pattern had also appeared on Janus's doors, and he was more willing to risk another run-in with Janus.

He came to a halt as he felt the black opal stirring again. This time it didn't ask. It simply spun its protective cocoon of color around him. Alasdair peered out of it. He couldn't see anything or anyone, but he felt energy reaching toward him and though it wasn't purely animal, it had the unmistakable quality of a predator stalking prey. He waited there motionless while his stalker's energy probed and bounced off the opal's net of colored light. At length, frustrated, the hunter receded. What did it want from him? And, he asked himself almost idly, would he have to die before it was sated?

He walked uphill through the city to its eastern edge where the streets narrowed to a maze of curving lanes and alleys. He found the labradorite bridge easily enough, its iridescent blue-grey stones quietly spanning a century. He gave silent thanks to the stones as he crossed it, wondering who else used the bridge between realms, whether someone like Lucinda or Tyrone would be able to find it at all.

The moment he stepped off the bridge the three emeralds he'd gotten off the boy slid into his hand. "Oh, so you like the old city better, is that it? Or is this where you came from?"

The skies were somewhat brighter on this end of the bridge, and the green oval cabochons drew in the light and glowed with it. Yet they were as opaque to him as a ream of blank paper. There was nothing in them he could read or even sense. Their history had been carefully masked so that no one with his skills—that is, from the Source Place—could divine it.

"What are you concealing?" he asked them. Some emeralds, Alasdair knew, were particularly useful in calling on the dark angels and spirits. Had these stones been used that way? Or were they masked simply to protect the identity of whoever had held them last?

As Alasdair stood wondering whether there was a way to open them, the emeralds stirred in his palm, became lighter, then hovered above the surface of his hand. Their green light grew brighter, more intense, and he blinked in astonishment as the three stones broke into tiny, glittering green particles that reassembled themselves into three glowing, green fireflies. For a heartbeat the fireflies hovered in front of him—he had the strange but distinct sensation that they were greeting him—and then swept into the skies and over the rooftops.

"Hera and Hermes," he breathed. "What was that?"

Although he'd witnessed many strange phenomena, he'd never known stones to change themselves into insects. Then again, it was exactly—or exactly the reverse—of what the boy had described. Besides, there was an old legend that the first emerald came into the world as a firefly hovering beneath the moon. Of course, there were other stories of how emeralds were originally drops of dew on lotus leaves or the bile of the demon god Vala. He glanced around for the fox, and seeing none, he headed for the lot where Janus had displayed his doors.

The lot was there, but the doors and the god were gone. Typical, Alasdair thought, trying to reconcile himself to the fact that he'd have to return to the market plaza after all.

Grimacing, he started back toward the bridge only to feel a familiar small presence nestling against his collarbone.

"You," he said softly. "I've been wondering where you were."

The dragon proceeded to traipse from his collarbone down his arm, lifting its tiny clawed feet high above the folds in his robe. It stopped on the flat of his wrist where it posed itself, as if it were the jade ornament on an expensive and showy bracelet.

"Yes, you're very handsome," Alasdair told it, smiling.

The dragon tilted its wings slightly, so that they seemed to gather the muted daylight. Lustrous and translucent, their jade color never altered, yet it now seemed to hold earth and water and sky. In the dragon's wings Alasdair could see shimmering clouds of pearl-green light, and he laughed in spite of himself. "Yes, you are even more beautiful than the emeralds that became fireflies," he admitted. "Were you jealous?"

The dragon gave an indignant snort.

"Silly question." Alasdair regarded him fondly, then his expression became serious. "I am seeking a pattern: diamond set within diamond. Have you seen it?"

The dragon blinked in affirmation.

"Will you show me then?"

The dragon took wing, and Alasdair began following him through the streets of the old city.

"SHIT, THIS IS not how I wanted to acquire a diamond necklace," Lucinda muttered. "I never even wanted a diamond necklace."

She had always thought of diamonds as fussy status symbols for overdressed dowagers. This one was so simple: the single uncut stone, like a rectangle of clear water, transparent yet somehow containing a world of flickering depths. One of Tyrone's ex-lovers, an older man from Brasília who dealt mostly in the black market, had once told her that the rarest diamonds were those that had come from India before they discovered the art of faceting stones. She had no doubt that this diamond was at least that old. After all, it had come from Madana's garden in a time out of time.

Lucinda's hand trembled as she held the diamond up to the light, casting long, slender rainbows across her bedroom wall. This was the closest she'd ever come to holding true wealth. She could sell the stone and pay Tyrone's medical expenses, make up any losses the business might suffer, travel in the heedless style she'd always fantasized, and never have to work again. She could live the kind of freedom that she had long ago resigned herself to never tasting.

And yet all of those sweet fantasies felt as remote as ever. Gifts like this didn't come without strings, she knew, especially gifts from Sebastian. He'd left the dress for her and now the diamond. He had somehow got into her flat when she was sleeping, and her dream of being with him had not entirely been a dream. Sebastian had been here, in her bed, with her last night. The sick part was that warring with a cold, paralyzing fear, she felt a perverse but definite twinge of pleasure. He still wanted her and she was glad. She still wanted him.

He had to have known that she would be disconcerted to find the diamond. Was he hoping that she would show up at his loft, grateful and smitten? Or was he counting on her to give it back to him? She thought of the much lesser diamond that Alasdair had taken from the boy. This one probably wasn't any healthier for her than that one had been for Tyrone. Weren't diamonds famous for being cursed? She really ought to throw the thing down the trash chute.

Lucinda closed her hand around the stone, resolving to get rid of it somehow, and heard the locked door to her apartment swing open.

She grabbed the knife that she kept in the drawer of her night table and stepped out into the living room. Sebastian stood in the doorway, his body relaxed, his eyes searching hers, questioning and still guileless.

She never knew why she didn't scream.

"It's the same necklace you wore in Madana's garden," he said. He was wearing a white linen shirt beneath a black vest, and slim black jeans tucked into soft, black leather boots. "Please don't throw it out."

That odd sense of lightness went through her again, as though her body were almost weightless, and yet everything was perfectly balanced and aligned and she was exactly where she was always meant to be. Had any physical sensation ever been so wrong?

She crossed the hallway to him and held out the necklace. "Take it back," she said.

Sebastian raised his open palms. "The necklace is yours to do with as you please. Sell it if you don't want to keep it. But don't waste it."

When she'd left home as a teenager she taught herself to handle knives. She'd endlessly practiced thrusts and feints and cuts, so even though she'd never actually drawn blood, the knife she now held felt like a natural extension of her hand, and it was pure reflex to press its tip against Sebastian's skin, just below his collarbone where his white linen shirt opened. "You break into my apartment, sneak into my bed and rape me—"

"No," he said, his voice far steadier than hers. "I would never do anything like that to you."

"I was asleep!"

"You were sleeping," he agreed. "I came in, sat on the edge of your bed, and just watched you. You sensed me there and reached out a hand. So I held it, stroked it." He smiled ruefully. "For a while I just petted you, which was lovely and more than I'd expected. And then you—you began to do the same to me and things . . . went on from there."

"Then why don't I remember any of that? I remember fucking—"

"Making love," he corrected her gently. He stepped back from the point of her knife and moved to stand beside the window. The light from the morning sky made his eyes seem lighter and even more alive than she remembered.

"Fucking," she insisted. "I remember that. And you leaving the necklace on my pillow."

"You remember it because it happened. It wasn't a dream. I don't know why you don't remember the beginning of it."

"How did you get into my locked apartment?"

For the first time he looked slightly embarrassed. "Locks don't . . . present a problem for me."

"You mean, you pick them. Apparently, with no concern for the fact that the person who locked the door might want it to stay that way."

Outside a layer of clouds moved over the city. The light in Lucinda's apartment suddenly dimmed, and the light in Sebastian's blue eyes went flat and his voice was cool as he said, "Picking them isn't necessary. Doors aren't locked for me."

"You mean, you approach any door and it opens?"

He nodded, looking at her steadily. "The god Janus has been kind."

"I'm just wondering," Lucinda said after taking that in, "how anyone who sounds so sincere could be so full of shit. Janus opens doors for you. And Madana opens women to you. Any other gods protecting your interests?"

He pursed his lips, hesitating. "There are others whom I work for, but it's best if we don't get into that now."

"No, of course not." Disgust made her suddenly weary, and she lowered the knife. "How do you expect me to believe anything you say?"

"I haven't lied to you," Sebastian insisted, and the rare defensive note in his voice made it clear to her that honesty was something he seldom gave.

She turned away from him, aware that she was still holding the necklace. "Tell me about the diamond," she said, her tone detached. "It's very valuable?"

"Isn't that obvious?"

"And what else?" she asked. "It has some sort of power, doesn't it?"

"Most stones have some sort of power," he said evenly.

"What about this diamond?" She returned the knife to his chest, pressing against his skin until she drew a perfect bead of deep-red blood. He didn't flinch, didn't seem to notice it all. "Is it cursed?"

"No!" He looked appalled. "I wouldn't give you a cursed stone."

"Then what does it do?"

"Bend the light, like any prism." Sebastian glanced down at the knife. "Are you going to slit my throat with that?"

"I haven't decided yet."

The lighter-than-air-feeling intensified. She felt weightless, insubstantial, as if he could breathe on her and she would drift across the room. Perhaps he sensed this, for he gently touched the hand that held the knife, and her hand floated away from him in a dancer's graceful curve and came to rest at her side. She watched, transfixed by her arm describing a curve that, though beautiful, was completely alien to her own instinctive way of moving.

"What are you?" she demanded, her voice jagged.

Sebastian pulled a red bandana from his pocket and stanched the bleeding cut. "You're very hostile for someone who expects me to reveal my secrets."

Realizing that the knife was useless, that she had no real defense against him, she folded the blade back into the handle.

"I just need to be clear about something," she said. "Are you playing with me? I mean, are you getting off on watching me flail about in your trap? Is that what this is? Because I'm trying to figure out what to do, thinking maybe I should just gnaw through my own foot now and flee, even if it leaves me a cripple."

He winced a bit at her words, then stood gazing at her with so much pity that her entire body began to shake. It took a minute before she could make her voice work again. "I can't get away from you, can I?"

He sat down in the wing chair, staring at the wood planks of her floor. "A while ago, after one of my disastrous love affairs, I resolved that if I ever fell in love again, I wouldn't use . . . the abilities that I have."

She let pass his assertion that he was in love with her. "But you have."

He nodded then glanced up at her. "It's my nature, instinct really. For me not to use my abilities would be like not using my own hands. There are things I do because they're as natural to me as breathing."

"Seducing me, stalking me, entering my flat when you knew damn well I didn't want you here—"

"Bringing you to Madana, taking you up to my loft when I could have taken you home, giving you the necklace," he countered.

Lucinda held out the diamond again. "Is it enspelled? Or is it some kind of spying device?"

"No, nothing like that." Sebastian's eyes traced the line of the molding that edged her ceiling, as if searching for an explanation. "That particular stone is a filter and a magnifier. It purifies and intensifies the energy that it takes in and reflects. I hoped that when you wore it, it would filter out your anger and mistrust and let you feel—"

"What? Some unfathomable love for you?"

He sat up straight. "We have a connection," he stated doggedly. "You're lying to yourself if you deny it."

"You're a great one to talk about lies."

"I haven't lied to you," he repeated. "But there are things I haven't told you."

"Why don't you start with what you are. Are you like Madana—a god?"

Sebastian gave a snort of surprise. "Hardly."

"Then what?"

"I'm an—animal." He struggled to get the words out.

She couldn't make sense of his confession but the fact that he was having so much trouble with it eased a little of her fear. Unwilling to make it any easier for him, she said nothing, only waited for him to continue.

"I change," he said, his voice a harsh whisper. "I create illusions. I make people lose their bearings. Sometimes I steal. And I've caused madness, but only once. To my mother's great-uncle."

She thought back to the story he'd told her in his loft. "He was the one who had the lions guarding his estate."

Something cruel flickered in Sebastian's eyes. "He would have needed more than stone lions to keep me out. Or to keep down the madness that was inside him. Actually, all I did was steal his defenses so that he dropped permanently into the chaos and terror that were already churning beneath that aristocratic veneer." Sebastian looked up at her. "That's the worst of it, the worst that I've done."

And what did he want from her, Lucinda wondered. Absolution? "I don't know what you're talking about," she said.

"You don't?" A hard tone entered his voice. "What did you see in the gazing ball in my bedroom?"

Fear gripped her gut as she remembered. "A fox, sitting in your kitchen, licking its lips."

He reached for her hand. She tried to pull away and couldn't at first. Then she could because something in the air around them wavered and bent, the way intense heat bends the air and creates mirages. She saw the sleeve of his white shirt fade away in the wavering air. Dark red fur covered his hands and his fingers blurred then became solid again as large paws with long black nails.

Lucinda jerked back from the large red fox that sat on her chair, its blue eyes watching her with Sebastian's wary concern.

She tried to scream but all that came out of her throat was a high-pitched whine. She couldn't make her voice work and her body's betrayal terrified her more than anything that had come before. Again, she tried to scream and got out only a strangled cry.

The fox touched her with a paw, the way a dog might when trying to comfort a weeping human, and she bolted clear to the other side of the room. She stared helplessly at her knife, lying on the floor where she'd dropped it. How was it that she dropped the knife and was still holding onto the diamond?

She deliberately dropped the necklace, not looking down when she heard it hit the floor.

The fox dropped down onto the floor, standing on its four legs. It was bigger than a fox ought to be, larger even than a wolf. It was beautiful, she realized, its thick fur gleaming in the dull light of the windows, a brush of white fur along its throat, its sides gently rising and falling with each breath, its blue eyes gazing at her with keen intelligence and an untranslatable question.

The fox shook itself and she saw the air bend around it again, distorting her vision, and yet she could see the fur on its head lengthen, change texture, and become human reddish-brown hair. She saw the fox's elongated face flatten and round into Sebastian's, the fur pelt seeming to recede beneath his skin.

Sebastian stood before her again, dressed in the black pants, boots, and white linen shirt. Only the expression in his eyes hadn't changed. His face had always had a fox's sharpness she realized, and his eyes had always held that animal light in them.

"That wasn't one of your illusions," she said at last, her voice quavering.

He shook his head. "I told you. I change."

"You're a monster."

"A trickster, actually."

"I want you to leave," Lucinda said.

"Why won't you believe that I won't hurt you?" Sebastian asked impatiently. "If I'd wanted to, I could have been at your throat in a heartbeat."

"That's a comforting image."

"I'm saying all the wrong things," he said, sounding distressed. "And look at you. I've got you backed up against the wall in fear." He ran a hand through his thick hair. "This is really going fucking splendidly."

"Tricksters play tricks," Lucinda said, thinking it was no wonder his other relationships ended disastrously. "Is that what this is?"

"No!"

"Then what do you want from me?"

"You know," he said. "I'm in love with you."

"You barely know me. How can you love someone you don't even know?"

"I don't know." Sebastian sounded surprised at the question. "Despite my time with Madana, I don't understand the first thing about love. I can only recognize it when it appears. And what I feel for you goes beyond lust or friendship or even tenderness. You have a heart-path inside me."

Lucinda's legs had stopped trembling, leaving her with a weariness that was kin to surrender. With her back still against the wall, she slid down until she was sitting on the floor. "I believe you that you don't have any intention of hurting me," she said slowly. "That doesn't mean you won't."

He nodded, his eyes holding hers. "Harm is often unintentional, especially between lovers. But if it's any comfort, I won't suddenly lose control, turn into a fox, and bite you. I'm not a werewolf, controlled by the waxing of the moon. I change only when I want to."

She couldn't find any words. She simply sat, trying to absorb what she'd seen, trying to grasp whatever it was that was the truth.

"Lucinda? Are you all right?"

"I don't know what to do with any of this," she told him at last. "I can barely figure out how to be with men who are human. I don't know how to be with a man who's really a fox."

"Who's *also* a fox," he corrected her. "I'm both equally."

"Fine. If you don't mind me asking, are there women who also change into foxes?"

"Oh, yes," Sebastian assured her, "though not so many here in the city."

"And you can't find a heart-path, whatever that is, to one of them?"

"I've tried."

"I think you really ought to talk to your friend Madana and ask him why he's such a sadistic bastard. He can help you. I can't."

"Granted, but beside the point." Sebastian settled himself on the floor, sitting cross-legged opposite her, once again looking relaxed and sure of himself. "That's like asking the gods to take away the color of your eyes. Once they've given it to you, the gift is yours."

Lucinda shut her eyes. Clearly, she was not going to reason her way out of this. She kept her eyes shut a moment, asking herself if her attraction to Sebastian was gone now that she'd seen him as a fox. No, she realized. He had scared but not revolted her.

She reached for a truth she could tell him, knowing he wouldn't accept anything less. "My life is crazed right now," she said finally. "The man I work with, who is also my best friend, is in the hospital. I don't know if he's going to make it. I'm not exactly feeling romantic."

"What happened to your friend?"

"He got stabbed by a sociopathic kid. I think it happened around the time I left your loft."

"What kid?" he asked, something guarded in his voice.

"His name is Michael something. About eleven. Hungry and mean. You know him?"

"I may have seen him," Sebastian said, sounding troubled.

"Did you send him to Tyrone?"

"No." Sebastian's voice had dropped so low, she could barely hear it. "I saw him after. He was running, with a companion, it turned out."

"The jaguar?" Lucinda asked. "You saw the jaguar?"

Sebastian blew out a long breath. "Whatever troubles I've had, at least I've never had one of those following me around."

"Do know how Michael got the jaguar?" she asked, for the first time wondering if there might be some connection between Sebastian and Alasdair.

"A caretaker assigned it to him, no doubt."

"A caretaker."

"That's a clumsy translation of the term, *cearu*. It's a title of sorts. It means someone whose role it is to care for those in need."

"And this is a role that the caretaker would choose?"

Sebastian gave a short, humorless laugh. "I suppose there are a few selfless souls who would choose such a thing without any encouragement. But the *cearu* are born to it. Not only is it hereditary, in the blood, bred for generations, but it's foretold in the stars. Their births are not random. Poor bastards have no real choice in the matter."

"Where?" Lucinda asked. "Where is this that the births of *cearu* are planned?"

"Ah, you don't know that, do you?" Sebastian's eyes roamed over her, cool and assessing. "Then I'm afraid I can't be the one to say."

She stood up quickly. "Get out," she said. "Just please get the hell out of here now."

He ran a gentle hand along the side of her face, leaning toward her and she felt herself moving into his arms. "No," she said. With effort, she pulled away, so that she stood well out of his reach. Gods, but she craved that tenderness. It was so hard not to go toward him when his touch was all she truly wanted.

"I see," Sebastian said, sounding regretful. "I'll go now but if you see this caretaker again, be very careful. It's remarkable how dangerous a creature can be when it's been bred to be the living equivalent of a saint. In fact, they tend to be more like"—a smile curled his lips—"guard dogs, and you know how it is with trained guard dogs. An unfortunate number inevitably have to be slaughtered because they go bad."

"Says the fox."

He smiled and brushed her lips with the lightest of kisses. "Exactly."

She latched the door behind him, knowing it wouldn't do any good.

Eleven

ALASDAIR FOLLOWED THE dragon through the streets of the old city, aware that they were even quieter than they'd been the morning after Carnival. It wasn't sickness, he told himself. He'd been in villages caught in plague, and that silence was different, a silence locked in grief and terror that he didn't sense here. And this wasn't the emptiness of a place deserted. Although he didn't see anyone out on the streets, he caught glimpses of employees behind storefront counters, and he heard the occasional voice through an open window. But there was a damped down, muted quality here, as if everyone were lying low, trying not to attract attention.

The warm, spicy scent of roasting peppers wafted toward him, and he hesitated. "Give me a moment?" he asked the dragon.

Annoyance flickered in the dragon's golden eyes, but it hid itself in the folds of his robe as he detoured from Luminaria Street down an alley. He followed the scent to a yard where, next to a shrine dedicated to the Virgin Mary, a man with a lined face and ropy, muscular arms turned a blackened metal drum over an open fire.

"You like chile peppers?" the man asked him.

"Sometimes," Alasdair said.

"I'll have some ready in a little while," the man told him. "My chiles are hot. You only need to use a little bit." He held a forefinger and thumb close together. "Then everything tastes better, wakes up. Even chocolate."

"I'm afraid I'm not much of a cook," Alasdair admitted. "Can you tell me why the city's so quiet? You're the first person I've seen on the streets."

"We have a trickster in the neighborhood," the man said. "He's causing confusion everywhere. People know that if they go outside, they might not find their way home again. Or perhaps they will get home but not recognize it. Or they'll go to work without their clothes. Or worse—" He chuckled in embarrassment. "An old man like me will fall in love with a young woman, only to discover she is really a lamppost. No one knows what to believe anymore. Excuse me." He took a bandana from his pocket and blew his nose loudly. "It happens in this part of the city."

"But you're out here, roasting your chiles," Alasdair said, deliberately averting his eyes from the topaz and amethyst that were nuzzling against the man's boot. "And you're not afraid?"

The man inclined his head toward his shrine. "I pray to the Virgin for protection. And I leave food out at night for the fox."

"The fox?"

"My neighbor, Mr. Kitamura, he prays to his god Inari, who watches over foxes," the man said. "I told him, this is the work of El Diablo, or maybe even a coyote or a crow, but he says no, it's a fox—a *kitsune,* the kind of fox who can change into a man—causing all the trouble. So he leaves offerings for this Inari, and he has no problems."

"I shouldn't wonder," Alasdair murmured. He knew beings who were both human and fox. Even those born on other continents seemed to fall under the benevolent gaze of the Japanese rice god Inari, who was the patron of foxes. "Thank you," he said, turning to go.

"You don't want any chiles?" the man asked.

"Not today," Alasdair told him with a smile.

He returned to Luminaria Street, where the dragon emerged from the folds of his robe, its eyes flashing indignation. "You're right," Alasdair said, already feeling the fool, "I should have known. Take me to the lair of this fox."

A short time later he stood on Luminaria, near Montague Street. The buildings here were all industrial, most of them given to manufacturing. According to their signs, one made ribbons, another was a button factory, and a third made chairs and tables. The dragon hovered by the one building that had no sign and didn't seem to be a working factory. There were no lights inside, no sounds of machines whirring. Alasdair studied the black cast-iron facade. Since there was also no doorbell, he knocked on the ground-floor door. He was not surprised when no one answered.

Curious, he went to the button factory across the street and rang its bell. A man in a stained apron and spectacles soon came to the door. "What can I do for you, sir?" he asked.

"I'm trying to find out if that building across the street is occupied," Alasdair said.

The man looked him over suspiciously. "Why? You looking to set up shop?"

"No, I'm looking for someone. I was wondering if he lives in that building."

"Well, the first two floors used to be a thread factory. But that shut down a year ago," the man told him. "The top floor belongs to a chap, sells furniture."

"Do you know his name?"

"Can't say it's any of my business," the man replied, peering at Alasdair over the top of his spectacles. "What do you want with him?"

"I'm not sure it's him I want," Alasdair hedged. "I'm looking for a relative, someone in my mother's family, whom I've never actually met."

"Then wait around," the man advised. "Maybe you'll see him."

"Thank you," Alasdair said as the door was shut in his face. He wondered if the man had been rude because he needed to get back to work or because the questions seemed intrusive. Or was it just that in a neighborhood with a trickster, any stranger was looked on with suspicion?

Alasdair walked around to the side of the building. Looking up at the third-floor loft, he saw that one entire wall was glass. Not for the first time, he wished he'd been born with the ability to shape-shift into a bird or better yet, had simply been born a bird. He'd always secretly believed that he would make a splendid hawk.

"Well, is our fox home?" Alasdair asked the dragon.

The dragon obliged by flying up and peering in through the windows. From the ground, Alasdair could just make out the tiny bit of green jade hovering high above. Moments later the dragon returned, calm and composed. The fox was nowhere near.

"Very well," Alasdair said to it. "Then let me see what I can find out."

Stepping into the shadow of the building, he cast his senses toward the loft three flights above him, hoping it contained stones he could read. Reading stones when he could neither see nor touch them, meant that he had little influence over the type of information they would give. Still, it was worth a try. Quickly, he took the black opal from his life stones and invoked its protection. This time the stone's power worked along more traditional lines, concealing him with a play of shadow and light that even a fox's keen eyes couldn't penetrate.

Returning his attention to the rooftop flat, the first thing Alasdair sensed was the glass in the windows. The sands that had been melted to make them were taken from the shores of the Aegean, he learned. He moved on, searching for what would resonate. He could feel textures of wood and fabric, ceramic and metal, none of which opened to him. Then he began to sense a familiar range of resonance—the objects made of stone, their rough forms and mineral composition. Two large pieces of granite, carvings of some sort, yielded the information that they had once graced an English manor house as guardians and now resided with the fox who stole them. Lapis inlaid in a frame revealed that it had been taken from a house in Afghanistan; an onyx box holding a family of crystal elephants informed him that the fox stole it from a Brahmin's house in Delhi, where it had once been a wedding gift; a chunk of sandstone offered that it had been quarried in a desert canyon, its sinuous strata shaped by wind and rainstorms; and a crystal bowl stated with great clarity that though the fox had taken it from a French chateau, it was originally taken from the earth and carved in Brazil.

Very helpful, Alasdair thought with a sigh. *I've learned that I'm dealing with a well-traveled fox.* What the stones had told him was the equivalent of a captured soldier giving the enemy only his name and rank. It was so similar to the firefly emeralds revealing their presence and nothing more that he was sure the fox was somehow masking things.

Alasdair put a general question to the stones: *What is the name of this fox?* The stones shut down; he could barely sense their presences.

Alasdair knew he should probably give up this futile exercise, and yet he was too stubborn to let it go.

He continued probing, grabbing onto the mildest hints of resonance, and finding more objects made of stone, all of which were happy to tell him how they came to be in the loft but not much else. At last, when he found himself returning to objects he'd already visited, he began to withdraw.

That was when he found the crystal gazing ball. He'd overlooked it the first time because it was shrouded in protective spells. His senses had been searching for stone, not magic, and he'd gone right by it. But now he picked up on the polished sphere of transparent blue quartz and found that the spells that surrounded it were familiar magic, the sort of thing he'd learned after his third initiation.

With one hand he traced symbols, reversing the spells already in place. Then Alasdair silently invoked a simple incantation, asking the sphere for a vision.

It would have been so much easier had he been able to touch the crystal or at least look directly at it. Briefly, he envied the fox its ability to slip through locked doors, then he returned his concentration to the chant until he could picture the blue sphere in his mind's eye. Its clarity startled him; the crystal was so fine, so flawless, and it had been used for divination for so long that its power went beyond that of most gazing stones. He forced his mind away from the character of the sphere and centered himself on the incantation again, until he felt something inside the crystal stirring, and he began to see the clouds that swirled in its depths.

You have my thanks, he told it. *Will you show me the one who now claims to own you?*

The clouds continued to swirl until, as if blown by a strong wind, they traveled to one edge of the sphere then vanished. In the center of the blue crystal was the image of an outsized red fox, with a swath of white fur down its chest, calmly licking a paw. No surprise there.

And in human form? Alasdair asked. The crystal's clear blue center clouded and paled. Now the cloud seemed to move to the very back of the sphere, showing the fox still sitting proudly, front and center.

Human form, Alasdair reminded it.

The fox turned and bounded into the mist with a jaunty wave of its tail; and Alasdair waited patiently until a new image stepped out of the swirling clouds. This time it was a slender, sharp-featured man with blue eyes, reddish-brown hair, and a reckless grin.

He's looking fit and young, Alasdair thought, *considering that it's been at least seventy-five winters since we last saw each other.*

LUCINDA RETURNED TO the hospital to find the little man in the plaid pajamas gone, his bed stripped, and Gabrielle sitting in the single chair beside Tyrone's bed.

"Hey," Lucinda said softly.

"No need to whisper," Gabrielle told her. "You're not going to wake him."

Lucinda nodded toward the empty bed in the room. "Do you know what happened to him?"

"He was gone when I came in. I hope he got better and some nice relative came to take him home."

"I hope so, too," Lucinda said, shrugging off a quick stab of guilt for having been a bitch to the man. "And how's our boy?"

"He's not awake, but they took him off the machine that was breathing for him."

Lucinda blinked as she realized it was true. Tyrone's chest was rising and falling with shallow but even breaths.

"Oh, thank goodness," she murmured, taking one of his hands between hers. She glanced at Gabrielle. "This is good news, right?"

"It's a good sign," Gabrielle said. "But it's no guarantee that he'll regain consciousness. They told me that he might have suffered brain damage."

"No," Lucinda said fiercely. "He can't. Do you hear that, Tyrone? You have got to come out of this as your impossible, ornery self, because I couldn't stand anything less."

"Shush, you're going to make him afraid to wake up," Gabrielle chided her gently. "So tell me, how are *you* doing?"

"I'm managing." Lucinda perched on the edge of the bed and stroked Tyrone's hand. "Did a tall man wearing long blue robes come by?"

Gabrielle arched one dark eyebrow. "Is this the redhead?"

"No, someone else. He helped Tyrone when he was stabbed."

"Well, if he came by, it wasn't on my watch."

Lucinda considered asking if Gabrielle had seen a small, flying jade dragon, but thought better of it. Instead, she said, "Gabrielle, have you ever heard of people who can change themselves into animals?"

"I celebrate Lilith," Gabrielle admitted with a smile. "Some say she's the mother of all demons, but I see her as the mother of all women who enjoy men but also enjoy their own power too much to surrender it. She likes to take the form of an owl or sometimes a wild cat."

"I'm not talking about myths. I mean real people. The kind you meet on the streets of Arcato."

"You've been on Madana's boat and you say that with a straight face. Girl, don't you learn?" Gabrielle pushed her unruly mass of hair off her neck, and her incredulous expression became sympathetic. "You were born out of favor, weren't you?"

"Tyrone told you?"

"You did. When we first met. You seemed—I don't know—almost proud of it."

Lucinda found herself unable to meet Gabrielle's probing gaze. How the hell had the conversation turned to this?

"It leaves you vulnerable," Gabrielle stated. "You need some protection. Especially if you're meeting up with shape-shifters."

"What do you suggest?"

"That you get over your own bitterness at being born out of favor and align yourself with one of the gods."

"No, thank you. I grew up having religion forced down my throat and you know what it always tasted like? A heaping serving of guilt."

"So?" Gabrielle asked. "Anything can be misinterpreted or skewed. That's your past. Now you're out of your mother's home, and you need to find a deity who doesn't repulse you and ask if he or she will look kindly on you."

"That's impossible," Lucinda said flatly. "It's not in my stars. Besides—"

"The stars aren't fixed," Gabrielle overrode her. "If they can change position in the skies, certainly your fate can change as well."

Lucinda looked down at Tyrone's still form. "It's too late. I feel like any luck I might have had has run out. The gods aren't going to want to hear from me now, not after I've spent my whole life resenting them."

"Try it," Gabrielle urged her softly. "You don't have to become an acolyte. Just don't walk around this city so abandoned and exposed. There are too many energies working on people. It's too crazy here."

"Well, that last part I agree with." Lucinda smoothed out a wrinkle in Tyrone's blanket. Tyrone was far too meticulous for wrinkles. "Ever since all those gemstones started turning up, this city has been nuts."

"Oh, it started before that," Gabrielle assured her. "The gems have added to general madness, but they're really the least of it. Did you hear about the boats? Early this morning at the north pier someone cut half a dozen boats loose from their moorings. A few of them collided, with deckhands going overboard and damage all around. According to the river gossip, the crews suspect each other and all sorts of old rivalries and grudges are surfacing. Of course, all the gods coming in and out of the port just add to the confusion, though I don't think they're the real problem, either."

"So what is it?" Lucinda asked, realizing that for a while now—certainly before the gems had started appearing—she had felt something off or wrong in the city. It had been one of those vague feelings that it always there but hovers so unobtrusively in the background that you get used to it, stop noticing, and it becomes part of the fabric of things, rather than the discordant element. Besides, Arcato was such a jumble of discordant cultures, interests, and buildings that it was hard to see what didn't fit, what might be a true deviation.

Gabrielle interlaced her fingers and stretched her arms overhead. "I don't know," she answered. "But the way I feel it, is that it's not a god or a person. More like something in between, but something, I don't know . . . dark. And it's searching for something. Waiting. And while it waits it can't help but stir up chaos, tear things apart." She unlaced her fingers, this time stretching her arms out to the side, the movements languid despite her words. "Who the hell really knows? I may be way off."

Lucinda had a fleeting vision of Sebastian and dismissed it, asking, "And Lilith protects you from this?"

"There are no guarantees but she's a hunter in her own right," Gabrielle explained. "I think it's like two predators who coexist, each respecting the other's territory. I think that's about the most protection you can hope to find here."

"Oh, that sounds like something worthy of worship," Lucinda said. She got to her feet impatiently. "Honestly, Gabrielle, no offense—it's just not for me. Look, I'm going to get something to drink. Can I get you anything?"

"No, I've got to get over to my studio soon."

"And stop looking at me with all that damn sympathy."

"It's empathy, hon," Gabrielle said, standing up. Again she put her arms around Lucinda. Her embrace smelled like ginger. "If you're in trouble, you let me know, okay? Don't go dealing with things like shape-shifters all on your own."

Lucinda felt the muscles in her chest tighten against the urge to let it all pour out into Gabrielle's comforting arms. What stopped her was the fear that what had happened to Tyrone had something to do with her. She had no proof. It was just a guilt-ridden guess, but it was enough to make her afraid that she might bring similar danger to Gabrielle.

She pulled herself out of the hug. "Thanks," she said. "I can't take you up on it, but that doesn't mean I don't appreciate the offer."

"Well, it won't go away," Gabrielle told her.

When Lucinda returned to Tyrone's room with another awful cup of hospital coffee, Gabrielle was gone. Lucinda sat down beside Tyrone and watched him breathe his light, shallow breaths.

ALL THAT DAY and all that night Alasdair remained in the old city, waiting for the fox to return to its lair. He used the opal to both conceal himself and sharpen his senses, but when a weak sun struggled to light a cloud-swathed noon sky and there was still no sign of the fox, he decided to quit the waiting game.

The wait, though, had given him time to think about the one he'd seen in the crystal ball. When they first met, the shape-shifter had gone by the name of Malachy. The strange thing, Alasdair now remembered, was that Hermes, patron of thieves, was not particularly fond of Malachy, but Janus was. It was Janus who had opened door for Malachy into the Source Place.

Malachy had been a young man then, in his early twenties and full of himself. He claimed he came from the Celtic Isles but said he'd rarely stayed in one place more than a moon. He said that his family was always on the move, that his upbringing gave him a restlessness he couldn't quench. He was cocky but charming, and he'd managed to win over the elders by reining in his innate tendencies to steal and wreak havoc. Instead, he humbly asked to be taught to work with the stones. And though Alasdair's people saw him for the fox and trickster that he was, they had treated him kindly. Malachy's true gift was to make everyone see the glimmer of goodness in him and want to nurture it.

Malachy spent seven years among them, during which time he caused relatively little trouble. Old Averill kept an eye on him. She was a shape-shifter herself, wiser, faster, and more powerful than most. Averill could change from woman to cat to boar to owl and back to woman again in a breath, and when she was in human form you could catch glimpses of all three animals looking out through her eyes. She awed even Malachy. She taught him herself, and though he studied with her a relatively short time, there was a quickness and agility in everything he did, and the stones responded to him. Whereas the stones tended to regard Alasdair as a peer, someone whom they argued with as often as they obeyed, they responded to Malachy as if they were loyal hounds, eager to do his bidding. Alasdair had found it extremely annoying at the time.

Now Alasdair wondered what other sorts of power Malachy had acquired in the intervening years. It was a safe bet that he knew about and had crossed the labradorite bridge into the city where Lucinda and Tyrone lived. It was a perfect setup, really. He could take what he wanted from their city and come home to store his goods in this one. Another, more disturbing thought occurred to Alasdair. Since Malachy was one of Janus's favorites, was he the one who had petitioned Janus to let Michael Fortunato out of jail? Certainly, he had been the one to give the boy the firefly emeralds. What, he wondered, was a creature like Malachy doing, playing with that forsaken, angry child? The fox usually took his pleasure from tricking those better able to defend themselves. Briefly, Alasdair wondered if Malachy was the one stalking him. No, he realized. Malachy knew how to open the stones. If he'd been the one to show up at Alasdair's flat, half the stones would have left with him. Happily.

Alasdair felt the dragon's cold jade nose press against his neck and realized he'd been moving too slowly.

He plucked the dragon from its perch on his collarbone and set it on his open palm. "You indicated that you knew who gave Lucinda the moonstone necklace. Was it Malachy?"

The dragon's wings fluttered in anxious affirmation.

"Then we'd better get back to her," Alasdair said, setting off for the bridge, "before he does."

ALASDAIR WAS ONLY a few streets from the labradorite bridge, striding down an alley called Helicon or Heliodor—the end of the name had faded from the sign—when a tapping on a window caught his attention. He looked up and saw a young woman beckoning to him. A sign propped in the base of the window read:

FORTUNES READ. CARDS. CRYSTAL. TEA LEAVES.

Alasdair shook his head, indicating that the last thing he wanted was to know his future. But the young woman beckoned to him again, and the dragon, who was now riding on his wrist, gazed up at him as if it thought going to see the fortune-teller was an excellent idea.

Reluctantly, Alasdair walked up the blackened metal stairs that led to the flat. The girl opened the door before he reached it, smiling provocatively. She had long, glossy black hair, and though she wore a simple fitted dress made from a rough grey fabric, her dark eyes were heavily made up. Purple and blue streaks lined her lids and kohl rimmed her lashes. He guessed her age to be no more than seventeen.

"Come in," she said, with another smile full of promise. "Let me tell you what the future holds for you."

Alasdair hesitated as he felt resistance from a protective spell over the doorway but it opened for him, and he stepped inside to a small parlor. A table covered with a flowered cloth sat in the middle of the room. On top of it sat a deck of cards and a gazing ball. It was polished glass, he sensed at once, and had neither powers of its own nor any spells surrounding it.

Alasdair took a seat at the table, wondering why on earth the dragon thought this was a good idea.

The young woman settled herself in the chair across from him. "It will cost you a gold coin," she informed him.

"I don't have one." Alasdair reached into his robes and found a piece of faceted, polished amethyst. "Will this do?"

She examined the stone critically. "Not for the Tarot. I'll read the crystal ball for you."

"Fine."

"Do you have any questions?"

He found himself laughing. "I have nothing but. Why don't you just start by telling me what you see?"

The girl waved her hands around the globe and muttered words in a language that he was not familiar with, if indeed it was a language at all. They both concentrated on the glass ball, Alasdair noting that it was not rock crystal but had been manufactured in one of the city's factories. Silently, he asked the glass what it saw. It answered that it reflected the tablecloth, the girl's face, and his own.

And what visions have you had? he asked it.

The crystal ball responded with a kind of incoherent confusion.

"I see that you are far from home," the girl began.

A reasonable assumption, given his robes.

"And you have left one that you love."

Many actually, he thought.

"You have come to this city to search for a new love—"

"That's not the case at all," he said as gently as he could.

She looked up at him reproachfully. "Don't interrupt my vision. You came to this city to search for love, and I see that it will find you."

"I suspect you're reading your own fortune," Alasdair said. He got to his feet, unwilling to waste more time. "You can keep the amethyst but I have to go."

He regretted his words immediately as he saw hurt and humiliation cross her face. "I'm sorry," he said quickly. "I appreciate you trying. I—"

"Katja," a sharp voice interrupted. "I finished the wash. Go hang it on the line."

The girl fixed him with an indignant look then left the room, and he turned to face a round, middle-aged woman. She had the girl's dark, glossy hair and dark eyes, and he knew at once that she saw things that the younger woman never would.

"Forgive my daughter, *cearu,*" the woman said. "She's young and inexperienced."

It was the first time since he came to Arcato that someone had addressed him as *cearu,* and the word stirred both regret and dread in him. He considered disabusing her of the notion but had neither the time nor inclination to explain. "What makes you think I'm a *cearu?*" he asked instead.

"It's in your eyes," she said simply.

"You've met others?"

"Thomas, Guillermo, Darragh, and Ysobel," she answered. She looked at him, almost shyly. "As you are a familiar of the gods, I am a familiar of the *cearu.* If they come to this city, sooner or later they all find their way to my door. Will you take a cup of tea with me?" She looked at the collar of his robe, precisely at the spot that concealed the dragon, who was once again resting in the hollow of his collarbone. "And I have sweet honey cake for the dragon."

Alasdair smiled. The dragon loved honey cake. "We can't stay long."

"I understand."

The rooms in the flat were laid out one directly behind the next. She led him through a living room crowded with books and bric-a-brac, into a small bedroom with lace hung over the windows that he took to be the girl's. The bedroom opened into a large kitchen. Wooden shelves stretched floor to ceiling, the lower ones containing the usual dishes and pots, the upper ones crowded with glass jars filled with herbs and powders.

"Have a seat, please," she said, pointing to a square wooden table with four chairs.

Alasdair took a seat, and the dragon emerged from his robes, stretching one clawed foot, as if just waking up.

The woman brought a pot of black tea to the table, along with cups and two dishes made of bright yellow ceramic. The larger dish held a slice of the honey cake for Alasdair, the smaller one held carefully broken-up bits of the cake for the dragon.

The woman poured the tea then stood with her hands folded over her stomach, seeming content as she watched the dragon nibble delicately at the cake.

"My name is Mariamme," she said.

"Alasdair."

"Thomas saved my great-grandmother's life," she explained. She took a rounded cup from one of the shelves and handed it to Alasdair. "He gave her this."

The cup had been shaped with a great deal of love. Its outer surface was smooth, the color translucent, halfway between gold and orange. The inside was blackened. "This cup was carved from Baltic amber," Alasdair said, "and it's blackened this way because it once held poison."

Mariamme nodded. "Thomas gave it to my great-grandmother. He told her that if poison touched the inside of this cup, the amber would burn it away. And it did. The women in my family have been friends to the *cearu* ever since."

"Thomas was one of my teachers," Alasdair said. "As was Guillermo. They were both very fond of amber. Thomas used to call it a 'most reliable substance.'" The dragon fluttered indignantly. "Next to jade, of course," he added with a smile.

"And Ysobel?"

"She left the Source Place when I was still a young boy, before I began my training. My mother speaks of her with great affection, though."

"Ysobel took a ship from this city to Madagascar," Mariamme told him. "She said there was a red stone there that she wanted to work with."

"Madagascar has very fine rubellite," Alasdair acknowledged, picturing a chunk of the deep red tourmaline. "It's useful in healing—and for those who struggle to understand love."

"Don't we all," Mariamme said with a laugh. "And you? How can I help you, *cearu?*"

"Tell me what you can about the trickster who lives in this part of the city."

Mariamme traced a sign in the air. "May the gods protect us. I won't let my Katja out on the streets alone. He deals in fine furniture and pretty trinkets, every bit of it stolen. The young girls find him handsome. He sweet-talks them, gives them some little box or vase or knickknack that they can't resist. Then he takes something precious from them."

"You know his name?"

"Artemis and Tara forfend." She drew the protective sign again. "I don't want to know that much about him."

The dragon, having finished the last of its honey cake, sat upright on the table, its tail flicking slightly, a reminder, Alasdair knew, that they couldn't afford to linger here long.

"One more question," he said. On the table's warm wood surface he traced a diamond inside a diamond. "Have you ever seen this—as a pattern or sign or decoration?"

Mariamme began emptying the dish drainer with nervous, hurried movements. Through the kitchen window Alasdair could see Katja in the yard, sullenly holding an empty laundry basket against her hip; she was waiting for him to leave before coming back into the flat.

He returned his attention to her mother, who still had not answered his question. "You have seen it," he stated.

"It's a . . . key," Mariamme said hesitantly. "If you know the right way to invoke it, it will open doors for you."

"Doors to?"

"That's beyond me, *cearu,*" she said, her voice barely audible.

"And do you know who wields this key?"

She shook her head, not looking at him.

He could see how uncomfortable this was making her, and yet he couldn't let it go. "What else?" he probed. "I wouldn't ask, except I'm afraid it's important, and I know almost nothing about it."

Mariamme began to put away silverware, still avoiding his eyes. "I don't know much more. Sometimes this key appears and when it does there's great pain in that place."

"That was certainly my experience of it," Alasdair murmured. He was thinking that keys and doors seemed to fit with Janus, and yet the god himself was not known for cruelty, at least not more than any other god. "When did you first see the diamonds?"

Mariamme stopped fussing with silverware and came to stand at the table. "My mother taught me symbols. She used to draw them in the dirt with a stick. She'd say, 'This one is a blessing, and this one a warning, and this one for the fire spirit, and this for wisdom, and this the sacred heart of love that burns eternal.' "

"And she drew the diamonds for you."

Mariamme nodded. "She told me what I told you, and said that if I ever saw it, I must run in the opposite direction as far and fast as I could."

"Excellent advice," Alasdair said, getting up from the table. The dragon flew to perch on his shoulder. "Thank you," he said, "for your hospitality and your help."

"It's nothing, *cearu*."

"May you and your daughter always be under the protection of the gods," he said, tracing the pattern of a blessing in the air.

"May the gods go with you," she replied.

He started out of the flat, stopping briefly in the living room to leave two deep-blue Indian sapphires on a doily-covered table.

LUCINDA, FRUSTRATED BY not being able to make Tyrone better, found she could not remain endlessly by his bedside. She became bored and restless, unable to concentrate on Tyrone, the novel she was halfway through, or even on the Dessalines work that she'd brought with her from his studio. She wound up pacing the halls, annoying the nurses, and irritating the other patients in his room. One of them pointedly asked, "Just who do you think you're helping by being here?"

The days at the hospital blurred into each other, and she was no longer sure about time, but she thought it had been two days since she last saw Gabrielle, and at least four since she saw Alasdair. On Carnival Night he said he was leaving Arcato, she remembered. Maybe he'd gone and was already in another port.

And she hadn't heard from Sebastian since his man-into-fox demonstration at her flat. That was two days ago. She'd gotten her period yesterday, right on time, which really hadn't been a surprise. Lucinda had scarring from an abortion when she was sixteen; she'd been told then that she could no longer get pregnant. Still, she felt relieved when the bleeding started. She couldn't have borne another link to Sebastian.

The connection between us should be gone by now, she thought during a day spent at Tyrone's studio doing finish work on samples. But she knew it wasn't. She felt certain that Sebastian would reappear, and she hated yielding him the element of surprise. So as she finished the last of the samples she decided quite impulsively that she would find Sebastian. She would go to his loft, return the diamond necklace, tell him it was over for good, and then try very hard not to jump his bones one last time.

It was late afternoon on the following day when Lucinda left her flat. The diamond necklace was tucked away in one of the inner pockets of a long, quilted black velvet coat that Tyrone had designed for her. She wore it over frayed denim jeans, and a loose blouse she'd made by sewing together old silk scarves. The scarves were azure and green, purple and gold, and somehow they seemed to call for her red leather boots. Tyrone looked so wan and grey lately that she felt nearly obliged to wear color, hoping that on some level he would sense it and it would draw him back to life.

She began walking toward the top of the city, taking the narrowest, steepest streets, aware of the sound of her boot heels against the brick streets. True to form, she hadn't bothered to check a map of the city for Luminaria or Montague Streets or the footbridge she'd crossed with the dragon. Arrogantly, perhaps stupidly, she was counting on her own street sense—or Sebastian himself—to lead her to him.

At first the streets were all familiar to her: Fulton Street near the water, crowded with cafés, bakeries, and restaurants; Lionscross Road, where art galleries, jewelers, and shops selling ceramics and hand-blown glass employed most of the city's art students; Linnea Street, which smelled of printers' ink and bookbinders' leather; Consolación and Haifong, the blocks given to music clubs and theaters; Vine, a street lined with optometrists, dentists, and herbalists; Vercelli, an alley devoted to lacemakers' shops; and Morro Street whose renovated flats were now studios belonging to graphic artists, calligraphers, and yet more clothing designers. Tyrone was right, she realized as she climbed higher; there were shrines everywhere—in doorways, niches, even in the windows of galleries that had renovated themselves into austere, minimalist spaces.

The streets wound uphill jaggedly, sending her into crowded streets and lanes, where there were no businesses or overpriced flats but tenements built nearly a century ago. She'd once known a dealer who lived in this part of the city. She still had vivid memories of a tiny, filthy apartment with cheap, rotting fixtures, a thriving roach population, and dim light filtering through a filmy window that looked out on another brick wall. She wondered if this was where Michael Fortunato grew up.

Lucinda climbed higher, heading vaguely east, looking for anything that she might recognize from Carnival Night or the route that the dragon had taken. Where were all the stairways that Sebastian used, the cluster of old industrial loft buildings and the little storefronts selling fabric and lamps? Lucinda felt herself breathing hard, covered in a light sweat. She stopped to get her bearings, maybe catch a glimpse of Sebastian's loft, but there was nothing familiar here, only an endless tangle of crooked streets and alleys.

When she was at the very top of the city, nearly in the foothills of the mountains that towered over it, she passed two long-abandoned brick factory buildings, their windows boarded up, their walls sprayed with graffiti. Cigarette stubs, shards of glass bottles, candy wrappers, and broken gelatin capsules littered the ground in front of the buildings, a particular kind of detritus that Lucinda recognized from her own adolescence. It was perfect, really: crumbling brick buildings and everyone's trash, a harsh ugliness that guaranteed isolation and privacy for a time in life when those qualities mattered more than nearly everything else. It seemed ironic to her now, but she knew that if she were fifteen, this would be exactly the kind of place that seduced with the promise that here you could begin to be yourself. She could almost picture the kids who would start drifting toward the buildings at twilight in self-conscious groups of two or three, cloaked in boredom and attitude and whatever clothes might conform to the prevailing ideal of cool, opening themselves to the night and all that darkness hid and promised.

She shook off memories of too many nights that burned on into dawn, too many hours spent doing nothing except numbing out and yet feeling somehow genuine, rebellious, and alive because of it. That part of her life was over and she had no regrets. So she didn't understand why she was reluctant to keep walking, why she felt drawn to the abandoned factories. She studied them more closely. They were approximately the same vintage as Sebastian's building. Maybe she was finally getting close. She gazed around again and noticed an alley running between the two old factories. She took a step toward it and felt the fine hairs along the back of her neck rise. There was something there, in or through the alley, that was working on her, pulling her. Wishing she'd brought her knife, she started between the buildings. She moved slowly, cautiously, ready to bolt at any second. She felt no menace, only a kind of magnetic pull that grew stronger with each step.

The alley opened into a square, and a rush of sunlight poured down into it, as if spring had just arrived in this one particular patch of city. Lucinda stepped into the square, dazzled by the light and warmth. She couldn't remember when she'd last seen so much sun. The air had been cold and grey and washed out for so long. Now the bricks of the buildings around her were a deep hearth-red and the ground in front of her sparkled with color, and the faint but distinct smells of earth and trees filtered down from the mountains.

Whatever force had been pulling on her had eased, she realized, as if she were now where she was meant to be. She started to open the long row of glass buttons on the black velvet coat, and stopped as she realized that the square was more than a gap between buildings. Broken stone columns stood on each of its four corners, as if they'd once held up a roof. And the ground was sparkling with color because she was looking at the remains of what must have once been a mosaic. It had been beautiful, she guessed from the remaining squares of turquoise, green, sapphire, deep red, and gold. The mosaic had to be ancient and yet the fragments were still so bright, the colors so rich that she could almost picture it as a whole, an intricate, shimmering carpet of stone and glass. Her heart quickened as she recognized a familiar pattern, the same pattern that was carved on Sebastian's bed. Fascinated, she knelt down and stretched out a hand to trace the diamond inside the diamond.

Something tugged at her cuff and she looked up from the mosaic to see the jade dragon pulling at the sleeve of her coat.

"You're back!" she said, delighted. The dragon continued to pull at her cuff. "What is it?" she asked it. "What do you want?"

"He's trying to tell you to get away from that damn mosaic." Alasdair strode toward her, looking even more irate than he sounded.

Bristling at his tone, Lucinda stayed exactly where she was.

"Look at him!" Alasdair demanded. "Can't you tell he's trying to protect you?"

The dragon was still frantically tugging at her sleeve, trying to pull her arm, and the rest of her, up.

Lucinda straightened and took a step back from the mosaic. The dragon stopped pulling on her but sank its little talons into her quilted sleeve and fixed her with an intense topaz glare.

"It's all right," she assured it. "I won't touch it."

The dragon's eyes flashed another warning, remarkably stern for such a small creature; then it released her and took flight, hovering between her and Alasdair.

"I've been looking for you," Alasdair said His voice became gentler. "I didn't expect to find you here. . . . How is Tyrone?"

"Not good. He's breathing without a machine but he hasn't woken up yet. His skin has this horrible grey tone. . . . I was wondering where you were, too," she admitted.

"I'll tell you," he said, glancing at the mosaic nervously. "But for your own safety, move a little farther from that thing."

She hesitated. "What is it?"

"I'm not sure," he admitted. "I touched it and I was hit with pain so intense I thought it was going to rip me in half. Please do as I ask." Lucinda stepped back, and Alasdair looked at her curiously. "Why *were* you trying to touch it? Did you feel something coming from the mosaic—some sort of pull?"

"No, nothing like that," she lied reflexively, then felt a pang of guilt. "I've seen that pattern before," she added more truthfully.

"Where?"

She hesitated, her defenses rising like a shield. She was about to once again tell him to mind his own business, but this time the shield felt heavy and useless. Maybe she was giving in to her own weakness, or giving in to the warmth and promise of the sun. Maybe she had actually begun to trust Alasdair.

"I saw it carved in the frame of a bed."

"Whose bed?"

"You would have to ask that, wouldn't you? Oh, hell, I'm tired of evasions. His name is Sebastian. He lives somewhere near here, at the top of the city"—she gestured distractedly toward the alley—"in an old cast-iron loft building. I was looking for it, and now I can't find it." Alasdair didn't say anything, but he was looking at her so intently that she felt impelled to go on. "He sells antiques. He's the one who took me to Madana's boat."

"Did you touch the diamond pattern on his bed?" Alasdair asked, the calm in his voice belied by the concern in his eyes.

"I didn't touch his bed at all," she said with a self-mocking smile. "Still, we were . . . lovers," she admitted, conscious that she was using Sebastian's term for it, because his came closest to whatever it was they had shared. "I think the dragon was in his loft with me. He helped me find my way back."

Alasdair regarded the dragon. "Well, that explains a good deal."

"You know Sebastian, don't you?" she asked, though the answer now seemed blazingly obvious.

"I haven't seen him for the last seventy-five years. When I knew him he went by the name Malachy."

"Seventy-five?" she echoed in a choked voice. "Neither one of you can possibly be seventy-five."

"Actually, we're quite a bit older," Alasdair said in that same calm voice. "I'm nearly twice that and Sebastian is roughly ten years younger than I am."

"He can't be. I've seen him—"

"He's not like you," Alasdair said gently. "Neither of us is."

"I know that." A kind of vertigo took hold of her, and she sat down unsteadily on the steps of the closest building to wait for the dizziness to pass.

She felt the tiny warm puffs of breath against her skin. The dragon was perched on her collarbone. Gently, she ran a finger along its narrow spine. It rubbed its little cheek against her neck.

Alasdair stepped toward her. "Are you all right?"

She gazed up, thinking it was impossible that Sebastian was more than a few years older than she was, or that Alasdair might be far older than that. There was a lightness, a centeredness, in the way Alasdair held himself that she'd only seen in dancers and athletes. His skin was unlined, his features sharp. Despite the grey in his dark hair, it was only his eyes that seemed ancient.

"Sebastian told me—showed me—what he is. And he told me what you are," she went on, her voice steadier. "He said you're a caretaker."

"More or less. Your language doesn't have a word for *cearu*. It's what I was born to and trained for. As it happens, I'm not very good at it."

"You helped Tyrone."

"If I'd been doing what I was born for, that never would have been necessary. I'd have gotten to Michael before he got to Tyrone. That boy has spent his entire short lifetime desperately needing someone to look out for him. And I saw that clearly and let him stay out there on his own, to be used by gods and—"

"And Sebastian?" Lucinda guessed. "Did he have anything to do with Michael?"

"I don't know for certain. I suspect he did."

Lucinda sat on the step, knees together, red-booted feet splayed in front of her, gazing down at the broken mosaic. "Why the fuck are the two of you in my life? I went for years with nothing more bizarre than the usual run of screwed-up boyfriends. Now I know a fox and a saint and you're both confusing the hell out of me."

"Don't make that mistake," Alasdair said sharply. "I'm about as close to sainthood as your friend Sebastian, and believe me, he has a long way to go."

She looked up at him wearily. "It doesn't matter."

Alasdair knelt down to face her. "What *does* matter?" he asked softly.

"That Tyrone gets better." The sun was almost hot. She unbuttoned her coat, wanting the soft spring air against her bare neck. "I can't think past that right now."

Alasdair shot to his feet, as though he'd been stung. "Where in holy heaven did you get it?" he asked hoarsely.

She blinked. "Get what?"

"That diamond you've got concealed in your coat. Do you have any idea of what you're carrying?"

"A big, pretty rock?"

"Don't be deliberately stupid."

"Then stop being so condescending."

Alasdair looked away, as if searching the brick wall for lost patience. "It's over fifty-six carats. Not priceless but you could probably buy half the city with it."

"Amazing," she drawled. "The stones not only speak to you, they give you their vital statistics."

"Actually, this place dulls my senses and my ability to read the stones. I didn't even know you had it until you opened your coat."

She shrugged, finding it hard to care whether or not Alasdair could read rocks. It didn't matter. This one was going back to Sebastian.

He spoke slowly and deliberately. "The diamond you're holding, I've seen it before."

"It's cursed?"

"No. I'm not sure what it can do. It's covered with protections; I've never been able to read it—"

"Are you going to take it from me?"

"It's not a stone that can be taken," Alasdair told her. "It's Kama's gift."

"He's right," said a voice coming from the alley. "It always has been."

Lucinda started as Sebastian emerged from between the two brick buildings, hands in his pockets, wearing his usual black jeans with a black jacket and a dark grey shirt, open at the neck. She didn't know why he was here, but she was certain it was no coincidence. "H-how did you find us?" she stammered.

He smiled at her. "I have a good sense of smell."

She stared, sensing a difference in him but unable to pinpoint it. He looked as relaxed and comfortable as ever. What was it that had changed? He seemed thinner and taller somehow, elongated and not quite real, like one of Tyrone's sketches.

She glanced from Alasdair to Sebastian. Neither seemed surprised to see the other. They were looking at each other with identical expressions of complete equanimity.

"You loathe each other, don't you?" she said.

"We have a history," said Alasdair.

"It doesn't matter," Sebastian said. He turned to Lucinda, his gaze full of warmth and promise. "Whatever I am, have done, or am about to do, believe that I love you."

The dragon, she noticed, had vanished again, and a number of polished stones—sapphires, emeralds, and amethysts—were rolling along the ground on a rather direct route from Alasdair to Sebastian.

Alasdair paid them no mind. "If she does believe that, she's going to have trouble understanding why you petitioned Janus to free the boy from jail on Carnival Night," he went on. "Without you, he never would have been out on the streets. He never would have met Tyrone. Actually, I've been wondering about that myself. Why *did* you ask Janus to free him?"

"You did what?" Lucinda was on her feet. "You got that little bastard out on the streets when he was safely locked away?" She studied Sebastian's face, trying to reconcile the man whose gentle touch had opened her with what she'd just heard.

"It wasn't exactly like that," Sebastian protested.

"Did you or did you not have Janus free the boy?" she demanded.

"I asked for help," Sebastian said carefully. "That first day we met I sensed your life was tied up with another's, that I would never truly have you as long as you were so close to this other person. And so I prayed to the gods—Janus and Kama—and asked—"

"You presumptuous, self-centered—"

"No." He put his hands on her shoulders. "I only asked the gods for help in making it possible for you to open to me. I never asked them to hurt your friend."

"Are you naïve or just blind? Don't you know the gods do as they please and don't give a damn who they hurt?"

"That's not true," Sebastian said gently. "Lucinda, please, you have to believe me. It was never my intention for that boy to hurt your friend."

She pulled away from him. "You set it up. You wanted Tyrone out of the way."

"Yes, but I never meant for him to die."

"Is that what's going to happen next—Tyrone dies?" Her voice was unaccountably steady, so controlled that she didn't quite believe it was hers.

Sebastian moved toward her, put out a conciliatory hand.

"Don't touch me. Just answer the question. Is Tyrone going to die?"

"That's not up to me. And you've got to believe that was never my intent."

"Stop telling me what to believe!" she shrieked. She caught her breath, pulled her voice back down to a normal register. "Okay, maybe you didn't order his death. But you did want him out of the way, and so you made sure that would happen in the most permanent way possible. I mean, you haven't prayed to Janus to heal Tyrone, have you?"

"No, I—" Sebastian ran a hand through his hair with a sigh. "You don't go to Janus for healing, anyway."

"So whom did you go to?" Alasdair asked. "You're asking her to believe you meant no harm. Tell her, then, what have you done to reverse it?"

Sebastian's gaze brushed over Alasdair quickly, as if he were no more than an annoying insect. "Stay out of this."

"That means you haven't tried to undo it," Alasdair translated.

Sebastian's eyes locked on Lucinda, as open and guileless as ever. "This is between me and Lucinda, and she knows what I am. There are no lies between us."

"Then I hope you've had the decency to explain to her that being a fox, you can't imagine getting what you want without resorting to trickery and deception. It's simply not in your nature."

"Fuck. You. *Cearu.* May your power wither and dry to dust. May your testicles recede into your cowardly gut and rot there. May even the stones, which are all you have left, abandon you."

"Was that supposed to be a curse?" Alasdair asked politely.

Lucinda took out the diamond necklace, deciding it was time to do what she'd originally intended. "Listen," she said to Sebastian. "I just want to give this back to you and—"

"Don't!" Alasdair cut her off.

"Why not?" she asked.

"The diamond is yours," Alasdair said in a more restrained tone. "I give you my word I'm not trying to take it from you. I'll return it to you later, but I strongly suggest you let me hold it for safekeeping now."

"That was my gift to you," Sebastian reminded her.

"Kama's gift to her."

"Through me," Sebastian said. "I brought her to Kama."

"And you're actually proud of that." Alasdair's voice was soft with amazement. "You can't get close to anyone without making them candidates for the madhouse, can you?" He held out his hand to Lucinda. "Please let me hold the diamond for now. If you don't, he'll use you to use its powers and I guarantee, you don't want that."

"*He* doesn't want that," Sebastian translated. "But he's really got no say in the matter. He has no right to the diamond. Madana gave it to you and you alone."

Lucinda let their arguments flow past her. She held the diamond in her open palm, watching it play with the sunlight, sending off shafts of color so brilliant, she could almost believe that all the colors of the world originated in that one stone. The colors seemed to whirl around her, bringing back the spice-heavy scents of Madana's garden, the feel of her body pressed against Sebastian's in the green light of the waterfall. . . .

Her eyes on the stone, she turned toward Alasdair. "You said he wants to use me to use the diamond," she reasoned aloud. "That must mean he can't do much with it on his own."

"That is not what I meant at all. Don't you see you're already caught in his power? He's a trickster. He lives to turn everything upside down, to steal, confound, and cause madness."

In a blur of motion Sebastian changed from man to fox. A detached part of Lucinda couldn't help admiring its glossy red pelt and white chest, as weirdly beautiful now as it had been in her flat. Then everything happened so quickly she had no time to react. The fox sprang for Alasdair's throat, jaws open. Even faster the dragon appeared hovering in front of Alasdair. Topaz eyes intent on the fox, the dragon opened delicate jaws and breathed a cloud of pale green mist into the fox's open mouth.

Lucinda watched as the fox fell back and dropped to all fours, coughing. It staggered in a circle, still coughing, then lay on the mosaic, wheezing painfully.

Lucinda stepped toward the fox, appalled. "What the hell was that?" she asked, her voice shaking.

"A toxin," Alasdair answered.

"You told me the dragon wasn't dangerous," she said, unwilling to have the one creature she believed to be good and harmless turn out to be as lethal as the rest.

"I said he didn't breathe fire." The dragon, looking exhausted, was perched on Alasdair's hand. Alasdair's eyes, fixed on the fox, had gone a hard flint-grey. "Every animal has some instinctive means of defense. You'd think a fox would know that."

The fox had gotten to its feet but its back legs were barely working. It was dragging its hindquarters, panting and desperately trying to move in a circle.

"How can you just stand there?" Lucinda demanded of Alasdair. "Help him! Isn't that what you're supposed to do?" She knelt, reaching a hand toward the injured animal. Her voice quavered as she asked, "What's he doing?" A painful memory surfaced: Jasper, a cantankerous cat and the only pet she'd ever had, desperately racing through her flat in its final hours. "Oh, gods. He's trying to find a place to die, isn't he?"

"Don't—" Alasdair's words broke off as the animal pulled itself to the center of the mosaic and pressed one weakened front paw against the diamond within the diamond. The mosaic shuddered then cracked. Lucinda stumbled forward only to be pulled back by Alaisdair as the ground beneath her heaved and the crack deepened into a fissure.

The earth gaped open to reveal a stairway carved from the bedrock. Candles set in the rock wall showed stone stairs spiraling downward.

The fox heaved itself toward the opening. Almost involuntarily, Lucinda began to follow. All her fury at Sebastian had dissolved into pity and the same terrified impotence she'd felt as she'd watched Tyrone bleeding. She turned to Alasdair, frantic. "You have got to help him!"

Alasdair seemed barely conscious of either her or Sebastian. He stared into the chasm with undisguised fascination, murmuring, "A key indeed."

The air wavered and bent around the dying fox and Sebastian's face emerged, as if he'd simply been hiding beneath the pelt all along. Lucinda pressed a fist against her mouth, holding back a scream. His weakened body hadn't been able to complete the change, and the human face on the fox's damaged body horrified her.

"Lucinda, I'll see you again," he promised, his voice caught in a freakish high pitch, somewhere between a human's range and a fox's shrill yelp.

"No," she pleaded. He was a creature out of nightmare, distorted, unnatural.

The fox lost control of its bladder then, peeing a blood-streaked yellow stream around its paws. The corners of Sebastian's mouth quivered in humiliation. He turned away from her, pulled his fox's body toward the stairway into the underground, and slowly began the descent.

Lucinda kept her fist against her mouth so that she wouldn't beg him to stop, wait, let her help him. She couldn't bear to see him like this but she couldn't bring herself to touch him.

"It's all right," Alasdair said.

"All right?" she echoed, incredulous. "He's in pain. He's *dying*."

"You have to let him go, Lucinda. He's a danger to you even now."

Ignoring him, she knelt at the side of the opening, searching for Sebastian on the candlelit stair. The fox was so far down that at first she saw only the thick red tail, but as if it sensed her, the animal turned and Sebastian's face peered up at her, pain and fear in his eyes.

She made an instant decision. Despite all his manipulations, they'd been lovers; she couldn't let him die alone. She gauged the distance to the top step. It was much farther down than she'd initially thought, a steep drop. She heard the fox whimpering. Holding onto the edges of the broken mosaic, Lucinda began to lower herself into the hole.

"Close now," called the fox in that odd high voice.

Then Alasdair was at her side, his hand clamping down on her biceps, jerking her up roughly, and hurling her out of the way.

Lucinda landed hard on her side, facing the brick buildings. "You cold-hearted bastard," she spat, wrenching around to see Alasdair dropping into the opening. She got to her feet unsteadily. The ground was shuddering again, the stones in the mosaic tilting up as if to catch the light, and the sides of the crevice were moving, inching closer together. Then the earth lurched again and sealed its opening shut.

Lucinda stood staring, stupefied. A hairline crack ran through the mosaic where only moments ago there had been an entry to an underground stair. The fragments of color that made up the pattern of the two diamonds seemed to grow brighter in the sunlight, as if winking at their own secret.

I was too slow. The knowledge vibrated through her like a humming wire. *Too slow to save anyone.*

She stood unmoving except for the hot tears that streaked her cheeks. She couldn't make sense of what had just happened. All she knew was she had to get out of there. So why wasn't she walking away? Did she really think that if she stood there long enough the mosaic would open again and Sebastian and Alasdair would emerge? *Shaking hands, no doubt,* she told herself wryly.

Maybe if she stayed until nightfall, the kids would come and take pity on her and feed her drugs and she wouldn't have to deal with any of this. It had been a long time since she last craved smack. She sank down on the broken back step of one of the factory buildings, willing to wait.

Something cool touched the palm of her left hand.

"Why the hell didn't *you* jump down there with the two of them?" she asked.

The dragon opened and closed its wings, regarding her with a steady topaz gaze.

"That's not a fucking answer. Did you have to mutilate him?"

Again the dragon opened and closed its wings. It was being patient with her.

"I trusted you," she said, her voice shaking. "I trusted you not to be vicious. You weren't supposed to be dangerous."

The dragon's expression didn't change.

She shut her eyes, remembering the warm, sweet rush of the drug moving through her veins. This could all go away. "Leave me alone," she told it. "I'm going to stay here a while."

The dragon moved to her wrist and used one clawed foot to tap against her cephalic vein. Not all that long ago, she'd been such a dedicated junkie, she'd memorized the names of the veins and arteries so as to better know the system she was using for transport.

"Now what?" she asked, opening her eyes.

The dragon tapped her arm again.

"You have something better to suggest? Maybe I should just mainline your green mist?"

The dragon gave her a reproachful look. A moment later it turned from a living, breathing creature to a jade carving that toppled from her wrist to the ground.

Lucinda scooped it up, her anger giving way to remorse. "Oh, don't do that. Look—" She hesitated, carefully choosing her words. "I hate what you did to Sebastian. It scares me. I can't help that. I also know you couldn't let him kill Alasdair. So it happened. I don't know where that leaves us."

The topaz eyes gleamed and the dragon's jade scales rose and fell with its breath.

"Not too much of a drama queen, are you?" she asked as it righted itself and took to the air.

Shadows crossed the square. The sun was dropping behind the western edge of the city. The day's warmth was gone, the promise of spring disappearing into the chill of another wintry night.

The dragon began to fly toward the alley. Resigned, Lucinda pulled her coat collar high and followed the little serpent out through the two factory buildings and down through the streets. Sebastian was dead or dying; Tyrone, not much better; and Alasdair was gone, sealed beneath the earth. The dragon was really the only one she had left.

Twelve

THE SUN WAS no longer visible, but its red glow reflected against the city's west-facing windows, tinting them deep red, as the dragon led Lucinda across the footbridge.

"Why are you bringing me back here?" she asked, irritation rising through her exhaustion. "I really do not need to see Sebastian's building again. And why couldn't I find this damn bridge on my own?"

But she continued following and soon realized that the dragon wasn't taking her to Sebastian's loft. Instead it led her through a series of winding alleys—more of the city that she didn't recognize—to a ramshackle apartment building, where a window held a sign advertising a fortune-teller.

"You're kidding, right?" Lucinda said. "Because if you're not, this is a terrible idea and I want to go home."

The dragon wasn't listening. It had flown up the single flight of metal stairs and was hovering there, beating its wings against the door, as if knocking.

"Maybe I do belong in a madhouse," Lucinda muttered, trailing after it. She knocked on the door, glaring at the dragon. "Happy now?"

The door cracked open and a teenage girl in a plain brown dirndl scowled at her. "It's late," the girl said. "We're closed now. Come back tomorrow."

A round middle-aged woman behind her pushed the door all the way open. She wore a high-necked brown muslin dress with tucks in the yoke that Lucinda pegged as Victorian, but it wasn't the sort of Victorian-era clothing that showed up in the vintage shops. The cloth was too rough, the design too workaday. "Can I help you?" the woman asked.

Lucinda gazed past her shoulder to see a typical cheesy fortune-telling parlor, complete with candles, fringed tablecloth, a deck of cards, and a crystal ball.

"I'm sorry," she said to the woman. "I made a mistake. I'd better go."

"You haven't made a mistake," the woman said. "Not if the dragon brought you here." She nodded over her shoulder to where the dragon sat on the table, examining its toes.

"Oh," Lucinda said, realizing that this was the first person she'd met since Alasdair who obviously knew the dragon.

"Come in, and I'll do what I can to help you," the woman said. "My name is Mariamme."

Lucinda walked over to the table but Mariamme said, "Not there. That's for more ordinary readings. Come with me."

She led Lucinda through a series of small, dark rooms to a cheerful kitchen lit by oil lamps. "Sit," she said, tilting her head toward a wooden table.

Lucinda sat at the table and the dragon perched attentively beside her. Mariamme unwrapped a piece of flowered cloth, uncovering a golden-brown cake inside. "Would you like some honey cake and tea?" she asked.

"That would be great, thanks," Lucinda said. She must be coming out of shock; she was actually hungry again.

Mariamme gave her a slice of the fragrant cake and a mug of black pekoe tea, and set another plate of cake crumbs in front of the dragon. Delicately but eagerly, the dragon dug in. "So that's why you brought me here," Lucinda murmured.

"He has his reasons," Mariamme agreed.

She went to a cabinet and took something from the top shelf. It was another, smaller crystal ball. From a drawer she took a bronze tripod. She set the tripod on the table and balanced the crystal on top of it.

While Lucinda drank her tea and ate her cake, Mariamme gazed into the crystal ball, turning it several times as if to get a better view. Lucinda didn't see any images in the crystal and was secretly relieved. She'd had more than enough magic for one day. As for Mariamme, she couldn't detect anything remotely mystical about the woman. Mariamme seemed as practical and straightforward as a broom.

Mariamme shook her head and frowned at the ball, which, from what Lucinda could see, showed nothing but clear glass.

"No future for me?" Lucinda guessed.

"You've met a *cearu*, haven't you?" Mariamme replied.

Lucinda put down her cake. "You know Alasdair?"

"He was here once."

Lucinda gestured toward the crystal ball. "Can you tell me where he is now?"

"No. This crystal can only tell me about those in close proximity. You, me, my daughter, the dragon."

"Tell me about the dragon," said Lucinda.

Mariamme gave her a look of fond reproof, the sort a mother might give a foolhardy child. Without looking at the crystal she said, "What you need to understand is that he is indeed a dragon, and though he's small for his species, that does not make him any less dangerous. There's a reason our kind have always feared dragons."

"I know all that," Lucinda said. "At least I do now."

"This dragon is a friend to the *cearu*," Mariamme went on.

"I know that, too."

Mariamme gave her another reproving look. "Am I wasting your time?"

Lucinda bit back an impatient reply. "I've had a . . . strange . . . day," she said. "I'm sitting in your kitchen now because I followed the dragon. I don't really know why I'm here."

"Then let me tell you," Mariamme said. She gazed into the crystal ball for what seemed a long time before pushing the tripod toward Lucinda. "What do you see?"

Lucinda looked into the crystal and blinked. "Flowers," she said, seeing a tall but delicate tree with pale purple blooms. "Lilacs."

"Lilacs," Mariamme echoed, nodding. "I see lilacs, too."

"And lilacs mean—"

"You follow the lilacs to the lost towns of the mountains."

Lucinda glanced at the dragon. Its eyes were closed in what seemed perfect contentment. She glanced back at Mariamme. "I have no idea of what you're talking about."

Mariamme shrugged. "I may not be much help to you. What I know is this: The *cearu* and their kind, they live in what my mother's people used to call 'the lost towns.' Our kind, ordinarily we cannot even find these places. Most of the time they're closed to us. But sometimes in spring, if you are meant to find them, you can follow the lilacs high into the mountains, and you will be allowed to enter."

"You're telling me I should walk up into the mountains, following lilac bushes?"

"It's what the crystal is telling you," Mariamme said. "I think that's why the dragon brought you here. He wants you to follow him to the lost towns, but he needs someone like me to say, 'Pack light but make sure you have warm clothing, comfortable shoes, and a good supply of food and water.'" She eyed Lucinda critically. "No velvet coats or blouses made of scarves. They're not practical. You should wear layers."

"You can stop worrying about my clothes because I'm not going," Lucinda said flatly. "I have a friend in the hospital, and I have to be here for him. I can't go traipsing off."

"The *cearu* needs your help," Mariamme said, getting to her feet. "That's why the dragon brought you here."

Her elbows on the table, Lucinda dropped her head into her hands and massaged her eyes. For a second she saw a river of dark red lines against her eyelids, which meant nothing, she reminded herself. Not everything meant something. Maybe the lilacs in the crystal were just a sign of spring, not marching orders.

She looked up at Mariamme. "You're asking me to choose helping someone I barely know over staying with my best friend, who may be dying. Besides, Alasdair didn't strike me as the helpless sort."

Mariamme began adjusting the wicks in the oil lamps so that they burned more brightly, and Lucinda realized that it must be getting dark outside. "I can't tell you what to do," Mariamme said, "only that you're being given a choice that's not given to most mortals."

"Why me?" The question seemed dumb even as she asked.

The woman's smile was sympathetic. "That's always the question, isn't it? Maybe it's enough that you know the *cearu*. They make few acquaintances among our kind."

"I think Alasdair probably is in danger," Lucinda admitted. Then she told Mariamme how both Alasdair and Sebastian had disappeared that day.

Mariamme's face blanched at the mention of the diamond pattern, and grew even paler as Lucinda told her about Sebastian changing into a fox. She began to rock and back and forth, almost as if she were keening.

"Can *you* help Alasdair?" Lucinda asked.

"I'd risk leaving my daughter an orphan." Mariamme rocked harder. "Forgive me for asking, but were you intimate with this fox?"

Lucinda nodded and voiced what she'd been telling herself ever since the mosaic closed up. "I think Sebastian's too weak now to cause any more trouble."

"A wounded animal is like a crazed, jagged blade, and the *cearu* is trapped with him," Mariamme disagreed, finally coming to a standstill.

"Well, how is my trekking after lilacs going to change that?" Lucinda asked in exasperation. "I can't read rocks or whatever it is Alasdair does. I was born out of favor, so if there are gods, none of them are going to help me. Alasdair works with things that . . . things I didn't even know existed," she explained. "Wherever it is he comes from, the people there are the ones who can help him."

Mariamme pursed her lips as she poured herself a cup of tea. Returning to the table, she sat down across from Lucinda. "If it were just a matter of summoning help from the lost towns, the dragon could do that on his own. He could probably fly there much faster if he weren't leading you."

The dragon flicked its pale green tail in agreement.

"Well, then that's what he should do," Lucinda said to them both. "I need to stay here with Tyrone."

The dragon shot Mariamme an alarmed look, and she said, "I understand your loyalty to your friend, and—"

Lucinda put a hand on her arm. "Honestly, the only thing I'm good at is knowing which fabrics will go together to make clothes that most people can't even afford. Find someone who can actually help Alasdair."

"And I understand that you still have a loyalty to the trickster," Mariamme continued.

"I don't—" Lucinda began to protest, but Mariamme waved away her objection, saying, "Hush, I know what it is when a man gets inside you. Why do you think I watch over my daughter like a hawk? Of course, you still care for him, and perhaps there is even a glimmer of goodness in him that is worthy of you. Nevertheless, you must know that there's something tearing at this city, something that will take many lives. The *cearu* is one of a very few beings who might be able to change that. That is why we must help him."

"He doesn't want to be a *cearu,*" Lucinda said. "He says he isn't any good at it."

"That's like the Lord Mayor saying he isn't any good at giving speeches when that's all he does."

Lucinda was getting tired of arguing with this dogged woman. "Look, I'll think about it," she said. "That's the best I can do for now. Why don't you give me your number, and I'll call you if I change my mind?"

"What number?"

"Your phone—" It suddenly occurred to Lucinda that Mariamme's apartment had no electric lights. What she'd assumed was some sort of half-refrigerator was actually an icebox. And the furniture, the dishes, Mariamme and her daughter's clothing—all of it belonged to an earlier time. Just as Sebastian's loft had. And the Lord Mayor? The city council hadn't had anyone answering to that title in over a hundred years.

Mariamme was looking at her with a baffled expression.

"What year is this?" Lucinda asked.

"Eighteen hundred and ninety-six," Mariamme replied in an any-fool-should-know tone.

"Oh, shit." Lucinda felt as though the floor were spinning beneath her chair, and her chair was spinning, too, in the opposite direction. She was afraid she was going to be sick. She gripped the edge of the table, as if it were her hold on reality.

"What's the matter? You look ill," Mariamme said in a worried tone.

"I need to get back to my friend," Lucinda said, managing to stand on shaky legs. None too steadily, she made her way through the flat, the dragon riding on her shoulder.

"What do I owe you?" she asked Mariamme at the door.

"Nothing," the woman told her. "Please, think about what you saw in the crystal."

"As if I could forget," Lucinda murmured.

Outside again, Lucinda looked around. It was dark out, and the streets were lit by the glow of gas lamps. She could smell wood and coal fires burning. She took the dragon from her shoulder and set it on her palm. "I need you to take me back to my own time," she told it. "You've got to get me back to Tyrone."

The dragon flew just far enough ahead of her that she could keep it in sight, leading her back to the footbridge. In the darkness the pale blue labradorite gave off a faint glow. "This is it, isn't it?" she asked. "The thing that connects the two different times."

The dragon didn't answer but kept moving. It crossed the bridge and led her down toward the Candra. Lucinda felt herself relax a little as she found herself on familiar streets. She kept up a quick pace, afraid that if she slowed, she'd have to think about all that had happened that day. She headed straight for Mercy Hospital. The dragon peeled off to the right two blocks before that, and for once she wasn't sorry to see it go.

THE BACK OF Tyrone's hospital bed had been raised. He sat up, his eyes open and blinking at Lucinda as she entered his room.

"Tyrone?"

"'Cinda." His voice was weak but unmistakable.

She approached his bed, grateful and disbelieving and frightened all at once. He looked reduced, as if there were very little of him left. "So you're back," she said, gently touching the hand that lay on top of the blankets. It was Tyrone's right hand, the hand he used to sketch.

"Seems that way."

Lucinda sat down, careful not to disrupt any of his tubes or wires. He was so thin, his skin stretched taut over his bones. "Do you hurt anywhere?" she asked.

"No. My body feels different—distant, as if I'm only remotely connected to it. I think, maybe it doesn't really belong to me anymore." He frowned. "How long have I been here?"

"Almost three weeks."

She had unbuttoned her coat when she entered the hospital. Now Tyrone looked her over with the appraising look he reserved for his trade. "You made that blouse last summer, didn't you? Those colors look good."

"You must be returning to life if you're noticing clothes," she teased him.

He turned his head away from her to stare out the window. "I'm just grateful to see colors like that again," he said quietly. "Don't mean any more than that."

An uneasy feeling began to wrap itself around her gut. "What do you mean? You know, the studio's still going, just waiting for you to come back. We filled the orders you had open and we've been taking new ones. Everyone and their mother wants to order that silk suit with the lace camisole."

"Back up a minute. *We?*"

"Gabrielle's been helping me out."

He turned back to her sharply. "What the hell is Gabrielle Oculara doing in my studio?" Lucinda was about to explain when he waved a tired hand at her. "Oh, never mind. It doesn't matter, anyway."

His first reaction was what she'd expected; like most designers, Tyrone had always been fiercely territorial about his work. It was his second reaction that seemed so blazingly wrong.

"What doesn't matter?" she asked carefully.

"Dessalines Productions. It's just a business, babe, mostly a place where I have both exercised and fed my overweening ego."

"Oh, Tyrone," she murmured, "what have they done to you in here?"

Tyrone's eyelids drifted down, narrowing his eyes to slits. "I almost died. Isn't that enough? Doesn't that entitle me to a few changes?"

"I suppose, but—"

"Lucinda, I need you to do me a favor. I want you to get ahold of de Brault."

"Your lawyer?"

"The same. Tell him I'm gonna close down the studio and I want him to draw up the necessary paperwork. And tell him to keep it simple. My head's been rearranged. Ain't no way I'm going to be able to penetrate his usual mumbo jumbo."

Lucinda drew in a sharp breath. "You don't know what you're saying. You can't dissolve—"

"I can't?" he asked mildly. "Why not?"

She reminded herself that he had just awakened from a coma, that he was bound to be scared and confused and feeling overwhelmed. She took his hand in hers. "Tyrone, I know this has all been traumatic. But it's temporary. You are going to get better. Don't go making decisions now when you're going to feel completely different a month from now."

"I won't, you know. Whatever comes next, couture is *not* going to be part of it." He gave her a wry, weary smile. "Could anyone choose a vocation that matters less? Tell me how you've been, 'Cinda," he said, his tone gentler. "You okay?"

"No, I am not okay. I feel like I've been in the middle of a long, drawn-out nervous breakdown ever since Carnival Night."

"Because of me?"

"You and other things," she admitted. "But you've been the worst of it. I can't bear the thought of losing you, Tyrone."

"You might have to," he said quietly. "None of us is anything more than temporary. You know that, girl. Hey, stop that," he said, and she realized she was crying.

Clumsily, she brushed away the tears. "I've been so worried about you. So scared—and so lonely."

Tyrone rested his head back on the pillow and closed his eyes but his fingers stroked the back of her hand. They had almost no weight. "Yeah, we've been quite a team, had some good times. It's hard now when we've got to go our separate ways."

"We don't," she insisted. "You're back now."

"Yeah, but something tells me it may not be for long. This feels like more of a reprieve than the real thing, babe."

"No," she said stubbornly. "You're conscious again and that means you can heal. You just need to get your strength back."

Tyrone cast her a sardonic glance. "You went and got yourself a medical degree while I was out?"

She gave him a prim smile. "Yes, you may now address me as Doctor, and I'll expect you to follow orders."

"I ain't that far gone."

For a while neither of them spoke. Tyrone's eyes were shut again, his breathing shallow. Lucinda watched him anxiously, wondering if he was simply resting or if he'd retreated back inside to wherever he'd been for the last three weeks.

"Dammit, Tyrone, are you dying on me?"

One eye opened. "You always were the soul of tact."

"Okay, maybe that was a little bald. But I can't help it. I've been going crazy for three weeks now. Please tell me the truth. Are you dying?"

"I don't know. All I know is something changed inside me and I can't go back to what was."

She nodded, trying to take that in and not attach too much hope to it. "Was it being stabbed?"

"No. That was the least of it. . . . What happened to the boy?"

"I don't know. I don't think he's in the city anymore. But it's you I'm worried about. Tell me what happened. Tell me what you mean when you say something changed inside you."

"Give me a sip from that water glass there," Tyrone said. Lucinda complied then counted her breaths so that she wouldn't implode as Tyrone sipped the water excruciatingly slowly.

At last he handed her the glass and said, "What nearly killed me was Ilyap'a. I had a god inside me. For just a split second and it was too much. I should have died then. Maybe it's happening right now. He might just be playing with me, prolonging things. I swear, it feels like he left something inside me."

"They said you had burns inside," she remembered, "like someone struck by lightning."

"No shit." He gave her a sad smile. "Why'd you let me go out in that crazy-ass costume?"

"You think I could have stopped you?"

The smile faded. "Probably not. But I wish someone had tried."

She took his hand. "It isn't fair."

"Oh, I think it's spectacular and fitting. Killed by the arrogance of my own designs. What more could a designer want? You make sure they write up my obituary that way, hear?"

She clutched his hand tightly. "No more morbid humor. I can't take it."

Tyrone snorted. "Oh, stop sounding like such a delicate flower. You can take a hell of a lot more than that. And you will," he went on, his voice a whisper. "Don't let it scare you, 'Cinda."

She was crying again. He patted her hand absently. "Maybe it won't be so bad. Feels sort of like Ilyap'a started something with me Carnival Night and now he's just going to finish it, collect what's his. And there's a kind of completion in that. Like taking the last stitch in a dress."

A nurse came in then, took his temperature and blood pressure and listened to his heart.

"How is he?" Lucinda asked anxiously.

The nurse peered down at her through horn-rimmed bifocals. "He's doing as well as can be expected but he needs rest. I suggest you wind up this visit."

Lucinda waited until the nurse had gone then she leaned down and kissed Tyrone's forehead. His skin was smooth and cool. "I'm not giving up on you," she told him quietly. "So don't you give up either."

"Not if I can help it," he promised.

ALASDAIR HELD HIMSELF motionless, letting his eyes adjust to the dim light of the shaft or cave or whatever it was that he was in. He stood on a stairway, carved from the city's bedrock and spiraling down into the earth. He supposed he should be alarmed by having the entrance above him sealed, but mostly what he felt was intense curiosity. Besides, he was surrounded by rock, which he always found to be a comfort.

Candles set in the crevices of the rock walls lit the stairway, their flames steady in the still, damp air. Given the effects of the dragon's poison, he rather doubted that Sebastian had been the one to light them.

So who else is down here? he wondered, feeling a shiver of trepidation. Each candle was embedded in a thick bed of congealed wax; candles had been lit here for a very long time.

He began to descend the stairway, admiring its workmanship. Someone had cut the stairs evenly then polished the limestone until it was smooth and gave off a dull white gleam in the candlelight. There were no other carvings or designs; whoever had fashioned the staircase had known its beauty would come from the perfection of its angles and surfaces, its purity from simplicity.

Alasdair queried the limestone about its purpose and got back only the idea of an entrance, with no response at all as to who had carved it or what it led to. Continuing down, he looked for tunnels, passageways, shafts that the fox might have crawled into, and saw only more stairs. They were steep and high, as if carved for beings with much longer legs, but he found a steady if uneven rhythm for descent. He saw no sign of the fox or the man it had been.

The farther he descended, the cooler the air became. The sounds of the city above him were muffled at first then faint; then they were gone. The stone that surrounded him was cold to the touch and smelled of damp and the candles' burning wax.

At great length the curving stair ended in a long tunnel, also illuminated by candles. He proceeded down the tunnel, feeling the muscles along his spine tighten as he saw that the walls here were etched with symbols. There was no obvious pattern to them. The symbols themselves were strange—shapes that suggested nothing, lines that seemed to have no reason for being grouped together. He didn't recognize any of them. Yet as he moved deeper into the tunnel, he began to identify images he thought of as old friends: the spiral, the diamond, the vine, sun and moon and stars, the lotus, the heart. Alasdair breathed easier. Malachy had called on whatever was down here and it had responded but perhaps whatever that entity was, was not in itself malign.

The smell of incense became stronger. Sounds began to filter into the tunnel from somewhere far ahead, voices low and rhythmic and melodic. He went toward them, certain that the sound of his footsteps would be carried back to the singers.

At last the tunnel opened into a great room with a high, vaulted ceiling and an altar at the front of the chamber. Hundreds of candles wedged into the rough walls illuminated the room. They revealed rows of hooded figures, seated on limestone benches, facing the altar and chanting. At first Alasdair wasn't sure what or whom they were singing to. The altar itself featured none of the usual religious icons. Two silver candelabras flanked a large heart carved from the cave's limestone and polished to a soft sheen.

Niches had been carved into the arch above the altar, a statue carefully set in each one. Like the symbols, many of these figures were familiar. Alasdair recognized a blue-green glazed Isis suckling the infant Horus; Demeter with her sheaf of wheat; a dancing black Kali, wearing her necklace of severed heads; Kwan-Yin carved from jade, carrying her flask of nectar; Lilith with her taloned feet and her owl familiars; a winged and horned Inanna; the warrior Durga, each of her many arms bearing a weapon; the ocean goddess Yemaya; Potnia, the Lady of the Labyrinth; a terra-cotta Ixchel at her loom. *The mothers, light and dark.* Some of the statues were rough, almost crude representations. The Virgin Mary was made from a block of wood, her painted features faded and chipped. Others, like Green Tara, who appeared to be carved from a single large emerald, were worked so finely as to be almost beyond mortal artistry. Even his people, given the gift of working with the stones, couldn't have brought forth an image like that. There were, Alasdair remembered, stories of sacred images that simply appeared, not crafted by human hands but formed by the energies themselves.

His fixed his attention on the singers, wondering if one of them might be concealing the fox. Slowly, he moved up the center aisle of the chapel. One of the cloaked figures turned to face him. She was ancient, her face deeply grooved, her eyes, dark and sharp and authoritative.

Alasdair inclined his head and pressed his palms together in a gesture of respect. It had no effect on her at all. The others were still singing and he sensed that to interrupt or ask questions would be a violation, and yet he hadn't come this far to lose Sebastian.

He walked toward the altar, stopping at each bench to gaze at the faces of the singers. They were all women, as diverse as the statues of the divinities. He guessed that some had traveled here from Africa, others from the Mediterranean, still others from Asia, the Andes, the Pacific Islands. To a one, the women seemed ancient, even by the standards of his people, as if they'd been down here for centuries. None of them seemed to be concealing a wounded fox.

The sharp-eyed woman pointed to an open space on one of the benches, indicating that he should sit. He did, his senses still searching for the trickster. There must be other chambers down here, he thought, and yet he could detect no doors in the stone. Had Sebastian somehow gained the power to shape-shift into a cloaked crone? Could he be sitting here among them?

Baffled, Alasdair began to pay attention to the chants. He had a smattering of languages and enough proficiency in four or five to know that these were the names of the goddesses, repeated in patterns, along with words of praise and welcome. When he recognized a chant to Durga, praising the Mother of the World, he joined the song.

It had been a very long time since he'd prayed this way. He'd forgotten the power residing in the names of the deities. The names themselves were ancient, their origins mysterious. They contained secrets as old as the stars. It was said that by chanting them again and again it was possible to open oneself to the gods, to feel their power lift the heart.

Alasdair joined the chants and gradually the sense of dread that had clamped itself around him when he first found the plaza loosened and fell away, as if someone had removed a confining cloak from him.

The chant quickened. The women were on their feet, swaying and clapping. A few took drums stowed beneath the benches and pushed the beat faster, harder. The sharp-eyed one turned back to Alasdair and motioned that he should get to his feet, too.

Alasdair did as he was bid. He stayed with it, following along as they sang to the different goddesses, trying to wrap his tongue around the words he didn't understand. And he began to notice that the image of whomever they sang to responded to the chants. The bronze Sita seemed to give off a glow as they sang her praises. The features on the worn, wooden Virgin became clearer, as if refreshing the original colors from paints that were no longer there. He swore he saw the jade Kwan-Yin lift her vial of golden nectar and pour it over the altar like a benediction. And the limestone heart at the very front of the altar took on a luminous sheen and seemed to become the focal point of the room, as if the songs were all about the heart and it was the heart that connected them all.

The women began to dance, mostly in place. Spry for such elders, they seemed immune to weariness. The songs went on and on, and the women didn't stop or even break between them to catch their breath. It occurred to Alasdair that they had been chanting like this for hours, perhaps days, and they would continue for many more. They were singing now about sinking into the arms of the goddess, surrendering to her embrace, feeling her healing touch.

The chant shifted again, this time to one insistent syllable repeated over and over. Alasdair tried to identify the name of a goddess in it but the sound was unfamiliar to him. Yet he sensed that they had come to the most important part of the ritual. This was what it was all building to.

He was suddenly conscious of something stirring above the altar. It was one of the icons, a goddess he'd never seen before. She was made of pure gold, her face blending African and Asian features into an expression of sublime serenity. Like Tara, she sat with one leg bent, one extended, as if to step into action. Her legs, torso, and head were as still as any statue. But one wrist moved backward and forward in time to the chant, the goddess's golden bracelets clicking softly against each other.

That syllable again, more insistent, and as if in response to its call, the goddess stretched, tilting her head to one side then gracefully arching her back.

And Alasdair understood that it was a seed syllable they were chanting. That one syllable contained the vibration and the essence of this goddess. It was calling her into being.

He watched transfixed as she woke fully, carefully extending each limb, and then stepped down effortlessly onto the floor of the chapel, her body growing to the size of an adult human as she moved. She gazed at the congregation with such beneficence that Alasdair found himself struggling to hold back tears. This then was always the promise of the gods, that they could send into you the pure, undiluted love that all mortals seemed to crave from the day of birth.

Now Alasdair, too, was intently chanting the syllable, wanting her presence, wanting her touch, desperately wanting her to stay.

A high-pitched keening rose above the sound of the chant, and the song broke suddenly and cleanly as a limb snapped from a tree. The chapel was silent except for the high, anguished cry.

Alasdair felt the hairs on his arm stand straight up as he recognized the fox's voice. From somewhere in the shadows near the front of the altar Malachy dragged his mangled form toward the goddess. He still had a man's face on a fox's body but his furred limbs were so grotesquely swollen that he could barely move them. The dragon's poison was killing him.

He was slow and tormented and completely vulnerable. *It would be a mercy to break his neck,* Alasdair thought, and yet in this place in the presence of the goddess, it would also be sacrilege. Here he could not interfere.

Malachy only had eyes for the goddess, and she gazed at him with an infinite compassion marked by the gods' equally infinite remove. She waited as he torturously made his way to her.

As clearly as if it were now being sung, Alasdair remembered the chant that had preceded the seed syllable. An invocation to the goddess, an image of sinking into her arms, surrendering to her embrace, feeling her healing touch. And as he heard it in his own mind Malachy manifested it.

Stunned, Alasdair watched the goddess's golden arms open to the trickster. Malachy crawled into her lap and she folded her arms around him and touched the top of his head with her lips. She stroked him, as one would stroke a beloved child. Her hand passed from the tips of his furred ears over the skin of his still-human face, and the face changed, became wholly fox again. Nose and lips to snout and muzzle, skin now sheathed in rich, russet fur. The torment left Malachy's eyes; the fox's blue eyes gleamed content and healthy. The goddess ran her hands over its swollen limbs and they returned to their own slender, graceful vulpine proportions.

She rose to her feet with the fox still curled in her arms and she sang her own seed syllable and golden light streamed out of her. She was so radiant that Alasdair had to shield his eyes. But he saw the air bend around the goddess and the fox, making them flicker and shimmer until their forms blurred into one then finally dissolved in a spiral of red and gold light.

The priestesses took up the chants again, happily sending up praise to other divinities. Alasdair sat down heavily on the bench, torn by an odd grief. He already missed the goddess who had come for Malachy. All that light that had been in her eyes, that had streamed out of her limbs . . . he felt bereft and, despite the presence of the women around him, achingly alone now that it was gone.

As for Malachy, Alasdair didn't know what to think. Was he disappointed that the trickster hadn't died of the dragon's poison? A little, though he had been so rigorously schooled in not wishing harm to any creature that acknowledging such a thought felt like a betrayal. In truth, he had felt some relief at seeing the goddess heal the fox—if that was what she'd done. Had she taken him somewhere—to her temple, perhaps? Had she returned him to Arcato? Or had Malachy's life just ended? Perhaps she was carrying him to the spirit world. That thought gave Alasdair pause. The last thing he needed was a visit from Malachy's spirit.

Alasdair had no idea of what to do next. With a slight bow to the women, he got up. He retraced his steps through the tunnel and up the steep, candlelit stair to the top step. Above him was a layer of extremely solid bedrock. He couldn't even see a trace of a line where it had once split. He closed his eyes, envisioning what had happened: The fox had pressed the sign of the diamond within diamond and the earth had opened. He'd said, "Close now!" and it had closed. It couldn't truly be that simple, could it?

Alasdair looked around for the diamonds or any other symbol that might be carved near the top of the stairway. There were none. "Open now," he tried, and when that didn't work, a more sarcastic, "Open, sesame!" which proved equally ineffective.

He sat down on the top step, forcing his mind to a place of calm. He placed a hand on the limestone wall beside him, tuning himself to whatever it would tell him.

Entry. Protection. It was here as entry to the chapel and to protect it.

Fair enough. Will you open for me?

He felt a stirring of resistance and the repeated message, *Protection.* It wasn't going to open for him.

I understand but then why did you open for the trickster?

Old debt, it replied, and then he couldn't get anything more out of it.

Not seeing any other option, he started back down. He paused in the tunnel, searching for the symbol of diamond within diamond, but the only diamonds carved into the wall were quite singular. He pressed on a few of those, as well as a number of the other signs, with no results.

In the chapel the chanting was still going strong, the women's voices resonating off the walls and filling the room. His space on the bench was still open; he took his seat. As far as he knew, he was trapped down here with an eternal goddess choir. With a sigh of resignation he joined a chant to Isis. There were probably worse things to do with his life than sing to the mothers.

LUCINDA TOOK A long, hot bath, brewed a cup of oolong tea, doctored it with whiskey, lemon, and honey, and stood by her window, drinking the tea and willing herself not think about Sebastian. Voices floated up from the flats below, a would-be opera singer practicing her scales, giggling teenagers, an older couple who couldn't seem to talk without haranguing each other. They all sounded so normal and safe, qualities she'd once scorned which she now thought she'd give almost anything for.

The charcoal night sky flared bright turquoise. She stepped out onto the balcony, not quite believing what she'd seen. The air was cool and moist. She held out a hand. No rain falling yet, no thunder. She could see patches of clouds floating like smoky grey brushstrokes over the Candra. The bright turquoise light burst through again, sheet lightning.

Lucinda whirled back into the flat and reached for the phone, punching in the number for the nurses' station on Tyrone's floor.

It rang seven times then a brisk voice answered. Lucinda didn't give the woman a chance to identify herself before breaking in, "I'm calling about Tyrone Dessalines. How is he?"

"Who's this?" the nurse asked suspiciously.

"You know who this is," Lucinda snapped. "I've only been there every day. I'm his friend. I—"

"You were here earlier this evening?"

"Yes, and he was sitting up and—"

"He's had a bit of a setback," the nurse said. "He's lost consciousness again."

"Another coma?" She was gripping the phone so hard, the plastic of the receiver protested with a squeaking sound.

"The doctors haven't said. We've moved him to Intensive Care, though."

Lucinda hung up, her body rigid with fear. *Ilyap'a,* she thought. *It's his lightning. He's come back for Tyrone.*

She was bone-tired and her brain didn't seem to be working terribly well, but she knew she had to do something quickly. She didn't know how much time Tyrone had left. Maybe just until the end of the storm.

A glimmer of light caught her eye. The diamond. She'd carelessly left it on her side table when she undressed. Alasdair had said it was powerful— powerful enough to heal Tyrone? No, she was certain that Alasdair would have told her if it could. He might be cold and oblique but he wasn't cruel. He knew how much she was hurting for Tyrone. He wouldn't have kept that from her.

Lucinda grabbed the diamond and brought it out to the balcony. She offered it to the sky on her open palm. "I know you gave Tyrone a diamond. Maybe you want one in exchange? Here, take this one. It's bigger and worth more and—" She felt like an idiot talking to Ilyap'a. You couldn't be born out of favor and expect the gods to listen.

But some people could get through to the gods. Alasdair and Sebastian, both of them gone. She remembered Sebastian telling her the story of the monk who interceded with Madana for him. What she needed was to find someone who could intercede with Ilyap'a for Tyrone.

She dressed quickly, paying no attention to what she put on, then flipped through the phone directory. Alasdair had said Ilyap'a was an Incan god from Peru, so all she had to do was find an Incan or Peruvian—what? She scanned for the words "Inca" and "Peru." No luck. She wracked her mind frantically. Sebastian had said that the monk who helped him was a true holy man, and so Madana was bound to listen. She hadn't gone near a church in years—they brought back too many memories of the religion she'd so resented as a child—but maybe a priest would do the trick.

She found the address of a church with a Spanish name. *Nuestra Señora de Lourdes* was close to the waterfront but a good ways from her neighborhood, on the edge of the industrial area of the city. Lucinda girded herself with a stiff shot of whiskey, locked up the flat, and set out, walking so fast she had a side stitch within minutes. She walked faster, passing a line of tired-looking people waiting at a streetcar stop. The wind swept off the river, whipping her hair into her eyes. She could hear thunder now, rumbling in the distance. Ilyap'a's storm was building. She pushed herself into a lope, her hands pressed against the ache in her side.

She was winded by the time she reached the church, a massive, forbidding Gothic structure that took up most of a block. Breathing hard, she pulled on the iron handle of one of the great double doors. It didn't budge. She yanked again then pulled and pushed on the other door. "Shit," she muttered. "Isn't this supposed to be a sanctuary? Don't they know they're not supposed to lock it?" It was only then that it occurred to her that it was nearly ten at night, and this was not the safest of neighborhoods. Of course, the place was locked.

Lucinda felt her mouth starting to quiver. She bit down on the insides of her cheeks, not allowing herself to cry. She didn't have a backup plan; she didn't know where else to go. She remembered that churches had priests, and they often lived in buildings close to the church. She walked around to the back of the church and was rewarded by the sight of a much smaller Gothic building with a sign on the front that said RECTORY.

Without hesitation, Lucinda began to pound on the rectory's wooden door. "Hello! Is anyone there? Please, I have to talk to a priest," she called out. "Will someone please answer the door?" She silently congratulated herself on not having said, "the damn door." She knocked again, making the rosette window at the top of the door rattle in its lead frame.

She was so immersed in the rhythm of her pounding that she nearly fell forward when the door opened a few inches—as far as the chain that held it would allow.

Two dark eyes peered out at her. *"Sí?"*

She spoke in a rush, terrified he would shut the door before hearing her out. "Please, I need your help. I need you to send up prayers to Ilyap'a for my friend Tyrone because he's dying, and I think Ilyap'a is the one killing him and—"

"Un momento," the man said. He slid the chain off the door and opened it.

He was a priest, all right, complete with black robe, white collar, and a large cross hanging on his chest. "Come in," he said, and led her to a parlor of sorts. "Please." He indicated a high-backed Gothic chair facing an empty hearth. "Have a seat."

The room smelled of frankincense and brought back memories of Lucinda's first and only Communion: the stiff, white frilly dress; the patent leather shoes that pinched; the unremarkable cracker that tasted dry, not godly; the tormented Christ on the cross, overseeing it all. She'd always been uncomfortable in churches. Obviously, growing up hadn't changed that, she thought, as she sat down.

The priest took the chair directly across from her. He was a tall, gaunt man with thinning black hair and dark, sad eyes. "Now what's the trouble?" he asked kindly.

"Do you know the Incan god Ilyap'a?" she asked. "He's from Peru."

The priest blinked. "There is only one God."

"Okay," she said, thinking it best not to offend him. "But there's also an Incan storm—spirit—named Ilyap'a, and if you don't believe me, take a look outside because he's the one who's causing that turquoise lightning. And he's about to kill my friend. That's why I need your help."

The priest leaned toward her and said, "Have you been drinking, my child?"

"What?" She stared at him, then realized. "Oh. I had a shot of whiskey. I'm not drunk, though. Please. I need you to pray to Ilyap'a for my friend Tyrone."

The priest shook his head, looking even sadder than he had at the start of their conversation. "That's impossible. I can't pray to a false god. It would be a sacrilege and it wouldn't do you or your friend any good." To her surprise he got down on his knees. "Kneel beside me," he said. "Together we'll pray to Jesus Christ and the Virgin Mary and ask for their protection."

"You're not listening." Lucinda tried to keep the hysteria out of her voice, but she could almost feel Tyrone's life slipping away from him. Frantically, she tried to think of an argument that would persuade a priest. "It can't be a sin to help someone," she reasoned. "All I'm asking you to do is send up one prayer to Ilyap'a and ask him to spare Tyrone. Why can't you do that?"

"Kneel beside me, child. We'll pray together."

"I can't." She glanced around, saw the poker by the fireplace and actually considered threatening the priest with it, she was so desperate, but she couldn't imagine that prayer extorted by physical threat would do much good.

"*Pater nostra . . .*" the priest began.

Lucinda didn't stay to hear the rest. She ripped past him, out of the rectory and out onto the streets. A steady rain was falling, covering the sidewalks with a dark sheen. She pressed back toward the center of the city, toward the hospital, the rain soaking into her wool shawl and melding with her tears. This section of Arcato was nearly completely dark. There were no stores open, no lights from apartments or lofts, only the occasional street lamp or a security light over a factory door. The turquoise lightning flashed erratically, as if Ilyap'a were taunting her: *I'm here, in your city, and when I leave I take Tyrone with me.*

Countless blocks later, she came to an all-night bodega. She went in, feeling absurdly grateful for the bright lights and respite from the rain. First, she called the hospital and was told that there had been no change in Tyrone's condition since her last call. Next, she bought herself a chocolate bar and after that, a notebook and a pen, oranges and candles and a bunch of tiger lilies. She left the oranges and candles and flowers as offerings at the various shrines she passed, along with notes, asking whomever passed by to petition the storm god for Tyrone. When she happened on a phone booth strung with rosaries made of colored glass beads she left offerings there, too.

As dawn broke she found herself back on the waterfront. She sat down on one of the empty benches, realizing that the rain and lightning had stopped. The storm was over. Her heart started to hammer with dread. Did that mean it had taken Tyrone's life with it?

She was suddenly so sick with fear she couldn't move. Was not knowing worse than knowing? At least this way she could believe that he was still alive. She stared at the Candra with glazed eyes until she realized she couldn't bear the uncertainty.

Lucinda found another phone booth. She could feel her pulse jumping in her fingertips as she dialed the nurses' station. Her stomach hurt and her voice cracked when she asked about Tyrone. She nearly fell out of the phone booth with relief when the answering nurse said, "There's been no change in his condition." *That's good news,* she told herself, still trembling as she hung up. That meant there was a glimmer of hope; at least Ilyap'a hadn't finished the job.

Still shaky, she returned to the bench and sat watching the sun touch the river with a soft silvery sheen. A lone tug slipped across the water, barely breaking the surface. The river and its city were quiet. All was deceptively calm. Lucinda appreciated the semblance of serenity, even knowing it for a lie. It soothed her, gave her a place to balance the small comfort of knowing that she had done what she could against the bleaker fact that she had not been able to find anyone to make the god listen.

Her hands were cold. She thrust them into the pockets of her pants and as she did she heard a faint tapping sound. She glanced down at the ground. Nothing except the usual stray gum wrappers and cigarette butts. The pigeons weren't up yet. She heard it again. The sound was coming from the bench beside her.

A small, compact, faceted rock was bouncing itself against the surface of the bench with what struck her as both determination and impatience. Tentatively, Lucinda reached out a hand to it. The rock launched itself higher and landed on her open palm where it rolled once then came to what seemed to be a grateful rest. It was a rough, deep-red crystal of sorts, the red so dark it was almost black. Though it wasn't transparent, there was a glitter to its surface that made Lucinda think it could be polished to some kind of gem-like quality. She counted twelve facets. Given that he was trapped somewhere beneath the city, she knew it was impossible, and yet all Lucinda could think was that Alasdair had sent the stone.

Alasdair, she thought. He had known exactly who Ilyap'a was. He seemed to be familiar with the gods the way she was familiar with nearly everyone in Arcato who worked in fashion. For the first time she wondered about the place he had come from. Was everyone there like him? If she actually did what Mariamme counseled and went to these lost towns, would she find someone who could help Tyrone, someone who could unlock whatever it was she and Tyrone seemed to be caught in? She rolled the crystal along her palm. *And what do you do?* she asked it silently.

The river's damp air seeped through the fibers of her shawl. She was chilled and exhausted and so delirious with desperation that she had a completely insane idea. She would go to the lost towns of the mountains and try to find Alasdair or someone like him. She would do whatever it was she was meant to do to help him—in exchange for getting Ilyap'a to give Tyrone's life back. Now all she needed was for that poisonous little dragon to show up. . . .

ALASDAIR GAVE HIMSELF to the chants, allowing himself to be blessedly unconscious of both time and his circumstances. He sang to Tara and Yemaya and Ixchel and Tiamat and Pele. He heard his voice deepen and become resonant as the chants moved through him. He heard himself going hoarse. He sang until he couldn't sing anymore and then without voice or sound continued to sing. The chants were inside him now, so deep in his heart that he could feel them sending blood and light through his body. They soothed his raw throat and frayed nerves. They gave him strength in the places where he was sure he had lost it for good. They worked on his heart, healing what was trampled and embittered and worn. And although the chants didn't lift the sorrow he carried, they made it seem bearable again.

He became aware of one of his life stones, the lapis lazuli, calling to him. He took the grainy blue stone from the deerskin pouch. The stone was darker, its blue deeper than usual, as if it were immersed in water. He felt its essence stirring and saw the golden veins of pyrite that ran through it gleaming in the candlelight. He looked up at the icons above the shrine, his eyes going first to the Virgin Mary. He knew that artists used to grind lapis lazuli to make the ultramarine paints that were used for the Virgin's robes; celestial blue *was* lapis. The wooden figure of Mary, though, was not what the stone was responding to.

What is it? he asked the life stone. *What's calling you?*

The lapis danced in his hand, and what he read inside it urged him toward an icon he hadn't paid much attention to. It was a wooden carving of a woman, kneeling with hands on knees, only instead of a woman's face she had a cat's head. He knew it couldn't be either of the Egyptian feline goddesses—Bastet or the lion-headed Sekhmet. The body was too voluptuous, its posture too relaxed and comfortable. This goddess seemed almost welcoming.

And the lapis in his hand wanted to go to her. Alasdair approached the altar, relieved that none of the singers seemed disturbed by this. Their chants went on, unbroken, almost pushing him along.

The cat goddess kneeled in a niche above the right side of the polished stone heart. Alasdair stood beneath her, wondering where she was from, whether her nature was cruel or compassionate or that peculiar divine blend that managed to be both simultaneously. The stone in his hand moved again; it was growing warmer.

Give me to her, it told him.

A selfish pang went through him. One didn't give a gift to a goddess and expect to get it back. It would be the second of his life stones he was losing. The lapis was the most ancient of the stones he carried. It was the stone that had opened him to the rhythms of the sacred texts of his people. He counted on it for awareness, for its help in understanding the more arcane messages that came his way, for protection from spectral attacks. Most of all, it had always quenched the fires of his anger, allowing him to see clearly. Without the moonstone's tenderness and the lapis to lend him its clarity, the best parts of himself would be gone.

The stone was restless in his hand. It wanted to be with the cat goddess, and Alasdair understood that its gifts were no longer meant for him.

"Thank you," he told it. "I've been fortunate to have you with me for so long."

He set the chunk of lapis in front of the wooden figure, and the kneeling cat goddess began to sway. At first the movement was infinitesimal, so subtle he couldn't be sure he wasn't imagining it. The movement increased, became more pronounced, until she was rocking side to side, back and forth, hard and fast and unrelenting. Until she fell from the niche, knocking into the life stone in front of her so that it, too, tumbled into the air.

Instinctively, Alasdair stepped forward and reached out to catch the lapis lazuli. Instead the cat goddess fell into his hands with the hard, heavy thunk of stone. He stared down at her with disbelief. She was no longer made of wood but of the deep blue lapis lazuli. And his life stone was gone.

Ancient, gnarled hands gently lifted the statue from him, and he looked up to see the crone who had bade him sit. She cradled the lapis cat goddess with a mother's tenderness and a devotee's reverence, singing to it all the while. Alasdair had the distinct sense that she was sending the chant into it, giving it some vital pulse. Only when the chant ended did she set the statue back into the niche it had fallen from. Then she touched Alasdair's arm with one hand and with the other gestured to the side of the altar.

There, in the wall that had been solid limestone, was an open door. It was a small door, no higher than his waist, made of thick timbers with ornate, beautifully worked brass hinges. It was, he saw, wide enough for someone of his size to pass through.

The crone touched him between his shoulder blades, gently nudging him toward it.

Alasdair inclined his head in thanks, took a last look at the chapel of the mothers, and with their songs following him, he bent and eased himself through the door.

He found himself in another candlelit tunnel, this one leading upward. He turned back one last time and saw the small door swing shut. The latch clicked into place and the door seemed to pull inward, into the surrounding limestone. "Oh, no," Alasdair murmured as the small door became smaller and smaller, until it disappeared altogether, leaving only a solid white wall.

Seeing he had no choice, Alasdair began to make his way through the passageway. It was just high and wide enough for him to travel on hands and knees. *Crawling out of the mother,* he thought. *How appropriate.*

PART 4

The Lost Towns

"And we follow weeks of lilacs up from the prairie
Into lost towns of the mountains . . ."

—THOMAS HORNSBY FERRIL,
"Waltz Against the Mountains"

Thirteen

LUCINDA WAS TEARING through her closet, searching for sturdy shoes. Sleek leather ankle boots, strappy sandals on pencil-thin heels, white ballet flats, teal satin pumps, bright red slides . . . didn't she have anything that was even remotely sturdy?

She sat back on her heels with a sigh. Packing. This was supposed to be the easy part, and here she was frantic because she didn't have the right things to wear. It seemed everything she owned was either tight and fitted or had long, sweeping skirts, and nearly all of it was made of silk or velvet or lace. She simply didn't have the wardrobe to pull off this practical look. It was almost a shame she'd incinerated the clothing that she'd borrowed from Sebastian.

She did have a roomy backpack left over from her student days; it was made of gold lamé but would have to do. She settled on two pairs of jeans, even though both were nearly threadbare, a thick sea-green sweater that her mother had once knit, a pale blue button-down cotton shirt that Tyrone once discarded as too boring, a wool scarf and her silk scarf, her wool shawl, and a jacket. As for shoes—she made one last dive into her closet and came up with a pair of lace-up suede boots with crepe soles that had been given to her by a boyfriend and never worn.

Now what? She tried to remember what Mariamme told her. She had to bring plenty of water, enough food to keep her. She realized then that she had no idea of how long this hike might take. Was she packing for a day, a week, a month? Did she need a tent, a sleeping bag?

Lucinda gave a little laugh of hysteria. This venture was beyond absurd. She was about to take off into the mountains with absolutely no idea of where she was going or how long she'd be gone in search of mysterious lost towns that were so well lost they never appeared on any map. Her destination was a place that most of the population couldn't even find. And she had no guarantee that these hidden places would open for her.

And she was actually hoping this insane quest would save Tyrone.

Shaking her head in disgust, she began to empty the gold backpack. Whether or not Tyrone woke up again, she would stay in Arcato and be by his side. At the very least she would see that he didn't die alone.

She took the two scarves from the pack to the Victorian coat stand, where she kept them. The dragon was perched at the very top of the stand, looking like an elegant jade ornament.

"Forget it," she said, draping the silk scarf over one of the upper hooks. "I just talked myself out of this craziness. I'm not letting you talk me back into it."

The dragon took flight, grabbed the silk scarf in its tiny talons, and dropped it back on top of the pack. Lucinda grabbed it. "I said no." Moving with great deliberation, she draped both scarves on the coat stand. "Don't even think about pulling that again," she told the dragon.

The dragon was no longer interested in scarves. He made for the top of her dresser where she'd put the dark-red stone that she found by waterfront. Grasping it in his talons, he flew it over to the pack.

This caught her interest. "So you approve of that rock?" she asked, curiously. She had had no real sense of whether it was a good, bad, or neutral object. The dragon nudged it with his snout so that it slid into one of the inner pockets of the pack. Lucinda felt a bit of relief. The fact that the dragon thought she should have the red rock with her seemed to bode well for—well, something.

Next the dragon went for the diamond on her side table, adding that to the pack as well.

"Give it up," Lucinda said with more weariness than irritation. "I can't leave Tyrone. You know that."

The dragon beat its wings against the cloisonné box containing the moonstone, obviously indicating that it should be the next item packed.

Lucinda sat cross-legged on the bed, waiting patiently for the dragon to stop its version of arguing with her.

The dragon, never less than perceptive, left the cloisonné box and came to perch on her knee. It gazed at her intently and she found herself holding out a hand, touching the smooth, leathery scales along its neck. "What if I don't go with you?" she said. "Will I ever see you again?"

The dragon flitted up and lit on her outstretched palm. And as it touched her she saw a vision of something she had seen once before in a dream. She was walking along a mountain ridge, following a vein of pale green jade. She followed the line of jade to the peak and looked out into a mountain valley. Cut into the rocks were the dwellings she'd seen before, only this time she saw more detail. They had towers and balconies and windows. Flowering vines climbed their walls. Terraced trails ran between them, with gardens and streams of clear spring water edging the terraces.

The dragon lifted itself from her palm and the vision was gone as quickly as it had come. "The lost towns," Lucinda said. "They're real."

The dragon hovered in front of her, its brilliant topaz eyes holding hers.

She took a sharp, aching breath. "Is there someone there who can help Tyrone?"

The dragon gave no answer. Perhaps it didn't like to make promises.

"Will they at least talk to Ilyap'a for me?"

At this the dragon inclined its head.

She got up, stuffed the cloisonné box in the pack, changed into the sturdier pair of jeans and her mother's thick sweater, then wedged the rest of the clothing into the pack along with a toothbrush and a hairbrush, and zipped it closed. She put a quick call in to the hospital, checking on Tyrone's still unchanged condition, and another to Gabrielle's machine, saying she'd be gone for few days.

She grabbed the wool scarf from the coat stand, looped it around her neck, and turned to the dragon again. "Okay," she said, "first we see Tyrone, then we go."

ALASDAIR HAD NO idea of how long he traveled through the tunnel. It went on and on, always wide enough for him to crawl and occasionally high enough to squat. It was certainly roomy enough to stretch out and rest, which he did periodically simply because his wrists and knees, unaccustomed to crawling, ached. His long blue robe, he found, was not a terribly practical garment for this pursuit. He wore holes in the area above his knees, and whenever he tried to kirtle it up, it would eventually fall down again and he'd wind up tearing the hem. Often, he thought of taking if off altogether but the tunnel was chilly and humid and he didn't want to add being cold to his general state of discomfort.

Like the stairway, the tunnel had been smoothly carved, almost as if a giant worm had spun through the limestone, boring it clean. There were no rough edges to the rock, just a sameness that he thought might drive him mad. Only the angle of the passageway occasionally changed. Although it always went upward, there were stretches that were steep, others that were more gradual, and still others where it nearly leveled out. Alasdair could not imagine where it was leading, but he had crawled so long that he was sure he was well beyond Arcato. The most curious aspect of it was that precisely one turn of the tunnel after he left the mothers' chapel, there were no longer candles lighting the way. Rather the light seemed to emanate from the stone itself, with different stretches of the tunnel glowing more intensely than others. The lighting was sometimes helpful, sometimes perverse. It dimmed on a particularly precipitous section of the passage, where he found himself gripping the smooth rock with his fingertips and toes, trying desperately not to slide down.

He kept traveling. When his knees bled he tore off swatches of the troublesome blue robe and fashioned bandages. Every so often he would find a pool of fresh water, fed by some sort of underground creek, he guessed, and he would stop to drink and clean himself. He craved food, of course, and yet his people could do without it far longer than most and he found that the water was enough to allow him to keep moving, to go wherever it was the mothers meant for him to be. They, after all, had healed him with their songs then opened the door to this, so he trusted there was some sort of intent guiding him. He wished very badly that he could stand up.

THE DRAGON DID not like the idea of leaving for the lost towns at once. It flew to the pillow on Lucinda's bed repeatedly until she finally understood that it wanted her to sleep for the night before setting off. Surrendering to the little reptile's persistence, she undressed and got into bed but sleep was impossible. Images danced before her closed eyelids like a lurid chorus line from a play she'd never wanted to attend: Tyrone in his damned Carnival costume, Madana on his boat, Michael clutching the diamond, Alasdair's cool grey gaze, Mariamme and her crystal ball, and the agonized half-man half-fox that was Sebastian as he fled into the earth. She wound up staring wide-eyed at the ceiling, and even then she saw them.

She felt only relief when dawn finally broke. She was out of bed, dressed, and out of the flat within the hour, the dragon riding comfortably on her collarbone. After a brief, wrenching visit with an unconscious Tyrone, Lucinda bought water, fruit, nuts, crackers, and a few wedges of cheese in a grocery store, and set off on her journey. Whether or not she actually found the lost towns, it felt good to be doing something, to have a mission other than watching Tyrone weaken, and she took pleasure in pitting herself against the steep streets as she made her way to the very top of the city. There weren't many people out at this hour. Most of those Lucinda encountered were straggling out of the tenements, heading down toward the waterfront for work. Almost no one headed uphill. She passed the abandoned factory with a shudder then veered off into streets lined with warehouses and industrial lofts which gave off the hum of well-greased machinery. At last the big industrial buildings tapered off to a few blocks of smaller, unkempt commercial buildings—offices for leasing companies and parts manufacturers—punctuated by the occasional bar, betting parlor, or newsstand.

Beyond these streets the city stopped. Lucinda looked around her in astonishment. She had spent her entire life in the city and others connected to it by the river. She'd never ventured to this place where there were no buildings or lights or people. The sky around her was open, the air cooler. In front of her the foothills rose green and broad, sloping up to steeper brown mountain peaks. Lucinda felt her first jolt of dismay since her visit to the hospital. The land spreading out in front of her was thick with brush, a wild tangle of shrubs and young trees and briars. "How am I supposed to walk through that?" she murmured.

The dragon emerged from its nap beneath her collar to fly just ahead of her. She followed it to what appeared to be a narrow footpath cutting through the brush. She hesitated, seeing thorny branches jutting into the path.

With a shrug, Lucinda started after the dragon, up into the foothills. Half a dozen steps later she was skidding downhill. She scrambled to her feet, peering at the ground. The top layer of soil seemed to be a sheet of tiny, round pebbles, all of which started rolling downhill as soon as she set foot on them. She resumed walking, concentrating on placing her feet firmly and carefully and pushing aside the thorny branches that seemed determined to grab hold of her. She had a sinking feeling that this journey was going to take a hell of a lot longer than she'd imagined.

The sun rose higher in the sky, the trail widened, and the day warmed. Lucinda took off first her shawl then her jacket. All around her birds were singing madly. It was the only noise other than her own footsteps, and that spooked her a little. She missed the city's constant rush and thrum. But she wasn't entirely alone. As she moved higher, the trees grew taller and thicker and she caught glimpses of rabbits and chipmunks and colorful lizards sunning themselves on the rocks. Wildflowers grew in small, brilliant clumps of yellow, orange, pink, and blue. And the higher they went, the happier the dragon became. His scales gleamed a deeper green and the thin line of his mouth curved up in what looked like a smile. This nature stuff really wasn't so bad, she decided.

As the day wore on, the wind became stronger, sweeping down from the peaks in gusts that would rake the land and rattle the trees and then suddenly go still. The wind made the walking harder, forcing her to lean forward into it, like a speed skater, but it also carried a familiar scent. "Lilacs!" she cried, and hurried forward, overtaking the dragon for the first time.

There were, indeed, wild lilacs, growing on the side of the trail, their scent sweet and heady with the promise of spring. Lucinda stood admiring a tall, wild-looking bush, covered with blooms. She reached up to break off a stem of blossoms. A frantic look from the dragon stopped her. "Okay, I won't," she said, wondering if there were other taboos in this place.

She climbed higher along the trail, nearly intoxicated with the scent of the pale purple flowers. The dragon stayed with her, sharing her lunch and leading her to a clear stream where she refilled her water bottle. As they left the foothills and traveled into the mountains the vegetation began to thin out. There were fewer trees and they were scrawnier with more space between them. It was easier to see animals now and she caught glimpses of rabbits and mice. A snake coiled on the trail gave her a start. There was no way to detour around it—large boulders on either side of the path made circling around impossible—so she sat down to wait. The dragon took care of the matter, hovering in front of the snake, its topaz eyes flashing a warning. The snake's tongue darted out, inquiring, then the serpent slithered off the trail and Lucinda and the dragon continued on.

The shadows grew longer, the air cooler yet, and the ground rockier. She was finding it required more effort to catch her breath. Still lilacs edged the trail, and Lucinda kept walking until the sun was nearly down and she could barely see. She hadn't thought to bring a light of any sort.

The moon rose, a thin silver crescent giving off just enough light for her to see the dragon who led her to another stream, where she drank and washed her face. As she fed the dragon bits of cheese, clouds gathered and hid the moon. Lucinda had never known a night so dark. Far below she could see Arcato's lights winking up, surprisingly golden. The city seemed so far away, so small and frail. She wondered if any of the lights were Mercy Hospital, if one of them might be Tyrone's room. She sent him a silent message: begging him to hang on, promising to get him help. At last, she settled down for the night, using her pack for a pillow and the thick wool shawl for a blanket. When she fell asleep the dragon was curled up beside her, one clawed foot resting lightly on her outstretched hand.

The clouds vanished before dawn, and the second day was much like the first except that her feet were hurting and her food was running out and her muscles were protesting all the strenuous exercise. The knowledge that Tyrone might not have much time left hovered over her, kindling a flame of anxiety that seemed to singe her nerve endings. Where were the lost towns and when would they open to her? When would she find someone who could intercede with Ilyap'a? She kept walking, rationing her water and food, now certain that she hadn't taken nearly enough.

Early on the third morning Lucinda passed the last of the lilacs. The slopes above her were green with scraggly evergreens, most of them growing at a downhill angle, bent by the wind. All of the plant life here seemed smaller and sparser and somehow twisted, and even when the sun was straight overhead, it never seemed to fully warm the air. And the air was thinner; she was working harder for every breath. Still, the sky was bright blue, brighter than she'd ever seen it, and the scent of the evergreens filled her lungs with something like hope.

By noon she was painfully aware of blisters on her heels, others on her toes, and the fact that she had no bandages or salves. "I packed like an imbecile. Why didn't you tell me I needed first-aid supplies?" Lucinda asked the dragon after stopping to examine her bleeding feet.

The dragon flitted off and returned a short time later with some sticky leaves, which when applied to the blisters eased the pain and drew the swelling. "Thank you," she told it, knowing it was doing the best it could. But for the first time she was starting to be afraid that they wouldn't get to wherever they were going. She simply wasn't going to last; she didn't have that kind of endurance or strength. *It was my choice to do this,* she reminded herself stoically, and she kept climbing though the blisters were raw and her back and shoulders ached from the weight of the pack and her skin was wind-chapped and sunburnt and she would have given just about anything for a long, hot bath.

On the afternoon of the fourth day, with her breath coming shallow and fast, Lucinda glanced up to see that ahead of her there were almost no trees and the ground was dusted with a thin layer of snow. In the sunnier spots where the snow had melted, she saw short, scrubby green plants and lichen covering the rocks in shades of bright green and deep red. She was above the tree line.

Lower down on the mountain she'd walked a trail through the brush. Here there was no trail at all, just an openness to the landscape that she found disorienting and disturbing; it meant she was now completely dependent on the dragon for direction. She was chilled and sore, her food was nearly gone, and she was having a hard time getting enough air into her lungs. Every step was a matter of concentration, of telling herself to take one more step, and then another and another. Just staying upright was exhausting.

The dragon kept urging her on, never straying far. She'd come to think of him as both friend and tormentor. If it weren't for him, she probably would have folded up to die two days ago. But he kept pushing her on, prodding her with affection and unrelenting stubbornness. He wouldn't let her give up.

As dusk fell on her fifth night in the mountains Lucinda began to sway on her feet. All her muscles were cramping and something tight in her chest made it hurt to breathe. She'd finished the last of her food the night before. Aside from some bitter greens the dragon had brought her that morning, she'd had nothing but water all day. Now a throbbing band of pain behind her forehead attested to the fact that it had been hours since her last meal. And despite having no food in her stomach, she felt nauseated.

She turned to look for the dragon. It was time to tell him that she just couldn't go farther. She'd tried her best but she could no longer hold herself upright. Even the dragon would have to agree it was time to quit.

She glanced around futilely. Naturally, when she wanted him, the infernal creature was nowhere to be found. Lucinda staggered over to the nearest boulder and sank to the ground. She managed to get her pack off her shoulders, then leaned back against the rock with her eyes closed. *I'm sorry, Tyrone,* she thought. She was too dehydrated to cry.

The perverse sound of someone whistling distracted her from her misery. She was losing everything, and some fool was up here whistling as if he hadn't a care in the world.

Lucinda was too spent to be wary. "Who's there?" she demanded in a raspy voice.

She heard the sound of footsteps approaching from the other side of the boulder. She didn't have enough strength to turn around and see who it was. So she just waited, eyes closed, wondering if she had enough courage to ask whomever it was to please to slit her throat so she could die quickly.

She heard the footsteps come to a halt. Then an uncertain voice said, "Are you all right?"

Lucinda opened her eyes. He was young and gawky, maybe eighteen at most, with a sprinkling of acne across his forehead. He wore thick, horn-rimmed glasses on his thin face, a down jacket over jeans, truly sturdy hiking boots, and an enormous pack. His lank brown hair was greasy and he smelled of sweat.

"You're alive," he said, sounding relieved.

"Just barely," she agreed.

He immediately knelt beside her, shed his pack, and took a water bottle from one of its many pockets. He offered it to her and she drank deeply.

"You don't look so good," he observed.

"Thanks." She handed the water bottle back to him.

"No, I mean—" He hesitated, flustered. "Are you hurt or—"

"I have a blazing headache. You wouldn't happen to have any painkillers, would you?"

"Sure." He got to work unzipping pockets, untying brightly colored stuff sacks, and rummaging through watertight containers. She was actually hoping for morphine but when he fished out two aspirin, she took them gratefully.

His eyes fell on her suede boots. The left one sported a gash in the side, ripped open by a thorn, and the suede upper on the right boot, having gotten soaked in one of the mountain streams, was peeling away from the sole.

"Those aren't real hiking boots," he pointed out.

"Look," she said, "I came up here in a hurry. And I didn't prepare very well, and I'm in trouble now and I don't need you to tell me—" She bit off her words. The kid looked like he was about to burst into tears. "I'm sorry," she said, finding it hard to be gracious when she had so little strength left. "I know you're just trying to help, and I . . . I appreciate that."

"I only meant that if your shoes aren't good, you might have blisters." He spoke in a rush, nervous and eager. "I can tape your shoes so they don't rip more. And I have a first-aid kit. So—do you have blisters?"

"Yes, I have blisters!" she snapped, but he seemed relieved at the information and instantly set to work removing her shoes and socks and treating the open wounds.

He was surprisingly gentle. Lucinda barely flinched as he cleaned the raw flesh and applied salve and bandages. Equally gently, he patched her shoes with wide metallic tape.

"What's your name?" she asked as he handed her shoes back to her.

"Elden," he said, blushing furiously. "It's a family name."

"I'm Lucinda."

"Are you hungry?" he asked, rummaging through the pack again.

"Not very." It was true, she realized. Even though it had been too long since her last meal and her stomach felt empty, she wasn't craving food.

"You've got altitude sickness," he told her. "But you should try to eat anyway." He promptly set up and lit a little camp stove, boiled a pot of water, dissolved a packet of dried something into it, then handed her what she thought was the most delicious soup she'd ever tasted. "Miso soup," he told her proudly. "It's made with dried soybean curd and chives."

She ate slowly but steadily, savoring the salty warmth of the soup. Elden didn't eat but sent her furtive looks. His cheeks reddened in the light from the stove when he realized she'd noticed, and he immediately began fussing with his pack—until his gaze strayed to her again. She almost laughed. It was clear he couldn't help it. He was so awkward and self-conscious and completely teenage that he made her feel very old.

"So, Elden," she said, feeling a little stronger. "What are you doing so far from civilization?"

"It's what I do," he explained. "I hike all over."

"You a masochist?"

"No, I hike because up here it's just you and the mountain and—" He stopped himself. "I sound like a dork, don't I?"

"No," she lied, not wanting to hurt him.

"I should have had some cool, clever comeback," he said, sounding completely dejected.

"Elden, you're fine exactly the way you are," Lucinda said, hating herself for lying yet again. He was clearly miserable being the way he was.

"You really think so?" he asked.

"Yeah, I do." This time it came a little easier because a smile was playing at the corners of his mouth, and she found she liked making him smile. "I think you're not a usual type of person and that in itself is cool. And the fact that you can survive up here is amazing."

He moved a little closer to her. "Sometimes I get lonely when I'm back-packing," he admitted.

"Not surprising."

"I guess. I wasn't counting on that when I took off by myself. Everything else, I prepared for."

"You're very organized," she said, still trying to shore up his shaky ego. "I mean, you seem to have everything you need in that pack."

"*Almost* everything I need." He gazed at her again with a heat in his eyes that was all too familiar, and she instantly felt herself drawing back from him. Great. Not only was she stuck on a mountain with a teenager but a horny teenager. Then again, the terms were almost synonymous. She should have seen it coming.

"So, where are you headed?" he asked, making an obvious but unsuccessful effort to sound casual. "Are you lost? Because I know these mountains really well and could probably guide you to—"

He broke off as she looked around for the dragon. The little serpent was making itself scarce. "I'm not lost," she said. "Just badly prepared."

"That's why I should come with you."

"Why in the world would you want to do that?"

He blushed again so deeply that she was afraid he was going to burst the blood vessels in his face. "You're—you look nice," he blurted out in an agony of awkwardness. "I mean, maybe you would like hiking with me and we could—"

"Shit," she said. She had to cut this one off fast. "Listen, Elden," she said, "it's sweet of you to want to help me but I'm not a terribly nice person. I used to eat guys like you for breakfast." At the alarmed look on his face, she added, "Metaphorically, of course."

"What did you do to them?" he asked, sounding genuinely curious.

"I mean, I've gone through more men than I can count, and I don't have much sympathy for any of them. I mean, *do not* for a minute think that there's anything in me you want. I'm a bitch even when I'm not half-dead, and walking up this mountain has put me in a truly vile mood. *Comprende?*"

He nodded so obediently she felt sorry for him.

"I really appreciate everything you've done," she finished. "But it's best if we go our separate ways." She hesitated, already regretting what she was about to say. "So, since you're the one who's more capable of moving right now, I think you have to be the one to leave. Now, please."

"No," he said. "If I leave, you won't survive the night, and I can't live with that on my conscience—"

"Fuck your conscience—"

"I'm staying," he said. "I'll see you to wherever it is you're going, then I won't bother you again. But you can't make me leave."

"You'd be surprised," she muttered, but she was secretly glad he wasn't leaving her to the mountain and didn't argue further.

Elden proved to be a camping whiz. Using a tarp and several expandable metal poles that he pulled from his pack, he set up a windbreak that sheltered them from the worst of the mountain gusts. He fed her dried beef jerky that didn't taste half-bad, brewed her a soothing herbal tea, and covered her with a reflective blanket before she went to sleep. It was the first night she slept on the mountain that she didn't wake up cold. It was also the first night that she slept without the dragon.

Just after sunrise Lucinda woke to find Elden lacing up his hiking boots. "I'll be right back," he promised. Quick and agile, he scrambled down the rocks and disappeared into a stand of trees.

"Dragon," she called softly when she was sure the boy was out of hearing range. "Are you there?"

The dragon appeared almost at once, lighting on top of a boulder.

"Well?" she asked it. "Can I trust him?"

The dragon didn't exactly say yes; neither did it look unduly alarmed at the prospect.

"Will you stay and show yourself to him?"

The dragon's topaz eyes narrowed, which she took to be a no.

That gave her a panicky feeling. "I don't think I can get rid of him. Not without killing him, at least. And how am I supposed to find the way without you?"

The dragon didn't seem to be concerned about the question.

"You want me to tell him I'm searching for the lost towns?"

To her amazement the dragon lifted one tiny pale green shoulder in a shrug, then flew off into the distance. Lucinda would have screamed with frustration if she hadn't been sure she would have to explain the scream to Elden.

It wasn't long before Elden returned, looking disgustingly cheerful and carrying a sturdy branch that was nearly as tall as Lucinda.

"What's that for?" she asked, as he began to strip the bark from it with a pocketknife.

"You. It's going to be your walking stick." There was so much eager puppy in his voice, she half-expected to see a tail wagging happily from the back of his khakis.

"Like a crutch?" she asked suspiciously.

"Like a walking stick," he told her. "It will make it easier as we go higher."

"How do you know I'm going up and not down?"

"I saw your tracks," he told her matter-of-factly. "How are you feeling this morning?"

"A little better," she admitted.

He nodded, still using his knife to smooth the surface of the walking stick. "Your body is acclimating to the altitude, getting used to having fewer oxygen molecules in the air. We'll have some breakfast and when you're ready, we'll get going."

Breakfast consisted of more jerky and a powder added to water that became a vitamin-infused fruit juice. Afterward, Lucinda stood up gingerly and walked around a bit while Elden watched her. "The nausea and headache are gone," she reported. "And I don't feel dizzy anymore."

He nodded. "Let me check your bandages and we can try going a little farther. If you feel worse, we come back down."

"Wait a minute. When did you start making the rules—"

"Irrational behavior is symptomatic of not enough oxygen reaching your brain," he overrode her. "So don't act irrational or I'll be forced to save your life and carry you back down the mountain."

"Screw you," she muttered, but she said it without venom, and Elden ignored it as he changed the bandages on her feet. He carefully repacked his pack, fastening its many compartments with drawstrings and zippers, then turned to her expectantly.

Wonderful, she thought, *he's waiting for me to lead the way.* Lucinda stared at the long, rocky slope above them and fervently wished the dragon would show his scaly little self. Couldn't he at least have left her a sign of some sort?

Elden shouldered the heavy pack. "It might be a good idea if you told me where we're heading now."

"I don't know," Lucinda replied, then added, "Actually, I can't talk about it."

"Why not?"

"Because . . . let's just say, there's something I have to find and it's personal."

"Cool," he told her.

"What's cool?" He was making her feel extremely old again.

"You not being able to talk about it. It's just like in all these books. You know, quest stories where—"

"It's not like that at all."

"Okay." He was quiet for a moment but she could see she hadn't managed to dampen his enthusiasm. "Question: How will we know if we're going in the right direction?"

"Up is a start," she said. She thought about what they could look for. "You said you know these mountains. Have you ever seen a place where there's a ridge of jade in the rocks?"

"That's a long way from here," he said, his voice unusually quiet.

His tone sent a shiver through her. "It's where I have to go."

He nodded. "All right then. That's where we'll go."

Although the *we* grated, her brain was still clear enough to know that she needed him. So she shouldered the gold lamé pack, which he seemed to find very humorous, and they set off.

It didn't take long to realize that the walking stick was making walking easier, and there was a certain comfort in Elden's goofy, young presence. As he'd said, she was getting acclimated to the elevation. Her breathing was deeper and more even, and the overwhelming exhaustion was gone. Despite her worries over Tyrone, Lucinda felt her spirits lifting.

"So, have you ever been in alpine tundra before?" Elden asked. "We're at about nine thousand feet," he went on, not giving her a chance to answer. "You can tell by the plants—we're still seeing sedge and grasses and some herbs. Actually, you lucked out. Normally, in spring this part of the mountain would be covered in snow but it was a dry year and you're on the southern face of the mountain. If you were up here in summer, there'd be all sorts of flowers—bluebells and dryads, even forget-me-nots. You ought to come back up then."

She gave him a look implying that he ought to be in a mental institution.

"Fact: The word tundra comes from Lapland," he went on, oblivious. "It means 'land of no trees.' It's a pretty fragile ecosystem. You need to be careful where you walk because just stepping on one of these little plants can kill it."

She noticed then that he was carefully stepping on bare rock face, avoiding the low spongy greenery that clung to the patches of dirt. She made an effort to follow in his footsteps.

"You won't see too many animals up here," he continued. "Mostly birds and little burrowing rodents, like voles, though occasionally one of the larger animals wanders up from below. And soon we may see snow. . . ."

She found that Elden made moderately interesting company. He knew a lot of facts—about hiking, camping, and nearly every creature and plant on the mountain—and seemed eager to share all of them. An eagle winged above them, and Elden treated Lucinda to a detailed discourse on the nesting habits of eagles and how they differed from hawks.

At one point she couldn't resist asking, "How long has it been since you've had someone else to talk to?"

"You haven't been doing any of the talking," he said, looking embarrassed. "It's my fault. My mother always said I communicated too much."

That struck her as a weird thing for any mother to say; then again, mothers were weird. "It's just that being in a conversation is hard for me right now," she explained.

"You want me to shut up?"

"No," she said honestly. She was finding that his chatter made the walking go faster. He didn't seem to mind if she didn't pay strict attention, so she felt free to drop in and out of his monologues, picking up bizarre pieces of information whenever she chose to listen.

For dinner that night he made them each another soup from his packets of dried ingredients and accompanied that with a dessert of roasted cashews and raisins.

"I shouldn't be eating your food," Lucinda said, feeling guilty. "You're going to wind up with nothing to eat because of me."

"No worry," he told her. "I can always scrounge up something. I've even eaten bugs when I had to. Grasshoppers aren't really bad, you know, and some varieties of beetles are tolerable if you like crunchy." Lucinda made a face and he smiled. "It won't come to that," he promised. "We'll be fine."

The *we* word again. Again she let it go unchallenged. He was so chipper she started to censor her innate cynicism, not wanting to hurt him. It was bizarre to feel so protective of someone she barely knew. It had to be because he was such a puppy—or because he was protecting her from cold and exposure and starvation. He even knew where the vein of jade was—he pointed it out to her on a topographic map—and from what she could tell with her limited map-reading skills, he seemed to have them traveling in the right direction.

She hoped so, anyway. She hadn't seen the dragon since it flew off the night before, and she couldn't help feeling betrayed. It was the dragon, after all, who had been so insistent that she go on this crazy quest, and now it was gone, as if it had lost interest in her with the appearance of Elden. She thought about her last conversation with the little serpent. He had seemed . . . ambivalent about the boy. He hadn't seemed afraid, and he certainly didn't consider Elden the kind of threat necessitating poison green powder. But the dragon hadn't stayed around to introduce himself either.

When darkness fell they bedded down, separately but comfortably, on spongy moss, sheltered from the wind by a granite ledge. It was dark of the moon, and the stars blazed so bright in the black sky that there was a crazy moment when Lucinda thought she might actually reach up and touch one.

That night she fell asleep to the sound of Elden playing a wooden pipe, its sound high and sweet and ancient.

THE SEVENTH DAY of Lucinda's journey brought them to a wide, sweeping plateau that rolled out toward jagged mountain peaks in the distance. They were in a world of pure rock—fragments, slabs, and chunks of granite covered the ground, which was more granite. The debris was talus, Elden explained, broken off from the peaks by freezing and thawing. They were very much alone; the raptors they'd seen farther down the mountain were gone. "They don't fly this high," Elden told her. "No prey for them up here."

A dry wind soared across the plain, sending elongated white clouds skimming across the sky, their shadows slipping so quickly across the ridges that it seemed as if the mountains themselves were moving.

"This is wild," Elden shouted over the wind. "There's always snow up here at this time of year—up to your knees or deeper. It should be all white. I've never seen it dry like this in the spring. I mean, this almost counts as summer."

"You've got a weird concept of summer," Lucinda shouted back. To her the snow frosting the boulders and the ice sheeting the granite slabs were plenty wintry. And the wind was cutting through her layers of wool so easily that it felt as if she had nothing more than lace between her skin and the freezing air. She was already shivering violently.

Elden dug into his pack and found a hooded down jacket much like his own. "Here, put this over your jacket and shawl."

"I can't believe you carry two of these," she muttered.

He heard her despite the wind. "Never know when you'll need a spare. I carry extra underwear, socks, and gloves, too." He handed her a pair of gloves made from a thick, fleecy fiber.

Lucinda grinned at him and donned the gloves and jacket, all of which were cozily windproof. Leaning into the wind, they pushed on. She wasn't sure if it was the altitude or the light, but everything on the plateau had a slightly surreal clarity that made her feel as if her vision had suddenly widened and sharpened. She saw every angle and gradation of color in the rock, was aware of the distinct shape of each cloud as it raced past. If Elden was experiencing the same thing, he never mentioned it. They kept walking, stopping only to eat.

"I feel like we've reached the top of the world," Lucinda said as Elden offered her a packet of nuts and dried apricots.

"Actually, you can go much higher," he told her. "In the Arctic, the tundra gets much colder and the temperatures drop to—"

"Hush," she said, putting a finger over his lips.

She felt a jolt go through him the instant she did. She snatched her hand away. "Sorry."

"You shouldn't have touched me," he said, the accusation curiously without emotion. "Not when you know I want you and you don't want me."

She flinched, unprepared for that much honesty. "You're right. It wasn't fair. I apologize."

"Why did you touch me?"

She wished he would just let it go but felt obliged to answer. "I don't know. I just did it. I didn't think about it."

"So mostly I bore you but you tolerate me because I'm useful and because you feel a little sorry for me. Does that cover it?"

"No, I—"

"No lies," he interrupted. "I won't have lies from you."

Although there was no menace or threat in his manner, there was an aggression in it that unnerved her, made her wish she could run from him the way she'd run from so many others. She saw that she had misread him, underestimated him—or perhaps overestimated his kindness. He was no different than any other man. She was dependent on him and he knew that gave him the power. And yet she could see no way out of it for now. "How much longer till we reach the jade?" she asked.

"Not that long." He inclined his head toward the snowcapped mountain peaks. "We just have to cross this plateau."

"And then you'll turn back?"

"If you still want me to." Beneath the thick lenses his dark eyes went liquid with hope.

"Please. Don't look at me that way."

"What way?"

"Like, I'm going to soften up and fall in love with you. I won't. It's not possible."

"A great many things are possible," he said. Just six words but his tone was so unlike his normal pitch of goofy puppy mixed with pompous professor that the hairs along the back of her neck stood straight up.

"Who are you?" she asked uneasily.

"Here's a hint." He sat down on a boulder, reached into one of his jacket's inner pockets, took out a small, roundish, dark-red stone and began tossing it from one gloved hand to the other.

"That's mine," she said, recognizing the stone that had found her by the river, the one the dragon had wanted her to take.

"It's mine now. Besides, how can it be yours? You don't even know what it is."

"It's a . . . ruby."

He gave her a look of pure derision.

"Okay, a garnet then."

"Good guess. Almandine, if you want to be precise. Note the twelve perfect sides. Only pyrite, diamonds, and garnets manifest in rhombic dodecahedrons, which are part of the cubic system and that, you should know, has the highest order of symmetry in all the crystal systems." Elden was back in professorial mode, providing more information than anyone could possibly want, and the familiar pedantry relaxed her. Until she heard his next words: "It was given to you because of your loyalty to your friend, Tyrone. Garnets have always honored bonds of the heart. And there was a special bonus for you and your friend." As he held the stone Lucinda thought she saw light flickering inside it.

"Lightning," he said. "There's a flare of lightning inside each garnet and, as like works on like, some garnets have the power to calm storms. That's why he survived that last sending from Ilyap'a. This garnet is why Tyrone is still alive."

She had never told him about Tyrone.

Lucinda stared at the pimply teenage boy for a moment of sickening disbelief then scrambled backward, putting distance between them. "You're another one of them," she said.

"Them who?"

"Like, Alasdair. You're a *cearu*."

"Hardly," he said softly. "I'm not half so tormented—or so kind."

"Why did you take the garnet?"

"Because it was there. Because sometimes stealing is the only way to get what you need."

Maybe it was the effect of clouds racing across the sky, but she was suddenly so dizzy she could no longer stand upright. She sat down heavily, feeling snow through the seat of her jeans. "You're a fox?"

That seemed to amuse him. One side of his mouth quirked up. "No, but the foxes and coyotes and ravens of this world are dear to me, and a great many are under my protection." He rubbed at his chin. She could see a faint shadow there, barely stubble. "They're not the only ones," he added.

She didn't understand at all. She felt dense and slow, as though the final piece to a puzzle had been handed to her and she couldn't even begin to fit it into its place.

The boy got to his feet. "Elden means 'old friend,' " he told her.

She shook her head. "You're not my old friend."

"I'm not?" He took off his glasses.

She forced herself back onto her feet, backed farther away from him. "Who are you?"

Elden changed before her eyes. The acne disappeared and the planes of his face became sharper, his features longer and finer. He looked as if an artist with the gift of exaggeration had sculpted him, working the clay to make him simultaneously more and less real, more and less human. And the artist had added a glaze: A silvery, reflective sheen glinted from his eyes and skin. She could still see the boy Elden in his features but the gawkiness was gone, and in its place was something beautiful and terrifying.

"Guess," he said indulgently. "Or are you still planning to eat me for breakfast?"

She winced, wondering how many spectacularly stupid things she'd said in the last few days.

"Do you have any idea of how arrogant you are?" he asked.

"I was afraid I'd hurt you. I didn't want to do that."

"Have I mentioned your sensitivity and compassion?"

"Go fuck yourself." It was out of her mouth before she could stop herself, and she wasn't even sure why, except maybe because she'd never been able to say it to Madana.

He didn't reply. His silvery gaze held hers until her sudden fury was gone, leaving a draining fear in its place.

"That was probably the worst thing I could say, wasn't it?"

"It was honest."

Lucinda took off the gloves and rubbed at her eyes. This strange vision in front of her did not vanish or alter. *I've already blown it,* she told herself. She didn't know who or what he was but at this point what did she have to lose? "You're not Ilyap'a, right?"

"You're quick. Nothing gets past you."

She ignored his mockery. "Well, if you know about Tyrone, then you know I need someone to intercede with Ilyap'a. Is there any way I could persuade you to talk to him?"

His beautiful mouth quirked the way Elden's had. "I'm sure there is, but it wouldn't do you much good. Ilyap'a and I have never gotten along. You're going to have to find someone else for that task."

She got to her feet and slid the gold lamé pack onto her shoulders. It was battered now, the shiny gold finish cracked and stained. "Then I'm exactly where I was before I met you," she said.

"Not quite," he pointed out. "Or would you like me to return you to that boulder where you sank down to die, two days' walk down the mountain?"

She shut her eyes, sure she was playing this all wrong but having no idea of what she ought to be doing instead. Honesty seemed to be all she had. She opened her eyes again. "I told you I was grateful for your help. That hasn't changed."

"And in return for my generous help, you'll do what?"

"I wasn't aware there was a price," she said stiffly.

"There's always a price. All transactions are commerce."

I used to know that, she thought. *When did I forget—when Sebastian came into my life and made me believe it could be otherwise?* "What's the price for Tyrone's life then?"

"I can't tell you. That one's not in my hands. We're highly specialized, you know."

She ran her bare hand through her hair. It was filthy, she realized, her mind latching onto the completely irrelevant detail, as it often did when her life was coming apart. She forced her thoughts back to a detail that mattered. "And the price for all the help you gave me—?"

"Haven't decided yet. I could force you to listen to years of Elden's endless prattle but I think we'd both get bored."

"I liked Elden," she said. "I thought he was a good person."

"More the fool you," he said softly.

"Obviously." She waited, wondering what he was capable of. Was he going to strike her dead? Would he punish her for her arrogance the way Ilyap'a had punished Tyrone? When he did nothing but watch her with those unreadable silver eyes, she decided that the next move was hers. "Can I have the garnet back?" she asked.

He laughed, the sound so deep she could feel it echoing in the rocks beneath her feet. "You think thieves return what they've stolen? I wouldn't have taken you for such a naïf."

"Fine." She had to get away, away from the searing contempt in his eyes and away from the power that radiated from every atom of his being. Lucinda couldn't bear standing there waiting for him to pass judgment on her. She turned her back on him, took a firm grasp of the walking stick, and started toward the mountain peaks. She could feel his eyes on her back as she worked her way across the plateau.

"Are you sure you want to do that?" His voice, though mocking, was distant, an echo carried on the wind.

She glanced back, frightened. *Now I'm going to pay the price for his help,* she thought, but he was gone, as if the wind had taken him.

Lucinda focused her attention on the plain of treacherous ice-covered rocks that lay before her. The wind roared down from the peaks, pushing against her so hard that the only way she could move was hunched over, almost crouching. She slid and scrambled and occasionally fell as she fought her way toward the peaks. Her face and extremities went numb. Though the walking stick somehow remained in her grasp, she couldn't feel her hand curled around it at all. Perhaps, she thought disinterestedly, it was frozen to the glove.

When the daylight began to fade and the violet light of dusk cloaked the snow-covered peaks Lucinda found herself breathless and dizzy again. More altitude sickness. She knew she ought to retreat to a lower elevation, but she could no longer walk that far. She sank down on the lee side of a boulder, thinking ruefully that instead of asking for the return of the garnet, she should have asked for food. Not that she was hungry but she was aware that there was very little left inside her. Every bit of energy, even fear, was gone. All that remained was the vague nonsensical notion that she ought to be pressing on.

Willing herself forward, Lucinda stumbled to her feet, managed a few more steps, then dropped to the icy rock beneath her. Too numb to feel pain, she reached for the walking stick and tried to pull herself up. She didn't even have enough strength to lift herself into a squat. And so she understood exactly what price Elden had decided to extract from her and how it would be paid. She had come all this way to die. There was no surviving this. An old memory surfaced: sitting snug in her room when she was a kid, reading a book about Arctic explorers. Even then she had known they were crazy and stupid and doomed. Now she tried to remember: What urged them on in the first place? Certainly not a fortune-teller or a jade dragon. Cursing the dragon and sending love to Tyrone, she surrendered to the mountain and sank into a place where there were neither thoughts nor sensations nor dreams.

Fourteen

WHAT ALASDAIR HAD come to think of as the Endless and Monotonous Tunnel changed without warning. Having learned to crawl at a quick clip, he rounded the corner of a stretch of steep burrow and abruptly found himself in a high-ceilinged room. The walls were a water-stained brown, which was wonderfully refreshing after the glowing tunnel.

Even more wonderful, there was plenty of room to stand. Very slowly, hands gripping one of the walls, Alasdair pulled himself to an upright position. His body screamed in protest and he instantly dropped back down to hands and knees. *Never again will I take standing upright for granted,* he thought.

Hunched over, he waited for the pain to ease. Then he began the slow process of stretching his cramped muscles. Upper and lower back, neck and shoulders, hips and groin, arms and legs—every part of his body seemed contracted and locked. He kept at it, gently and patiently reacquainting himself with muscle, ligament, tendon, and bone until at last he was able to get to his feet, keep his balance, and walk, albeit stiffly.

He started as something on the wall beside him moved. It was only a salamander, reddish-brown and no bigger than his thumb, the first living creature he'd seen since leaving the chapel. He nearly scooped it up to kiss it.

While the tunnel had felt like a passage carved by—he still couldn't imagine what—this cave was natural. Translucent white stalactites hung from the ceiling. As he had when he was a boy, he saw other forms in them: a bear's claws, a sickle moon, a cow's udders, a skeletal finger, and what might be either a long, spiraling seashell or a unicorn's horn. For once he didn't read the stones or ask them for information. He had no need to. The vibration emanating from them was as familiar as his own heartbeat. He did consider turning back in the direction from which he'd come, but he couldn't quite face the idea of going back into the endless tunnel. Besides, he didn't think the mothers would allow it. Resigned and half-laughing at his inability to direct his own fate, he began to seek a way out of the cave.

He heard the sound of running water. On the opposite side of the cavern, beneath a travertine shelf, he saw a dark line of water. He drank from the underground stream, not minding the slightly metallic taste, then followed the stream into another room, which opened into another where the stream flowed into a crystal-clear pool. This time he stripped off his ragged blue robe and bathed himself. The water was too cold to stay in longer than it took to quickly rinse his body, but the luxury of being immersed in water was delicious. He dressed again and entered the next cavern, skirting a large colony of sleeping bats, the floor beneath them thick with guano. That was a good sign. If there were live bats in here, then he couldn't be too far from an exit.

Two more large caverns—one filled with rounded limestone pillars, the second edged with undulating stone drapery—and then a final chamber, smaller and brighter than the others. It was interesting, he reflected, that he had never been in these particular caverns before. He'd thought he knew every nook and cranny in these mountains.

Alasdair stepped into the last of the rooms and rubbed his eyes. He'd fully expected to have to climb his way out of the cave and that it would be a long arduous process, but directly in front of him was an archway leading out. Sunlight and the smell of fresh air rushed through.

Can it really be this easy? he wondered.

Alasdair stepped out of the cave and blinked at the sunshine pouring down on a rock-strewn hillside and on a familiar, burly figure, sitting comfortably, across from the cave's entrance. The man nodded to him and said in an amused voice, "I've been wondering when you'd work your way back."

SOMETHING SMALL AND cool and moist pressed against Lucinda's outstretched hand. Lucinda forced one eye open. She was lying on smooth, brown rock bisected by a ridge of translucent, pale green rock. She felt the cool, damp pressure again. The dragon was nudging her with its little snout.

Her mind was still surfacing from the thick fog of unconsciousness that had claimed her. It seemed to take too much effort to form words but she curved her hand so that her fingers touched the dragon's side. In answer, the dragon pressed its narrow flank against her fingertips.

She shut her eyes again, peripherally aware that she was no longer cold and that was nice.

"He's right, you know. You've slept long enough. It's time you got up and started moving."

The voice was disturbing in a way that the dragon's presence hadn't been. Lucinda tried to drop back down into the warm darkness where nothing had been asked of her. A hand smoothed back the tangle of her hair, and the voice spoke again, gentle but unrelenting. "Come on, get up. There's something here you're going to want to see."

She opened her eyes to see the silver-skinned Elden kneeling beside her. "Here, have something to drink." This time he didn't offer her one of Elden's plastic water bottles but a flask made of opalescent blue glass. He lifted her to a sitting position and placed the flask in her hand.

"What is this?" she asked. Now that she was more or less awake, she felt surprisingly clear headed.

"Spring water."

She drank, looking from the otherworldly Elden to the dragon, who sat perched attentively on her knee, to her surroundings. She couldn't figure out where she was. On rock, obviously, but if she was still on the mountain, what had happened to all the ice and snow, and why wasn't she freezing to death?

She asked her next question aloud. "Why are you here, helping me again? I thought you wanted me to die."

"No," he said. "I told you thieves aren't the only ones under my protection. I've long been a friend to travelers." He held out the garnet he'd stolen from her. "I took your garnet and it reminded me of my loyalties. You're a traveler in need of help. And in your own way you befriended Elden, so according to this pebble, I must acknowledge that bond. To that end, you'll find more food and water in your pack." He looked at the garnet with an expression of wry distaste. "Despite my natural tendencies to keep what I take, I think it's time I returned this meddlesome rock to you."

Lucinda closed her hand around the small red stone. Of the stones she'd been given the garnet was the least impressive in size and beauty, probably the least valuable, and yet the one that had kept Tyrone alive. She held it tight, a little dazed by the realization that she'd been given something truly powerful and precious.

He looked at her and smiled, the silver of his skin gleaming. "Yes, you know its worth. That's good."

She gazed back at him, searching for the traces of the awkward boy in his sculpted features. Something of Elden's generosity and humor was there in the edges of his smile, but the being in front of her was so clearly not of this world that the rest of the boy seemed erased. Lucinda felt herself missing Elden and yet curious about this creature who, while terribly beautiful, no longer frightened her.

He lifted both brows in a parody of inquiry. "You have a question?"

"Yeah," she said, unable to suppress a smile of her own. "Who the hell are you?"

His answer was serious, spoken in the rhythm of ritual: "I am messenger and diviner, healer and shepherd, musician and thief and trickster divine. I am the protector of travelers and merchants and thieves. I cross all boundaries and guide those who journey to Hades."

"Hades," she echoed. Bits of mythology she'd learned in secondary school, and promptly forgotten, were surfacing. "That's the Underworld, isn't it?"

"Yes, the realm of the dead."

She looked around wildly. "Is that where I am?"

He laughed so loud and long that the dragon started to look very irate and finally flew up to glare into his eyes. That seemed to sober him. "I'm sorry," he said. "I didn't mean to be rude."

"It's okay, as long as I'm not dead or about to be dead," Lucinda said, feeling more relief than embarrassment. Another bit of long-forgotten school lore surfaced and her breath caught. "Oh. I do know who you are," she said, her voice coming out a little strangled. "Hermes."

He inclined his head to her then lifted it, his eyes mocking. "How else do you think you got over the mountain and beyond the snows so quickly? Given what a hiker you are . . ."

Lucinda didn't answer. According to both Sebastian and Alasdair, she'd met a god before—Kama—but she hadn't known it at the time, so in a way it hadn't counted. But now a self-confessed god was standing before her and she had no doubt that he was exactly what he claimed he was.

"I don't know what to do," she said haltingly. "Am I supposed to bow or—"

He waved the suggestion aside with an indolent hand. "You are supposed to go to the lost towns. We've wasted quite enough time here. The dragon is already impatient with me."

It was true. The dragon, now looking extremely cross, was sitting on Hermes's broad silver shoulder, tapping one tiny clawed foot.

"Then I guess I'd better go." Lucinda looked around her again, this time focusing on the pale green line running though the brown rock. "The vein of jade."

As if to confirm her words the dragon left the god's shoulder and settled on the translucent green stone. Lucinda knelt down, touching first the rock then the serpent. "It's exactly the same color that you are. This is where you're from, the place you dream of."

The dragon closed both eyes, seeming pleased that she understood.

"And if I follow this vein, it will take me to the lost towns?" she finished.

In answer the dragon flew ahead, following the line of jade. Lucinda, though, had one more question for the god. "You must know I was born out of favor. Why did you help me?"

"You called on me."

"I couldn't have. I didn't even believe you were real until about two minutes ago."

"You left me a message," he said, and when her face registered only bafflement he sighed with exasperation. "The shrine in the phone booth. I rule, among other things, all messages and communications. Whom did you think a shrine in a phone booth would address?"

Her lower jaw dropped. "I—" She shut her mouth.

"You're at a loss for words," he said, sounding bored with her. "We'll talk again when you're more capable of holding a conversation."

Lucinda nodded, and just for a moment the god's features changed back into the goofy teenage boy. "Fact: I'm still your friend, Lucinda," Elden said. Blushing, he leaned forward, kissed her lightly and swiftly on the cheek, and then he was gone.

Lucinda turned to see the dragon hovering a distance ahead of her, waiting for her to catch up. She picked up her pack and followed him along the line of jade, finally allowing herself to breathe in the sweet elixir of hope.

THE REMAINING LIFE stones in the deerskin pouch were stirring, tumbling over themselves in a flurry of excitement at being back in the Source Place. Alasdair was aware that he should really let them out, let them touch earth here, but his eyes were fixed on the short, brown-skinned man who sat watching him, eyes lit with amusement.

"Welcome home. You've been gone from us too long."

"Nicodemus." Alasdair kept his voice level. "Thank you for the welcome. Have you been waiting for me or is this a happy accident?"

"Oh, no, we knew you were coming. The stones told us."

"Undoubtedly. And you were posted here to make sure I didn't turn and hightail it back into the cave as soon as I realized where I was?"

Nicodemus ignored that. "We asked the stones to keep an eye on you in Arcato," he said in the tone of one confiding a closely guarded secret.

"Oh, they did. They did everything but transport me back here and I'm sure they would have done that, as well, if someone could have only figured out the proper spell for it."

Nicodemus shrugged. "Unfortunately, our talents are limited. We could not bring you back ourselves, Alasdair, only trust that you would return when the time was right."

"I didn't return because of timing, and you know it. I returned because I was given no other option."

"By whom?" Nicodemus asked, wide-eyed.

Alasdair grinned. "Don't you ever tire of asking questions whose answers you already have?"

Nicodemus got to his feet, looking as thickly muscled as ever. He was wearing pants made from a light, stiff linen, sandals, and a sleeveless shirt whose front panels crossed over his broad chest. "Averill has had premonitions about you. Ever since you left us she's been saying that you were in danger, especially lately. Then this morning she woke at dawn and proclaimed that today you would return to us."

Alasdair groaned. "Is there anything that any one of us does that Averill *doesn't* have a premonition about? I swear, there hasn't been anything resembling privacy here since the day that woman was born."

"How would you know? She saw a hundred and fifty winters before you were even called into being."

"I'm sure of it," Alasdair muttered darkly.

"Now, now. You almost sound as if you don't want to be back."

He didn't. And he did. Despite the memories, it felt good to be back in the Source Place, to feel the rocks and gemstones all around him, alive and vibrating to the breath and hum of the earth. And though he'd always had conflicting feelings about Nicodemus, it was good to be back in a place where people knew exactly what he was and what the stones were. Here he no longer had to hide his abilities or struggle to make others understand, and he was surprised to discover what a relief that was. Living in other places, he hadn't even realized how much effort that required.

They walked over a ridge and down its other side to a trail that led to a slot canyon. After an hour's hike between steep canyon walls, they emerged on a terraced hillside. The sound of goat bells filtered up from one of the paths below them. Alasdair had forgotten how beautiful the place was at this time of year. Flowering vines climbed the walls and the terraced gardens were green with spring's first plantings. He hadn't thought he'd be able to set foot here without the intense pain of loss. To his surprise all he felt was a gentle melancholy mixed with a genuine gladness. He supposed he had the mothers to thank for that.

"Al-as-*dair!*" A young boy pelted down from one of the houses and raced onto the path. He launched himself at Alasdair, wrapping his arms around Alasdair's legs and hugging him hard.

"Gervase!" Alasdair ruffled his fine black hair then bent down and opened his arms to him. He held the boy's skinny frame, thinking of Michael Fortunato. Gervase, who had just passed his ninth winter, was well loved by all who lived here. Alasdair tried to imagine Michael racing to embrace someone this way, trusting that arms would open and hold him. It would never happen, he knew, certainly not in the remnants of Michael's childhood.

Gervase finally released him, looking up at him with curiosity. "Who were you just thinking about?" he asked.

"A boy I met in the city," Alasdair answered, both pleased and a little alarmed that the boy had intuited his thoughts so clearly. Gervase was always precocious but he hadn't been this accurate when Alasdair left.

"Tell me where you've been," Gervase said. "I want to hear everything."

"He can tell you later." Nicodemus cuffed the boy affectionately. "I need Alasdair to come with me now. Make yourself useful and go tell the elders that he's back."

"I want to show you my carvings," Gervase told Alasdair, deliberately ignoring Nicodemus. "Wait until you see what I've done with the chalcedony that Hesper gave me." Alasdair worked to keep a straight face. He'd spent a good deal of his own adolescence defying the adamant Nicodemus and he sensed the pattern beginning again.

"I do want to see your carvings," Alasdair assured the boy. "Later, all right?"

Giving Nicodemus an irate look and Alasdair another wide smile, Gervase went off.

The two men didn't speak as Nicodemus led Alasdair up one of the side paths to a wooden gate set in a stone wall.

Nicodemus opened the gate to a courtyard that Alasdair remembered well. Nicodemus's wheel sat in the very center of the yard beneath an oak tree that had been growing there for centuries. It was here that Nicodemus, master stonecutter, shaped, faceted, and polished stones, drawing out of them what had lain hidden in the bedrock. Alasdair still felt a bit of the awe that he'd had for this place as a child. No one had ever worked the stones as Nicodemus did.

They did not pause at the wheel but went up a staircase that wound along the outer walls of Nicodemus's house. They climbed three levels to where the stairway ended. A narrow walkway stretched out before them. In one direction it led to a wooden door into the house. In the other it led to a garden, this one planted around huge faceted stones. There were lobelias, lupines, forget-me-nots, delphiniums, and cornflowers surrounding a pale-blue celestite crystal; roses, cosmos, hibiscus, and trillium all in brilliant shades of red, surrounding a deep-red sphalerite; purple flowers for an amethyst; pink for pink kunzite, and yellow planted around a brilliant, yellow heliodor. Stonecutters tended toward consistency, Alasdair reflected.

Nicodemus hesitated. "Would you like to come inside first? I can offer you tea or wine or—"

Alasdair shook his head. "No, better to get it over with."

Nicodemus gave a brief nod, and they crossed a footpath through the garden and out through a second gate. They followed another path higher until they reached a dwelling so simple it seemed little more than a cleaned-up cave. The door, though, was a thin sheet of banded agate whose swirling lines, a pattern of black, cream, brown, grey, and lavender, had fascinated Alasdair since he was a boy. The door, he had known from the first time he saw it, held great power and the being who lived behind it, even more.

Nicodemus cleared his throat, the door swung open, and they stepped into a high-ceilinged room. A window, made of square panes of blown glass, took up the entire east wall, overlooking the footpath into the towns and providing the room's only source of light. Alasdair was instantly aware of a pulsing coming from the stone walls, the glass windows, even the dirt floor—they were all vibrating with the power of the one who lived here.

A large grey cat sat at the window, staring out at the mountain valley below.

Alasdair and Nicodemus waited.

At length the cat swung around to face them. Her green gaze fixed first on Alasdair then Nicodemus, then Alasdair again. Without warning, she let out a great, angry caterwaul, startling both men, then leapt to the trunk of the alder tree that, against all laws of botany, grew indoors out of the bare dirt floor. She scaled the trunk quickly and crouched in one of the upper branches, glowering at them.

Dear gods, Alasdair thought, *she gets worse with every year.*

The cat let out another furious yowl. She arched up, thick grey fur standing on end.

Alasdair watched with weary patience as the cat's erect grey fur darkened, taking on inky tones, and then became fuller, broader, flatter, changing from fine silky hairs to grey-and-brown feathers, except for the throat which was snowy-white. The cat's muzzle flattened and hardened into a curved black beak. Its wide grey forehead became wider and more rounded, its face disk-shaped, its ears tufted. The green eyes lightened to bright yellow though the fury in them remained unchanged. Within moments he and Nicodemus were staring at a great horned owl, huge wings spread wide.

"Averill—" Alasdair began, but the owl screeched and he wisely shut up. He'd crossed her once when she was in owl form and she'd torn a chunk out of his arm that had taken months to heal.

The owl screeched again and this time the change happened so fast that Alasdair didn't even see it. A slender woman, as tall as he was, stood before them, hands pressed together, as if trying to contain her rage between her palms.

Well, Alasdair thought, refusing to be rattled, *at least she didn't change into a boar.*

Averill glanced at Nicodemus, said, "Leave us," and the master stonecutter, who'd grown visibly nervous during the transformations, left.

She began to pace the room, long grey robe swirling around her bare ankles, iron-grey hair swirling around her hips. Alasdair stood motionless, feeling absurdly like a small disobedient child awaiting punishment. Which was, of course, exactly what she'd intended. Averill had always had a very precise command of theatrics. Very deliberately, Alasdair banished the feeling of dread, returning to weary patience.

She must have sensed it because she stopped her pacing and came to stand in front of him again. Her face had more owl in it than boar or cat, with a short, curved beak of a nose, a thin mouth, and piercing amber eyes. She had never been pretty and yet she had an undeniable animal beauty, simultaneously fierce and soft. You never quite knew what you would get from Averill.

"Did you have to leave?" she asked.

"You know I did."

"And did you find whatever it was you were seeking?"

"No," he admitted. "I wanted escape."

"I could have told you that wasn't possible."

Alasdair sighed heavily. "I'm sure you could have told me a great many things if I'd had the sense to ask."

Though her mouth remained a severe line, a hint of a smile played in her eyes. "So what did you find in that city?"

"Electric lights. Moving pictures. An abandoned child. More complications in every direction, chief among them, Malachy."

Her eyes brightened at the name of her onetime apprentice. "Malachy? Where is he?"

Without invitation, Alasdair took a seat in one the chairs carved from cream-colored soapstone. "I was hoping you could tell me."

TO LUCINDA'S RELIEF the vein of pale green jade only ran uphill for a short distance. She followed it to the top of a rounded peak and then saw that the line of jade curved down the other side. She couldn't resist looking back once. She was now so high up that she couldn't see Arcato at all, only the smooth brown rock flowing down to a snowier stretch below.

The dragon tugged impatiently at her sleeve. "Okay, okay, I'm coming," she told it, and followed it up over the peak and down. Although the ascent had been steep, the slope on the other side of the mountain was gentler, and she was able to follow the jade vein fairly easily. The ground beneath her changed from sheer granite to a layer of dark topsoil dotted with green seedlings and small shrubs. She still needed Elden's walking stick but the footing wasn't treacherous and wherever it was she and the dragon were going, it felt as if they were making good time. They traveled this way for hours, stopping once to eat— the god had left them honey cakes and crisp apples and goat cheese—then continuing down. To Lucinda's surprise and relief, the lilacs reappeared. They were not as thick here as on the other side of the mountain, just a few scattered bushes, always growing close to the jade. But they were an undeniable sign of spring which, after the winter that swept the mountain peaks, seemed a good omen. The thought made her smile. When had she started believing in omens?

The jade vein ended abruptly in a wide jade slab. It was taller than Lucinda, rounded on top, and nearly transparent. In places the green pigment was so light she could almost see through to the other side. For a moment she ran her fingers along its smooth surface, thinking it was one of the most beautiful things she'd ever seen.

Now what? she wondered. The slab was quite thick. It took her a while to walk around it, but when she did she discovered that the vein didn't pick up on the other side, where there was only black earth and a sprinkling of new plant life. The jade really ended with this slab.

"Dragon!" she called, trying not to sound alarmed. The dragon, as was his wont, had done one of his periodic vanishing tricks. She had learned not to take them personally or ascribe any meaning to them. He disappeared from time to time; it was simply what he did.

The dragon did not come at her call, though she tried several times. She felt a familiar heated mix of frustration and anger building inside her. She hadn't felt this way since marching away from Hermes, ready to die on the slopes. She'd almost forgotten that this used to be the way she felt nearly all the time. That, too, brought her up short. She hadn't realized that had been her norm. *Lordy, how did Tyrone or anyone else stand me?* she wondered.

Not knowing what else to do, she sat down to wait for the dragon. Idly, Lucinda began to go through her pack and spread the contents on the rock before her. Then she put everything back except the moonstone, the rectangular diamond pendant, and the garnet. All gifts, she thought. And she'd only begun to understand the powers of the garnet.

She picked up the diamond. The sunlight danced through it, casting a dazzling rainbow. She let herself play with it, turning the perfectly clear stone so that bands of color flashed on the slab. Guided by an instinct that she had no explanation for, Lucinda held the diamond in front of her and moved it along the jade, tracing the slab's shape: two long sides and a curve on top.

The third time she did this she heard a slight grinding sound coming from the jade. She tried it again, realizing that the lines she was tracing with the diamond's reflected light seemed to be lasering into the jade, as if the diamond's light was burning through it. Lucinda traced the lines again and again. Each time she heard the slight grinding and saw more of a groove in the jade—in the shape of a door.

For a long moment she sat absolutely still, trying to be sure that she wasn't imagining things. It was too wild to be believed, so why was adrenaline shooting through her body, making her shaky and speedy? "Oh, please work," she murmured to the diamond and the jade. "Oh, please open the way to the lost towns for me."

At that point the dragon reappeared. It didn't stop to acknowledge Lucinda but flew directly to the outlined shape of the door and began to beat its wings against it.

Nothing happened. The little creature beat its wings even more furiously.

"Stop that. You'll hurt yourself." Lucinda stepped forward, reaching for the dragon. She never saw a door actually open. Her eyes were focused on the dragon, and she watched him fly straight ahead, out of her grasp, and through what was now an opening in the jade slab.

Lucinda had just enough presence of mind to grab her pack and the three gems before following the dragon through. She stepped over the threshold and caught her breath in a gasp of delight, barely conscious of the jade door shutting behind her.

Before her, in the mountain valley below, lay the lost towns: Towers and terraces, balconies, stairways and footbridges, all carved into cliffs and outcroppings of steep brown rock. Gardens with streams running through them and gemstones glittering in the sunlight. She heard the sounds of bells and wind chimes, caught the scents of lilacs and wisteria and honeysuckle.

The dragon nuzzled her neck with its cool, moist snout and settled itself on her shoulder. She stroked it gently in thanks. Then together they started down the switchback trail that led into the towns.

"YOU WERE IN the Shrine of the Mothers," Averill said when Alasdair finished telling her where he'd last seen the fox. For the first time in the nearly hundred and sixty years he'd known her, there was something close to awe on her face.

"You've heard of it?"

"Heard rumors of it." She gave him one of her rare unguarded looks. "Women who journey into the mysteries of the Goddess, in any of her manifestations, have always sought it. There have been legends about it for centuries. But you—you actually found it." She grimaced in disgust. "Women seek it and it opens for two half-crazed men. And to think, it's been hidden under that foul city all these years."

"The city's not so bad," Alasdair said quietly.

She cast him a sharp, skeptical look. "Look at what it did to you. You, a *cearu,* with all the power of the stones, needed the dragon to save you from Malachy."

"That's because I wasn't interested in saving myself. And that started here. It had very little to do with Arcato."

She knelt by a small stove, lit it, and set an iron kettle on its grill. "I don't see that same desperation in you now."

"No," he admitted, "something happened in the shrine."

She gave a harsh laugh. "You bull's prick of an ingrate. The mothers healed you, *that's* what happened. The least you can do is acknowledge their power."

"You're right," he said, realizing it was inevitable that Averill would chastise him for something. The oldest and most powerful of the elders, she considered the rest of them foolish children in need of frequent correction, though some she indulged more than others. He wondered if there had ever been anyone she fully approved of; Malachy's was the only name that came to mind.

"I suppose that finding the shrine proves that you were meant to leave here," she added more graciously.

"The goddess who came for Malachy, do you know who she is?" he asked.

Averill poured the tea she'd brewed into two onyx cups, adding a pinch of herbs and dried flowers to each. "Not from what you've told me, no," she said, handing him one of the cups. "And I really can't guess as to whether he's still alive and if so, in what form."

"Will you look for him?" Alasdair asked. "You're the only mortal I know who has a chance of finding him."

"I'll think on it," she said, and sipped at the tea. She was gazing out her window, ostensibly not focusing on him, and yet he could feel tendrils of her power extending toward him, searching, questioning. "You returned without two of your life stones," she said, her eyes fixed on something distant. "And the spirit is gone from your quartz."

He nodded, not wanting to elaborate. He hadn't told her about the lapis insisting on being given to the cat goddess. Nor had he told her about the moonstone going to Lucinda. It was a disgrace among his people to lose one, let alone two, life stones. He sat there, willing himself not to tense as he waited for her to tell him how stupid and careless he'd been.

"I hope you had good reason for letting them go," Averill went on, "because there's no time for regrets now. Something's coming after you, Alasdair. I've felt its energy in my dreams. I couldn't see a form, but I can tell you that it's male and that it may be a shape-shifter. He's got animal energy all wound up in human. And he's a strong one."

"That was my impression, too," Alasdair said. He peered into the onyx cup. The tiny dried flowers that Averill had added to it seemed to have come into bloom; bright blue blossoms swirled through the hot tea. "What on earth did you put in here?"

"Never mind that. You have to know that it wasn't Malachy I sensed in the dream," she went on, a shade defensively.

"No, I'm sure it wasn't," Alasdair agreed. "Whoever he is, showed up at the flat I rented in the city. I wasn't there at the time. He tried to get in using some sort of magic, and the stones stopped him. They wouldn't have stopped Malachy."

"No," she said, sounding pleased, "they wouldn't." She peered at Alasdair over her beak of a nose. "You still carry the obsidian knife, don't you?"

"Always. It's not the sort of object you leave lying around."

"Good," she said. "That may be some protection. What kind of enemies have you made lately?"

"It's a question," he said, rubbing his chin. "None that I know of, though I did manage to irritate both Janus and Kama."

Averill dismissed this notion with an impatient flick of her hand. "Neither one is petty by nature. If they were angry with you, you would know it. There would be no doubt at all."

"I suspect you're right."

"Well, at the very least, you should be safe while you're here," she said.

With amusement he noted her implication; Averill was too canny to expect him to stay. He said only, "I hope you're right about that, as well."

She surprised him, gently reaching out and touching his face. "I'm glad you're back, my difficult one. Now drink your tea."

He inhaled the strong scent of herbs warily. He'd once taken one of her teas and wound up hallucinating for days.

"Oh, come now," she said, seeing his hesitation. "I'm drinking it, too."

"That's not much comfort. You're immune to things that would slay an army."

She flashed him a smile, and he was sure he saw a cat's pointed canine tooth in it. "Drink, Alasdair. I offer it only to welcome you back. I promise it will do you no harm."

A promise that left great room for interpretation. In truth, the hallucinations hadn't actually hurt him. With a shrug, he did as she bade him. He was back, after all.

HAVING FINISHED HIS tea with no obvious ill effects, Alasdair took his leave of Averill. Although he no longer feared her the way he used to, he was glad the meeting was over. To be in Averill's presence was to have her covertly working on you. She was incapable of anything as simple as a friendly social visit.

He followed the path that led downhill from Averill's, choosing not to take the turn that went through Nicodemus's garden. He continued on, past a high wall covered with purple wisteria. Beyond it was a series of three open doorways. They weren't built into the cliffs like most of the dwellings; these doorways were fashioned from flat pieces of stone, carefully laid and fitted like bricks. The doorways were simple rectangles, each directly behind the one in front of it. He glanced at the three thresholds with a shudder and walked on.

Not far from the three thresholds he took another stairway up to a two-story dwelling that had been carved into a particularly beautiful rhyolite outcrop. The stone that served as the outside of the house was flow-banded; shades of chocolate and a lighter reddish-brown swirled through it in gentle waves. Two intricately carved columns supported a balcony on the top floor. Bright flowers in even brighter ceramic pots flanked the entrance. In the windows he could see the reflections of mobiles made with gemstones, mobiles he'd fashioned when he was a boy.

His life stones were stirring again, so he stopped before he reached the door and took them out of the deerskin pouch. Carefully, he set them in a hollow in the rhyolite wall: aquamarine, opal, topaz, red coral, turquoise, emerald, sapphire, and the empty quartz crystal. They seemed incomplete, lonely, without the moonstone and lapis, but he dismissed that as being his own feelings rather than the stones'. "Welcome home," he told them.

He pushed open the door, entering the first room with its high, rounded walls and the sweet, familiar scent of sage. Something deep inside Alasdair relaxed. What he'd felt in Averill's walls was her power, penetrating everything, overwhelming all. Here, in the house where he'd grown up, what he felt was the rhyolite all around him. Originally part of a volcanic flow, the rhyolite still contained movement in its essence. It was the finest tonic he'd ever known for moving through difficulties. It wouldn't allow you to stay in a place where you were stuck. It was the rhyolite, finally, that had convinced him that he had to leave the Source Place, that only the act of moving on might move him out of paralyzing grief. It quietly urged him toward change and resolution, offering its own energy and strength to aid him. He'd grown up so used to its support that it wasn't until he left the Source Place that he realized what it was to live without it.

From years of habit, Alasdair went first to the shrine where his mother gave offerings—flowers, crystals, bits of calligraphy, and a series of exquisite, miniature watercolors—to a number of gods she was particularly fond of. He lit more of the sweet sage incense and paid his respects to Ganesh, Tara, Bastet, Hermes, Kwannon, Dagda, and Vishnu, of course, who ruled all crystals.

A familiar, soft presence wound against his ankles. He knelt to hold his hand out to the silver tabby cat. "Moura," he said, scratching the side of her neck. She was a genuinely sweet-natured creature, something he'd begun to think was a biological rarity. "How've you been? Do you know, you're one of the few beings I've missed." The cat purred appreciatively as he continued to pet her.

"Alasdair!" He got to his feet as his mother, a small woman whose long, black braid was streaked with grey, rushed into the room. She swept him into her embrace. "Thank the gods, you're back safe."

"Did you doubt my safety?"

Vita pulled back and fixed him with a shrewd look. "What I doubted was that you would be back."

"I couldn't stay away forever," he said, realizing it was the truth.

"But you wanted to."

"When I left, yes."

She shook her head with mock disapproval. "Go upstairs and change into some clothing that isn't shredded, then come back down and let me fuss over you."

Upstairs, he found several of his robes in a cedar trunk. He changed quickly, not taking the time to reacquaint himself with the room that used to be his.

He found his mother in the kitchen, a wide sunny room that opened onto the veranda and looked out on the garden. She'd gained weight since he'd seen her last but her movements were still deft and quick as she set a pitcher of cold tea on the wooden table.

"Are you hungry?" she asked, filling an amber cup with the tea.

"I am."

"You sound surprised."

"I can't remember the last time I craved food."

Something like pity flickered in her eyes but she didn't comment, only set out tomatoes and goat cheese and thick slices of freshly baked bread. Her skin was sun-browned, her eyes the same grey as his own. She wore a soft lavender robe and a necklace of amethysts.

"It's good to see you," he said as he watched her spoon black olives into a shallow alabaster bowl.

"Have you seen Averill yet?"

"First thing. She fed me some of *her* tea, so don't be alarmed if I sprout wings and a tail and suddenly take to hovering 'round the ceilings." He helped himself to the olives then concentrated on slicing the tomato.

"She wouldn't do that."

"Oh, wouldn't she?"

"No," his mother said, and something in her voice made him look up. "She knows better."

"That's an unusual statement concerning Averill. Did something happen between you?"

"How could you think a thing like that?" she asked innocently.

"Mother."

The edges of her mouth turned up.

"Did you really go up against Averill?" he asked.

"That hasn't been necessary, at least not yet." Vita frowned at the table. "I'm going to go out to the garden to get some mint for the tea."

"Not before you tell me what you're talking about," Alasdair protested.

She leaned down and kissed the top of his head. "All in good time, my dear."

Alasdair rubbed his eyes and laughed to himself. Vita paused at the door. "What's so amusing?"

"In Arcato I met a young woman who was forever accusing me of being oblique and deliberately mysterious. At least I know where I get it from."

"Don't be so certain. Your father had a talent for the most circuitous answers I've ever heard."

"Did he?" Alasdair asked. His father had died before Alasdair reached his second winter. He had no memories of him at all. And Vita, who was loving but not in the least sentimental, rarely brought him up.

Vita nodded, as informative as ever, and went out into the garden, leaving Alasdair to his meal.

AS LUCINDA DREW closer to the lost towns she began to wonder what it was she was actually approaching. She could only see one small town, which was more like a village. There was no obvious center or marketplace, no public space where she could introduce herself, ask questions, find someone who could help. With only private dwellings evident, the task seemed more daunting. But the jade door had opened for her, and even Hermes said she had to go here.

The dragon nuzzled her again. "And you're with me," she added. She was finally beginning to believe that she was fated for this journey—but she couldn't let herself dwell on the idea because it scared her.

Her steps slowed as she reached the final turn on the switchback trail. A tall woman with long grey hair was striding briskly and purposefully toward her.

"Hello," Lucinda said, wondering for the first time whether she and the people here spoke the same language.

The woman came to a halt, towering over her and standing so close that Lucinda involuntarily took a step back. "Who are you and what do you want?" the woman demanded.

Lucinda took another step back, feeling as if she'd just been slapped. Somehow she'd assumed that everyone in the Source Place would have Alasdair's unfailing natural courtesy. "I'm—"

"What makes you think you have any right to be here?" The woman cut her off. "You certainly weren't invited."

"I—" Lucinda wasn't sure how to respond, and her brain immediately fired off a series of self-accusatory questions: Why hadn't she thought this through on the long journey here? Why hadn't she asked Hermes about the Source Place when she'd had the chance? Why had she assumed she'd be welcomed? Fortunately, at that moment the dragon lifted off her shoulder and hovered in the air between her and the furious woman.

"Oh." The woman's voice softened. "So he brought you."

Lucinda nodded. "From Arcato."

"I see." The woman's amber eyes bored into her. "Well, then. Why did he bring you? What are you hoping to gain?"

Lucinda met her eyes but resisted the temptation to reply with equal rudeness. She had to get help for Tyrone, she reminded herself. Antagonizing the locals was probably not the best way to go about it.

"Perhaps you want our gems," the woman suggested, her tone neutral and poisonous.

"I doubt that's why she's here," said Alasdair's familiar voice.

Lucinda had been so locked into trying to stare down the woman that she hadn't even noticed him coming toward them. Now she pushed her way around the woman to look at him. He wore a different robe, this one sage-green, she noticed, but otherwise looked fine, better, in fact, than he had in the city. "You're alive," she said, genuine gladness in her voice.

"It seems that way." The dragon sat on Alasdair's outstretched palm and the *cearu* was smiling more broadly than Lucinda would have believed possible.

"You know each other," the grey-haired woman stated, not sounding pleased.

"We do," Alasdair said.

Lucinda had to ask. "When you went into that cave . . . did you find Sebastian down there?"

"Sebastian?" the woman repeated.

"Malachy," Alasdair translated before answering Lucinda's question. "When I last saw him he seemed healthy and content. I'll tell you about it in a bit. Come on." He took her gently by the arm. "You've had quite the journey, I'm sure. You could probably do with some food."

"Alasdair," the woman intoned.

"Forgive my shoddy manners. Averill, may I present Lucinda. Lucinda, Averill."

Lucinda could not bring herself to extend her hand. The woman didn't seem to expect it. She drew herself up even taller, looking down at Lucinda over the curve of her nose.

"You are now and will always be an outsider here," she stated. "You're being allowed to enter our lands because the dragon brought you and Alasdair seems to consider you a friend. But do anything that violates this place, and neither one of them will be able to protect you. Do you understand me?"

"I do," Alasdair said before Lucinda could answer. "And I find it a very curious form of greeting. If I didn't know it was beneath you, I'd think you were trying to frighten her."

Averill stepped back from him. "Oh, you're thinking now, are you? Then tell me how it is you think you can walk away from your calling and still have the right to interfere here?"

Alasdair let the accusation go. "I'm only asking for the courtesy we extend to any traveler," he said. "Would you dishonor Hermes and deny comfort to those he protects?"

Averill snorted. "Hermes also protects thieves."

"Lucinda isn't a thief," Alasdair said evenly. "You know the dragon wouldn't have brought her if she was. Besides, I can think of at least one thief you've looked on kindly."

Averill fixed her amber eyes on him and when she spoke her voice was cool and controlled. "I've looked kindly on you as well, Alasdair, which is why there is still breath in your lungs. You'd be a fool to forget it." Giving Lucinda a dismissive glance, she turned and strode back toward the village.

"What did I just do?" Lucinda asked uneasily. "Did I get you in trouble with her?"

"I've been in trouble with Averill over one thing or another for years now." Alasdair took Lucinda's pack from her, shouldering it easily. "And we haven't killed each other yet, so we'll probably survive your arrival here."

"She's not—your wife?" Lucinda asked.

He struggled for a moment to take the question seriously then burst into laughter. "No. Thank the benevolent aspects of the Goddess, Averill has never been anyone's wife. She's—"

"A harridan?" Lucinda suggested, grinning.

"There have been times I've been sure she's one of the Greek Harpies—or the Furies," Alasdair confessed. "But the truth is she's one of our elders, and she's a shape-shifter, like Sebastian, only more so."

"You mean, she's better at it?"

"Well, yes," Alasdair said as he began to walk down the footpath. "She can change into any one of three animals—cat, owl, and boar—all intensely territorial creatures, mind you. And she has other abilities. She's quite prescient. In fact, I suspect that's why your arrival angered her so."

"That doesn't make sense." Lucinda was once again having trouble following what passed for logic in Alasdair's bizarre mind.

"Well," he said thoughtfully, "strangers usually don't rattle Averill. She's far too powerful to be threatened by most mortals. Normally, she doesn't even bother with the few travelers who manage to find us. So the only reason I can think of for her greeting you the way she did is that she never saw you coming."

"Then she couldn't have been looking very hard. I wasn't trying to be inconspicuous or stealthy. I walked straight down the center of the trail."

"I expect you did. I also expect something"—he ran a fingertip between the ears of the dragon, who was now perched on his shoulder—"kept you cloaked." At Lucinda's confused expression, he added, "As a safety precaution. When the dragon decides to guide someone, he takes his responsibilities very seriously. So Averill, who normally would have sensed you the moment you walked through the jade door, didn't know you were here until you were so close that she saw you from her window." He gave Lucinda a sympathetic look. "I'm afraid she isn't used to surprises."

"Well, I hope she won't hold it against me," Lucinda said, "because I came here for a reason." She explained her theory about Ilyap'a and needing Alasdair or someone like him to intercede for Tyrone.

Alasdair listened, his eyes grave. "You may be right," he said. "Unfortunately, I've never dealt with Ilyap'a. I'm not sure I can reach him, much less get him to listen to me. But we'll see what we can do."

"We?"

"Me, others here, the dragon. . . . You should know that there's something else he cloaked for you."

"What's that?"

"The diamond," Alasdair said. "Averill should have sensed it at once, and if she had, you would have known it." He touched the dragon's side. "Can you keep it masked?" The dragon pressed its head against Alasdair's finger, which Alasdair took for an assent. "Good."

"You're saying that people here shouldn't know about the diamond," Lucinda interpreted.

"It would be recognized," Alasdair told her, "and it will be much simpler for us both if it isn't. So, if you can, keep it on you but keep it hidden and for pity's sake, don't mention it to anyone."

Lucinda stopped walking. "You can't keep doing that to me, giving me half an explanation and expecting me to do what you say. Why would people here recognize it?"

Alasdair's grey eyes darkened. "Do you think you're the first one Kama gave that necklace to?" His voice was tight with control, reigning in anger or grief or both. It was the way he used to sound in the city, she realized. And up until she'd asked that question he'd seemed different here, easier, maybe even happier.

"I don't know. I never thought about it." She was already half-regretting having asked.

"Before it was yours, it was given to someone from the Source Place," he said, his voice flat. "Her name was Gioia. She's dead now. Does that answer your question?"

"I'm sorry," Lucinda said, feeling badly but also wondering for the hundredth time just what it was she was walking into. "I don't mean to pry but . . . she's not dead because of the diamond, is she?"

"No," he said. The dragon lifted itself into the air to press its cheek against Alasdair's in what was clearly a gesture of comfort.

Lucinda took it as a chance to shift the direction of the conversation. "I didn't notice him doing anything special when I came through the jade door. How did he manage to 'cloak' the diamond?"

Alasdair let the dragon settle on his wrist and his mood seemed to lighten as he regarded the little serpent. "Think of it as something that runs in his family. Dragons have long hidden and guarded the earth's treasures. One diamond probably didn't present much of a challenge to him."

Lucinda reached out a finger to stroke the dragon's back. "Thank you," she told it. "I had no idea you were taking such good care of me."

"Look," Alasdair said a bit awkwardly, "things here are different from what you're used to, and there may be a lot of things you don't understand. It would help if you would trust me. There are . . . obligations . . . that I have to honor but I'll try not to be so oblique. As much as I can, I'll be a friend to you."

Lucinda took a breath. "I'd like that," she said. "I have a feeling that I'm going to need a friend here." The dragon gave her an indignant look. "Besides you, I mean."

They drew near to the dwellings and Lucinda saw that the cliffs and outcroppings were not formed of what, from a distance, had looked like solid brown stone. The rock here had a lighter curving pattern in it that made her think of ocean waves. "Oh," she breathed. "The stone here is so beautiful."

This seemed to amuse Alasdair. "Most outsiders who visit us have eyes only for the gemstones but you noticed the rhyolite. It's a felsite, in the feldspar family, like moonstone. Rhyolite contains feldspar and quartz. It's softer than quartz, easier to carve."

She looked at him suspiciously.

"What?"

"The way you were talking, it reminds me of someone I met recently. A . . . sort of a teenage boy named Elden."

It was one of the few times she'd managed to shock him. "Hermes? You met the god Hermes?"

"That's how I got here, more or less. Hermes and the dragon."

"You *did* have protection," Alasdair said, sounding impressed.

They fell quiet as Alasdair led her through the village. Lucinda couldn't get over the beauty of the place, and she soon realized what it was that affected her so strongly. She'd never been anywhere where everything was fashioned either by geology or by hand. Nothing here had been made by machine. Everything in this place was skillfully, lovingly wrought, unique and idiosyncratic.

"This is where I grew up and where my mother still lives," Alasdair said as they started up the stairs to Vita's house.

Lucinda caught his sleeve before he could go any farther. "Is your mother . . . anything like Averill?"

"Yes and no. Don't worry. She'll be very glad that you've brought the dragon with you. And she and Hermes are old friends; unlike Averill, she places great value on the mores of hospitality. I think she'll make you welcome."

Vita did indeed make Lucinda welcome, sitting her down and feeding her a light meal, then leading her up the hill to soak her aching muscles in a hot spring. Finally, Vita took her to a small room on the second floor where a bed was tucked onto a shelf carved in the rock wall. "Get some sleep, child," she said. "We can talk when you've rested."

LUCINDA WOKE AS the setting sun streamed in through the window, turning the rhyolite walls a deep red. She'd lost track of how many nights she'd slept on the hard rock of the mountain. Now, lying on a feather mattress tucked beneath clean sheets and a soft wool blanket, she was feeling drowsy and luxuriously comfortable. It took her a moment to realize that she'd only slept a few hours, that this was not the morning of the next day.

Someone had a left a basin filled with water on the malachite table directly across from the bed; she could see the water's reflection wavering on the ceiling. She got up, rinsed her face, and dried off with the linen towel that was folded next to the basin. Earlier, before they went up to the hot spring, Vita had lent her a plain linen robe, which now lay folded across the bottom of the bed. Unable to face the idea of putting on her dirt-caked clothing again, Lucinda slipped on the robe and made her way downstairs.

She followed the sound of voices to a veranda that faced the garden behind the house. Vita, Alasdair and a girl, whom Lucinda judged to be about fifteen years old, sat on brightly colored cushions at a low table made of a smooth cream-colored stone. A fifth, very small cushion covered in lavender silk sat on the table. The dragon was curled up on it, head tucked inside his tail, gently snoring.

"Lucinda, please join us," Alasdair said, indicating an empty pillow. "Were you able to sleep?"

Lucinda confirmed that she was.

"Will you have some wine?" he asked. She nodded as she took her seat, and he poured dark red wine into a crystal goblet. She couldn't quite get used to what she'd begun to think of as Alasdair-at-home. In Arcato he'd often been distant and irritable. Here, he seemed to have turned into the soul of courtesy. Was it his mother's influence? she wondered with amusement.

"Lucinda, this is Hesper," Vita explained, waving a graceful hand toward the younger woman. Vita had changed from the lavender gown with amethysts into an even simpler ivory-colored gown. A round golden topaz, with a light blue topaz beneath it, hung from a long braid of gold around her neck. Similar topazes were set in bracelets on each wrist, smaller ones in her gold earrings. Vita had the kind of effortless elegance that Tyrone adored, Lucinda thought wistfully. She glanced down at her own silver bracelets, which suddenly seemed cheap and common.

Hesper was dressed in loose pants and a V-necked top made of some sort of linen. The pants were dyed bright red, the top bright turquoise, and she wore a leather string around her throat bearing a single chunky red coral bead. She had short, straight, white-blond hair and a young girl's small, even features.

"Alasdair told us about your friend Tyrone," Vita began. A silver tabby cat leapt into her lap and she ran her hand down its back before continuing. "He said that you journeyed to us because you realized that you needed someone like Alasdair to reach Ilyap'a."

"That's right." Lucinda tasted the wine. It was light and sweet and smooth.

"And he said you were fortunate enough to have help from my lord, Hermes. What he didn't tell us," Vita went on, "is how you knew this place existed."

Lucinda put the glass down, suddenly feeling wary. "When I was in the city the dragon brought me to a woman named Mariamme," she explained. Alasdair and his mother exchanged a glance at the mention of Mariamme's name. "She gazed into a crystal for me," Lucinda went on, "and she—we both—saw lilacs. She told me I had to follow the lilacs up into the lost towns. That was the first time I'd ever heard of them."

"But she didn't tell you to come here for your friend," Vita guessed.

Lucinda shook her head. "No. I told her I wasn't going. I wanted to stay in the city with Tyrone. But she said that Alasdair needed my help. Probably because I'd told her about seeing him swallowed up in the ground."

"So she knew I was trapped beneath the city and yet she sent you here to help me?" Alasdair asked.

"Yes, but Mariamme lived in an older part of Arcato. I mean, she was living in the eighteen-eighties." Lucinda realized with relief that her audience didn't seem to find this weird or even questionable.

"The labradorite footbridge," Alasdair said. "It leads to the city in an earlier time."

"So maybe the danger she saw was in that time, not ours," Lucinda went on, trying out an idea that had occurred to her while walking up the mountain.

Alasdair and Vita exchanged another look, then Vita said, "When a seer reads a crystal for someone, what she sees reflects the subject's world. She was reading your time, Lucinda, not her own. Now please, try to remember exactly what Mariamme told you."

Lucinda closed her eyes, trying to recreate the reading. "First she told me you needed help, then I told her what happened that day. She knew about Sebastian, too, that he was a fox and a trickster." Lucinda opened her eyes. "That's all I remember. I was pretty freaked at the time."

"Try the andalusite," Hesper suggested.

Before Lucinda could ask what that was, Alasdair inclined his head toward a transparent crystal resting on the end of the table. "It can enhance memory," he told her. "Hold it and see what happens."

Feeling increasingly nervous, as if she were performing in a play and had never been given the lines, Lucinda reached for the oval crystal. Looking at it carefully, she realized she had no idea what color it was. At first she'd thought it a smoky grey-brown but as she turned it in her hand it changed color, going from brown to red to green.

Alasdair, seemingly reading her thoughts, said. "That's just the way it refracts the light, revealing different colors in different directions. It works with memory by reflecting different facets of what we've known."

Lucinda held the andalusite in the open palm of one hand and stared at it, seeing nothing but a pretty, polished rock. At length she cupped her other hand over it, thinking maybe she was supposed to feel something, but all she felt were three pairs of eyes fixed on her, waiting for the revelation. "I can't do it like this," she blurted out, "not with all of you watching me. Turn around or something. Please."

Vita raised one black eyebrow and the cat meowed loudly, as if to say it wasn't going anywhere.

Lucinda pushed herself away from the table. "Okay, I'll go back inside and—" Her protests were cut short by a vision of Mariamme saying, "The *cearu* needs your help." Mariamme went on and Lucinda began to relay her words exactly as she spoke them: "If it were just a matter of summoning help from the lost towns, the dragon could do that on his own. . . . You must know that there's something tearing at this city, something that will take many lives. The *cearu* is one of a very few beings who might be able to change that. That is why we must help him."

Not wanting any more memories, Lucinda dropped the andalusite. It rattled against the stone table. Darkness had fallen. The garden was quiet and black.

At length Vita got to her feet. She turned to Lucinda, put a comforting hand on her shoulder, and said, "Oh, child, I wish you'd never come."

Fifteen

VITA REACHED INTO a niche in the wall of the veranda, struck a flint, and began to light the oil lamps that were set in sconces.

"More wine?" Hesper asked, but no one took her up on it.

Lucinda's throat was thick with dread. She had the feeling that she had just done something awful, though she wasn't quite sure what it was.

Alasdair picked up the andalusite and rolled it in his hand. "What Mariamme told Lucinda isn't news to me. So"—he glanced pointedly at his mother—"let's not blame the messenger. Averill's already had dreams about this . . . being. She thinks he may be a shape-shifter. And when I was in Arcato, I knew he was following me."

"But you came back here," Vita said, resuming her seat at the table.

"Not by choice or plan. It was what the mothers ordained for me."

"You would have stayed in Arcato then?" Vita asked.

Alasdair set the stone down abruptly. "I was planning to take a boat out—to another city. And yet I knew about that—presence—and I hadn't quite decided to run from it. When I wound up in the Shrine of the Mothers I was going after Malachy, because I had a feeling that he knew what it was."

"Shrine? And whose mothers?" Lucinda asked, lost.

"I'll fill you in later when I tell you about Sebastian," Alasdair said.

Vita spread both hands flat on the table. She hadn't brought a lamp to the table but she didn't have to. The topazes she wore gave off a soft glow, making her look radiant, almost ethereal. "Mariamme seems to think it's up to you to fight this thing in Arcato, and yet she sent Lucinda here to help you."

"And Lucinda came seeking help from us," Alasdair reminded her. "With the aid of both the dragon and Hermes. She didn't show up here accidentally."

With those words the dragon woke from its nap, stretched its front toes, and flew over to Lucinda to settle on her wrist. She took this as a sign of encouragement. "I'm willing to do what I can if you'll help Tyrone," she told them. "But what Mariamme said doesn't make sense to me. I mean, I don't know anything about stones or gods or—" She broke off, frustrated, and faced Vita. "It just seems that all of you know things and have powers, and what Alasdair actually needs is *your* help."

"He'll have it," Vita assured her in a cool tone. "That doesn't disqualify you. So there'll be no more 'Why me's?' Whether or not you're aware of it, you obviously have something to contribute."

"What about Tyrone?" Lucinda asked stubbornly. She was rapidly starting to dislike Alasdair's mother.

Vita tilted her head toward the blond-haired girl. "Hesper has an affinity for storm gods."

"I was born during a storm and I've been struck by lightning," Hesper said blithely.

"So, that means you can reach Ilyap'a?"

"Don't know. Never tried but I'll find out."

Lucinda held her tongue. As far as she could tell, Vita was shuffling her off on a teenager who was entirely too casual about the matter of Tyrone's life.

Alasdair got to his feet. "There's not much more we're going to accomplish here tonight, and I need to talk with Lucinda."

"Of course, dear." Vita was again the epitome of graciousness. "I'll see all three of you tomorrow."

"MY APOLOGIES FOR my mother," was the first thing Alasdair said as Vita and Hesper went back into the house. "I've been away a long time, she's barely seen me, and then you show up with a message from a seer, telling her I have to go back to the city to deal with some sort of murderous monster."

"That's not what I said," Lucinda protested.

"That's the way it looks to her at the moment. She'll calm down. Vita knows enough about fate to recognize it when she sees it." He studied Lucinda curiously. "If we lend you some clothing, would you like to take a walk?"

"Yes," Lucinda said. She'd been dreading going back into the house with Vita.

A short time later Lucinda, dressed in a pair of the loose pants and a knit tunic top, followed Alasdair back onto the terraced trails. A golden half-moon had risen and she found once her eyes adjusted she could see fairly well. She inhaled deeply, taking in the sweet scent of wild fennel growing along the sides of the path. "Are there other towns up here?" she asked. "This seems like one teeny little village."

"I'll show you," Alasdair said. He led her along a series of footpaths until they dead-ended at a massive wall of rock. "Give me your hand."

Back in Arcato she would have balked at that, but she realized that she did trust him. She took his hand and let him lead her toward the rock wall. It was actually two huge rocks with a gap between them that was about the width of Alasdair's shoulders.

He walked through the passage between the rocks and she followed close behind. Just as it got so dark that she had to put out her hands to feel her way, the moon's light came streaming through again, and they were out of the gap and looking over another mountain valley.

Lucinda couldn't see the houses clearly but there were dozens of windows lit with the glow of oil lamps and a few torches blazing on the lower paths. Music drifted up from below, a stringed instrument and more pipes.

"This is Second Village, the largest of the towns," Alasdair explained. "That's a marketplace down there to the right, and if you look straight ahead and drop down one, two, three . . . four terraces, you'll see an amphitheater."

"How many towns are there?"

"Just three and we're all very closely linked. You weren't wrong. It's really more like one village that's spread out along the slope of the mountainside."

Alasdair led her to a grassy ledge and they sat down, looking out over the larger town. She listened as he told her about the Shrine of the Mothers and Sebastian's healing and disappearance.

"I hate him," she said when he finished. "But I'm glad he's not caught in that awful half-man half-fox state."

Alasdair nodded. "I just wish I knew where the goddess took him. . . . I thought Averill might. She says she doesn't."

"Does Averill lie?"

"Rarely."

"What about Hesper?" Lucinda asked. "How am I supposed to believe that that teenager—"

Alasdair cleared his throat. "That 'teenager' celebrated her fiftieth birthday last summer."

"Jeez, you all age well," Lucinda couldn't help saying. "How long do you people live, anyway?"

"Averill is one of the oldest among us, and she's somewhere near three hundred," Alasdair answered. "Her mother was almost four hundred when she died."

"Maybe I ought to relocate," Lucinda muttered. "I wouldn't have to worry about old or even middle age."

"Do they worry you?" Alasdair asked, sounding curious.

"Not that much," Lucinda admitted. "For a while I was on track to leave a young corpse. So when I finally cleaned up and decided to live a little longer, the idea of aging seemed kind of quaint and okay." She turned to face him. "I got the feeling that Hesper was at your mother's house for a reason. Was the reason connected to me?"

Alasdair was silent a moment before answering. "Hesper has a more dangerous calling than most who live here. She's a storm-bringer, the one who calls down our rains and who keeps them from being too destructive. She can't always rein in that kind of power but more often than not the storm gods favor her requests." His quick smile lit his face. "Who better to petition Ilyap'a?"

Unexpectedly, Lucinda found her throat thick with unshed tears. "That means there really is a chance to save Tyrone?"

"A chance, yes."

"And what else?" she asked. "What is it your mother thinks I'm supposed to do?"

"At the moment Vita has no more idea than you do, which is why she was on edge. She's another one who doesn't like surprises."

"Al-as-dair!" The voice was young and male, calling from a distance.

Lucinda started. "Who's that?"

"I'm here, Gervase," Alasdair called back. "A friend," he told Lucinda. "Hesper's son."

Lucinda peered into the night, hearing rapid footsteps coming toward them. Moments later a young boy darted into the swatch of trail that was lit by moonlight. He stopped inches from them.

"Alas—who are you?" he asked bluntly, seeing Lucinda.

Alasdair made the introductions, and the boy looked Lucinda up and down. "You don't work with the stones, do you?"

"No, not at all. I work with fabric."

"Oh." That apparently didn't interest him. Gervase gave her a brief nod of acknowledgment and settled down on the ledge next to Alasdair. He seemed to have no inhibitions about talking in front of a stranger and immediately launched into a long monologue about how Nicodemus had been teaching him stonecutting and Nicodemus insisted that he work on faceting when it was easy and boring and any six-year-old could do it and what he really wanted to do was carve animals.

"And Nicodemus won't show you how to carve animals?" Alasdair guessed.

"I already know how. He won't even look at them. He tells me I'm too young and I'm not ready and I can't possibly know what I'm doing," the boy went on indignantly. "Nicodemus is an ass."

"I see," Alasdair said. Lucinda glanced at him; in the moonlight it was hard to be sure but it seemed he was struggling for a serious expression. "I suppose I should remind you that Nicodemus knows a great deal, and that to cut a stone properly is worth the years of training, but—"

"You'd be lying," Gervase said confidently.

"No, I'd be telling the truth. But I remember how set in his ways Nicodemus can be."

"Diamonds yield more easily than he does," the boy muttered.

"Maybe you should study with your mother instead."

"She says she'd rather teach a slab of basalt to multiply fractions. She thinks I'm recalcitrant."

"You are," Alasdair assured him. "You said you had carvings to show me?"

At that the boy reached into a pouch at his waist. He first took out a faceted stone and handed it to Alasdair.

"Blue topaz," Alasdair told Lucinda as the stone began to glow with a pale blue light.

Lucinda shook her head, unused to gems that acted like night-lights. "What makes them glow like that? I never heard that topaz was phosphorescent."

"It's not, but it has a natural radiance which it will emit when it's in a place where it feels safe," Alasdair explained.

"So topaz doesn't feel safe in Arcato?" she guessed with a touch of skepticism.

"Of course not," the boy said. "Your people don't have the first idea of how to properly care for the stones."

Alasdair hooked an elbow loosely around his neck. "Don't be rude, Gervase."

The boy wriggled out of Alasdair's hold, protesting. "It was only the truth. Honesty isn't rude."

"It is when it's meant to make someone else feel diminished."

Gervase didn't respond at first and Lucinda felt a tense stalemate between the boy and the man. Gervase was the one to break it. He bent his head to Lucinda and said in formal tones, "My apologies. I hope you'll forgive me and feel welcome here."

"Um—apologies accepted," Lucinda said as graciously as she could.

Gervase gave Alasdair a hopeful smile and thrust a chunk of stone at him. "What do you think of this jasper?"

Alasdair examined the carving. "That's a very passable goat." He handed it to Lucinda, who thought the miniature goat more than passable. Although the boy hadn't managed to give a sense of the goat's silky coat, the head, musculature, and stance were all rendered so realistically, Lucinda wouldn't have been surprised if the little goat had lowered its horns and tried to butt.

The boy then showed them a tortoise with a beautifully detailed shell and what looked like wrinkly skin on its outstretched legs and neck. His third carving was a cat made of blue-grey chalcedony with narrowed emerald eyes. Though it was half the size of her thumb, the carving was so precise that Lucinda could tell it was a very bad-tempered cat.

"Averill," Alasdair said with a snort of recognition.

"Don't tell her!" Gervase said. "I sketched her first and if she ever found out that I watched her long enough to draw her . . ."

Alasdair looked down at the boy. "These are more than good, you know that."

"They don't have breath in them," Gervase said, sounding discouraged.

"No, but you're close. Be careful what it is you carve from now on. I'm not sure you want to give breath to this cat, for example." He gave a mock shudder. "Having a miniature feline Averill in your life might be more than even you could handle."

The boy grinned and began to stuff the carvings back into the pouch. "Will you work with me then? Show me what Nicodemus won't."

Alasdair hesitated before answering. "I'd like to, Gervase, but I don't think I'm going to be here long enough."

"What do you mean?" The boy sounded betrayed.

"You know Lucinda traveled here from Arcato. She has to go back soon and I'm going to see that she gets there safely."

That was welcome news to Lucinda. So far she hadn't let herself think about the journey back down the mountain.

It wasn't welcome to Gervase. "Why? Why is she more important to you than we are?"

Alasdair's voice was soft. "You *have* been spending time with Averill, haven't you?" He touched the boy's shoulder. "It's not that there are others more important, only that there are things I am bound to do."

Gervase slipped the topaz back into the pouch and their faces fell into shadow. "I wish you weren't a *cearu*."

"So do I," Alasdair said. He stood up and reached out a hand to help Lucinda to her feet. "We'd better go back, too."

They walked with Gervase until they were through the stones and back in the upper village where the boy sprinted off for his home and Alasdair and Lucinda headed toward Vita's.

Lucinda tried to piece together what she'd overheard. "When you and Gervase were talking about giving breath to the carvings . . . is that how the dragon . . . I mean, you carved him and gave him life and that's why he's so loyal to you?"

"No," said Alasdair. "Although it's not acknowledged in your scientists' geology, there are some rare beings who are born of stone. And no, not all dragons are; most hatch from eggs laid by other dragons. Both sorts are very different from what Gervase was talking about. If I'd taken a piece of jade, carved a dragon, and breathed life into it, it would be . . . a more limited creature. It would contain what I knew of dragons and what memories the jade itself might hold, but not much beyond that." A smile flickered across Alasdair's face as he considered the possibility. "A dragon I carved might be a great deal more biddable than our friend but not nearly as interesting."

"So you can bring a stone to life?"

Alasdair frowned. "It's more a matter of recognizing what is already alive in the stone and encouraging it."

"Of course," Lucinda muttered. "That should have been self-evident." Alasdair, she knew, was genuinely trying to be helpful and informative; it was just that when she thought about it, nothing he said actually made sense.

She hung back as Vita's house came into sight. "I have an idea," she said slowly. "If the diamond necklace Kama gave me is so important, why don't I give it to you or your mother or someone who will know what to do with it? I don't need to keep it. I was going to give it back to Sebastian anyway."

"We could hold it for you," Alasdair agreed, "but none of us could call on its essence. I can't even read it. The only one you can give it to, who could work with it, is Kama. That's the way it is with his gifts. It was meant for you and so it's yours to use and care for until he chooses to give it to another."

Lucinda refused to be put off so easily. "What if I just leave it somewhere? Here, on the side of the path, for example. Someone would come along and find it and—"

"And it wouldn't matter," Alasdair assured her. "You'd wake up one morning and find it clasped in your hand or—"

"It was on my pillow," Lucinda said, shaken.

Alasdair shrugged. "It's the way he works. Eros is fond of beds."

Lucinda felt a familiar surge of exasperation at the gods. She began to tick them off on her fingers: "Eros is fond of beds and Hermes likes thieves and Ilyap'a isn't so hot on people impersonating him. How can you stand them, much less keep them straight—all these gods in your life?"

"What choice do I have? It's simply seeing and acknowledging what's all around you."

"Now you sound like Sebastian," she muttered.

"Well, there are a few things he and I have always agreed on." Alasdair studied her, his gaze focused and curious, as if she were an exotic organism beneath a microscope. "Why are you so angry at the gods? Didn't Hermes help you?"

"He did and I'm grateful, but he also made me feel overwhelmed and powerless, like I was completely at his mercy."

"You were."

"That's just it. You say we're at their mercy, so you believe in them and fear them and pray to them. How can you feel anything but manipulated? I look at that shrine in your mother's house and it gives me the willies. I think: She's trying to placate them or bribe them to keep them from ripping her world in half."

Alasdair gave her a sideways glance as he started up the stairway. Lucinda stayed where she was for a moment, her eyes following the graceful lines of the stone house that rose above them. She could smell the pots of hyacinths that flanked the door. Oil lamps in the windows gave the rooms behind them a warm, golden glow. If she didn't know better, she'd swear the place looked welcoming.

"Bribing the gods," Alasdair mused as she reluctantly caught up to him. "That's a rather negative interpretation."

"Not after what Ilyap'a did to Tyrone."

"I suspect it has more to do with your own fears than with the reality of the shrine," he went on as if he hadn't heard her. "After all, we're at the mercy of so many things—disease, old age, other people—and these things we can't always address. But the gods are sentient energies."

"Okay," Lucinda said, regrouping her thoughts, wanting to sound reasonable if not actually logical. "So if your mother isn't trying to bribe them to do her will, then what is it she's doing?"

"Vita sees it more as being in a daily dialogue with them," Alasdair explained. "Conversations with loved ones, if you like. She's always believed that on a certain level the gods are not so different from us, that they delight in the sensual. So, among other things, she offers up the flowers and the paintings."

"What if someone doesn't have something delightful to offer?"

"We all do," Alasdair said matter-of-factly. "Everyone has some part of their selves worth cherishing. That's what the gods respond to. So why not ask for their help and protection? Especially now that you've seen that they sometimes give it. They're always listening, you know."

Lucinda gave an overly dramatic shudder. "That is an eerie concept, omnipresent eavesdroppers. Besides, they're not supposed to be listening to me. I was born out of favor."

"Do you know, you only find that phrase in the cities along the river. I've often thought some misguided mortal wallowing in self-pity dreamed it up."

"And I always thought it was the gods whom misguided mortals dreamed up," Lucinda replied. She stopped on the top step, crossing her arms over her chest.

Alasdair pushed open the door. When she didn't move he asked, "Aren't you coming in?"

Her reply was deliberate and stiff. "I guess."

"You make it sound like a necessary evil."

She gave him a wan smile. "It's just hard for me to be here, asking for your help. I hate asking anyone for anything."

That," he said, "is something you're going to have to get over. Now think good thoughts as you pass the shrine," he added with a grin. "You wouldn't want to annoy the deities."

ALASDAIR DID NOT attempt to sleep that night. He spent the hours between midnight and the coming of dawn searching the scrolls and books in Vita's study, trying to answer the questions that had plagued him since he first found the ancient plaza in the city: What could strip stone of all memory? What would want to? And what was the meaning of the diamond-within-diamond symbol that he found there?

Over the years his mother had acquired what he considered a decent reference collection. Faded manuscripts carefully penned by his people contained the basic lore of the stones—the old stories of how the stones came to be, and the accounts of how his people had been taught to open themselves to and work with these bones of the earth. Illustrated manuals contained detailed instructions for the proper methods of identifying, cutting and carving, polishing and setting the stones. Copies of Hindu scriptures delineated the relation of gems to the planets and the parts of the body, the way in which those correlations could be used to heal, and how to array and wear the gems for the most propitious planetary influence. Wafer-thin volumes held lists of which gods favored which stones and which stones were ruled by which elements. And there were the more recent books that Vita had purchased in her travels, thick texts on geology and the chemical composition and internal structure of rocks and minerals. Alasdair found the geologists' worldview accurate, as far as it went, but limited. Although they had a solid grasp of how chemistry and physics combined to form and shape rock, the scientists had only the most limited idea of what the stones were capable of.

His eyes fell on Vita's most prized manuscript, a thirteenth-century copy of the thirty-seventh volume of Pliny the Elder's *Naturalis Historia,* which dealt with rock crystal, amber, and gemstones. Alasdair had always been fond of Pliny for dismissing the notion that amber was formed from bits of crystallized lynx piss; he also couldn't help being fascinated by the fact that Pliny, ever the scientist, had calmly taken notes on the cloud of volcanic ash spewing from Mt. Vesuvius, then bravely sailed into Pompeii to study it more closely and died of asphyxiation from what his nephew, Pliny the Younger, described as "the thickening fog."

Sitting at his mother's desk, Alasdair began skimming the familiar texts, remembering all too well the frustration he'd once felt at the wealth of conflicting, often inaccurate, information. Rubies were thought to store heat. One writer went so far as to advise tossing a ruby into water if you wanted it to boil. *And wait a millennium for your cup of tea,* Alasdair thought. Opals allegedly prevented blond-haired women from going grey, as if you could get an opal to care about such a thing. And several sages were sure that if you placed two diamonds together, they'd mate and produce offspring. Then there was confusion about the stones; some texts cited sapphire when they really meant lapis, mistook green marble for jade, peridot and olivine for topaz, and red spinel for red diamonds. Yet over the years Alasdair had come to believe there was at least a germ of truth in all of these works, that none of them could be completely dismissed.

He read for hours and found nothing that answered his questions. Again, he tried to grasp at the fleeting images that he'd seen when he touched the diamond-within-diamond pattern but all he clearly remembered was the excruciating pain.

An inlay of malachite, lapis, sugilite, and turquoise covered the top of Vita's desk. He traced its intricate pattern, then, still troubled by his questions, he took a sheet of cream-colored paper and a fountain pen and drew the diamond-within-diamond pattern, reviewing what he knew: Mariamme said it was a key and was afraid of it. And in the mosaic it was indeed a key to the shrine, though Lucinda said it also appeared on Sebastian's bedpost. And when he'd seen it on one of Janus's doors the god had steered him away from it. Based on all of that, he'd assumed that the pattern was connected to the being who'd caused him that excruciating pain in the ruined plaza in Arcato.

Idly, he picked up the large, flat amethyst crystal that served as Vita's paperweight and turned it over in his hand. Amethyst was always a good stone for clarity and now he could feel it working with him, helping him through the thicket of his own ignorance, helping him to turn the problem in his mind. What if instead of assuming that the diamond-within-diamond pattern signaled something evil or dark, he assumed it was merely a key to the Shrine of the Mothers? Sebastian having some alliance with the mothers—an old debt, the limestone told him—kept the pattern close as his protection. Mariamme feared it but she had no idea of what it led to, only warnings passed down over the generations. After all, the mothers would have put protections on the shrine, kept it hidden and safe from the city above it. If the wrong person attempted to use the key. Alasdair could well imagine that the consequences would have been dire, and the diamond-within-diamond symbol would have been feared.

Which was not at all the same thing as whatever it was that had stripped the memory from the stones of the plaza above the shrine and nearly killed him. That was a different entity altogether.

If the diamond-within-diamond wasn't the problem and was, in fact, a protected key, then maybe what he'd sensed in that plaza—whatever caused so much pain and wiped out everything else—maybe that entity was there because it knew about the Shrine of the Mothers, was searching for it, and yet couldn't find the way in. Perhaps what the entity left there at the door it couldn't open was all the fury it couldn't unleash at its target. Could it have been simple luck that the entity wasn't there when the passageway opened for Sebastian and allowed him in as well?

So, Alasdair asked himself, *what is it that's still lingering in Arcato, waiting for its chance to destroy the mothers? And is it connected to whoever was stalking me?*

A brisk knock startled him out of his reverie. The door to the library opened and Vita peered in. She was dressed in the long wool cloak she wore for traveling. "I thought I might find you here. We need to set out if we're going to get there by sunrise."

Alasdair nodded. "I'm ready. We should wake Lucinda and take her with us."

"No," Vita said. "You know Averill would never permit it. I've already arranged for Neelam to drop by later this morning and take care of her."

THEY DIDN'T TRAVEL far. It was little more than an hour's journey since both Alasdair and Vita moved swiftly across the dark, rocky terrain. For them the route out of the towns and east into the mountains was as familiar as the stairway to Vita's house. Once the terraced footpaths ended the climb became steeper but a pale gold line of light was burning across the charcoal-grey horizon, and it was enough to allow them to see the markers: the round, nearly flat granite boulder inscribed with a spiral; the first of the obelisks, this one clear red carnelian; and beyond it a rounded bluff overlooking the towns. As they passed the bluff the sun's crown edged above the horizon, turning the charcoal sky a pale violet with just the beginning of blue coming into it. His mother's face, Alasdair saw, was composed, as usual, betraying none of her thoughts.

They climbed higher to the next marker. From a distance its black basalt back looked like a slender hooded figure, nearly as tall as Alasdair. Its front, though, revealed an open geode, an amethyst "cathedral," its inner walls covered with dark amethyst crystals, their points catching the morning light. Vita stopped momentarily and held out a hand to the cathedral. Alasdair could feel her sending the crystals her deep love of their purple light and in return, the crystals sending her their clarity and protection from sorcery. Alasdair smiled, admiring his mother's thoroughness, then he, too, held out his hand to the amethysts, greeting them after a long absence and thanking them for the help their kin had given him in the library.

He felt a kind of happy confusion moving through the crystals in the cathedral—a mix of delight at his return and conflict as to how to respond. He could feel some of the stone's calming influence coming his way, along with some of the protection against sorcery, then Vita touched his shoulder and nodded toward the ground where a small hexagonal amethyst was rolling toward him.

He stooped and picked up the crystal that had just been given him. Its widest surface bore an engraved image of a bear. Alasdair stared at it, not quite believing what he held. Since Renaissance times it had been known that a bear engraved in amethyst was a powerful protection. Nicodemus, who could carve nearly any form into nearly any crystal, had tried to fashion this very charm more than once without success. Something always went wrong—the angle of the head, a paw that was too big or small for the rest of the animal, a split in the crystal. He'd carved an entire series of bears—sleeping, playing, running, even a pregnant sow nursing her cubs—in topaz.

"Oh, Nicodemus will have a fit if he sees that," Vita murmured, sounding quite pleased.

"You have my gratitude," Alasdair told the amethysts, humbled by their unexpected gift.

They continued climbing, passing other markers. A dark green tourmaline column, an arc of crescent moons carved into the black of a black-and-white striped gneiss boulder, and beyond that another boulder with a serpentine pattern adorning its face. Alasdair heard the sound of running water as they dipped down into a fold in the mountain. They traveled down to where a stream bisected the shallow mountain valley, its banks lined with wildflowers opening to the dawn light. His mother lifted the hem of her cloak as they crossed the stream, smiling at the profusion of flowers. "Oh, Alasdair," she murmured, "how could you have stayed away so long?"

He knew she didn't expect an answer so he didn't bother to give one. Then they were climbing again, out of the valley to another peak and to the gateway—two massive rectangular stones, serving as posts, with a third laid across the top, the lintel—that led to the higher reaches of the mountain. Even his people's legends held no clue as to who had built this massive open doorway or who had carved the great stags that stood on hind legs on either post, their outstretched front legs almost touching the sun that was carved in the center of the lintel.

They passed beneath the gateway, feeling its benediction, then began winding their way through the colonnade of pillars that led to the upper peaks. As a child Alasdair had always thrilled to this part of the climb, memorizing the order of the pillars: first deep red almandine garnet, then orange citrine, olive-green peridot, pale blue aquamarine, deep blue sapphire, violet-blue tanzanite, the lighter violet iolite, ruby spinel, lilac kunzite, red rhodocrosite, pink topaz followed by yellow heliodor and golden topaz, smoky quartz, black tourmaline, emerald, dark green alexandrite, even darker dioptase . . . there were thirty in all. They were irregular in height and texture, most quite rough, and yet they were dazzling. Over the years he'd had favorites, been drawn to one stone or another, but Vita had taught him well: You weren't meant to linger here and read any one stone. You were meant to wind through the gemstone columns; it was as much a passage as the gateway. On ceremony days the people of the towns would form lines that danced through the pillars like a long, joyous snake. This, at least, he knew the reason for.

Their stories told of a young woman, Helice, who'd lived in the towns during a harsh winter when there was little food, warmth, or light. Even the gemstones had no light in them and could give the people no aid. The people stayed in their houses, grieving those they lost to starvation. Only Helice refused to give in to grief. Instead she made her way up the mountain to this place and danced joyously, some said madly. Their most powerful elder followed and called her down, insisted she stop her crazed dance, claiming it was an affront to the gods. But Helice kept dancing, through day and night and cold winds that ripped the rock into shards. Again the elder commanded her to stop and again Helice ignored her, whirling and spiraling up the mountain. No one knew if the elder struck her down or if Helice simply died of exhaustion and exposure, but when she at last fell to earth it was said the gemstone pillars sprang up, honoring the path of her dance. And when the elder returned to the towns she found that the winter had broken. For generations, each year before winter set in, the people traced Helice's dance through the pillars, asking the blessings of the mountain spirits.

Beyond the gemstone colonnade the mountain leveled out. Here Alasdair and Vita faced east, gazing across another steep valley to a ridge that arched up in the shape of a bull's horns. The sun was just resting between the horns.

"Perfect," Vita said with relief. Lifting both arms she sang a chant to the rising sun, inviting it to send its rays into the earth and the stones, to give them light and life. Alasdair echoed the chant. As he sang the last line Vita began a second chant, this one asking the sun to reveal the secrets of the stones. Alasdair sang that one as well, and then they sang both chants together, their voices falling into the easy harmony they'd practiced over the years, soaring toward the sun.

This more than anything made him feel as if he were not only home but rooted to the place, his mother's songs as much a part of it as the rock beneath his feet. The last note lingered in the chill mountain air. Alasdair and Vita stood perfectly still, waiting.

"Now," Vita said. They turned to see a crack in the high, solid wall of white granite behind them. Gradually, silently, the crack widened, revealing a stairway cut into the crags, each step worn smooth by centuries of use. On the side of the stairway, run-off from a mountain stream trickled down the rock face into a stone basin. Alasdair and Vita washed their hands and faces in the icy water and began to ascend.

They followed the stairs up the cliff face to a broad plateau that extended back to where the mountain rose in yet another sheer rock wall. Alasdair always found himself amazed by the plateau's lush greenery. A stream rippled through it, fed by its source near the peaks. Alders, evergreens, and wild sage and fennel grew thick in its rich, black earth. And in the rock wall, close to the stream, was the opening to the birthing cave, where the women of the villages gave birth. It was still a wonder to him that any woman who was nine months pregnant managed to safely make it up the steep route to the cave, and yet they all did and all the children of the lost towns emerged into the world from the mountain. It was said that every child was born to two mothers: the woman who gave birth and the mountain herself who gave mother and child sanctuary.

One last set of stairs led up from the plateau to the mountain's summit. Vita raised an eyebrow, asking Alasdair if he was ready. He nodded and they climbed up through the granite passageway to the peak that Averill claimed as her second home. She stood on bare rock face, wearing a white robe. Alasdair wasn't certain whether it was the color of her robe or the harsh light of the morning sun, but for the first time the shape-shifter looked old, deep lines around the sides of her mouth and eyes, arms too gaunt beneath the loose white fabric.

The elder's glance slid over Alasdair and Vita, then with arms stretched wide, she arched back, looking up at the sky, and uttering odd, high-pitched cries. Alasdair wondered if she were about to shift into an owl and take flight. He glanced down at his mother. Vita stood calmly, regarding Averill with her usual inscrutable gaze.

The odd cries continued, echoing off the rock walls until, without warning Averill snapped upright. She took in deep gulps of air then turned to her right, and crouched low to the ground. "Don't move or make a sound," she told them, and again began the animal cries.

It was all Alasdair could do not to turn his head when he heard the sound of light footsteps—they had to be paws—on the rock. Then Averill's voice was soothing, speaking what sounded like tender endearments in a language he didn't recognize.

"If you move very slowly, you can look this way," she told them.

He and Vita turned to see Averill murmuring her endearments to a red fox, who stood with its head between her hands. She was scratching it behind the ears, running her hands along its flanks, and the fox was rubbing against her, its eyes closed in contentment.

Sebastian? Alasdair wondered. No, this fox was smaller and didn't have the same blaze of white on its chest.

From inside her robe Averill drew a silver chain bearing an engraved bead of smoky quartz. She fastened it around the fox's neck, giving it what seemed to be further instructions in the strange language and the fox, seeming to understand, butted her once with its head, then loped away, disappearing into a cleft in the rock.

When it was gone Averill turned to them and shrugged. "It's my best hope of reaching Malachy. I flew all night searching for him and couldn't find a trace. If we're lucky, the foxes will know where he is and deliver my message."

"Lucky," Alasdair echoed. "You sound certain that finding him will be a good thing."

"For me it will," Averill said. "Whether he is help or hindrance to you, I've missed him."

"We appreciate you searching for him," Vita said with more diplomacy.

Averill raised a dark, skeptical eyebrow. Wordlessly, she led them back down to the plateau. They sat beside the stream, the sun filtering through alders and evergreens, extracting a warm, sweet scent from the leaves and needles.

"I intend to help Malachy when I find him," Averill said bluntly.

Alasdair didn't respond. It was somehow typical that he had come to her for help, and Averill had turned it into a quest to help Malachy. He should have known.

If any of this bothered Vita, she didn't let it show. "Of course," she said. "We wouldn't expect otherwise. In the meantime, though, we need your help."

Averill smiled her feline smile. "I hear there's a seer in Arcato. Perhaps you and Alasdair should visit her."

"Don't send me in circles." Alasdair couldn't keep the irritation out of his voice. "You know I don't have time for that."

The elder stretched her arms above her head, as if just waking up. Alasdair felt alarms going off in every cell of his body and instinctively reached for the amethyst charm. He wasn't quick enough. Averill's arms swept down again and as they did a pins-and-needles sensation ran through his arms, and he felt his limbs stiffening. He tried to fight it, to touch the amethyst despite the paralysis that was sweeping through him. He couldn't make his arms work at all.

Vita touched him lightly on the back, a piece of rhyolite between her fingers and his shoulder blade. He felt its call to movement, felt it lending him strength, helping him fight Averill's power. The rhyolite's essence damped the pins-and-needles prickling, insisted he feel the sensations of his own muscle and bone. His hand closed around the six-sided amethyst crystal, and the last traces of the paralysis vanished. Averill was watching him dispassionately. Vita's touch was still on his back.

His eyes locked on Averill, Alasdair opened his hand.

Averill glanced at the amulet and arched back as if she'd been struck. "Where in the name of the Kali did you get that?"

He knew why she'd called on Kali but refused to take the bait. "I don't think Kali had anything to do with it," he said. "Artemis perhaps—she's always been partial to bears—but more likely, it was simply the amethysts' kindness."

"Or foresight," Vita suggested. "They must have known he'd need protection."

Averill's golden eyes were hot with contempt. "He was in no danger from me. You know I'd never do anything to one of my own that causes lasting harm."

"No, you just try to bully us into submission," Alasdair said, rubbing at his arms. "Can't you trust us to listen to you without the tiresome theatrics?"

Averill's chest seemed to swell with anger, her eyes grew round, her arms stretched out, and the folds of the white robe flattened into feathers. In the space of a breath the great horned owl was hovering over them, talons extended.

"You spend too much time as predator, Averill." Vita spoke in a light casual tone, as if she were noting it was time for the evening lamps to be lit. "You've become too used to inspiring fear in others. You seem to think it's an acceptable way to treat everyone, and now your insist on your own power taking precedence over all. And that may harm my son and others. You do understand, I can't let that happen?"

Alasdair barely had time to reach for his mother before the owl attacked. Vita, though, slipped out of his protective grasp and out of reach of Averill's talons. Quick as the raptor, she opened her hand, revealing a large, smooth cabochon of red carnelian, a symbol inscribed on its surface. The owl let out a furious scream and retreated to a branch above them.

Alasdair stared at the translucent red stone, trying to suppress a feeling of awe. Carnelian was linked to blood and so to energy and power. And it had an ancient connection with Seth, the volatile Egyptian god of the desert and of storms. Embodying opposites, carnelian could still the very qualities Seth was known for: envy, hatred, and rage. The stone's connection to the god had also given it the potential to deflect psychic attacks. Vita, who wielded the stones with more skill than most, had not only found a carnelian with tremendous power of its own—this one, he read, had been used as a protector for centuries, buried with the dead in Egypt and again later in Japan—but bound it to her with her own blood. As if that weren't enough, she'd also engraved it with Tara's seed syllable, so that as long as it was used with compassion and wisdom, it would invoke the protection of the goddess of compassion. Now the carnelian was not only keeping the raptor at bay, it was drawing Averill's fury from her. The owl was sitting in the tree, blinking sedately, as if it had just woken from a lengthy nap.

"We've always been on the same side, Averill," Vita went on calmly. "There's no reason for antagonism between us. We need your help." She fixed the owl with a reassuring gaze. "It's really best if you're in human form for this. Do come down and change."

The owl fluttered to the ground. The change took longer this time, as if the carnelian were slowing the owl's wits, disorienting it somehow, and Alasdair felt a moment of concern for Averill, but she managed the shift and soon stood before them, white robed and erect.

Averill seemed riveted by the carnelian. "Where did you get that stone?" she asked. It was a question Alasdair would dearly have loved the answer to. When his mother didn't reply, the shape-shifter gave a surprised little shrug and said quietly, "It's enspelled me."

"I prefer to think of it as a balancing," Vita said. "You're free to do as you like. I haven't weakened you; in animal form you'll still have your kills. I've only shifted the way you reach for power."

"You stopped my attack," Averill reminded her, her voice mild.

Vita nodded solemnly. "That's a change you'll have to adapt to. You can no longer use your power to attack your own. It's destructive and a waste of your gifts—self-indulgent, really. We have no time or room for that."

Alasdair watched the exchange between them, fascinated by the ease with which his mother was assuming control over the woman who had ruled them for generations. He was as aware as Averill that this betokened a power shift within the towns, that while she might be the oldest and most re-spected among the elders, from now on it would be Vita they deferred to. He studied his graceful, diminutive mother, wondering if he'd ever truly seen her for what she was. Had she been planning this all along? And given that she'd adapted the carnelian into a charm of almost frightening power, what other stones had she been working?

"Tell me what gives you the right," Averill said.

"Necessity," Vita answered. "We need you to find Malachy but not for your own purposes."

Averill smiled her feline smile. "You're the one with all the power now. You find him."

"You know I can't," Vita said. "I don't have the connection with the ani-mals or with Malachy." She held out the carnelian again and when she spoke her voice was gentle. "When I invoked this stone I left your essence un-touched. You've always had such a strong spirit. I don't like the idea of hav-ing to weaken you."

The shape-shifter backed away from her. "You have no right—"

"No, of course not," Vita agreed. "One never has the *right* to take power from another, but survival sometimes demands it, and you know that better than most. What will it be, Averill? Will you help us?"

Averill's golden eyes danced between Vita and Alasdair, and for a long moment Alasdair thought she would defy Vita and make everything much worse, but at last she nodded and said reluctantly, "But only because your son is dear to me, too."

Alasdair then cleared his throat and explained the theory he'd come up with in the library about the diamond-within-diamond symbol being a protective key for the mothers.

"You may be right," Averill allowed.

"So you must get Malachy to tell you what he can," Vita said. "Maybe he knows who's trying to destroy the Shrine of the Mothers . . . or who was trailing Alasdair in the city."

The shape-shifter stretched her back the way a cat would, and Alasdair sensed that she couldn't wait to change into animal form, that it was painful for her to be standing here as a human, compelled to respond to Vita's summons, but all she said was, "I'm curious about that one myself."

"One other thing," Vita said. "You've met the girl who is staying with us?"

"Lucinda," Alasdair prompted, seeing Averill's face go deliberately blank. Clearly, she still held some sort of grudge against Lucinda.

"Who came in with her?" Vita asked.

"The dragon," Averill answered.

"And?"

The shape-shifter pulled her long grey mane off her neck and twisted it into a knot. "Hermes was with her earlier, before I saw her." She frowned. "He never liked Malachy, you know, even though Malachy's a trickster after his own heart."

"Apparently not," Alasdair demurred.

Averill shot him a warning glance but a look from Vita quelled it. "She had two other spirits with her," Averill went on, her eyes half closed. "One from the living—her mother. The girl has no notion that she travels with her at all, doesn't even see the bonds her mother feels. The other spirit is also from the living but just barely."

"Meaning?" Vita asked.

"It's a man's spirit. Not a father or a lover, a friend who also loves her fiercely. He doesn't have much left for himself so he's traveling with her, wanting to give her what protection he can. It's draining him."

"Tyrone," Alasdair said softly.

Averill lifted her thin shoulders in a shrug. "He won't be with her long. He's dying."

"Can you send him back to his own body?" Alasdair asked. "It's the only chance he has of surviving long enough for Hesper to help him."

"I suppose," Averill said reluctantly. "The girl will lose a layer of protection, though."

"We'll do what we can to address that." Vita pressed her fingertips together, a gesture she used when she was thinking through a problem. Alasdair realized that she'd put away the carnelian without his noticing. "According to Mariamme, there's something the girl can do here to help Alasdair. Do you know what it is?"

Averill chuckled. "No, but finding out is easy. All he has to do is take her through the three thresholds."

They left her on the mountain. When Alasdair turned to look back Averill stood on the edge of the green shelf watching them. A mountain lion flanked her right side, a wolf her left.

Sixteen

LUCINDA SAT AT the table in Vita's garden, feasting on freshly baked pastries stuffed with nuts and spices. Neelam, who was Nicodemus's daughter and the baker of the pastries, sat across from her. Nicodemus sat next to Neelam and a slender, quiet young man named Than sat on Neelam's other side. They were there, Lucinda realized moments after meeting the trio, to babysit her until Vita and Alasdair returned from wherever they'd gone.

Neelam, who looked to be about fourteen, didn't resemble her father at all. She was a lively dark-haired girl, who seemed to have a predilection for spectacular rubies. Though she was dressed simply in a gold linen shift, deep-red faceted stones flashed from her throat, wrists, and ears. Lucinda had to work not to stare. Vita's amethysts and topazes had been beautiful, even exotic. Neelam looked as if she were wearing jewels stolen from someone's crown.

"So in the city, can you really see moving pictures every night?" she wanted to know.

"Every day, too," Lucinda assured her. "Movies are pretty common. At least in my part of the city," she added, thinking of Mariamme.

"Oh, I've always wanted to see a movie," Neelam said. She looked at her father imploringly. "Don't you think it's time I was allowed to go to Arcato?"

"I most assuredly do not," he told her with a fond smile. "When you're older perhaps."

Vita's cat sprang onto Lucinda's lap and Lucinda stiffened. Seeing her expression, Nicodemus chuckled. "Moura's just a cat. She won't shift into a hawk or a pig."

"You sure?" Lucinda muttered, petting the cat.

"There's nothing to worry about." Neelam continued in her efforts to persuade her father. "Than would come to Arcato with me."

The startled look on Than's face made it clear that this was the first he'd heard of this plan. Neelam didn't let it discourage her. "And you won't have to worry about where I am. I'm sure I could stay at Lucinda's house."

Lucinda choked on her pastry, startling the cat who bounded off her lap. She had to drink several glasses of Vita's fennel tea before being able to say, "I don't have a house exactly. It's a flat, an apartment," she added when Neelam looked at her blankly. "Just a bedroom and a tiny living room and a kitchen." She gestured to the garden. "It's not beautiful, like this place. In fact, the city is crowded and pretty grimy. You might not even like it there."

"I'll like it," Neelam said with a determination that somehow reminded Lucinda of Vita.

Nicodemus shrugged his expansive shoulders. "All our young ones want to see Arcato," he said. "And most of them get there sooner or later. But not until they've passed their third initiation," he reminded his daughter.

"Have you been there, Than?" Lucinda asked, both to divert Neelam from her campaigning and because Than hadn't said a word since his arrival at Vita's house and she was curious about him. He had a slight build, straight black hair, and Asian features; he didn't seem to be related to Neelam or her father.

"No," he replied.

"Than is visiting from Mandalay," Neelam explained. "He's apprenticed to my father. Miraculously, he hasn't gotten bored with this place yet."

"Perhaps that's because he actually applies himself to stonecutting," her father suggested.

Idly, Neelam turned the bracelet on her right wrist, a chain of oval rubies, each set in delicate gold filigree. "I've had more than enough stonecutting. I need to try something new." She glanced up at Lucinda. "What sort of professions do you have in the city? I hear women can make a lot of money dancing without clothes."

Nicodemus flushed bright red and began coughing violently, Than got up and began pounding his back, and Neelam, concentrating on Lucinda, said, "Have *you* ever danced without your clothes?"

Lucinda was spared from having to answer by Alasdair and Vita's arrival. They greeted their guests and inquired after Lucinda's sleep, appetite, and general state of health. Alasdair, she noticed, looked drained while Vita looked as if she'd just won a lottery. She was positively beaming with good cheer. Lucinda found it all a little maddening. No one was really talking about what was going on and when she tried to ask Alasdair where they'd been, Vita said, "All in good time, child," effectively putting an end to that conversation.

It was sometime later that Nicodemus, Neelam, and Than departed, and Vita left Alasdair alone with Lucinda. Lucinda didn't waste time. "What's going on?" she asked.

"Many things," Alasdair told her, "some of which are just internal politics. I won't bore you with those."

Lucinda grinned in spite of herself. "You have politics here in Shangri-la?"

Alasdair grimaced. "We do, and believe me, you don't want the details. Suffice to say that we saw Averill this morning. She's trying to find Sebastian and she gave us some information."

Lucinda looked at him expectantly, aware that the dragon had reappeared from wherever it had been and was perched on the edge of the table, listening intently.

Alasdair hesitated before saying, "There's an agreement of sorts between you and us. We'll do what we can to help Tyrone, and you'll do what you can to help me against that entity in the city, right?"

She nodded, fear suddenly wrapping itself around her gut.

"Well, Averill took the first step in helping Tyrone."

"Averill, who nearly scratched my eyes out when I showed up here?"

"She sees spirits," Alasdair said gently. "She said that when she saw you yesterday, you had two spirits traveling with you, both of them protective: your mother's and Tyrone's."

"My mother?" Lucinda choked out. "We barely talk. We make each other miserable."

"None of that affects what Averill saw. Wherever you go, a part of her goes with you, looking out for you."

"Yeah, probably waiting for me to fuck up."

He shrugged. "Perhaps. But the love is real and so is the protection she gives you."

"And Tyrone?" It was easier to ask about Tyrone than to contemplate her mother's love.

"That's more serious," Alasdair said quietly. "There's so little left of Tyrone that for him to send his spirit to watch out for you—it's all but killed him. Averill can send his spirit back to him. You, however, have to agree. It means you'll have less protection."

Lucinda leaned back, stunned. "I never thought I had any, anyway. Tell her, yes. Tell her to do it this minute."

Alasdair looked at the dragon. "Will you convey that?"

The dragon cocked its delicate head, as if considering the request, then lifted into the air and flew out of the terraced garden.

Lucinda felt tears welling again and rubbed at her eyes. *Tyrone, you idiot,* she thought, *stop taking care of me and take care of yourself.*

"The other thing Averill said was that to find out what you have to do in this bargain of ours, you and I have to go through the three thresholds together. They're literally three open doorways made of stone."

"And you do what when you cross them?"

"Nothing. You simply stand inside each one. And see what it shows you."

Lucinda's eyes narrowed. "Do you have any idea of what they'll show us?"

"Usually past, present, and future. They're a very linear phenomenon."

"Dangerous?"

"Not physically, no. The danger is that you'll be asked to view something you'd rather not see."

"And Neelam was so keen to see our movies," she murmured.

"The thresholds aren't like that at all."

"Can the dragon come with us?" Lucinda asked, suddenly aware that though she hadn't known it at the time, she'd had quite a bit of protection and now felt more vulnerable than ever.

"Not into the thresholds, no."

"And Hesper's still working on talking to thunder gods?"

"Yes," Alasdair assured her.

Lucinda found she'd been holding her breath. She released it in a ragged sigh. "It sounds as if the thresholds are the next step. When do we go?"

"They only open at night," Alasdair told her. "So we go tonight. In the meantime, I'm badly in need of a nap."

LUCINDA PASSED THE afternoon in a state of mild anxiety. Vita, who visited with her briefly, told her there was nothing to be afraid of, that the people of the towns often visited the three thresholds when they needed guidance. Vita's casual tone made going to the thresholds sound like going to a telephone directory for a phone number, which Lucinda didn't quite trust. Still, she told herself it was silly to get worked up when she didn't even know what it was she was getting worked up about. So she took a long, luxurious soak in the hot springs above Vita's house, wondering if Averill had succeeded in sending Tyrone's spirit back to him. He was still hanging on, she told herself. He had to be. Despite her entrenched cynicism, she couldn't even contemplate the idea that she had come all this way and it might be for nothing. She didn't know if it was naïve hope or blazing denial, but she believed Tyrone was still alive; she wouldn't allow any other possibility.

She did, however, have some skepticism about the other part of Averill's message. Was some part of her mother traveling with her, looking out for her? No, she decided. Her mother wasn't the sort even to admit to having a spirit, let alone send hers out to protect the daughter she so deeply disapproved of. Maybe Averill was right about Tyrone—he was just enough of a gallant fool to try to protect her when he was barely holding on to life himself—but she didn't know the first thing about Lucinda's mother.

Sinking deeper into the water, Lucinda let the heat soothe her frayed nerves. Eyes closed, resting her back against the earthen wall of the pool, she felt the anxiety slipping away. She had a moment or two of delicious tranquility, and then her sense of peace gave way to an odd and disquieting sense that she'd forgotten something. She was certain that it wasn't a mundane something—she hadn't forgotten to brush her teeth or pay her rent. It was something larger that hovered just on the edge of consciousness, and it was something, she was fairly sure, that would never have even occurred to her in the city.

LUCINDA AND ALASDAIR set out just as twilight fell, when the skies were a soft violet and the stone of the mountains and houses pulled a deep red hue from the setting sun. The air was softer than it was during the day, and night-blooming flowers along the sides of the footpaths were just beginning to open, giving off a sweet, summery scent. The moon was not yet up.

Alasdair hadn't said much since waking from his nap. He seemed preoccupied as he led the way uphill from Vita's house. They hadn't walked more than ten minutes when he stopped in front of what looked like ruins: a rectangular doorway in a wall built of flat stones, and behind it two others, identical and freestanding; no roof or other walls connected them.

"This is it?" Lucinda asked, a little disappointed. She'd thought the thresholds would at least be some exotic site, reeking of ritual and magic, but the wall of another house was just a short distance away—they were still firmly in the upper town—and what she was looking at seemed decrepit rather than mystical. "These are the three thresholds?"

"I'm afraid so."

Lucinda leaned forward, peering into the first doorway. Although the fading sun cast deep shadows, it was still light enough to see that there was nothing inside the first doorway—just a "floor" that had once been paved with stone and now had grass straggling over and between the broken pieces of the foundation. "It's empty," she reported.

"It usually is," Alasdair said.

The tension she'd been feeling since Alasdair first mentioned the thresholds ebbed. The place was just too . . . nothing. She glanced at Alasdair. He didn't seem to be in any hurry to enter.

"So what was this?" she asked, and when he didn't answer, added, "I mean, before it fell apart. Was it originally built as a house or a school or—"

"We don't know who built it," Alasdair said. "The three doorways were here when our ancestors first came to this place. As far as we know, it's always been just like this. My guess is that it's not the ruins of anything but that it was built this way, quite deliberately."

"How many times have you gone in before?"

"Once when I was a boy and too stupid to resist the mystery of it. Again when Gioia asked me to and at least once before each initiation."

"And how many of those have you had?"

"Seven." He smiled at her. "That why I've had other names. You're given a new one each time you pass a new level of initiation."

"That must get fucking confusing." She said it without thinking and was startled when he laughed out loud.

"It does. Especially since everyone who lives here goes through multiple initiations and has multiple names. I've often thought we should appoint someone whose sole job it would be to keep all the names straight. A scribe of sorts. We have scribes, of course," he went on. "Unfortunately, none of them are terribly interested in sorting out initiation names."

Maybe they were both just delaying the inevitable, but it felt good to talk so easily with this man who still seemed so—other. "So your mother has multiple names, too?"

"At least a dozen. I don't think I've ever remembered all of them. Let's see . . . Sadira, Iolanthe, Dalila, Maeve, Jessamine, uh . . . Rosabel—"

"Rosabel?" Lucinda sputtered. "That's so adorable. It sounds like a fat, fluffy kitten."

"Well, that was one of her younger names."

"I love thinking of your mother as Rosabel. My mother's is Gertie," she added, feeling she should offer some tidbit from her own life.

"As in Gertrude?" he asked politely.

"No, just Gertie. She likes it but it always made me think of girdles, so I thought it was a very embarrassing name for a mother to have." She considered him. "I'll bet Vita, or whoever she was when you were a kid, was never an embarrassment."

"No, I wouldn't use that word for her. Still, she could be difficult in her own way."

"And now?" Lucinda asked, curious about the small, regal woman who was both charming and domineering.

Alasdair gave a short, hollow laugh. "Now she scares me."

"Does she really?"

"Let's just say that this morning when we met with Averill, I was extremely glad it was my side she was on." The sun dropped farther and a shadow from the first threshold stretched out across the ground in front of them. "It's almost dark." There was something wistful in his voice, as if he didn't want the conversation to end. "We should go in."

Lucinda delayed a moment longer, wanting reassurance. "You went through the thresholds nine times," she said. "So if you've survived it nine times, it can't be too terrible."

His grey eyes studied her, and again she had the sense of someone truly ancient looking out at her. It was more than that, she realized, more than his hundred and sixty-odd years. What she now saw in his eyes was unfathomable pain coupled with a steady and detached resolve to bear it. How was it that she'd never recognized that before?

"You've been through hell," she said. "Was it the thresholds?"

"No more than anything else."

The fear was back. "You don't want to go through them again, do you?"

He didn't answer; something impassive came into his eyes and she sensed that he was girding himself. "No," he said at last. "Except for that first time, it's never been my choice. But as you pointed out, we all survive it."

"Let's go then," she said, and though she meant it to sound brave, her voice came out small and childlike.

He took her hand and they walked through the first doorway.

They stood between the first two walls. Above them the sky was nearly dark. "Now what?" Lucinda asked.

"Now we just stand here," he said. "And we see what it wants to show us."

What it showed them first was a young woman with nut-brown skin and short, straight black hair. It wasn't as if they were watching her on a screen. She seemed real, three-dimensional. Lucinda could even smell the sweet dusky scent of sage that emanated from her. Only the fact that they were standing in the darkness of twilight and the young woman stood in clear, bright daylight made it clear that she was not actually there beside them. She had a strong face with wide, dark eyes, a prominent nose, and a dazzling smile. And she seemed so purely, radiantly happy that Lucinda grieved for herself, knowing she had never felt that unfettered joy and never would.

Why, she wondered, were some people given the gift of happiness when others weren't? Was it a talent, like the ability to sing? Was it simply that she had no talent for being happy? Beside her Alasdair stiffened and released her hand, and Lucinda snapped out of her self-absorption, suddenly noticing what the woman wore and understanding who she was.

She wore a simple white silk sheathe, adorned with a familiar necklace: a rectangular, flat-cut white diamond suspended from two white-gold chains. Alasdair had said that Kama gave it to someone before he gave it to Lucinda, and her name was Gioia.

Quickly, Lucinda felt for the velvet pouch she wore at her waist. Kama's diamond was still there. This was just a vision from the past. Lucinda dared a glance at Alasdair. He had dropped to a crouch, as if to shield himself from a blow.

When Lucinda looked up again the background had changed. Gioia no longer stood with the crude stone wall of the second threshold behind her. She was on some sort of portico—there were columns carved of what looked like amethyst and jade—and she was holding an opal goblet; Lucinda could see the fire in it. She was toasting a tall, familiar-looking young man—Alasdair before he had all the grief in his eyes. He, too, was beautiful then.

And they were lovers. Lucinda could see it in their eyes: love and trust and delight, connection and spark. They stood there, barely touching and yet she felt as if she were watching a great intimacy. Again, she felt an odd stab of jealousy, this time because she'd never had the chance to look at Sebastian that way, because she'd never known that kind of trust with anyone.

Something else was there between the columns, a dark smoky form that had no definition, almost like a cloud except that its shape was rapidly, continually changing. Lucinda stared at it a moment. The cloud was roiling, almost as if it were gathering itself, dark and hovering over the lovers and neither of them seemed aware of it.

Another woman came toward them. She was more of a classic beauty with cascades of long, coppery hair and a wide mouth that turned down slightly at the corners. She was as tall as Alasdair and her close-fitting green gown revealed high, full breasts, a long waist, and rounded hips. She was one of those women born to seduce, Lucinda thought. Her every movement was vibrant with the awareness of her own sexuality.

She strode up to them and began speaking and gesticulating angrily. Lucinda couldn't hear any of the words—this was like watching a movie with the sound turned off—but it was clear that she was demanding something from them. From Gioia actually. The argument was between the women, and though Alasdair tried to interject, neither of the women paid him any mind. Gioia seemed to be trying to explain something but as she spoke the taller woman reached for the diamond. Her hand closed around it and she yanked hard. The diamond slipped out of her grasp. She reached for the diamond a second time. Gioia put out a hand to stay her, and the copper-haired woman drew a knife and plunged it into Gioia's belly.

Lucinda gasped as Gioia collapsed to the ground, her eyes wide with shock, a thin ribbon of blood streaming from her mouth. Alasdair was on his knees, cradling her in his lap, frantically drawing out the coral from his life stones, trying to heal her. And even as he tried to heal Gioia the other woman was clawing at the diamond necklace. He pushed her away, and she came at him again. Her knife flashed a second time, this time opening a diagonal line between the corner of Alasdair's eye and his mouth. He turned back to Gioia, working with the coral, seeming indifferent to his injury, not bothering to touch the wound or wipe away the blood that ran down his face and neck. The other woman raised the knife to strike again. In a movement so fast Lucinda couldn't follow it, Alasdair had a black stone knife in his hand. The copper-haired woman stepped back, seeming wary. She and Alasdair exchanged words, and she, seemingly reluctant, dropped her own knife but it was a decoy gesture. With uncanny speed, she darted in for the necklace, one hand shoving Alasdair out of the way, the other reaching for the diamond. Alasdair reacted with equal speed, reaching up to pull her head down against his chest. For just a second he paused, holding her there almost gently, and Lucinda wondered if they, too, had been lovers. Smoothly, expertly, like one who had done it many times before, he drew his blade in an arc across her throat. He released her and she fell to the ground, and the jade column behind him went red with her blood.

The dark energy that had been hovering there all along now took a shape and form so immense and horrific that Lucinda began to gag. And finally Alasdair saw her. She held a bloodied sword in one hand, a severed head in another, a lotus in a third, shears in a fourth. Snakes writhed along her blue-black skin. She wore a garland of severed heads, a girdle of corpses. Her long, blood-smeared tongue stuck out and her eyes were alight with a wild joy. Naked and grotesque, she towered over them. Lucinda saw terror in Alasdair's eyes, saw him throw himself over Gioia's body, trying to shield it. But the dark woman snatched her from him, held Gioia's corpse aloft on one blue-black hand, lowered her fanged face into the ripped abdomen and began to drink. She drank long and hard and Lucinda saw that her thirst could never be slaked. She stopped only for a moment to rip the diamond necklace from Gioia's neck. Heedlessly, she tossed it from her, not even noticing that it was caught by a bright blue parrot who carried it away, winging through the open thresholds behind it.

Lucinda flinched at the first sound she heard since the dreadful scene began. Alasdair was crouched beside her, rocking back and forth, and sobbing. For a long moment Lucinda couldn't move. Terror held her pinned. Her breathing was so shallow it felt as if her lungs were afraid to take in the air, as if by breathing, they'd take the horror into her. Unable to think, she dropped down beside Alasdair and put her arms around him and held him as he wept. She stroked his back, not daring to murmur the usual rote words of comfort. He was shaking violently.

When his sobs finally stopped the sky above them was black and the vision was gone. They would have been sitting in darkness except that on either side of the second threshold a crystal glowed, giving off a soft bluish light.

Alasdair drew in a jagged breath. "Ever since it happened—that's *always* what the first threshold shows me. You'd think I'd be used to it by now."

"So you won't forget?"

"I don't forget things like that," he said quietly. "But the thresholds seem determined to sear it into me anyway." He lifted his head to look at her. "And obviously, they wanted you to see it, too."

"Why?"

"So you wouldn't be deceived. So you'd know the worst of me."

"That you tried to protect your lover and yourself?"

"That I'm capable of taking life as easily as you would brush back a strand of hair."

"She pushed you," Lucinda said.

"That's a charitable interpretation, but it doesn't excuse or change it. . . . The one who wore the diamond, that was Gioia."

"I know."

"And the one I killed, Noelle."

"Why was she so desperate to take the diamond? Did Kama give it to her?"

Alasdair laughed mirthlessly. "Kama's no fool. He gave it to Gioia, knowing she'd use it wisely or not at all. Noelle had a different . . . orientation. She believed that power exists to be wielded, not held in reserve. And years before Kama gave the diamond to Gioia, he gave it to Noelle's mother. So she saw it as her birthright."

Lucinda felt her pulse racing. They were talking about Gioia and Noelle but what she couldn't wrap her mind around was the horror of the blue-black demon, the devourer. And though it was beyond her understanding she felt it imprinted on her, deep in the fiber of her being. *Every night for the rest of my life,* she thought, *that's what I'm going to see when I close my eyes.*

"Are you all right?" Alasdair asked.

"That monster—"

"The goddess Kali, one of the great divine mothers. She's the energy of the cosmos cutting through illusions and severing attachment. And she feeds on most of us sooner or later." He straightened up as he spoke, gently detaching himself from Lucinda's embrace.

Lucinda wrapped her arms around her rib cage, needing the comfort of an embrace even if it was her own. "I-I've never seen anything like that," she said, then cut a wry glance at him. "How's that for understatement?"

He gave her a sympathetic smile in return.

She forced her mind into a diversion. "So. What we just saw—that's why you left here?"

"Part of it. Murder is hard on the spirit; lots of unfinished business. Neither Gioia nor Noelle moved on easily. They both haunted me and, being a *cearu,* I had to find ways to lay them to rest. By the time I finally did—it took years—I'd had enough of ghosts and grief, and all I wanted was to leave this place where nearly every stone held the memory of them."

Lucinda reached for the velvet pouch once again and this time took out the diamond necklace. "You lied to me before. At least two people have died for this thing. Why didn't you tell me?"

"Because that wasn't the diamond. That was Noelle's arrogance and greed. There's no reason to think that sort of drama will repeat itself."

Even in the dim light of the crystals, the fire inside the diamond danced, casting slivers of light on the rough stone walls. Lucinda shuddered; it was almost like holding something live in her hand. "Seems to me," she said slowly, "that a stone like this is a magnet for all sorts of drama."

"Only if others know you have it," Alasdair said. "Put it away."

She slipped it into the pouch and held it out to him. "I never wanted it."

He ignored her offering. "That's probably why Kama trusted you with it. It can be used for good, you know."

"How?"

Alasdair got to his feet and started toward the second threshold. "Maybe this will tell us. It will show us something of the present, in any case."

They stepped through the second doorway. This time they weren't touching. Lucinda looked up at him. "I'm sorry Gioia died. She looked . . . wonderful."

"She was."

They stood between the second and third walls. Two more glowing crystals, on either side of the third threshold, provided just enough light to see by.

"I think I'm going to sit down this time," Lucinda said. She sat cross-legged, bracing herself with her hands, telling herself nothing could be more horrific than what she'd just seen. She felt Alasdair sit down beside her and rest a hand on top of hers, but she didn't look at him. Her attention was focused on the square of white shining on the wall in front of her.

The square shone brighter, whiter. It grew taller, wider, until they were looking into a room with white walls, a white ceiling, and a white tile floor. At the far end in a metal bed with white sheets Tyrone lay, thinner and greyer than ever, his eyes shut, machines monitoring his every breath. One hand poked out from the covers, curled inward unnaturally, like a claw.

"They've moved him," Lucinda said. "That's not the same room. There's no window. It must be Intensive Care or something." She knew she was babbling but couldn't seem to stop. "Do you think he's sleeping or still comatose?"

"I don't know," Alasdair said. He turned to her as she breathed in sharply. "What is it?"

"Someone's with Tyrone, sitting beside the bed."

At first all she could see were the hands. One cupped Tyrone's twisted hand; the other gently stroked it. Then more of the visitor was revealed. Her eyes followed the line of the cuff to sleeve to shoulder to a smoky quartz bead on a silver chain at his throat. For a moment she stared uncomprehending, unable to trust her eyes, and then she was on her feet, rushing back toward the first threshold, her blood turned to ice in her veins.

Alasdair caught her by the shoulders. "Lucinda, wait. We haven't gone through the third doorway yet."

She whirled on him, wild-eyed. "Fuck the third doorway. Tyrone's dying and Sebastian's in the room with him."

Alasdair's voice was maddeningly calm. "Sebastian being in the hospital room doesn't mean that he's going to hurt Tyrone."

"Are you nuts? He set him up. He got that sociopathic kid out of jail. And he tried to kill you. Now he's there to finish the job on Tyrone." Lucinda tried to wrench herself free of Alasdair's hold and settled for kicking him soundly in the shins.

Alasdair didn't appear to notice. "Lucinda." He stopped, seeming at a loss for words. "What do you intend to do? Race back down the mountain to the hospital? If Sebastian does mean to harm Tyrone, you don't have time to stop him."

She stopped fighting, sickened by the truth. She wrenched herself free of his hands. For a few moments she paced, examining the options that she didn't really have. "Why don't you people have phones? If I could call the hospital, I could get a cop or someone into that room."

"Do you really think one of your police officers would stand a chance against a fox? Sebastian would have him wandering lost and out of his mind before he even stepped into the room."

She massaged her temples. "I never should have come here. I should have stayed with Tyrone."

"Then we should go through the third threshold," Alasdair said. "The sooner we're done with this, the sooner you get back there."

"I'm done now." She turned toward the first doorway again.

Alasdair gently turned her back. "The third threshold holds the future," he reminded her. "It's why we came here. It may give us some key to what we need to do in the city."

"I don't have time for this crap. I need to get back to Tyrone now." Lucinda was mortified to realize she was crying. She felt helpless and scared and stupid. She'd been insane to make this journey to the lost towns. She'd wasted days for what—Alasdair's hocus-pocus? "Please let go of me."

"If you go back through the first threshold, there's a danger of getting stuck in the past," he said as he released her.

She brushed the tears from her face, looking down the length of the brick wall. It was open on both sides. Why not just walk out the side of this second threshold?

"Don't you know you did the right thing?" he went on. "Tyrone needs the kind of help that you won't get from physicians or police officers. I can't make any guarantees, but you came to a place where at least we've got a chance of turning aside what's killing him."

"But Sebastian—"

"—may not do him any harm. After all, one of the mothers healed him and Averill's sent him a message—"

"I don't think Averill has all that much interest in helping me."

"No," Alasdair agreed. "But she has a definite interest in not antagonizing Vita. Please, Lucinda. We don't have time to waste. Won't you trust me on this?" He held out a hand to her.

She hesitated then took it and together they crossed the third threshold.

Lucinda held tight to Alasdair's hand. Now she was the one trembling, terrified of what this third threshold might reveal. She tried to reason herself out of fear: What could be worse than Sebastian at Tyrone's side? Kali at Tyrone's side, she realized, and the thought nearly made her start retching again.

"Is Kali always there when someone dies?" she asked, managing to calm her queasy stomach.

"No. Sometimes it's Hathor or Hermes or one of the other gods connected with death—Yama, Sucellos, Hekate, Astovidad, Ixtab, Morrigan, Todote—and some, though not all, are gentler than Kali."

"If this third vision is Tyrone dying, I don't think I can watch."

"Well, perhaps you'd better try," Alasdair said a bit testily, "because the future can be changed, especially once you have a hint of what it might be."

"Can it?" she asked, her voice hollow. "What difference can I make if Kali's hovering in her black cloud, just waiting for a corpse to devour?"

Alasdair clasped her hands between his. She felt his warmth and strength pouring into her, steadying her. "Some of what we do is futile. There are many things beyond our control," he acknowledged. "But other things we can and do change. The rub is, we often don't know which things are which, and so we've just got to blunder along and hope that what we're working on can indeed be altered. If you give up now, then you give up all hope of change. Do you see?"

She did. "All right then," Lucinda said, more to the threshold than to him.

Alasdair released her hands, and the vision came at once. "It's Arcato," Lucinda murmured, recognizing one of the benches by the waterfront and feeling immensely relieved that she was not watching Tyrone die in a hospital bed. A burly man with wiry grey hair sat on one of the benches. Although no one else was visible, he was talking and this time they could hear every word.

"You think you can sneak up on me like that? You think I don't see you. I know you've been following me. I know you put poisons in me while I sleep. I've seen your needles. You think you're so damn tricky but you left a needle in with my cigarettes. You thought I wouldn't notice. . . ."

The man's voice trailed off and the scene shifted. This time they were looking at a small girl with butterscotch-colored hair, also talking to someone who couldn't be seen. "Please don't make me go with you." She began sobbing. "No, please, don't hurt me again. Please—" Her voice broke off in a wail of rising terror.

Lucinda didn't know either of these people, couldn't make sense of any of this. She shot a glance at Alasdair. He was staring at the image of the frightened child, his body rigid and perfectly still except for one muscle twitching in his lower jaw.

A third image appeared: Marcus, leaning on crutches, looking hunched and thin from his hospital stay. "Oh, no, no, no," he was saying. "I ain't gonna dance with you, my friend." As in the earlier visions, whoever it was he was speaking to remained concealed. Marcus used the crutches to swing his body backward, touch ground, and then swing back again. "You got *co-jones*, coming on to me twice," he said. "What kind of whore you take me for? You think I'm gonna turn tricks for the likes of you?" He held out one hand, rubbed his thumb over his fingertips in a gesture of greed. "You still ain't giving me nothing I like. I've met pimps who cut a better deal than you."

Lucinda decided to sit down as she watched this scene play out. Who the hell was he talking to with that phony street-thug act? And where was he? Marcus was outside somewhere—there was a lavender twilight sky behind him—but he didn't seem to be either on one of the streets or down by the waterfront.

Beside her she heard Alasdair mutter, "Thank the gods Michael is out of the city."

"What?" Marcus sounded outraged. "What do you mean? Now hold on." His voice became nervous, quicker. "Wait, wait a minute, man. You don't have to take it that way. I'm only saying, if this is going to be a deal, we need a little quid pro quo here, right? So don't go getting all—" Marcus swung himself backward again. His voice rose, arrogant but also fearful. "Just calm down. No need for this irate attitude because we can come to an accommodation. I— you crazy? Put that thing away!" He swung back again, this time looking over his shoulder but the look was too late, became one of terror as his feet swung out over the edge of the roof and he plunged toward the street, limbs flailing, crutches flying, and a desperate scream echoing through the streets.

Lucinda pressed her face into her knees and covered her ears. It didn't help. She still heard the awful, hard cracking sound of Marcus's body hitting ground.

She felt Alasdair's hand on her shoulder. "It's changed again," he said.

She forced herself to look at a fourth scene from the future. Although this one seemed relatively benign—it was simply Alasdair, seen from the back, walking through Arcato's streets—she tensed, waiting for some awful thing to happen. Alasdair continued walking, and she recognized him approaching then entering her building. The thresholds showed him ringing her buzzer and then climbing the stairs to her flat. They showed her door opening to him. Then the scene winked out altogether, and she and Alasdair were standing on the far side of the third threshold, the night's darkness covering them. Lucinda whirled around. The glowing crystals that had illuminated the three walls had gone dark.

"We should go," Alasdair said. "They've shown us what they meant to. There's nothing more for us here now."

A cool wind swept down from the peaks as they left the thresholds. Though the night sky seemed heavy and low, the wind felt good, cleansing somehow. For the first time since Lucinda started up the mountain she saw no stars in the night sky, just swaths of clouds scudding across the moon.

They wound their way downhill, back toward Vita's house. Lucinda concentrated on the footpath, making sure she didn't step off it in the darkness. The vision of Marcus's fall was still with her. Marcus's fall and the deaths of Gioia and Noelle, a dying Tyrone with Sebastian hovering over him. Everyone seemed terribly fragile to her, capable of being snapped from life in the space of a breath. Unsure of what to make of it all, she decided to ask the easiest question first. "Why do you think we saw that vision of you walking into my flat?"

"I'm not sure." Alasdair gave her a faint smile. "Are you bothered by the idea of me paying you a visit?"

"Not now, no," she admitted. "What bothers me are the other parts of that last vision. Do you know any of those people?"

"Not well, but I recognized the first two. The man is someone I talked to in one of the riverfront cafés. He told me he works at the fish market. The little girl lives in the old city, across the labradorite bridge. She helped me once, brought me a piece of chalcedony that I needed."

"I didn't recognize the first two, but the third one was Marcus. He's the one who gave Tyrone the elixir on Carnival Night. He's the one who found the wolf costume, the way I found my costume—just waiting at his door."

"I see."

"That's it? That's all you can say?" She was still feeling shaky and the jitters made her blather on, as if she could talk them out. "You know, I absolutely loathe Marcus, I have from the first time I saw him. He's completely reprehensible but seeing him fall like that—"

"It doesn't have to work out that way," Alasdair reminded her gently. "The vision of the future was shown to you, because you may be able to change it."

Lucinda gave a short, bitter laugh. "Oh, they showed it to the right one. If it were me up there on the roof with him, I probably would have pushed him off. Wait a minute," she said, puzzled. "Who *was* up there with him? And who was with the man and the little girl? They were all afraid. I think, in their own way, each one of them was being driven over the edge. And all of them were talking to someone who was hurting them or scaring them."

"Or not," Alasdair said. "I've been wondering why that particular vision was shown to us, and I've got an idea but I need to do some checking to see if I'm right." A sound like ocean waves rolled down the mountain. "It's just the wind going through the trees and canyons," he told her.

Lucinda rubbed her arms, chilled. "I didn't even hear all these gusts when we were in the thresholds."

"The thresholds are a protected space, though if the rain had started while we were still in there, we probably would have gotten wet."

"You think it will rain? It doesn't even feel damp."

"Look up," Alasdair said softly.

A thin vein of turquoise lightning flickered in the distance. She turned to him, afraid to make assumptions, but his words warmed the embers of hope in her: "Yes, I think it's safe to say that Hesper's made contact with the storm gods."

THEY CLIMBED THE steps to the house just as the rain began in earnest. Alasdair led her straight to Vita's library. It was a beautiful room, Lucinda thought, proportioned like all the rooms in the house to feel both spacious and sheltering. Four of the six walls consisted of bookshelves cut into the stone. The fifth wall framed a window seat that looked out, Lucinda guessed, on the side of the house. It was impossible to tell now; outside there was only the black night and the sound of the rain hurling itself against the windows. Moura was curled up on the window seat's cushion, sleeping contentedly. On the sixth wall, across the room from the window seat, a small fireplace held logs wound with sage, ready to be lit.

Alasdair took a seat at the stone-inlay desk in the center of the room, indicating that Lucinda should take the big comfortable chair. She did, gazing up at the books that surrounded her. Most were leather-bound; many bore gold-stamp lettering on the spines. But there was also a shelf holding a glass case containing scrolls and another glass case that held an old yellowed manuscript whose pages had ragged edges.

That was what Alasdair brought to the desk, along with two leatherbound books. Handling the manuscript with great care, he began to leaf through the vellum pages. "It's medieval," he explained, "a copy of the thirty-seventh volume of Pliny's *Historia Naturalis,* which was first published in A.D. 77." He glanced up at her. "More than you wanted to know?"

Lucinda shrugged. "You haven't told me what this is about."

"Here it is." He pointed to a page lettered in thick black ink. "Well . . . it's written in Latin, but roughly it translates as, . . . the diamond drives away madness, and protects against fascination and night spirits and evil dreams."

He closed the manuscript and picked up one of the leather-bound books. "And this one is an eighteenth-century reprint of Chevalier Jean de Mandeville's *Le Lapidaire,* written in the fourteenth century. Mandeville says diamonds work against enchantment and sorcery and aid those who are plagued by devils, among other things."

He picked up the third book. "The *Speculum Lapidum,* by Camillus Leonardus, published in Venice, 1502, says that the diamond counters fear and phantasms.'"

"Okay, they agree," Lucinda said. "Or the latter two basically repeated what the first one said."

He nodded. "That's possible. Pliny was considered the authority for centuries, and a great deal of what was written in later centuries just expanded on his works. But what I'm getting at is the diamond. I think that what will happen in the city—actually, it's already started—is that people are seeing phantasms. Those people in the third vision, I don't think they were each arguing with someone who was simply out of view. I think they were all arguing with someone who wasn't there, a phantasm or chimera, if you will. A hallucination."

"What do you mean, it's already started?"

"On Carnival Night," Alasdair said, "I found the woman who runs a newsstand dancing with her dead husband, much to the dismay of her grown daughter. At the time I assumed she was suffering some sort of brain disturbance. Now I think it was just one incident of many. People in the city are seeing things that aren't there, and it's not because there's anything wrong with their brains."

"Yeah, but they're also seeing some strange things that are real," Lucinda pointed out. "Like men who change into foxes and flying jade dragons. It gets hard to tell the difference." She drew her knees up, wrapped her arms around them, and thought about what they'd seen in the thresholds. The man, the child, and Marcus. It was possible that there was no one there with them, that each was afraid of something imaginary. "Okay, maybe they were seeing illusions," she allowed, "except for the very last bit. What about you walking up to my flat? What was hallucinatory about that?"

"Oh, that," Alasdair said quietly. "That, I suspect, is connected but also a bit different. I'm not sure how it fits just yet. In the meantime, though, here's a theory: You were given that vision of people being tormented by chimeras because you hold Kama's diamond, because you have the way to dispel fear, to counter the phantasms."

Lucinda wasn't sure how to respond. The idea of having to use the diamond scared her. She wasn't the sort of person for that sort of job, and yet she'd agreed to help Alasdair. "How can you be sure any of those books are right?" she asked. "I know stones have all sorts of power—at least when *you* hold them—but what you just read to me sounds like a collection of old superstitions."

Alasdair shut the third book. "Admittedly, there's a lot in these volumes that's just that. Folk beliefs are handed down from one generation to the next whether or not there's truth in them. Diamonds have always been treasured for their clarity, so having the power to distinguish phantasm from reality is a natural connection for people to make."

"Is it wrong or right?" she asked impatiently.

"It all depends on the diamond," he replied. "Stones are as individual as we are. And while you can make broad generalizations—coral can be used to staunch bleeding; opal, the thief's stone, can grant temporary invisibility—what the stone will actually do depends on the stone itself, its history, and the person who wields it."

"And Kama's diamond?"

"Even if it hadn't been given to you by a god who has, by the way, a habit of infusing gems with his power, it's an extraordinary stone, large and pure with excellent transparency, fire, clarity, and incandescence. I have no doubt that at least some of what Pliny believed in is possible with that diamond."

"*If* you know how to work with it," she added. "I *don't*."

"You figured it out when you came to the jade door."

With all that had happened since her arrival, she'd nearly forgotten about that. "I did, didn't I . . ."

"I'm going back to Arcato to find whoever it is I sensed by that mosaic. It may be the same being who's causing people to see phantasms. Will you use the diamond to help me?"

Lucinda gave him a pained smile. "You do realize I have no idea of what I'm supposed to do or whether I'm capable of doing it?"

Alasdair touched the back of her hand. "You have far more strength than you think. Have I told you how lucky Tyrone is to have you for a friend?"

His faith in her was so genuine that it took her aback, made it impossible to look him in the eye. "What about Sebastian?" she asked.

"In the vision he was wearing the smoky quartz that Averill sent him. That's a good sign. Smoky quartz aids communication. I expect she's using it to get messages to him."

A light rapping sounded on the library door, then it was pushed open. Vita stepped in, her hair and cloak wet with rain.

"There you are," she said, sounding pleased. She looked around. "Why haven't you lit the fire?" She shed her cloak, revealing a wine-red dress adorned with a ruby choker, and busied herself lighting the kindling. The sweet smell of dried sage soon filled the library. "That's better," she said, turning to face them. "I see you both fared well with the thresholds."

"That's a matter of opinion," Alasdair said darkly.

"Lucinda." Vita reached into the pockets of her dress. "Gervase asked me to give this to you."

Lucinda stared at but did not take the pale blue carving of an extremely cranky-looking cat. "That's Averill," she said.

"Well, yes and no," Vita hedged. "It's more accurate to say it's a carving inspired by Averill. Perhaps it would help if you gave it a different name."

Alasdair took the carving from Vita's hand and set it on the arm of Lucinda's chair. "Chalcedony is a stone that's long been connected with victory in both arguments and battles. That's why you see it in the old cameos depicting military leaders. It's also been known to open pathways where there's resistance. You might find it useful."

Lucinda gazed distrustfully at the cat that bore Averill's nasty disposition in every fold of its miniature body.

"It's a gift, child," Vita told her. "Go upstairs and befriend it before you need to call on its powers."

Lucinda shot Alasdair a look, silently asking if his mother was trying to get rid of her.

Alasdair gave a barely perceptible shrug then said, "You might as well try to get some rest before we leave for the city."

"Where's the dragon?" Lucinda asked. She would much rather travel with the dragon than this cat she didn't even like.

"He's with Hesper," Vita replied. "I expect he'll be here soon."

The rain was still pounding against the window. Both Alasdair and Vita were looking at her expectantly. The stubborn part of Lucinda wanted to tell them she didn't like being dismissed and wasn't going anywhere, but the reality of what she faced sobered her. "Fine," she said, taking the cat with an inward shudder. "I'll be upstairs."

"AND THE VERY last image you saw in the thresholds?" Vita prompted.

Alasdair sat in the comfortable reading chair, Vita at her inlaid desk, facing him. The Pliny manuscript and the two lapidaries had been returned to their places. He and Vita each held a crystal goblet filled with wine as red as the ruby at her throat. She looked, he thought, extremely businesslike. If she lived in Arcato and wore the type of suits that the women there wore, she'd be right at home taking over corporations. And she'd probably be a raging success, because she wouldn't hesitate to make whatever sacrifices were necessary.

"Alasdair," she said with a tinge of impatience, "please answer my question."

"The last image was me walking through the city to Lucinda's flat. Seen from the back," he added.

"That's all?"

He nodded and took another sip of the wine. "I've told you someone's been following me in the city. Averill says it's another shape-shifter. I suspect that last vision was from the shape-shifter's point of view. What we watched was the shape-shifter following me to Lucinda's flat."

Vita's grey eyes seemed to darken in the flickering light. She set down the crystal goblet and pressed her fingertips together. "Since that vision was given to you along with the visions of people being beset by phantasms, they must be related."

"That would be my guess," Alasdair said in a bitter tone. "I'm asking Lucinda to use the diamond to help destroy the phantasms. Meanwhile, unless I'm careful, I'm going to lead the one who's creating those illusions right to her door."

"You can't," said Vita. "You're going to have to protect the girl."

"I know. I'll use the opal and make sure I'm not followed."

"That may not be enough. She doesn't have a clue as to what she's up against."

"Oh, she has a clue, all right. She's watched a god nearly destroy her best friend, and she's been seduced by Malachy. Speaking of Malachy . . . he wore Averill's quartz bead in the visions. Has Averill heard anything back from him?"

"Not yet, which may be her fault and not his. Averill's not as strong as she used to be. Things get past her now."

He let that one go. Instead, he said the thing that he wouldn't say to Lucinda. "It was worrisome to see him with Tyrone. The fox in the chicken coop."

His mother inclined her head to the window. "I was with Hesper when Ilyap'a answered her call. I take it he finds her quite entertaining. He's never come across a storm-bringer with a sense of humor before. They're always so solemn, walking around with their rain-sticks and rain crystals and the like." She smiled at him. "Though I have seen some rain dances that worked marvelously well."

"Do you think he'll spare Tyrone?"

"Hesper hadn't gotten that far in her negotiations when I left to come back here. And as gods go, he's a stern one. But Hesper hasn't given up." Vita drank deeply of the wine, her expression brooding. "There's too much about this that's murky. You still don't know who it is that's searching for the Shrine of the Mothers, creating phantasms, and possibly stalking you."

"No. And it could be nearly anything—a demon, a god, a shaman, a trickster—"

"I was hoping Malachy might give us some information by now. Still, there is one more thing we can try." She opened one of the drawers in her desk and took out a box carved of green turquoise. Lifting the lid, she pushed it across the desk toward Alasdair. Its inside, he saw, was lined with red silk. Nestled in the silk was an egg-shaped quartz crystal, each of its many facets bearing an inscription.

Alasdair stiffened. "Where did you get that?"

"It came to me through one of the traders," she replied vaguely.

"I'll bet," he muttered. It was the sort of ancient gazing crystal he'd only heard rumors of, one whose different facets would simultaneously allow you to gaze into different times and different worlds.

Vita adjusted the lamps in the room so that only the one on her desk remained lit. "Hold the crystal in one hand," she told Alasdair. "You can open it."

"Can I?" he asked, his voice soft with skepticism.

"Stop it, Alasdair. Stones have been opening for you since you came out of my womb."

"Then when I was in the womb you must have been teaching me your secrets. Why am I suddenly sure that there's a slew of them you never even hinted at?"

"Maybe you've just been away too long and you've forgotten things."

"No," he said. "I'm sure that's not it." He took the crystal in his hand and nearly dropped it, it contained so much energy. The first thing he sensed were the inscriptions, some of them symbols, some of them names, some of them blessings or protections. Each was a way to open what the crystal held. Each had its own vibration, a kind of low hum. Holding the crystal was almost like listening to a cacophony of different voices, some emanating quietly, others ricocheting off the quartz surfaces. It made him think of market day, with different sellers all calling out, hawking their wares. Beneath the inscriptions the quartz itself was bafflingly complex. Whereas most quartz crystals contained only one spirit, this crystal held so many, he felt as if he were holding a little community in his hand. They were all protective spirits, from what he could tell, but some were so fierce that calling on them could be nearly as dangerous as any threat he might face.

"I don't even know where to start," he said.

Vita was watching him, her grey eyes sharp. "There isn't a right or a wrong place."

He sent up a prayer to Vishnu for guidance, then he let himself go into the stone, searching out different facets, trying to sense what each one held, whether or not it would open to him, whether or not he wanted to deal with the protective spirit that resided inside. He felt interest stirring within the crystal—the spirits were curious about him, too. He stilled himself, quieting his breathing, clearing his mind, opening himself to the spirits, letting them see for themselves what he was. It was almost a ticklish sensation; he could feel them exploring, invisible tendrils of energy probing, wanting to know how he meant to use the crystal. He kept the message simple, telling them he needed information about the present, that he was searching for someone.

One by one, the facets and what they held inside began to make themselves known to him. He asked additional questions, hoping for facets that would tell him of one who hid and dealt in illusions, who sought the mothers and left pain and rage in his wake.

He held the stone in his hand, turning it slowly, and its cut planes winked up at him in the light from the oil lamp, almost as if they held a diamond's fire. As he turned the quartz he began to see images in the crystal. Some showed him the Source Place, others the mountains that looked down over the city. He saw an image of the Shrine of the Mothers, looking exactly as he'd left it, and he sent up a prayer of thanks. They were still safe; they hadn't been found by the one who was tearing through Arcato, searching for them.

He turned the crystal to an inscription that intrigued him. It was Inari's name, the Japanese rice god and patron of foxes. Alasdair invoked the inscription to Inari and the facet beneath the god's name gleamed deep cinnabar red. The red soon delineated itself as two unusually large foxes, running side by side down the streets of Arcato. They ran through the night and though Alasdair could see people on the sidewalks, no one seemed to notice the two oversized animals bounding through the streets. It could have been that the foxes were casting an illusion that hid them, or simply that everyone in the city was, as usual, both accustomed to strangeness and preoccupied with their own lives. In Arcato it took a lot to attract attention.

Alasdair squinted at the crystal, trying to determine where the foxes were. Haifong Street, he decided as he saw well-dressed theater patrons pouring out beneath a marquee, side-by-side with punked-out kids waiting to get into a club. The two foxes came to a stop in the middle of the street, mouths open, panting with that peculiar fox grin. One had a familiar white chest; the other, even larger, was pure russet. Alasdair watched as the fractured light from the street lamps seemed to bend around them and they changed shape, became men. Still, no one on the sidewalks noticed. The fox with the white chest became Sebastian; no surprise there. The other, though, was someone Alasdair had never seen before. He was taller than Sebastian and rail-thin. He seemed younger, too, though that might be because he was dressed for the clubs in an artfully tattered shirt and leather pants that fit like skin. His hair was the same russet his fur had been, long on one side, hacked short on the other, and his features were beautiful, almost too perfect to be real. It was his skin, though, that shocked. It looked as though someone had taken razor blades to every inch of his body. His face, hands, and what Alasdair could see of his neck and chest were scored with black lines. Not only cut but something had been rubbed into the open wounds to ensure that they scarred black. Sebastian said something to him and he laughed. He reached beneath his shirt and pulled out a bronze amulet that hung from a chain on his neck. He spoke a few words and rubbed the charm, and the scars receded into his flesh, disappeared, leaving a sweet-featured young man in their place.

A girl who looked to be in her late teens hurried toward the two men. She wore stiletto heels, a very short skirt, and a fringed jacket. She began talking with them, tossing her mane of blond hair and smiling at Sebastian's companion in a way that could only be flirting. Then she looped an arm through each of theirs and steered them toward the club. Alasdair sent up a prayer to Kwannon, asking her to protect the young woman from the two foxes.

So this scarred shape-shifter was the one he had to find. And when he did, what then? He sent the question to the crystal, turning it once more in his hands, searching for the facet that would answer.

Abruptly, the facets of the crystal went dark, as if black ink flooded their surfaces, as if the clear quartz had turned to black marble.

"What just happened?" Vita asked uneasily.

Alasdair didn't reply but examined the crystal again. The inscriptions were all there but their voices silent and the spirits within, still. Wordlessly, he held it out to his mother.

Vita turned the crystal in her hands. He could feel her trying to invoke the inscriptions; he could hear their answering silence. Vita's eyes were troubled as she placed the crystal back in its turquoise box. "I've never known it to shut down that way," she said. "That shouldn't have happened. Something knew it was being observed and struck at the crystal." She stood up and began to pace. "You know what sort of defenses surround the towns and this house. How could anyone have gotten through them?"

"Maybe he didn't have to," Alasdair suggested. "Maybe he sensed me observing him and was able to strike directly to the means of observation."

"I don't like this," his mother said.

"Well, it's certainly distracting us from the vision," Alasdair observed. "Tell me. Did you see the one with the scars?"

She nodded, the tip of her tongue touching her upper lip. "I've never seen him before."

"Nor I. But Malachy's obviously in league with him."

"It looks that way." She stopped pacing to stand directly in front of him. "There's got to be something I can give you that will protect you in Arcato. I don't like you going into this without three of your life stones."

"I have the amethyst amulet now," he reminded her.

"That may not be enough. After all, it didn't counter Averill's paralysis on its own."

He tried not to let that worry him. "Only because I didn't reach for it quickly enough."

"I don't like trusting your life to reflexes."

"I have the obsidian knife."

"No." There was more force in the word than he expected.

Alasdair finished his wine, using the time to try to determine why Vita was so upset. Was it the crystal going dark or was she genuinely frightened for him? "Why shouldn't I use the knife?" he asked her. "It was an initiation gift. And it's already saved my skin more than once."

His mother rubbed her temple with her fingertips, looking confused. The expression was so at odds with Vita's usual demeanor that Alasdair almost didn't recognize it. "I can't give you a good reason," she said, "but I've never trusted that knife. Perhaps I should return to Arcato with you."

"After declawing Averill that way? The towns can't be ruled by someone so vulnerable."

"The towns do need help," she agreed after a moment's pause. "Stay here, Alasdair. I've never asked that of you before. But we need you now, and I can't bear to think of you in that city being hunted by that being. Besides, if you stay here, sooner or later he'll lose interest in you. Maybe he'll even leave Arcato."

"You're the one who raised me to be a *cearu*," Alasdair reminded her gently. "You know I can't walk away from that, though the gods know I've tried."

"Then bind one of the gemstones to you," Vita said fiercely. "One of your life stones. Give yourself a protection that no one else can—"

"No," he cut her off. "That's not an option."

"I did it." Her voice was cool and without regret.

Alasdair studied his mother, the lovely familiar face and the adamantine will beneath it. "How long were you preparing for that little showdown with Averill?"

"I bound the carnelian to me to a while ago," she replied evasively.

He'd been surprised and alarmed when he'd read the carnelian and realized Vita had bound it. When you bound a stone to your blood, your power mingled with its essence and its essence with your blood, so that you were both connected for life and the power of human and stone each magnified the strength of the other. After that the stone would only respond to your call; no one else could use it. But the act of binding wasn't easy. It could only be done through one of the gods and for this service a sacrifice was required. "At what cost?" he asked quietly.

"Ten years."

"From your life?" he asked, aghast.

"We're given so much more time here than most mortals. With the carnelian, power that was being abused can finally be reined in. In light of that, it seemed greedy to cling to a few extra years." She regarded him again, her eyes narrowing. "Are you afraid to give up years from your own life?"

"No," he said, realizing it was true. "I simply don't believe stones should be bound that way. I think they should have more freedom in their fates, even if we don't. For me to bind a stone would be an abuse of my power."

"And in my case?" she asked, a dangerous edge to her voice.

"In your case, I grieve for the lost years. I don't want to see my mother die before her time. You wanted to overpower Averill that badly?"

"Oh, Alasdair, I have no interest in ruling." Vita sounded weary. "I'm content to let the others be who they are, do as they will. But I won't sit by and countenance the ones who go power mad, like Averill."

"And you're certain that you won't turn into one of them?"

"That's always the danger," she admitted with an evenness that indicated she'd already thought it through. "If I do, I give you my permission—no, I command you—to end me."

He went rigid, furious and disbelieving. "Don't you think I have enough blood on my hands? Did you somehow not notice what I went through with Gioia and Noelle?"

"Alasdair, it wouldn't be like the others." She stood up and put a hand on his shoulder. When she spoke again, her voice was tender, the way it had been when he was a child. "Do you think I'm capable of haunting my own son?"

"I don't know what you're capable of anymore. I'm afraid to even guess. But I'm not going to be your executioner. If you think you need that kind of check on your power, find someone else to do it."

"It won't come to that." Her voice was as soothing as honey dissolved in hot tea. She leaned down and dropped a kiss on the top of his head. "Trust me, Alasdair. I want what's best for us all."

When she left the library, she left him with his head in his hands. It was definitely time to return to Arcato.

Seventeen

LUCINDA WAS STARING at the cranky-looking chalcedony cat, trying to convince herself that befriending it was possible. She had changed back into traveling clothes: her jeans and the sweater her mother had knit, and a pair of rope-soled shoes that Vita had given her. Though she'd barely been here two days, her own clothing seemed like something from the distant past, from another life. She felt clumsy and awkward in it. It didn't help that Gervase's little carving seemed to be looking at her through slanted eyes, radiating disapproval.

A knock on the door distracted her from ruminations on cat and wardrobe. She opened it to find Alasdair with the dragon perched on his shoulder. The dragon peered into Lucinda's room, then flew in and neatly knocked over the chalcedony cat.

"See?" she said to Alasdair as she retrieved it from the floor. "The dragon doesn't like it either."

"He's got a jealous streak, I'm afraid. He wants to make sure you're not about to replace him in your affections."

"Do you really think I'm that fickle?" she asked the dragon.

The dragon flew to her collarbone and pressed its little snout against her neck.

"It's a good thing you're not a man," she muttered, running her finger along its side. "I'd hate myself for caving to this kind of manipulation."

"Are you ready to go?" Alasdair asked.

Her stomach clenched at the thought. Everything about going back to the city scared her. "Yes," she said.

"It's too bad it took a crisis for you to find your way here. If things weren't so dire, there are places I would show you, things you'd like far better than the thresholds."

"That wouldn't take much." Lucinda looked at the cat in her hand. "I even like this thing better than the thresholds."

Alasdair smiled. "I only meant that there are other sorts of experiences here. I think you'd enjoy the performances in the amphitheater. And the gemstone rooms."

"Where you keep the most valuable jewels?" she guessed, imagining a treasure hoard from the *Arabian Nights*.

"No, they're rooms carved from the gems. We have rooms of tourmaline, emerald, sapphire, ruby—"

"Rubies don't come that big," she said. "I remember Tyrone had a wealthy client, who was outraged because she wanted a large ruby for a gold bracelet she designed, and no jeweler could find a stone big enough to satisfy her. They kept trying to sell her on red spinel."

"The jewelers weren't wrong," Alasdair said. "In your world rubies never even reach the size of a goose egg. These rooms are in a place that's not quite in this world. They're between dimensions, if you will. But they're linked to the towns and you can enter easily enough from here."

"Maybe next time," Lucinda said, knowing it was glib but not sure how else to respond. She looked at Alasdair more closely. "Except for the thresholds, you seem happier here," she said. "Do you really want to leave?"

He gave her his quicksilver smile. "I don't know. The mothers healed something in me; they made it possible for me to love this place again and it's been a gift to feel that. But there are the other things. The politics, which I want no part of. And whatever it is we must deal with in the city."

She glanced at the window. Sheets of rain were still falling against the glass. "Hesper is already doing what she can to help Tyrone. I still don't really understand how I'm supposed to help you."

"Nor do I," Alasdair admitted. "But I expect it will become clear. In the meantime—" she saw an uncharacteristic uncertainty fill his eyes "—do you think you and I might be friends?"

"Yes," Lucinda said, surprising herself with the immediacy of her response. "We are already." She held a hand out to him and he clasped it between both of his.

For a long moment, she stared at him, fascinated by what he was letting her sense. The sorrow and resolve were still there, but also great warmth and the curiosity and natural empathy that allowed him to open the stones, and a strength that would have been frightening if she hadn't trusted him. He was revealing himself to her, she realized, the way shy men took off their clothes, an act of vulnerability, unsure that what he was showing her would be welcome.

She pressed his hand back, saying, "It's okay," and feeling a fool for it; could she have come up with a more inadequate response?

He didn't seem to notice. "Good," he said, releasing her hand. "We should go."

They went downstairs where Alasdair said, "I'm going to say good-bye to Vita. Would you be willing to rummage through the kitchen and grab some food for the journey?" When Lucinda looked doubtful he added, "Take anything you like. My mother won't mind."

Lucinda found a fresh loaf of bread, a round of cheese, and a bowl of pears and grapes. She carried the lot over to the table where she made a concerted effort to fit it all into the gold lamé pack.

"Do you have to mash it?" a voice asked. "I hate mashed bread and mashed cheese is revolting and mashed fruit is just pulp, you know. It's messy."

"Elden?" she asked in happy disbelief. Elden leaned against the kitchen doorway, fixing her with a critical gaze through his thick glasses. He shook his head in mock disapproval and came over to the table. "Didn't anyone ever teach you how to pack a backpack? Here, let me show you."

"You're still giving me camping advice," she said, grinning at him.

"Well, you need it, obviously. Next trip I teach you how to freeze-dry your food."

"Next trip?"

"Travel is good for the soul; stasis, death. Actually, even in death there's a certain amount of travel, at least when I'm involved." He began rearranging the contents of her pack, his hands big and raw-boned, his gestures awkward. "There should always be a next trip on your horizon."

"Do you really appear when someone dies?"

"Well, not for everyone and not in this form. But yes, that's one of my jobs, to lead the soul to the Underworld."

"And do you make sure they're not afraid?" she pressed.

He stopped fussing with the pack and gave her a sharp look. "What's this about?"

"My friend Tyrone. He may be dying, and if he is . . . I don't want Kali to be the one who comes for him. Will you do it?"

"You sound like you're choosing funeral directors," he muttered. "It's not that simple. Besides, Kali-Ma embodies not only death but triumph over death. And when we do come for the dying, it has to do with who the person was, in this lifetime and others, and how he walked the earth. You don't just pick one of us."

Lucinda refused to be put off. "I don't see why not. Isn't that what praying is? Someone picks you as their patron and then if they're lucky, you respond."

Elden frowned at her. "You don't know what's involved or what you're asking. I can't give you promises for your friend."

"Good my lord Hermes." Vita and Alasdair spoke as one. They were standing outside the kitchen door and clearly had just seen him. They both bowed their heads but Elden waved a hand at them. "That isn't necessary. We're all friends here. Besides, this one—" he nodded at Lucinda "—is extremely casual in how she addresses me. We seem to have established a very informal relationship."

"That's because whenever you show up you look like a geeky teenager," Lucinda pointed out.

Elden gave her an indulgent look but she saw Hermes's silvery gaze shimmering out from his eyes, and when he spoke it was in Hermes's resonant voice. "Yet you ask a god's favors."

"Only for my friend," she insisted, fighting back a sudden rise of fear.

Hermes glanced out toward the play of the lightning that could be seen through the windows. "Your friend is being given more help than most mortals."

"I know that," Lucinda admitted. "Can you tell me what happened when Ilyap'a answered Hesper's call?"

"He's agreed not to take anything more from Tyrone or do him further harm. He won't help him either. Now it's up to Tyrone."

"But he's better, right?"

"He's—" Elden hesitated, seemingly to choose his words, "not worse. You know, he took a lot of damage."

Lucinda found that her legs suddenly felt like rubber bands. She put a hand on the kitchen table, not wanting to stumble. It had worked. She'd come all this way, and Hesper had gotten Ilyap'a to leave Tyrone. And now it seemed that wasn't close to enough.

Elden touched her shoulder. "Tyrone should have died days ago," he said. "Fact: That he didn't is a freakin' miracle."

"I know." She couldn't say the rest, that the thresholds had shown her a present with someone nearly as dangerous as Ilyap'a sitting at Tyrone's bedside, someone she had once trusted, and there was nothing she could do about that. Except go back to the city.

Elden reached into the pocket of his khakis, pulled out a shiny, silver key and held it out to Alasdair. "Present from Janus."

Alasdair regarded the key warily. "Why?"

"Don't know. He didn't say." Elden tossed the key lightly on his palm. "Best guess: Janus never apologizes or even admits regret, but this is his way of trying to make something up to you."

"Alasdair, did you berate Janus?" Vita sounded highly amused.

"I did," Alasdair admitted. "And he nearly killed me for it."

"And now he sends you a gift," Elden said. "You might as well take it. It's bound to come in handy."

Still looking reluctant, Alasdair took the key. The dragon began to flutter about frantically. "We should go," he said.

Vita stepped forward and embraced him. "I'll miss you. Don't be so long coming back."

They held each other for a long moment, though Alasdair said only, "I'll miss you, too."

Releasing him, Vita turned to Lucinda. "I wish you luck, child."

"Will you thank Hesper for me?" Lucinda asked.

"Of course." Vita kissed each of them, including the dragon, then the dragon lifted off Alasdair's collar and flew toward the door, and Elden and Alasdair and Lucinda followed.

Outside, the rain had lightened to a drizzle but lightning still broke the sky in sporadic flashes of turquoise light. Was this Ilyap'a leaving some sort of message? Lucinda wondered. A sign-off to his conversation with Hesper? An echo of his presence?

She looked at Elden hopefully as they started toward the footpaths that wound back up to the jade door. "Are you coming with us?"

"Maybe." He sounded distracted. "There are other places I have to be, and Alasdair can find his way back to Arcato." He smiled at her. "This time I don't have to worry about you losing your way or collapsing halfway up the mountain."

"I know," Lucinda said carefully. "And I'm incredibly grateful for all the help you gave me last time. I wouldn't ask for more except for Tyrone—"

The god looked at Alasdair. "Perhaps it's time you told her the story of how the gems came to the Source Place."

"What are you talking about?" she said suspiciously. "Are you changing the subject?"

"Only indirectly," Alasdair answered. "Keep walking. And listen: Long ago, when the winters were much colder and the nights much longer, and when the people who lived in the mountains heard stories of gems with fire inside them but had never actually seen one, there lived a kind hunter named Vania who adopted a young orphan girl named Dara and her cat, Moura."

"Vita's cat?" Lucinda asked.

"Vita's cat was named in honor of this one, who was also a silver tabby," Elden explained.

"The three of them lived in Vania's little hut on the mountain," Alasdair went on. "Every winter Vania would hunt deer and bears and wolves for their pelts. Each day when Vania went out to hunt, he would leave Dara and the cat in the hut. She would cook and clean for them, and Moura would chase mice. And every night Vania would tell Dara and Moura stories about the deer he'd been searching for since he was a young man, the one he'd never glimpsed and the one he'd never kill—a small stag with five-point antlers and one silver hoof. Of all the stags on the mountain, this stag was the only one who didn't lose his antlers in the winter. He was known as Silver-shod, and it was said that when he touched the ground with his silver hoof, sparks rose into the air then fell to the earth as jewels."

They were walking companionably on the switchback trail that led out of the village, the scent of fennel strong in the air. Lucinda concentrated on the steep footpath, wondering why Elden thought she needed to hear this story.

"Now Dara was only six years old," Alasdair went on, "so naturally she was fascinated by the story of Silvershod. She, too, wanted more than anything to see the stag. It happened that it was a good winter for hunting, and soon Vania had so many pelts that he had to go down the mountain to the village to sell them.

"That very first day that Vania was gone, just as dusk fell, Dara went to the window of the hut. The setting sun was shining red on the snow. Something darted out from the trees. It was a small, perfect stag with five points on his antlers.

"By the time Dara ran outside the stag was gone. 'Did you see him, Moura?' she asked the cat. But Moura was curled up, sleeping on the bed. And Dara thought she must have imagined the deer.

"The next day at sunset Dara made sure she was sitting by the window, but she didn't see anything except snow and trees. That night, though, as she got ready to sleep, she heard a sound—a light clattering on the roof. The sound moved across and down the steep sides of the roof, and finally tapped against the door.

"Dara threw open the door to see a small, perfect stag with five-pointed antlers and a silver hoof. The stag looked at her then bounded away with a laugh."

"Deer don't laugh," Lucinda pointed out.

"This one did," Alasdair told her. "Just listen. The next day Dara began to feel lonely. She'd thought Vania would be back by now. And as the day wore on, she realized Moura wasn't in the hut either. That night when the moon rose and Moura still hadn't come home, Dara went out to search for her. She called and called but the cat didn't come.

"Finally, she started back. Beneath the full moon, not too far from the hut, she saw the cat, sitting next to the five-point stag. The stag's head was bent to the cat's. They seemed to be conversing. Dara called to her cat, and the cat did something she'd never done before. Moura ran away from Dara, higher and higher up the mountain slopes, and Silvershod followed. They ran farther and farther, until Dara could no longer follow or even see them.

"Finally, the girl started back alone, her heart heavy with grief. She had been without her parents for years, but she had never been without Moura. Then just as the hut came into sight they came back, the deer and the cat racing past her, down the snowy slopes to the hut. Silvershod bounded to the top of the hut with one leap and struck the roof with his silver hoof. Deep blue sparks blazed from his hoof—and fell to the ground as sapphires. He struck the roof again and again. Green sparks became emeralds, red flared into rubies, purple became amethysts, and white sparks burst into blazing white diamonds.

"As pale blue sparks leapt into the air and fell as aquamarines, Vania returned from the village. He looked up and saw the stag on the roof, striking his hoof and sending gems flying to the ground. Vania and Dara watched in wonder until Moura suddenly dashed up to the roof and let out a wild cry that rang through the night. And then she and the stag vanished."

"That's it?" Lucinda asked a little breathlessly. The muscles in her legs were already aching.

"You okay?" Elden asked sharply.

"I don't remember the trail being this steep on the way down," she admitted. "Shouldn't we have reached the jade door a while ago?"

"That's not the way we're going," Alasdair said. "And no, that wasn't it for the story. There's a bit more, which is that Dara and Vania filled his hat with jewels and went inside to sleep. As they slept it snowed, and in the morning the rest of the gems were gone. They had only the jewels in Vania's hat, but those were more than enough to keep the two of them comfortably for the rest of their days. Moura and Silvershod were never seen again. And though Vania and Dara now lived in a fine house, bought with Silvershod's jewels, this was very hard on Dara. She missed her cat terribly.

"Until she began to dream. Every night when she slept she saw Silvershod and Moura in her dreams. She traveled with them as they raced along mountain ridges and through canyons and across wide, open plains. They ran through winter and spring and summer skies. They ran all autumn, and everywhere the stag's silver hoof struck sparks, they left gems in their wake. And each time they left jewels, Moura would give that wild cry that meant it was time to move on. . . ."

Alasdair's voice trailed off, but it didn't matter because now Lucinda was staring at the night sky, seeing a silver-and-white striped cat and small five-point stag running through the darkness, tearing across the mountainside. She saw them head downhill to the lost towns, saw Silvershod spark gems along the footpaths and houses, circle round the three thresholds, touch stairways, chimneys, and rooftops and then sprint toward the mountain's peaks.

She heard a light clatter of hooves, saw cat and stag bound along the steep grade beside her and then leap into the night sky to run toward the stars. Lucinda found that she, too, could follow them as they ran. It was as if the stars were pulling them all up into the cool spring night. They skimmed through the darkness, always climbing higher, until the stars seemed to whirl around them, until the moon seemed so close that she was sure it would be the next surface Silvershod's hoof would strike. As they raced through the night sky, the stag's silver hoof struck a bit of rock in the tail of a passing comet, and Lucinda saw the sparks of light become gems and the gems fall to earth like angels.

Then the stag and the cat were bounding down a pale wash of moonlight to the other side of the mountain, where they chased each other in a mad rush across bare plateaus and through scrub forests and then down through thicker woods. They leapt streams and gorges, they pelted along trails. . . .

"There you are," Elden said, startling her from the vision. "I knew you would like that story. It's a good one for traveling, eh?"

Lucinda blinked. The city lay spread out below them. She—and Alasdair and Elden and the dragon—had somehow followed Silvershod and Moura up over the mountain and down the other side.

"Sorry," Elden said without a trace of apology in his tone. In fact, he sounded tremendously pleased with himself. "No offense, Lucinda, but you're such a slow hiker. And, despite the divinity thing, I simply didn't have the eternal patience to watch you struggle over the mountain again."

Lucinda was too amazed and too grateful to bristle at the insult to her hiking. "You do have a unique approach to travel," she managed to say.

"My specialty." Elden kissed her lightly on the cheek. "Go see your friend. He needs you."

LUCINDA AND ALASDAIR went directly to the Intensive Care ward. Tyrone was no longer there. A nurse explained that he'd been moved that evening. The new room wasn't a ward like the last one, and it wasn't the room with white walls that Lucinda had seen in the threshold. This room was beige, and there was only one other bed in the room and it was empty.

Tyrone was lying on his back. Something inside her relaxed as she realized that neither of his hands was twisted into the horrid curled position she'd seen in the thresholds. His eyes were open. They focused on her as she moved toward him.

"Hey," she said softly.

He didn't answer, and she felt fear clamping down on her again. Had he lost the ability to speak? Averill had said that his spirit had followed her to the lost towns, trying to protect her even as he struggled for his own life. Lucinda hoped it hadn't cost him dearly.

She sat on the edge of his bed, grasping his hand, not bothering to hold back her tears. Tyrone's hand lay cool and limp in hers.

"Can you hear me?" she asked.

Tyrone's eyes moved to the right and when he spoke his voice rasped. "Who's he?"

She'd forgotten Alasdair was there. "A—my friend," she said. "This is Alasdair. He helped you that night you were stabbed. And he's helped us both since then."

"Hello, Mr. Dessalines," Alasdair said with his usual courteous formality. "Would you rather I left you two alone?"

Tyrone's eyes met Lucinda's again. "He can stay." His voice was so weak she had to bend close to hear him. "Thought something happened to you. When they told me you stopped coming by—"

"Things did happen. I left the city to get you help."

He considered that for a while then with effort asked, "Did you?"

"Yes. Ilyap'a's gone from you and won't hurt you anymore. All you have to do now is get well."

Maybe she'd been expecting Tyrone to look happy at the news. He took it with a neutral expression.

"Tyrone, when I was gone, did someone visit you, a man with reddish hair—"

"Marcus visited," he said. "Just before you."

"What did he want?" she asked, her voice sharp.

"Don't know. Show off his new crutches?"

She and Alasdair exchanged a glance over the bed. So Marcus was on crutches. So far the vision of the third threshold was accurate. "What about this other man?" Lucinda asked.

"Don't remember," Tyrone said. "Just woke up today." His eyelids began to drift down. "I'm tired."

Lucinda immediately went to get a nurse and cross-examined her as to whether Tyrone was sleeping or going unconscious again. The nurse came, prodded Tyrone, got a baleful glare, and pronounced him sleeping. "I think you'd better let him sleep," she finished. "You two can come back in the morning."

Lucinda hesitated outside of Tyrone's door. "I'm afraid to leave him," she told Alasdair. "Sebastian may come back."

"I suspect Sebastian was here looking for you," Alasdair said. "If you really want to keep him away from Tyrone, then I'd advise you to be somewhere else."

The idea of Sebastian looking for her made her skin crawl. He'd found her flat when she'd never given him her address. She could still hear his voice, mocking and truthful, when she'd asked how he found her: "I have a good sense of smell." Now that she was back in Arcato there would be no hiding from him. Still, better that he come after her than Tyrone.

"Maybe you're right," she said to Alasdair. "But I still don't feel good about leaving Tyrone. He's so weak and he's got goddamn Marcus dropping in on him."

"Marcus is someone we should probably try to find," Alasdair observed. "If we don't find him, he may not have much time left. At the very least, we owe him a warning. Besides, I'm hoping he'll know something about the phantasms."

"If he does, he won't tell us," Lucinda predicted. "Marcus wouldn't help his own grandmother if she were having a heart attack in the middle of his kitchen."

"Be that as it may, we have to try. We can't afford to overlook anyone who might know the one we're seeking. This being who creates phantasms, he's after something. I don't know what it is, but I suspect he'll become more desperate and more dangerous as he closes in on his goal."

"I can't leave Tyrone on his own here."

The dragon emerged from somewhere in Alasdair's cloak, and Alasdair smiled. "I believe we have a bodyguard."

Lucinda did not find that reassuring. "After that green toxin? If Sebastian comes back to the hospital and finds the dragon, he'll try to kill him."

"Sebastian's never struck me as stupid. A fox is no match for a dragon and he knows it."

Lucinda held out her hand and the dragon lit on her forefinger. "Are you sure you'll be all right?" she asked it.

The dragon stiffened with an expression that could only be high dudgeon.

"Okay then. I'm—incredibly grateful."

The dragon relaxed at once and tapped her finger with a tiny clawed foot, as if to say, "It's nothing," then flew off into Tyrone's room and perched on the headboard above the sleeping man.

THEY WENT TO Lucinda's flat first, so that she could change, drop off the pack, and collect her mail and phone messages. In the morning she'd check in with Gabrielle on the studio. Now, though, the question on both Lucinda and Alasdair's minds was whether Sebastian had tried to contact her.

"So if I do find something from Sebastian," Lucinda said, as they entered her building's familiar, gloomy lobby, "what do I do?"

"What do you want to do?"

"Nothing. I don't want to see or talk to him ever again." She unlocked her mailbox, removed a sheaf of envelopes, and started up the stairs. "I don't want him dead or tormented. I just wish he'd disappear. I want him out of the city, away from Tyrone, out of my life."

"You could try telling him that," Alasdair suggested mildly.

"Have you ever tried telling Sebastian no? He doesn't discourage easily. He acts like he's backing off, like there's no pressure and you could walk away at any time, but all the while he's looking for a way in."

"He cares for you," Alasdair said as they started up the stairs.

"Are you defending him?"

Alasdair seemed to consider this very amusing. "That would be a change. Maybe I've finally found something that would manage to shock both Averill and Vita."

"Is that a goal of yours?"

"It was when I was much younger. I suppose I'd still find some entertainment in it."

She reached her door, fitted the key into the lock, and hesitated.

"What is it?" asked Alasdair.

"Just something I remembered Sebastian saying: 'Locks don't present a problem for me. . . .'"

"Do you want me to go in first to make sure he's not there?"

"No, I'll do it." She refused to be spooked out of entering her own flat. Her hand steady, she turned the key and opened the door, but she was unnerved thinking that her home was open to the trickster, that she couldn't keep him out.

They found no sign of Sebastian inside. Though the rooms smelled slightly musty and there was dust on every surface, it felt good to be back inside the familiar confines of her apartment. She dropped her pack on the floor and played her phone messages. A few from Gabrielle reassured her that the studio hadn't yet fallen apart. One of the fabric sellers down by the waterfront called to say she'd just gotten in a shipment of antique saris that Lucinda had to see. Maxine called to report that she was closing Indigo for a spell and taking a leave of absence from the city. A man Lucinda didn't remember invited her to a gallery opening. The final message played: "*Lucinda, it's your mother. Where are you? I stopped by your building and your super said he hadn't seen you in days. Call me.*"

Lucinda glanced at Alasdair. "Tyrone didn't seem to know his spirit went to the lost towns with me. Do you think my mother knows about hers?"

"Tyrone was probably still in a coma when his spirit was drawn to you. That level of spirit energy often works subconsciously. So it might have worked that way for your mother, as well."

"It must have," Lucinda agreed. "I can't imagine her consciously sending her spirit anywhere."

Alasdair didn't comment on that. Lucinda rubbed her eyes. "Do I have time for a bath before we go do whatever it is we do next?"

"Go ahead. I'll make some coffee. You do have the fixings for coffee, don't you?"

"In the cabinet above the sink. Help yourself."

The water in the building's aged pipes was tepid that day, so Lucinda bathed quickly, staying in the water only long enough to clean herself. She emerged chilled and cranky. As she dressed in loose black pants and a high-collared white silk jacquard shirt, she cursed the building's super, the geriatric water heater, and the other tenants who had so thoughtlessly used up her nice, hot bath water.

"I miss the hot springs," she told Alasdair when she stepped into the kitchen a few minutes later.

Alasdair glanced at her. "Well, I've missed coffee. It's one thing that the towns are sorely lacking."

"Why don't you just bring some back from the city? It sounds like enough of you visit here. You could stock up."

"We'd need to set up a real system for transport if we were going to bring up nearly enough. And the towns don't like to establish any connection with Arcato that's too permanent. We prefer to visit individually, trade as we see fit, and bring back only what the individual can carry."

Lucinda waved a hand toward her coffeepot, which was making little snorting noises, indicating that the drip process was almost done. "Well, you're welcome to as much of mine as you like."

"Thank you," Alasdair said solemnly. He filled a mug for each of them, which they took into the living room.

Lucinda curled up in the cushions on the big wicker chair, still reveling in the comfort of being home again. Alasdair sipped his coffee, gave a sigh of profound contentment, then said, "There's something I haven't told you."

She gave him a resigned smile. "For a change."

He had the grace to look embarrassed. "Bad habit," he said, staring into his coffee. "I'm sorry."

"So what is it this time?"

His grey eyes met hers, level and without emotion. "Before we left Vita showed me a gazing crystal, and in it I saw the one who I believe is responsible for the phantasms. He's another shape-shifter who takes the form of a fox. I saw him on Haifong Street with Sebastian."

"Oh, Jesus." She felt sick, realizing that there'd been a tiny part of her that believed that Sebastian had changed when he was healed, that wanted to believe he might not be evil. Though she'd never said the words to herself, she'd believed that if Tyrone was better, then Sebastian hadn't hurt him, maybe had even helped him. "And you didn't tell me this because?"

"You'd seen Sebastian at Tyrone's bedside. I thought you were already frightened enough."

"Well, I was," she admitted. Unable to remain still, she slid off one of her silver bracelets and put it back it on again. "Do you know who this other fox is?"

"No. Vita didn't recognize him either. He's not from the towns. And he's something more than Sebastian."

"The way Averill is something more than Sebastian?"

"No." Alasdair hesitated, as if searching for the right words. "When I first saw this fox shift into a man he was covered with scars. So many that his skin looked like it was covered with hatch marks. Then he made the scars vanish so he looked like any of the young people who go to the clubs."

"He made the scars vanish," she repeated.

"They seemed to recede into his body, leaving him smooth-skinned. Averill's capable of shifting forms but not of changing her own that way."

"And what did this shape-shifter look like without his scars?"

"He looked like he was in one of the bands that play on Haifong Street," Alasdair told her. "A ripped jacket, reddish hair, down below his shoulder on one side, razor-cut short on the other, eyeliner and earrings, fine, even features, more classically handsome than Sebastian. Almost pretty."

"Oh, do I know the type," Lucinda said. "He's the kind of bad boy teenage girls crave. I can still see the ones I fell for . . . hot and very male but with a hint of the female. They have this soft thing about them that makes them seem accessible, safe. And it's always such a lie."

"Maybe not always," Alasdair said, "but in this case it is."

She was feeling sicker by the minute. "If he can make the scars disappear that way, is it possible he can alter his other features? I mean, what if there's no way to recognize him?"

"There might be a way to get some sort of alert if he—or one of his phantasms—is near."

Alasdair put the coffee mug down, extended one hand, and stared hard at his open palm. He closed the hand and when he opened it again, a bracelet rested on his palm. It was a slender but solid silver band imprinted with a few simple designs—single diamonds on the ends, triple banding on either side, and waves and arches on the raised bezel that enclosed a rectangular sea-green crystal. "Tourmaline set in sand-cast silver," he said.

"You know, if you ever want to give up this *cearu* business, you could pull off a hell of a magic act."

"That wasn't magic. I called the stone to me, that's all."

"And got a bracelet?"

"I specified that the tourmaline be in a form that would make it easily available to you. Tourmaline is known as a 'teller' stone. It can tell you who the source of evil is."

"How?"

He handed her the bracelet. "The same way all the stones work. You have to open yourself to it and listen."

"What if there's no time for that?"

"Make time," he said curtly. "The tourmaline may be the only thing that will be able to tell you whether or not you're dealing with the shape-shifter. Now please, put the bracelet on."

They decided to go off in search of Marcus. Alasdair had a hunch that Marcus was already engaged with the phantasm, and he wanted to see if he could find out more about that. Lucinda wanted to know why Marcus had visited Tyrone.

He wasn't hard to locate. The advertisement in the phone directory read:

MARCUS
SCULPTURE AND FINE ART

"Notice he doesn't use his last name," Lucinda said. "It's Tuttle, which he finds embarrassing. Besides, he's convinced he's so hot that everyone should know him by first name only. Also notice that he doesn't claim his sculpture *is* fine art."

Alasdair just glanced at the ad and said, "The studio is on Lionscross Road. Do you think he'll be there now?"

For the first time since returning to the city Lucinda looked at a clock. They hadn't had clocks or watches in the lost towns, and the very act of checking the time now seemed slightly alien to her. It was just past two in the morning. The exhaustion she'd been keeping at bay with adrenaline rushed in at her. She pushed it aside. "I think his studio is also his home, the way Tyrone's is. He used to go out to the clubs a lot, but the crutches should have slowed him down." She smiled. "Let's go wake his ass up."

"Malice doesn't suit you," said Alasdair.

She shrugged, not particularly caring. "It might be better if we catch him unawares, not give him a chance to spin his usual bull."

"And maybe he won't bother to answer the door at this hour," Alasdair said. "I don't like barging in on people in the middle of the night."

Lucinda let her jaw drop. "You're the one who's made it sound like finding this shape-shifter is so all-fired important. And you won't disturb someone's sleep for it? Oh, now I get it. You only fight evil as long as you don't have to do anything impolite."

Alasdair's quicksilver smile flashed. "That's certainly the way it would be if I were writing the rules. I've always found rudeness to be tawdry, very bad form."

"That's kind of a limited view," she said, enjoying teasing him. "I find it pretty damn refreshing."

"You would." He looked at the clock and then back at her. "You're right though. This is serious. We'll have to risk disturbing Marcus's sleep."

They set off through a quiet city. Most of the shops and businesses were shut down, the apartment windows dark. They passed few people; the streets were for the most part empty, dark slicks of rainwater reflecting beneath the streetlights.

They followed the streets uphill to Lionscross Road. Although all of the galleries were shut for the night, some of the windows were still lit. Above a gallery featuring a show of dioramas of famous murders, Lucinda found a bronze plate with the word MARCUS inscribed on it. She pushed the buzzer, holding it down.

"That's enough." Alasdair took her hand off the bell. "He's got two broken legs and he was probably asleep. Give him a chance to get to the door."

After what seemed an interminable wait Marcus's voice, thick with sleep, came through the intercom. "Yeah? Who is it?"

Alasdair spoke up. "My name is Alasdair. I'm a friend of Tyrone's. I know what happened to him Carnival Night. There's a chance you may be in similar danger. Please, I need to talk with you."

"Then come back in the fucking morning," was Marcus's irate reply. "Now get away from my door before I call the cops."

"And you were worried about *me* being rude," Lucinda muttered.

Alasdair grimaced with distaste then jiggled the door's handle. It didn't move. With a resigned shrug, he reached into a pocket and withdrew Janus's key. Lucinda wasn't even surprised when the key slid smoothly into the lock and the tumblers clicked into place. Alasdair pushed open the door, and Lucinda led the way to the top floor that Marcus had converted into his loft/studio/gallery. She paused as they reached the top landing. "Do you think we should tell him we're here?"

"No. That would only give him time to grab a weapon," Alasdair said. He walked to the door, inserted Janus's key in what seemed to be an altogether different sort of lock. Again, the door opened easily.

Lucinda followed him into a large, rectangular room with polished oak floors and tiny spotlights hanging above Marcus's sculptures. Her trepidation was quickly replaced by revulsion. Everything Marcus sculpted reminded her of giant spiders or lobsters, including one that seemed to be a shiny black arachnid sticking a long, spindly leg into the vagina of a female manikin. The metal plate on its red plastic base gave its title as CONNECTION.

"Gods, he's vile," she murmured. "Who buys this shit?"

"That's not the question."

A door at the end of the room was abruptly flung open, revealing a rectangle of bright light; Marcus stood in the doorway. Lucinda felt a pang of grief go through her. Even hunched over on crutches, Marcus's resemblance to a healthier Tyrone was striking. It was almost as if she were looking at a vision of what Tyrone used to be.

Marcus blinked at them. "Who the—"

"Hi, Marcus." Lucinda forced herself to speak up with false cheer. "It's just me and my friend Alasdair. We came to visit you. How ya doing?"

Marcus swung himself into the gallery. "You evil hell-bitch. What are you doing here?"

"Tut, tut." She couldn't resist reminding him of his name. "Where *are* your manners?"

"Manners, my ass. You tried to push me down a staircase when I was in a wheelchair."

"Only because you gave Tyrone the elixir on Carnival Night and then didn't even have the guts to tell me until I threatened you."

"Both of you, stop it," Alasdair said with a notable lack of patience. "Marcus, we didn't come here to argue with you."

"Actually, I'd like to know why you visited Tyrone today," Lucinda put in.

"Because he's in the hospital," Marcus said, enunciating each word. "And it gets lonely in there. Which you might have picked up on if *you'd* been visiting. Where have you been anyway? The nurses said you haven't shown in days." His eyes narrowed. "Guess you're too busy breaking into other people's places."

"You left your doors unlocked," Alasdair said calmly. "Check them if you like; you'll see the locks haven't been tampered with." When Marcus made no move to check the locks he went on. "Now I'm sure you'd like to go back to bed, so we if could all just talk for a few moments, we'll be happy to leave you in peace."

Marcus hobbled over to one of the brushed-aluminum couches and gingerly lowered himself onto its shiny surface. Alasdair sat on the facing couch. Lucinda chose to remain standing. It was like breaking bread, as far as she was concerned; you didn't take a seat in your enemy's house.

"Is there anyone who's come into your life recently?" Alasdair asked.

"What?"

"Someone you've met since Carnival."

"A shitload of doctors and nurses."

"How about your dealer?" Lucinda asked. "And I don't mean for your so-called art."

Marcus straightened one of the crutches in preparation for standing up. "I'm calling the police and asking them to remove you from my loft. You two are trespassing on my private property."

"You think we *wanted* to come here?" Lucinda demanded. "I could think of a lot of places I'd rather—"

"We actually came here to help you," Alasdair interjected quickly. "Or at least give you fair warning."

"Of what?" Marcus asked suspiciously.

"You received a costume for Carnival the same way Lucinda did. It just showed up. Did you ever find out who sent it to you?" Alasdair asked.

"Never."

"Well, there's someone you know—or will meet in the near future. I suspect it's the same person who sent you the costume. And this person is someone you'll be making some sort of deal with. Up on a rooftop."

Marcus looked at Lucinda. "Where's he getting this shit?"

"We saw a vision," she answered. "I can't tell you how, but we saw you on a roof at night. You were on your crutches and you were talking to someone, saying how you weren't going to turn tricks for him. Like there was something he or she—we never saw who it was—was trying to get you to do."

"And it ended badly," said Alasdair. "This other person advanced on you, probably with some sort of weapon. And you backed up, over the edge of the roof."

"You're telling me I fell off a roof." Marcus's voice held too much scorn to even frame it as a question.

Alasdair said, "We're telling you that's what *may* happen. It was a vision of the future we saw. It's possible for you to change your actions so that things don't turn out that way."

Marcus shook his shaved head in disbelief. "You wake me up in the middle of the night for this crock of—"

"Fine, don't believe it," Lucinda said. "But don't say you weren't warned."

"And for pity's sake, as long as you're still on crutches stay away from rooftops," Alasdair added, getting to his feet. "I'm sorry we had to disturb you." He and Lucinda started for the door.

Marcus hobbled after them. "Wait just a goddamn minute." When neither of them slowed their steps, he grabbed Alasdair's arm and pulled him around, nearly losing his own balance in the process.

Alasdair watched Marcus struggle to right himself. "You should go back to sleep."

"You're holding out on me," Marcus said accusingly. "You don't get to break into my loft in the middle of the night and give me some half-assed warning. What else is there?"

"You don't deserve to know anything else," Lucinda told him. "You're right. We shouldn't have come. We should have left you to fall off your fucking roof and—"

"Could we have a little less vitriol all around?" Alasdair looked from one to the other with exasperation. "Do you both have to make things more difficult than they already are?" For a moment his glance rested on one of the sculptures, and a look of revulsion flickered in his eyes. Schooling his expression to neutrality, he said, "What we left out is that whoever was up on the roof with you wasn't actually there."

Marcus tucked one of the crutches under his armpit so he could rub his forehead. "You know, I'm getting one mother of a headache from all this double-talk."

"There's someone in this city creating phantasms, illusions," Alasdair said. "He's making people see things that aren't there. If you go up to that roof, it will be a phantasm that you will meet and that will kill you."

For once Marcus had nothing to say.

"Please be careful," Alasdair finished, "especially around anyone who might make some sort of deal with you. And if such a person does surface, would you please call Lucinda and tell her who it is?"

Marcus nodded and they took their leave of him. Back on the street, Alasdair didn't speak and Lucinda took it as a justified accusation. "I'm sorry," she said. "I shouldn't have dropped to his level, but I can't seem to help myself around Marcus. I can't forgive him for what he did to Tyrone."

"Which is?" Alasdair's voice was cool and remote.

"I told you. He gave him that elixir. He drugged him and if he hadn't—"

"Someone else would have," Alasdair said. "Don't you see that Marcus is just a tool for one of the larger forces who've orchestrated all this? Tyrone is now fighting for his life because assorted gods willed it that things turned out that way. I'm fairly certain that Janus released Michael from jail at Sebastian's behest. But even before that, the boy was Hekate's pawn. Ilyap'a took offense at Tyrone's presumption, and Sebastian had Kama's help in separating you from Tyrone that night. That's at least four gods and one shape-shifter involved in this mess. And it's possible that this second shape-shifter had a hand in it, too."

"You mean he was the one who sent Marcus the wolf costume?"

"Possibly. The point is, in the face of that kind of power—gods and tricksters and who knows what else—Marcus becomes nearly irrelevant. And while he may have certain loathsome aspects to his character, you don't have the luxury of wasting time or energy blaming him."

Stung, Lucinda didn't respond. She concentrated on the sound of the foghorns floating up from the river, on the ever-present humidity that clung to the city streets like a skin. And she tried to ignore the exhaustion that had her muscles quivering and chills playing along her spine and the back of her skull.

They walked through the empty streets in silence until Alasdair stopped at the corner of Warren and Linnea, where they would turn downhill to Lucinda's street. "I'm sorry if I was harsh," he said. "I'll walk you back to your flat so you can get some sleep."

"Where are you going?"

"In the vision the shape-shifter was on Haifong Street. He's probably long gone but the clubs should still be open. Someone there might remember him. I'd love to find that young woman who was so eager to take his arm."

"I should go with you," Lucinda said at once.

"You're so tired you can barely stand upright," he said gently.

"I know. But look at you in your green robe." She hesitated. "I don't mean any offense, but you don't look like the kind of person who frequents the clubs. You'll have a hard time getting anyone to talk."

Alasdair gazed at her, questioning. "And you have the right . . . look?"

"Could be better if I had time to go home and change, but it'll do. Besides, I know the guy who owns the Kingfisher, and the bartender at Ravenna. We should also check the Dome and Guthrie's down by the waterfront. They're all open till dawn."

A faint smile crossed Alasdair's face and she saw that he was nearly as weary as she was. "To Haifong Street, then."

HAIFONG STREET WAS jumping. The theaters were dark but club kids streamed in and out of the clubs, and bone-jarringly loud music pumped out onto the street every time one of the doors opened. Lucinda took in the skinny leather-clad boys and the girls glittering in deliberately ragged splendor. They stood in small groups, heads bent as they lit cigarettes with a casual sense of cool so studied that any one of them could have conducted a course in it. It wasn't that long ago that she'd ended most of her nights on Haifong or Consolación. Why did it now seem so distant, a part of her life all but closed to her?

Alasdair, too, was assessing the crowds. "I see what you mean," he said.

He looked so woefully out of place that Lucinda had to smile. "It's not so bad," she kidded him. "Maybe long robes will be the next trend. You could be the next big look."

"No," he said darkly, "I don't think so."

"Want me to go in on my own?"

"Hunting shape-shifters? Not on your life."

They went to the Kingfisher first, standing on line only a few minutes before the imperious man monitoring the line spotted her and ushered them inside.

"How are you, darling?" he shouted above the music while kissing her on both cheeks. "Long time, no?"

"Too long, Claudio." She, too, was shouting as she returned the kisses. "You're looking dazzling as ever. Is Ronny around? I need to talk to him."

"He's in his office, love. You know the way."

Lucinda led them through a room packed with gyrating bodies. On the stage a band slammed out music so raw and strong and weirdly beautiful that Lucinda felt as if it sucked the exhaustion from her pores, filling her instead with its own unrelenting energy.

At the back of the dance floor a narrow metal stairway led up two flights to an almost equally narrow hallway, lit by a bare red lightbulb. Lucinda and Alasdair walked to the very end of the hall where she knocked on a nondescript door.

"Enter!" bellowed a deep voice.

An overweight man with a mop of frizzy brown hair sat behind a desk, studying an open ledger, his face grim. His glanced up and his expression lightened as he realized it was Lucinda who'd barged into his sanctuary. "'Cinda, baby, where you been keeping yourself?" He got up and enfolded her in a bear hug. He smelled of sweat and shaving lotion. "I've missed you, girl."

"I've missed you, too," she said honestly. "Ronny, this is my friend Alasdair."

Ronny gave Alasdair a fleeting glance; if he found him an unlikely patron, he didn't let on. "You two come for the band?" he asked. "They've had this place packed to the rafters every night for a week now. Me, I look at them and think: They're so loud, so angry, so cynical. Does every song have to be a 'fuck you' to the universe? And then I hear myself saying those things and I think: Ronny, you've turned into your mother."

Lucinda grinned. "I've met your mother. I think you're still safe." She turned to Alasdair and explained, "His mother heads the board of trustees at the city opera. You can't find a more refined lady."

"Lady? Please, we're talking about a dowager," Ronny said. "Every time I see her she tells me how much money I'm not going to inherit. She's terrified that the fortune she faithfully bedded my father for will wind up funneled into the club, den of iniquity that it is." He shook his head, helped himself to some chocolates from a box on his desk, then offered the box to Lucinda and Alasdair, who each took one. "So, what can I do you for?"

"We're looking for someone," Lucinda said.

She described Sebastian then Alasdair described the shape-shifter's human form and the girl who'd led him toward the clubs.

Ronny chewed thoughtfully on another chocolate. "Haven't seen either of the guys, and I'm out on the floor most nights. I'll ask around. But the girl—"

"What about the girl?" Alasdair asked.

"I'm not sure," Ronny said. "To tell you the truth, she could be any one of hundreds that come through here every night. They all have the short skirts, the heels, those manes of hair. But that jibes with the description of a girl who's been missing these last few days." He opened his desk drawer and pulled out a snapshot. "Name's Janna Powell. Her roommate says they got separated here on Haifong and she never came home. The police left this with me. Look familiar?"

Alasdair glanced at the photo and frowned. "That's her."

Ronny returned the photo to his drawer. "Maybe it's the police you should be talking to."

Alasdair stood up. "Yes, apparently it is. Thank you for your help."

Lucinda gave Ronny another hug. "We'll catch up another time, okay?"

"Don't be a stranger, girl."

Lucinda didn't mention it when she saw a handful of transparent stones make themselves at home in a dark corner of Ronny's office as she and Alasdair were leaving. Outside the Kingfisher, though, the first thing she said was, "What were those stones that stayed with Ronny?"

"Amethysts and alexandrites, mostly, with a few tanzanites thrown in. They liked your friend. If you noticed, none of them bothered to show themselves at Marcus's."

She hadn't noticed, but she felt oddly pleased that stones shared her general view of character. "We should try Ravenna next," she said.

Lucinda started toward the club but Alasdair pulled her back. "If the police are searching for the girl, then you and I can't be marching into clubs, inquiring about her. Not unless we want to do a lot of explaining to the authorities. And they would never believe what I told them anyway."

"Why not?" asked Lucinda. "I mean, everyone knows about the gems in the city."

Alasdair's expression hovered somewhere between amused and appalled. "Certainly, people in this city know that strange things have been happening, and some have even heard rumors of the lost towns. But if I explain that the problem is two renegade shape-shifters, they'd lock me up for a lunatic."

"Then I'll go to the police. I don't have to say anything about shape-shifters. I'll tell them I saw the girl on Haifong with a guy whose hair is long on one side, cropped short on the other, and I'll give them Sebastian's description as well. At least they'll be able to look out for them. It could help."

"Do you really want to send in police officers against a being whom they have no chance of containing? You could be setting them up for . . . disaster."

He was right, of course. The exhaustion she'd been fending off returned in a wave, so strong that Lucinda was tempted to sink to the sidewalk and fall asleep where they stood. She fought for a coherent thought and finally said, "Okay, going to the police is not optimal. I've only got one other idea: I go home and go about my life and wait for Sebastian to find me."

"In that case I'd better go with you." When she looked hesitant he added, "I'll make sure we're cloaked. I have a black opal among my life stones that's particularly good at concealment. No one will follow us to your flat."

"That isn't what I was worried about," she told him. "You can crash on my couch, but you can't shadow me or be my bodyguard. Sooner or later I'm going to have to be on my own. Besides, Sebastian hates you. There's a chance that if it's just me, he'll tell me what happened to that girl."

ALASDAIR LEFT LUCINDA'S apartment just after dawn the next morning. As agreed, he'd spent the night on her couch. She'd left the door to her bedroom slightly ajar, an act he didn't dare interpret. But he peered in before he left and was comforted to see her sleeping soundly.

Finding that he was hungry, he headed toward Josefina's. His eyes swept the streets as he walked, wondering where the shape-shifter was now. Could he be disguised among the groups of longshoremen, making their way down toward the waterfront? Or could he have morphed into another shape altogether—the spindly woman watering the violets in her window box, the young boy unfurling the awning over the spice shop, or any of the older men who now sat at Josefina's counter, nursing mugs of coffee? It was futile to suspect everyone, Alasdair decided, as he entered the café.

He ordered eggs and toast and coffee then found a table in a darkened corner and began to scan the paper for stories that might suggest phantasms. He knew he would have to go back to the ruined plaza at the top of the city, but he was hoping for more information first. Maybe the girl had been found. Maybe someone had seen an oversized red fox. He didn't look up as a waitress brought his food to the table, his attention caught by an odd story. Manjusha, a small but fine jewelry store, had been vandalized during the night. None of the jewelry was missing. The most expensive items were in a safe; the rest were found scattered on the floor. The vandal had wrenched open the locked glass counters and gone after the velvet display cases inside, slashing them to shreds. The owner, Rudelle Udovitch, had not been in the store when it was broken into, but shortly before the damage was

discovered, neighbors reported a high-pitched sound, so piercing and painful that many were still complaining of head- and earaches. Alasdair stared
at the newsprint, feeling sick inside. This couldn't be random coincidence,
and he—

"Excuse me." A woman's melodic voice interrupted Alasdair's thoughts.
"Would you mind if I shared your table?"

The woman who asked the question was of medium-height and build.
She wore a long, dark blue skirt and over it a man's linen shirt, its rolled-up
sleeves revealing sinewy forearms. Her skin was tanned and weather-beaten,
with deep creases at the edges of her eyes. Her long hair was tied back at the
nape of her neck, a soft halo of windblown silver-blond strands escaping the
cloth tie.

"No," Alasdair said, aware he hadn't answered her question because he'd
been staring. "Please, have a seat."

She sat down in the chair across from him, and each studied the other
with open curiosity. Alasdair noted that she wore thin gold hoops in her ears
and a round bronze amulet around her neck. And then he knew. "Johari sent
you?"

She nodded, seeming pleased that he'd guessed. "He said I might find
you at Josefina's. My name is Teja." She looked around the dingy café with
an amused expression. "Apart from the waitress, I seem to be the only
woman here. Am I violating a taboo?"

"Not that I know of. I suspect it's by default that Josefina's is somewhat of
a men's gathering place."

"Well, I won't stay long. I wouldn't want to scare off the regulars," Teja
said good-naturedly. "Johari asked me to find you because he's received
more information about the topic you two discussed."

"What's been set loose in the city, you mean," said Alasdair. He felt both
heartened and mildly alarmed: heartened because Johari was enough of
friend to help despite his travels; alarmed because the news couldn't be good
if Johari had found it necessary to send a messenger. "Johari said it was
something familiar, something used for good but turned to another purpose."

"Perhaps." Teja's gaze was direct. She had hazel eyes that seemed amber
one moment, green the next. "The reason it—he—felt familiar to Johari is
that he may be one of ours."

"The shape-shifter?"

"I know." She anticipated his next question. "We don't have many shape-
shifters among us, and we're glad of it. It's visceral, really. Although we
grow up with horses and most of us take to nearly any animal we encounter,

to see a creature that's both human and animal . . . it repulses. Your people revere shape-shifters; we consider them aberrant and dangerous."

"This one is," Alasdair said softly.

"Perhaps," she said again. "If he is the one Johari suspects."

"If?"

"We have no proof," Teja said carefully. "But there was a shape-shifter born to our people. Before his birth an oracle foretold that he would have tremendous power, so his mother gave him the name Sangeet, which means music, hoping he'd turn to the healing sounds. And he was a remarkable student, absorbed everything he was taught. By the time he was six he could alleviate all but the most severe pain." She hesitated, then said, "It's been years since he's been among us."

"What happened?"

She shrugged. "Nothing unusual, really. Like many of our people, when he came of age he wanted to see the world. He left our camps, didn't maintain contact at all."

"Then why does Johari think . . . ?"

"Stories have filtered back to us. That Sangeet took our knowledge and perverted it. Instead of using sound to heal, he used it to do harm and take things apart."

She didn't have to elaborate. Alasdair knew that the Sinpiedras healed with sound vibrations, balancing and aligning the energy in the body, restoring to health what was damaged. If someone had that capability and chose to invert it—

"What Johari sensed when he was in Arcato fits with those stories," Teja said. "However, I must emphasize that they are stories only. When Sangeet left us he was an exemplary student, a fine healer. And it's more than a hundred years since any of us have seen or heard from him, thirty years since the last rumor came to us. His mother believes he's dead."

"Why?"

Teja traced two stick figures on the tabletop—one female, the other a smaller male—then drew a line between them. "There's a kind of auric connection between mother and child that exists as long as both are alive. Sangeet's mother says that cord between them was severed nearly ninety years ago. She mourned him then. These rumors of his being alive, doing evil, make her furious."

"Do *you* think he's dead?" Alasdair asked.

"I would need some sort of evidence to believe otherwise."

Alasdair thought about that. "When he was with your people, aside from shape-shifting, did you have any evidence that he was a trickster?"

Teja smiled ruefully. "Other infants cause mischief. Sangeet caused madness, even before he could crawl. But we schooled it out of him quickly, and he learned to restrain his impulses to shape-shift. He was never a danger when he was with us. That's why, despite Johari's intuition, I'm not sure he's the one you seek. I'm here as a favor to Johari, not because I agree with him."

Alasdair pointed to the newspaper article. "Recently, there have been a number of incidents in Arcato—objects being slashed, people seeing phantasms. Both are often preceded by an excruciating sound. Does any of that sound like Sangeet?"

Teja quickly skimmed the article. When she looked up at him again her eyes were troubled. "I don't know about the cutting. The sound—yes, that's what I meant by a perversion of our techniques. As for the phantasms—" she hesitated, as if weighing what to tell him "—when he was an infant, that's exactly how Sangeet caused madness. He made people see things that weren't there. At first the things were amorphous—just dark shapes—but soon he was casting the illusion of whoever was nearby. His mother once looked up from bathing him and saw her double on the other side of the basin."

"And you need more proof?" Alasdair asked, an edge in his voice.

"I can't believe his own mother would make a mistake about the auric connection between them being severed."

Alasdair considered that. "Maybe she's not wrong," he said. "For whatever reason, this shape-shifter's got a penchant for slashing things. Maybe that was one of the things he cut."

Teja blanched. "That's unheard of."

"But not impossible?"

She pursed her lips, considering. At length she said, "Not for an adept, no. If the stories about him are true and he's here in Arcato—"

"Will you help me stop him?" Alasdair asked.

"I'll have to go back and speak with the elders. We're not permitted to act against our own unless it's been sanctioned by the elders."

"We don't have time for procedural niceties."

"I've taken vows. I'm bound by the rules of my people. I'm sorry."

Alasdair tried to keep the anger out of his voice as he said, "So your shape-shifter is my problem."

"You have one advantage," she said gently. "You're not one of us. He's familiar with our powers and probably more than able to counter them. You have abilities that are foreign to Sangeet."

"The stones."

She nodded. "We can feel their vibrations but have never been able to get the stones to respond to us. So we journey in other directions. But from the time Sangeet was a child, he's hated the stones for that. He has his charms, you know. Most beings respond to him. He's never been able to bear being so completely defied. Perhaps that will be useful to you."

"Let's hope so," said Alasdair.

"I'll speak to the elders. Perhaps we can help. In the meantime, go carefully, and may the gods go with you."

Teja stood then, made what he took to be a symbol of blessing over him, and left him to his now-cold breakfast.

Eighteen

LUCINDA SLEPT IN. It was nearly ten by the time she woke, and she came to her senses groggy and disoriented. City sounds filtered through her windows: the bell on a streetcar and someone shouting after it to stop; a messenger pounding on a door, calling up that he had a delivery; a vendor hawking bargain "designer" watches. It was hard for her to comprehend that just yesterday morning she'd woken in the Source Place. She forced herself out of bed and stumbled into the living room where she found that Alasdair was gone. He'd left the sheets and blankets he used folded neatly on the couch, the considerate houseguest. He hadn't left a note but she trusted that they would find each other again.

The first item on Lucinda's agenda that morning was a visit to Tyrone, so she dressed quickly, drank a hurried cup of coffee, and set off for Mercy Hospital. She found the corridor outside Tyrone's room a swirl of activity. Patients were being rolled through the hall on gurneys, doctors were giving orders at the nursing station, and nurses were going in and out of rooms with trays bearing hypodermics and small paper cups with pills in them. Compared to other times she'd been in the hospital, when Mercy seemed all but deserted, Lucinda found this encouraging. At least there was the possibility that Tyrone was actively being cared for.

He was asleep in the beige room, still its sole occupant, breathing peaceably without the aid of a machine. The dragon was walking along the headboard, deliberately stretching its front leg with each step, as if taking its daily exercise. It saw Lucinda at the door, lifted its little snout, and flew to her at once, landing on her hand. "How are you?" she asked, happy to see it. "And how's our patient?"

The dragon gazed up at her with a contented expression, which she took for a positive report. She sat down in the chair next to the bed and watched Tyrone, feeling grateful for the even rise and fall of his chest. He looked positively sweet when he slept, though she knew he'd be annoyed if she told him as much. He was so dear to her. Whatever it was she had to do with the diamond, it would be worth it if only Tyrone would get better.

She looked up as a dark-haired nurse in a crisp white uniform entered the room, closing the door behind her.

"How is he?" Lucinda asked as the nurse glanced at the chart clipped to the foot of Tyrone's bed.

"He's weak but holding on," the nurse said, smiling at Lucinda. She was young and pretty and wore a small brass disk on a chain around her neck. "Your friend is a fighter." She reached into a hip pocket and withdrew a packet holding plastic tubing and scissors. "I have to change the tubing on this," she said, nodding to the IV stand.

The dragon suddenly materialized from wherever it had been hiding and flew at the young woman, claws extended.

"Stop it!" Lucinda found herself shouting. "Leave her alone!" The dragon paid her no heed. It ripped into the nurse's face, front claws raking bloody gashes in her skin. The young woman backed up with a muttered oath, and Lucinda lunged for the little reptile, apologizing profusely. The dragon flew toward the ceiling, evading Lucinda's grasp. "What's gotten into you?" Lucinda demanded.

Her voice died in her throat as the woman in the nurse's uniform smiled a ghastly blood-streaked smile and began to shift. Her dark hair lightened until it seemed a dark, burnished red, and then thickened into fur that covered her face and hands, which were elongating into a fox's muzzle and paws.

The dragon attacked again, darting toward the fox's head, talons reaching for its eyes. The fox flattened itself against the floor. It was still shifting: white-clad torso into a furred one, a woman's long, slender legs into vulpine haunches. And all the while Lucinda stood there, paralyzed with the knowledge that she was looking at the second shape-shifter, the one who was creating phantasms, the one they'd come back to Arcato to search for. Fear and stupidity held her in an inexorable grip. What could she do? How was she supposed to fight this thing that had come for Tyrone?

In the next instant the room's door thrust open and the shape-shifter completed its transformation. The fox opened its mouth, emitting a shrill, high sound that made Lucinda clamp her hands over her ears. The awful sound rose in pitch and the fox whirled and bounded out of the room, knocking into the orderly and the male nurse who were rushing in.

The room went blessedly silent and Lucinda felt the pain in her head fade. She glanced at Tyrone, at first disbelieving and then frightened as she realized he'd slept through the hellacious noise.

The orderly recovered first. "What the—?" He shot a quick, alarmed glance at the nurse then started after the fox, which had bolted into the hallway.

The nurse, whose name tag identified him as Dominic Finch, rushed over to Tyrone's bed. Hurriedly, he felt for Tyrone's pulse then began checking the tubes and monitors connected to him. "What happened to the nurse who was in here?" he asked Lucinda, as he adjusted the IV bag. "She was young and pretty, with dark hair. Did you see her?"

"She was in here but she left," Lucinda said, being as truthful as she could. She was conscious of the dragon having disappeared again. "I think she heard you and the orderly coming."

"Thank the gods she didn't cut anything in here," he said, seeming satisfied that everything was working properly. "Your friend was lucky. She sliced through another patient's oxygen line, IVs on two others. I don't know who she is, but the guards in this hospital had better wake up."

Tyrone stirred and opened one eye. "What's going on?" he asked in a weak voice.

"Nothing," Dominic told him, taking out a stethoscope. "You're fine. I just came in to check on you."

"You didn't hear anything?" Lucinda asked.

Tyrone shook his head. Dominic Finch checked Tyrone's blood pressure then listened to his heart while Lucinda clasped Tyrone's hand. As she did the cuff on her sleeve slid up and she noticed the tourmaline bracelet Alasdair had given her. Had the stone tried to warn her when the shape-shifter was in the room? She'd been so panicked she hadn't even thought to look at it. It was a wonder Tyrone was still alive. She was going to have to do better.

"Heartbeat's normal," the nurse told Tyrone, returning the stethoscope to its place around his neck. He raised the back of the bed and helped Tyrone to a comfortable sitting position. "You didn't see a name tag on her, did you?" he asked Lucinda.

"No," Lucinda said, realizing for the first time that all of the nurses at Mercy wore name tags and she hadn't bothered to learn any of their names.

Dominic was studying the now-upright Tyrone. "How are you feeling?"

"Weak. Tired. Cranky."

"All to be expected." Dominic assured him.

"And the cranky's normal," Lucinda added, forcing a grin.

Tyrone shot her a ghost of his usual smile. "Don't you think you ought to be doing something with your life besides hanging around a hospital room?"

"I should actually," she admitted, thinking of the studio she'd neglected. "But I don't like leaving you."

"I'm going to get a guard on this floor," Dominic told her. "We're not going to have any more fake nurses visiting patients."

That was all very well, Lucinda thought, as Dominic left the room, but what could a guard do against a shape-shifter?

Tyrone waited until Dominic was out of the room before saying, "Tell me what just happened. Who's this imposter he was talking about?"

Lucinda took a breath, for the first time empathizing with Alasdair and his oblique explanations. How much did you tell someone when the explanation was so bizarre?

"There was someone who came into this room and others, dressed as a nurse. She cut oxygen and IV lines." Lucinda hesitated, wanting to tell him about the dragon, but the dragon was still nowhere in sight, and she knew that particular explanation would be easier when the dragon chose to be seen. Instead she said, "Dominic and an orderly came in here before she could cut yours."

Tyrone shut his eyes. "Why do I think that's not even half the story?"

She couldn't stand lying to him. "Tyrone, that nurse who was cutting things is a shape-shifter. Do you know what that is?"

"My granny used to tell stories about shape-shifters," he said softly. "Ravens who were enchanted princes, deer who were young women under a spell."

"This one isn't enspelled, I don't think. He's a man who can change into a fox—or a woman—and he's doing a lot of scary things all over the city."

Tyrone's voice was weary, barely audible. "You'll forgive me if I'm not scared. Ilyap'a about took the fear right out of me."

"That's okay. You don't need to be scared." She sat down beside him, took his hand again. "The hospital's getting security on this floor. And I'll stay here with you for a while." She didn't tell him how badly both she and hospital security matched up against the shape-shifter, but Tyrone drifted into sleep again, and the dragon returned from wherever it had been and perched attentively on the bedside table.

"If I go over to the studio, will you be all right watching him on your own?" she asked it.

The dragon's steady gaze told her it would, so she kissed them both and set off for Dessalines Productions.

Twenty minutes later Lucinda let herself into the studio. Gabrielle, bless her, had left things in excellent shape. The mail was sorted with bills, new orders, and deliveries of fabric and notions all carefully noted. There was a long list of calls to return, though, so Lucinda sat down at Tyrone's glass-topped desk and began making calls. She didn't let herself think about Tyrone getting rid of the business. Instead she told people that he was recovering and, when they pressed her for answers, made what interim decisions she could. She hoped she wasn't being overly optimistic when she agreed to purchase a fairly expensive shipment of antique Belgian lace. Dresses, shawls, blouses, perhaps even long summer jackets . . . Tyrone would find a way to use it, she told herself. Working quickly, almost mechanically, she finished with phone calls and bill paying then set about unpacking the shipments of new fabric.

One by one, she brought the bolts of cloth into Tyrone's cutting room, where a custom-made cabinet held the bolts in tiered rows. Although Tyrone's original designs were usually made from the fabric that Lucinda found in flea markets and antique shops, she would then later find something similar that could be ordered by the bolt for the pieces that went to the stores. It was one of her favorite parts of her job, finding fabric with a similar weight and texture to the silk in a nineteenth-century morning dress, or finding a flowered print similar to the print from a 1940s summer dress. Even now, when everything in her life was such a mess, she felt soothed by the fabrics' colors and textures.

She was setting the last of the bolts into place when the loft's buzzer rang. She went to the door, peered through the peephole, and felt her stomach start to churn. Sebastian stood there, leaning comfortably against the railing. He was alone.

She hesitated then ran back into Tyrone's office where she pulled up her cuff and stared at the tourmaline bracelet. "Okay," she told it, "I'm counting on you. Is he evil?" She sat for a moment, trying to quiet her thoughts, to open herself to the stone, whatever that meant. The green tourmaline crystal sat in its silver setting, as inanimate as, well, a stone. It didn't pulse or light up or send psychic warnings. It didn't do a damn thing. "Thanks a lot," she said, and pulled the cuff down over it.

He didn't ring the buzzer again. He knew she was in there and he was waiting. She'd sounded so matter-of-fact when she'd talked to Alasdair about this the night before: Sebastian would appear and she would deal with him.

Then do it, she told herself, though her heart was in her throat. *You know you can't hide from him.* And that thought—knowing he could make her confront him, knowing he could still manipulate her—brought a vision of Kali. Lucinda had no desire to do Sebastian physical harm, but she suddenly understood that she could relish shredding what was before her, devouring anything that remained, severing the last bond, leaving nothing except emptiness, and finding purity in that. It was that terrible strength she wished for, though she still had enough fear, or maybe sanity, to refrain from actually calling on the goddess.

She opened the door. He looked much as she remembered him. The reddish hair and the high cheekbones in the narrow face, blue eyes that had always held the wild. Why hadn't she seen the fox in him from the start? And what was different about him now? Maybe nothing except that for the moment she wasn't afraid.

Sebastian's eyes locked on hers. "Oh my," he said softly. "Someone's been through a sea change."

"We're a long way from the sea," she said. "What do you want?"

"I was afraid you wouldn't answer when you saw it was me out here."

"What choice did I have, considering a locked door can't keep you out?"

"I wouldn't—won't—do that to you again."

She thought about the implications of what he'd said. "So if I tell you I don't want to see you, that I just want you out of my life and Tyrone's, you'll go and not come back? Don't answer unless you can tell me the truth," she warned.

"If that's what you want. But it might be best to wait a bit before banishing me." He fingered the inscribed smoky quartz bead that hung from his neck. "Averill asked me to help you, and Averill is one of the few beings in this world to whom I'm indebted. "I've sent a message telling her I'll do as she asks."

"How can you expect me to believe anything you say?"

He scratched his chin. "It's a point. I've lost all credibility with you, haven't I?"

"Are you surprised?"

"Look, could I come in so we could talk about this? It's hard, standing here on the doorstep."

That he could even ask seemed proof he hadn't changed. "This is Tyrone's place. You don't have the right to set foot in the home of the man you nearly killed."

"Then take a walk with me?"

"No. Say whatever you have to say right there. And start by telling me why you visited him in the hospital."

One reddish brow arched. "How did you find out about that? Did a nurse tell you?"

"Just tell me why you were there."

"I went looking for you. I wanted to apologize to you, Lucinda. And when you weren't there I took a good look at him. I felt something I haven't felt for a very long time—remorse. He seemed so broken and alone. I don't have the gift of healing, so I couldn't undo what had been done to him but I thought that if I sat with him, at least he wouldn't be so alone."

"And that's all you did when you were there?"

"Yes." He shifted on his feet, looking uncomfortable. "So back to that apology. I'm sorry for all the hurt I've caused you. That was never what I meant to happen. I was very careless with you and yours."

"Careless? You played me. That was too deliberate to be called careless."

He looked at her, blues eyes measuring, reading between her words. "I see," he said at last, and she could have sworn she heard genuine grief in his voice. "This thing between us can't be mended."

To her amazement the words tore at her. There was some insane, undoubtedly masochistic part of her that wanted to hold out a bit of hope to him, that desperately wanted to believe it wasn't over. There was a part of her that still longed for the warmth in his eyes. But the possibilities were gone. She couldn't risk opening herself to him again.

"All right," he said. "You want me to let you go and I will. I promise I'll leave your heart alone. So the only question remaining is, do you want the help I told Averill I'd give you?"

"If I thought I could trust a word you said . . . the thing is, you might genuinely try to help and you'd still gut me in the process. I don't think you know any other way—"

"I know who you're looking for," he interrupted. "The girl, Janna, is alive but she's not in good shape."

"They never are when you're through with them, are they?" Lucinda crossed her arms over her chest, unwilling to give him the least opening, and yet how could she refuse information about the girl? "Okay, then, where is she now?"

"She's—" He stopped speaking at the sound of heavy footsteps on the stairs below them.

"Lucinda, is that you up there?" called a woman's voice. The footsteps came closer, now accompanied by labored breathing.

Lucinda shut her eyes. "Oh, gods," she murmured.

"You know her?" Sebastian asked quietly.

"Lucinda, why haven't you returned my calls?" the woman demanded as she reached the landing below them. She was squat and heavyset with thinning, wavy brown hair and small brown eyes heavily rimmed with eyeliner. The tan trench coat she wore was pulled tightly across her breasts and belly. "You scared me to death. I called your apartment and—" She broke off as she caught sight of Sebastian.

Lucinda wondered briefly if she could possibly keep the truth from him. Resigned to the fact that she couldn't, she said, "Mother, this is Sebastian Keane. Sebastian, my mother, Gertie de Francesco."

"Hi." Sebastian held out his hand to her as she reached the top stair. "It's nice to meet you, Mrs. de Francesco."

Gertie shook his hand and beamed at him while Lucinda winced. "I got your messages," Lucinda said to her mother. "I was going to call you today."

"Was going to? Half the day is already gone. How long did you plan to wait?"

The truth was Lucinda had forgotten about her mother's messages. "I was away and got in very late last night," she said.

"You don't owe me any explanation," her mother said, suddenly proud.

"Why have you been trying to get in touch with me?" Lucinda asked. "Is something wrong?"

"I don't owe you explanations either." Gertie's innate belligerence, never far from the surface, was about to erupt.

"I was just curious," Lucinda said mildly. She glanced at Sebastian who was studying her mother with apparent fascination. *Oh no,* she thought. *He wouldn't use her, would he?*

Gertie looked around, glancing through the open door into Tyrone's loft but not finding much to hold her interest. "This is a hell of a climb to get to work every morning. You couldn't find a job on the ground floor?"

"Actually, I was just closing up for the day," Lucinda said. "And Sebastian was just leaving. Would you like a glass of water or something to drink before we go?"

Gertie waved her hand in a dismissive gesture. "Let's go. The sooner I get off these stairs, the better. I'm getting vertigo up here."

Lucinda grabbed her things and locked up the studio, shooting Sebastian a warning look.

Following Gertie, they slowly made their way down the metal staircase.

"Good-bye, Mrs. de Francesco," Sebastian said politely when they'd reached the ground.

"You look like a very nice boy," her mother pronounced.

"I try," Sebastian said, sketching her a short, charming bow.

"Not very fucking successfully," Lucinda muttered.

He gave her a wide-eyed, innocent look and moved off, leaving her with her mother, who said at once, "Why do you talk that way about people? Is that nice? Is that how I brought you up?"

"Um—Mother, are you all right?" Lucinda asked. "I mean, I'm sorry I didn't get back to you and—"

"I'm fine," said Gertie, eyeing her daughter critically. "You're too skinny. Aren't you eating?"

"I eat."

"Eat what—that terrible diet food? It's all chemicals, you know."

"So are we," Lucinda said. "Listen, I eat just fine. Now won't you tell me what made you climb that staircase looking for me?"

Her mother glanced around the street, as if to make sure no one was listening in, and Lucinda saw the small gold cross she always wore catch the sunlight. For the first time Lucinda didn't find the cross off-putting. It occurred to her that this was her mother's pathway to the gods, embodied in her holy trinity. Her mother's faith, although different from Lucinda's experience of the divine, no longer seemed unreasonable; in fact, Lucinda saw a kind of beauty in it.

Gertie swallowed hard. "I dreamed about you, Lucinda," she said. "You were climbing up into the mountains all alone, and you didn't pack enough clothes or food—you never have, not even when you were a little girl, going on a school trip—and I thought you were going to die."

"You dreamed that?"

Her mother nodded, the anger gone from her eyes. "Ever since I had that dream, I worried about you."

Lucinda thought about what Averill had said about her mother's spirit journeying with her and being a protection. She touched her mother's wrist, and said quietly, "You know something, Mom? I'm really glad you did."

LATER THAT AFTERNOON Lucinda sat in one of the riverfront cafés, drinking an espresso and trying to absorb the meeting with her mother. Were they really going to try to have a relationship after all this time? Was it even possible? Lucinda drained the espresso. She didn't have the first idea.

"May I join you?"

She looked up to find Alasdair standing beside her table, holding a demitasse cup on a saucer. The query was so polite, his expression so respectful, that she nearly laughed aloud. "Sure, have a seat," she said, using her foot to nudge the other chair away from the table. "It might even be a relief to deal with your kind of weirdness instead of my own."

"What happened?" he asked, taking no perceptible offense.

"Oh, my mother showed up. Averill was right."

"Yes, that's the problem with Averill. She usually is. So," he said after a swallow of espresso and a sigh of contentment, "you have a mother who's giving you gifts of a sort that you don't want or aren't ready for."

"Something like that."

"I know the feeling," he said wryly. "It's probably best to accept those gifts with as much grace as you can muster, though the gods know I've failed with Vita often enough."

Lucinda shook her head in wonder. "All these years I told myself I didn't care that we had this rift between us. I mean, when we lived together we drove each other mad. I had to get out of that apartment, for both our sakes. Then today, we talked for a bit, and I realized that all along I'd been missing her. Go figure."

"You have genuine bonds of love with her," said Alasdair. "That's nearly inevitable with one's mother, no matter how good or bad the relationship."

"I—" Lucinda finished her espresso, deciding to confess something she'd never even told Tyrone, something that now sounded blindingly stupid. "Day in, day out, all I got from her was how she disapproved of me, how bad I was, how I needed the church to cleanse me and make me good. I didn't think she ever really cared about me. But maybe she did and telling me I needed to go to the church was the only way she had to say it." Lucinda's voice was barely audible as she finished. "Christ, it's taken me twenty-eight years to figure out that my mother loved me all along."

"Yes," Alasdair said simply. "It can be surprisingly difficult to be the object of love."

Something in his gaze made Lucinda uncomfortable and she found she had to change the subject. "I was in Tyrone's hospital room this morning," she said, "and so was the shape-shifter we're looking for." She told him about the fox-nurse.

"Thank the gods for the dragon," Alasdair muttered. His eyes sought hers, and for the first time she thought she saw shame in them. "I owe you an apology, Lucinda. This is my fault."

"How is it your fault?"

"I haven't been making the connections. Among the incidents, I mean. So this morning he pulled one that even I couldn't possibly miss. He went after Tyrone."

"We don't know that. She, I mean he, was in a number of rooms cutting through medical equipment. What makes you think it was Tyrone he was after?"

Alasdair's grey eyes hardened. "It was a message for me. I'm the link. Do you remember when we met in the cemetery and you told me there was someone watching me at that boy's funeral? You were right."

"That was him?"

Alasdair nodded heavily. "His name is Sangeet, and he's from the mountains, though not one of our people. I'm the one he's after, the one he's been trailing."

"But why would he be after you? Does he want the gems?"

"Not that," Alasdair said. "In fact, I'm relatively certain he has no interest in stones at all. But he has—what do your films call it?—several M.O.s: He creates these phantasms, he likes to cut things, and he uses sound to create intense pain. Since he hasn't been able to get to me directly, he visits these M.O.s on other people. People connected to me, no matter how tangentially."

"That can't be right," Lucinda said. "This stuff has been going on all over the city."

"Add it up. The woman I saw who thought she was dancing with her dead husband was the woman who runs the newsstand *I* frequent. Mrs. O'-Donnell, who heard a piercing sound before her dog's leash was slashed was *my* landlady. The people we saw in the thresholds: I've met both the man and the little girl. And I know Tyrone as well."

"What about Marcus?"

"The shape-shifter may have followed me to the hospital and seen you with Marcus. I'm sorry, Lucinda. I've put you in terrible danger."

Lucinda wasn't having any of it. She pushed forward her own copy of the daily paper. "This jewelry store?"

"I've been there."

"The boats on the north pier that were cut from their moorings?"

"Who else had a boat on the north pier?" Alasdair inquired. "I'm thinking of a rotund Indian god in a red scow whom we both visited. The shape-shifter couldn't touch Kama, of course, but he got as close as he could."

"Look," Lucinda said, "before I even met you, I found out about two of these slashings—the stage curtain in the Teatro up on Consolación and my friend Maxine's club, Indigo—"

Alasdair just lifted his dark brows.

"You can't possibly have—"

"I attended a performance in the Teatro Descardo. We can probably assume that was sometime before its curtain was slashed."

"And you were clubbing at Indigo?" she scoffed.

Alasdair's expression became almost pitying. "You don't know very much about your friend Maxine, do you?"

"What do you mean? I've known her for—"

"She's our mail-drop," he said. At Lucinda's stunned silence, he went on. "Whenever someone from the Source Place comes to Arcato, Maxine is our first stop. She takes messages for us. And if we want to get a message back and can't do so by other means—Averill's smoky quartz, for example— Maxine sees that our messages get back to the Source Place."

Lucinda, aware that she was gaping, tried to compose herself. "She's not one of you, is she?"

"No. But her grandmother, who owned an antique shop in the city, performed a similar service for us. You might say, Maxine inherited the job. We have contacts like that in most of the cities along the Candra. In any case," Alasdair went on, "the pattern I see is that everyone so far who's been affected by the shape-shifter has known me or, by extension, you."

Lucinda wasn't quite sure why she was fighting this theory so hard, except that she was sure it couldn't be right. "Not the girl who disappeared the other night, Janna Powell."

Alasdair brooded over this for a moment. "You might be right about that one. Though the girl approached him when he was with Sebastian, whom we're both connected to."

Lucinda groaned and rubbed her forehead with her fingertips. "Sebastian's all mixed up in it, isn't he?" Alasdair's answering silence affirmed it. "He came to Tyrone's loft today," she said. "We talked a little and then my mother showed up. But when I first saw him there, I actually remembered to check this." She touched the tourmaline bracelet. "And *nada.*"

"That could mean you have nothing to fear from him."

"Or I don't know how to read the bloody thing."

"The stones have ways of making themselves understood."

"So that means Sebastian's *not* evil?"

The unscarred edge of Alasdair's mouth quirked up. "Sebastian tends to occupy a nebulous territory that's neither good nor bad. Which isn't to say that he can't cause harm. But morally, he's an ambiguous creature; tricksters often are."

"He said he knows who we're looking for and he knows where Janna Powell is. He said she's not in good shape. Should we trust him?"

"No, but that doesn't mean he's lying."

Lucinda again had the sensation she'd had in the Source Place, that there was something she was forgetting, something integral. She let the sensation sit in her mind for a few moments and when there was no hint of a solution, she drew the conversation back to that morning.

"You know what I can't figure out," she said. "Why didn't the dragon just blast Sangeet with his green poison powder? Then this would all be over."

"So would Tyrone," Alasdair told her. "He's too weak to be anywhere in the vicinity of that toxin, and the dragon knew it. That's why he held back. He still managed to protect Tyrone and alert you."

Lucinda folded an empty sugar packet into an accordion pleat. "I was worse than useless," she admitted. "I just stood there, frozen. I didn't even remember to look at the tourmaline bracelet."

"It's to be expected." Alasdair's voice was gentle. "It was your first encounter with an enemy. But I don't like the fact that he came for Tyrone. Or that the girl is still missing. We're going to have to find this other shapeshifter. I need you to call Sebastian."

"That's a terrible idea. Don't you have another gazing crystal or something? Or we could go see Mariamme."

"No, we can't. Vita's got a veritable armory of protections around her house. If her crystal went black after glimpsing him, I don't even want to contemplate what might happen to Mariamme. We can't ask her to risk that kind of danger. Last night, after you went to sleep, I tried to scry for Sangeet with a moonstone. It didn't work." He signaled to the waiter for another espresso then turned back to her. "I need you to call Sebastian."

"He doesn't have a phone," Lucinda said stubbornly.

"Not that way. He's still connected to you. That he showed up at Tyrone's loft this morning proves it. If you call out to him, he'll hear you and I wager he'll answer."

Lucinda swirled the dregs of her coffee in her cup. "It hurts me to see him," she said quietly.

"I know that. And I'm sorry for it but it can't be helped."

She looked up at him. "When?"

"Now."

LUCINDA PACED THE riverwalk, picking her way through a flock of pigeons on the hunt for bread crumbs. Alasdair remained in the café. She knew she was passing in and out of his line of vision as she waited for Sebastian to answer her call.

She'd sat in the café, trying to ignore the father at the table next to them who was imploring his son to drink his milk, and the couple on the other side who were arguing about symbolism in French films, and she'd sent out a silent call to Sebastian. Could calling him possibly work, she wondered, when so much of her didn't want it to? It had been a half-hearted effort at best.

She stopped pacing and stood at the railing, gazing out over the dark expanse of river. She'd never been able to pin down its color. It had murky blacks and slate-greys and bottle-greens in it; sometimes she even caught a touch of midnight-blue. Once a trick of the light had made it seem the clear pale blue of aquamarines. She liked that it was unknowable and ever-changing. To her the Candra was one of the few honest things in the city.

"The city council's been talking about cleaning it up for years, and they never do a blasted thing. There are probably river monsters mutating down there, and no one will ever know it till they rise up one night and swallow the mayor's office." Sebastian was standing beside her. She hadn't seen or heard him approach. One moment no one, the next Sebastian there, elbows on the railing, staring out at the water.

"You pay attention to city politics?" She kept her tone neutral.

"Occasionally. I have been a resident for a very long time."

"In this city or the old one?"

"Both. I come and go between them and between Arcato and the mountains. I couldn't live in a place where I didn't have wilderness nearby. The fox in me craves it. And the antique dealer finds a port equally vital. I do travel, you know."

His determination to cast himself as a legitimate businessman amused her. "Do you ever buy things or is it all stolen?"

"Some things I buy, some I trade for, some I take." His voice made no distinction among them, giving her the impression that he considered all three methods of acquisition equal and interchangeable, all valid means of doing business.

"And your clients don't care?"

"Most of those who can find me know what I am." He was still facing the river but his eyes slid to the side, glancing at her. "Seems you know how to find me now. You called me."

"I didn't think it would work," she admitted.

"I told you, you have a heart path in me. I can't change that. Even if you go for years without seeing or talking to me, you'll always be able to reach me."

"And you'll always be able to reach me?"

"Yes. The connection is there, can't be broken as long as we both breathe.

But if it's not what you want—as I believe you've stated—then I won't try to reach you. I'll leave you alone."

"Sounds like the best I can hope for," she said with a sad smile. Despite all that had happened, she had to keep wrenching herself away from the current of attraction that still hummed between them. Sebastian, she decided, was just additional proof of the universal law she'd been trying to ignore ever since she gave up junk: If it's bad for you, you will crave it.

As if a ray of sunlight had suddenly broken through the clouds, Lucinda felt a focused warmth along her back. Alasdair, she realized; he was watching. The thought brought her back to her purpose. She faced Sebastian with what she hoped was detachment. "The reason I called you is because we never finished our talk this morning. About the girl."

"She's with me."

His candor caught her off guard. She'd expected more serpentine answers. "Doing what?" she asked carefully.

"I'm keeping her safe, actually." That made her laugh and Sebastian shot her an irate look. "She needed a place where she wouldn't be found."

"By?"

"He's another shape-shifter. And a shaman of sorts," he added almost reluctantly.

"Who creates phantasms."

"Sometimes. He's from the mountains, like Alasdair's people."

"And he works with the stones, too?"

"No, not at all, but he has other powers."

"And his name is—"

Sebastian's blue eyes narrowed. "Never mind that. But the girl is at my loft."

"Why does that not surprise me?"

"I only brought her there because she needed a haven," he said a bit defensively.

Lucinda couldn't keep the skepticism out of her voice, "So she feels safe with you."

"Actually, she's terrified. She spends all day huddled under blankets on that Biedermeier sofa, and whimpers if I even come near her. I have to set her food on a table about ten feet away. If I go any closer to her, she gets hysterical. It's like trying to tame a rodent that's been beaten. This morning I brought her toast and she bared her teeth at me."

"Was she beaten?"

"In a manner of speaking."

"Are you going to let her go?" Lucinda asked.

"As soon as I figure out how," he muttered. "Believe me, she's no joy as a houseguest." He turned from the water to give her a sharp look. "You're with the *cearu,* aren't you?"

"Why?" She was instantly wary.

"Because I don't know if I can get Janna out of my loft safely—without the other fox knowing about it. But Alasdair could."

Lucinda took a step away from him, putting necessary distance between them. "Why do I feel like I'm walking into a trap?"

"Because you have a suspicious and paranoid nature," he told her. "Look, if I were a danger to you, that thing would let you know." He pointed to the tourmaline bracelet on her wrist.

Should she have kept it hidden? Too late now. "What will it do exactly?" she asked.

"Can't say. Stones react differently to different people."

"You're as helpful as Alasdair."

He rolled his eyes. "Back to my point. I gave you my word I won't hurt you."

"Or Alasdair?"

Sebastian didn't answer at once. "He can take care of himself, you know. He's actually quite formidable when he wants to be."

She did know. The vision of Alasdair quickly, easily slicing Noelle's throat came back to her. She pushed it aside. "Give me your word that you won't do anything to harm him or set him up in any way, and I'll tell him you want him to take Janna off your hands."

Something calculating flickered in Sebastian's eyes. "I thought you were keen on helping the girl. Seems what you're keen on is Alasdair."

"He's my friend."

"You and your bloody friends."

"You're protecting this other fox, aren't you?"

"No!" The vehemence of it surprised her.

She met his eyes. "Prove it to me."

A look of self-loathing crossed Sebastian's face and he turned away from her to face the river.

Deciding it was time to call his bluff, she began walking away from him.

"All right." His voice stopped her before she'd gone a dozen steps. "Tell Alasdair to come get the girl tonight, and you have my word that I won't set him up or do anything that might harm his precious self." He turned to gaze at her, and this time she couldn't read anything in his eyes at all. "There's just one condition."

She waited.

"You come with him."

JUST AFTER SUNDOWN Alasdair led Lucinda across the labradorite bridge into the old city and up through the winding alleys to Montague Street. She felt her heart contract as the cast-iron loft building came into sight. For a few sweet deluded hours she'd been happy there. She had surrendered her anger and cynicism, what Tyrone once called her prophylaxes against disappointment, only to find that she'd been right the first time: Romantic love was just illusion and the longing for it, a snare.

Alasdair glanced at her as they approached Sebastian's building. "Are you all right?"

"There's this thing I've been trying to remember, and well, I just remembered something else. When I first met Tyrone he accused me of working negative magic. He said I was acting like his grandmother when she was trying to fool the gods. She thought if you were hopeful, the gods would take notice and decide you needed taking down a peg. They'd make sure you got disappointed. So instead you tell yourself that what's real is an indifferent universe, all the while secretly hoping the gods will take it as a challenge to prove you wrong by giving you all those good things you never dared hope for."

"And *is* that what you were doing?" Alasdair asked.

"Not consciously, no. I didn't really let the gods figure into anything in my life then. But I did try to make myself proof against disappointment."

"And did you succeed?"

She stopped a few feet from Sebastian's front door and stared up at the windows of his loft. "Seemed that way. Until recently. And now it all just feels completely fucked up. I can't sort any of it out."

"You were caught in a trickster's net," Alasdair said.

"Yeah. And I feel like I'm about to step right back into it."

"You won't. Those nets are only invisible when you don't know they're there. Now, well . . . you're a bit more educated."

She winced. "It was a hell of an education."

Alasdair chuckled softly. "I know. I've never understood why learning is so often twined with pain. Are we mortals so stupid that pain is the only thing that makes a lasting impression?"

Lucinda turned to him then, about to say, most uncharacteristically, that she'd learned plenty from pleasure, when the outer door to Sebastian's building opened. Sebastian stood there, his eyes flicking from one to the other. "I've been waiting for you," he said with mock graciousness, but his eyes met Lucinda's with something softer.

"Where is she?" Alasdair asked.

"Upstairs."

They followed him up the three flights. For the first time Lucinda noticed that neither Alasdair not Sebastian made any noise when they walked. It was as if hers were the only footsteps climbing the metal stairs.

Alasdair seemed to have no reaction at all to Sebastian's collection. He barely spared a glance for the surroundings as Sebastian led them through the maze of furniture to a graceful Biedermeier sofa upholstered in a green-and-ivory striped satin. Very little of the upholstery showed, though. Most of the couch was hidden beneath a thick, plaid, wool blanket. Someone lay beneath the blanket, sniffling loudly.

Alasdair lifted an eyebrow.

"You try talking to her," Sebastian said. "She's made it clear that she doesn't want anything to do with me."

Alasdair shot him an "And you're surprised?" look but refrained from comment. He knelt beside the sofa. "Janna," he began softly. "Are you all right?"

The sniffling stopped.

"My name is Alasdair," he went on in a gentle voice. "I've come to get you out of here. I'll take you home if that's what you want."

Silence followed, and it occurred to Lucinda that after whatever happened with the other shape-shifter, the girl was probably scared to death of men or foxes or both.

"Janna," she spoke up. "My name is Lucinda and if you'd like, I'll go with Alasdair and make sure that nothing else bad happens to you. Sebastian will stay here. You don't have to see him anymore."

"Thank you very much for that vote of confidence," Sebastian muttered.

"Just tell us where you want us to take you," Lucinda went on.

More silence.

Lucinda knelt down next to the sofa. "Listen," she said. "I don't know what happened to you the night you met Sebastian and that other—"

"Guy," Sebastian filled in helpfully.

"But I know it must have been something awful, and something that you never would have believed possible. I've had stuff like that happen to me, too, lately."

Another lengthy silence, then slowly the blanket was pulled back, revealing a young, blond-haired woman with swollen, red-rimmed eyes. Lucinda turned to the two men. "Can you give us a few minutes?"

"Certainly," Alasdair said, and he and Sebastian retreated to another part of the loft.

"Hi," Lucinda said, not really knowing what else to say. The girl seemed too shaken for questioning.

Janna swallowed hard and sat up, pushing the heavy mass of hair away from her face. She still wore the short skirt Alasdair had described, but what was probably one of Sebastian's big flannel shirts was buttoned over her top. Lucinda could see that though the girl looked ravaged, she had that clean-scrubbed-but-ripe prettiness that men found so attractive. Tyrone had once defined it as "cheerfully and healthily fuckable."

"Are you in school?" Lucinda asked, hoping it was a neutral question.

Janna nodded. "Third-year, university. I'm studying statistics."

"So you live in the city?"

"With my roommate, Carly. She's probably worried out of her mind." Janna pulled a handkerchief from the pocket of the shirt and blew her nose. "What kind of weird shit happened to you?"

"Oh, gods," Lucinda said. "So much, I've lost track. . . . How about, for starters, I slept with Sebastian."

Janna snorted and they both started to laugh.

"Are you still—"

"Are you crazy?"

"I don't know," the girl said, suddenly sober. "I can't take in what happened. I can't believe it was real. But it must be." Her voice quavered on those last words, and she pulled up the flannel shirt and her own much tighter top beneath it.

Lucinda pressed a hand against her mouth and managed not to cry out. Janna's belly looked like it had been scored with a razor. A hatchwork of raised black lines ran across her pale skin. "The man who was with Sebastian did this to you?" asked Lucinda.

Janna shut her eyes. "I think so. I don't remember much. I know it wasn't Sebastian. He's the one who got me out. It—it burns like crazy. All the time. Like it will never stop."

"Has Sebastian given you anything for it? A salve or—"

"I want to go home," Janna said. She opened her eyes and there was a deliberate, hard-won blankness in them. "I need to be in my own flat, in my own bed."

Lucinda found the request a relief. It was a concrete task, something they could actually do. "Then we'll go right now," Lucinda told her. "Alasdair and I will take you."

Janna stiffened. "Sebastian said it wasn't safe, that—that monster would sense me."

"That's why Alasdair's here. He can shield you." She gave Janna a weak smile. "He's another one of the strange things that happened to me lately, but you can trust him."

Janna nodded and rooted around under the sofa, drawing out two spike-heeled pumps.

"Do you want me to see if Sebastian has some other shoes you could borrow—"

"No. I don't want anything from him. He—" She stopped because her lower jaw was trembling so hard it looked like someone was working it up and down with a marionette's strings. She forced herself to talk through it. "He was with that monster. I mean, Sebastian wasn't there when I was hurt, but he knew what that other one was and he let me go with—"

"I know," Lucinda said. "I'm so sorry. I think he is, too. That's why he brought you here."

"I want to go home." Janna's voice rose an octave with the repeated demand.

"Put your shoes on. I'll get Alasdair."

Lucinda followed the low murmur of voices to the far end of the loft. She found Alasdair and Sebastian in one of the little "rooms" Sebastian had defined with an arrangement of furniture. This one featured a barrister's case, a gold love seat with a heart-shaped back, and a pedestal end table, the pedestal being a bust of a nude woman with exceedingly large breasts.

Neither Sebastian nor Alasdair noticed her come in. The glass door of one of the barrister's cases was open, revealing an array of amulets on a black velvet tray. "Where did you get it?" Alasdair asked, his tone hard.

Lucinda followed the line of his gaze and felt the fine hairs on the back of her neck stand straight up. Alasdair was gazing at a round brass amulet that looked like an old, stamped coin. It looked exactly like the amulet that the shape-shifter had worn that morning in the hospital.

"Where did you get it?" Alasdair repeated.

Sebastian hesitated several beats before saying in a vague tone, "I think I traded someone for that. It was a long time ago. Can't remember now."

"Try," Alasdair said. "Or better yet, tell me where the other fox is."

Sebastian's blue eyes danced with mockery. "And reveal the secrets of a fellow shape-shifter? I thought you knew me better than that."

Lucinda started as the air around her shifted. Again it had happened so fast that she never saw either one of them move. Moments ago they'd stood several feet apart. Now Alasdair had the back of Sebastian's collar gripped in one hand and he was forcing Sebastian to arch backward. Alasdair's other hand pressed the blade of the obsidian knife against Sebastian's exposed throat. "Tell me where you got the amulet and where the fox is."

Sebastian shook his head.

Alasdair jerked hard on Sebastian's shirt collar, forcing a strangled sound from Sebastian's throat. "The gods demand sacrifices," Alasdair went on evenly. "You know I'd have no regrets if I offered you up. Perhaps if I spill blood—"

"Stop it!" Janna's voice rose with hysteria as she pushed past Lucinda to grab Alasdair's arm. "I can't stand any more blood! And I don't want anyone tortured—even that bastard. Now get me out of here."

Lucinda put an arm around the girl's shoulder, gently pulling her away from Alasdair. "We'll go now," she said soothingly. She glanced at Alasdair. "Are you coming with us?"

Alasdair gave the slightest shrug of his shoulders. His concentration remained focused on Sebastian. Alasdair bent the trickster backward until the crown of Sebastian's head grazed the floor. "Where did you get the amulet?"

"The Sinpiedras," Sebastian coughed out, then fell awkwardly as Alasdair released him. "But that one wasn't his. I stole it from someone else. At one of their gatherings."

Alasdair held up the bronze amulet and examined it. "What kind of protection does it give?"

Sebastian remained on the floor. "The one you're holding is a protection against dark spirits. You know how the Sinpiedras love their rituals."

"And the amulet that Sangeet wears?"

Lucinda saw something like respect cross the trickster's face. "You know who he is?"

"Where is he?" Alasdair repeated.

Sebastian eased himself up into a sitting position. "I don't know where he is now," he admitted. "Only that he hasn't left Arcato. Sangeet's amulet is a 'manifold,' as in 'many fold blessings.' It contains an image of a minor spirit, who intensifies the effects of rituals that the wearer performs."

"And the point of Sangeet's rituals?"

The mockery returned to Sebastian's eyes. "You should know the answer to that one," he chided Alasdair. "The usual. Power. And he's nearly gotten what he wants. I don't think there's much that can stop him."

"Did you try?"

"I tried to distract him when he took the girl. It didn't work."

Lucinda felt Janna's hand clamp onto her upper arm, fingers digging in. "In a minute," she promised her. "I need to hear what they're saying."

"And yet you managed to get Janna away from him."

A fox's sly expression came into Sebastian's eyes. "I never said he was proof against theft. Even gods can be robbed."

"And what will you do when he comes after you for stealing from him?"

Sebastian traced the diamond-within-diamond pattern on the floor then gazed up at Alasdair with a guileless smile. "The same thing I did when you came after me."

"I need to get out of here now!" Janna sounded as if she were seconds away from detonation.

"Yes, I see that," Alasdair said, turning a level grey gaze on her.

It occurred to Lucinda that though Alasdair was a *cearu,* who genuinely lived by an obligation to help those in need, there was something so dispassionate in his manner as to make him seem almost callous. "We'll go right now," she said, hoping he wouldn't contradict her.

He didn't. Janna removed Sebastian's shirt, putting on her own fringed leather jacket, and they left the loft. Downstairs on Montague Street, Janna looked around in dismay. "Where are we? I don't recognize this part of the city."

Alasdair and Lucinda exchanged a glance and Lucinda said, "Where do you and Carly live?"

"Our flat is on the High Road."

"Then we're about twenty minutes away," Alasdair said. *And over a hundred years,* Lucinda added silently. "There's a shortcut, a footbridge, we can take," he went on. "It's this way."

They began walking, with Lucinda and Alasdair on either side, the girl between them. Janna was all nerves. She jerked around at the slightest sound, as if she expected to be jumped. Lucinda wondered if Alasdair had cast some sort of protection over them. If he had, he was damned subtle about it. Maybe he was using his opal to conceal them, she thought, but then she realized that people were making way for them on the street. Obviously they weren't invisible. Still no one stopped them and if anyone was following, she certainly couldn't detect it.

"Can you tell us any more about what happened that night?" Alasdair asked as they stepped off the footbridge into the city of Lucinda and Janna's time.

"Oh, there's Morro Street," Janna said, and seemed to relax a bit as the city again became familiar. "That night . . . Carly and I decided to go the clubs. Haifong Street was mobbed. All the clubs had bands playing and the theaters were letting out. Somehow in the crowds Carly and I got separated. I wasn't worried. Lots of times we go out and come home separately." Her voice quavered. "I always felt safe in Arcato. And that night I was—" She hesitated, giving Alasdair a defiant look. "I was up for fun. I'd just finished spring exams and all I wanted to do was party. So I when I saw these two guys standing in the middle of the road—I was so stupid; I thought they were cute!—I went up to them and invited them to go to Kingfisher with me."

"Sebastian and this other guy?" Alasdair prompted.

"He said his name was Robert."

"Robert?" Lucinda snorted.

"It's actually Sangeet," Alasdair interjected. "Please, go on."

"He started hitting on me and it was fun. We danced, drank. He had some powder, and we did that too. He was ... insanely good-looking. At one point I looked up at him and thought he was the most beautiful man I'd ever seen. And he was a phenomenal dancer. You should have seen him move."

Janna fell silent and neither of them pushed her. "I don't really remember what happened next," she finally said. "Sebastian was gone for a while. He said he was going to the bar to buy a round of drinks and never came back. And—the other one—he told me he wanted to show me something special. Next thing I knew I was in a cramped room with a mattress on the floor, I don't know where. He pushed me down on it. He took off his shirt. He had real white skin, except his entire body was covered with these straight black lines. At first I thought they were tattoos. Then I realized they were all scars, thousands of 'em. I remember I asked what had happened. Real gentle. You know, the way you talk to someone who just had their house burned down." She shook her head in amazement. "I felt so sorry for him."

"And?" Lucinda asked.

"He said—" Janna stopped walking and put her hands over her face. When she spoke again she spoke into her hands and her throat was thick with tears. "He said, 'I'll show you.'"

Nineteen

LUCINDA FELT COMPLETELY wrung out by the time they reached Janna's building on the High Road. She also felt vaguely guilty because she'd been glad when Janna couldn't remember the worst of it. She already knew that whoever they were hunting was sadistic; she didn't want details.

Janna looked up at the brick apartment building and said nervously, "This is it."

"We'll see you up to your flat," Alasdair said.

Janna thought it over. "Only Lucinda," she said. "Carly's probably already upset. I don't want to make it worse by bringing a strange man into the apartment."

Alasdair asked Lucinda if she was comfortable with that, and Lucinda said she was, and she walked up the two flights of stairs with Janna to her flat.

Janna let them in with her key. The apartment was dark and Janna felt along the wall for a light switch. When she found it Lucinda saw classic student décor: bookshelves made of boards and bricks, two mismatched couches with bedspreads thrown over them in the place of slipcovers, a big, wooden industrial spool for a coffee table, and posters plastering nearly every inch of wall.

Janna slipped off her jacket, seeming calmer here. "Do you want something to drink?" she asked, leading the way into a small kitchen where an elderly refrigerator was covered with photos of Janna and her friends.

"No, thanks. Alasdair's waiting—" Lucinda broke off as a small, wiry, dark-haired girl burst out of the bedroom and flung her arms around Janna.

"You're back! Are you all right? I've been so friggin' worried. I called the police and of course, they did dick-all, so I've been bugging the shit out of every club on Haifong and—" She caught sight of Lucinda and abruptly shut up and let go of her roommate.

"I'm okay," Janna said. "And this is Lucinda. She helped me get back here."

"Hi," Carly said stiffly. "Thanks, I guess." She turned back to Janna. "Well, what happened to you?"

"It's a long story." Janna gave her roommate a weary smile. "I'll tell you tomorrow but right now I really need to sleep."

Lucinda took that as her cue. "I'd better go." She hesitated. "Look, I'll give you my number. I can't guarantee that I can help but if anything else weird happens, you can always call." She rummaged in her bag for something to write with and found only a scrap of blank paper. "Do you have a pen I can borrow?"

"Sure." Carly took a pen from a kitchen drawer and handed it to her.

"That's a pretty bracelet," Janna said as Lucinda wrote down her name and number. "What stone is that?"

Lucinda nearly dropped the pen as she saw the tourmaline was glittering, glittering the way a diamond would, throwing sparks of sea-green light along the surface of the white kitchen table. Though she didn't know much about tourmalines, Lucinda was certain that this was not what they usually did. "Um . . . it's glass, actually," she told Janna. "Austrian crystal." Her heart was racing. She had a good guess as to what was going on. Quickly, she held out the paper to Janna. The stone stopped sparkling. Now it was just a rectangular blue-green crystal, beautiful but quiet.

"And here's your pen," Lucinda said, handing the pen back to Carly. The stone came to life again as she did. Carly saw it, too, and something calculating and deadly slid into her eyes.

"Cool. Must be the way the light hits it," Janna said, oblivious to the change in her roommate.

"No, it's not," Lucinda said. She was too frightened to continue the charade. "You and I have got to get out of here now. Come on!" She grabbed Janna's arm and began pulling her toward the door.

"Are you crazy?" Janna tried to pull out of her grip. "Let go of me."

"You heard her." Carly darted past them to plant herself in front of the door. "Get your friggin' hands off her."

Janna was struggling wildly. Lucinda let go with one hand but kept pulling her toward the door with the other. "Janna, please. You've got to be-lieve me. It isn't safe here. Come back downstairs with me and I'll explain everything."

"No. No more weird shit. I can't take any more. I want you and Sebastian and Alasdair and everyone else to just leave me alone!" Janna yanked hard, deliberately wrenching Lucinda's shoulder. Lucinda swore at the pain but didn't let go.

Carly smiled at her. "You won't get through me. You know that."

Lucinda froze. How was she supposed to fight a phantasm? Could she just walk through her?

Carly started to move toward them. "I know what happened to you, Janna," she crooned. "You always act so innocent, like you're the victim. But I've watched you. I know how you picked him up, how you tried to make him think you were so hot, how you wanted everyone in the club to see that he was yours. You won the prize, didn't you? And I know how you went with him, how you let him do whatever he wanted—"

"No!" Janna shrieked. "Make her stop!"

"That's not Carly." Lucinda kept her voice steady. "It's a phantasm, some-thing that *he* sent. You've got to ignore it. We just have to get out of here."

But Janna was kneeling on the floor, arms wrapped around her rib cage. "I never wanted him to hurt me like that. I never would have spoken to him if I knew what he was. It wasn't my fault!"

"I know that." Lucinda crouched down and with her hands on the girl's shoulders, tried to urge her to her feet. "That's not Carly, so don't listen to her. Everything she says is a lie. It's what *he* wants."

"It was your idea for him to cut you, wasn't it?" Carly was standing on the other side of Janna, her eyes alight with malice. "Admit it. You wanted him to do it. You asked him to."

Lucinda let go of Janna and slapped Carly hard—and her hand con-nected only with air.

The phantasm's smile widened. "You can't fight me," she said. "There's nothing to fight."

Lucinda knew she was right. And Janna wasn't budging. Now she was curled up on the floor like an embryo, rocking herself back and forth, re-peating endlessly, "I never wanted him to hurt me. I never wanted him to hurt me. I never wanted him to hurt me. . . ."

"Shit," Lucinda muttered. She didn't know what to do. Where was Alas-dair and why the hell hadn't he charged up here to the rescue? Again, she had the clear sense that she was forgetting something with no idea of what it might be. Desperate, she reached into the velvet pouch she wore at her waist. Her hand closed on the chalcedony cat. What had Alasdair said—something about chalcedony being connected to victory and pathways? She pulled it out, gripping it tightly. *I need a pathway out of here,* she told it silently. *And I need to win this now. Give me some of Averill's strength. Show me how to fight this thing.*

She knelt in front of Janna and gently touched her shoulder. "Please get up and come downstairs with me," she said. To her amazement Janna got to her feet. "Good," said Lucinda. Fighting her own sense of panic, she moved slowly, taking Janna's hand and leading her toward the door.

The phantasm in Carly's form was blocking it again. "You're going to have to go through me," she said. "And when you try, I'll feed on you both and leave you dead at my feet."

Lucinda didn't take her eyes off the phantasm. Behind her, she felt Janna stiffen with fright.

"She's lying," Lucinda said to Janna. "She doesn't have any real form. She's just a bitch of a vision. We're going to walk through her. There's nothing she can do about it."

"You're wrong. She's more than a vision. She handed you that pen." Janna's voice was high and shaky, but she was making sense and what she said scared the hell out of Lucinda. The phantasm wasn't just a vision. She did have some corporeal reality. Could she really feed on them?

"I don't care," Lucinda decided. "I'm getting out of here now."

Again she pulled on Janna's arm. Janna sank her teeth into Lucinda's wrist. Reflexively, Lucinda spun and sent the fist that was clenched around the chalcedony cat into the girl's jaw. Janna stumbled back with a cry and Lucinda made for the door again, yanking the stunned girl after her.

Carly stood facing them, her back to the door, arms outstretched.

Instinct took over and Lucinda opened her palm. For a quick flickering moment Carly's face vanished beneath a wash of pale blue. The blue wash vanished. The phantasm was still there, staring at the chalcedony carving with an expression of puzzlement, as if she couldn't quite believe what she was seeing.

Words that could have only come from Averill surged through Lucinda. "In the name of Kali-Ma, I cut you off from the one who gave you life. I sever you from this earth and your own cruelty. Everything you are Kali-Ma will consume."

And the blue chalcedony cat sprang from Lucinda's palm, pale blue claws extended. Lucinda saw the tiny stone feline land on the phantasm's throat. Carly grabbed for it, and as her hand closed around the cat, she broke. She broke into pieces of colored light, like bits of glass falling to the floor, and then she and the cat winked out of the room, as if they'd never been.

Sending up silent thanks to both Averill and Gervase, Lucinda turned back to Janna. The girl's pale face had gone chalk-white. Even her thick golden hair seemed drained of color. "How much of that did you see?" Lucinda asked.

Janna opened her mouth and closed it again. When she was finally able to summon her voice, it was barely audible. "All of it."

Lucinda ran a hand through her own hair. Her legs were trembling, weak in the aftermath of the fight. "I'm sorry I hit you," she said. "You do know that wasn't Carly, right?"

Janna nodded. "Wh-where is the real Carly, then?"

"I don't know but we'll find her," Lucinda promised. "Look, it's not safe for you to be here alone. He knows where you live. Please come with me."

This time Janna didn't argue. They went down the staircase together, Lucinda's arm around her.

At first Lucinda didn't see Alasdair. There was no one in front of the building's front door, where she'd left him. But there was a crowd gathered on the corner, forming a ring around something.

Janna came to a halt. "Oh, I've got a bad feeling about this."

"There's Alasdair," Lucinda said, spotting his tall figure on the edge of the crowd and nudging the girl in his direction. "Let's find out what's going on."

"I don't want to see whatever they're looking at," Janna told Lucinda in a small voice.

"I know," said Lucinda, keeping an arm around the trembling girl. Janna's dread seemed to pass directly from her body into Lucinda's. And Lucinda knew that Janna was right; whatever had caused the crowd to gather wasn't good. *Maybe I should just call out to Alasdair,* she thought, and at that moment Alasdair turned and walked toward them. "There you are." He sounded relieved. Lucinda thought she saw a glimmer of surprise in his eyes at the sight of Janna, but he didn't question why she'd come back downstairs.

"What's going on?" Lucinda asked.

"A young woman was found. She was cut up. Lines all over her, just like the shape-shifter."

Lucinda began to ask what she looked like, but Janna already seemed to know. She pulled away from them, her eyes terrified and focused on the crowd. "No."

Lucinda took a step toward her. "Janna, just listen—" she started, but the girl darted out of reach. She ran straight for the corner, shoving her way into the crowd. Alasdair and Lucinda ran after her, but both were too late.

A moment of silence fell over the street, then Janna's voice rose in a heart-rending cry, "Carly. Oh, my God, Carly, what did he do to you?"

JANNA TOLD THE police that the body was Carly's and Carly was her roommate, but she didn't say much more and the police seemed wary of questioning the overwrought girl. Moments after the body was taken away she became completely unhinged, tearing through the crowd and screaming at a Robert who wasn't there. It was decided by the officers on the scene that Janna should be taken to the hospital for observation, and neither Lucinda nor Alasdair attempted to intervene. Privately, Lucinda thought that a few nights' worth of sedatives might be exactly what the girl needed. But she and Alasdair followed the ambulance to Mercy Hospital where they did the requisite waiting in hallways, talked to physicians, left messages with the statistics department at the university, and finally saw Janna safely settled in a bed. She'd been drugged and was sleeping peacefully.

"Why don't I stay with her? You go visit Tyrone," Alasdair suggested.

Lucinda was glad to take advantage of the suggestion. A day ago she hadn't even known Janna Powell existed; now the girl and her problems seemed to be at the forefront of her life. How did a stranger do that, come into your world so suddenly and overwhelm everything? Sebastian had done it, and Alasdair, too, to an extent. It had been so long since Lucinda had had what she considered her "normal" life that somehow she was beginning to doubt it would ever resume. Did you go back to spending your days poring over fabrics after traveling with Hermes and vanquishing a phantasm? What *did* you do? Truthfully, it wasn't as if she wanted more trafficking with tricksters and shape-shifters and gods. They overwhelmed her and she was getting awfully tired of feeling overwhelmed. Visiting Tyrone in the hospital wasn't exactly what she would call normal, but at least he was a part of her life that she'd chosen.

She found Tyrone sitting up in bed, staring at the tiny TV screen positioned above his bed. He still had the room to himself.

She leaned forward to kiss his cheek. "How are you doing?"

He made an unintelligible noise in response, more growl than grunt.

"You look a lot better," Lucinda said, in what even she could tell was a nauseatingly chipper tone. She made an effort to bring her voice down to its usual register. "When did they let you sit up?"

"Earlier."

"Your color is better. Are you eating solid foods again?"

"Lucinda, I'm trying to watch a program here." That sounded so much like the cranky Tyrone she knew that she was heartened by it and couldn't take offense.

She sat down in the orange plastic chair beside the bed. The people on TV were screaming at each other. After the scene in Janna's flat, it was the last thing she needed. "Well, I had a hell of a day," she said in a conversational tone.

Tyrone, riveted by the TV screen, didn't reply.

Lucinda grabbed the remote and shut off the TV. "Why are you acting this way?"

"Could I have my remote please?" he asked in a cold voice.

She handed it to him and he turned on the television, restoring his program.

"This is ridiculous," she said loudly. "You've been dying, I went—well, never mind where—but it wasn't easy getting Ilyap'a out of you so you could recover. And now it's worked and you're not talking to me? Now you, who used to ridicule the tube and anyone lazy enough to watch it, *you're* turning into a TV junkie? What is going on? Damn it, Tyrone, talk to me."

He switched off the TV to glare at her. "Happy?"

"No. Tell me why you're so angry. Aren't you glad you're better?"

"You want the truth? Not really."

Lucinda forced herself to count to ten, but even after the count her words came out in a stream of anger. "Oh, I get it. You were so resigned to dying that now it's kind of a letdown to come back to life and have to deal with the world again. Is that it?"

Tyrone slammed his hand against the mattress. "No, that is not it. Christ, Lucinda, I expected you of all people to be more perceptive, to show a little bit of understanding. Were you just so selfish—so afraid you'd be left on your own—that you couldn't see what was happening?"

Lucinda felt her face go red with hurt. "Okay, tell me what it is I missed. What is it that I was too self-centered to see?"

Tyrone closed his eyes, and she saw tears starting to make their way out from beneath his lids. He brushed the tears away impatiently then opened his eyes to look at her, and the anguish she saw in them took her breath. "It's my boy, Winston. I was so close to being with Winston again. I heard his voice calling me. I could feel him in the room with me, right beside my bed. He was holding out his hand for me, Lucinda. And I was so close to taking it. The more I let go of life, the closer I was getting to Winston, and that was right. He was happy and I was happy. It was the way it was supposed to work out for us both. And then you and those damn doctors did whatever it was you all did, and now he's gone again."

"Oh gods." She was staring at the pattern on his chenille bedspread, unable to see anything beyond its ridges and swirls.

Tyrone laid his cool hand on top of hers. "I know you meant well. I know you did it because you love me. It's just that now it feels like it's going to be a long, long time before I see my boy again. Ever since he died it tears at me every day. It just seemed I was finally getting to the end of waking up ripped open like that, you know?"

"Excuse me." Alasdair was standing in the doorway. "I couldn't help overhearing," he said, coming into the room.

Tyrone turned his head away, clearly not wanting any further intrusions on his grief.

Alasdair reached into the folds of his robe and removed a thin collar of beaten silver with a clear, perfect quartz crystal set in its center. "In the Vedic tradition," he said quietly, "if you offer a libation to the dead while wearing white quartz, then you give the dead the gift of happiness wherever they are."

Tyrone's head snapped around. "What do you know about it?"

"Quite a lot, at least where the stones are concerned. Wear the quartz, make an offering to your son's spirit, and see what comes back to you."

Tyrone looked as if he were searching for another combative remark, but he took the silver collar.

"Do you want me to put it on you?" Lucinda asked.

Tyrone didn't object, so she fastened the torque-like necklace around his neck.

"It suits you," she said. "I mean, beyond 'looks good.' It looks like it was made for you." She studied him for a long moment, taking in the odd juxtaposition of his leonine mane, hospital gown, and the silver torque. "You know, if I believed in reincarnation, I'd swear you'd worn it in another lifetime."

"He did," Alasdair said. "When we die we must give up all our possessions, but some have a way of returning to us. Sooner or later we recognize them."

Tyrone scowled. Then he touched the crystal and his expression softened. "Thank you," he told Alasdair. "I hope you're right."

Lucinda glanced around the room. "I just realized. I haven't seen the dragon. Where is he?"

"You mean that shiny green insect you left with me?"

"He isn't an insect," Lucinda said indignantly.

"Well, I haven't laid eyes on it up close but I could feel it buzzing around. And Marcus was standing at my door this afternoon, yelling something about how it wouldn't let him into my room. The nurses kicked him off the floor, he made such a racket."

Alasdair and Lucinda exchanged an amused glance. Alasdair tilted his head as if listening to something then made a sound in his throat that sounded like a note played on a piccolo. Moments later Lucinda noticed a tiny commotion beneath the bedspread at the foot of Tyrone's bed.

"He must have been sleeping," Alasdair explained. "He likes to open and close his wings when he first wakes up. Sort of serpentine calisthenics."

Lucinda lifted the edge of the bedspread. The dragon fluttered its wings and peered up at her with bright topaz eyes. "Won't you come out?" she said. "I think it's time we introduced you to Tyrone."

"WHAT DID YOU say to Janna's parents?" Lucinda asked as she and Alasdair left the hospital that night. Shortly after meeting the dragon, Tyrone had fallen asleep. When they'd gone back to Janna's room, they'd found her parents keeping watch over the sleeping girl. Alasdair had spoken with them briefly.

"Probably the same thing the police did," he answered. "I told them that I was there on the street when she found her roommate's body, and it might be best if she didn't have to return to that apartment again, especially not on her own. I think they saw the reason in that."

"I hope she'll be all right."

"I think she will," Alasdair said.

"You didn't see her when the phantasm was taunting her. She was almost apoplectic."

"Probably. But in Sebastian's loft, after being tortured by the shape-shifter and then being held captive, more or less, by Sebastian, she still marched in and stopped me from slitting Sebastian's throat."

"You were just bluffing. You never would have done it."

"Wouldn't I?" he asked softly. "Did you forget what the thresholds showed you?"

"I haven't forgotten, but I still don't think you would have killed him."

"The point is, Janna has strength," Alasdair said. "She'll be traumatized for a while, but I think she'll find a way to heal."

By unspoken agreement they were walking back to Lucinda's flat. Though Lucinda couldn't see or sense it, Alasdair assured her that his opal life stone was concealing them. She found this idea kind of charming, and realized she also didn't mind the idea of his spending another night at her flat. The night before he'd slept on her couch and while she'd been conscious of him being in the next room, she'd felt perfectly comfortable having him there.

Back in the apartment the hot water was running again, so they each took a bath, first Lucinda, then Alasdair. Lucinda put on an old, comfortable nightgown, ankle-length white cotton with a square neck edged in lace, and tiny pearl buttons down the front. Alasdair emerged from his bath, swathed in one of her bath sheets. The long lavender towel clung to his damp, tanned skin, making him look both strikingly handsome—for the first time she could see that he had a runner's long, lithe musculature—and absurd. She chose to focus on the latter, unable to resist teasing him. "I've never seen you in lavender. Makes you look kind of spring-like, you know, like an Easter bunny—a *tall* Easter bunny but—"

"You never told me how you dispelled the phantasm," Alasdair reminded her.

She sighed. "I was trying to tell you that you look cute for once, instead of grim and foreboding. You're changing the subject."

Alasdair immediately resumed his grim, foreboding look. "Agreed. And if 'cute' is a compliment, thank you . . . I suppose." His look became slightly perplexed. "I've never aspired to cute. That aside, you need to tell me—"

"The chalcedony cat Gervase carved. It's gone now," she said bleakly. "It leapt at the phantasm and they both disappeared." She looked up at him. "It felt as if Averill's words came through me when I held it. It was eerie. I destroyed the phantasm in the name of Kali-Ma. Not exactly an option that would occur to me on my own."

"Gervase must be doing better than he thinks if so much of Averill came through his carving."

Lucinda made a face. "That's probably why he gave it away."

"Possibly," Alasdair conceded. "You might take comfort in the fact that both the chalcedony and the tourmaline opened to you. And obviously, you to them."

She looked at the tourmaline bracelet on her wrist and again felt the now-nagging sensation that she was forgetting something. "What do I do the next time it starts sparkling?"

Alasdair, too, stared at the tourmaline, dark brows drawn together in concentration. After another moment of focus on the stone, he said, "It suggests turquoise." And at her baffled expression added, "Turquoise is apotropaic, useful for averting evil."

"I'll try to remember that." She got to her feet, wondering why most of her conversations with Alasdair left her feeling slightly dizzy. She looked at him, still wrapped in the long, lavender towel. "My robes will probably be too small for you, but I can lend you my biggest one—"

"Thank you, but I'll put on my own robe," he said, and returned to the bathroom to dress.

Lucinda wondered what he'd been like with Gioia—equally formal and distant? No, from that glimpse she'd seen of them before Noelle's arrival, Alasdair had once been easy in love and ardent. An ember of jealousy that Lucinda hadn't even known was there suddenly flared. She quenched it at once, telling herself it was crazy to be jealous of someone who was dead. Still, she couldn't help wishing she'd known him before all the sorrow came into his eyes.

Restless, and not at all comforted by the suggestion of turquoise, Lucinda went into her bedroom. On her bed, beneath the window made of violet glass, she spread out the stones she'd been given. The chalcedony cat was gone. She hadn't liked it when it was given to her, had been uncomfortable with its resemblance to Averill, and yet it had destroyed the phantasm. The one stone she'd figured out how to use and it disappeared. Was she perverse for now wishing she had it back?

She still had the garnet, a small, dark red stone—nothing showy about it—that had saved Tyrone from Ilyap'a's second storm. She peered at it but didn't see the lightning that she'd seen when Hermes held it.

Hesitantly, she took out the diamond necklace. She hadn't really looked at it since she'd seen the vision in the thresholds, since she'd seen Gioia wear it and die for it. No matter what Alasdair said, she was convinced that without the diamond Gioia would still be alive. It was too large, too perfect, too gorgeous not to endanger whoever owned it. Even in the lost towns it led to murder. You really couldn't hope to wear a thing like that unless you had a phalanx of armed guards surrounding you.

But oh, it was so beautiful. She remembered wearing it in Kama's garden. And it had opened the jade door to the lost towns for her. Maybe that was all it was meant to do. She held it up to the little lamp on her bedside table, savoring its cool, solid weight and the fiery rainbow that danced inside. It was an extraordinary jewel. If it wasn't so fraught with baggage—Kama and Gioia and Noelle and Sebastian and the gods only knew who else—she might have actually loved it.

Finally, she opened the cloisonné box and took out the moonstone. It still gleamed like a pale blue drop of seawater, a thin arc of silvery light reflected in its smooth surface. "You were the first," she said to it, half-fondly, half-resentfully. "All the craziness started with you."

"An old friend." Alasdair stood in her doorway, clothed in his sage-green robe, watching her. "That moonstone used to be one of my life stones."

Lucinda stood up, crossed the room, and held out the moonstone. "Then it's yours. Here."

He didn't take it but said, "Do you know how it came to you?"

"I just found it in my flat one day. In the cloisonné box."

"The dragon," Alasdair said. "He's always had an affinity for seeing that gifts are properly presented. The cloisonné box is his version of gift wrap."

"The dragon?"

"He decided you had more need of it than I."

"That doesn't make sense. It's yours. And life stones are special somehow, aren't they?"

Alasdair smiled. "Being given life stones is almost like being given guardian angels. Yes, they're very special."

"Then you've got to take it back. It's meant to be with you."

He moved slightly and the light in the room emphasized the scar on his face, the scar that she'd all but forgotten he had. Funny how parts of a person could disappear as you got to know them. "The dragon decided otherwise," he told her, "and dragons have always been wiser about the earth's gems than we humans. Especially jade dragons." Alasdair closed her hand over the stone. "Gems aren't meant to stay with one person for eternity, sometimes not even for a lifetime. They're meant to move, to change hands and grace many. The moonstone was with me when I needed it most. Now it's meant to be yours, so we'll have no more discussion about it."

"What will you do without it?" she asked, ignoring his dictum.

He shrugged but his eyes betrayed the grief inside him. "I think my time for the moonstone's gifts is past. Put it back in its box," he said, "for safe-keeping."

She started toward the bed, where the open cloisonné box lay beneath the fan-shaped window, but stopped and turned to face him again. "You once said the moonstone brings tenderness."

"It does."

"So that means that since your moonstone came to me, you've gone without tenderness?"

"I hope not entirely," he said. Something in his grey eyes softened. "Have I been . . . harsh . . . with you?"

She thought it over. "Now and then. Really, it's no big deal. Mostly, you've helped me." Honesty compelled her to add, "And I'm grateful."

"I'm glad of you, too," he said. "You're what has made it bearable for me to return to Arcato. Everything else I've come back to here is hard and sad and harrowing. And then there's you—an innocent in the realms I've always taken for granted and cursing your way through most of it, but also going straight through. Not shutting down or turning to run. If it were my choice, you wouldn't be mixed up in any of this. But given what is—you're, well, exactly what you were named. You're the light in this for me, Lucinda."

Lucinda stood perfectly still, like a woman afraid that if she moved or even spoke she'd shatter the crystalline web of happiness that had suddenly been spun around her. At last, though, she had to ask the question that was ringing through her. "Are you sure?"

Alasdair began to laugh and laughed until he gasped for air. "Yes," he finally managed. "Gods above, yes!"

The crystalline web dissolved but Lucinda found the sense of happiness remained, not nearly as fragile as she'd imagined. She grinned at him. "It's not that funny."

"Probably not," he admitted, smiling back at her with a new openness. "I've just never seen you look so uncertain—and about something that I assumed was more than evident."

"It wasn't," she told him. She looked at him, thinking that she had never quite felt this way before. There was that delicious thrum of desire vibrating between them, but desire was a familiar feeling. This other feeling had to do with what they'd gone through together, with her sense that Alasdair was one of the more extraordinary beings she'd come across, and with a new, almost overwhelming tenderness for him. Lucinda found she wanted him, not just his cock, but what he was, his essence, deep inside her.

She took a step toward him and held out the moonstone again. "I think you're wrong," she said. "Your time for the moonstone's gifts isn't past."

His voice caught. "What are you saying?"

"I'm saying that it's now. I want you to come to bed with me."

He stepped back from her, his grey eyes wary. "Is this out of pity?"

"I don't do pity fucks," she assured him. "Not for you, not for anyone. I've never seen fucking as a consolation prize."

"No wonder Kama likes you," Alasdair said with a trace of a smile. "But I don't fuck."

She couldn't hide her surprise. "You're a eunuch?"

That brought another laugh. "I mean, as a *cearu,* I can't be that close to a person and keep the kind of distance that renders it fucking. I'm not, as your people would say, 'wired' that way. If I'm with you, it will be . . . complete."

"You're talking about love," Lucinda said, uneasiness steeling over her.

He nodded, calm and almost neutral. The choice was hers.

She thought about it—what already existed between them: trust and friendship that had become intimacy, and now unexpectedly, desire and this new tenderness. She held out a hand to him. "Then come love me."

He didn't move. "I don't do one-sided couplings either."

She took his hand in hers, the pale blue stone of moonlight pressed between their palms. "Then let me love you."

This time he was the one to ask, "Are you sure?"

Hands still clasping the moonstone between them, she led him to her bed. He sat facing her and then when he read the answer in her eyes, he slowly began to open the tiny pearl buttons on her nightgown. She couldn't look away from him. No one had ever looked at her with so much desire, a desire that went beyond sex, that seemed to see through her defenses and weaknesses and fears and still want her wholly.

Lucinda wasn't conscious of the moment when they released their clasped hands and let the moonstone fall to the bed between them. She was too caught up in the sensations of Alasdair's hands on her bare skin, of her hands on him. To touch Alasdair was to drink from waters she'd been thirsting for her whole life. They moved carefully at first, then eagerly, then with a need that welled up from the deepest parts of them to open into pure abandon. For the first time nothing in her held back, and she knew it was because she trusted him as she'd never trusted any man, and that trust was both balm and aphrodisiac.

Making love with Alasdair was a matter of recognition rather than of surprises. It all felt familiar, as if they already knew each other's bodies, as if they were somehow picking up where they'd long ago left off. There was none of that intoxicating first-time thrill. Lucinda had always craved the friction of sex, the moments of conquest and surrender, the intense rush of pleasure that was just across the threshold from pain. Now she found herself on terrain that felt as if it were a landscape she'd known for years that had somehow become concealed from her. Now the light was flooding into it again and warming every fiber of her being, loosening her limbs, opening her eyes and her heart. Everything in her was aware of him, connected to him. And he to her. Every sensation was heightened. Neither one of them, it seemed, could make the smallest movement without giving the other pleasure, and the pleasure was infinite. No one had ever been so gentle with her, had loved her so thoroughly and completely. She felt as if she'd been taken up by the sea.

THEY WOKE AS dawn light filtered in through the window above her bed. She was lying on her side, curled in his arms. He pulled her closer and through half-open eyes she noticed the sculpted line of muscle in his arms. She'd never seen his arms before last night. He had perfectly beautiful arms and she'd barely noticed, she'd been so lost in sensation.

"How are you this morning?" he asked drowsily.

"Reborn," she admitted.

He laughed softly.

She decided she trusted him enough to risk an idea that made her feel terribly vulnerable. "When I was in the Source Place," she began, "I had this sense that there was something—something important—I was forgetting. And since we returned to the city, I've gotten that same feeling again and again. Making love with you felt so familiar—so wonderfully familiar—that I can't help thinking *that* was the thing I'd somehow forgotten."

Alasdair's hand traced the line of her hipbone. "It was like we've been lovers before. Or have always been lovers."

"So it felt familiar to you, too?"

He turned her in his arms to face him. "As it never has with anyone else."

"That must be it then, what I was forgetting and needed to remember."

"Maybe." He kissed her lips. "If that's it, I'm awfully glad you remembered."

She pushed herself up onto one elbow. "But maybe that's *not* it?"

"I don't know," Alasdair told her. "I suspect that whatever it is you're sensing is a soul memory. Some bit of knowledge that you've known in another lifetime or dimension. Or perhaps an earth memory, something transmitted from the earth itself."

She shot him a wry grin. "Trust you to take something perfectly straightforward, like sex, and make it oblique and complicated."

"Perfectly straightforward?" he echoed. "When has lovemaking ever been uncomplicated? Even for animals I suspect there are layers—territory and survival and family and affection—that get mixed in with all the rest." A smile played at the corners of his mouth. "Besides, soul and earth memories tend to emerge obliquely. It's not as if you can simply will yourself to remember."

"What I don't want to forget," she said, taking his hand, "is last night. That wasn't the moonstone, was it?" she asked, suddenly afraid that what they'd felt was all due to a bit of translucent rock.

"The moonstone and probably a bit of the diamond's influence, and I'd say we had Kama's blessings, as well," Alasdair answered. "It was certainly proof that the moonstone went to the right person. I'll have to remember to thank the dragon," he added, almost as a note to himself. "But mostly, it was you and me and all that connects us."

That thought unsettled her, too. "Sebastian says that he and I have a connection."

"You probably do." Alasdair seemed unbothered by this. "You'd have to live an extremely insulated life to have intimate connections with only one person, especially looking the way you do. You're extravagantly beautiful, you know."

Lucinda registered the compliment and passed over it. "But what you and I had last night was different," she insisted. "I've been with a lot of men, and it's *never* been like that for me."

"Nor for me. It was like touching something we've always known, that's always been part of us." His voice became hoarse as he drew her close. "Lucinda, I think you just gave me back part of my soul."

Much later she got up to make coffee and they drank it in bed. Gradually, as the morning's light filled the room their talk drifted from intimacy to what awaited them.

"Do you want to return to the lost towns?" Lucinda couldn't help asking.

"Eventually, when Vita's secure in the power she wants and has stopped her machinations."

"What machinations?"

"She's displaced Averill," he told her. "Or started to. It's going to be a process and she's going to meet resistance. I'd rather not be drawn into it as she fights it out."

Lucinda found this facet of Alasdair's life fascinating. "Why? Aren't you on her side?"

"That's just it," he said, frowning into his coffee. "I don't want to be forced to take sides. Averill may be a harridan but she's led our people for a long time and she's done well by most of us. And taking power from another is never pretty. Maybe I just want to hold onto a few illusions about Vita. I'm loath to watch my own mother be as ruthless as she's going to have to be. As she is," he corrected himself.

"And Vita won't feel betrayed by you not coming back to help her?"

"Vita doesn't need my help. That's the crux of it. She doesn't truly need anyone. She'll probably be vexed with me, but she'll get over that. She always does." He glanced at her. "Did you ever call your mother?"

"Not yet but I will." She laughed. "We sound like an old married couple, discussing our mothers."

"Not many in the lost towns have that kind of domesticity," Alasdair mused. "It's always been a clear matriarchy and in most households, on the woman's instigation, the men and women live nearby but apart. They come together mostly for childcare."

"And lovemaking?"

"That, too, but they rarely share the same home."

"Then I might have to keep you in the city with me," she said lightly, marveling at her own daring even as she spoke the words.

"You just might," he agreed, then added distractedly, "The wind chimes are making a terrible racket. We should see what's going on."

"It's probably windy," Lucinda said, feeling a trace of her old exasperation with him.

Wrapped in a sheet, Alasdair stepped onto her narrow balcony. She followed him out. As she'd predicted, it was windy, with gusts howling down the streets and sending the city's detritus—hats and newspapers snatched from pedestrians, empty cans and wrappers and dead cigarettes—in a careening dance to the river below.

"You have quite a view," Alasdair said.

"If you like watching the city go mad. I always seem to have a ringside seat for that."

He turned his head sharply and asked, "Do you hear it?"

"What, the wind?"

"No, something is calling. If you listen hard, you can hear a voice in the wind."

Lucinda listened. "I think you're just hearing echoes off the buildings. It always sounds like that during a windstorm." Dust blew into her eye then and she stumbled back into the flat to rinse it out. When she emerged from the bathroom, Alasdair had come inside, too, and though he'd shut the French doors that led to the balcony he was staring though the glass panes, seemingly absorbed by the storm.

" 'Something comes through the stones heralded by the call,' " he murmured.

"What are you talking about?"

He started, as if he'd forgotten she was there. "It's a bit of our lore," he explained. "I always thought it was about the Source Place. There's a colonnade of gemstones there, up in the mountains where most of our ceremonies take place. And since many of them begin with a call, I always assumed that's what that phrase described."

"And now?"

"Now I think it may be about something else altogether. And I think it means I have to go back up to that plaza. I'm fairly certain that Sangeet, the shape-shifter, was there," he went on.

She didn't say anything. She'd known they were going to have to return to the hunt for the shape-shifter; she'd just been hoping to postpone it a little longer.

Alasdair raked his fingers through his dark hair. "I keep coming back to the fact that he stripped the stones of their memory. Concealing memory is one thing and fairly easy to do. But stripping it . . . I thought it was simply his rage. But now I'm wondering if it wasn't a more deliberate act."

Lucinda tried to match his cool tone. "For example?"

"I'm wondering if something didn't happen in that plaza, something he was part of, something so terrible that he's ensured that no one will ever know what it was." Alasdair stared at the window again, his body tense and alert. "I have to go back up there."

"Can't it wait?"

"No, I have to go now while I can still hear that call in the wind."

"Then I'll go with you," she said at once. "After all, I'm supposed to do something with the diamond, right?"

Alasdair took her hand. "Lucinda, there aren't many things that scare me. That plaza does. Let me at least find out what's going on up there before you come riding to my rescue."

"What if he's up there waiting for you?"

"Then I'm the one who's meant to confront him. Besides, you really ought to check on Tyrone and Janna. We know Sangeet's been making rounds in the hospital."

She hated being reminded of it. "You're not really giving me a choice."

"No." He drew her into his arms. "Please stay away from the plaza."

Lucinda held him tightly, loving the feeling of being in his arms and aching with the fear that she might never be in them again. "I'm not making any promises but I'll go to the hospital first," she finally offered.

"I suppose that's a start." Reluctantly, he released her then drew her back for a very thorough kiss.

"Be careful," she called as he left the flat. It seemed terribly unfair that he was always giving her various sorts of protection and she had none to offer him. Especially when moments after he left she felt an unfamiliar weight against her collarbone and realized she was now wearing a strand of bright blue turquoise beads.

PART 5

The Plaza

"He says, 'There's nothing left of *me*.
I'm like a ruby held up to the sunrise.
Is it still a stone, or a world
made of redness? It has no resistance
to sunlight."

—RUMI,
"The Sunrise Ruby"

Twenty

AGAINST THE PREVAILING winds, Alasdair made his way to the top of the city. He wished that the dragon weren't guarding Tyrone; he could have used the company. It was desolate up here. The streets became steeper, and the commercial and residential areas of Arcato fell away, as if the city were shedding itself as it reached for the foothills, as if it couldn't quite shake concrete and brick and yet the earth beneath the cobblestone streets had already returned to the wild. The mountain reclaimed its own, whether or not the city chose to acknowledge it.

He recognized the alley between the two abandoned factories at once, and wondered only at the fact that he'd reached it so quickly. Both of the times he'd been here before, it had seemed much farther from the waterfront.

Alasdair stopped for a moment, centering himself with his breath, identifying his fear as terror of the pain he'd suffered the first time he was here, and pushing it to the edges of his mind. Fear had its uses; he meant to keep its heightened awareness but he would not let it rule him.

He walked between the two factory buildings that opened onto the ancient plaza. The first thing he felt was the curious damping of his senses. Although he could sense his life stones reaching toward him with reassurance, even their essences—which he knew as well as his own—were dissipating, becoming weaker as he drew closer to the square. The broken mosaic at his feet caught the sunlight, highlighting the diamond-within-diamond pattern, and he sent greetings down through the earth to the mothers below. Though he could identify the bits of gold and colored stone—turquoise, lapis, carnelian, coral, malachite—again he could find no memory in them.

The wind whipped through the four columns, as if trying to push him back downhill, back into the bustling, congested streets of the city. An excellent suggestion, Alasdair thought, but he stayed where he was, studying the remnants of what had once been. Why had the factories left this bit of an ancient city here? Nowhere else, as far as he knew, was there anything else remaining from this time. Perhaps the mothers were protecting their key but somehow he sensed it was more than that. After all, there were other keys to their shrine; Lucinda had told him there was one in Sebastian's loft.

He directed his attention to the four dark columns that marked the edges of the plaza. Had they held up a roof? And what sort of structure had it been—a temple, a marketplace? Again, he found himself frustrated by being unable to read them. He had to push that aside; it was ego and it wouldn't do him any good.

Think, he instructed himself. Ego resurfaced. Having spent as long as he had working with the stones, he had to be able to determine something about them, even without their active cooperation. He refused to be gainsaid.

Start with what's obvious. Each of the broken columns was rounded and fluted. They'd been carefully carved. He examined the stone more carefully. When he'd been here before he'd been so focused on the mosaic and then Sebastian that he hadn't paid much attention to the columns. He'd known the stone they were carved from was imported, assumed it was a grey granite, grimy with the city's fumes. It was granite, all right, but now he realized it was black granite, which was much rarer. He looked around again. So close to the foothills, it was likelier that this would have been the site of a temple rather than of a marketplace. And situated on top of an entrance to the Shrine of the Mothers it seemed even more certain that before the city had claimed it, this had been a holy place, a gateway to the mountains and the spirits who dwelled in their peaks.

A memory came to him of the only black granite temple he'd ever seen, a temple devoted to the Egyptian cat goddess Sekhmet, a warrior goddess and the embodiment of the destroying heat of the sun. Known as the "Crusher of Hearts," she was also one of the most bloodthirsty deities in any pantheon. When Ra initiated the Slaying of Mankind, Sekhmet killed so eagerly and savagely that even Ra, who had asked for her aid in the slaughter, saw that if she continued, humankind would be eradicated. He had to trick her in order to stop her, but that was hardly the end of Sekhmet's influence. In the millennia that followed she was worshipped as a deity of fate, associated with magic and sorcery. It was said that she never lost her taste for blood and that what she craved was the sacrifice of children.

Surely, this couldn't have been a temple to Sekhmet, Alasdair told himself, not here, so far from her native land. Importing deities to a foreign city was one thing, usually tolerated. Importing deities who required ritual human sacrifice was quite another; the foreign cities tended to take great exception to the practice.

The wind rose and again the voice inside it called. Alasdair listened carefully, then pitched his voice to imitate the call. As a child he'd learned to imitate the calls of coyotes and foxes and wolves to the point where—with the exception of shape-shifters—he could usually summon them at will. This felt very similar, except that he had no idea of what it was he was summoning. He called, high and sharp, until his voice was indistinguishable from the wind itself, until his throat was raw and his voice was nearly gone. But as he uttered a last hoarse croak the call was answered.

At first it wasn't that a presence entered the plaza but that the plaza itself began to change. The four columns were growing. Alasdair stood in the center of the plaza, fighting a feeling of alarm as they rose to three times his own height, each one crowned with simple capital. At his feet the mosaic was no longer cracked and broken but a jewel-like pattern of color, the diamond-within-diamond pattern at its center with the citrine that had originally led him here at its heart. To his profound relief there was no image of Sekhmet. Had it all just transformed, he wondered, or was he being granted a vision of what it had once been?

Perhaps the stones remembered after all. Perhaps the call woke their memory, and it was that memory that he was being shown.

Warily, Alasdair stepped back outside the mosaic and the columns. The Shrine of the Mothers he considered a good influence; the black granite columns he was unsure about. What had happened in this place?

Something comes through the stones, heralded by the call. The line nagged at him.

Surrendering to its insistence, he again joined his broken voice to the voice in the wind.

This time a fox's shrill call answered. He waited, hearing the animal's cries moving closer, as if like the wind, it was racing down from the mountains. Moments later the large russet fox he'd seen in Vita's crystal bounded through the black granite pillars and into the center of the mosaic. It was too large, he thought, with a wide, thick ruff over a deep chest. Aside from the coloring and the shape of its head, it seemed more wolf than fox.

As Alasdair watched, the fox lifted itself onto its hind legs. It stood comfortably, needing no effort to balance. This, too, was most unfoxlike.

From the ground up, the fox began to shift into a man. First the paws became bare feet, the hind legs and waist a man's legs and waist, covered in a long, straight bloodred skirt. The wide chest became a man's powerful chest, the skin bare and covered by a hatchwork of scars that also covered arms and hands and feet and face. The round bronze manifold amulet hung from his neck on a leather thong and over it, a necklace of other amulets, all of them images of deities. Alasdair recognized a steatite Sekhmet; a bronze Shiva in his aspect as the Destroyer; the African sorcerer-god Heitsi-Eibib, carved in serpentine; and a red jasper image of the wolf Fenrir, waiting hungrily for Ragnarok.

The shape-shifter held up his hands and let out a cry that reverberated, its echoes changing the air, shifting things in the plaza. Alasdair could feel energy gathering, revolving, and gradually taking on color and shape. It became a dark, whirling oval. And as Sangeet continued to sing to it, it solidified into a wide bronze bowl, coming to rest in the shape-shifter's open hands. He knelt, reverently setting it in the center of the mosaic.

Then he stood and sang the song that was in the wind, the same song that Alasdair had sung. He was softening it, making it gentler, more melodious, a song to attract. Alasdair watched uneasily, wondering who else was being summoned.

A young, pale-haired boy, maybe five years old, came through the black granite columns, stumbling with the unseeing movements of one who has been drugged or hypnotized. Alasdair watched as Sangeet bid the boy kneel over the bowl and the boy obeyed.

The shape-shifter began an incantation in the language of the Sinpiedras. Alasdair understood enough to make out the gist of it:

You must have no fear
For I travel with your spirit
I will tell the gods how bravely you died
Have no fear
Die with courage
For your strength and spirit will live on in me.

Alasdair's breath caught as he realized that the shape-shifter held a terribly familiar obsidian knife. The boy seemed oblivious, his unseeing eyes focused somewhere beyond the bowl. Without thinking, Alasdair summoned black tourmaline and started toward the boy, determined to break the shape-shifter's spell.

The instant Alasdair set foot inside the stone columns, Sangeet, the boy, the sacrifical bowl, and the changed plaza vanished. It was all as he'd seen it before: broken columns, crumbling mosaic, a ruin of a place haunted by a peculiar lack of spirits. He then did what he should have done first; he reached for his obsidian knife. It was there in the folds of his robe where he always carried it. Blinking, Alasdair stepped back outside the columns.

The vision—for clearly that was what it was—reappeared, continued. It had happened in the past, he realized, and there was nothing he could do to alter it.

"*It is an act of joining.*" Sangeet's chant became tender, almost loving. "*I would not cut you if I did not first cut my own flesh.*"

Alasdair watched in fascinated dread as Sangeet used the familiar obsidian knife to press hard into his arm and make a long slice across a row of scars on his arm. He stood unflinching, his blood pouring over the boy and into the bowl. Had every scar on his body come from a human sacrifice? The number of his victims would be almost beyond reckoning.

"*We stand above the Shrine of the Mothers,*" the shape-shifter chanted. He gripped the boy's pale hair, pulled his head back, and raised the knife high. His own blood streamed down his elbow and onto the boy's passive face. "*We consecrate our blood to them and ask their favor, ask that they bless us with their own immortality—*"

The wind screamed and became a whirlwind, spinning wildly in front of the shape-shifter. It sucked the knife from his hand and pulled the boy from his grip. Alasdair saw first dismay then amazement in Sangeet's eyes as the boy's inert form was lifted and gently set down, and a blue-skinned cat-headed goddess stepped out of the spiral of wind. It was not Sekhmet, Alasdair saw, but the voluptuous cat goddess who had claimed his lapis in the shrine.

"How dare you ask our blessings when you deface us with your greed?"

Sangeet fell to his knees, forehead pressed to the mosaic. "Hear my prayers, infinite Mother. Look kindly on me. I seek only to please you. I—" Trembling, he sat up on his knees, raising his eyes to the goddess. "I only ask for more life, more years to serve you."

The goddess began to prowl the edges of the plaza, long blue legs moving with a leopard's lethal grace.

Sangeet held open hands out to the boy. "I swear to you he will feel no pain."

She struck him then, a blow that ripped four deep gouges from shoulder to groin, cutting through veins and exposing bone. "Have I given you what you wanted?" she asked as the shape-shifter crumpled to the ground.

"You tire us," the goddess went on. "We are tired of your insatiable demands, of you killing in our names. We are tired of you claiming to intercede with us on behalf of those you murder. So now you will wander, always wanting, always craving, and knowing that the gods will never again answer your call. Do you understand? You are no longer our familiar. You will never again even come close to what you seek."

Alasdair watched as she knelt and gently took the boy in her arms. One blue hand touched the boy's eyes. Alasdair saw the boy's eyes focus, no longer caught in Sangeet's spell of blindness. "Yes," she told him, a mother comforting a frightened infant, "I'll show you a better place." Still cradling the child, she stepped back into the whirling spiral of wind.

The shape-shifter lay on the bloodied mosaic. A low crooning sound was coming from his chest. Alasdair watched with unwilling admiration. A true Sinpiedras, Sangeet was summoning frequencies whose vibrations would align what had gone disastrously awry when the goddess ripped him open. They would restore harmony to a body that otherwise would have disintegrated into the entropy of death. He was healing himself from a blow that should have killed him.

Sometime later Sangeet slowly got to his feet. The gouges were still open, and though the bleeding had stopped, he was covered in blood. His eyes, Alasdair saw, were the amber of a fox's eyes and they burned with hatred as he stared at the diamond-within-diamond pattern.

"Then I curse you, Mothers." He opened his mouth, releasing an excruciating, high-pitched scream that shattered the mosaic at his feet. The citrine bounced out unnoticed, rolling beyond the pillars. "And I curse the stones that witnessed this." The shape-shifter let out another piercing cry. Alasdair felt something inside him recoil as the horrifying sound penetrated the stones of the plaza, obliterating all memory, light, and sense. Finally, Alasdair understood. It wasn't the use of the plaza for blood sacrifice that Sangeet concealed when he stripped the stones. Rather, what Sangeet was determined to erase was the memory of his humiliation at the hands of the goddess.

The vision ended then, and Alasdair was once more looking at the broken pillars that bordered the empty plaza and its long-broken mosaics. He felt his muscles ease out of the tension that had held them rigid since the vision began, a vision he'd clearly been given by the mothers.

"Couldn't you do better?" He put the question to any of the goddesses who might be listening. "Why didn't you simply put an end to that madman? Why did you leave it for me to clean up your mess?"

As was often the case, the goddesses didn't deign to answer.

LUCINDA WENT FIRST to Janna's room only to find that her parents had taken her home. To their home, a nurse told her, out of the city. Lucinda silently thanked the gods for small favors and headed for Tyrone's room.

Tyrone was awake, sitting up in bed, drawing with charcoal in a black, cloth-bound sketchbook. The dragon sat on his shoulder, watching intently.

"Where'd you get the charcoal and sketchbook?" Lucinda asked as she settled herself on the edge of the bed.

"Gabrielle brought them to me last night. She said too much television would rot my inspired mind."

"And what are you inspired to sketch?" Lucinda asked, cheered by the sight of Tyrone seeming so much like himself again.

He held the sketchbook out to her. "Start on the first page."

Lucinda flipped back to the beginning. She wasn't sure what she expected—clothing or silhouettes maybe; sometimes Tyrone didn't know if he wanted to make a dress or pants or a jacket but simply started playing with shapes, gradually working them into garments. But what she found were drawings of a young boy, with Tyrone's wide-set eyes, slightly bow-legged stance, and curly hair. Although the boy was clearly beautiful, the drawings weren't sentimentalized or prettified. In some he had a stubborn, determined set to his mouth; in others, his clothing was covered with stains, his face unwashed. A sketch of him sleeping showed an angelic expression but also a thin line of drool stretching from open mouth to pillow. The last sketch showed him standing in a downpour, umbrella pointed to the ground, laughing with gap-toothed delight as rain plastered his hair against his scalp.

"Winston?" she guessed.

"That's who I saw when I was halfway to death," Tyrone said. "Figured I might as well draw what was on my mind."

"He was beautiful," she said.

"Wasn't he, though." Tyrone reached for the sketchbook. "These don't even begin to do him justice."

"I wish I'd known him."

Tyrone grinned at her. "Do you? He was a pain in the butt. Always clamoring for attention, like most young kids. But gods, he was sweet, had a big, generous heart. Smart, too. I could barely keep up with him."

Lucinda looked at the quartz necklace that Tyrone wore. "Maybe Alasdair had a point. Maybe when you get out of here, you should think about making some kind of offering to Winston's memory. Something more than tiger lilies on his grave, I mean."

Tyrone pursed his lips and began another sketch. "I'll think on it," he said in the clipped tone that meant he was now doing Important Creative Work and did not want to be disturbed.

She ventured a question anyway. "Tyrone, how did he die?"

He didn't look up from his drawing. "Got pneumonia, never got better. When that kid Michael was in my loft, hacking away with his cough, I thought I was being given a chance to make it right. Ain't it a bitch the way that worked out? Gotta be careful next time I get one of those stupid-ass philanthropic urges."

If it were Alasdair sitting at Tyrone's bedside, he probably would have responded with one of his discourses on the gods and fate, but all Lucinda could do was give Tyrone's shoulder an affectionate squeeze. She had no idea of whether he'd done the right or wrong thing, whether there had been a correct or incorrect action to choose.

"You still thinking about giving up the studio?"

"Not the space. Just the business."

"What will you do?"

"Don't know." He looked up to scowl at her. "Would you please let a man draw in peace?"

"All right, all right. I'll go."

"Nice turquoise choker, by the way," he commented.

"I didn't you think you noticed."

"I always notice. Just like I noticed that you got some good lovin' recently."

"Tyrone," she warned, "don't start—"

"'Cinda, we've known each other too long for bullshit. So listen, I'm fine here with the jade bug looking out for me. You go find that man you're so worried about."

LUCINDA WAS HOT and suffering a severe side stitch by the time she reached the street where the abandoned factory buildings perched at the top of the city. At least the winds had subsided. Sun shone through the cloud cover in a warm haze, and she unbuttoned her suede jacket as she began to grow warm. The factory buildings came into sight and she slowed her pace, mostly because the sight spooked her. What would she find this time when she went through that alley? Instinctively, she reached for the velvet pouch at her waist. Her hand closed on the diamond necklace. For the first time since she wore it in Kama's garden, she put it on. Lucinda stole a quick glance in a storefront window on the other side of the street. She hadn't dressed with any particular care that morning. She was wearing a simple black knit top over loose pants of smoky-purple raw silk. The strange thing was the extravagant gem didn't look absurd, even though she wore it with the turquoise choker. It looked much as Tyrone's quartz necklace had looked on him, as if it were made for her. That actually gave her a little courage. Still, despite being sweaty, she buttoned her jacket over the diamond necklace.

Steeling herself, she walked through the alleyway. Lucinda was prepared for anything from gaping chasms in the earth to pyrotechnics. The sight that greeted her was strangely anticlimactic.

Alasdair sat on one of the broken pillars in the empty plaza. There was no one else. He looked up as she approached and frowned. "What are you doing here?"

"You know."

"Please go back. While you still can."

"This is my half of it. I promised I'd help you in exchange for your people helping Tyrone. He's better now. That means you've got to let me do my part. Besides, I'm not leaving you up here alone." She glanced around the empty plaza, knowing she should be wary and yet unable to find anything to be wary of. "I can't even see the place where the ground opened up last time," she admitted. "Has anything happened yet?"

Alasdair gave her a wry smile. "That all depends on which time period you're discussing. In the past quite a lot happened here. So far I just caught a glimpse of it. And you're wearing the diamond," he went on, his gaze focused on her jacket.

She nodded. "So you're just up here waiting? For what?"

Alasdair opened his hand and she saw the small, deadly obsidian knife, its grey-black blade translucent against his palm. "I was given this on my third initiation," he said.

"Who gave it to you?"

"The rocks. Or that's how it seemed at the time. At the end of the initiation when I'd been out in the mountain wilds for weeks, it was waiting for me, lying on top of a white granite boulder. No one in the Source Place could identify it when I brought it back. And all I could read of its history was that it had somehow been cleansed. It fit my hand perfectly and I became adept with it in a very short time, which was when I understood something else about it. Someone deliberately left it open."

"You're losing me," Lucinda said.

He touched her cheek briefly and smiled. "That's the one thing I don't want to do. What I mean is, when we read a stone we open the heart of the stone. It's something that happens quickly and when we withdraw our intent from the stone, it closes back up again. The obsidian in this knife was opened by someone who could read the stones, and that person left it open. I don't know how he or she did it. It's never occurred to me to do such a thing myself. But the stone was left open for a specific purpose—to be filled by whomever it belonged to." With a bemused look he hit the flat of the obsidian blade against his other palm. "The reason I could use this blade so easily and unerringly, the reason it's always felt like an extension of my own hand is because I filled it." He looked up her. "Do you see?"

"It was . . . possessed by you?" she translated uncertainly.

One of Alasdair's dark brows rose. "I wouldn't have chosen that term but it comes close. Yes, the owner of the knife sends his spirit into the open heart of the stone, and the obsidian becomes an extension of him. Today—" Alasdair's voice faltered slightly, but he continued. "Today I discovered that in the past the knife belonged to Sangeet, the shape-shifter we've been seeking. He used it for human sacrifices. And to scar himself of course."

Lucinda took an unconscious step away from the knife. "And it's still filled with him?"

"No. The mothers took him from it and cleansed it. I'm now fairly certain they were the ones who left it for me. And—" Alasdair's voice broke and for a second Lucinda thought his composure would break as well, but he recovered himself, saying, "I finally understand why it was given to me."

"To keep him from using it again?" she guessed.

Alasdair laughed mirthlessly. "Janna is proof that he's able to find other blades. No, it was given to me because he wants it back."

Lucinda thought she might be sick. "You're the bait."

"Essentially."

"And you're luring him to—?"

"That remains to be seen." She wanted to run to him, to fling her arms around him, but something in his eyes held her back. "Please go home, Lucinda. I don't want you here when he comes for it."

"No." Lucinda touched the diamond beneath her jacket. "You can't use this and I can."

"That may not be enough to protect you."

"I don't care. You asked me to use the diamond to help you."

"Then help me some other time, when this business with Sangeet is settled. I can do without it now."

"No," Lucinda said stubbornly. "I'm not going to let you face him alone."

"Lucinda, please. You have to go back—"

"A lover's quarrel? How bittersweet!" a familiar, mocking voice rang out. As he had before, Sebastian strode out of the alley, a smile of gleeful anticipation lighting his face.

"I didn't call you this time," Lucinda said, dread roiling through her.

"No," Sebastian agreed, "but I smelled him on you and I just had to see for myself if it was true. It is, isn't it? You're fucking the *cearu*."

"You told me you'd leave if I wanted you to," she said, her voice unsteady. "Well, I want you to leave right now."

"And miss the show?" Sebastian turned toward Alasdair. "Isn't it charming to watch her try to pretend she's a good person when she's always been a self-centered whore?"

"That's enough," Alasdair said.

Sebastian held up a hand, as if fending off an argument. "She just about has herself convinced—and maybe even you—but the truth is she's never given a damn for anyone or anything except her own looks, comforts, and lust. Especially her lust. Not to put too fine a point on it, she assumes every man wants to fuck her. That's how she gets her own. And to prove she has it, she has to fuck a lot of them. Anything less and she loses her identity. Do you start to see a pattern here?"

Alasdair was on his feet now but it was Lucinda's hand that connected with Sebastian's face. The sound of the blow rang through the plaza; the force of it reverberated through her arm. Lucinda's mind flashed back to slapping Carly, her hand slicing through air. Sebastian was real.

"And you're telling yourself you actually care for the *cearu*," he leered. The imprint of her hand reddened on his pale cheek. "Who do you think you're fooling? You're not capable of love. He's just another passing fashion."

"You're jealous," Lucinda said, seeing the truth. "You're jealous because I could never love you."

The fox glowed through Sebastian's blue eyes, territorial and scenting prey. "And you're lying to yourself again. Don't you think it's time you faced the truth? You don't deserve anything more than a trickster. We were meant for each other. We *belong* to each other. For the rest of your life I'm yours and you're mine."

"You couldn't be more wrong."

It occurred to her to wonder why Alasdair wasn't rushing to her defense. She risked a glance away from Sebastian and saw Alasdair staring at Vita. Dressed in an ankle-length wool cloak, Vita looked wind-burned and thinner than when Lucinda saw her last.

"I've been traveling through the mountains for five days now," Vita was saying to Alasdair.

"And why is that?" Alasdair asked, his voice polite and curiously remote.

His mother gave him an exasperated look. "Must I spell it out for you? Very well then. I came here to bring you back with me. You've done all you can in this city and you're in danger. This is no time to be heroic, Alasdair." She shot Lucinda a cursory glance. "The girl has Kama's diamond. You know it will protect her."

"Actually, I don't know what it will do," he pointed out.

"Then bring her with you." Lucinda thought this a rather grudging invitation. "Just leave this—" Vita glanced around "—place of hurt and come home to us."

"And why are you so determined to have me back?"

Vita moved toward him, one hand outstretched and as she did Alasdair touched the oblong crystal that he wore at his throat. A cloud of darkness, like the stone, shimmering greens and blues and purples wrapped itself around him and his mother, cloaking them completely. Lucinda gaped at the cloud, her jaw dropping.

"Let them work it out." Sebastian spun her back to face him. "I love you," he said. "I have from the day I first saw you."

"Stop it." She wrenched herself free and looked past him, desperately searching for Alasdair and Vita and seeing only the dark cloud. "Alasdair!" she screamed.

"He can't hear you now. It's an *oscuras,*" Sebastian said impatiently. "You can't penetrate it and it won't lift unless the *cearu* wills it. Or unless he's dying. Now back to what matters. I love you," he repeated. "There's nothing you can do to change that."

Lucinda blinked, unable to believe that after everything that had happened, Sebastian still wouldn't give up. She had to put an end to this now.

"You didn't treat me with love," she said as plainly as she could. "You drew me in and you manipulated me. So now if I can't change anything, it's because there's nothing to change. Except more of your lies. That's the thing with tricksters, isn't it? Eventually, you trick even yourselves."

He reached out and grabbed her wrist and that's when she saw it, the tourmaline on her wrist sparkling as if the diamond had lent it its own brilliance. Why hadn't she thought to look before?

"Oh, thank the gods," she said softly. "I hated it that Sebastian was turning out to be so deranged."

The phantasm Sebastian smiled at her. "Believe me, I can't do anything that he wouldn't do or at least contemplate. That's the way we're designed. We're called up from the very worst impulse, the ones most mortals—even tricksters—entertain yet never dare enact. I'm the worst of Sebastian but Sebastian to the core."

Still, one thing didn't make sense. "But I touched you and you're—"

"A more solidly constructed phantasm than others? Some of us do have substance, you know."

Lucinda's mind was racing. She no longer had the chalcedony cat, but she figured it couldn't hurt to try the words anyway. "In the name of Kali-Ma, I sever you from what gave you life and . . ." What was the rest of it?

"Chocolate milk?" the phantasm suggested irreverently. "I'd be devastated if you separated me from my chocolate milk." His eyes seemed to narrow and she saw the fox, sly and ravenous, flickering in their depths. "You really think you can appropriate Averill's strength without help? You wouldn't even know where to start when it comes to calling on her sort of power."

"You're right," Lucinda admitted, ordering herself not to panic. There had to be something she could use against the phantasm. She looked at him curiously. "So what do you want? To hurt me?"

He seemed surprised by that. "No. Even the worst in Sebastian never wanted to harm you. I just want you back in my arms."

He reached a hand out to her, tentatively this time, and she took his hand and pressed his fingertips against her throat, just under her jaw, at the pulse point where Sebastian had touched her that night in his loft. She saw Sebastian's desire come into his eyes. Still holding his hand, she slowly unbuttoned the top button of her jacket, watched a smile begin at the corners of his mouth, then pressed his palm firmly against the turquoise choker.

He jumped back from her with a cry, shaking his hand as though he'd been scalded. "You deceptive bitch—"

"Right. I forgot. Only tricksters are allowed to play the tricks. They're very poor sports when anyone else turns the tables."

The phantasm stared at his hand. Ugly red blisters were rising across the palm.

"I'm impressed," she said. "You're much more realistic than Carly was. You even blister."

"I'm vulnerable to you because Sebastian is vulnerable to you," he muttered, cradling his burned hand. Then he looked up at her and smiled, and in that instant she knew she'd underestimated him. "And like Sebastian," he went on more calmly, "I know a thing or two about the stones. The old stories say turquoise stole its color from the sky. And like attracts like, you know, one of those universal rules. Those who steal open themselves to other thieves. So thief to thieves, I bid them come to me."

He held out his uninjured hand, and Lucinda felt the necklace of turquoise beads open and slip from her neck. It slid beneath her jacket, by-passed the diamond necklace, and landed with a soft clatter at the mosaic at her feet. She lunged for the necklace but it now had a snake's movement and speed. It slithered across the broken bits of stone to the phantasm's feet. Reaching into a pocket of Sebastian's jacket, the phantasm grabbed a ban-dana, used it to pick up the turquoise necklace, and stuffed it back into the pocket.

"That's better," he said. "Now there's nothing to stand between us."

ALASDAIR RELAXED A fraction as he realized the *oscuras* was holding. Whatever happened next, Lucinda would not get caught in it. He sent a quick prayer to the mothers to watch over her then turned to face the figure that claimed to be his mother. "Who sent you?" he asked it.

"Oh Alasdair," she said, her voice perfectly mimicking Vita's tone. "No one had to send me. I told you I wouldn't let you come here unprotected."

"You also wouldn't so much as leave your bedroom without wearing pro-tective stones of your own," he said. "But interestingly you've journeyed—what was it, five days through the mountains?—without your gems. No earrings, no necklaces, no rings. Why is that?"

Vita drew herself up with unself-conscious dignity. It was, Alasdair saw with a tug of sadness, a gesture that was perfectly characteristic of her. This imposter might be the last image he would have of his mother. Perhaps he ought to be appreciative of the attentiveness to details.

The *oscuras* glimmered around her slight figure, an ever-changing cur-tain of dark, colored light. If she noticed it, she didn't remark on it. "I saw a vision of you in the crystal, Alasdair. You were in terrible danger. I didn't stop to worry about what I was wearing. I came straightaway."

He didn't answer, lost in thoughts of how infuriating his mother could be and how powerful the ties between them remained, how it was impossible to look at this pretender without a surge of tenderness for the true Vita. Did Sangeet actually believe that this chimera would fool him? Perhaps he didn't. Perhaps Sangeet was just buying time—or using this as a distraction from whatever was going on between Sebastian and Lucinda.

Alasdair addressed the vision for the last time. "You're not Vita. You're a phantasm created by a Sinpiedras, by someone who couldn't give you any-thing even resembling Vita's gems. So where is he?"

"Alasdair—" she pleaded.

He turned away from her, meaning to dissolve the *oscuras,* and that was when he saw him. Sangeet sat inside the very edge of the curtain of dark light, golden eyes watching Alasdair. He was squatting, bare feet flat on the ground, chest bare, thin, sinewy arms hugging his knees. Every inch of his skin was scarred with the pattern of hatchmarks, and yet he had a kind of beauty. Fine features, the glossy deep-red hair; though he was generations older than Alasdair, it was still possible to see the boy in his face. He looked more mendicant than threat, except for his eyes. They were glittering, burning with fever or madness or both.

"*Tk, tk aaa tk, tk, tk, a tk, a tk, a tk, tk, tk aaa . . .*" So quiet that it was barely audible, a rhythm came from the back of the shape-shifter's throat. Though it was a different sort of sound entirely, it made Alasdair think of a rattler's warning. Alasdair felt his life stones stirring, each of them sending up its own protections to shield him. He reached for the amethyst bear amulet and then let it go, deciding to save it for a measure of last resort. The Vita phantasm, he noticed, had vanished.

"You—" Sangeet spoke, his voice reed-thin and yet melodic. "You have my knife."

"The mothers gave it to me," Alasdair told him.

Sangeet nodded. "I've looked for it. Looked for you. Nothing cuts like my knife."

"I believe that. Where did you first get it?" Alasdair asked. He knew he was taking a risk, but he couldn't help being fascinated by the shape-shifter, wondering if he was in as dreadful shape as it seemed or if this was another ruse.

Remaining in the squat, Sangeet clapped his hands together then spread them wide, like a child playing a clapping game. "I went to your people. One of them carved it for me. Another opened the stone for me."

"Who?" Alasdair asked. If someone in the Source Place had actually aided Sangeet, he had to warn Vita. "Who opened the obsidian for you?"

Sangeet clapped his hands shut again, and Alasdair felt the sound reverberating in his bones. "Can't tell." He tilted his head to one side, the movement fox-like and disarmingly innocent. "Will you show me the knife?"

"It's different now," Alasdair said. "Before the mothers gave it to me, they cleansed it. I think they were giving you another chance—to live without it. So it no longer contains what you put into it."

Sangeet was making the soft, disturbing rhythmic sound again, and Alasdair knew he couldn't play this out much longer. He wasn't getting any information from him.

"I—" The shape-shifter's voice was breathy and labored. "I need my knife. It contains me. *This* is my chance." He nodded, encouragingly, as if he were explaining something that Alasdair would understand. "I bound it to bloodshed. Forever. Wholeness."

Alasdair blinked, wondering if he should even try to make sense of that.

Sangeet got to his feet, the movement so quick that Alasdair barely caught it. He was tall and terribly thin. Alasdair saw pain in his amber eyes and also a fox peering through them, wasting and ravenous.

"My knife. It has thirsts." The shape-shifter's voice was breaking now, the words alternating between the melodic human tones and high-pitched fox's yelps. He touched his scarred chest. "I put them there. And you felt them."

"You're ill," Alasdair said, hoping to divert him. "You need help."

Sangeet wouldn't be diverted. "Even you, a *cearu,* gave it what it thirsted for. Even you fed it blood."

Holding an outstretched hand toward Alasdair, Sangeet sang out a long, sweet, melancholy note, and Alasdair felt the obsidian knife leave the folds of his robe and slide through the darkened air to the shape-shifter's outstretched hand.

Alasdair sent a silent call to the obsidian and another to the goddess Pele who had formed it, and then he used everything he knew about rock to destroy the knife. He asked all that was locked and hardened and harnessed in the obsidian to soften and flow, to return to its source. He called for the cooled vitreous lava to return to Pele's liquid fire, and failing that—

Sangeet gave a wild, disbelieving cry as the knife shattered on his open palm. Tiny shards of smoky-black obsididan leapt to the mosaic floor and lay glimmering in the light of the *oscuras*. The shape-shifter dropped to the ground with a keening sound, his scarred hands running over the bits of broken glass and becoming newly bloodied as he gathered them up.

Alasdair couldn't move for a moment. He felt like a man who has unforgivably struck a loved one. He'd destroyed stone. It had hurt him to take it apart, especially because the knife had saved him. Not only from Noelle but from attackers who'd found him sleeping alone in the desert and others who set upon him when he was traveling. Once, when he'd gone two weeks without anything solid to eat, the knife brought down a rabbit for him. It was because of the knife that he was now alive.

Sangeet cried out again and dropped the obsidian shards. They were glowing red, molten. Pele had answered Alasdair's call. Alasdair sent his thanks to the goddess as each bit of obsidian became liquid again. Sangeet crouched low, rocking back and forth, grieving for the knife as a mother might grieve for a dying child. Alasdair could see the web of energy that surrounded the shape-shifter; it was broken now, with gaping holes. It was the part of Sangeet's spirit that he'd bound to the knife.

Alasdair stood watching the shape-shifter, knowing he should strike.

This was why he'd been given the knife all those years ago, to lead him to this moment when Sangeet knelt before him, vulnerable. All this had been set in motion by the mothers so that he might put an end to some of the harm being done in this world. And yet he hesitated.

Maybe it *was* the knife that made him a killer, Alasdair reflected, because without it all that circled through him now was the great truth that had shaped his life since his first initiation, since he first understood the term *cearu: You are here to care for others, as the stones have always cared for you. You are here to care for others . . . you are here to care. . . .*

Sangeet moved so quickly that his form blurred, springing from the mosaic floor into the air, hurling himself at Alasdair. Alasdair tried to move out of range but wasn't nearly fast enough. The shape-shifter landed on him, knees clamping around Alasdair's ribs, clutching him with tensile strength. Sangeet raised a bronze dagger high overhead. His other hand circled Alasdair's throat and squeezed. Alasdair could feel the long fingers digging in, cutting off his wind, slowing the flow of blood to his brain. And the hand holding the dagger arced up and plunged down.

The instinct to survive overrode everything else. Without thinking, Alasdair reached down, grabbed Sangeet's balls and twisted, and as he did hundreds of needle-fine slivers of black tourmaline appeared in the *oscuras* and flew at the shape-shifter, embedding themselves in his emaciated body. Sangeet released Alasdair with an outraged cry and fell to the ground, desperate to pull one of the tourmaline needles from his eye. Alasdair watched appalled as Sangeet rolled away from him, howling in pain. He hadn't called the tourmaline, hadn't even consciously known it could be used that way, but something in him had summoned it.

Wild with pain, Sangeet frantically tried to pull out the tourmaline needles. Alasdair stood, trying not to feel pity, trying to summon the will to end him. The shape-shifter gave another anguished cry. He seemed more wounded animal than man. Then he stopped fighting and went absolutely still, as if calming himself. He struggled to a kneeling position. Head bent, he began to sing.

From deep inside, the shape-shifter's body began to ripple. It was a subtle movement, like gentle waves rolling beneath the scarred skin. Gradually, Alasdair saw, the waves were easing the tourmaline needles out from beneath the skin. Sangeet was healing himself.

Swiftly, Alasdair sent a prayer to the mothers. "Let your will be my will," he entreated them, moving toward the shape-shifter, knowing he had to get the bronze dagger away from him. He focused on Sangeet; it was only on the periphery of consciousness that he sensed the *oscuras* falling away and sunlight pouring down on them both. There was no help for that. He couldn't waste energy maintaining it now. Out of the corner of his eye he saw Lucinda exchanging angry words with Sebastian. Not a comforting sight but she seemed to holding her own. Lucinda . . . he wanted to survive this.

Sangeet remained kneeling, as if unaware of anyone else. Alasdair didn't believe that for a second, and wondered whether he should summon the tourmaline again. At that moment Sangeet's song changed, became high and discordant and piercing, and Alasdair doubled over in a blaze of agony. His mind reverberating with pain, he could no longer sift reality from illusion. So it might be true what he felt: His tendons were being stripped from his bones.

SEBASTIAN'S PHANTASM MOVED toward Lucinda with the air of the inevitable. He was the fate that couldn't be escaped. Like Sebastian, he walked soundlessly.

Not daring to take her eyes off him, she backed up until she felt the cool, rounded surface of one of the pillars behind her. Then Alasdair cried out and she forgot all about the phantasm. The dark light that had enveloped him was gone. He and Sangeet were still on the plaza. Sangeet, seeming frail and ill, with what looked like black needles sticking out of him, knelt on the ground, incongruously, singing. Alasdair lay a short distance away, crumpled in on himself, writhing in pain.

Lucinda started toward him but Alasdair, seeing her, called out in a broken voice, "No. Don't come any closer. Please."

Sangeet lifted his head, gave Alasdair a mild look, and sang a high, clear, bell-like note, and Alasdair convulsed with a scream.

Instinctively, Lucinda tore open her jacket and held up the diamond pendant. The stone drew in the sunlight that filtered down to the plaza and threw a spectrum of color across the ground.

The phantasm jerked her around and Lucinda struck him again, furious. Again his cheek reddened, but this time he didn't let go of her. "Kama's diamond," he observed. "Pity you don't know how to use it."

Somehow through her red blaze of fury came words she remembered from the night in Vita's study: " . . . *works against enchantment and sorcery . . . protects against fascination . . .* " Silently, she asked the diamond to do just that, to banish the grinning phantasm that held her.

Nothing happened.

"It's not that easy," the phantasm taunted her. "Clearly, Alasdair hasn't taught you the first thing about working with stones. Did you think that you just tell a stone to do something and it obeys? They're not slaves."

"Go to hell." She jerked free of his grasp and turned back to Alasdair, Alasdair who was being tortured, Alasdair whom she loved. Another possibility for invoking the diamond's power occurred to her. It might be as ineffective as simply asking the stone to work but she had nothing to lose.

She forced herself to push aside her fear and panic, imagining the light of the diamond dispelling her terror. That helped a little but seemed more her own mind than anything emanating from the stone.

She concentrated on the source of the diamond, on Kama. She made herself remember what it had been like the night before when she felt Kama streaming through Alasdair and streaming through her own body, and the sense of wide-open generosity that had held them both. Eros, she thought. She'd known so little of him when she assumed he was just about sex. What she knew now was that Eros was about letting yourself love another life, about loving life itself. Willingly, she opened herself to the god, to his power to connect and join. She felt her heart opening like a flower to the sun. She felt herself laid open to love of this world and all the joy and pain that carried.

Lucinda started as something unexpected came to her: the love that both Kama and Alasdair bore for the stones. She could feel it pulsing inside the diamond: the way they both delighted in the stones' beauty and strength, listened for their stories, handled them with empathy and respect, tenderness and humor. She understood why the stones came alive for them, wanting to be read, reveling in being understood. She used to think Alasdair had some sort of X-ray vision that allowed him to see inside them. Now she understood it as an exchange.

She felt Kama's bright energy moving inside her, rising from the base of her spine through womb and belly, filling heart and throat, streaming out the crown of her head and yet continuing to fill her. Everything in her felt awake and connected and open to the stones. In the next moment the exhilaration of Kama's energy moving through her was replaced with a sense of desolation as she suddenly, overwhelmingly became aware that the stones that surrounded her were empty, stripped of sense and memory.

What she had to do was clear. Knowing she could guide it, Lucinda sent all of Kama's energy that was pouring through her body into the diamond. "Give it back to them," she told it. "Give them Kama's light." She felt a gladness stirring deep in the diamond's ancient heart. It gathered Kama's light into itself, intensifying and infusing it with its own beauty and strength, then it sent all of that pure radiance back into the empty stones of the plaza. The colors of the spectrum flashed through the diamond and played on the broken shards. Malachite and carnelian, lapis, coral, and turquoise, they drank in Kama's light, took in his vibrant life force and let it renew the life inside them. The ancient memories that defined them reverberated through them; the mosaic became whole again, a carpet of gems. Lucinda focused the diamond on the black granite columns, and they began to gleam with dark beauty, to stretch toward the sky. The courtyard was trembling. The mosaic beneath her feet, the columns that surrounded them, life was pouring back into all of it, and she knew that a temple had once stood there, understood that this had always been a sacred place.

"You're a quick study," Sebastian's phantasm said.

His voice snapped her out of the trance of light. She could still feel the life in the stones. She could also feel the life draining out of Alasdair. Kama's light left her and fear and dread replaced it. She ran to Alasdair, barely registering the odd, relentless melody that was coming from the shape-shifter.

Alasdair lay on the mosaic, writhing in pain. Lucinda knelt beside him, put a hand on his shoulder. "What's he done to you?"

"He uses sound vibrations. Specific to my body. To take me apart."

"I'm going to take you home now," she said, making an instantaneous decision. "I need you to try to stand up. We've done what we came here to do. Come on, the stones will help you." She had no idea of whether those last two sentences were true; she hoped, though, that Alasdair would believe them.

"Wrong again." Sebastian's phantasm was moving toward her. "Or do you think an emerald wheelchair is suddenly going to spring up to cart him back to your flat? You can't just make this stuff up, you know. It doesn't work that way."

Lucinda edged away from him.

"I know I told you Sebastian wouldn't hurt you," he said smoothly. "But I'm Sangeet's creation and so I have considerably less discretion." He reached for her again, but she ducked low, stepping out of his grasp. It didn't faze him. The phantasm continued to advance on her, his voice patient and fond. "Come on, we can't play cat and mouse here forever. Just be a good girl and stop fighting me. You can't win, you know."

The words from the lapidarium returned to her. "... *works against enchantment and sorcery ... protects against fascination.*" And this time she sent them as a question into the open heart of Kama's diamond, silently asking, *Can you do this? If this is in your power, will you use it to help us?*

She held up the clear, rectangular stone and let the diamond's refracted light hit the phantasm. A streak of banded rainbow light—deep orange, yellow, green, and blue—played along the phantasm's hand and an odd, disbelieving expression filled Sebastian's eyes. "You're not supposed to have that kind of power," he told her. Lucinda watched in amazement as Sebastian's features and body attenuated and lightened. The phantasm was fading. Within moments what was left of his image had become transparent, like a filmy bit of nylon floating on the air.

"Oh, thank you," she murmured to the diamond. She turned back to Alasdair and was relieved to find that he was no longer writhing. "You're better," she said.

Alasdair opened his eyes, and she saw a trace of the expression he'd had in Vita's library, a kind of intellectual fascination with the nature of rock. "You returned life to the stones." He could barely speak but pushed on. "That's what Kama's diamond was meant for."

Lucinda blinked back tears. "I'm such an idiot. That could have waited. I should have been helping you. Come on, we're getting out of here now." She grasped Alasdair beneath his arms and began to pull him up. His eyes drifted closed again. His body was heavy and inert. It was like trying to lift a sack of wet cement.

"You have to help me here," she pleaded with him. "Even if you can't stand . . . can you at least sit up?"

"Leave him." She'd forgotten the shape-shifter. Now he was on his feet, tall and gossamer-thin, grotesque and weirdly beautiful, with something still innocent in his scarred face. The black needles seemed to have fallen out. "He's dying." His voice was high-pitched, somewhere between human and fox, overlaid with a weird buzzing.

"What do you want?" she asked.

"He destroyed mine." His amber eyes darkened as he started toward them. He crossed the plaza slowly, fighting for each step, as if he'd been crippled. He started to sing again, and Lucinda felt blinding pain rip through her. Stumbling, she fought through the pain to hold the diamond up a third time. Wasn't it also supposed to heal the insane?

The clear stone flashed in the sun and Sangeet's voice broke then went silent. Lucinda drew a deep breath. The pain was receding and disbelief flickered in the shape-shifter's eyes. He opened and closed his mouth soundlessly, like a landed fish gasping for oxygen.

Lucinda crouched over Alasdair's inert form. How long did they have before Sangeet recovered his voice? Could she possibly get him out of here before then?

A look of horror came over Alasdair's face. "Don't let him—"

The shape-shifter was kneeling now, drawing a bronze dagger across his own arm, slicing open scarred skin, seeming mesmerized by the blood that flowed.

"When he cuts himself—" Alasdair began. Then something spun end over end through the air, and Lucinda cried out as a burning sensation streaked through her left arm, the pain blazing up through her shoulder and down through her fingertips. The hilt of a bronze dagger was sticking out of the arm of her suede jacket, its blade embedded deep in her biceps. For a second she thought she might throw up, then frantically she began to pull on the hilt of the knife. It was stuck. And her arm felt like it was on fire.

For a long, horrifying moment Lucinda gave in to paralysis. She couldn't think, didn't know what to do, didn't even know what to be most afraid of: the searing pain and the blood streaming down her arm—she had to get that fucking blade out and stop the bleeding; or Alasdair, lying senseless, possibly dying, at her feet; or the shape-shifter, lips peeled back to reveal a fox's canine teeth. "Oh, gods, what do I do?" she murmured. "Please," she prayed to any deity who might listen. "Don't let him die. I'll never ask for anything again. Just let him live."

"Lucinda." Alasdair's voice was frighteningly weak but his eyes were open. She knelt beside him, running the hand that wasn't washed with blood gently through his hair. *This is what I have to do,* she thought wildly. *I have to just be with him now. The rest doesn't matter.*

"Hand," Alasdair whispered. At first she thought he meant her bloody one, but then she realized he was holding one of his hands out to her. She took it, pressing palm to palm, and felt something hard between them. It was a flat, dark purple hexagonal amethyst carved with the sign of a bear.

"What do I do with it?" she asked.

He didn't answer but she felt something similar to Kama's energy streaming through her, only this time it was Alasdair's. Grief wracked her as she understood. The things he was giving her now—his strength, his understanding, even the remnants of his power—they were all things his body could no longer use.

"No," she said, choking back a sob. "I won't take anything from you."

"Use them," he urged her. His words seemed to be coming a little easier. "Use them now. I don't know how much longer I can last. First, get that dagger out of you."

Feeling a surge of Alasdair's strength inside her, she grasped the handle of the bronze dagger. She pulled hard, and this time it came out with one sickening tug. She gagged for a moment and fought not to black out. Managing to stay upright, she took off her jacket, used the bloodied blade to rip a strip of cloth from her top, and clumsily bandaged the cut. Her arm still burned but the pain was no longer consuming.

Getting to her feet, she faced Sangeet, the amethyst amulet clenched in her fist. She could now see a web of dark light around the shape-shifter. The web was broken and yet trying to re-form, to keep its integrity. His body too weak to shift, he had no access to the fox; but she understood that didn't make him any less dangerous. His voice was coming back. He hummed a broken, discordant snatch of notes, and the web of dark light around him billowed, some of the broken areas weaving odd, shapeless patches, mending itself. He was getting stronger.

Lucinda felt no fear, only repulsion mixed with an odd sense of sadness for the shape-shifter. That was Alasdair's, of course. Only Alasdair could find room to understand the monster who was even now, killing him. The shape-shifter, she saw, was being consumed by a hunger he'd tried to sate with his own blood and the blood of others. The hunger was with him day and night. It never ceased. It clawed at him, burned inside him because, of course, it couldn't be sated with blood. He'd been mistaken from the first, had refused to consider any other way. And so for generations now he'd hungered in pain and fury. Lucinda didn't fight any of this. She let herself feel compassion for Sangeet and as she did, Alasdair's energy streamed into her even more strongly. Mixed with the compassion she felt a cool, unyielding resolve. She glanced down at him to be sure. Alasdair nodded, and she didn't question it again.

She opened her hand, holding out the amethyst amulet, watching the sunlight glint on the carving of the bear.

Sangeet was watching, too, his eyes bright with fascination. "Give me that," he said. "Trade. His life for the purple rock."

She felt Alasdair inside her: *Don't bargain with him. Ever. Use the amulet now!*

Lucinda quieted her own doubts, waiting for some sense of how she was supposed to invoke the power of the amulet. Sangeet held out his hand, and the bloodied dagger that she'd pulled out of her arm returned to him. Why hadn't she thought to hold onto it? She and Alasdair would both die here, of her stupidity. She saw Sangeet reaching back to throw the bronze dagger, and as he did another kind of energy rippled through the plaza. She'd given life back to the stones, and now they were sending their strength into the amulet. Malachite, turquoise, lapis, coral, and carnelian, and Kama's blazing diamond, they were all calling on the amethyst to open, calling on its power to awaken.

Lucinda could feel the amethyst growing warm. And she felt the black granite pillars adding their energy to the call, sending their strength directly into the small purple hexagon. It stirred on her palm, stirred again. Lucinda had a weird memory of being a kid on Christmas morning, waiting for one of those Christmas balls to open and spill out the little presents inside. The memory of Christmas faded as the scent of wild fennel surrounded her, bringing with it a vision that lasted no more than a heartbeat but a vision she recognized nonetheless, the soaring granite peaks of the Source Place.

The amulet split into two neat halves, and an immense dark shadow with the shape of a bear materialized directly in front of the shape-shifter. The knife dropped from Sangeet's hand. Lucinda stared, not sure what it was she was looking at. It wasn't a real bear. It was a shadow. And it was a great deal more than that. It was born from the mountains in the Source Place, she was sure of it. It contained all of the wildness of that place and all its fierce magic. The bear padded toward Sangeet, the great arc of its shoulders towering over the granite columns. Sangeet backed away from the shadow, looking frightened and small.

The shadow bear attacked with blinding speed, claws lashing out. To Lucinda's astonishment, Sangeet managed to dodge it. Eyes glittering, he intoned an odd, almost funereal, chant. Lucinda could sense the black granite columns trembling with the rhythm of the chant. He was going to bring the pillars crashing down on them, she was sure of it. Sangeet was standing upright now, the chant was growing stronger, and Lucinda had a terrible feeling that he was somehow winning. He added a higher refrain to the chant and Alasdair cried out, writhing in agony. Sangeet turned to him, fixed him with an eerily benevolent smile and said, "Because you took my knife." As the shape-shifter gazed at Alasdair the bear struck again, its claws ripping into his throat, tearing out a chunk of flesh that left the white knobs of his cervical vertebrae exposed. Sangeet struggled to fight, and perhaps he attempted some magic of his own, but this time he had no chance to heal himself. The bear knocked him to the ground. Another swipe of its claws opened his stomach, ripped out his guts. Lucinda couldn't watch as the shadow creature opened its massive jaws and began to feast.

She ran back to where Alasdair lay on his back, eyes shut. She didn't see blood or wounds, but his pulse was so faint she knew he couldn't last long. She sat beside him, gently resting his head against her thigh. "Tell me what to do," she pleaded. "Tell me which stones to use to heal you."

"You can't." His voice was more breath than sound.

She called on Kama again and on her own love, and sent it through the diamond. She could see the colored bands of light streaming into Alasdair.

He gave her the faintest smile. "Thank you," he said. "A gift for the journey."

"You're not going anywhere," she told him. She cast about with her mind, asking the stones which ones could help her. And she felt them responding—the coral, the carnelian, the malachite, the lapis, the turquoise, the citrine, and Alasdair's own life stones. Other gems appeared in the plaza. Citrines, garnets and white quartz, fluorite crystals and amber beads nestled in the folds of his robes. Emeralds and amethysts, pearls and iolites, aquamarines and peridots, opals, and smooth rounds of moonstones arrayed themselves around him in a ring of gleaming color. Rubies and sapphires, topaz and tourmalines, chrysoberyls and rose quartz settled on his chest, arms, legs, throat. Lucinda felt all of them sending him strength and protection. Alasdair, though, wasn't responding. Lucinda could still feel him inside her but what was there was very quiet, gradually shutting down.

Tears streaked her face. She'd used the diamond, and she'd even used the amethyst amulet, and now it seemed every stone in the city was doing its best to heal him, and none of it was enough. Alasdair lay there, dying. She touched his face, pushing back strands of dark hair. His skin was already cool. The color was draining from his skin.

"You can't die now. I won't let you," she said stubbornly.

"No choice," he told her.

She felt a shift in the stones as they aligned themselves slightly differently. Now they were no longer trying to heal him. Instead they were sending him their thanks and their love. "Surrounded by friends," he said, sounding content. One of his hands reached for hers but didn't have enough strength to reach that far. She took his hand, holding it fiercely, as if by holding it she could pour life back into him.

"It's all right, Lucinda."

But it wasn't. All she could do was huddle over his body, whispering endearments, loving him completely for the few minutes that were left to them.

SEBASTIAN FOUND HER there as the sun was setting, still holding Alasdair's body. She hadn't moved, though the gemstones that appeared in his final moments had all dispersed. The bear shadow, having devoured most of Sangeet, had inclined its great head toward Alasdair in a gesture that struck her oddly as the amulet's spirit paying its respects. Then it had ambled off toward the mountains.

"Oh, Goddess," Sebastian murmured. She noticed, irrelevantly, that the phantasm hadn't been wearing the smoky quartz necklace; the real Sebastian was. He knelt beside her, his eyes going to the grisly remains of the shape-shifter, a few feet away.

"You or Alasdair?"

"Both." She didn't even recognize the hoarse, croaking voice that came out of her. "Sort of. A bear amulet."

"And Sangeet killed Alasdair?"

She nodded brokenly.

"I'm sorry, Lucinda."

"Are you?" She looked at him and saw that he was sorry, if not for Alasdair, for her. What had the phantasm said? That there was nothing in Sebastian that wanted to harm her. She believed that now but found no comfort in it.

"I thought I could stop him," he said.

"Alasdair?"

He shook his head. "Sangeet. He was another fox. I thought I could trick him, beat him at his own game."

"You got Janna away from him."

"After nearly handing her over. I—" He shook his head, seeming baffled. "I underestimated him. Or overestimated me. I'm sorry."

"I was right here," she said, disbelief beginning to set in. "Alasdair was dying and I had Kama's diamond, all his power streaming right through it. And what did I do? I gave memory back to the stones. You'd think that could have waited ten minutes."

"It wasn't in error and it wasn't in vain. You finished Alasdair's work, for which the mothers are grateful." Lucinda's head jerked up at the sound of the god's deep voice. Hermes, all shimmering quicksilver, was kneeling on the other side of Alasdair.

Sebastian's eyes widened with fear as he saw the god, and he fell prostrate on the ground. "Forgive me, Lord," Sebastian murmured.

Hermes gazed at him dispassionately. "Your hubris knows no bounds. You thought you could out-trick Sangeet. You saw what he was and you treated it like another one of your games."

"I know, and I know I was wrong." Lucinda heard a note of shame in Sebastian's voice that she'd never thought him capable of. "Let me atone for it. Please, give me that chance."

"You, who've abused so many gifts, dare ask for more?"

"Only—"

"I have nothing to give you." Hermes cut him off. "Get up." Sebastian got slowly, hesitantly, to his feet, his eyes downcast. "Leave us," Hermes said. "You don't have the right to grieve for him."

Sebastian sent Lucinda a complex look that she was too worn to begin to interpret. She could only return a blank gaze. She felt nothing as he left the plaza.

"That one may yet be a friend to you," Hermes said with obvious distaste, "but do not be too quick to give him your trust."

Grief clamped itself around her heart as she realized why Hermes was there. "You've come for Alasdair."

"Yes."

"Not yet. I—" she began, then swallowed the rest of her protest. A glimmer of rationale in her benumbed brain knew she couldn't fight the god and knew she couldn't continue to sit there clasping Alasdair's corpse. And yet she couldn't bear the thought of losing all that she had left of him.

Wanting just a little more time, she changed the subject, inclining her head toward what was left of Sangeet. "Will you take him, too?"

Hermes didn't even spare him a glance. "He doesn't interest me. Someone else will come for him. Perhaps Sekhmet will appreciate his remains."

"And you'll take Alasdair." She knew fairness was beside the point and yet she couldn't help feeling it was savagely unfair. Just when they'd opened to each other, he'd been taken from her. "Why couldn't Alasdair have lived?" she asked, unable to stop herself. "I prayed to the gods. Why couldn't you save his life?"

Hermes's voice was gentle. "His body was so badly hurt, he couldn't recover. The only thing I can tell you is that he wasn't cut off before his time."

"What does that mean?"

"Alasdair had topaz among his life stones," he told her.

"Topaz." Her brain wasn't working. ". . . Glows in the dark?"

"Sometimes," Hermes said. "It's a fire stone, a healing stone, and a powerful protection against untimely death. Alasdair lived out his allotted days. It was his time, Lucinda."

Her eyes were dry as she pulled Alasdair to her for a last embrace. Where was he now, she wondered. Was his spirit still there in the plaza, hovering above them? Or was it already far away, embarked on that final journey, just waiting for Hermes to catch up with him? All she really knew was that earlier in this very day Alasdair had been alive and inside her. Now he was dead and she was empty.

"I have to take him," Hermes said. "But see, I've brought another mourner to grieve with you." He opened his hand. The dragon sat there, its small body trembling. Slowly, the god lowered his hand and the dragon stepped onto Alasdair's shoulder.

Lucinda gasped a little as a fresh wave of pain and regret surged through her. "He was guarding Tyrone when he should have been with Alasdair. He'll never forgive himself—or me."

"Tyrone had more need of protection than Alasdair," Hermes told her. "In any case, the dragon did what Alasdair asked of him."

The dragon was nuzzling Alasdair's face with its snout, as if it might nudge him awake. Lucinda closed her eyes, unable to bear the tiny creature's grief. Then, feeling ashamed, she opened them and let herself weep for them all.

"It's time," said Hermes.

"You won't let him be afraid of whatever comes?"

"In life, Alasdair gave fear short shrift. In death, his spirit won't be that different. And I'll accompany him as far as I may," Hermes assured her. "We're old friends, after all."

"And Vita?"

"I'll tell her. She already senses he's gone, though not how."

Lucinda watched as Hermes gathered Alasdair into his arms. He held him easily, as if Alasdair weighed nothing at all. The dragon still clung to Alasdair's robe.

"Dragon?" Lucinda said. She held a hand out to him. For an endless moment the dragon didn't move, and she thought he might accompany Alasdair's body to the Underworld, but at last the dragon stepped onto her outstretched hand. Slowly, almost painfully, he made his way up her arm to her collarbone and pressed his trembling head against her neck.

Twenty-one

ALASDAIR HAD BEEN dead for three weeks on the morning that Tyrone came to breakfast at Lucinda's flat. Lucinda had not attempted to go to work during that time. The first few days she'd careened from grief to shock to a jagged pain that felt like a hot iron, searing her nerve endings and burning through what was left of her heart. By comparison, the pain from the knife wound was negligible. And none of it seemed to affect what she'd begun to think of as the invisible inner tendrils that had connected her to Alasdair. It seemed another cruel joke that she'd only become aware of them after his death. Now they were as real and self-evident as her hands. She could feel them nights when she lay down to sleep and in the mornings when she woke. In every hollow of her body the tendrils reached for him and were left bewildered and aching when he couldn't be found. When, she wondered, had those tendrils come alive—when she and Alasdair became lovers or during those moments in the plaza when she'd felt his spirit inside her? Or had something in her reached toward him from the very first moment they met?

She found her greatest need was to be still. Though she did manage several phone calls with Tyrone and one with her mother, she had little need to talk with anyone and no interest in work. What was the point anyway? Tyrone was in the process of closing down Dessalines Productions, spending his days either in meetings with his lawyer or reviewing sheaves of legal documents. She'd been glad he was preoccupied. She couldn't have borne him fussing over her. A few times she tried going to her books of poetry for comfort, and though some of the poets wrote eloquently and truthfully of loss, none came close to the grief that held her. She felt as if it were scouring her of everything but those damned tendrils.

She couldn't bear to look at the stones. They reminded her too much of Alasdair, and she still couldn't separate the memories of Alasdair from the memory of his death. She tucked the diamond necklace away in the safest place she could find, sure that one day Kama would want it back. The garnet she dropped into a cup, which she put high on a shelf along with the tourmaline bracelet and the moonstone in its cloisonné box. She couldn't even bring herself to wear her own jewelry.

The dragon stayed with her through those three weeks. He, too, spent hours being very still. Only the rise and fall of his chest gave any sign that he was more than an expertly carved piece of jade. Something had gone out of him, too, with Alasdair's death. And though Lucinda was too shell-shocked to worry about herself, she worried about the dragon. It was partly why she'd agreed to let Tyrone come for breakfast. She thought the dragon needed distraction.

The dragon did, in fact, look marginally livelier when Tyrone walked into the flat, embraced Lucinda, and held out a hand to him saying, "Get over here. I've actually missed you, you green bug."

The dragon flew onto Tyrone's hand, and Tyrone stroked its head while watching Lucinda with concern. "You seem to be moving that arm all right now."

"It's almost healed." She set the fruit salad she'd made on the wooden kitchen table. She gave the dragon his own blueberry in a tiny saucer designed to hold tea bags.

"No widow's weeds?" Tyrone asked gently.

She was dressed in white painter's pants and a worn blue denim shirt, sleeves rolled to her elbows. That was another thing that had gone in the last weeks: She no longer cared what she wore. She glanced down at herself, bemused. "I haven't done wash in weeks. This was what was in my closet."

"I guess that counts as widow's weeds."

"Maybe. It wasn't a deliberate choice."

Tyrone took a seat at the table. "You made *any* choices lately?"

"Yes," she told him smugly. "I chose to invite you to breakfast. Now don't make me regret it. Eat your fruit salad."

Tyrone obediently ate several bites of the salad, then said, "You haven't been out much lately, have you?"

"You know I haven't."

"You ought to give it a try. It's different out there now. The city doesn't feel half so crazed. People stopped seeing all those hallucinations. And of course, they've stopped finding gems, too. So there isn't that gambler's edge of hope on every corner, but that's all right. Things are settling down."

"I guess that's good," Lucinda said. She made an effort to sound interested. "Have the gods up and left, too?"

"I never said the city was sane." Tyrone let himself be momentarily distracted by the dragon strolling along his outstretched finger. "The gods and their ever-multiplying shrines are still with us. Makes for delicate maneuvering. You gotta be careful whom you might offend but there's benefits, too. A couple of nights ago, someone set up a big, elaborate shrine to some river god, right on one of the piers, and damn if the Candra wasn't cleaner the next morning. You can actually see the bottom."

Lucinda smiled. "Now that might be worth venturing outside for."

"You should come see me, 'Cinda." Tyrone's voice was uncharacteristically quiet. "I've missed you."

She'd been too caught up in mourning Alasdair to say she'd missed anyone else. Instead, she took his hand. "I will," she promised.

He poured them each a cup of coffee. "And, while I'm updating you on the state of the city, you'll be glad to know I figured out my next step. I'm going to teach life drawing at the art college for a while, and they're giving me a show for the drawings I did of Winston. Got a bunch more I want to do, then I got to mat and frame the things."

"I'm glad for you," she told him sincerely. "That's wonderful."

"Well, it won't pay the rent unless I find another sideline, but I'm solvent for a while. What about you, girl?"

"I don't know," Lucinda said. She got up and cracked five eggs into a bowl. Though she generally resisted all forms of cooking, she'd somehow learned to make a mean omelet.

Tyrone stared into his mug, as if fascinated by the sight of coffee. "Well, since I took away your livelihood, without even a 'by your leave,' seems I owe you something. How about I pay your salary for the rest of the year while you sort out your next move?"

She turned from the stove, amazed and a little appalled by the offer. "You can't do that. One, it's ridiculous and unnecessary; two, you'll go broke."

"You saved my life, Lucinda. I figure you're worth a sacrifice or two."

"No, it's not right," she said, beating the eggs a little harder than necessary. "Don't worry about me. I'll figure out something."

"Gabrielle already told me that she'd love to have you on board at her studio if you're game."

Lucinda considered it briefly. "I don't know," she said. "You and I had a partnership. Gabrielle's got a whole staff. I'd just be another hired hand. Besides, I'm not sure I want to work in fashion anymore. It did somehow come to seem . . . pointless."

"Maybe, but you're damn good at it. You've got an eye, 'Cinda. Talk to Gabrielle," Tyrone urged her. "See what she says."

"I'll think about it," she lied. She put a few generous pats of butter in the frying pan, lit a flame under it, and quickly sliced some Black Forest ham to go into the omelet. Her head jerked up sharply at the sound of someone knocking on her door.

"You expecting visitors?" Tyrone asked.

"No. Could you get it and tell them to go away? I'm in the middle of omelet creation here."

Tyrone obligingly went to the door. A few minutes later he was back in the kitchen, giving her a perplexed look.

"Who was it?" she asked, concentrating on the asiago she was grating.

"No idea. They wouldn't give their names. Just said they had to see you. He's tall and quiet—didn't say a blessed word. She did all the talking."

"She?"

Tyrone put his hand level with his chest. "About so high, dark hair, dark eyes, intense teen type, and unless I'm sorely mistaken, she's wearing a king's ransom in rubies."

Lucinda forgot about the omelet and hurried to the door in happy disbelief. "Neelam! Than!"

Neelam beamed up at her and said, "I told you we'd visit."

"So you did," Lucinda said, remembering with a bit of apprehension that Neelam had also planned to stay with her.

"Invite them in," Tyrone called from the kitchen. "I'll add more eggs to the pan."

Than, looking uneasy, took a seat on Lucinda's sofa but Neelam walked through the small, crowded flat, her neck craned in delight as she examined the framed prints on the wall, the mirrors and lamps and knickknacks and the shelves of books. "Oh, I love your home," she said to Lucinda. "You have such marvelous things!"

"Thank you," Lucinda said, trying not to smile. Only a teenager romanticizing the idea of living in the city could be so enthusiastic about her flat. "This is my friend Tyrone, and we were just about to have some breakfast. Will you join us?"

Than shot Neelam an alarmed look but Neelam smiled and said, "We'd love to."

So Tyrone cooked multiple omelets and Lucinda set two extra places at the table. She heard Neelam coo, "Oh, here he is!" and turned to see the dragon on the girl's wrist, looking happier than he had since before Alasdair's death. Lucinda's heart gave a little tug as Neelam ran a finger along the dragon's spine. Would he want to go back with them?

Tyrone brought the eggs to the table, and Lucinda set down a basket of croissants and poured more coffee and juice. Everyone dug into the food, seeming relieved, Lucinda thought, that they didn't have to talk. Neelam and Than eventually did speak but only to compliment Lucinda and Tyrone on the meal. The dragon, watching them all eat, walked across the table to Tyrone's plate and stood on its rim until Tyrone offered him a bite of egg. The dragon gave him a deeply offended look and turned his little head away.

"You snob!" said Tyrone.

"It's not that," Neelam said quickly. "Dragons won't eat eggs. It's too close to eating their young."

"Oh," said Tyrone. "Sorry." He reached into the fruit bowl and scooped out a grape. This the dragon took with alacrity.

Tyrone's eyes went back to Neelam. "Well now," he said, "I met Alasdair before he died, and that dragon there and I are just about what you'd call friends. I understand they both came from a place on the other side of the mountains. You two are from the same place, aren't you?"

Lucinda saw both Neelam and Than blanch, and Than said quickly, "I'm from Mandalay."

Something in his tone made Lucinda certain she'd violated a taboo. Alasdair had never said that the Source Place was a secret but she remembered now how he, and even Sebastian, wouldn't mention it before she'd been there. These last few weeks she hadn't given much thought to details like that. She'd told Tyrone a little about the lost towns over the phone, because there had been moments when she had to talk to someone. "Tyrone is my dear, dear friend," she began to explain.

Neelam held up a hand and her eyes fastened on Tyrone, grave and dark and so unquestionably authoritative that for a moment Lucinda thought she was catching a glimpse of the young Vita. "Tyrone," Neelam said, "it was because of you that Lucinda journeyed to the lost towns."

Tyrone nodded.

"That much you certainly had the right to know," the girl continued. "So yes, we came here from the Source Place. However, that is not something we wish to make public. Do you understand?"

Tyrone's expression was equally grave. "You have my word. I'll keep your secret," he promised.

Neelam nodded, quite regally, then once again seemed to morph into a teenager as she twisted her hair into a knot at the back of her neck, making her ruby earrings seem even more dazzling. Again, Lucinda got the feeling that there was something important she was forgetting. Something to do with Neelam or Than? No, that didn't make sense.

"How is everyone back there?" Lucinda asked, realizing she very much wanted to know. "Vita and Hesper and Gervase? And your father?"

"Vita's still grieving. My father is fine and Hesper is well. Gervase— Gervase is angry that Alasdair is dead."

"I know the feeling," Lucinda said. "And," she hesitated, "Averill?"

Neelam made a sour face. "Who knows? The rumor is, she saw Alasdair's death just before it happened. It's probably true. She sees almost everything connected to the towns. But she's been in owl form ever since so no one's been able to get a word out of her."

"Is that a problem?" Lucinda wondered.

"So far, no," Neelam said. "But we depend on Averill for certain protections."

For the first time Lucinda wondered if the towns had also depended on Alasdair. "Are there other *cearus* in the Source Place?"

To her surprise, Than answered. "Three others, currently. But they're more like . . . monks. They keep themselves apart from everyone else."

Neelam fed the dragon a bit of her croissant. "Alasdair was different."

"Certainly different than anyone I ever met," Tyrone put in. He touched the white quartz crystal he still wore. "He gave me this. Helped me make peace with something that had been tearing me up for years."

Neelam gave him a knowing smile. "Yes, he was wonderfully good at that sort of thing."

Lucinda knew her next question was rude but she had to ask: "Why are you here?" She immediately tried to soften it by adding, "To see the city?"

"We'll be here three whole days." Neelam was effusive by nature, but even for Neelam, she sounded thrilled. "Than has purchased rooms in a hotel for us!"

"Reserved rooms," Than corrected her.

"I want to see everything," Neelam said dreamily. "All the shops, all the clubs, all the motion pictures, all the boats, all the tall buildings—"

Tyrone began laughing. "All that in only three days? Sounds like you could use a guide. Tell you what. You cover up those rubies, so we don't wind up inviting muggers along, and I'll be glad to show you around Arcato."

"That's sweet of you," Lucinda observed. Tyrone shot her a humorous look that seemed to say, "Well, someone's got to watch out for them."

Than dipped his head and said solemnly, "We would appreciate that."

"And you must visit us in the Source Place," Neelam told Lucinda. "You weren't there long enough to really see it. Than and I could show you around."

"Thanks," Lucinda said, genuinely touched by the offer. "But I'm not sure I'd make it over the mountains again. I had help last time."

"If you're meant to come back, you will," Neelam assured her.

Than, who'd been concentrating on the dragon as it explored the back of his wrist, looked up at Lucinda. "We both wanted to see Arcato but that's not why we're here."

"Vita sent us," Neelam said.

"Alasdair's mother," Lucinda explained to Tyrone, feeling her pulse quicken. She had a terrible feeling that Vita blamed her for Alasdair's death.

"Vita asked us to bring these to you." Neelam handed Lucinda a familiar deerskin pouch, its soft leather yellowed and creased with years of handling.

Lucinda felt her eyes becoming glassy with unshed tears. "These were Alasdair's," she managed.

Neelam nodded. "His life stones."

"Why would Vita give these to me?"

Than answered. "She said you would have need. And now they're rightfully yours."

"Is that as ominous as it sounds?" Tyrone asked.

Neelam gave a careless shrug. "With Vita there are always at least three layers to any statement. You can't let it worry you. Besides, you know Alasdair's life stones will bring you good things."

"Will they?" Lucinda wondered.

Neelam flashed her brilliant smile. "Of course. They're all from the Source Place. They're Silvershod's gifts."

THAT NIGHT LUCINDA sat cross-legged on her bed, the dragon perched on her knee, watching with keen interest as she spread Alasdair's life stones on her comforter. A clear quartz crystal, a golden topaz, a smooth piece of red coral, an emerald, a sapphire, a black opal, an aquamarine, and a chunk of bright blue turquoise. She wasn't familiar with all of the stones. The coral, though, brought back painful memories of Alasdair trying to stop Tyrone's bleeding. And the quartz. She picked it up, remembering its jaguar spirit. She looked at the crystal more carefully. Was she imagining it or did the quartz actually feel empty, waiting for the jaguar's return? She touched the golden topaz and felt the warmth of honey and of evening fires banked low. Her hand shook a little; she hadn't imagined that. Carefully, she put two fingers on the emerald and sensed the ever-present spring in its green crystal, vibrant with the promise of rebirth. She made herself pick up the coral and was given a vision of the sea, the coral reef growing among the water spirits. The opal was a trickster's stone; in its flickering colors she sensed concealment and illusion and a delight in both. The sapphire, she found, was a companion for long winter nights and a protection for travel.

Lucinda reached out a tentative finger, let it rest on the dragon's pale green chest, and for the first time understood that jade was a stone of good fortune, a link to the ancestors and their blessings. "I thought I knew what you were and I was missing at least half of it, wasn't I?"

The dragon's steady gaze seemed to affirm that.

She swallowed hard. "I wish Alasdair were here now. Can you imagine his expression if he saw me actually reading the stones—" She fell silent as the dragon fixed her with a look of reproof. "What? What did I say? *Oh.*" She had to steady herself as the realization hit. This was the soul memory, the earth memory, Alasdair had talked of. This was what had been tugging at her, the thing she knew she had to remember: her own connection to the stones, through other lifetimes, through the earth itself.

Lucinda sat perfectly still, half-afraid that even breathing might make this newfound awareness vanish. At length she touched the aquamarine crystal. A cool wave of protection flowed from the gem, and in it she sensed a connection with water, with spirits of light, and with courage. Moreover, she understood that this protection was hers for as long as the life stone was with her.

"Oh, Alasdair," she murmured, beginning to understand what these stones had been to him. And a hint of what they might hold for her. She had known that a phase of her life was shutting down. She hadn't seen a future for herself beyond the present grief and emptiness. Now, though she wasn't sure what the ability to read the stones would bring, she felt as if a door were opening. The strange thing was she also felt as if the door had always been there, an essential part of herself, concealed but always beckoning, waiting for her to step through.

Lucinda touched each of the life stones again. This time she sensed them missing something. "The moonstone," she said.

The dragon took off from her knee at once, used a delicate claw to lift the top of the cloisonné box. Moments later he added the pale blue stone to the array on the bed. The other stones stirred, glad to have the moonstone back among them.

Lucinda held the moonstone in one hand. She'd thought it would break her heart to touch it again. Instead, she felt a great tenderness stealing over her. The bitter sense of loss and aloneness, the ragged ache of mourning was easing, and in its place she felt a sense of connection to the city outside her window, to the mountains beyond the city, and to all the beings, mortal and divine, that they held. The stones were open to her and she to them.

Above the city the stars wheeled through the night sky. Lucinda could feel them calling to the stones and the stones resonating in response, ancient memories and connections flowing through them. And each of them, it seemed, connected her back to Alasdair. Reflexively steeling herself against the pain, she let herself picture him, as he'd been with her in this room. This time, though, there was no pain wound through the memory, only gratitude that he'd been part of her life.

The dragon took the moonstone from her palm and set it next to the sapphire, where it clearly wanted to be. Then he came to rest on her open hand, a translucent bit of pale green jade, alive with the light of the earth.

ACKNOWLEDGMENTS

My deepest thanks to: Beth Meacham, for the genesis of this book, and who, along with Tappan King, Terri Windling, Annita Harlan, and Thomas Harlan, was so welcoming to those early pages; Julie Fallowfield who took me on; Patrick Nielsen Hayden, Jim Minz, Natasha Panza, and all those at Tor, who have been patient and supportive beyond belief; and Terri Windling for continued faith, inspired suggestions, and the deft, graceful editing that is every writer's dream.

Lorna Soroko and Kasia Yuska read and reread the roughest drafts and offered invaluable critiques, ideas, and support—without you two I'm not sure I would have found my way through. My gratitude also goes out to the brave and perceptive volunteers who read through the first draft: Erica Swadley, especially for her knowledge of the stones; Linda Byberg for clarity; Liz Marraffino-Rees for so many details and good ideas and the bead book; Delia Sherman for her expert editorial eye; Doug Lantz for the tundra; and my cousin Judith Grodowitz for Hekate's true nature and for the suggestion of what tugs at you from behind. Thanks also for generous encouragement from Mimi Panitch; Alan Lee; Christopher Schelling; Krystal Greene; Ari Berk, whose amazing discourse on the stones inspired Vita's crystal; and Tappan King for solving the title crisis.

Doug Lantz has been a source of unstinting, loving support, and my sisters, Phyllis Steiber and Barbara Steiber, have been unwavering in their belief in me and in this book. Finally, love and gratitude to two who are no longer with us: Dorothy Sternberg, my aunt, who fed my soul with wonderful books, particularly the Adrienne Segur *Fairy Tale Book,* from which the story of "Silvershod" has been adapted, and Steven Chernesky, healer and magic man.

BIBLIOGRAPHY

The following is a partial list of books I referred to in writing A Rumor of Gems. *A more complete and annotated bibliography can be found on my Web site: www.ellensteiber.com.*

Andrews, Carol. *Amulets of Ancient Egypt.* Austin: University of Texas Press, 1994.

Bauer, Jaroslov. *A Field Guide in Color to Minerals, Rocks, and Precious Stones.* Translated by Zdenka Náglová. London: Cathay Books, 1974.

Bhairavan, Amarananda. *Kali's Odiyya: A Shaman's True Story of Initiation.* York Beach, Maine: Nicolas-Hays, 2000.

Brown, Norman O. *Hermes the Thief: The Evolution of a Myth.* Great Barrington, Mass.: Lindisfarne Press, 1990.

Budge, E. A. Wallis. *Amulets and Talismans.* (Original title: *Amulets and Superstitions,* 1961.) New Hyde Park, N.Y.: University Books, 1968.

Cavey, Christopher. *Gems & Jewels: Fact & Fable.* London: Studio Editions, 1992.

Cooper, J. C. *An Illustrated Encyclopaedia of Traditional Symbols.* London: Thames and Hudson, 1978.

Daniélou, Alain. *Gods of Love and Ecstasy: The Traditions of Shiva and Dionysus.* (Original title: *Shiva and Dionysus,* 1984). Rochester, Vt.: Inner Traditions International, 1992.

David-Neel, Alexandra. *Magic and Mystery in Tibet.* New Hyde Park, N.Y.: University Books, 1965.

Dubin, Lois Sherr. *The History of Beads: From 30,000 B.C. to the Present.* New York: Henry N. Abrams, 1987.

Eliade, Mircea. *Shamanism: Archaic Techniques of Ecstasy.* Translated by Willard R. Trask, Bollingen Series LXXVI. Princeton: Princeton University Press, 1964.

Gump, Richard. *Jade: Stone of Heaven.* Garden City, N.Y.: Doubleday, 1962.

Hall, Cally. *Gemstones: The Visual Guide to More Than 130 Gemstone Varieties.* New York: Dorling Kindersley Publishing, 1994.

Hall, Judy. *The Crystal Bible.* Cincinnati, Ohio: Walking Stick Press, 2003.

Hyde, Lewis. *Trickster Makes This World.* New York: Farrar, Straus and Giroux, 1998.

Ions, Veronica. *Indian Mythology.* London: Paul Hamlyn, 1967.

Johari, Harish. *The Healing Power of Gemstones: In Tantra, Ayurveda, and Astrology.* Rochester, Vt.: Inner Traditions, 1988.

King, C. W. *The Natural History of Gems or Decorative Stones.* London: Bell and Daldy, 1867.

Knuth, Bruce G. *Gems in Myth, Legend, and Lore.* Thornton, Colo.: Jewelers Press, 1999.

Kunz, George Frederick. *The Curious Lore of Precious Stones.* New York: Dover Publications, 1971.

———. *The Magic of Jewels and Charms.* New York: Dover Publications, 1997.

Leach, Maria. *Standard Dictionary of Folklore, Mythology, and Legend.* Vols. I and II. New York: Funk and Wagnalls, 1949.

Melody. *Love Is in the Earth: A Kaleidoscope of Crystals.* Wheat Ridge, Colo.: Earth-Love Publishing House, 1995.

Mookerjee, Ajit. *Kali the Feminine Force.* Rochester, Vt.: Destiny Books, 1988.

Newman, Harold. *An Illustrated Dictionary of Jewelry.* London: Thames and Hudson, 1994.

Pliny. *Natural History X: Books XXXVI–XXXVII,* Loeb Classical Library. Edited by G. P. Goold and translated by D. E. Eichholz. London and Cambridge, Mass.: Harvard University Press, 1962.

Raphaell, Katrina. *Crystal Healing: The Therapeutic Application of Crystals and Stones.* Vols. I, II, III. Santa Fe, N. Mex.: Aurora Press, 1987.

Read, P. G. *Dictionary of Gemmology,* second edition, Oxford, England: Butterworth-Heinemann, 1982.

Scully, Vincent. *The Earth, the Temple, and the Gods: Greek Sacred Architecture.* New Haven and London: Yale University Press, 1962.

Turner, Patricia, and Charles Russell Coulter. *Dictionary of Ancient Deities.* New York: Oxford University Press, 2001.

Untracht, Oppi. *Traditional Jewelry of India.* New York: Henry N. Abrams, 1997.